# BOOKS BY BRE

**The Realn**

*The Crimson Court*

**Realm Reacher Novellas:**

*The Amber Dame*

**The Frostmarked Chronicles:**

*A Dagger in the Winds*

*The Trials of Ascension*

*The Daughters of the Earth*

*The Deathless Sons*

**Frostmarked Tales:**

*The Rider in the Night*

*The Lady of Rolika*

**The Prism Files:**

*The Fractured Prism*

*Crimson Reigns*

*Pridefall*

*White Crown*

*For Andrea.*
*You convinced me to start writing and have been my greatest supporter ever since. What have you done to me?*

# AUTHOR NOTE: TRIGGER WARNING

*The Crimson Court* contains elements that may be triggers or traumatic to some readers, so please proceed with caution if any of the below are so for you. I have done my best to treat these serious topics carefully and with respect.

- Mental illness
- Suicidal thoughts
- Death
- Torture

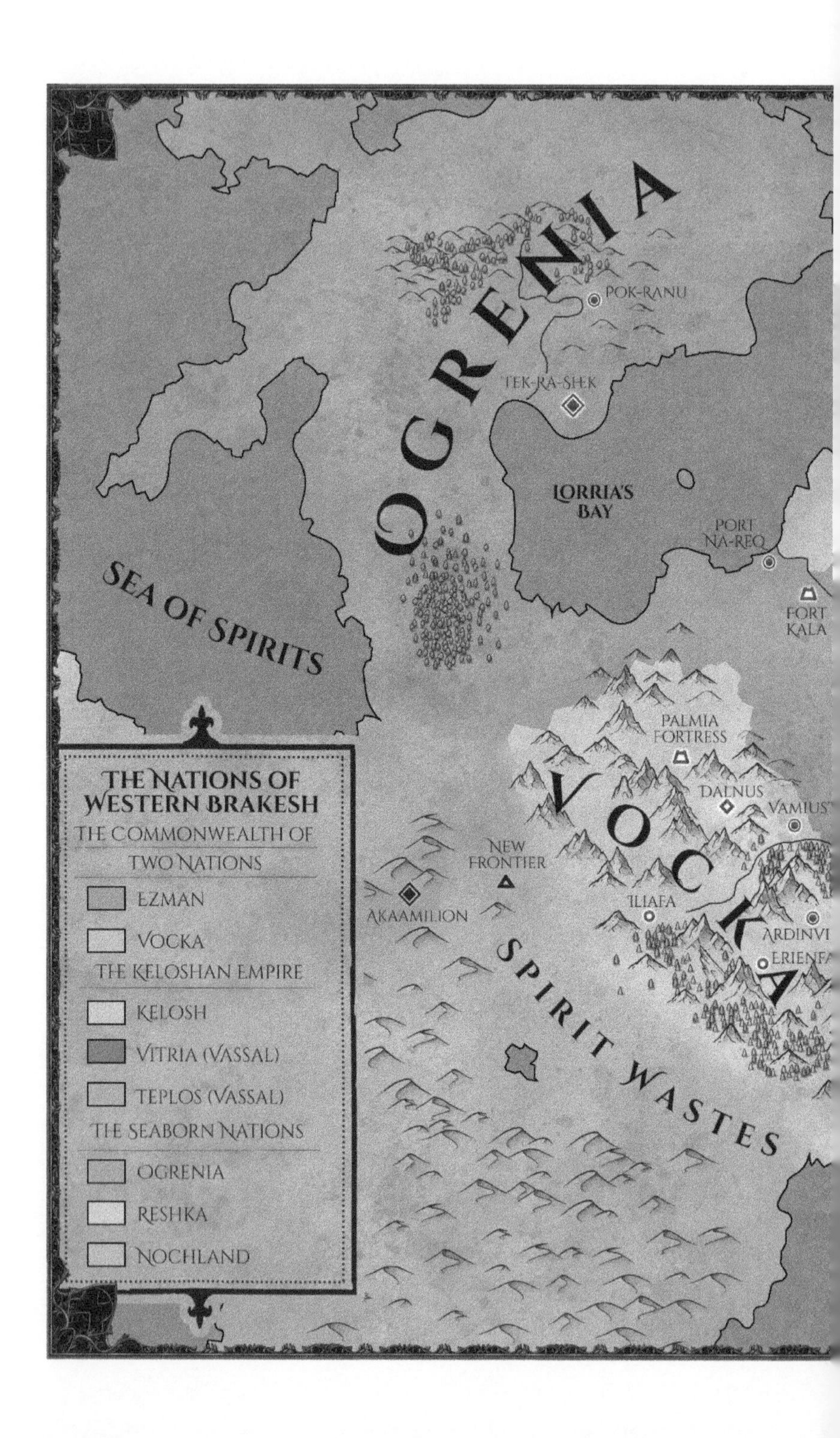

OGRENIA
POK-RANU
TEK-RA-SHEK
LORRIA'S BAY
PORT NA-REQ
FORT KALA
SEA OF SPIRITS
PALMIA FORTRESS
DALNUS
VAMIUS
VOCKA
NEW FRONTIER
AKAAMILION
ILIAFA
ARDINVI
ERIENFA
SPIRIT WASTES
THE NATIONS OF WESTERN BRAKESH
THE COMMONWEALTH OF TWO NATIONS
EZMAN
VOCKA
THE KELOSHAN EMPIRE
KELOSH
VITRIA (VASSAL)
TEPLOS (VASSAL)
THE SEABORN NATIONS
OGRENIA
RESHKA
NOCHLAND

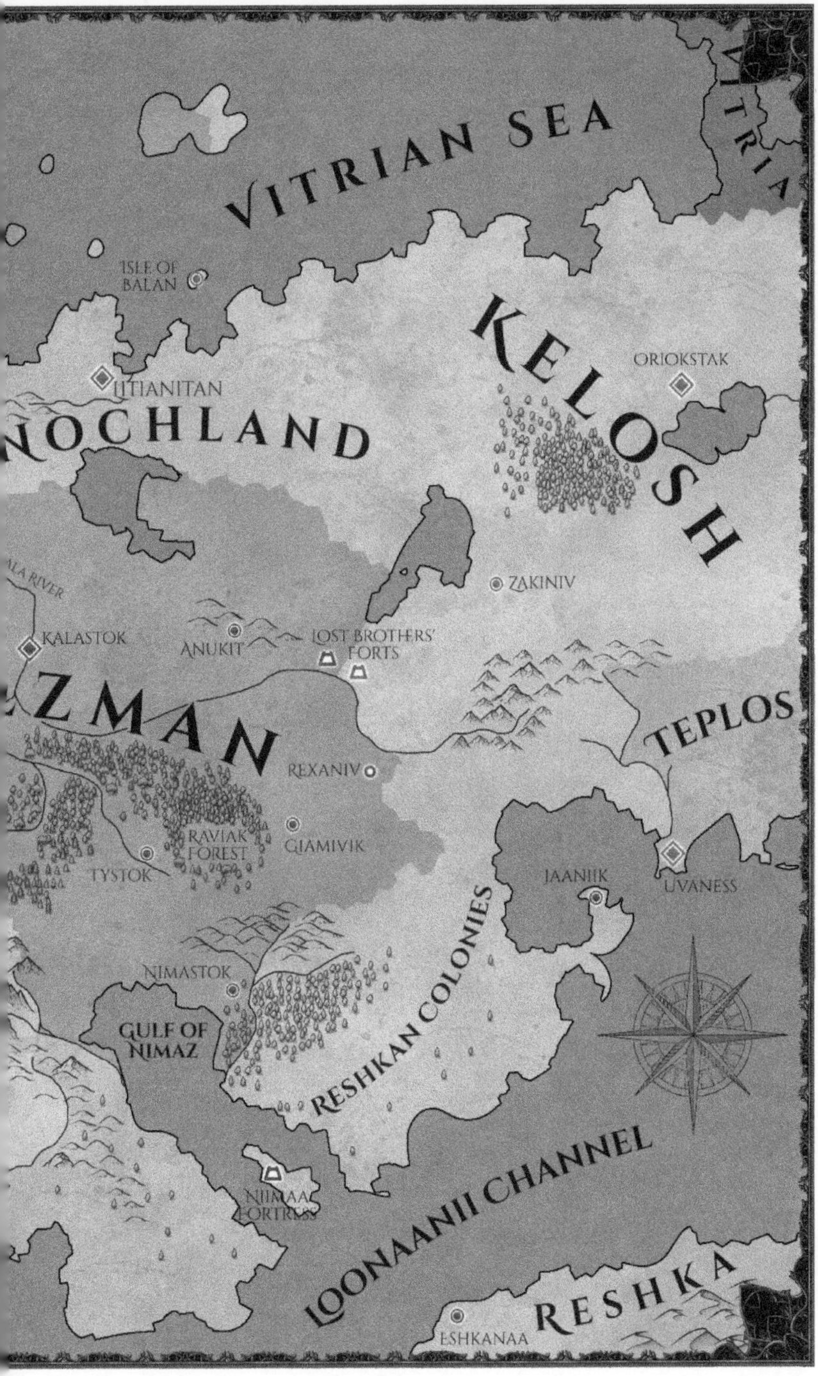
VITRIAN SEA
VITRIA
ISLE OF BALAN
KELOSH
ORIOKSTAK
LITIANITAN
NOCHLAND
ALA RIVER
ZAKINIV
KALASTOK
ANUKIT
LOST BROTHERS' FORTS
ZMAN
TEPLOS
REXANIV
RAVIAK FOREST
GIAMIVIK
TYSTOK
JAANIIK
UVANESS
RESHKAN COLONIES
NIMASTOK
GULF OF NIMAZ
LOONAANII CHANNEL
NIIMAA FORTRESS
RESHKA
ESHKANAA

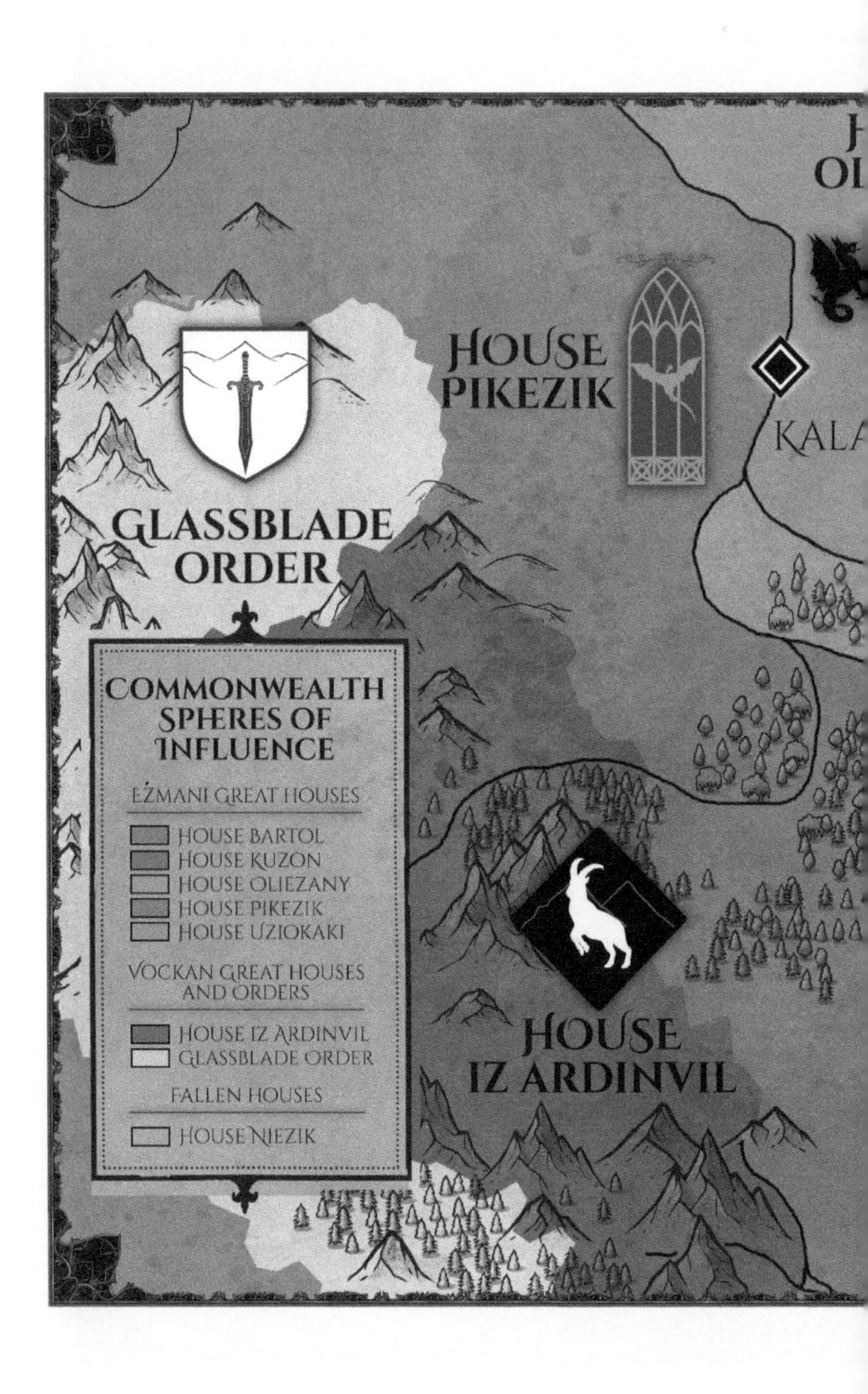
HOUSE PIKEZIK
GLASSBLADE ORDER
COMMONWEALTH SPHERES OF INFLUENCE
EŻMANI GREAT HOUSES
HOUSE BARTOL
HOUSE KUZON
HOUSE OLIEZANY
HOUSE PIKEZIK
HOUSE UZIOKAKI
VOCKAN GREAT HOUSES AND ORDERS
HOUSE IZ ARDINVIL
GLASSBLADE ORDER
FALLEN HOUSES
HOUSE NIEZIK
HOUSE IZ ARDINVIL

OUSE
EZANY

HOUSE
BARTOL

TOK

HOUSE
UZIOKAKI

HOUSE
NIEZIK

HOUSE
KUZON

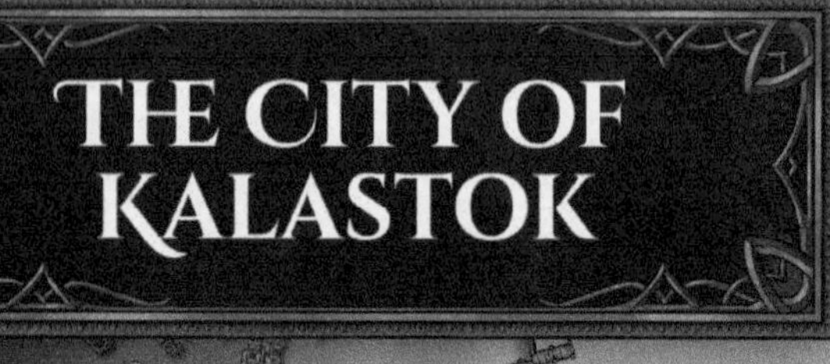
THE CITY OF
KALASTOK
PARZINAK'S
CAFE
NEX'S
APARTMENT
KING'S BRIDGE
REACHER
TOWER
SHADOW
QUARTER
HOMELESS
ENCAMPMENT
KING'S BRIDGE
THE HOPE
OF LINARIUS
BEG AVE
KALA RIVER
INDUSTRIAL DISTRICT
IRON ALLEY
PUB
NEW BEGINNINGS
BRIDGE

ON DISTRICT
BURIED TEMPLE
KALASTOK COLLEGE
PIKEZIK ESTATE
CRYSTAL PALACE
CRYSTAL REACHER TOWER
UNIVERSITY DISTRICT
HAXON'S HALL
KALASTOK ARENA
DRIFTERS' QUARTER
NORTH MARKET REACHER TOWER
IZ VAMIUSTOK TOWNHOUSE
TEXTILE ALLEY
KET DISTRICT
NOCHLAND CONSULATE
OLD MARKET REACHER TOWER
OLD MARKET CLOCKTOWER
LAZIK STREET TAVERN
HE
LUENCE
OLIEZANY BRIDGE REACHER TOWER
ANY
GE

# THE KNOWN REALMS

| Realm | Reacher Power | Color |
|---|---|---|
| Air | Summon and control air/wind | Sky Blue |
| Body | Heal and strengthen bodies | Blood Red |
| Dark | Summon complete darkness and see within it | Black |
| Death | Kill target's body and spirit | Purple |
| Earth | Manipulate earth, alter metals, call earthquakes | Brown |
| Fire | Summon and control fire | Orange |
| Force | Call force fields and blasts of energy (or smaller pushes) | Bright Red |
| Life | Create plants and encourage their growth/Grant life energy to a target who is near death | Green |
| Light | Summon pure light and see no matter how bright | Yellow |
| Mind | Manipulate a target's thoughts | Pink |
| Possibility | Alter odds/Summon objects | Rainbow |
| Shadow | Summon shadows and see through them | Dark Gray |
| Spirit | Repel spirits or guide them into newborns | Silver |
| Truth | Compel target to speak the truth or halt/Mend broken objects (inorganic) | White |
| Water | Summon and control water | Navy Blue |

# HOUSE EMBLEMS

*Not Great Houses. Included for reference

# FLAGS OF WESTERN BRAKESH

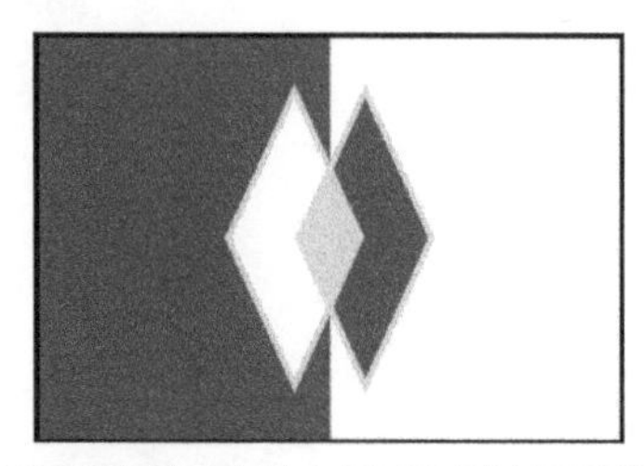

THE COMMONWEALTH OF TWO NATIONS

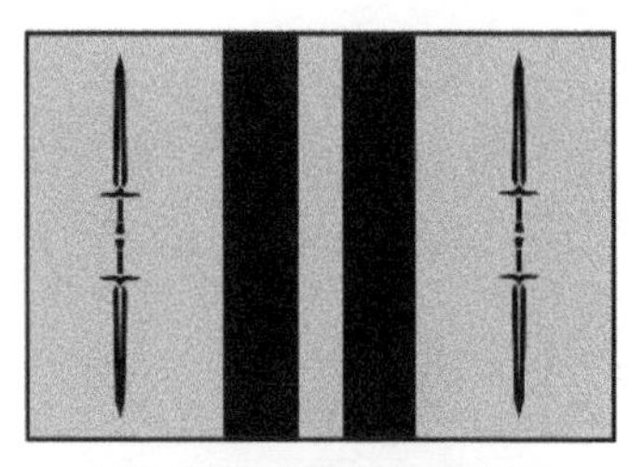

THE KELOSHAN EMPIRE

THE OGRENIAN HEGEMONY

THE KINGDOM OF RESHKA

THE MERCHANT REPUBLIC OF NOCHLAND

# ACKNOWLEDGEMENTS

This was such an exciting book to write and design, and I could not have done it without the help of so many amazing people. *The Crimson Court* was a project I had imagined for many years but had not been ready to create until now. Still, though the words are mine, so many others impacted this book.

Firstly, I would like to give a huge thank you to my amazing beta readers. Their feedback has allowed me to remove what wasn't great and add more of what was. Each of them has their own way of adding to the story, and each is appreciated: Ross H., Andrea W. N., Rebecca C., Brandon S., Ryan W., Lora C., Rachel S., and Ann D. Many of these wonderful people have beta read for me for many years, and I am so grateful to have each of them with me on this writing journey.

I of course must mention the artists that brought the story with so many wonderful pieces. Kateryna Vitkovskaya's stunning cover is beyond words, and I'm honored to have it on book along with her art of Kasia in a certain fractal location (read and find out), Radais in the Spirit Wastes, and the cityscape of Kalastok too. Joni Matoz's character portraits have also been *so* fun to work with. I hope it brings you as much joy as it does me to see the characters whom we spend so much time with in this story. Deranged Doctor Design has also been with me since the start of The Frostmarked Chronicles, designing all the text for the covers to finish them off right.

An extra thank you goes out to my wife, Andrea, as well for her support, beta reading, and design assistance with the in-world newspapers and posters. I would've spun my wheels on many things if it wasn't for her helping me think out loud.

Of course, I cannot go without mentioning all the amazing backers of the Kickstarter! I am still amazed at how many of you backed a new series, and I am determined to make every book in The Realm Reachers all it can be for you. Now, without further ado, the backers:

Chris Behrsin
Tanya Young
Maria Mejia
Emma Adams
Delancey Stewart
Francesco Tehrani
Christina Stoddard
Gianna C.
Christa Niehot
Trevor Jerome
PunkARTchick
Hope Terrell
Wouter de Wit
Heiko Koenig
Craig Francis
Marte Myrvold
Ian Bannon
Diane
John Idlor
Lexie Valverde
Andy99000
Becerra
Nick Mandujano III
Paul Staples
Nicole Sanders
Mandy Wetherhold
Richard Böddeker
M. H. Woodscourt
Mary Ann
Silvia Morris
Kirsten Johnson
Phoenix17
Dan Kawecki
Querard Onasys
ALB
Taylor McGinnis
Sean Reilly
Dylan H.
Senthil Kumaran Rajasekaran
Akos Nagy
Sydney
Dfeajq38
Renee Portnell
Lorenzo G.
Hannah Wilkinson
Morgan G.
Brian Grimes
Silverbreeze
Katherine Leslie
Burt Struble
Thomas Vaultonburg
Paz
Danielle Riccardi
Lewis Dix
Apinya Wong
Zeb Berryman
Z.S. Diamanti
Caitlyn Price
Cortney Babcock
Christina Bloszinsky
Elizabeth Mellas
Diana & Rudie N.
Breana N.
Stacy W.
Amanda Kwieraga
Matt Baron
Anna Liang
John Halbig
Kassie H.
Sarah-Jane Baird
April Ayton
Amanda Eschmeyer
Billye Herndon
Metthea W. Ross
Susan Yamamoto
Jordan Polly
Patricia Horton
Ringmaster
Quinn Giguiere
In loving memory of Basil Martin
Adam Nemo
Ryan H.
JP Rindfleisch IX
Merle Schlanke
Kris Marchesi
David Dehaan
Josh & Kelli Luebke
Josh O'Brien
Metal
Kasia Nowak
Kalin Nabiof
Franchesca Caram
Adam M. Myers
Michael Sugarman
Joe Rixman
Faye Quinn
Joel Freudenberg
Bill Kong
Jose Vicab
Chris Bernardo
Drew Gohmann
Ryan Scott James

Mike Olson
Justise Briones
Jeffrey M. Johnson
Flemming P.
Elias Rondou
Anja Peerdeman
Mike Malloy
Andrew Barnett
Cat Parker
Kelly Stirling
David Wolfson
Katrina Gilles
Tallulah
Spencer Wright
Kate Malloy
Nancy Richey
Hugo Essink
Stephanie Fischer
Krystie Hollifield
Mariëlle van Zelst
Rachel
Dawn Marie
Michael J. Sullivan, author
Alex Dummer
Ashley Byrd
Michael B. Mitchell
Anders Sørensen
Cody L. Allen
Covington
Christopher Clayton
Paul Davis
Eric Vilbert
Jordan Newman
Ricardo Monascal
Arwyn Cunningham
Robert Brown
Ariel S
Joe Barros
Paul Hijmans
Heather Cooper
Kelsey Stenberg
Jay Mullen
Xiomara Reyes
Henry Bacuilima
Nick Fragosa
Georgina Nicholls
Vanessa Mohr
Raúl Aguilar López
Aldchad
Christiana Falcon
Shanon M. Brown
Karissa W.
Izaak
C. Gendreau
Mark Salud
Sean Lovely Ramsey
Brandon Ngo
Cheyenne Thomspon
Charles E. Norton III
Nicholas Paynter
Elly T.
Trevor Roelfs
Kaitlyn Sterrett
Kailey B.
Michelle L. Sanchez
Matt R.
Nicolas Breton
Iris Juylyenne
S. Loges
Terry M. Hulett
Alexander Edwards
Tyler Cheek
Jezza
Jonathan Hamm
Ashley Gibson
Joshua McGinnis
Megan Kell
Christopher Wesselstam
Kristyna Fiserova
Jairo Rosado
Walter E. Alvarez Jr.
Vannessa Goodwin
Heath D. Alberts
Dori
Zack Newcomb
Briana Fowler
Ryan Wearmouth
Wendy M.
Nathan Daleness
Jesse Nicholas
Spyros Ravanopoulos
CJ Denhard
Quinn & Manda Johnson
Charlie and Sarah Baker
Cathy McLoughlin
Michael Johnson
Eryn
Justin Rose
Jamie & Thaila Cook
Rumen Ganev
Kailey
Emily Chaffin
Steff Martin
Keith Dolan
Alexandra Corrsin
Megyn "Sapphi" MacDougall
Niota

BOOK ONE OF THE REALM REACHERS

# THE CRIMSON COURT

BRENDAN NOBLE

# PROLOGUE - THE AWAKENED

*"The Awakening changed everything. Spirits struck in the everdark until dawnrise came to reveal the meager remains of our glorious empire. May the Crystal have mercy on us all…"* – Horaton Pariniat, final scribe of the Piorakan Empire

Leonit Niezik stared down at the massive tome before him, desperate for an answer. The old grandfather clock in his study's corner chimed for midnight, but the slowly aging lord gave it only a passing glance as he pushed up his spectacles with a shaking hand. Time meant little, as he had little left.

A far softer noise from across the lavishly furnished room pulled him away from the book. His ashen haired daughter, Kasia, swung her legs impatiently as she tapped a piece against their game board.

Of course, he'd forgotten his promise to continue their game before bed. It was a secret tradition of theirs, as her mother believed the twelve-year-old was nestled in her chambers on the floor above. She was a tricky thing. Few men of the court could match Leonit's cunning, let alone a girl so young.

"I will join you in just a moment, my love," he said, his voice dampened by the room's rug-covered floors and bookshelves, full of histories and tales from before the Awakening and after. Hundreds of books collected during his two lives. If only one could tell him how to stop what was coming.

Kasia groaned, tucking her hands defiantly under her legs and leaning back in her chair until it hung at the precipice.

*Always on the edge, that girl,* he thought. *Too much like me.*

"You said that an hour ago!" she complained. "Father, what is that book anyway? *Surely* it can't be better than losing to me again."

Leonit sighed and removed his spectacles. He rubbed the bridge of his nose, which ached from wearing the readers for so long. "What have I told you about using such informal language? You are my heir, and one day, when you join the Chamber of Scions in my place, the other patriarchs and matriarchs will not tolerate it."

She furrowed her narrow brow. Her skin was a pale gray, like Leonit and the other scions who carried Realm Reacher bloodlines, and it made the silvery blue in her eyes as radiant as the quarter-year everbright, despite the devious thoughts she held behind them.

"I will do what I must," she said, forcing a more noble tone, "but I doubt members of the Chamber appreciate false promises either."

That spurred a chuckle from him. Leonit knew he kept his daughter closer than most fathers, who preferred specialized tutors to teach their heirs the arts of science, literature, and eventually magical Reaching, but Kasia reminded him why he fought for the Commonwealth of Two Nations when the country was obsessed with destroying itself. It wasn't about him. Not anymore.

"This book is the story of the Awakening," he said, closing it. "It, unfortunately, has offered little insight into why the spirits awoke and destroyed Piorak."

"King Yaakiin has you reading about ancient history? You are the minister of glass. Does he not have scribes?"

Leonit snatched his spectacles and circled his desk to Kasia, countering her most recent move without even sitting. "The king trusts few, and I consider myself lucky to be among them."

She perked up and made her next play, advancing a seemingly harmless peasant—a spy in disguise. The haataamaash board resembled a battlefield, and it was a flanking maneuver he'd taught her to disrupt an opponent's strategy. Her position could now threaten his throne if he wasn't careful. "It is a secret, then?"

"Glass is our best defense against the awakened," he replied, sending his dragon straight over her defenses. It put him a single turn away from victory if she failed to see how he'd exposed himself to her weakest piece. "It is my responsibility to understand them if we are to remain safe."

"We are safe, aren't we?" she asked, hesitating on her next move.

It was rare for her to reveal any wavering of her confidence, but Leonit took heart in it. With how she acted, one could forget she was only a child. He wanted her to learn, yes. The enjoyment of juvenile pursuits was important too, as he had no desire to see her experience adulthood's burdens too soon.

A grin crossed her face as she reached for her peasant and placed it behind his throne, revealing the spy's true power. "You left your back exposed."

He chuckled with pride, bowing his head before ceremoniously tipping over his throne to signal defeat. "So you did. Well done, my dear."

"Did you let me win?"

Leonit crouched beside her. Though his knees ached, he smiled and pressed his hand to her cheek. "Like that spy slipped through my defenses more easily than a dragon, we cannot always see those who threaten us. There is always danger among the great houses. The king has his allies and his foes, and there are those who—"

A crash came from outside, stopping Leonit mid-speech.

*Have they come so soon?* There was still so much to be done, so much he had planned.

"Father?" Kasia asked, grabbing his arm. "What's happening?"

Another crash shook the entire mansion. A scream followed. Leonit took a shaky breath, then steeled himself. "Keep your voice down and come with me."

"But—"

"Defiance can be a worthy trait, but you must listen to me now. Do you understand?"

Kasia stared at him with her usually narrow eyes as wide as saucers. "I do," she whispered.

"Good." He yanked her toward his desk, tearing back the rug beneath it at the rear of the room. A glass trap door wrapped in iron was set into the floor. "Climb in, and do not leave until either your mother or Uliusa retrieves you."

"Why? What about you?"

More screams sounded throughout the house as he yanked open the latch and gestured toward the ladder heading down into the darkness. His mind spun, fighting his heart. Oh, how he wished he had told her everything. But there was no time for such things now. "Please, Kasia. I need you to trust me."

She hugged him tight, and he returned it, squeezing with every ounce of will he had left. It took everything he had not to follow her down. He was no fool, though. They had come for him and would end the search once he was found. If he hid, it would only lead to more death. Still, some primal part of him clung to life.

"I love you," Kasia whispered. Her tears wetted his vest, and his own trickled down his cheeks. Spirits, how had it come to this?

"You are everything to me," he replied as a *thud* came from the double doors across the room. "That is why you must go. Hurry!"

She scrambled into the opening, and Leonit slowly shut it behind, making as little noise as possible as he returned the rug to its place, then grabbed his flintlock revolver from the desk's hidden drawer.

Flexing his left hand, he dragged the gray blade upon his index finger through the air. It was made of winding crystal that covered the finger from knuckle to tip, and blades like it were called talons among the scion nobility due to its resemblance to a bird's claw. The talon tore through veil as he Reached into the realm of Shadows. Deep gray wisps circled his arms, and he commanded them to cover the rug with a heavier darkness than the candlelit room would normally allow.

The doors shook. They were nothing more than wood, as the exterior walls had enough glass to keep out any rogue spirits. No, the Crimson Court had finally come, and he was too late to stop them.

He raised the revolver as the wood splintered. Many scions were well practiced with a gun, but Leonit had neither served in the army nor been much of a shot. The battles of the king's court took more skill with one's wit than with weapons. Words could disarm a nation, but they were useless in the face of his house's demise.

His finger squeezed out of instinct alone when the doors burst open. The resulting shot sent a ringing through his ears as the bullet ripped through the doorway and embedded itself in the wall across the dim corridor.

"You have your mark," he called out, inching further from the desk. "Come out, and let this escapade be complete."

No one replied.

The hairs on Leonit's arms raised, and he shivered at the familiar horror before him. He'd not seen battle, but he had lived long enough to meet his share of awakened spirits. He lowered the gun. Bullets would do nothing against this foe, and neither would his Shadow Reaching.

"So they have finished their research, then?" he asked.

The lamps flickered near the door as misty gray tendrils spiraled forth. Soundless, they surged toward him faster than any man could run, all light extinguishing around them.

Leonit could only stand and face the end with pride. He had built House Niezik into a powerful name, hoping to one day live a second life like the most powerful magnates, but as he stared at the menace crossing his study, he knew this life would be his last. The Crimsons would be sure of it.

His breaths fogged the air as the tendrils met to form a human-like figure. Neither solid nor entirely air, it resided somewhere between, unable to be harmed by material weapons… except for glass.

Leonit struck in turn with the awakened, pulling a glass-bladed dagger from a hidden pocket in his vest and slashing at the spirit's chest. Normal spirits would flee at the slightest hint of glass, but the awakened plunged forward, undeterred. Its tendrils pierced Leonit's chest and throat as he desperately tried to wound his attacker. Though the dagger found its misty torso, it only hissed and released more tendrils into him. His vision began to fade.

*I should have stopped this. I should have saved the Commonwealth.*

But he had failed. Any hope of stopping the destruction to come vanished as the awakened's tendrils drew his spirit from his body. He collapsed, and with one last breath, he whispered into the darkness.

"Find them, Kasia."

# The Hunters and the Huntress

*"Parqiz Uziokaki, the Spirit Reacher. He knows the names of the rest."* –
Leonit Niezik, former patriarch of House Niezik

TWELVE YEARS LATER

Wind and a cold rain greeted Kasia as she stepped from her carriage, clutching shut her high-collared coat and glaring at the mansion before her. House Uziokaki had made their fortune in hunting and forestry, and their estate resembled an overgrown hunting cabin. She grinned at that.

The only one hunting tonight would be her.

"Lady Katarzyna, should we not hasten our way inside?" Tazper asked, rushing beside her with an umbrella. Her rounded koilee fur hat had done its job well, though, and she quite appreciated the rain. It announced the arrival of the everdark season—far more fun than the unending light of everbright.

"Haste would make it seem as if we wanted to be here," she replied to her friend.

A poorer scion with a gentle face and a swoop of chestnut hair, Tazper could not afford a Reacher talon, so Kasia had taken him as her house footman to help him earn his way. He was a bit of a klutz and his cravat spilled over his shirt like a waterfall, but he was one of the few people she could trust. On the day she intended to kill her father's murderer, that mattered more than ever.

"Don't we?" he squeaked, slipping out of his formal tone.

Kasia faked a smile at a group of passersby who were headed in to join the gala. The Ephemeral Storm of Everdark was an annual celebration of the quarter-year darkness that would soon arrive. Such events were hosted by many of the great houses, and none of the minor scions wanted to miss their chance to converse with the most powerful aristocrats. It was all a game, much like the one Kasia had played nightly against her father, and after twenty-four years of life, she'd learned her lessons well.

"Never let your opponents know your true intentions," she replied before straightening the amber chains that connected the buttons along the front of her coat.

The peasants of House Niezik's estate had called her the Amber Dame ever since her scouts discovered large reserves of amber in an ancient forest basin near the border of House Uziokaki's lands. The Uziokaki claimed the reserves should be theirs, so wearing amber in their mansion would be considered an insult. Kasia sincerely hoped they noticed.

Before Tazper could stumble through his reply, she started toward the gate. It was made of intricately carved wood and crested with a golden-antlered stag—the Uziokaki sigil—and archways resembling interwoven branches lined the cobblestone path to the mansion itself. Guards stood on either side of the gate with rifles shouldered. Such guards were little threat to scions, most who were Reachers capable of drawing magic from other realms, but they still eyed her as she passed.

"They are watching us," Tazper whispered once he'd scrambled to Kasia's side.

"If you are worried about guards doing their jobs," Kasia said, "then you should turn back. I can't have you panicking."

He held his chin up. "I will have poise."

With an amused huff, Kasia led the way to the mansion's double doors. A butler awaited them behind a podium.

"Lady Katarzyna Niezik, what a pleasant surprise." He dipped his quill in ink and crossed her name off his parchment before turning to Tazper. "And who might you be?"

"This is Tazper of House Janka," Kasia said. "He is my footman for this evening."

The butler scribbled something down, then took a long breath and pointed behind him. "You may deposit your coats and hats to the left before making your way to the grand hall. I am sure they are *dreadfully* sopping amid this weather. However, before you go, I must examine your gloves."

Holding back a smirk, Kasia held up her hands to reveal her long black gloves and the amber jewels embedded along her knuckles. The one on her right hand was a formality, but the butler examined the left closely. Scions could only Reach if the crystal talon on their left index finger remained uncovered, allowing them to tear the space between their realm of Spirits, called Zekiaz, and the one they were Reaching into. It wasn't just impolite to remove one's gloves during gatherings such as this. People had been killed for less.

Tazper did the same, despite not being a Reacher, and the butler waved them both past. Kasia laughed to herself at the irony of the check. Yes, they had ensured she was wearing gloves upon her entry, but nothing stopped her from removing them when the time was right.

The mansion's interior tore away the illusion of a rustic cabin and replaced it with rural displays of wealth. Wooden pillars with glass-carved patterns lined two curved staircases that headed up to the next floor. Rustic chandeliers led the way to the stairs, exuding a dim glow that made the floors shimmer like copper as their footfalls echoed through the hall along with an ever-growing hum of conversation. Only a roll of thunder broke the ambience before surrendering to the constant drum of heavy rainfall.

The pair dropped their coats and hats, then followed the other scions to the stairs.

Kasia gripped the handrail as her skirts clipped at her heels. Her outermost layer was a cutaway jacket, belted at the waist to reveal a sleeved cream dress beneath. Like her coat, the jacket flared open at the torso with thin amber chains connecting the buttons on either side. It was a combination of domestic Ezmani stylings and foreign Ogrenian ones from the northern coast. Among the nationalists at the party, it would be yet another affront, but she'd intended so.

*Keep their eyes on the dress,* she thought, *and they'll miss the dagger in your hand.*

Tazper took the lead as they reached the top of the stairs, but it wasn't him who drew the crowd's stares. In the twelve years since an awakened commanded by Parqiz Uziokaki killed her father, neither Kasia nor any other remaining members of House Niezik had stepped foot within their rivals' estate. It was far from public knowledge that the attack hadn't merely been a rogue spirit, but whispers had spread among the scions. If House Niezik was stepping back into the fold, what did that mean for those who'd replaced them?

There wasn't a smile among the near hundred faces beneath the chandeliers pulsing with Fire Reacher flames, except Kasia's. Most of the ones she gave nowadays were feigned to hide her grimace or hidden smirks. This one was genuine. For tonight, she would take her largest step since she'd discovered Leonit's list of names two years before. Her father's list had been left for her, hidden in a secret compartment of his desk:

*Raniana Laxis, the peasant spy.*

*Fantil Tozki, the traitorous sergeant.*

*Parqiz Uziokaki, the Spirit Reacher. He knows the names of the rest.*

*Find the Crimson Court. Find those who killed me.*

Kasia carried the list at all times. She'd already ridded Zekiaz of Raniana and Fantil, but they had offered little information regarding these elusive Crimsons.

Parqiz was her last target… and last hope.

Her talon seemed to hum at the thought of killing the assassin. She was a Death Reacher, a rare type technically banned in the Commonwealth, but no one had any way of knowing her power. That made her a scion's worst nightmare.

Spirit Reachers, like Parqiz, were far more common, keeping rogue awakened away from populated areas and guiding gentle drifter spirits into newborns so that they didn't become empty husks. This was Zekiaz's cycle. When a person's life ended, their spirit became a drifter until it found a newborn and forgot its old life. Only the six great houses could break the cycle and truly live again.

When a great house heir bore their first child—still empty of spirit—the magnate, heir, newborn, and a Spirit Reacher would retreat to their house's obscenely expensive glass room. The heir killed the magnate with the house's ceremonial Inheritance Blade, trapping the magnate's spirit in the room of spirit-resistant glass. The Spirit Reacher then guided the magnate's confined spirit into the newborn. This newborn carried a new name and was given a moniker of *the Second* or however many times the spirit had passed through the Initiation Ritual. They remembered nothing of their past lives until they touched the Spirit Crystal and became a Reacher in their teenage years, allowing them to develop their own personality, but rule with experience when it came their turn to be magnate of their house again.

The Initiation Rituals ensured the six great houses ruled through the generations and never feared death. Even if a magnate incurred a mortal wound, they always had Body Reachers nearby to heal them before they died. Only a Death Reacher could kill both a person's body and spirit, making it impossible for them to return.

Kasia's existence threatened their glass houses, and they didn't even know it.

"Ah, Katarzyna!" a woman called out in a tone oozing with conceit. Kasia swallowed a groan as Qaraza the Second, the mid-thirties heir of House Uziokaki, strode over with her brows rising impossibly high up her light-gray forehead. She wore a high-collared dress of the Ezmani style with a neckline that was deep enough to make Tazper blush. "I am not alone when I say your attendance tonight is quite the surprise."

"I thought it best I start venturing out more," Kasia replied flatly. "Especially with your father pressing an unfounded claim on my amber, it is ever-so important that I remind the scions in our region that rumors of House Niezik's demise are greatly exaggerated."

Qaraza took a sip of white wine from her glass goblet. "Are they? My father says House Niezik's voice has been all but silent in the Chamber of Scions for a decade. I am pleased to see you managed to dust away the cobwebs coating your carriage. It is quite the antique. As is this *rare* dress of yours. Have you forgotten that dastardly Reshkan is no longer king?"

She referred to King Yaakiin, Leonit's old ally who'd been assassinated not long after Leonit himself. The Commonwealth's scions elected their kings, and often, they preferred to select a weak, influenceable foreigner over a rival house's scion from within the Commonwealth. Yaakiin had been neither effective nor popular during his reign—a fact no one let Kasia forget.

"Of course not," Kasia said. "My dress is of Ogrenian inspiration, not Reshkan, but who could forget how conveniently your family took charge of the southeastern lands following my father's death?"

Kasia scanned the balconies above, where her informant among the Uziokaki servants claimed Parqiz spent the galas as a reclusive nephew of the house patriarch, Sazilz the Second. Then she dropped her gaze to the massive green stone hanging from her counterpart's neck.

"If only that tragedy were as forgettable as that jewel which I dare not call an emerald," she quipped. "Now, if you will excuse me, I must find someone whose conversation will help this storm pass without granting me a similar thunder in my head."

Kasia barely caught Qaraza's disgust out of the corner of her eye as she slipped away, but that moment brought her immense pleasure. One day, Qaraza would take charge of her house and challenge Kasia herself. She was but a nuisance until then, dealt with by nothing more than petty quips.

"Is it proper to insult the host?" Tazper whispered as Kasia weaved her way between round standing tables full of scions, both significant and not. She would do business with many of them another day. Tonight, only one scion mattered.

"Father would not have approved," she replied, glancing at the balconies again. "But I didn't come here to make friends with House Uziokaki."

A quintet of woodwind musicians took to the stage at the far end of the room. They soon filled the air with an upbeat tune, and couples took to the open center of the floor, some out of lasting love and others pursuing new attractions. Kasia's heart ached watching them dance from afar. She'd tried to court many times in past years, but some scars seemed to never heal. When it came to her memories of Aliax, her last lover, they refused to stop bleeding.

*"This won't give you what you want,"* Aliax said, haunting her mind. *"You were always more to me than a matriarch seeking vengeance."*

The distraction tore her from her surveillance, and her wandering led her straight into the path of a gaggle of young men. They donned tailored suits, well-cut with exposed fittings of colored glass along the trim. Jewels were fine and well, but in a realm where glass was one's best protection against the awakened, it was more expensive than many diamonds. Why appear rich when one could appear both rich *and* practical? At least, that's what the scions of more minor houses believed.

The men swapped nervous grins before one stepped forward and removed his tricorn hat. Such a style was odd so far from the sea, especially with its cut favoring that of the northern Ogrenian tradesmen.

"Could I interest you in a dance, Lady Katarzyna?" the man asked. "It would be an honor to spend a moment with the Amber Dame."

Amber had changed everything. Just a few years before, Kasia had struggled to find any house of repute willing to negotiate with House Niezik's barley farms and gambling halls. Now... Well, she would have hardly disliked the attention any other night.

She bowed her head. "Thank you, sir—"

"Hazat, patriarch of House Tozki," he said.

She swallowed, instantly wishing she had a drink to hide her nerves, but she'd sworn off alcohol long ago in an effort to keep her mind fitter than her target's. This was the son of Sergeant Fantil Tozki, the second name on her father's list. Based on Hazat's fashion, though, he appeared to be far less of a nationalist.

"A pleasure to meet you finally," she managed. "I am sorry to hear about your father, however."

He chuckled. "You need not pretend to be sorry. It was no secret that our fathers stood on opposite sides of the Chamber of Scions, and I surely do not miss him."

"Oh?" Kasia barely held back her own laughter. "It would be my pleasure to dance with you, then, but I must abscond to the powder room after our lengthy journey here. I will find you upon my return."

Hazat nodded, then stepped back with an arm extended to the side. "Of course. I will eagerly await your return, then, my lady."

Without replying, Kasia stepped away, recollecting herself. House Tozki was minor, but a dance with its patriarch would still provide cover upon her return, as Parqiz's body would inevitably be found before the gala's end. First, though, she needed to find him.

Tazper tugged on her sleeve. "Kasia, look."

She followed his gaze up to a balcony on the third floor, where a heavy blond man leaned over the wooden rails with a liquor glass in hand. He sneered at the dancers before downing his drink and raising it for a servant to take. When none came, he barked something over his shoulder.

"He isn't alone," Kasia said, starting toward a side hall which her informant had claimed led to the balconies.

"Then this cannot be the time," Tazper said from close behind.

"There is no alternative."

The narrow hall led to a set of stairs. Guards patrolled, but none expressed concern at a stray couple wandering the lower level. How else could the Uziokaki and other scions sneak away for gossip and affairs?

Tazper protested as Kasia ran to the landing, then began up the second flight, but Kasia had none of it.

"I am tired of waiting for answers, Taz," she snapped. "When we reach the balcony, distract the servants by ordering a drink for me. Make it something complex, so I have more time."

"But you do not partake."

"Do you believe the servants know that?"

He shrugged. "Likely not."

"Then do as I ask, *please.*" She tried to say it nicely, but her insistence overrode any pleasantries. Luckily, Tazper wasn't one to take offense.

Hearing no further appeals, she finished climbing the stairs, then found another staircase up to the third floor. A guard gave her a questioning look mid-way, but if he had objections, he did not voice them. Giggles from a hiding couple echoed through the halls. A quiet scion woman going about her business was hardly his greatest concern.

Laughter surrendered to shouting as Kasia reached the third floor. A servant cowered near the balcony Parqiz had been on, shattered glass at his feet.

"He breaks enough glass to feed us for a season," the servant muttered before collecting the sizeable pieces and hurrying toward them.

Kasia grabbed Tazper and ducked behind a pillar, holding her finger to her lips until the servant had passed. When he had, she released her friend and nodded down the stairs. "Remember what I told you about my drink?"

Again, he tried to complain, but she was already gone, noting a cracked door to a bedroom nearby before she reached the balcony's edge. She kept along the wall and didn't step upon the balcony itself. There would be others watching, and it would be difficult to explain if she was the last one seen with Parqiz before he died.

"Now *that* is haste!" Parqiz called over his shoulder. In his mid-forties, he had not taken well to being far from House Uziokaki's center of power. He'd been a lighter, and tamer, man the last time Kasia had seen him over a decade before. "Give it here, boy."

"There is no serving boy here," Kasia said, crossing her arms.

Parqiz turned with a start. "Who are you? A suitor? A consort perhaps, sent by my uncle to keep me sated?"

*Not the tactic I intended, but easy enough to utilize.*

She smiled wryly. "Why don't you follow me and find out?"

As she spun away, she gave him a lingering glance. Leonit had been an adequate politician, but the real skill he'd taught her was using her opponent's perceptions against them. Politics was a game, sure. More so, it was theatre, and the greatest actors were the ones who came out on top.

Parqiz followed her into the nearby bedroom at a speed greater than she'd believed him capable of. She slipped her left glove off, hiding the hand behind her as she playfully danced around him and pulled the door shut.

Then she latched it.

"Oh, so Sazilz did send you?" Parqiz said, undoing his shirt buttons.

She swept her taloned hand toward him. "No, Leonit did…"

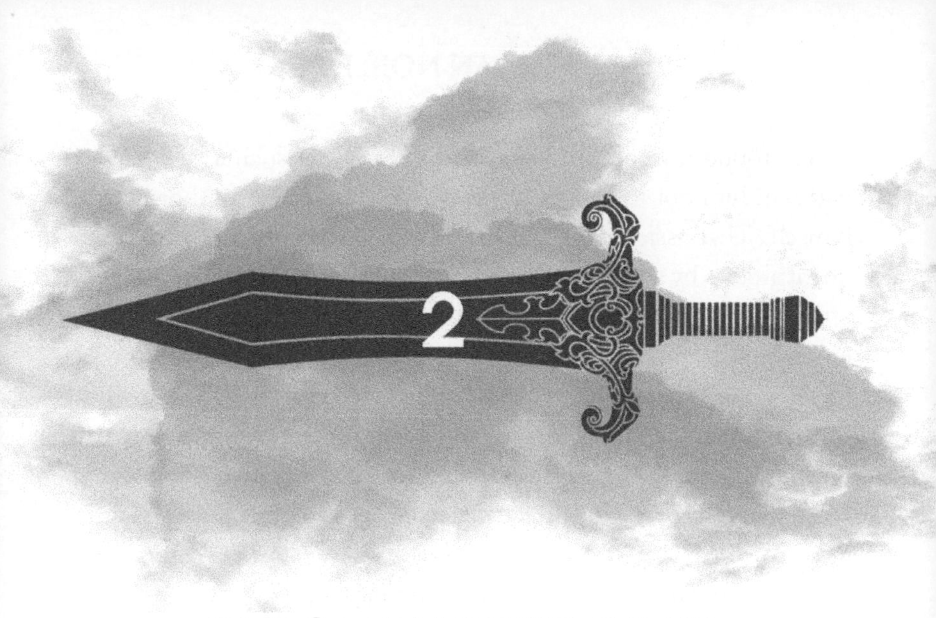


# Red Among the Gray

*"A Glassblade shall never be without his sword. To lose one's armor leaves one vulnerable, but when a defender loses their blade, they become defenseless."* – An excerpt from *The Code of the Glassblades*

The Ephemeral Storm fell heavily upon Radais as he rode tall. Beneath him, his ibex, Vuk, huffed and lowered his horned head, but there was no protection to be found from the chilled rain. They were far from the mountainous protection of Vocka.

"You tired already?" Radais asked, patting his mount's head. With the storm, the quarter-year everdark had come, but the glass upon his gauntlet refracted the light of his lantern into a rainbow across one of Vuk's curved horns.

Vuk gave a goat-like bleat in either response or frustration. Radais knew the animal couldn't understand him, but he swore sometimes it felt as if Vuk truly was trying to have a conversation. Miv, his commander, claimed Glassblades heard all types of things when traveling the Spirit Wastes alone.

*"Solitude is good for the spirit and toxic for the mind, if not moderated,"* she'd said.

He found it ironic that moments after saying such a thing, Miv had sent him out to protect a few villages at the Wastes' border by himself. That assignment had led him to a series of unusually frequent attacks by awakened. With those spirits fleeing into the Wastes after striking at random, Radais had ventured into the seemingly endless sea of deep gray sand to find his marks. It was against protocol to leave the villages undefended, but he needed to understand why these awakened attacks were increasing, and then put a stop to it.

A Glassblade's first responsibility was to protect the innocent from the awakened. As a mercenary order made almost entirely of Vockans from the western mountains of the Commonwealth, they worshiped untainted spirits, those the Ezmani called drifters for their harmless wandering through the air.

Awakened were far less docile. The Ezmani scions considered them nuisances, but the Vockans believed them to be an affront to the purity of the Spirit Crystal itself.

"Alright, alright," Radais muttered to Vuk, removing his helmet of finely crafted glass and allowing his wavy, Vockan-red hair to fall over his shoulders. "We'll rest for a while, but the storm won't pass for a few days."

It had been nearly twenty days since he'd left the village of Iliafa in search of awakened. He'd believed he would easily find where the spirits were hiding before the Ephemeral Storms began, but the traces of spirit dust only led further into the Wastes with each passing hour.

In truth, he didn't know what he was doing anymore. His father was dying back home in Erienfar—and there were plenty of people to protect back in his assigned villages—but he refused to surrender his search. At the age of thirty-five, he'd been recently inducted as the youngest master within the Glassblade Order, and he had immense freedom to pick his targets. An itch at the center of his back told him he was going the right way. His instincts had never failed before… at least with spirits.

Slowing Vuk, he dismounted and set camp. Vockans had bred ibexes for hundreds of years to be rideable up the steep slopes of their lands, but Radais had found Vuk just as formidable as a horse on level terrain. They had traveled across half of Vocka and the Wastes together over the last decade, and Vuk had never wavered.

Radais's tent was a tiny thing made of wood and leather, backed with bits of glass. It was formidable, but the downpour had the sand soaked. Within minutes of him removing his armor and lying down, his bedroll was already wet. He could tolerate the dampness of recent nights, but this was too much.

"Why did I do this?" he mumbled to himself as he sat up, grabbing his sketchbook and charcoal from his bag. "Dalnus or Kalastok have enough rich scions to hire artists, but no, I had to venture into the uninhabitable wasteland."

He scratched his bearded chin before flexing his fingers, grateful to be free of his gauntlets. The lanternlight exposed cracks in his dark skin. The valleys between his fingers looked like war zones, but he was far from any potions, salves, or Body Reachers to mend such minor ailments.

Survival mattered to a Glassblade, not comfort. Theirs was the work of warriors so that others could sleep through the night.

With a sigh, he took long strokes across the page. His book was filled with pages of the mists that usually covered the Spirit Wastes, but the wind had scattered much of it in recent days. He'd caught glimpses of distant mountains to the northwest before the everdark, not on any map, and he sketched them with a longing for home. Like towers, they broke through the rain and pierced the clouds in his mind. Maybe they hadn't looked like that in reality, but what was art if it only portrayed what *was* instead of something greater?

Radais sketched mountain after mountain for what felt like an eternity until Vuk bleated from outside. The ibex's hoofs stomped hard into the sand as he backed away from the tent, and Radais unsheathed his glass sword before rushing out to see what was the matter.

Rain stung against his shirt, only thick enough to stop the edges of his armor from scratching his skin, and the everdark fell heavy over the land. Though he raised his lantern, the storm obscured his sight of anything much further than the edge of his camp.

"What is it?" he asked Vuk, trying to follow the ibex's gaze. "What spooked you, boy?"

But Vuk just backed away further as he stared at something ahead. That had Radais's heart racing. Glassblade ibexes were trained not to spook at the sight of spirits, awakened or not, and Vuk had certainly never done so before.

He grabbed Vuk's halter and pulled him back to the tent, keeping his sword ready. Its glass was so thin that it was nearly translucent at the right angle, and it would shatter upon impact with any human defense. Against a spirit, though, it was the greatest weapon one could have.

"Stay here. I'll go investigate."

Vuk pawed at the wet earth as Radais crept forward. Awakened were quiet things, and with the wind whipping past his ears, he couldn't hear anything out of the ordinary. Not that anything in the Wastes was ordinary. It was said to be the home of the spirits since long before the Awakening, and no one knew why its ground refused to sustain life.

A man yelled from ahead. Not one of rage, but terror.

Radais burst after it. With the storm, it was difficult to tell how far it had come from, but he was quick. By the time the man cried out again, Radais was nearly upon him. He immediately wished he wasn't.

Eight awakened swarmed a man robed in red, their wispy tendrils drawing his spirit from his body. They were distracted by the man, but Radais lacked his armor. Though his glass sword could cut them down easily, attacking alone and unarmored was suicide. He could only grit his teeth and watch the man suffer his horrible fate.

*I need to leave.*

The realization struck him like an ibex at full charge. Awakened needed to feed on spirit energy to live, and this man was the only living target for a hundred miles. Except for Radais.

He bolted toward Vuk as the closest awakened turned its misty form. It could only devour a share of this man, but none of its allies had attacked Radais. So it chased after him far faster than he could stumble through the sand.

Radais lashed out at the last second, slicing his blade through the spirit's scattered form. Neither iron nor steel could pierce a spirit, but glass shredded its very being. The awakened shrieked as it dissolved into nothing more than a faint silvery dust. One spirit was simple, but based on the hissing back near the body, the others had heard.

Radais whistled for Vuk and leaped onto his ibex's back as it approached at speed. There was no time to collect his tent. He'd have to circle back once the awakened had dispersed. For now, escaping was all that mattered.

The wind carried strange noises as he pushed Vuk into a gallop. They sounded almost like words in a whispery language he couldn't understand. Awakened couldn't speak, yet the sound grew as the fastest ones closed in. They flanked him instead of making a direct chase, rounding him to the east and blocking his escape. When another strayed too near, he slashed at it, but could only send it reeling away.

The chase continued for a long time, but ended quickly. One moment, the awakened were diving at him, and the next, they veered overhead, flying into the distance without so much as a passing strike.

Radais slowed Vuk and watched the awakened go, catching his breath as he wrapped his head around what had happened. None of it was normal. He had strayed far into the Wastes, so there shouldn't have been anyone near. Who was that man the awakened had killed? Why had they attacked tactically instead of seeking to devour Radais with their usual greed?

He shook his head, suddenly aware of the rain that fell cold upon his head and shoulders. Answers would only come from a further inspection of the man. Miv would want him to bring the body back to seek an identification. The Commonwealth, Ogrenia, and other nations had sought to venture into the Wastes before, but they had been grand, announced expeditions. None had done so for nearly a decade.

He shuddered at the countless things this could mean. Politics was not his path, but if someone was secretly sending expeditions, this discovery would send shockwaves across the continent of Brakesh.

Vuk let out a deep breath as Radais pushed him back toward their camp and the place the man had died. It took longer than he expected for his tent to appear in the distance. They had galloped for some time away from the awakened, and he didn't know how long they had chased him for. In the end, it didn't matter. He had survived to tell the tale.

Radais armored up and packed the tent into the bags strapped to Vuk's side. More awakened could be lurking, and he had no intention of facing them unprepared again.

A Glassblade's armor cost more than a hamlet of peasants made in their lifetime, but it was worth every kena the Order spent to craft and maintain it for their soldiers. His set had saved his life more than once. Likely, it would do so again, if not sooner than he hoped.

The patter of the rain against the sand surrounded him as he rode Vuk slowly in the direction the red-robed man. He raised his lantern and kept his sword at the ready, but no awakened stirred. Nor did he hear the voices from before.

Then the red appeared ahead. The man lay still, drained of his spirit. Not dead, but empty. It was a terrible fate, as the mind lingered without a spirit to direct it. A killing blow was considered a mercy for such victims, and Radais delivered it swiftly, driving an iron dagger through the man's head. Once he'd cleaned up the blood, he threw the man behind his saddle and began his journey to Palmia Fortress.

*Spirits have mercy.*

# THE STAG'S RAT

*"Find the Crimson Court. Find those who killed me."* – Leonit Niezik, former patriarch of House Niezik

Parqiz Uziokaki's fingers trembled against his shirt buttons as he gawked at Kasia. "You are her," he stammered. "How… How did you know I would be here?"

"I didn't understand at first why your servants would so willingly give me information about you," Kasia replied, forcing her foe toward a wardrobe on the far side of the bedroom with her taloned hand extended before her.

She didn't Reach, not yet. The power would fade quickly if unused, and Reaching too often in a short period would inflict her with increasingly worse Realm Taint, draining from within herself the essence that she pulled from her realm. The Taint's cost was clear for realms such as Fire or Water, which would take the Reacher's heat or make them infinitely parched if they pushed too far. But as a banned realm, Death's Taint was less researched.

"It makes sense now," she said. "A fat, drunken fool like you is too much of a coward to face his own family's guests, let alone reveal himself to those he slaughtered."

"What are you—"

"Do not speak!" She shoved him into the wardrobe and grabbed his throat. Her talon dug into his skin as the stench of alcohol and body odor washed over her, and she grinned knowing it would only take a single Reach to rid Zekiaz of him. "You commanded the awakened. My father knew it, and so do I. You assassinated him."

Parqiz curled his lip. "You cannot kill me. Sazilz will destroy what remains of your pathetic house once his Body Reachers heal me!"

Her smile only grew. "Do you see my talon? Can you guess what realm it binds me to? Possibility? Force? Or is it Death?"

"Bah! No one Reaches Death."

"Would you like to test that hypothesis?" She squeezed tighter, but his neck was too thick to choke with a single hand. "Or are you going to answer my questions?"

He studied her for a few long moments. Even if she were lying, Leonit had trained his daughter well in the art. House Niezik was known primarily for its barley, but its true profits lay in its gambling halls. Kasia had studied well, and whether it was cards, dice, or negotiations, she'd yet to find someone who could tell when she was bluffing and when she had a full hand.

Kasia's patience soon ran out. She punched Parqiz in the gut, then slammed him against the wardrobe again. "What do you know about the Crimson Court?"

"I have never heard of such a group," Parqiz mumbled. "I swear it upon my mother's spirit."

"Then who told you to kill my father? You are far too lowly to assassinate the minister of glass by yourself."

His sneer returned, but Kasia's glare turned it to fear. "Sazilz demanded I do it! He gave me an awakened trapped in a glass prison, claiming that it could be commanded for long enough to kill Leonit. Our houses have been rivals for generations, so I did not question him further. All of Ezman is better for he and Yaakiin's deaths. They preferred us to become a runt state rather than a proud nation that fought for its lands."

"You don't regret it?" Kasia's fury burned within her chest. Though she tried to hold it back, Parqiz had insulted her father's honor after he'd killed him without the courage to look him in the eye.

"Why would I? He was a disgrace, just like his spawn."

She yelled and raked her talon across his neck, deep purple wisps trailing blood as she Reached. The vapors poured into the wound. Purple banished red, spreading through Parqiz's veins as he staggered, gasping for air.

Kasia finally had her revenge.

But a cold sweat struck her as she watched death take her father's killer. Memories flashed through her mind. A young man clung to her as those same vapors spewed from his mouth, the whites of his eyes turning scarlet as his body spasmed. Aliax called her name with his final breaths, but there was no saving one stricken with Death's power. Tears raced down her cheeks. They could do nothing to mend the brokenness she'd caused, and a scar opened in her heart as Aliax felt limp. Gone forever because of her.

Reality pulled Kasia back as she stumbled into the bedpost and held it to keep from falling. Parqiz lay still. His mouth foamed and blood seeped from the wound upon his neck, but both his body and spirit had succumbed to her Reaching.

The final target on her list was dead. Yet she felt empty.

*"I told you this wouldn't change the past,"* Aliax said in her mind. *"Killing the Crimsons won't bring Leonit back."*

"Shut up!" she spat, gripping her head. "I have to stop them! It was Father's last wish."

A quick knock came from the door. "Kasia, we need to leave," Tazper whispered from the other side.

Kasia pushed back her hair, knocking part of it free from one of the braids wrapping around her head. She reminded herself where she was and the danger she faced. There was no time for memories or regrets. Sazilz, a great house magnate, had ordered her father's death. She'd figure out what that meant when she was far from the Uziokaki mansion.

Tazper gave a sigh of relief when she slipped her glove over her talon and met him in the hall, pulling the door shut behind her. He nearly dragged her down the main hall to a side passage just before echoing footsteps reached the top of the nearby stairs. Parqiz was not visible behind the closed door, but it would not be long before someone discovered the body. She needed to be back in the grand hall before that happened.

The footsteps soon faded, so Kasia led Tazper back down the stairs as quickly as she could without appearing suspicious. As the party grew louder, the guards had decided to watch the festivities rather than keep their posts. Their attentions were turned toward the balconies and the dancing beyond, allowing Kasia to slip by unnoticed until she emerged in the grand hall again, searching for Hazat Tozki in hopes of taking him up on his offered dance.

Her heart sunk at the sight of Hazat twirling some scion girl across the dance floor. No others nearby expressed any interest in dancing with Kasia instead, likely out of fear of facing the wrath of House Uziokaki, and she considered leaving until she spotted an elderly man staring at her from the far corner.

"Stay here," she told Tazper, then swept across the grand hall before he could stop her.

The man wore a brown suit of an older cut, his cravat blood red at his throat. His face was wrinkled, and his neck protruded so far forward he resembled a turkey with its feathers puffed. At her approach, the man faked a cough and stepped away from the group he'd been standing with.

"Forgive me, sir," Kasia said with a faked smile. "I could not help but notice your gaze. Would you care for a dance? My father believed one was never too old to partake in life's enjoyments, even if it requires a slower pace."

The man smirked. "A rare truism from a man so focused on foreign nations that he lacked the ability to see what was directly before him. I am Gragoz of House Rakazimko, and it would be a pleasure to forget that Reshkan ass kisser while I dance with his daughter."

Kasia swallowed a dozen insults as he took her arm and led her to the dance floor. Luckily, the band was in the middle of a song, meaning she wouldn't have to spend a full dance with Gragoz. That was good, as he wore such heavy cologne that she could barely breathe, and when they reached the floor, he moved with less grace than anyone she'd ever shared a danced with. It was almost impressive. Kasia had spent enough time with awkward teenagers who tripped over their feet with each spin, yet at least they hadn't made her want to pull herself away out of revulsion.

The dance brought them closer to the center of the floor after a few turns, and she caught Hazat watching her over his partner's shoulder. Was his affection true, or did he lust for her family's wealth, however damaged its reputation? It didn't matter. She had no intentions of courting the son of a man she'd assassinated. It was burden enough to see flashes of her past scars without reopening others.

Despite Kasia's discomfort, she took pride in the gazes their unusually slow dance earned as they missed nearly every beat. The more people who saw her in the grand hall, the less who would consider her a suspect once Parqiz was discovered. Dancing with Hazat wouldn't have drawn such attention.

When the song soon ended, Kasia gave Gragoz a hasty curtsy, then sought a place to avoid further advances. She'd done her part. Now, all she needed to do was wait until guests started leaving so that she could do the same.

Hazat had a different idea.

"Lady Katarzyna," he said, once again removing his tricorn hat as he nearly slid to a stop at her side. "I must apologize that I missed your return. Would you like to—"

"Gather, dear embodied ones of the Crystal Mother!" an exuberant voice carried through the great hall. A priestess stepped onto the band's stage, tasseled robes of deep gray draping around her as she raised her arms. "Let us experience the changing of the seasons as we shift our spirits to follow Her."

Kasia was far from religious, but as a large group of scions grumbled and turned to leave, she'd never been so grateful for a priestess's appearance. A part of her pitied leaving Hazat. In the end, though, one young suitor's opinion was irrelevant, especially with her next target being the patriarch of a great house. It had taken her a year to find an opening to strike at Parqiz. Sazilz Uziokaki the Second would be surrounded by Reacher guards in the capital of Kalastok, and even Death Reaching wouldn't be enough for her if she wasn't careful.

She locked eyes with Tazper and gave a slight nod. "I am sorry, Lord Hazat," she said. "It appears that neither fate nor the Buried Temple wish for us to dance this evening. Perhaps another time."

"Very well." He gave his hat an elegant flip and placed it back on his head. "I shall hope that eve comes with haste."

Once Hazat was gone, Tazper joined Kasia again, and they headed back toward the mansion's entrance along with a few dozen other scions. Time had passed quickly through the night. Kasia's watch read nineteen-thirty, half-an-hour until the end of their realm's twenty-hour day. She'd stayed long enough to have made an adequate appearance at a rival house's mansion.

A tingle ran down her spine as she collected her coat and returned to the mansion's cabin exterior. Were the guards watching her more this time? Had they found Parqiz's body?

She resisted those questions to the best of her ability, straightening her back and keeping a noble smile. It came out crooked, but it was all she had as the storm buffeted her. It was only a hundred strides to her carriage. She could hold her composure until then, counting each step as Tazper glanced over his shoulder.

"Don't do that," she snapped. "Even if we make it out without drawing suspicion, we should not give them any additional reasons to question us afterward."

He took a shuddered breath. "Such as being spotted heading in the direction of his balcony?"

"I said *additional* for a reason."

Neither of the guards at the gate stopped them, and when Kasia's covered carriage appeared in the circular dirt path leading from the main road, she threw herself into it without Tazper's help. Her footman followed, settling across from her with a relieved smile.

"I cannot believe we succeeded," he said.

"I had hoped this would be the end of my search for the Crimsons," Kasia replied, hands held tight in her lap. "Instead, it appears I have been chasing threads in the country, when the true dragon rests in the nation's den."

Tazper furrowed his brow. "My apologies. I don't follow."

"Kalastok, Tazper." She sighed and stared out the small window. Rain streaked down it, obscuring any sight of the Commonwealth's southern forests beyond. "Whoever ordered my father's assassination is in the capital, and if Sazilz Uziokaki is involved, it means the conspiracy runs deep. Even King Jazuk could have had a role in it." She shook her head. "Shit! I thought this would end it."

He leaned forward and rested his elbows on his knees. "Lady Katarzyna, may I speak frankly?"

"Cease with your formalities. We've gone through far too much for you to call me a lady, especially after I assassinated the nephew of a great house's patriarch."

"It is best that you abandon this quest, perhaps?" he insisted, tapering into a question when she glared at him. "You have killed Leonit's assassin. You have done the same to his accomplices in Tystok. House Niezik is regaining its significance through its amber. Why risk the stability you have brought your house and the people you protect? Why not allow the Amber Dame to rise out of her father's shadow?"

Kasia clenched her fist and raised it to her chin. His questions were valid, but he didn't understand what it was like to be hidden away as one's father died mere feet above, what it was like to lose everything. No, she couldn't stop.

"You need not follow me to Kalastok if you fear the risks," she said. "I cannot forget the past to enrich my future."

"And if the Crimsons destroy you in the process?"

She flexed her taloned hand. "Then I will kill as many of them as possible first."

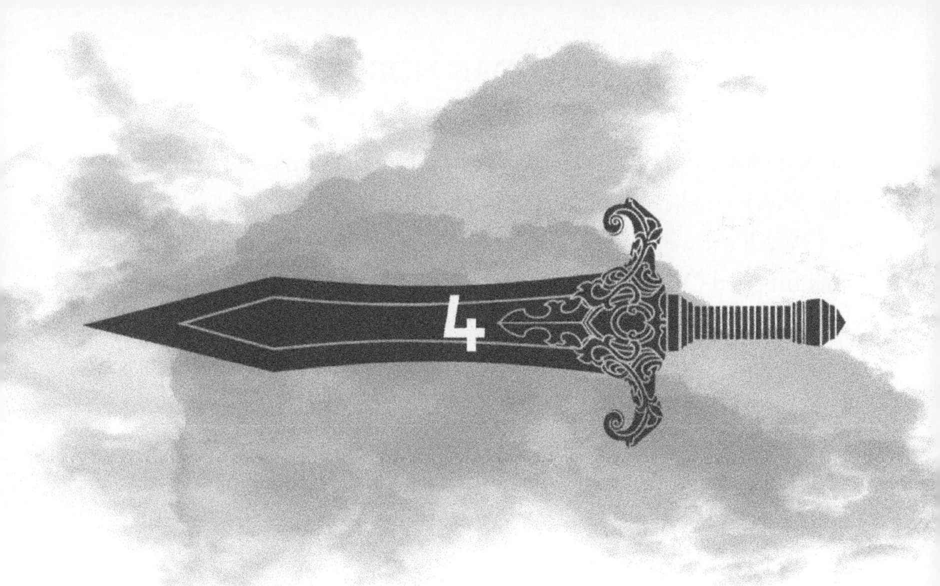


# THE FINAL FORTRESS

*"It is said that the Glassblades saved the living from the awakened at the Siege of Palmia. From upon towers of glass and stone, they slayed spirits of a number lost to time. So too, have we forgotten our saviors of ages past."* – Harianus iz Ramiona, former Vockan general

Radais shifted in his saddle, stretching his arms as he searched the horizon for any sight of home, or at least, what was the closest thing he had to one anymore.

The trek east from the Spirit Wastes had taken him back into the snow-covered Vockan Mountains of his homeland. Even with the southern wind blowing the cold highland air over him, he didn't shiver. He would reach Palmia before he had to make camp again, and thoughts of fires, beer, and a real bed were enough to keep him warm until then.

Lanterns twinkled in the distance as Vuk carried him around the eastern edge of the dark pass. In the everbright, he'd been able to see the western half of the Commonwealth, but now, even Palmia Fortress was only visible because of its glass walls amplifying the lanternlight. With a flat roof of glass-imbued metals stretching over its top, it resembled a cube from this distance. The sight was beautiful nonetheless, and he stopped to sketch it in his book. He exaggerated the fires to make the bastion a blaze amid the darkness.

"We'll eat well tonight," Radais said, patting Vuk's neck when he was finished. "And then I'm going to give both of us much needed baths."

He was no stranger to nose blindness through his travels, but he knew full well that days in the Spirit Wastes left a lingering stench unlike anything else. Another Glassblade had described it as a mix of soot and sorrow. That had once seemed a bit dramatic to Radais, but after returning with a rotting corpse behind him, it was starting to feel all too real.

The man in red's reasons for being so far in the Spirit Wastes lingered on his mind. No explanation made sense. The man had been an Ezmani scion of a great house based on his gray skin, crystal talon, and the glass imbued into his finely woven robes. He'd carried a pistol with a dragon carved down its barrel. King Jazuk had a dragon, but did that mean something about this man? Hopefully Supreme Defender Miv could at least offer some insight into his identity.

Snow gave way to muddied earth as Radais descended toward the fortress. He had taken this route more times than he could count, connecting the fortress to the Spirit Wastes and various settlements at the edges of civilization. After so long, riding it had become a trance in his exhaustion.

The village of Palmia rested at the base of the fortress with two mountains straddling it to either side. It made the position highly defensible but also a pain for anyone who wasn't a Vockan to get to. Luckily, almost every Glassblade was Vockan.

Palmia's dirt paths were still bustling through the homes and shops of deep gray stone, despite the clocktower ringing for midnight. Radais huffed at that. Without a mechanical watch—which only scions or well-off lowborn merchants could afford—he hadn't been able to track the passing of time in the constant darkness. Exhaustion and experience traveling gave him only a rough estimate. Hours meant little to Vockan workers, though, as they'd only accepted Ezmani standards for measurable hours upon their union into the Commonwealth of Two Nations. Still, it was disconcerting not knowing how long he'd truly been gone.

Men and women alike carried tools and drove ibexes that pulled ore from the mines. All gave Radais space.

The only difference between day and night in Vockan villages was the absence of children in the later hours. Adults took shifts at various tasks, but it was the communal responsibility of the village to ensure children were looked after when they woke. That was hard enough with them waking together, so one of the elders traveled through the village at the change of shifts, ringing a bell to tell the children it was time to rise. For now, they rested. Radais envied that sleep.

"Hello there, Glassblade," an elderly man said from upon a wooden stool.

The flames of the forge behind Gargas gave his deep red hair the glow of embers over his shoulders. He fiddled with the hair tie he'd use when he was smithing, then dropped it onto the leather apron in his lap. Radais knew that look well. On nights like this, Gargas had always been willing to tell many a tale whenever Radais was sick of being trapped in the fortress.

Gargas's firm expression shifted to a grin as Radais removed his helmet. "Ah, if it isn't Miv's favorite warrior himself."

"I am a Glassblade master now," Radais replied, pulling his hair free of the ponytail he wore beneath his helm. Relief came with it. The glass helmet protected him against awakened, but it also made it feel as if every strand of hair was being pulled from his head at once.

"Is that right?" The blacksmith chuckled. "They handing out titles like bread to the starving now?"

"I'll never be a true master like you with your hammer, but the Glassblades are far from generous with our titles. Took me twenty years to get mine, and I'm not even a commander." Radais dismounted and stretched his legs. "Have you heard anything I should know before I speak to the supreme defender?"

Gargas mimicked the stretching, revealing his leg of iron below his right knee. Radais had discovered the hard way that Gargas would talk about anything except that accident. "Miv's in a bad mood, like always. Apparently, Keloshan soldiers are mobilizing outside some town in eastern Ezman. Got anyone important wound up tighter than my stomach when the meat's too well cooked."

Radais stiffened. "They're preparing for an invasion? Has the king responded?"

"Think I know? We're as far from Kalastok as you can get without dumping yourself into the Wastes." Gargas groaned and scratched at a scab on his forearm. "Might as well some days with all 'em flying about."

A few drifters circled overhead, their wispy forms like a light gray smoke, but they kept their distance. Even when they didn't, they could do little harm. "What's wrong with a few spirits?" Radais asked. "We need them to ensure children aren't born empty."

The twenty-hour deadline before a newborn became a husk defined the length of a day. Scions could afford Spirit Reachers to ensure a drifter quickly found their child, but most were not so wealthy. Vockans instead placed newborns on their rooftops in hopes a drifter would see the spiritless child and decide to return to life through it. Beside the child, the family left a gift of goat cheese or woven nightjar birds, which were said to fly among the drifters at night, scaring awakened. Radais had only heard tales of lowborn Ezmani practices. From what he'd heard, though, they preferred to keep the child inside a room with no windows or glass so that the spirit would not be frightened. Their gifts were nothing but buried prayers for their so-called Crystal Mother.

"Not them… The awakened. Been more while you've been gone." Gargas nodded to the man slumped over Vuk's back. "He a victim?"

"I found him deeper in the Wastes than anyone has a right to be. I'm surprised nothing got to him sooner. He's…" Radais let his voice trail away. Gargas didn't need to know the man had been a Reacher. With his gossiping, half of the Commonwealth would know by the end of the hundred-hour—a five-day unit used to track time.

Gargas stood, pulling a canteen out of his pocket and taking a swig. "So, you didn't kill him? Shame. Wish you Glassblades would cause some problems instead of solving all of 'em for once. Would make this town a lot less spirit-damned boring."

"Better bored than invaded by Kelosh."

Radais grabbed hold of his reins and pressed in his heels, pushing Vuk onward as Gargas headed back into his smithy. No one else stopped him, but with his helmet off, many gave surprised glances in his direction.

Master Glassblades like him were rare sights in Palmia, as the fortress mainly served as a training camp for initiates and a base for the commanders. Everyone in-between was out protecting various villages in Vockan and western Ezmani lands. It seemed an eternity ago that Miv had led Radais through his initiation, and though his family had all but cast him out for joining the Glassblades, his years in the Order had treated him well.

The walls of glass mixed with stone reached to the sky as Radais reached the bridge headed to the fortress itself. Passing over a gully, it had been designed to be covered in a slippery or flammable liquid ahead of a siege, disrupting the advancing army's surge and forcing them through the gully, where other traps lay hidden. That vulnerability tickled the back of his neck as Glassblade archers peeked out from arrow slits in the wall—the only holes in the entire fortress. They had both glass-tipped and steel-tipped arrows in their quivers, but with his approach, Radais had no doubt which they had nocked.

"I am Master Radais ik Erienfar," he shouted to the archers, stopping before the gate. "Inform Supreme Defender Miv that I have returned and have urgent news from the Spirit Wastes."

"Radais?" a female archer called back. "You know she's going to hate this, right?"

Of course she would. No matter who you were, you simply didn't wake Miv unless you wanted to face her fury, but Radais didn't have a choice. If he'd seen what he was damn sure he had, then she needed to know.

"She'll hate me more when she hears my story," he replied. "But her wrath is mine to endure. Let me in and I'll wake her myself."

The archer shook her head but signaled for them to open the gate. "It's a shame we'll have to handle your corpse along with that one you've got there."

Radais dropped his head as the gate rose to reveal the empty training courtyard. Unlike most Vockans, the Glassblades kept to a regimented schedule when inside the fortress, and there was nothing more than a skeleton crew defending it outside of training periods. The targets and straw dummies lurking about the muddied field made Radais itch to grab his blade. Letting down his guard for a moment in the Spirit Wastes could've meant death against awakened. Safety would take some getting used to.

He headed down a side path, dropping Vuk off at the stables and throwing the corpse over his shoulder. He'd get his things later. One of the first rules of the Order was to never steal another Glassblade's possessions unless through a joke approved by a commander. Those had become much rarer ever since Miv's appointment as supreme defender.

The path led him past the initiate barracks and toward the commanders' chambers. More archers guarded the fortress from the towers in each corner, but the towers themselves were mere remnants of an ancient age, when the fortress had been intended to stop a human siege.

Legends told of the ancient Piorak Empire pouring its remaining funds into Palmia as a place for the Glassblades to make a final stand against the awakened that swarmed the world. They raised the walls to the tips of each tower, building a roof unlike any other castle's so that no awakened could swoop from above. Spirit Reaching to dispel awakened hadn't been fully understood then. No Glassblades were Reachers anyway, as no one of pure Vockan blood could wield the powers granted by the Spirit Crystal. No one knew why that was, but it made their glass walls, armor, and weapons Vocka's only hope, both in the ancient past and now.

Pillars rose throughout the fortress to hold up the roof, but the buildings themselves were no more than two stories. It was a city in itself, dwarfing the population of Palmia at full capacity. If only its barracks were ever full…

Radais soon reached the door to Miv's chambers, huffing from carrying the corpse up the two flights of stairs that climbed the side of the commanders' hall. He considered pounding on the door before thinking better of it. It was unlocked, so he pushed his way into the dark room and threw the corpse onto the stone floor.

Miv snored from her bed, unmoving. Most Glassblades would be aghast at Radais's actions, but he'd spent years training with Miv as his mentor in the day, and bedding her in the greatest nights of his life. Though their relationship had ended poorly, he knew where she hid her dagger.

He crept across the room, keeping to the long rug to muffle his steps. Only a few streaks of lanternlight entered through the window over the bed. Any other intruder would've tripped over her scattered gear, maps, and books, but despite her disorganization, she was a creature of habit. Her armor always ended up heaped in the same spot on the floor, and she'd bought no extra belongings upon her promotion. All was where it had been back in her days as a master Glassblade.

All except the Glass Wings.

Radais's boot struck the symbols of the supreme defender with a *clang* loud enough to wake the heaviest sleeper. He cursed under his breath, expecting what came next.

Miv spun from the bed amid a tangle of sheets, drawing her dagger from beneath the mattress in one sweeping motion. Her curly, bright orange hair flashed through the light from the window, along with her off-white undergarments. Glassblade women didn't wear dresses, but she wouldn't have even if she'd never joined the Order. Some women found power in a gown. Others found it clad in armor.

The tip of her steel blade pressed against his throat but a moment later. He chuckled. Many warriors lost their touch after years of command, but she'd never stopped training. In her heart, she'd always be a fighter, and Radais wished she'd held that same will to fight for him.

"Who are you?" she snapped through the darkness. "You wear our armor, but no Glassblade would step foot in my room unannounced."

"I'm sorry, Miv," he said softly, reaching to guide her arm away. "I knew you'd attack, so I'd hoped to take the dagger first."

She removed the dagger from his throat, then drove her knee into his crotch. "Radais? What the fuck are you doing here? And *what is that smell*?"

He staggered and fell to a knee, winded. "I likely deserved that." Coughing, he returned his gaze to her. "I found a man deep in the Wastes. Awakened swarmed him before I could get there, but I brought him back."

"You brought a corpse into my bedroom?" She scoffed. "Always the romantic."

"He's a scion, a Reacher of some kind."

She fell silent, pacing across the room to strike a match, which she used to light a lantern over her desk. Scrawled notes covered the papers upon it, but Radais couldn't catch a glimpse of what her panic was about.

"Any idea who he is?" she asked, arms crossed. She'd turned forty in Radais's absence, her red eyes heavier than when he'd seen her last. Still, they burned bright against her dark skin.

Radais shook his head. "I'd hoped you would."

"You dump a body on my floor and expect me to know who he is?" She crouched and examined the body's face, then his talon. "He carrying anything?"

"Just a pistol." Radais held it out for her to take, and her eyes widened as she ran her fingers along its barrel.

"Shit."

"What?"

She stood, lips pursed as she leaned against her desk with her neck craned. "It's an Oliezany pistol."

"The great house?" Radais eyed the dragon carving. "You can tell that from just looking at it?"

"They've got the best gunsmiths in the whole Commonwealth, and I doubt anyone else could make this." Miv shook her head. "What were you even doing out there? You were supposed to be helping the villages around Mount Lakinan. Iliafa's mayor will have my head."

"I was." He pulled out his drawings of the awakened the villagers had described, tossing them onto the desk. "There were constant attacks against the villages. More than I could handle. So, I decided to do something about it."

"Walking into the Wastes alone is an initiate's folly, not a master's plan."

Radais locked his hands before him, nose wrinkled. "Would you rather me send for reinforcements next time, Supreme Defender?"

"Spirits help me…" She snatched the first drawing and held it in the light. "Cut the bullshit. We've known each other far too long for you to play that game with me. Where did you discover the scion, and did you figure out what he was doing?"

He scanned the floor for a map of the known sections of the Spirit Wastes, pointed out the approximate spot. "It was hard to tell with the Ephemeral Storms, but it was somewhere just southwest of the old Ogrenian camp, north of New Frontier." Both Ogrenia and the Commonwealth's attempts to settle the deep Wastes had been failures, leaving spirit towns behind.

"You went that far by yourself?"

"Yes, but I have Glassblade armor. This man had only his robes and a pistol. No food and no water." Radais looked back toward Miv. "You know what that means?"

"He wasn't alone." Miv tapped her foot, eyeing the pistol. "What in the realms was House Oliezany doing that deep in the Wastes?"

They pondered that in silence until Miv groaned and yanked open a drawer, grabbing a sheet of parchment. Her quill scratched furiously against the paper as Radais approached.

"What are you doing?" he asked.

"Writing a letter to our allies in Kalastok. The government needs to know about this, but most Ezmani scions won't listen to us."

"Who, then?"

She stopped for a moment, taking a deep sigh. "Ivalat iz Ardinvil. His wife is King Jazuk's daughter, and his is the last great house that hasn't *completely* forgotten about us."

Radais recalled what little he knew about house politics in the Commonwealth. The Vockan scions—marked in their surname by *iz* and the city they were from instead of the lowborn *ik*—had all but ignored actual Vockan interests in return for marrying into scion bloodlines and gaining the ability to Reach. While the Glassblades had dwindled in the past century without Commonwealth aid, the Vockan scions had sat back and prospered.

"Why do you think they'll listen to us now?" he asked. "You've petitioned them dozens of times."

"Because no one else will. The Glassblades have been claiming the awakened will return in force for too long, and every king in-turn has grown sick of our pleas." She finished the letter, then folded it and stamped it with her seal. "No one else can read this."

He took it, rubbing his thumb over the seal. Maybe he'd be supreme defender someday, or someone more than a wanderer, fighting ghosts in the middle of nowhere. "Why? Don't we want everyone to know?"

"Politics is complicated. I've learned that the hard way." She paused. "There's more to this than just one scion, but I don't know what yet. Your villages aren't the only ones reporting increased awakened activity, and now with this disease—"

"What disease?" Radais interrupted. "I haven't heard anything about it."

Miv groaned and ran her hands through her mangled mess of hair. "It's too damn early for this! There's this Vockan professor at the College of Kalastok, Professor Etal iz Noshok. He discovered a disease called the Spirit Plague is spreading throughout Vockan and western Ezmani villages. It eats at the connection between people's bodies and souls, killing them slowly until their spirit splits from their body and becomes an awakened."

Radais wavered, stumbling back onto the bed. This was a nightmare. Glassblades spent their whole lives fighting awakened, but if ones could simply form from diseased people… "Can we stop it?"

"Apparently not."

"Then it's happening again?" he asked. "A Second Awakening?"

"The empires of the world have Spirit Reachers now. If the worst comes, which is far from a certainty, it will be different."

Radais scratched his stubbled chin. Spirits, he needed a trim, a bath, and a stiff drink. "I take this letter to Kalastok, and then what? They question House Oliezany about a scion found in the Wastes? What does that give us?"

"It turns those selfish pricks' attentions back to the real threat. If House Oliezany has people that deep in the Wastes, then they're up to something. I doubt it's a coincidence that this Spirit Plague showed up at the same time."

He shook his head. "Send someone else. I'm just a man with a blade, and at times, I barely deserve that. You want someone else in Kalastok."

"You're wrong. This was your discovery, and there are few people I trust more to handle this." Miv shot to her feet and threw on her commander's jacket, its glass epaulets rattling upon her shoulders as she dusted it off. "You've given me a lot of work, but thanks, Radais. Never thought I'd be happy to see you in my bedroom again."

"We could fix things between us," he replied with half a smile. "I'm not that initiate with his head in the clouds anymore."

"No." She nodded toward the desk. "There's a letter there from your brother that arrived a couple hundred-hours back. Didn't open it, because unlike you, I understand the concept of privacy. Once you're done with it, wash up, get some rest, get that damn corpse out of my room, and stop by the quartermaster for some decent attire before you leave. I won't have you representing me by smelling worse than the dead."

Before Radais could defend himself, she threw open the door and trudged outside, shouting for someone to wake the other commanders. He watched her go with a pang in his heart. Yes, their relationship had been years ago, but his time on the move had made it impossible to find anything stable since. And neither man nor woman could entangle his heart like her. He considered sketching her from the picture dawdling in his mind, her unruly hair radiant in the lanternlight and her scowl as sharp as a dragon's claw. The letter pulled his thoughts elsewhere.

He shuffled through the papers on the desk until he found the letter addressed to him. His hands shook, and he sat again, dreading what lay inside.

Markarial, his older brother, hadn't sent him a letter in the twenty years since he'd left home. Radais had visited his family in Erienfar when he'd found time, but that had not been often in recent years. If Markarial was writing now, it had to be because of their father. He'd been ill with a condition the spirit shamans claimed would slowly take over until nothing remained of his mind. Had the time finally come?

"Spirits have mercy," he whispered, sliding his finger across the seal and pulling out a single piece of paper.

*Radais of the Glassblades,*

*Jajia and I have cared for Father as long as possible, but I fear his time will soon come to rejoin the spirits. Come with a Reacher capable of helping him, or do not come at all. You are not wanted when we hold the funeral.*

*Markarial ik Erienfar*

Radais swallowed as tears welled in his eyes. Every decision he'd ever made ran through his head. The fear he'd felt when he left home in pursuit of something more with the Glassblades, the weight that lifted off his shoulders the moment he stepped foot in Palmia Fortress, and heartbreak when he'd returned home, only for his father not to recognize his second son. All of it hit him like a punch to the gut. Markarial had refused to call him his brother or even an ik Erienfar in the letter, and he'd signed it with his formal name—salt in a wound that had festered for decades.

He dropped the letter, picking up the one Miv had given him instead. Kalastok had more Reachers than anywhere else in the Commonwealth. There had to be a Body or Mind Reacher capable of helping his father, and if he brought one home, maybe he could earn his family's forgiveness for leaving. It was a distant hope, but one he clung to nonetheless.

"I'm coming, Father," he said to the lantern, refusing to look away from the light as his eyes throbbed. "I will do my duty to the Order, and then I'll find the money to hire a Reacher. You'll be whole again. I promise."

# THE FALLEN HOUSE

*"People whisper of what happens within the walls of the Niezik mansion. We have seen much of the Amber Dame, but what of her mother? One must question how severely Leonit's death has broken the once great house."* – Yoxan Kiutok, The Ty River Herald

"It is a shame you must go away, Mistress Katarzyna," Uliusa said as she folded yet another of Kasia's dresses into a leather suitcase, the nearby lantern casting a shadow over half her wrinkled face. "Your mother needs you here, as do we all."

Kasia sighed from her seat before the vanity, where her handmaiden, Kikania, was finishing a thin braid around her head. She leaned forward and stared into the mirror. It was the only one she owned and likely one of two in all of Tystok—her mother's being the other—as few people could afford glass for protection against awakened, let alone use it for looking at their reflection. Strands of silver hair hung down to frame her face in a way Kikania claimed was stern without losing her "natural beauty." Though Kasia despised being told there was a better way for her to look, she couldn't question the results of Kikania's idea.

"Mother has never needed me," she said, continuing to stare. Men and women alike had described her eyes as a blue-gray, like clouds parting in the everbright sky, but all she saw was two dark voids. "She will be fine, and Gregorzon can handle business while I am in Kalastok… maybe. It doesn't matter. What choice do I have?"

Uliusa muttered something under her breath before closing the suitcase—one of many—and rounding the bed to Kasia. "You have sought to avenge your father since before you knew what it was to lust after a boy or to pursue any of life's many pleasures, my dear. Because of you, his assassin will never see the everbright again."

Kasia shot to her feet, leaving her hair half-braided, and rubbed the scar on her left forearm. Her younger brother, Gregorzon, had burned her years ago when he'd become a Fire Reacher. It had been the last time she dared trust him, but leaving him in charge of the house was her only choice with their mother all but infirm ever since Leonit's death.

"Do you blame the bullet, the gun, the one who pulls the trigger, or the one who hired the assassin?" Kasia asked, hand still gripping that old wound.

Uliusa groaned. "You should not waste your life on this."

"My life is already wasted! Since I became matriarch, I've spent every moment trying to regain some semblance of what we lost. Even amber wasn't enough."

"My lady," Kikania said, head bowed, "you are revered among the peasantry for discovering that amber. There are more jobs than ever, and they pay enough to allow lowborn some luxuries."

Kasia's rage waned. "Is it enough?"

"We are peasants. We make do with what we have. Every bit more allows for more comfort." Kikania looked down at her hands. "At least people aren't starving anymore, as they were in the aftermath of Leonit's death."

"Stay," Uliusa said. "Do not go to that hateful city and spoil yourself on those bickering scions in the Chamber. Politics killed your father. I shan't watch it do the same to you."

Kasia shook her head, then paced over to her writing desk and snatched her father's note. "*The Crimsons* killed my father. Sazilz Uziokaki forced Parqiz to do it, and if the patriarch of a great house was involved, he certainly wasn't alone. Yes, this is about revenge, but it is about finding the truth too. Father's assassination was part of a quiet coup that put Jazuk Bartol on the throne. I need to prove it."

"Very well." Uliusa bowed. "Your bags are packed. Shall I call Tazper to bring them to the carriage?"

"That's it?"

The nurse frowned. "I have known you since you were a mere babe, Kasia. By now, I have learned when you are too stubborn to convince. Go to Kalastok if you wish, but you must cut your informal speech before you arrive. The scions of the court will tear you apart if you are unprepared."

"I can contend with them."

"Your father thought the same." Uliusa approached, laying a hand on Kasia's cheek. "Please, be careful. You may have not felt your mother's love in this home, but many of us do love you. I could not bear losing you."

Kasia tried to catch her hand, but Uliusa was gone swifter than the old woman should've been able to move. She slammed the wooden door behind her, and Kasia bit her cheek as the sound echoed through the room. She hated saying goodbye to Uliusa like that. The nurse had been like her mother for years, her opinion meaning far more than that of Kasia's actual mother. But on this, Uliusa was wrong. Kasia had to go to Kalastok and face Sazilz for ordering her father's murder. It was not a waste.

"Um..." Kikania stuttered. "Lady Kasia, may I finish your braid quickly before we leave? It is dangling like a wet fish."

Kasia chuckled at the rare joke from her handmaiden. "That would give them all the more reason to accuse me of following in my Reshkan-loving father's footsteps. Fine, I'll sit."

She closed her eyes while Kikania finished her work, pondering the news that the Keloshan Empire had mobilized outside the eastern village of Rexaniv. Kalastok would be in a hell of a fuss when she arrived. International affairs weren't usually her business, but the possibility of a full-scale war had her bouncing her leg so much that Kikania insisted she sit still for a moment longer.

Kasia couldn't help it. The surrounding empires had cut the Commonwealth in half through the three Reduction Treaties, and if any of them decided they'd had enough of the Ezmani and Vockans being independent, there would be little her castrated nation could do to stop them.

"There," Kikania said, stepping back. "You look as gorgeous as a princess and as deadly as that talon of yours makes you."

Kasia examined her crystal talon, shades of gray swirling through it. She'd been a Reacher for almost ten years now, but it still mystified her. Researchers had concluded the Spirit Crystal's essence allowed Reachers to literally pull powers from other realms in exchange for essence from one's own self, which fascinated and frightened her all at once. Their realm, known as Zekiaz, was the Spirit realm, so were people in other realms Reaching into her world to call spirits?

The thought gave her a headache, so she pushed herself to her feet and smiled at Kikania. "You never fail. Are you packed as well?"

Kikania nodded.

"Then go ahead to the carriage. There are a few things I need to retrieve before I go, and I should say goodbye to my mother and Gregorzon."

Her handmaiden departed, only for Tazper to step immediately into the room. "Uliusa informed me you are ready for me to bring your bags down. She was in quite the mood."

Kasia gritted her teeth. "I don't want to discuss it."

"Very well." Tazper grabbed the first two bags in sight, but set one down a moment later, wincing. "Did you pack dresses in here or perhaps the entire amber reserve?"

"I have enough amber to suit my purposes, and it is hardly the heaviest of jewels. Should I help, or can you manage on your own?"

He wiped away a bead of sweat. "Go on and give your parting words to Lady Yazia. Her temper this morning makes Uliusa look like a gentle drifter."

*Wonderful…*

Kasia took one last look in the mirror and straightened her simple traveling gown before heading into the hall with a parting word, reminding Tazper to bring the mirror along. She'd be traveling for days, so her appearance shouldn't have been all that important. For now, though, she had to deal with her mother and the gazes of the peasants outside who'd come to bid her farewell.

The hallways of the mansion's second floor were sparsely populated. Kasia remembered the days when servants and visitors had bustled about all day and much of the night, the wooden floors creaking from the commotion and dozens of conversations whistling through the air.

She'd overheard many tales with her ear pressed up against the door or wall. Scandalous gossip from Kalastok and other cities, negotiations continued during casual walks to the balconies, and the noises from the other bedrooms that no one thought she'd hear. That seemed a distant past now. Most of the rooms lay vacant or used only for storage, and her family had no need of so many servants when only three scions of House Niezik lived in the mansion anymore.

Her fingers met the glass railing out of instinct when she neared the open room surrounding the stairs. A multitude of colors swirled through the spiraled banisters that Leonit had installed during the height of his wealth. Kasia grinned at the memory of picking out each color with her father, how she'd stare during the dawnrise and everbright seasons as the skylights above made the glass glimmer like diamonds. They were beautiful even in the everdark, with only lanternlight to give them a dull glow.

She stayed there a moment with her memories, gripping the cold railing. Her mother's room was across the stairs from her, and Yazia's crazed shouts echoed across the high pyramid ceiling. Kasia had to say farewell, but part of her wished to skip duty and go on her way. Her heart just hoped her mother would be sad to see her go.

The shouting stopped when she knocked at the bedroom door. "Mother?" she asked. "May I come in? I wanted to bid you farewell before I left."

"Who is it?" she heard Yazia hiss at her servant. "Is it that woman again?"

"Mother, it's your daughter, Kasia."

"Oh, so Katarzyna has come! She is too ashamed of her given name to be called it, so she shortens it to another. *Kasia*! Pitiful girl!"

Kasia clenched her fists so hard her talon bit into her palm. She didn't care as she threw open the door without asking for permission again. The sweet, middle-aged servant greeted her, expressing her concern about Yazia's ever-deteriorating condition, but Kasia just patted her on the arm. "You have dealt with her enough for the moment. Take an earned rest. My mother will not regain her sanity in the time you are away."

The servant held her arm back, and Kasia flinched at the touch against her burn scar. "May the Crystal Mother bless you, Lady Katarzyna."

Despite her lack of belief, Kasia nodded at the gesture before continuing into the dark room beyond. Artwork from the most famous Ezmani artists covered the wall, surrounded by fake golden frames. They had been real once, but paint peeled off the frames now and the portraits no longer held their sheen.

Yazia lay on the massive poster bed, staring at the portrait of their family that Leonit had commissioned just hundred-hours before his death. It hung askew over a dresser, so Kasia went to adjust it.

"STOP!"

Her mother's voice came like a nightjay's shriek. It rung in her ears as she fixed the portrait anyway, but Yazia continued to demand she stop until she released it. In Kasia's rush, she had left it still a bit off center, but she didn't bother to touch it again. Obviously, her mother had no desire for her help.

"I am leaving for Kalastok, Mother," she said, biting her lip out of nervous habit. "Whoever ordered Father's assassination is there, and I am going to find them."

She raised her head to meet Yazia's gaze. Her mother's eyes were sunken, her pupils wide like obsidian, reflecting the dim lanternlight. Leonit had told Kasia many times that she held her mother's beauty, but she saw nothing beautiful about the woman before her. Not now, not then. Though they shared small ears and strong cheekbones, Kasia believed she looked nothing like Yazia. After all, one could wear the same clothes as another and bear no resemblance. Why would this be any different?

"You run!" Yazia stammered. "Leave your darling brother to do your work while you dance with the elites in the capital. You killed your father to take his place, and now you cannot bear his burdens."

"I have told you a thousand times," Kasia snapped. "I didn't kill him!"

"Yet you bear Death upon your finger like a wife bears her ring. You always flee, Katarzyna, because you know you will fail. Aliax knew, so you killed him. What did your father know?"

Kasia trembled, her entire body rigid as she glared down at the woman who'd despised her from birth. Images of a young brown-haired man flashed before her, his eyes bleeding as he whispered his love for her. *Aliax…* She closed her eyes and tried to force away the heartache that followed, but it never worked. Six years hadn't changed a thing.

"Why do you hate me?" she whispered to her mother. "Why did you never give me a chance?"

But no reply came. Yazia's infirmity had returned, emptying her mind between fits of rage. She'd never been the same since Leonit's death, and though doctors claimed she would eventually recover as the grief faded, Kasia had lost any hope of that long ago.

With a look toward the ground, Kasia muttered a half-hearted prayer for the Crystal Mother to carry Yazia on. She didn't believe in the goddess the priests of the Buried Temple called the Crystal Mother, but proof of the Crystal's power was wrapped around her hand. It was better for all their sakes if Yazia passed soon.

She fled the room.

*Maybe I do run from everything, Mother,* she thought as she rushed down the stairs and toward the study, *but you ran from life when it got hard. You ran from us.*

Gregorzon was lounging on the sofa when she barged into the room. He'd been playing with an Ogrenian toy made of swinging magnetic rocks, but he scrambled to put it down at the sight of her.

"I thought you hated everything from those 'smelly northern sailors,' " Kasia quipped, snatching the toy and putting it on her father's old desk—now hers. "What? Do your nationalist friends not have fancy gadgets?"

He rolled his eyes, then tugged on his vest as he stood. It was a deep gray, and he wore it unbuttoned to reveal a similarly dull shirt beneath, its collar puffed like his cheeks when he was frustrated—all the time around Kasia. She hated how much he looked like her. The same narrow eyes. The same uncomfortably gaunt torso and ghostly long arms. And the same stupid upper lip that was too big for its own right.

"You do know that the national-conservative coalition has a majority of the Chamber, right?" he asked, hands stuck in his pockets. "Nothing happens in Kalastok without our approval."

"*Our* approval?" Kasia shot him a glare as she grabbed various notes from her desk. "It is a good thing, then, that you lack the two-thirds majority to pass any laws without approval from the other factions." She raised a sheet on the voting habits of the various members of the Chamber. "I did my research too, Brother. I hope you have been paying as much attention to the family businesses as you have to politics, because I will not tolerate you burning down everything I have built."

His lip curled. "Take that back."

"Some things can never be undone." She pulled up her sleeve to expose the gruesome pinkish markings stretching across her left forearm, but he looked away. "Did you know that it still hurts sometimes? I'll wake with flashes of burning, but nothing stops the pain."

"I told you I was sorry."

"After you told Mother that I tricked you into Reaching."

"Do you know what she would have done if I told her the truth?"

Kasia slammed her fist into the table. "I lived it! Whatever icy relationship we had shattered because of you. Now she scorns me for trying to find the person who ordered our father's death."

"I wished often that you had fallen to the awakened instead of him," Gregorzon replied. "I would apologize, but Father once told me that 'one cannot apologize for their childish dreams, no matter how foolish.' Though a swindler, he was right about that."

"Can you do the job while I'm gone?"

"The answer to a vague question like that has to be no, because if you are asking, it means you do not trust me."

Kasia sighed. "I know I can't trust you. I'm asking if you can do the job."

He approached the desk and ran a finger along the scattered books strewn across it. "Are you certain I will not do better than you, that you will not return to find peasants who wish me to replace you permanently?"

"Try."

She slipped a key into the third drawer on the left, opening it and grabbing Leonit's flintlock revolver from within. The same one he'd held that night twelve years before.

Unlike most weapons' utilitarian intents, Leonit had traded for only the most elaborate Ogrenian revolver he could find. More advanced than traditional single-round pistols, it had an oakwood handle, silver patterns weaving down its barrel and a different skull engraved onto the edge of each chamber. He'd purchased it immediately upon hearing the rumors that it was the last revolver of the famous Nochlander pirate known only as Stormrider. Kasia had rarely seen her father purchase anything without negotiating, but each time she'd held the gun in her hand, she couldn't help smirking at the tales of Stormrider's journeys across the Vitrian Sea.

With a sharp look at her brother, she tucked the revolver into a hidden pocket on the inside of her coat and made for the door. "Do not try to smuggle away any of our money," she said over her shoulder. "I have every kena accounted for, and I have eyes everywhere."

"We should be more worried about you," he replied flatly.

"The Crimsons damn well need to be."

She threw open the study doors and headed down the main halls to the foyer. Decorated glass windows lined the ceiling and walls of it, arranged specifically to reflect the light of the few lanterns around the room's edges and make it feel far brighter than it should've been during everdark. They were an Ogrenian design, and with most of the mansion's expensive furniture and artwork sold in the aftermath of Leonit's death, they were one of the few reminders left that House Niezik had once been as powerful as any other in the Commonwealth. Kasia took heart in that. Not all things were lost, and she would claw back her family's prestige if it killed her.

First, she had her own killing to do.

Tazper met her at the door, quickly falling behind as she rushed down the steps and reached the carriage before him. "Lady Katarzyna, please, let me help you in."

A small crowd of peasants had gathered across the mansion grounds to watch her go, so she stopped and allowed him to do his job. There was no time to waste, but appearances mattered. House Niezik employed and oversaw thousands of lowborn. They needed to believe she was poised, elegant, and working in their favor. A hasty young woman ignoring her servants and defying tradition would not do.

So, she smiled and waved at them with her free hand. Many returned it, but a few shook their heads at her. Were they upset at her leaving or just at her? She didn't know, but she would have plenty of time to ponder that on the journey, not at the carriage door.

She climbed into the carriage, joining Kikania inside as Tazper followed. The maid tapped her feet and stared out the opposite window before giving Kasia a forced smile. "Are you excited to see Kalastok again? I have never been, and I've heard there are *so* many things to see."

*Am I excited?*

Kasia swallowed, clenching and unclenching her taloned hand. Each person she'd killed had brought more memories of why she hated her own power. Though Leonit's list was done, she doubted defeating the Crimsons would be possible without Reaching again. Kalastok held hundreds of thousands of people. What would happen if she lost control again, as she had with Aliax years before? Success against a faction powerful enough to quietly kill the minister of glass and the king would require risks, but when would she become too much of a danger to the innocents of the capital?

"No," she finally replied as she crossed her legs and pounded the wall of the carriage, signaling that she was ready. "But this is what I have to do."

# THE PRINCESS

*"Kelosh has refused to move its troops from the border. Please advise how we are to proceed."* – Tazak Aminnar, captain of the 4th Ranger Company.

Darkness hung heavy over the cobblestone streets of Kalastok. Princess Nikoza Bartol leaned upon the balcony railing of her grandfather's study, three stories up from the narrow, lamplit street called Textile Alley. Spirits floated over the Kala River in the light emanating from the towers scattered across the eastern half of the city.

Only *half* the city.

Drifters like these spirits were harmless, but their awakened cousins threatened Kalastok daily in their need to feed. When they neared the eastern riverbank, the Spirit Reachers upon those towers would send them back to the west with ease. Right into the lowborn Industrial District. Nikoza had no doubt what happened to the defenseless lowborn those awakened encountered.

With the Keloshan Empire lurking in the east, though, awakened were not the only threat they faced. Nikoza considered her grandfather's many teachings about the Commonwealth of Two Nations' foes as a Light Reacher illuminated an awakened over the Market District. A Spirit Reacher's gray wisps shot through the light, sending the spirit away.

*What fascinating creatures.*

As the king's granddaughter and ward, Nikoza had hoped he would help her gain entry to Kalastok College to study Reaching, spirits, and the sciences. Countless lessons on politics had met her in the capital instead. Every faction's leaders. Every great house's interests. Yet they had not held a single discussion about the nature of spirits, or how Reachers could aid even the lowliest of the Commonwealth's people.

The ringing of her grandfather's cane against the stone balcony tore Nikoza from such thoughts. King Jazuk Bartol the Fourth often paced here as he overlooked what he called his "true dominion". Their house ruled both Kalastok's clothing industry and the entire nation from its townhouse in the middle of the Crimson District, but its control over the former was far stronger than the unruly scions of the Commonwealth. Nikoza loathed that Jazuk preferred to handle his business here instead of in the Crystal Palace. Why be monarch if not to occasionally enjoy the beautiful luxuries that came with it?

A cigar dangled from Jazuk's free hand as he continued a rant she'd heard a thousand times. "How am I to defend our borders when King Yaakiin dismantled them? Kelosh has steel and artillery, the Ogrenians have advanced their technology far beyond our own, and Reshka possesses enough glass to slaughter the whole damned Spirit Wastes. What do we have against such foes? I cannot even convince the scions of the threats against us!"

Nikoza pinched her nose as Jazuk took a puff from his cigar and blew the smoke over the street. It curled ever upward, toward the Reachers who protected the wealthy half of the city.

"We have clearer access to the Spirit Crystal than anyone else, granting us more Reachers and a dragon," she said with her shoulders back and her chin raised. She had Jazuk's light gray hair, almost white, and soft jawline, but that was where the similarities stopped. While he was a war-wounded hunchback with enough scars to make many revile him, Nikoza had the splendor of a fawn. Purple-eyed, innocent, and—as Jazuk constantly reminded her—completely unprepared for the horrors of the world.

"That may have been enough once, but no longer." He glanced at her gloved left hand and the talon it concealed. "Many Reachers are like you. Do you believe you could wield the realm of Water to drown armies at will?"

She dropped her head, fiddling with the end of her dress's sleeve. Of course she couldn't. It took all her Reaching ability just to summon a trickle of water.

"Fix your posture," the king insisted as a knock came at the door. "We have company."

Nikoza complied and headed through the study, opening the door for a studiously dressed woman. She bowed to Nikoza before doing the same to Jazuk. "My king, I have brought the report from Professor Etal iz Noshok that you requested, along with the count of those killed by the Spirit Plague so far."

Jazuk took another puff, drawing out the breath before exhaling. "You are worried about lowborn lives when Kelosh is threatening war? Why does it matter if they die from some strange illness or a bullet through their brain?"

*Oh Grandfather, why must you forget your people?*

The woman clicked her tongue, but Jazuk cut her off before she could reply.

"I have no desire for more death among our populace," he said. "However, you academics have yet to give me a way to convince the Chamber of Scions to care, nor a way to fix it."

"From what we can tell," she replied, "the disease is unlike any other we have seen. Body Reachers cannot rid it from victims, and neither Life nor Spirit Reachers can keep the deceased's spirit from becoming an awakened when they pass."

A sudden chill struck Nikoza. Everdark always brought colder temperatures, but this was sudden, drawing goosebumps across her skin. "Awakened?" she breathed. "By the Crystal Mother…" Until now, the Spirit Plague had been all but rumor among lowborn of the Commonwealth's scattered villages. If it was truly turning people into the awakened spirits that had destroyed civilization eight-hundred years before, they were all in danger.

Jazuk shot Nikoza a scathing glare before looking back at the woman. "Do you have a way to stop it yet?"

"Well..." the woman stammered. "No, we have yet to find a cure. Perhaps if you were to provide experienced Reachers to the populace, however, we could research—"

"Our Reachers are engaged with the activities of the state and the great houses. Kelosh marches to our door!" He stomped his cane. "Inform Professor iz Noshok that I will send lowborn investigators to uncover the source of this disease."

"The source—"

Jazuk extinguished the cigar, dragging it along the rim of his ashtray. "You are dismissed."

With a huff, the woman hurried toward the door, but Nikoza followed her, softly catching her arm in the hall. "How many Reachers do you believe you would need?" Nikoza whispered.

"Any that could be offered," the woman replied. "Our students are mere neophytes, and we require far more experience to address the situation."

"I will press my grandfather, but I can promise nothing."

The woman smiled. "Perhaps you should join us as well at the college. You are the right age, and it would be better than learning from a stubborn old man."

Nikoza's eyes widened. "If you put in a word for me, I would love to apprentice for Professor Etal iz Noshok. I would be of greater use with him than with my grandfather."

The woman nodded before leaving, and Nikoza held back a hopeful smirk. At eighteen she was still young, but she would one day be the matriarch of House Bartol. It seemed a distant prospect, but with the premature death of her father, Lakuzk, just hundredhours before her birth, she was the Bartol heir. Except most great house heirs had the spirit of their ancestor to guide them. Jazuk had mourned Lakuzk greatly, swearing that this life would be his last. He did not conduct an Inheritance Ritual upon Nikoza's birth, and now, Jazuk taught her what it was to be a great house magnate.

But what did power matter when the Spirit Plague was spreading among the lowborn? Could she not seek her purpose at Kalastok College instead, allowing her uncle, Chatik, to become patriarch?

"That sounded quite frightening," Nikoza said, returning to her grandfather as he ruffled through the papers on his intricately carved desk. Every Bartol magnate for centuries had signed contracts and treatises upon it.

"If you have something to say, Nikoza, then say it."

She took a long breath, anticipating for the spurs in his rebuke. "The people suffer from the Spirit Plague, and it may worsen if Body Reachers cannot cure even scions of it."

"This is not the first disease that has struck during my reign," Jazuk replied. "Sickness does not threaten our existence. The Keloshan Empire does."

Nikoza yelped as a cough came from the door. She held a hand to her chest, collecting her breaths as Grand Secretary Votzan entered. With a bushel of books in his arms, the frail man looked as if he would be crushed by their weight.

"Lady Nikoza is right, your highness," Votzan said, his spectacles sliding down his nose. "When matters of national interest are brought before us, should we not seek answers?" He hefted the books onto the whiskey table between the sofas, and it creaked beneath the weight. "Regarding the *other* matter, here are the historical records of Kelosh's past invasions of its neighbors that you requested."

Jazuk eyed them, then reached for his cigar, but it was already out. "There is no time for such research now. The Chamber is meeting soon, are they not?"

"Indeed they are."

"Then inform them that I intend to make an address. Someone needs to before House Oliezany decides to whip their armament factories into a full war economy. Once those bastards have bullets, they will demand I give them someone to shoot."

Votzan cleared his throat. "Um, your highness, are you certain that we should act without speaking to Lord Gornioz Oliezany or the other ministers?"

"Do you take me for a fool?" Jazuk shuffled toward the door, leaning heavily on his cane.

"I do not," Votzan said. He was not the tallest man, but he was broad shouldered with a sharp black beard. Nikoza smirked at him cowering before her shriveled grandfather.

Jazuk patted Votzan's arm, unable to reach his shoulder. "I am prone to making myself a fool, Votzan. That is why I need good men like you to tell me when I am doing so. Gornioz is not one to be trifled with, and I have no intentions of drawing his ire. In fact, I am certain he and I will see this the same way in the end."

Nikoza helped him make his way down the stairs. Jazuk had once been a revered Spirit Reacher of the city watch, but even with the help of Body Reachers, age came for magnates who chose not to conduct Inheritance Rituals. One day, Nikoza hoped she would make him proud.

They soon reached the door of the lavish townhouse. Though far smaller than House Bartol's estate in the northeastern town of Anukit, Nikoza preferred it here. The city grew more with each passing year, and to be apart from it was to lose touch of time's forward march—the only power no Reacher could control. Its bustle filled the air with the raucous sound of two hundred thousand people going about their lives. Kalastok was miniscule compared to Kelosh's metropolises, but nowhere else in the Commonwealth came close.

Their carriage awaited them. Instead of horses, it had three sails fastened to its rear: one on the top and another on each side. Two Air Reachers stood on a platform behind them to push the carriage along with their gusts of magic. Jazuk tipped his tall felt hat to them before climbing the steps and throwing himself onto one of the benches within.

Nikoza held a hand to her heart and bowed her head to the Reachers, then climbed into the carriage and sat across from her grandfather. "What is your plan for the Keloshans? My friends say we are sure to lose a war if it comes to that, and your comments have not inspired my confidence."

"Young scions gossip," Jazuk replied, spinning his cane between his hands. "On a normal occasion, I would have the opportunity to meet with my advisors before addressing the Chamber, but most members will have heard of the news. If I do not speak, they will make a decision without my direction. My friends in the nationalist wing would not be pleased if the opposition gained the first word."

" 'Gossip is what runs a court when men quarrel over trifling things.' That is what Mother says."

Jazuk chuckled. "On that, she is right."

Their carriage pushed through the crowded streets closer to the heart of the city. It was early evening, and despite the darkness, people were flooding from their places of work and heading toward the many gambling halls, pubs, and—more discreetly—brothels spread across both halves of the city. Nikoza watched the gazes of scions and merchant-class lowborn alike. Some glared while others cheered for their passing king.

It was not long before they neared the Crystal Palace, its walls of both decorative and protective glass imbued with deep red Ezmani hues and streaks of Vockan white. Commonwealth flags of the same designs hung from each of the six archways that surrounded the palace. Those archways stuck out from the building so that from above, it resembled a six-petaled flower with a street stretching from each. It ensured that the scions' Chamber resided at the heart of the city and that the palace could be seen from every plaza in the Crimson and Market districts.

A sense of awe came over Nikoza each time she saw the palace. It was a perfect design of form over pure function, like the beautiful dresses her family's skilled seamstresses made. The Commonwealth deserved a beacon whose glory could be pursued.

If only the scions ever strove to match it.

Jazuk had taught her well that the king was not the sole source of strength in the Commonwealth. The aristocratic Chamber of Scions elected the king for life, but they, too, often chose when his life ended. Considering Jazuk had taken the throne after King Yaakiin's assassination twelve years before, that thought was ever-present in Nikoza's mind. The scions had elected the Reshkan lord in a desperate attempt to ensure none of the great houses gained too much power. In the end, all that had done was make the Commonwealth ripe for the neighboring empires to tear apart. Jazuk had worked tirelessly to pick up the pieces ever since.

She looked away from the palace, flexing her fingers in gloves made from domestic linens. Her talon pressed against the fabric over her left index finger. Oh, how Jazuk had hoped that she would be a powerful Water Reacher, but not even the king could sway the Spirit Crystal's gifts. Unlike him, though, she didn't care for power from another realm. There was still so much to learn from their Spirit realm of Zekiaz.

"Stay by my side once we are within the palace," Jazuk said. "All will be watching me, and as long as you are by my side, everything you say or do will reflect upon me."

She cocked her head. "I have visited the Crystal Palace before, Grandfather."

"You come today to join me beside the throne. It is a far different place than the shadows around the Chamber's rim."

*Beside him?*

She pressed her lips together, holding her poise the best she could on the outside. But her heart raced. Never before had Jazuk asked her to stand beside the throne. The most influential scions in the country would be there, able to see her for every moment of the meeting, and she could say nothing as they debated war.

"I will do what I must," she said, straightening her posture as he would want.

He smiled. "You make a fine princess, and if you continue to do so, you will make a fine matriarch, maybe even a queen."

She averted her gaze to the window as the carriage rolled to a stop behind a line of royal guardsmen dressed in red and gold. They had their rifles shouldered, and Jazuk hoped it would stay that way for many years to come.

"When I am matriarch, it means you have perished," Nikoza replied, opening the door before the servant outside could do so. "I do not wish for such a thing to happen soon."

Street lamps and ones hung from the palace's pillars illuminated the southern archway as Nikoza waited for her grandfather outside the carriage. She checked her watch, its golden hands ticking away and showing that they were five minutes late—precisely as Jazuk preferred. It was all but law that the king was to be tardy to a session of the Chamber, allowing him to bring calm to the inevitable chaos that resulted from two hundred prideful scions filling the same room. Such a silly tradition.

Guards filed in behind them as they entered the palace. Their footsteps echoed through the halls of marble and glass while they neared a statue of the Crystal Mother. Nikoza stopped before it, touching the crystal at the goddess's feet and then holding her fingers to her lips.

"May your wisdom guide us," she prayed.

Jazuk just huffed and tapped his cane against the stone platform at the goddess's feet. The anointed sister of the Buried Temple had demanded that he build it, but despite his acceptance, he'd claimed the Temple was merely a powerful institution bending the government to its will. That confused Nikoza. Why should such religious guidance be scorned?

A woman approached them before the hall's end, where wooden double doors marked the entry to the Chamber of Scions. The glass emblem of the Commonwealth of Two Nations stretched across them. Formed from two interlocking diamonds, one white for Vocka and the other red for Ezman, they resembled overlapping shields which guarded the Chamber. For beyond, there would surely be war among the factions.

"King Jazuk," the woman said softly, her head bowed in reverence. "Could I have a word with you regarding an agreement between Nochland and the Commonwealth that could address both of our problems?"

Jazuk raised his gaze to meet hers. Alyniana of the Wayfarers, Nikoza recalled her grandfather calling her before, the ambassador from the Merchant Republic of Nochland.

"How many times must you bother me with this matter?" the king grumbled.

Alyniana pursed her lips. Donning a forest green headscarf and a floral-patterned dress of a far looser style than her Commonwealth counterparts, she could hardly be mistaken for a talon-wearing scion. That was her job, after all. It would be suspicious if she too closely resembled the people of the nation she was assigned to, and just as suspicious would be the conversations she'd held with Nikoza beyond Jazuk's many serving ears.

Another voice interjected before the ambassador could reply.

"Have you not heard the immense trials we face?" Gornioz Oliezany the Eighth's voice boomed as he approached with a group of his nationalist allies in his wake. If Jazuk was a dwarf compared to Alyniana, then he was a mouse to Gornioz. The magnate wore strappings of gold and carved glass across his suit and vest like a general's, and his mouth was a narrow line beneath his trimmed white beard. "Nochland is but a speck on the map. Neither you nor your government can rid us of Kelosh, so do not waste his majesty's time claiming you can be of any significant aid to us in these dire times."

Jazuk gave a hesitant nod, then followed Gornioz and his allies to the side to whisper among themselves. Why did they always whisper? Nikoza was to learn from her grandfather, but that was quite difficult when she couldn't hear the most important conversations.

So she would find her own.

"Excuse me, Ambassador," she whispered, touching Alyniana's arm.

Alyniana had turned away, and she jumped at the sudden voice beside her, blushing as she held a hand over her heart. She turned to see Nikoza smiling sweetly. "My apologies, Princess Nikoza. I had not expected you to tarry behind."

Nikoza glanced over her shoulder. "Forgive my grandfather. He is far too prone to adhering to mutterings of magnates when answers lie before him, but I always have an ear for those seeking ideas beyond those trapped in these halls. You said you may have a way for Nochland to help us?"

"There is." Alyniana reached into a hidden pocket in her dress. "There are things that should not be spoken in public, but please, if you could deliver this letter to the king, I would be incredibly grateful. All of Nochland would be."

Nikoza studied the letter as she picked it from Alyniana's grasp with two fingers, as if fearing it would bite her. "I cannot promise anything, but I trust your candor. If my grandfather refuses to listen to reason, I will read the letter myself and attempt to convey its message through other means."

"Thank you, Princess."

"Do not thank me for what has yet to be done." Nikoza tucked away the letter before glancing at her grandfather, who headed toward the chamber with Gornioz. "I must have my leave. Thank you, Alyniana of the Wayfarers. I hope that we may find some solution together."

She hurried to Jazuk's side and took his arm. His absent smile said he was too focused on politics to notice her absence, so they headed toward the doors as Gornioz led the others into the chamber. A guard on either side held the doors open, their gold-trimmed infantry uniforms matching the colors of their respective diamond emblem. They saluted Jazuk with their off hands as he entered with Nikoza.

Beyond the doors bellowed the Chamber's cacophony, scions shouting from the raised seating which encircled a massive pit. Air Reachers stood along the pit's edge to carry the most important voices and drown others. Two hundred scion representatives from land-owning houses both great and small filled the Chamber, and Nikoza's ears rang with each of their attempts to be heard.

She calmed her nerves by admiring the stained-glass windows that lined the room's rounded far wall and ceiling. During the everbright of her first arrival to the palace, golden light had cascaded from the windows upon the Chamber, but now, only the glow of the Light Reachers' orbs above banished the darkness that seemed to emanate from the pit.

Nikoza's nerves returned as Jazuk led her along the narrow path that spanned the pit to a marble platform at its center. A high-backed throne of deep red and gold glass rose from it, surrounded by the pit's eternal depths and the scions' greedy gazes. Both the center of attention and the target at the Chamber's heart.

But she gave no attention to the throne. Instead, she smiled at the crystalline dragon curled around it like a rattlesnake prepared to strike. A majestic creature, birthed by the Spirit Crystal, it raised its head at the sight of the king.

The Chamber erupted further with every step they took toward the throne. Those to the left looked upon Jazuk with scorn, and those to the right held gazes ranging from envy to pride. Not pride in him, but in themselves. Jazuk's election as king had worked much to the favor of the nationalist and conservative factions of the Chamber, and he often mused to Nikoza that they saw him as a puppet to make them richer as the nation crumbled.

They were halfway to the throne before the Chamber fell silent. Gornioz Oliezany had been seated, but now he stood amid the heart of the nationalist faction on the right, quieting his allies without a word.

*Ironic,* Nikoza thought, *that when they seek to take power from the king and distribute it to the scions, they choose instead to follow the whims of a single magnate.*

The patriarch of House Oliezany nodded to Jazuk. Nikoza followed her grandfather's lead and returned the gesture, then took her place beside the throne as the dragon breathed out, sending wonderfully warm air through the room.

Nikoza raised her head, watching the king's brow furrow as he stared at her uncle, Chatik Pikezik, seated among the conservatives. Chatik smiled instead at Nikoza and pressed his fingers to his lips in a silent blessing. As Jazuk's second son, Chatik had taken the house name of his wife, Lilita the Third, upon their marriage, but he had always remained a true uncle to Nikoza. The same could not be said of his relationship with Jazuk.

"Scions of Ezman and Vocka," Jazuk began once he looked away from Chatik. His voice already sounded heavy, but he soldiered on as he leaned upon his cane. "We face a threat who seeks to destroy our great nation, so I call upon you at this hour to forget your factions and heed my words. The Commonwealth stands at the brink, and only unity can save us now."

# ILL TIDINGS

*"It is yet a mystery why pureblooded Vockans or lowborn of any race cannot bear the Spirit Crystal's power. Scion blood connects us to the Crystal Mother, empowers us."* – Argais iz Ardinvil, the first Vockan magnate

Among the shouting reformers sat a half-Vockan, half-Ezmani scion who watched the Chamber with his steel-forged foot tapping away against the marble floor. If the room were empty, the sound would have carried all the way to the Spirit Crystal at the bottom of the pit below. Instead, it was inaudible over the masquerade the scions put on before him.

Zinarus iz Vamiustok shook his head, topped with combed waves of flaming red, before straightening his purple and gold-trimmed suit coat. He was only twenty-five, but he'd served in the Commonwealth's Chamber of Scions long enough to know it barely functioned during normal sessions. And today of all days was *not* normal.

"For once, I wish for the presence of our dear king," Zinarus whispered to the man seated beside him.

Tiuz held the smallest of grins. A gentleman of middle age, his tight jacket and expression alike resembled a cavalry commander's more than a politician's. One could take the general out of the military, but the military never left the general.

"I'm not one for omens, my friend," Tiuz replied, "but if we don't speak against war, it will come."

Zinarus eyed the doors as Gornioz Oliezany entered with his entourage. "I fear war with Kelosh as much as the next reformer; however, I wish we could oppose it in a more orderly manner. In times like these, we appear as the rabble Lord Gornioz claims us to be."

The doors had barely closed behind Gornioz before King Jazuk Bartol the Fourth plodded his way into the Chamber with his granddaughter, Nikoza, following close behind. Late as always. For once, though, it wasn't the king's tardiness but the princess's presence that drew Zinarus's attention. Jazuk had earned the ire of the great houses for not conducting the Inheritance Ritual, so parading the girl who should have held his spirit was a bold decision.

The nationalists and conservatives across the deep pit quieted at Gornioz's signal, spurring the reformers and moderates to do the same out of respect for the crown. And out of fear of what lay ahead. The Commonwealth found itself at the brink of war with the mightiest empire on the continent of Brakesh. What action would the king suggest?

Jazuk began his speech with a call for unity, his crystal dragon eyeing the last of the opposition to sit. This, Zinarus had expected. King Jazuk was known as a pragmatic nationalist who would change his mind to avoid divisions among the ruling houses, yet over his half-decade in the capital, Zinarus had instead seen factions grow within the Chamber and beyond. All sides saw the king as a weak puppet to be bent to their will. What remained to be seen was whether he could lead against an external threat.

"We find ourselves in the season of everdark once again," Jazuk continued as he leaned upon his silver cane. "It is a time which our kind feared before we learned to Reach into the realm of Light. Overcoming the obstacles we face is what makes us human, what makes us scions as the inheritors of that great ability to channel the elements both of our realm and others. I stand over the Spirit Crystal today with the knowledge that our nation was built with the Crystal Mother's gift, granted to us so that we may Reach and become more. We cannot allow strife among us to ruin that treasure in the face of a mighty foe."

"Then what would you have us do?" someone shouted from the reformers near Zinarus. He could not tell who, but the outburst was greeted with a chorus of boos from the nationalists and conservatives until Jazuk raised a hand.

"Though out of line," Jazuk said, "the question is valid. I am sure you have all heard the reports by now that the Keloshan Empire has mobilized, claiming we occupy territory that is theirs under the Third Reduction Treaty. This is why I will be sending a force of our own to meet the Keloshans and seek negotiations to end this debacle. I do not seek war, but I find it suspicious that they would act upon the arrival of this new disease some call the Spirit Plague. While the negotiations begin, my government will launch a full investigation into the source of this disease and whether the Keloshan Empire had a part to play in its arrival within our borders.

"We will propose further action in due time, and I ask that those with alternative ideas present their plans in this Chamber as we gather throughout the following hundred-hours. Together, we will stand strong against all who oppose us. Survival is no longer enough. Whether our foes be Keloshans, Reshkans, or Ogrenians, they will learn once again that the Commonwealth is not to be trifled with."

The nationalists and conservatives burst to their feet with applause, but many among them did so with reluctance, likely hoping for a firmer response to the Keloshans' advance. Jazuk's tempered response, though, had earned nods among the moderates and even scattered applause throughout the reformers.

Zinarus gave a half-hearted clap himself, not rising. It would be difficult to do so with his mechanical left leg—a replacement for the one that had been amputated not long after his birth—and doubts about the speech lingered in his heart. He had seen many a promise come and go within these walls of marble and glass. Would investigations find the truth or what Jazuk's allies hoped to hear?

Formal debate followed for hours as the Chamber sought to address a variety of issues that Zinarus had researched thoroughly. Except House iz Vamiustok—meaning *from Vamiustok*—was a minor one among those represented in the Chamber. His mother, Lady Sania, owned one of the few sand mines not controlled by the great houses for their precious glass, but the village of Vamiustok was small. As her heir, Zinarus had a voice in the Chamber, but the Air Reachers would quiet him the second a greater scion began to speak.

Zinarus gripped his cane in his usual frustration by the time the Chamber voted to recess for the evening. Another session. Another chance to speak. And another reminder that he was no great house heir.

Someday, he would change that.

The scions waited for Jazuk to hobble his way over the pit and up the stairs with Princess Nikoza's aid. His speech had inspired confidence, but his fragile constitution countered much of those gains. Should war come, would Jazuk have the strength to lead? Was allowing himself to age instead of completing the Inheritance Ritual the right decision, not allowing the scions to elect a new ruler until his true death?

Zinarus glanced at the factions to his right, a majority of the Chamber. Perhaps a weak king was better than one too strong-headed to see that the Commonwealth would fall if it continued in the same old ways.

Change was coming. As Zinarus rose and tested his mechanical leg, he prayed to the Crystal Mother that it would be for the better.

# LONGING

*"To lose a possession brings sorrow. To lose oneself brings despair. To lose both brings vast amounts of beer."* – Anonymous contribution to The Kalastok Gazette

Shadows and cigar smoke hung over Radais as he lurched back to a table at the far end of the Iron Alley Pub, another mug in hand. Ironically, it was copper, and it had long since faded to a dirty turquoise. He didn't care. The beer was cheap on Kalastok's west side, and he needed it. After a hundred-hour ride from Palmia Fortress, he'd failed to get past Ivalat iz Ardinvil's butler, and he had far too little money to pay for a Reacher to heal his father.

"I ran away..." he mumbled to himself. No one else was at the table. There had been, he thought, but he couldn't remember if they'd left recently or long ago. Even strangers didn't want to deal with him when he was drunk.

"What are you running from?" a young woman asked, sliding into a chair across from him. She wore a wide-brimmed felt hat angled down over one of her eyes—the color that copper was supposed to be—and a duster that clipped against the bottom of her work boots.

Her face was unwrinkled, her skin the light brown of an Ogrenian northerner.

Radais slumped back, his expensive Glassblade jacket wrinkling against the chair. What did it matter? He was a failure to his family. Miv hated him already. She couldn't hate him *more* if he came back having failed with the scions.

"My father," he blurted out.

"We all run from things," she replied sweetly.

"Yeah? What did you run from to end up on the wrong side of Kalastok?"

She grinned. "I took something that wasn't mine, but the *Suava Petovi* don't cross international borders for petty theft."

"Swav-what?" He took another swig. "What are you talking about?"

The woman slumped back, mimicking his posture as she spun a betting chip between her fingers. A few men were shouting across the room amid a game of cards, but all of them that had come and gone lacked this woman's mild manners. She sat half in shadow, and when her left hand entered the light, a ring made of deep gray crystal glimmered upon her index finger.

"They are the Ogrenian special police force, called the Sea Patrol in your tongue," she said with a huff. "You Vockans have your Glassblades, the Ezmani have their Crystal Brigade, and we Ogrenians have our Sea Patrol."

"The Crystal Brigade is nothing like the Glassblades."

She smirked. "Would you say the same to the families on Kalastok's west bank? None have ever seen a Glassblade protect them from an awakened. Of course, ignoring the lowborn Ezmani is far more innocent than what the great houses pay the Crystal Brigade to do."

Something was off about her, but Radais couldn't tell what as he took another drink. It was as if her voice were shifting between hers and someone else's. He shook his head. Wasn't right to be suspicious of the woman just because she was a foreigner trying to match Commonwealth accents.

"The great houses?" he said, voice slurred. "Why… They killing people?"

"A pit surrounds the throne, but in truth, many say the pit is not to threaten the king but to protect him from those seated around it." She set down the chip. "Would you fancy a game of cards…" She gestured for him to fill the gap with his name.

"Master Radais ik Erienfar of the Glassblades."

Something twinkled in her eyes. "Fascinating, so you are one of the famed Glassblades. You may call me Naniana-Li." She hopped to her feet and snatched his free hand. "Come, Radais. Gambling is a much more enjoyable way to spend a tiresome evening than drinking by one's self."

For a moment, Radais considered lingering in his well-deserved sulk, but something about Naniana-Li intrigued him. She was far too young for any romantic interest. Radais had traveled much in his time with the Glassblades, though, and it was obvious she had a story to tell. He joined her at the gambling table, where the dealer was preparing the next hand.

"Buy-in is twenty keni," the dealer—a stout, rugged man—told them both.

Naniana-Li pulled out the money quickly, and the dealer slid her a set of colored chips. Radais hesitated again. Gambling seemed like a fun distraction. If he won, it would bring him closer to paying for the Reachers his father needed. Except the Glassblades had sent him with a limited allowance, and he'd have to stay longer than expected after House iz Ardinvil's rejection. Spending too much now could mean sleeping on the crime-ridden streets of Kalastok's west side, but in his stupor, all he saw was opportunity.

"Twenty it is," he said, sliding the bills across the table to the glee of the three players that had already been seated.

The dealer handed Radais his chips and then quickly began the game. It was a strategic one, built around odds that were difficult enough to consider when sober, and Radais could barely read the cards in his hand. While Naniana-Li won round after round, ridding the table of two other players in quick succession, Radais bet wildly.

He blinked and then had only two kena chips left. Eighteen keni gone—enough for a hundred-hour in a decent inn. Miv would be furious.

But Miv wasn't there, and as long as he had chips, he could claw his way back. Sure, Naniana-Li was on a streak. All luck came to an end eventually, and his turn would come next.

Naniana-Li played aggressively the next round. Both Radais and the other player countered, but she giggled before covering her flared nostrils. "Oh dear, Master Radais. It appears you are about to fall upon your last chip."

The other player was in a worse position, his final chip resting in the betting pool as he tapped his cards against the table, but Radais focused on Naniana-Li. It felt nice to hear someone laugh, even if he couldn't.

"Can we just show our hands?" the man said, wriggling his cleft chin. "I've got this."

"Such confidence." Naniana-Li laid her cards upon the table. A full set of Reachers—a perfect hand.

The man stuttered, glancing from his hand to her before slapping down his own cards. It was a solid hand, but nowhere near enough to best hers. "She's a cheat!" he shouted at the bartender. "Throw this bitch out, will ya? Ogrenians think they can just walk in here and take everything from us with their lies. She's probably got some kinda magic."

Naniana-Li displayed her hands, the crystal ring now missing. "I bear no talon, nor the crystal eyes of my people's Reachers. You, sir, simply are incapable of losing with dignity."

He spat in her face.

Radais was to his feet in a heartbeat, grabbing hold of the man and throwing him into the wooden wall so hard that the decorative sledgehammer mounted upon it dropped to the ground beside him. The man eyed it, but Radais punched him square in the nose. Dull pain met his knuckles. The alcohol numbed enough, and he raised his fist again.

"Go home!"

The man muttered something, but stopped fighting. When Radais released him, he scrambled out of the pub and into the raucous streets, full of other drunkards singing and fighting about their days. Radais shook his head. None of their problems mattered if the awakened were coming again, but that didn't stop him from thinking about his father. Besides, diseases came and went. Who knew if this Spirit Plague would even stick around?

"Thank you, Master Radais," Naniana-Li said with a wide smile. "I hate when people are sore losers."

He eyed his single remaining chip and clasped his hands before him. What a hero. Wasting his money and then starting a bar fight.

*I should cut my losses.*

"I'm done," he said.

Naniana-Li furrowed her brow. "But why? You are not finished, and you haven't told me why you're here."

There it was again, that casual tone. What Ogrenian noblewoman spoke like that? Why was she even on the west side?

"You first," he replied.

She gestured for him to sit, so he did. The dealer gave them each their hands, and Naniana-Li looked from her cards to Radais. "I am skilled at many things, Master Radais, but I wasn't always. My mother left me at a young age. My father was killed by Ezmani. Neither of these things I could stop, but I can control my life now, in each moment. Ogrenia holds nothing for me."

"I'm sorry," Radais mumbled. "My father's dying. I get it. Just wish I could get the money to hire a Reacher to help save him."

"A master of the famous Glassblades cannot afford to hire a Reacher?"

"The Commonwealth forgot we exist."

She bet a single chip, enough to force him to go all-in or fold. "A shame."

With a glance at his hand, he matched the bet. It was a decent set, three-of-a-kind, but he doubted he'd beat her. At least he could go to bed early and sleep until his inevitable hangover failed. His spare money for a Body Reacher to mend it was in Naniana-Li's stash.

She revealed her cards—a bluff.

"Spirits be damned," Radais whispered, collecting the two chips.

"See, Master Radais. Your luck appears to have changed already."

And it continued to change as Radais went on his own streak. Naniana-Li kept quiet until the table was even at fifty chips each. "I gave you my reasons for coming," she said with a childish giggle. "Now, it is your turn. There must be more of a reason for a Glassblade to walk into Kalastok than to play cards and mope about his father."

He sighed, staring at the ceiling. How long had it been since his last drink? Things seemed to spin less, and his cards were finally clear, but his mind was still fogged. "I tracked an awakened into the Spirit Wastes. It had killed someone in a village I was supposed to protect, so I followed it deeper than anyone should go into the Wastes alone. Then, one night while I slept, there was this noise outside that spooked Vuk."

"Who's Vuk?"

He smirked. "My ibex. I don't go anywhere without him."

Naniana-Li looked around and shrugged.

"I couldn't go walking through Kalastok with an ibex all day," Radais said. "No food for him here, so I had to drop him at a stable with a bunch of nasty horses."

"What happened next?"

He cocked his head, then realized what she was talking about. "Oh, right. There were a bunch of awakened attacking some man dressed in red robes. Had a talon and every…" He bit his tongue. "I… uh… I'm supposed to send a letter from the supreme defender."

Naniana-Li stood, setting down her cards without looking at them. Her gaze never left Radais, and she drummed her fingers across the table before asking the dealer for her keni. "I have a friend who might interest you," she said once the dealer had handed both her and Radais their money. "Ask for Tiak-Kath Lori at Haxan's Hall on the east side tomorrow night. Make it worth his time, and you'll have your Reacher."

Then she left before Radais even had the chance to comprehend what she'd said. He picked at the bills laid out before him, pondering his winnings and the woman's intentions. A headache was his only reward, so he raised his hand toward the bartender. "Another."

He'd won his share. Tomorrow, he'd figure out what pit he'd fallen into.

**NEX STUFFED THEIR HANDS INTO THEIR DUSTER'S POCKETS** as they skipped from the pub's threshold and into the muddied street of Iron Alley. Smoke rose from the chimneys of the forges less than a quarter-mile west, and soot rained upon the entirety of Kalastok's west side. They coughed as their duster's hem clipped at their heels, too long for someone as short as them. It did its job. And tonight, so had their disguise as Naniana-Li.

Hardened steelworkers eyed Nex but kept their distance as Nex pulled down their wide-brimmed felt hat. Black, like their duster, they liked how it made them blend into the emptiness created by the everdark. Wasn't life an attempt to mold oneself into someone that belonged where they were at the moment?

That question weighed upon Nex as they passed onto New Beginnings Avenue. Bullet holes riddled the wooden sign, making it read *Beg Ave.*

Nex smiled up at it as one would an old friend, and why couldn't it be? That sign gave them more joy than any friend they'd ever had. Except Vinnia, but calling her a friend was like calling a spirit a person—pieces were there, but the heart of it was missing. Beg Ave was something else. It didn't give Nex the thrill of a tumble late at night or the soft whispers afterward, but it reminded them that no matter how shitty life got, there was always humor.

Years ago, the Chamber of Scions had ordered someone to change the sign every time the kids or workers of the west side shot it for fun. It had become a game, destroying the ironic wooden sign at the corner of an alley named after iron, and the Chamber had eventually given up. So Beg Ave remained.

Nex's smile failed as they passed the reason for the name. Homeless lined the street, holding out tattered caps and bags in hopes of someone giving them enough to eat.

Tens of thousands of people had flooded from the countryside in search of work in Kalastok's growing Industrial District, but hope and reality rarely met. Many never found a job, and even some who did ended up in the Shadow Quarter slums or on the street, their wages too little to make rent. There were few west of the river who could spare change for these poor folk.

One particular beggar smiled at the sight of Nex. A lanky Ezmani man named Jax, he shook a tin cup that matched his tanned skin, rattling the few coins deposited within it. "The child of Possibility has come." He smiled with many of his teeth missing, and those that remained were as rotten as a scion's heart. "How'd you fare down Iron Alley?"

"Almost made eighty keni," Nex replied, thinking back upon their game with the Glassblade, Radais. Why had they let him take the money back? "Beat out a few idiots who couldn't keep their cards hidden. Probably could've won without my Reaching."

"Good lass."

But Nex wrinkled their nose, fiddling with the crystal ring they wore upon their left index finger. Of Ogrenian design, they'd stolen it from a black-market dealer years ago in hopes of selling it themselves.

Most Ogrenians Reached through Spirit Crystal infused with one of their eyes instead of using Ezmani talons, but Nex's Ogrenian father had told them about a new design in his homeland that could pull from another realm with vibrations, similarly to how the eye crystals worked. It had opened new opportunities for poorer Ogrenian scions to access Reacher abilities, but lowborn lacked the bloodlines that allowed them to Reach, even if they bought a ring. That's why Nex had been shocked when they'd been able to alter their luck and summon cards the moment they put the stolen ring on.

Somehow, Nex had scion blood, and every day since, they'd used their Possibility Reaching to survive in Kalastok's west side. They were hardly a talented Reacher. For them, it was enough, giving them a few limited uses each day.

"How much you need today?" Nex asked Jax.

He glanced down at the cup and sighed. His wrinkles showed in the motion, the nearby fires revealing the marks across his bald head. "Whatever you can give. I know you got Vinnia to take care of too."

That only made deciding harder. Some beggars would chase anyone with a hint of money down the street, but Jax… Jax wouldn't accept more than he needed to live. He'd keep a small portion and give the rest to someone he thought needed it more. Nex had considered bringing the old man into their apartment, but it was barely big enough for Vinnia and them already.

"Here," Nex said, handing him fifteen keni—half their profits after the buy-in, and a much-needed chunk of the rent they'd soon need to pay. "Keep at least ten of it, Jax. There's some spaces opening up on my block. They might have a room for you if you share with a friend and give 'em ten up front."

"My friends are here. Can't fit them all in one apartment, and I ain't going to ask you to help with rent each hundred-hour. Besides, can't trust them landlords. Even the ones that aren't scions will throw you out if they don't like the smell of you."

Nex nodded, understanding what it was like to be trapped like that. Money could help, but then came the struggle to keep what you'd fought so hard to get. No landlord would find pity on Jax if he missed a payment. Not when every tenant was the same, and there was a line of workers hoping to find a decent place.

"Still, keep it," Nex said with a forced smile. They studied the tents and make-shift buildings of wood and metal scraps filling the muddied plot behind him. Jax had been there long enough to claim a spot that would keep the everdark snow off him, but that was it. "I need to go home to Vinnia, but I'll see you around."

He returned the smile. "You know where to find me. Tell your girl I say thanks for the mittens. Best ones in all of Kala." He raised his hands into the light. Nex hadn't seen Vinnia's knitted mittens before, but it didn't surprise them that she'd given some out to the beggars. At least they recognized her talents.

"I'll let her know. Night, Jax."

Nex crossed a few more blocks before turning down a dirt path with no name. Warehouses lined it, full of goods both legal and not, and Nex headed toward the worst of them. The stench of rotting wood filled the air as they climbed the ladder on the back wall and up to the third floor. Four doors met them once they'd clambered to the top, each bearing a letter. Nex fished a key from their pocket and headed toward the door labeled *C* and opened it with a creak.

"Vin?" they whispered, stepping into the dark room beyond. "Vinnia?"

A match pierced the darkness, and a young woman looked back at Nex with bleary eyes. "Everything okay?" Vinnia asked. "You're later than normal." She lit a candle on the nightstand, its wax all but burned out.

Nex yanked off their boots and breathed in deeply at the relief that came with it. They tossed them in the corner of the room—barely large enough for a one-person bed, stove, and wardrobe—before collapsing alongside Vinnia on the bed. "I met a Glassblade and doubled my money at cards."

"A Glassblade?" Vinnia cocked her head, her wavy locks of amber falling onto Nex's face. The young half-Vockan, half-Reshkan woman smelled of cocoa mixed with smoke, and Nex breathed in deeply.

"A master," Nex replied. "Said he was looking to pay for a Reacher to save his father, so I let him keep some winnings. Took this, though."

Nex pulled a letter out of their bag. It bore an official-looking seal of a sword beneath a mountain, and Nex was sure it had something to do with the man in red that Radais had spoken about. If the man had actually been a scion, it was probably important, so someone as experienced as a Glassblade shouldn't have left it so easily grabbable in his bag. Nex hoped he'd meet with Tiak-Kath to tell him what he knew, but even if he didn't, that letter could earn Nex a good payout from the Ogrenian spy.

"What is it?" Vinnia asked, reaching for it. "That looks like the Glassblade emblem. Spirits… You stole from a Glassblade master?"

Nex shrugged. "The Glassblade said he found a scion in the Spirit Wastes. He was so scammered that he didn't even notice me grabbing the letter." They mimicked Radais's unsteady drinking.

"And scammed because of you."

"What? Are you mad I stole from the Vockans' little glass army?"

Vinnia tucked her legs, shivering in her thin shift as a breeze came through the shuddered, glassless window. "Mom used to say they protect us from awakened, just like they did in the old days."

"This letter could give us the money we need. Tiak-Kath—"

"Shh! The Crystal Brigade will kill you if they find out you're meeting with a spy."

Nex shied away. "I just want you to be safe, happy. Maybe Tiak-Kath can help do something about the awakened. Maybe he knows about the Spirit Plague."

"Don't talk about that," Vinnia whispered, averting her gaze before coughing.

"Why?" Nex laid a hand on her leg. "What's wrong?"

"A woman at the mill came in all wobbly today. She was ranting about all kinds of things, and just before my shift was over, she collapsed. Her spirit came out of her just like that and started attacking the other girls. A few of us had glass pendants to drive it away, but…" She sniffled, clutching the small shard of glass she wore tied to a leather necklace. "It killed Annia and Tarkiaala."

Nex fell back into the wall. "Shit. You're not infected, are you?"

"I…" Vinnia shifted away with another cough. "I'm scared, Nex."

Nex sat in silence for a while, fear gripping them as they stared into the darkness beyond the candle light. The Spirit Plague had everyone scared, but what could they do to stop it if it had Vinnia? Running wouldn't help. The villages outside Kalastok apparently had it too, and they doubted even the east side would be safe if more people kept dying.

"I'll go to Tiak-Kath before the Glassblade shows up and see if he knows anything," Nex insisted. "If we can get some money, we can pay for a Reacher or something. They can always fix things!"

"Maybe…"

Nex climbed alongside Vinnia, tucking their head into her shoulder. "I promise we'll figure it out. We always have."

*And I always will.*

# THE CRYSTAL CITY

*"Kalastok was birthed from the Spirit Crystal, formed around its bounty during the height of the Piorak Empire. What remains is a shadow, and one can only blame the scions for such blight."* – Jack Himolox, lowborn writer

The bumpy roads of southern Ezman had Kasia aching by the time Kalastok's smoke and spirits appeared on the horizon, lit by the Reacher towers protecting the eastern half of the city. Her stomach fluttered at the sight. She so badly wanted to rest somewhere that wasn't an inn stinking of manure, but few scions would welcome her appearance in the capital. Leonit's old rivals lurked everywhere, making her already perilous mission all the more dangerous.

But no great change came without a chance of failure. Leonit had taught her that lesson many times, both during their games and her tutoring sessions. The Crimsons awaited her in the streets of Kalastok, and she would do whatever it took to uproot their tendrils and avenge her father's death.

Kikania pressed her face against the window, gawking at the massive towers. "Is it true that they use Spirit Reachers to keep awakened from crossing the river?"

"And Air Reachers to keep the smog over the west side, yes," Kasia said, legs crossed as she did her best to keep her poise. She was *not* excited, but there was a thrill that came with leaving Tystok and finally returning to the capital after more than a decade. The newspapers claimed it had doubled in size since then. She'd yet to decide whether that boded well or not. "The scions prefer not to choke when they can make others do it for them."

"Couldn't they just push it out of the city?"

"That would require the Chamber to build Reacher towers on the west side of the river and then send Reachers to man them." Kasia shook her head. "It would probably help a hundred thousand workers breathe and keep them safe from awakened attacks, but why would the great houses care? They have labor to spare thanks to them telling everyone that their future will be better in Kalastok."

That last part may not have been a lie. Kasia's family oversaw amber mines and countless farms, and though she did her best to ensure they remained profitable while not overworking the peasants, it was a precarious balance. Most scions wouldn't care about a few lowborn falling dead in the fields, quarries, or mines. At least in the city, lowborn had some choices—all bad ones, but choices nonetheless.

The carriage soon rumbled onto the cobblestone streets of Kalastok's east side, filled with people and other carriages going about their early afternoon business. Horses pulled Kasia's carriage, but many here had sails as Air Reachers on the back pushed them on.

A Reacher talon was a great expense for the poorer scion families, so serving a great house was worth it for many in return for the chance to Reach. It seemed such a waste. They had power that even the richest lowborn merchant could never wield, yet these Air Reachers were nothing more than glorified footmen.

They wound their way through the streets until the carriage pulled to a stop at a tall brick townhouse. Nestled between the eastern bank of the Kala River and southern bank of the meandering Vazinarik Stream that cut through the Market District, Leonit had named it

The Confluence. He'd told Kasia many times that it was a vibrant place where both rivers and ideas met, as he hosted many travelers and scions within its walls. The townhouse's exterior had once been covered with flowers from every nation. Now, only a few small plants huddled around the gas lamps, all else lying fallow.

"Which one is ours, Lady Kasia?" Kikania asked, combining formality and familiarity in a way that made Kasia uncomfortable. Not that she didn't do it often herself.

Kasia pushed open the door before Tazper could run around to her side. "Furthest one on the right. Father claimed it had a better view of the Crystal Palace than anywhere else in Kalastok."

"Did Lord Leonit want to become king?" Tazper asked, barely getting to her in time to help her onto the cobblestone.

*Did he?*

She pondered that as she fixed her dress's skirt that had bunched up during the last day of sitting. A shame. It was a simple gray one, but there were few dresses that fit the way she liked: not too tight to suffocate her and not loose enough to ruin the appeal. Despite House Niezik's increase in funds since her amber discoveries, the last thing she wanted was to waste money for the sake of vanity. She'd have been lying to claim she didn't care how she looked, though. It was a form of power.

When she finished, she took a long breath of the humid air, the breeze carrying a chill from the Kala River as clouds rolled through the light of the Reacher towers. "I doubt Father would have wanted to be at the center of attention. He quite enjoyed his wealth, but his art was knowing how to operate quietly, even when people thought he was working only for their aid. It was easier for him to influence King Yaakiin than take his place."

She grinned as she looked north, where the tip of Crystal Palace's peak rose above the surrounding buildings, lanterns illuminating it in a golden glow. "Knowing him, though, he surely considered what it would be like to wear the crown."

Another voice interrupted them as a potbellied man hobbled out of House Niezik's door, leaning heavily on a golden-tipped cane.

"Oh, Katarzyna, I have awaited your arrival since I received your letter!"

Her great-uncle, Faniz, beamed from ear to ear with patches of pale skin dotting his otherwise scion-gray face. His hair had receded since she'd seen him last, and little remained of it except for a silver strip along the back of his head. What memories she had of him involved exaggerated stories and the heavy smell of cigar smoke. They flooded back as he embraced her.

"It has been far too long," she said with a smile. "I hardly remember what The Confluence looks like, except for the stairs I used to throw myself down when Father was too distracted with work to play our nightly game."

Faniz patted her cheek, examining the side of her head. "Good, good. We had feared for a time that the scars you had earned during those falls would never heal. Poor Yazia thought you would knock your brain out of your ear!" He stepped back as Kasia unintentionally glared at the mention of her mother. "I figure your relationship with her has not improved them? How is she?"

Kasia bit her cheek. "She is still having fits." Tazper handed her a coat to help keep away the cold, and she stuck her hands into its pockets, silently thanking the footman for the distraction. "Let us speak more inside. It has been a long journey, and I do not wish to tarry in this wind."

"Of course! Come, dear child. We have much to discuss."

"Remember, Uncle, that I am the matriarch of our house now, not a child," Kasia replied as he led her into the first floor of the townhouse, where a finely-carved wooden staircase greeted them alongside a narrow hallway that led deeper into the building.

Kikania hung Kasia's coat on a rack nearby, her mouth ajar as she stared at the chandelier of assorted colored glass that lit the foyer before the ceiling sloped up toward the higher levels. Sometimes, Kasia wished she still had her handmaiden's sense of wonder. The Crimsons had stolen that from her long ago.

Faniz laughed with his hands over his belly. "My apologies! Though it has been many years, it was not right of me to resort to such language with you. Let me show you to your chamber on the upper floors, as the rooms down here are for the servants. Except for the everbright room out back, of course, but you shall not have use of that for many hundred-hours."

He hauled himself up the stairs, one hand firmly on the banister and another clutching his cane. Kasia offered her assistance, but he waved her off with claims that his "old back was having one of its days." So, she followed in watchful silence as he explained the layout of the house and the history behind the few paintings that remained.

One caught her attention: an oil on canvas portrait of her family from her last visit to Kalastok a year before her father's assassination. Her mother and brother sat regally with neither smiles nor any joy in their eyes, but Kasia gave a wry grin with her father's hand on her shoulder. When she closed her eyes, it was as if she could feel his grip again—firm, but reassuring. He'd been proud of her then. What would he think of her now?

"Now we come to Leonit's favorite room," Faniz said from the second-floor landing, not realizing Kasia had fallen behind. He opened a wooden door adorned with golden patterns resembling the barley that had been House Niezik's staple for its entire history.

Beyond was a rounded study with bookshelves covering the walls. A desk sat on the far side beneath a stained-glass window depicting a man whispering into the ear of a robed figure, whose chin was raised. A modern gas-lit chandelier dangled overhead to provide reading light, but the room's true beauty came from a wooden spiral staircase heading up to the third floor, its banisters like twisted barley-stalks. Kasia traced them with her talon before sprinting up the stairs like she had many times as a child.

Faniz stuttered at her sudden glee. "Katarzyna? Your chambers are… Oh my, she has vanished."

Kasia bounded into her father's *true* favorite room. A rounded opening allowed her to see into the study below, and tapestries from Reshka, Ogrenia, and other nations east of Kelosh hung around her, depicting battles, weddings, and other key moments of history. Narrow windows lined the conical ceiling, and during the everbright, Leonit had leaned against the railing with her many times to recount the tales of places far away. It was dim now, and Kasia furrowed her brow at the dust and cobwebs that covered many of the tapestries.

"Why have you ignored Father's world room?" she called down to her uncle. "He would be aghast to see it in such a state."

"I struggle to climb the curved stairs," Faniz replied, "so I thought it best for the maids to focus on the more used rooms, considering our limited funds these days."

Kasia rolled her eyes at the obvious lie. "That changes now." She stomped back down the stairs to him, towering over the shorter man. "Now, where are my chambers?"

His eyes widened. "Right… Right this way."

As Faniz hurried as best he could out of the room, Kasia smirked at Tazper by the door. The footman had kept quiet, but he failed to hide his satisfaction at her telling off the old man. "Are you trying to prove a point already?" he whispered. "At this rate, I am certain all of Kalastok will know of your arrival by morning."

"Good. Let them gossip and wonder what I want. In fact, that is a fine idea. We should let the papers know the matriarch of House Niezik has returned to Kalastok after so long. They enjoy drama, so why don't we give them some?"

Tazper wriggled his jaw. "Are you certain that is best? My comment was meant in jest."

She patted his arm. "Yes, and it ignited an idea that I have no intentions of dousing."

Catching up to Faniz, she held her tongue as he nodded toward his chambers and the guest room before heading up to the third floor. His mood had dampened considerably, but she didn't regret her statement. House Niezik was hers, and she wouldn't have her great-uncle burying her father's past out of fear of nationalist reactions. Those tapestries' stories were woven into her spirit. She wouldn't let their ends fray.

"Here, then, are your chambers," Faniz said between heavy breaths.

Kasia took her time passing through the single door opposite the stairs. Her father's chambers had been the one place in the townhouse she'd been barred from entering, and now they were hers. Luckily, Faniz had kept them maintained, as Kasia stepped into a sitting room before a fireplace of carved marble. The doors on either side of the sofa along the back wall led into the bedroom itself, but Kasia turned back to Faniz.

"Have you seen Sazilz Uziokaki recently?" she asked.

He raised his brow but shrugged. "Of course. We are both members of the Chamber of Scions, and he will be there at the gathering this evening. He and I have had little interaction besides him shouting ludicrous complaints that we have no right to the lands that hold our amber."

*Not so ludicrous.* But Leonit's falsification of the border between Niezik and Uziokaki lands had yielded far more than he could've known at the time. Kasia had fought for that border and won once already, and she'd do it again if it saved all she'd hoped to build.

"Very well," she said. "I will attend the meeting, then."

"Oh? I had been planning to continue attending in your stead until you were settled."

She glanced at Tazper and then Kikania behind him. "I will be settled soon enough. Besides, I hear there are discussions regarding the Keloshan Empire, and I cannot sit idly by while the great houses stir up a war that kills us all." She extended a hand toward one of the chairs. "Let us sit so that you can inform me of what I have missed."

# SAND TO GLASS

*"If we are to march to war against Kelosh, then domestic glass shall become all the more important. Be careful, my son. Spirits haunt the crystal halls…"* - Sania iz Vamiustok, matriarch of House iz Vamiustok

The crowd of scions roared as two knights galloped across the arena, lances couched and horses kicking plumes of dust into the Reacher light that pierced the darkness. They struck in a thunderous clash of wood and steel. Lances shattered upon impact, and each knight clung desperately to their horse as they reeled from the blow.

Neither fell from their steeds.

From high above in the half-filled audience, Zinarus leaned forward in his seat, drumming his fingers across his metal left leg. The knight clad in purple and gold raised his gaze to him, then nodded. He was far too confident. Zinarus was still a young man, but he had seen many great jousters fall because of their arrogance. After all the time and money he'd spent to fuel Tiuz Hazeko's career, he could not afford for it to end now.

The horses grew reckless as the knights rounded the list. Tiuz held his steady, but his opponent faltered. From nothing, the horse burst forth, throwing the knight off-balance as Tiuz waited, then pushed forward.

Tiuz couched his lance, but his opponent barely managed to point the tip in his direction before they met with a *crunch* that rang through Zinarus's clenched jaw. Someone shot to their feet in front of Zinarus as the crowd cheered, signaling one of them had been dismounted.

*He has won, surely,* Zinarus thought, cursing his mechanical knee as he struggled to stand. Its newly greased gears slipped, and he was forced to grip the back of the chair in front to catch himself. It was worth the effort.

Tiuz bowed his head as he rode around the arena's rim with his helmet held at his side. His shield was nicked and battered, but the purple flaming sands of House iz Vamiustok still burned across it. Zinarus grinned at that sigil as he straightened his bright purple suit with a matching pin upon its lapel. His mother would be proud that his investments in the old cavalry commander had paid off, as the winnings would allow them to finally expand their sand mines in Vocka. Now more than ever, the Commonwealth needed it for glass.

"Regizald," he yelled over the crowd to the servant next to him. "Please help me down the stairs to Tiuz. I wish to celebrate his victory with him."

Regizald sprung to his master, grabbing hold of his arm too eagerly.

"Careful!" Zinarus exclaimed as he staggered. "Your job is to keep me on my feet, not throw me off them."

"So-Sorry sir!" the built man replied, his light gray locks hanging down to his shoulders. Only a few years younger than Zinarus, he was a scion from a minor family who had hoped he would learn some confidence. His Earth Reaching was a great help with crafting the intricate metal gears in Zinarus's knee, and shy or not, he had become one of Zinarus's closest friends.

The pair made their way down the stairs, tailing those seeking an autograph from Tiuz or simply wanting to see him closer. Zinarus chuckled at that. There was not much to look at in his opinion, as Tiuz showed his age with wrinkles across his Ezmani gray skin and a hairline that had receded to near nothing. Age had been enough to convince Tiuz to retire from war, but Zinarus's backing had ensured it was less of a retirement and more a new career opportunity. Besides, the old commander was a renowned member of the Chamber's reformers. Investments in a man like him paid off in many ways if one was patient.

When they reached the ground level, Zinarus took his cane from Regizald and thanked him, despite the initial error. "Please ask them to pull my carriage to the side gate. With a crowd like this, one has to believe the main streets will be as dense as an Oliezany's brain."

Regizald gave a passing grin before hurrying off through an opening. Zinarus had no such luck.

The crowd surrounding Tiuz showed no signs of thinning, and though the knight had caught a glimpse of Zinarus, he'd dismounted and was as trapped as anyone. This fame was not new to him. All of Ezman had heard of Tiuz's cavalry charge that had ended the last Keloshan invasion over twenty years before. It was a golden point in Commonwealth military history, but the nation had not won a major victory since. Zinarus's mood soured at that thought.

"Please make way!" he asked the minor house scions after what felt like an eternity—lowborn weren't even allowed in the arena. "My apologies, but I am his sponsor."

Many of them regarded his red hair with disdain, but he gave them a smile as he passed by. His mother, Sania, had raised him never to think less of himself because of his mixed blood. He was a scion of a land-owning house. They were not among the great houses yet, but with persistent effort, he believed that could change. Part of that change meant earning the favor of those less fortunate than himself.

"Quite the duel," he said as he reached the wall and shook Tiuz's gauntleted hand. Zinarus's half-Vockan blood had given him significant height and darker gray skin than most Ezmani, and the knight appeared far less threatening when he was a head shorter than his sponsor. "You had me concerned for a moment, but your experience in battle repaid you immensely."

Tiuz gave a slow nod, standing rigid with his hands behind him. "I did what I had to."

"This is not the army. Enjoy yourself! One more victory and you will be the Commonwealth's champion. If that is not a reason to celebrate, then I fear there is not one."

"Celebration comes in times of peace." Tiuz took a sharp breath. "I fear those leading us seek to cut it short."

Zinarus glanced over his shoulder, stomping his cane in the dirt. "Do be careful, Lord Tiuz. There are many in this wretched city who would seek to depose the both of us." He patted the jouster's shoulder. "We will speak more come the meeting of the Chamber. Should you seek to discuss matters more in private, then you know where to find me."

"I do."

"Then take a moment to relax and enjoy the victory." Zinarus handed him a stack of kena bills. "That is for the drinks, but your winnings will be enough to buy an army of horses."

Tiuz accepted the money without reply, then returned to shaking hands with the crowd. Zinarus studied the interaction, and his heart ached at how well people responded to his mere presence. How did he do it so easily?

Zinarus pushed away his thoughts and headed toward the side gate behind the stables. Such worries distracted him from his business for House iz Vamiustok, and Sania would be displeased to hear of them. As long as he had work to do, he would soldier on as a commander would in the face of a larger army. Except his own foes were the other houses, not an opposing nation. He doubted that was any better.

His carriage awaited him on the other side of a metal gate typically used to bring competitors and animals discreetly into the arena. Despite not owning the arena, his investments in Tiuz had earned him the right to come and go throughout its hidden passages as he pleased.

*"Money opens many doors, my young flame,"* his mother always said. She'd intended it figuratively, but sometimes wise sayings meant exactly what they stated. Regardless, he did own his carriage and the two horses pulling it, and he greeted each with a blow into their noses before tipping his hat to Regizald.

"I appreciate the haste."

Regizald opened the door with an elaborate wave. "Haste implies carelessness, my lord."

"Then I appreciate your speed. It seems you have learned something from your time with me after all." Zinarus stepped into the carriage with help from Regizald, his mechanical leg creaking. He'd need to return to his workshop and tweak it again. The schematics from his contacts in Ogrenia had improved his design of the leg, but it was far from perfect yet. With Regizald's help, he was sure they would figure it out. "Thank you, my friend. I do not *hasten* to wonder what I would do without you."

He shut the door and unbuttoned his suit as he sat on one of the cushioned benches. It was dreadfully tight nowadays, but he pondered what lay ahead before worries of his weight distracted him.

All the world seemed to pull him from his work—especially on days like this. Many a scion believed his time spent at the jousts was for recreation. They were wrong. Beyond his investments in Tiuz, there were connections to be gained at the arena, and one day, he hoped to reap the ticket profits himself instead of relying on bets. It was difficult enough to make a profit when so many of the fights were determined in smoke-filled rooms before the competitors stepped foot in the arena. Shameful. Sport was meant to be played with honor, but few had it.

Something shifted in the darkness across from him.

Zinarus tensed, only catching it out of the corner of his eye. Had it been a trick of the mind? Light was inconstant through the windows of the now moving carriage, but he could have sworn he had seen something. Swallowing, he reached out to flick the air, sure he would find nothing and calm his fears.

A force struck his arm. He pulled away, only to find himself bound by an unseen foe squeezing his right wrist so hard he was certain it would break.

"Who are you?" he stammered, trying to thump against the carriage door to alert Regizald and his driver.

Like a veil dropping, a figure robed in red appeared, shadows creeping across his sharp, clean-shaven chin and narrow lips. The darkness remained over his eyes and nose, enough to conceal his identity as his talon dug into Zinarus's wrist.

Zinarus's breaths caught in his throat. But he had Reaching of his own.

He wriggled his free hand, trying to remove the glove from over his Truth Reacher talon. It was no use. His house seamstress had made them fit near perfectly, and he accomplished little before the man spoke.

"We have been watching you, Zinarus the half-blood."

Zinarus gritted his teeth. "I… I am a scion of House iz Vamiustok! My father is Uzrin Ioniz, and he would not appreciate you accosting his—"

"His bastard son?" the Dark Reacher replied, lip curled. "I doubt he would care in the slightest. Perhaps he would even thank me for ridding him of a burden like you—not that we need a petty house like Ioniz to approve of our actions."

"What do you want from me?"

The man released him and leaned back on his bench, as if to relax. The window light made his robe seem to grow and shrink around him, but the dark strip where his eyes should have been remained fixed upon Zinarus. "Your pitiful family has one resource to provide the Commonwealth, and it cannot be trusted to one with tainted blood."

Zinarus rubbed his wrist. It throbbed as feeling returned to it, and he traced the line where the man's talon had marked his skin. "You seek our sand mines? Well, they are not for sale, and do not for a moment believe that veiled threats will deter my will." His mother was the matriarch of the house, but she'd placed most business decisions in his hands as heir.

"You will find a generous offer for your house's properties on your desk. Consider it well. We are not patient, and failure to accept will not end well for you or your precious mother."

"Don't touch her!"

The Dark Reacher cackled. "Remember this fear when you make your decision." Then he vanished into darkness.

Zinarus ripped off his glove and Reached into the realm of Truth to compel him to stop, but the Dark Reacher threw open the door and jumped free. Or at least Zinarus thought he did, based on the sound of boots striking the cobblestone outside.

Regizald shouted for the carriage driver to stop moments later. He scrambled into the carriage, grabbing Zinarus's arm.

"Sir, is everything alright?" he asked, his own glove gone to reveal his talon. He likely believed his master's mechanical leg was malfunctioning.

Zinarus sat deathly still, forehead wrinkled as he glared at the empty space across from him. He trusted Regizald completely, but the Dark Reacher may have lurked nearby. "Everything is fine. Please, just ensure we arrive at our townhouse."

"Then you will be pleased. We were about to stop in a few moments' time before the door flung open. I feared your knee needed to be mended."

He helped Zinarus out of the carriage, but Zinarus continued from there on his own, his cane thudding against the cobblestones as he approached his Kalastok home. A crescent-like structure, the building wrapped around a fountain that fed spiraling pools that filled the park. His family's townhouse lay behind a pool to the left.

A woman stood by the door.

*What have I done to deserve such a bother today?*

Zinarus held his composure despite his shock and greeted the woman as kindly as he could muster. She gave a curtsy, tugging upon a dress with floral patterns spiraling up it like vines choking a tree. That was plenty to tell Zinarus she was a Nochlander. The matching scarf covering her hair only confirmed it.

"You must be the ambassador from Nochland that my mother has told me so much about," he said, removing his hat and bowing. His tufts of bright red hair must have been in disarray from the hat, but she either did not notice or was too kind for her gaze to linger upon it.

"Correct," she replied with a gentle tilt of her head. "I am Alyniana of the Wayfarers, Nochland ambassador to the Commonwealth of Two Nations. My apologies for intruding outside your home, but I had hoped we could speak before the Chamber's assembly this evening. I have a proposition that my country believes will benefit us both greatly."

*Is this the Dark Reacher's proposal?*

Zinarus hid his question behind a bow. "Of course, Ambassador. Come inside, and let us speak."

Alyniana held her hands before her, covering something on her left hand as Zinarus led her into his townhouse. Its foyer was modest by scion standards, but pristine. Not a single strand was out of place on any of the woolen rugs that covered much of the floors as they passed a staircase before turning into a small room. Most scions left the first floor of their townhouses to the servants, but despite Zinarus's correspondences with his Ogrenian friends, they had yet to design a stair-climber for him that did not fail as often as it succeeded. His office would've been a servant's bedroom, and it was barely wide enough to hold a desk and an overstuffed bookshelf.

Zinarus set his cane against the shelf, then scooted into the chair behind the desk. It was rigid, uncomfortable, but he preferred it that way. Better than dawdling over paperwork for too long when there was much to be done for his workshop and family business negotiations.

An unopened letter lay on the desk, bearing the House Oliezany sigil of a thorned rose. He covered it instinctively, but despite his attempts to hide his discomfort, sweat trickled down his brow. Had the Dark Reacher sent Alyniana to see how he reacted to the letter?

"Niniaxi!" he called out to his maid. "Could you bring a goblet of Nochlander red for Ambassador Alyniana and myself?"

The stout Ezmani maid tucked her head into the room to eye the visitor before hurrying off as Alyniana sat in a chair that matched Zinarus's. She shifted, as if expecting more cushion than she found. "I appreciate the gesture, Lord Zinarus. It has been over a year now since I have been home, so every taste of it is a gift."

He glanced at the letter, then slid open a drawer and placed it inside. Out of sight, though, it was hardly out of mind. "What did you wish to speak to me about, Ambassador?"

"Your sand mines are among the few remaining on the continent of Brakesh that are not under the control of the empires or great houses," she said, her speech slow and deliberate. "Though Nochland has much to offer, we have a great lack of fine sand, and the increasing occurrences of awakened attacks have stressed our supply of glass to its limits. The merchant guilds are focused entirely on countering this Spirit Plague that haunts your nation as well. We need aid to replenish our supplies before the awakened overrun what remains."

Zinarus leaned forward as Niniaxi arrived with the wine. The goblets were metal, as House iz Vamiustok's few glass ones were reserved for their estate, but he found the taste of Nochlander red like a sweet kiss no matter the vessel.

"My apologies," he said, taking a gulp rather than a sip. His mind was still spinning from the Dark Reacher's attack, and he'd take whatever he could to dull it. "I wish to help those in need, as you have likely seen in the Chamber, but my family lacks the funds for such charity from our cornerstone business."

"I seek not charity but trade," she insisted. "We have the funds necessary to pay for such glass at a premium higher than any other buyer you have today."

He raised his brow. "Then why do you come to a supplier of minor repute such as myself instead of seeking aid from the empires? They say Ogrenia has glass far purer than anyone else's, and we need not discuss Reshka's and Kelosh's vast reserves."

She tugged on her left glove, revealing that her index finger was missing. "The Keloshans know nothing of my people. When I was a medic during the last war, they sliced off my finger during a raid because they believed I wore a talon like the Reachers of your nation. If they do not understand we use wands to Reach, what else will they—or any of the empires—fail to grasp of our culture when they attempt to gain dominion over us? The Commonwealth has faded because of its failure to understand the manipulations of its rivals, and Teplos has shown what Kelosh imposes upon its vassals. Ogrenia shows a kinder face upon the surface, but I promise you, no nation understands the threat of the privateer kings more than Nochland."

"I understand your plight, Ambassador." Zinarus pushed himself to his feet and paced across the narrow room, his leg making a horrible sound as its mechanical knee screamed to be fixed. Why did she have to pick such an inconvenient time? "If you would allow, I would prefer some time to consider this arrangement, as many Ezmani do not appreciate businessmen like myself dealing with foreign entities."

"Of course." She pulled a letter from her satchel and placed it on the desk—right where the Oliezany one had been. "You will see in these details that we do not ask for your entire supply, but it is surely enough to aid House iz Vamiustok in its wish to be named among the great houses."

"Why do you assume we have such a desire?"

She gave a knowing smile before sipping her wine. "Please, Lord Zinarus. I have spent enough time among your people to know it is what every house desires." That brought a chuckle out of him. "If there is nothing else you wish to discuss on the topic, I will leave you to prepare for the Chamber meeting this evening. After the king's speech, I am sure it will not be a dull one."

Zinarus returned to the desk, still without his cane, and traced the letter, his gaze distant. What was he to do? "Very well. Thank you, Ambassador. I shall let you know my decision soon. In the meantime, I wish the best for your nation, and if I find the king's ear—which I doubt due to my position among the opposition—I will seek to mention Nochland's plight."

Alyniana stood and curtsied. "I am grateful, as are the millions who live at risk of the Spirit Plague and the awakened attacks. We should stand together in this."

Then she left with Regizald hurrying after her to open the door.

Zinarus stared down at her letter before pulling the Oliezany one from his desk. *What are the odds?* he wondered. Two offers on the same day: one forcing the sale of House iz Vamiustok's mines, and the other sending the sand to aid a nation in need. At the right price, such a deal with Nochland could change everything for his family's fortunes. But the Dark Reacher's warning hung in his mind.

"Mother would say to be brave," he whispered to himself.

He grabbed his letter opener and sliced through the seal of Nochland's Merchant Council. Though he would write to Sania to explain his decision, it would take at least a hundred-hour for the letter to reach her, let alone for her to reply. He was here to make business decisions for the good of their house.

That was exactly what he would do.

# A Glassblade in a Haystack

*"When the Glassblades knock upon any door in the lands of old Piorak, they will receive a hero's welcome until the end of time."* – Harianus iz Ramiona, former Vockan general

Radais's hands shook as he sauntered down what felt like the thousandth street that day. Remnants of his roaring hangover lingered in his head and stomach, but it was hard to tell whether it was due entirely to his drinking or at least in part because of his absolute failure.

Miv had given him one instruction—give the letter to Ivalat iz Ardinvil and tell no one else. He'd lost the letter, and House iz Ardinvil had turned him away at the door *again*. Spirits, he was a fool. After hours of knocking on every great house door in hopes of finding someone who would listen, he was in the same place he'd started the day: hungover, hopeless, and without a Reacher to save his father.

A stray thought led Radais down this street near the Kala River. Few respected House Niezik, who'd made their bed with King Yaakiin the Reshkan, but the commanders had spoken highly of Leonit, the house's former patriarch. A fallen great house still had a voice in the Chamber. It was better than nothing, and he was desperate.

He checked the address on the scribbled note a House Kuzon butler had written for him. The darkness made it difficult to read both it and the signs posted before each townhouse, even in the lamplight, but when he crossed a narrow bridge over a stream, he soon found what he thought was the right building. A footman was unloading a carriage in front of it.

"Excuse me," Radais said, clearing his dry throat. "Is this House Niezik's residence?"

The footman's head popped out from within the carriage. A scrawny young man of middling height, russet hair streaked with strands of gray slipped out from his fur hat. "May I ask who is asking?" He thought for a moment, nose wrinkled as he scratched his head. "My apologies. I could have phrased that better. Who are you?"

Radais tapped the scabbard at his back. "Master Radais of the Glassblades, seeking a scion willing to hear a warning from Supreme Defender Miv."

"The Glassblades?" The footman gasped, his eyes darting from the sword to the building. "Er, yes. I believe Lady Katarzyna would want to hear about this."

"Lady Katarzyna? I was told the matriarch hasn't been in Kalastok for over a decade."

The footman lifted a suitcase with some effort. "That changed today. Follow me."

Radais followed him into a small foyer, then waited as the footman proceeded to half-drag, half-carry the suitcase up the steps with his face growing increasingly redder. A maid soon came to take Radais's woolen overcoat, a Glassblades patch sewn on its shoulder, and Radais thanked the spirits for the distraction. It discomforted him to wear a formal shirt and jacket under his coat, but at least Miv had allowed him to travel in one familiar piece of clothing. His blade and coat were the only things that felt normal about his situation.

Sometime later—after many thuds upon the stairs above—the

footman returned with his mop of hair stuck to his sweaty brow. He cleared his throat. "She will see you in the study. Right this way."

Radais's chest tightened as he climbed to the elaborate townhouse's second floor. After seasons spent in remote villages and the Spirit Wastes, Palmia Fortress had felt like a luxurious escape, but it couldn't match the rich designs spread throughout every crevice of House Niezik's rooms here. His eyes darted from piece to piece—he'd have to sketch them later.

If this was a house fallen from glory, what then did the townhouses of houses Bartol, Oliezany, and Pikezik hold? How much wealth was confined within scion walls, never to see the light again? He hadn't made it past their front doors, but his imagination alone had him in awe.

Thoughts of anywhere else faded at the sight of the study. Like an ode to literature, books were everywhere, but unlike in Miv's chambers, they weren't thrown haphazardly across the room. He chuckled to himself. Both ways had their beauty.

"Welcome, Radais of the Glassblades," a woman in a fine gray dress said, standing behind the desk at the far side of the room.

Radais bowed before returning his gaze to the woman. She had light, ashen hair like the remnants of a roaring flame that had long since extinguished. The waves framing her face failed to dull her sharp features, and her voice cut no softer.

"I am Katarzyna, matriarch of House Niezik," she said, "but you may call me Kasia if you wish. Tazper tells me my fellow scions have been hardly welcoming. Forgive me for saying that I am not surprised. They play games around the throne, and matters become complicated when people like you and I enter the fray." She extended an open hand toward one of the sofas in the room's center. "Please, sit. Have you been offered refreshments?"

She called for a maid before Radais could appeal, but when the maid appeared, his thirst got the better of him. It had been a long day with little rest. "I am here strictly on business," he said. "Water will do."

Kasia nodded to the maid with a wry smile, then rounded the desk and sat on the sofa closest to the wall. A gridded game board rested on a small table between them. Each of its wooden pieces resembled figures such as monarchs, dragons, knights, and peasants. Radais caught Kasia staring at him as he studied the pieces and sat.

"Are you familiar with haataamaash?" she asked, picking up a piece painted in red and rolling it between the fingers of her gloved left hand. It depicted a child with a hand up to its mouth as if to whisper.

"I am not. My family had little time for games, and the Glassblades value honor and strength over wit."

"That is a mistake that has led them to an unfortunate position. Honor can take you far until you face a foe without it." Kasia set the piece down, then adjusted it to ensure it was in the center of its square. But he caught her eyes flicking to him, as if judging his honor. "My father tried to teach me through games like this, which he believed represented a portion of the dynamic strife that is the balance among the great houses. This particular game is a Reshkan one, and we used to play it each evening. My mother despised me breaking my curfew, but that was half the fun of it."

The maid returned with a pitcher of water and a metal goblet for each of them. She gave Radais a kind smile, which he returned before gulping it down. Where was this woman headed with her story?

"My apologies, Lady Katarzyna, but I do not know much about house politics," he finally said, dropping his head. "That's probably why I found myself at your doorstep."

"Impeccable timing that you did, too. I have been in the city for merely a few hours; however, you are not here to discuss games and my travel." Her smile faded as she leaned forward on her crossed legs. "What brings a Glassblade all the way to Kalastok, knocking upon the gates of the great houses?"

Radais sighed, that tension in his chest returning. "I was to deliver a letter from Supreme Defender Miv to Lord Ivalat iz Ardinvil, detailing what I found in the Spirit Wastes a few hundred-hours ago, but he turned me away."

"May I see this letter?"

He scratched the back of his neck. "I believe it may have been stolen."

She rubbed her left forearm, lips pursed. "Unfortunate, but luckily, you still have your voice to tell it yourself. I assume Ivalat was not so accepting of a fellow Vockan?"

"No. His butler said that he'd hear no more requests from the Glassblades, because we 'give little, but ask for much.' " He shook his head, jaw clenched. "They are Vockan nobility, yet they sit in Kalastok instead of listening to their people."

Kasia took a sip, the ends of her mouth flicking up for a fleeting moment. "Ah, a political statement nearly slipped off your tongue, Master Radais. Careful. Your order is supposed to be neutral, and I doubt many in this city would look fondly upon you changing that."

He winced. "Yes, of course."

"I jest," she said with a chuckle. "But most scions would not do so. Please, continue with your story."

He recounted the events leading up to his discovery of the scion in red and the fight against the group of awakened. It felt crazy for him to mention voices, as the awakened never spoke, but he knew what he'd heard. Glassblades often returned from the Wastes with strange stories. None of them, though, had ever matched what he'd experienced, and his heart raced as memories followed his words.

Throughout the story, Kasia remained silent, her gaze fixed upon him. It was neither longing nor bored, and he hoped that meant she was taking him seriously. The days' rejections had hit him hard enough when he'd been rejected at scion doors. To fail now would mean she didn't believe him, and he had no way to change her mind.

"Supreme Defender Miv thought my discovery could be connected somehow to the Spirit Plague," he finished, "so she sent me to try and get the Chamber's attention. I don't know who that man was, but he was a Reacher for sure."

Kasia leaned back, biting her lip and squinting at the bookshelves behind him. "You are certain this scion was with House Oliezany?"

Radais reached into his bag and pulled out the pistol bearing the dragon across its barrel. "Miv… The supreme defender said that this is their work."

"They are master gunsmiths, yes. May I hold it?"

When he nodded, she took the pistol eagerly, examining it and tracing the dragon with her gloved fingers. "Its design is immaculate. Likely, it was crafted at an Oliezany forge, but it could have been for a buyer. If you are willing to part with it, I could send my footman, Tazper, to investigate who crafted it, and then who purchased it. That should help us narrow down who your corpse was."

"Why don't you just ask House Oliezany directly?"

She scoffed and set the pistol aside. "The only discussions House Oliezany and I could have about pistols would be where to duel with them. Their magnate, Gornioz the Eighth, hated my father, and he is the reason King Jazuk sits upon the throne. I am certain they would have preferred I never come to the capital." She paused, drumming her fingers across her leg. "You said the man wore red robes, correct? Would you describe them as crimson?"

"I..." He hesitated, thinking back to the encounter. "I'm not one for colors. It was a purer red than my hair, not too bright or dark."

Kasia took another sip. "I believe you, Radais, and I agree that it is at least an odd coincidence that you discovered this man around the same time that the Spirit Plague began to spread like wildfire. Second Awakening or not, it concerns me. I admit, some of it is selfish, knowing that the disease affects we scions too, but I have no desire to watch the lowborn suffer from it either. If there is a conspiracy here, I will help you uncover it."

Radais took a deep breath, a great weight lifted off his shoulders. "Thank you, Lady Katarzyna, but my role was to deliver this message, not to investigate further. I am a Glassblade master. I belong in the villages, where I can protect people from awakened. Besides, I must find a Body Reacher to heal my father of his illness."

"Your role is to protect people from awakened wherever you go, is it not?" She plucked a knight from the haataamaash board and spun it in her fingers. "Stay a while longer. I insist. You have traveled a long way, and it would be a waste for you to return to Palmia Fortress after a single conversation. I will fund your Reacher when I am finished with you."

Radais pressed his knuckles into his palm. A part of him wanted to fight further, but his thoughts returned to his father. Spending a few more days in Kalastok in return for a Body Reacher would change everything.

"Thank you, Lady Katarzyna," he said. "I will leave the address of my inn with your footman so that you can let me know if you need anything."

She set down her goblet and stood quickly. "No, if we are investigating House Oliezany, then we must be careful. They control most of Kalastok's Spirit Reachers and who knows how many other factions in the city. You will stay in one of the guest rooms here until you are ready to go."

Radais shook his head, sure he was mishearing her. "Are you sure?"

"Perfectly." She checked her watch. "If you will excuse me, I must prepare to attend a meeting of the Chamber of Scions. My handmaiden, Kikania, will help you settle in. Feel free to send Tazper to fetch any of your bags from whatever inn you were staying at."

The maid from before showed Radais to a room down the hallway. Small but well-furnished, it was superior in every way to the smokey inn from last night. Not that he remembered much about it between his rough sleep and spinning head.

At least now the brunt of his hangover had passed, but clarity brought anxiety with it. Completing his task in Kalastok would not bring the end of his time here, and Miv would question his involvement with an Ezmani house. But he'd faced enough in his life to know that no plan ever worked to perfection. This would do until he could think of something better. Until then, he had a free place to rest, a sponsor among the scions, a potential Body Reacher, and a lead with this Tiak-Kath that Naniana-Li had directed him toward.

He dropped his bag onto a desk against one of the bedroom's walls, pulling out his sketchbook and flipping to his sketch of Naniana-Li. The young woman, if not a girl, had confidence beyond her age. Whether he could trust her, he didn't know, but a shaky lead was still a lead.

Awakened had led him down fainter trails before. Hopefully, this one would get him information about the spirits and maybe even the money to save his father. His heart ached not knowing which to value more.

With a sharp breath, he flipped to the next page and drew a few of the townhouse's rooms from memory. Working without a reference was a skill, but he took joy out of creative interpretation and how the mind could twist what it had seen. There would be a chandelier in one instead of a lamp. The stairs could head the opposite direction. And the confident matriarch could have either a shadow draped over her face or a convincing smile.

The clocktower chimed for the seventeenth hour from across the Market District. Radais's stomach rumbled at the realization he hadn't eaten since leaving the inn that morning, but he needed to find Haxan's Hall soon if he didn't want to miss his meeting with Tiak-Kath. He promised himself a heavy meal and a heavier drink once that was finished.

He gave Tazper the name of the inn on the west side of town before he left. There was something off about that boy, he thought, but it was better than the brutes that had greeted him at many of the other houses. All powerful houses had enforcers ready to stop an incursion from rivals or gangs. If House Niezik had the same, though, he had yet to see it.

*Unless Tazper is the enforcer?* he thought to himself before laughing it off. The boy didn't have a Reacher talon. Even Radais's glass sword would be more effective against people than him, and it would shatter after a few good swings.

He headed east through the city, crossing street after cobblestone street in search of Haxan's Hall. There were so many people. It made that tight feeling in his chest return as he longed for the open air of the mountains or even the Wastes. At least there, he could travel without worrying about bumping into someone, and each person he passed here gave a worried glance at his sword. Had they never seen a Glassblade before? They were far from rare in Vockan lands, but people here acted as if he were an awakened who'd come to attack them.

Those gazes intensified as he entered the northernmost square of the Market District. Scions and the few richer lowborn gave him space despite his hope of asking for directions. People crowded around dozens of booths and stores that ringed the plaza. It was louder than battle, and Radais clenched his fists until he spotted a sign down a side alley.

*Haxan's Hall*, it read. *Cards, Drinks, and Merriment for the Finest Folk.*

He huffed and headed inside the red-brick building, where upbeat music met him. Dancing couples filled part of the L-shaped hall space before giving way to rounded card tables, not unlike the ones he'd played at the night before.

Except instead of grumpy workers, everyone here was dressed in long, fashionable suits and dresses. Younger men and women gathered in groups and whispered to each other as red-faced ones crossed the hall to ask for a dance or a drink. Radais smiled, watching them for a moment before his thoughts turned to his own failed romances.

The bar was at the opposite end of the hall, around the corner from the performers, and Radais was grateful for that. He'd thought the plaza to be loud, but this had his head throbbing already. How did the youth stand this for so long?

The bartender matched Radais's Vockan height, standing high above the crowd and smirking as he met Radais's gaze. "Rare that we see swordsmen here. Didn't you hear that guns were invented?"

"I'm a Glassblade master," Radais replied, leaning upon the bar, which resulted in a group of scions scampering away.

"That's great," the bartender replied as he cleaned a metal wine goblet, "but I can't have you scaring off my customers."

"You don't believe me."

The bartender scoffed. "Not every fool with a sword is a Glassblade, pal."

Radais took a deep breath, already regretting what he was about to do. He backed away from the bar and drew the sword enough for its glass to become visible. "Believe me now?"

What scions hadn't already scattered did so at the sight of the weapon, and curious murmurs echoed through the hall behind him. He had pointedly not wanted to draw attention. There was no hope in that anymore.

"I'm looking for an Ogrenian named Tiak-Kath Lori," he continued. "Where is he?"

"He… Uh…" the bartender stammered, stepping back. "Look, I'm sorry. He's in the private room down the hall, but Nex already came to see him. Not sure what else you want, but just put the sword away, alright?"

Radais shook his head as he sheathed the blade. "Who is Nex?"

"You don't know them?"

"Them?"

The bartender sighed. "Yeah, don't call Nex *she*. They walk their own path—just like how you should walk out of here. Nex doesn't like being talked about."

*So much for getting a drink.*

Radais opened the door at the end of the bar, heading down a hallway with angular wooden and metal artwork hanging on the brick walls. The art was unlike anything he'd seen. Strangely beautiful, he would've had to stand there for longer to figure out what it was meant to show, but there was no time for such things as he reached a closed door at the end of the hall.

He knocked. "Hello?"

"Come in," a woman's voice answered.

He tensed at that, but could Tiak-Kath have been a pseudonym? Was this whoever Nex was supposed to be? The door had no answers, so he opened it and stepped inside.

The light was dim within, and it took his eyes a moment to adjust as the door clicked shut behind him. When he finally took in what lay before him, he reached for his blade, but a gun cocked to his side.

"Do not move," the same woman said as she pressed the gun to his head.

Radais stared at the corpse in the room's center. An Ogrenian man was slumped back over a card table, his throat slit and one of his eyes missing as blood pooled around him.

*Why did I ever leave the mountains?*

MARCH AGAINST THE PLAGUE
DEMAND RELIEF
THE DEAD
RISE
THE KING IGNORES OUR PLIGHT!
The dead turn to awakened as the scions keep their Reachers to themselves. Towers rise in the east to protect the rich, but what have we? The Chamber must act, or they will face our fury!
ONLY PARAS HELPS US NOW

# DISEASE AND DISMAY

*"It is decreed that, by the approval of King Jazuk Bartol the Fourth and the Chamber of Scions, all those of Keloshan blood be hereby exiled from the Commonwealth of Two Nations and barred from reentry until this emergency ceases."* – An excerpt from The Keloshan Act

Chanting filled the streets of Kalastok. Lowborn marched across the river, swelling across the Market District as their torchlight cast an eerie orange hue over the buildings. Their voices echoed and they held signs stating their demands, but from atop House Bartol's balcony, Nikoza need not hear their voices to know what they wanted.

Except even the king could not cure the Spirit Plague.

Royal guardsmen, city watchmen, and great house mercenaries alike blocked the crowd's path to the Crimson District. So far, no shots had been fired, but Nikoza feared that would change. As long as none were fired at her grandfather's carriage, then they would be lucky.

Jazuk took a puff of his cigar, and its smoke swirled through the air to join that from the many torches. "What would you have me do?" he asked.

"It is the scions who elected you," Nikoza replied, waiting at the balcony door with her arms folded. "Yet you are called king of all people of the Commonwealth. Perhaps it is best to listen to their pleas."

"If only it were so simple."

The Spirit Plague spread further by the day, and reports of the increasing death count among lowborn and scion alike covered Jazuk's desk. The disease was bad enough by itself. Victims returning as awakened only made problems worse, and with no Spirit Reachers on the west side to repel such attacks, they would surely continue. Nikoza's Uncle Chatik claimed that Kelosh was the source of the accursed disease. That left her grandfather with little choice, but she would have her say.

"Grant Reachers to the Industrial District and Shadow Quarter," Nikoza replied, stepping to his side. Her voice was meek, but she held her shoulders back and her chin high. "Petition the anointed sister to send priestesses of the Crystal Mother to comfort the dying and the mourning, or at least listen to this alchemist, Paras ik Lierasa. They say he has a cure and that he should lead. Speak to him, and you can show the lowborn that you care for *all* your people."

"I am told Paras is a con-man and a fool," Jazuk replied harshly. "There is no cure, and the disease will spread if we do not contain it across the river. Scions will perish. Our reserves of Reachers will fail, allowing Kelosh to gain the upper hand in this war to come."

She rested a hand upon his and gently guided the cigar from his mouth. "Is this what you wish to be remembered for? Exiling foreigners out of fear and quarantining the most vulnerable lowborn in the west side?"

He huffed. "I wish for peace of mind, a strong smoke, and your grandmother's head to lie upon my shoulder once again. Understand, child, that wishes are for drunk men and foolish girls. Our realm does not grant wishes—it destroys them. It is only natural. As is war."

"You do not believe such things, Grandfather."

"I believe in what must be done to protect the scions of Ezman."

Leaving Nikoza calling after him, Jazuk snatched his cane and headed through his office. Votzan awaited him there as Nikoza sauntered behind with her head bowed. The chill had seeped into her bones during their time on the balcony, and she took her coat as Votzan helped Jazuk with his. It was not a patriarch's finery but a scarlet general's jacket with golden epaulets and glass chains across the chest. A lie. Jazuk had guarded Kalastok from the towers, but he had never served in the army. Nor, however, had many kings in the Commonwealth's century-long history.

"You do not approve?" Jazuk asked Nikoza as he adjusted the well-fitted jacket.

"Emperor Mataron wears military garb when he speaks," she replied.

Votzan raised a brow. "And is he not the respected and feared leader of Kelosh? One must dress like their station. Your advisors believe you have appeared passive for far too long, so we made a change."

"I must be seen as a king prepared for the trials ahead," Jazuk confirmed. "Get me to the Chamber meeting before these lowborn burn the city to its foundations."

Guards kept the protestors at bay as Nikoza followed at Jazuk's coattails. She gave a nervous glance toward them, so he took her hand. "It will be—"

A shot rang out, followed by a mighty cry from the crowd. They burst through the thin line of guards as many shouted Jazuk's name and enough slurs to make Nikoza blush. Jazuk pulled her inside, calling for the Air Reachers outside to push on with haste. Votzan had barely clambered into the carriage by the time it got moving, but it was too late.

Faces appeared in the windows. Crazed desperation filled their eyes as they clung to the carriage and pounded upon its doors. Outside, the Reachers demanded they cease their attacks, but for many, they believed their pleas to be life or death. Nikoza winced as they dragged one of the Air Reachers from his perch, causing the carriage to lurch with it only being pushed from one side.

"This must cease!" Jazuk stammered as the remaining Air Reacher's footsteps shifted toward the center of the carriage. She cried out at the crowd's attacks, but the carriage soon outpaced them, allowing Jazuk to take a long breath before he stomped his cane.

"These mindless fools must be banished from the civilized sections of our city, or we will become a madhouse far before this disease takes us all."

"You will only anger them further," Nikoza said, looking to Votzan for aid, but the assistant shook his head. "We must search for a cure, not punishment."

"The king speaks well," Votzan said. "We must have calm in the city if we are to survive these times."

Guards swarmed past the window and headed to intercept the protestors. Mind and Truth Reachers led the charge upon horseback, their bracers of glass marking them as members of the Crystal Brigade. If force and gunpowder could not quell the crowds, then commands would have to do.

Jazuk smiled at their deployment, but Nikoza averted her gaze, tears stinging her eyes. Her grandfather believed that ruling would be far simpler with lowborn minds free from revolutionary sentiments. Such problems would not disappear with the wave of a Reacher's talon.

Enraged scions met them upon their arrival at the Crystal Palace. Some demanded executions, others a complete lockdown of Kalastok's west side, and Jazuk matched their fury. Nikoza could barely keep up as he found Gornioz Oliezany beneath the statue of the Crystal Mother, the patriarch's head bowed and his tall hat removed until he heard Jazuk's approach.

"We find ourselves in trying times," Gornioz said, turning with a wry smile. "You realize now that the law must be amended further to protect what truly matters."

Jazuk met the tall man's gaze. "Kelosh stirs unrest among the peasants from within our borders. I should have listened to you sooner."

Nikoza twitched at the lack of proof beyond her Uncle Chatik's claims, but what right did she have to deny the results of his investigation? Kelosh sought to invade. It was only logical they would use every means at their disposal to weaken the Commonwealth.

"What matters is that we still have time," Gornioz said. "The Chamber will accept a quarantine, appeasing the bloodthirsty and preventing a revolt from the reformers with hearts who bleed for the lowborn."

"We have the votes, then?" Jazuk asked.

Chamber rules dictated all laws be passed with two-thirds of the vote of those present to ensure the king could not overrule the scions with a slim majority. Despite Jazuk's constant complaints about the threshold, Nikoza was glad for it. A single man's whims could not overturn the will of the scions.

Gornioz scanned the gathering members of the Chamber. "If we do not, then we will bring the measure again after some persuasion. There are few in these halls whose minds cannot be changed."

As Jazuk replied, Nikoza noticed a young woman entering the hall. Dressed in a long high-collared coat trimmed with amber chains and a hat of dark koilee fur, she was an unfamiliar sight in Kalastok. However, rumors had spread of Lady Katarzyna Niezik's arrival, and Nikoza had a keen interest in what Leonit's heir intended during her first meeting of the Chamber.

"The Niezik girl could be quite useful to us, Jazuk," Gornioz whispered, following Nikoza's gaze. "Introduce yourself before the speech. My spies say she can be quite the foe, so let us keep her from becoming one unless necessary."

The king nodded, then made his way across the hall to meet the one they called the Amber Dame with Nikoza trailing behind.

**SMOKE FROM THE RIOTERS' TORCHES STUNG KASIA'S EYES** as she emerged from her carriage and glared up at the towering Crystal Palace, draped in the red and whites of Ezmani and Vockans alike. Its colors were yet another reminder of the Crimsons whom she sought, but she was certain her father's note meant more than pointing a finger at King Jazuk. Her encounter with Parqiz had only deepened those suspicions.

She glanced over her shoulder at the chaos that consumed much of eastern Kalastok. This Spirit Plague had spread rapidly during her travels according to Faniz, and based on the chants she'd heard, they blamed the king for his inability to stop it.

It had not been her intent to enter Kalastok's political fray during a time of such turmoil, but both Kelosh's mobilization and the Spirit Plague provided plenty of cover for her arrival. Finding Sazilz Uziokaki would be simple from here. As the magnate of a great house, he would have plenty of scions surrounding him in hopes of earning his support. Kasia's appearance at House Uziokaki's celebration of the Ephemeral Storms had accidentally provided another reason for her to meet with Sazilz. They were neighboring houses, and she could play the part of a struggling matriarch seeking aid to reestablish her family.

First came making herself known in the Chamber of Scions.

Eyes fell upon her the moment she stepped through the palace doors. Leonit had taken her to the Crystal Palace only once, stating that the scions there were like "ravenous wolves, lurking until the weakest prey is on their own," and her memories had failed to capture the beauty of it. Glass seemed to weave between the pillars of crimson and walls of marble, creating a pattern that glimmered in the lanternlight. It took her breath away.

The hall soon gave way to a rotunda where the six entryways met. Amid its center rose a statue to the Crystal Mother, and Kasia shied away from its gaze as she skirted toward the entrance to the Chamber itself. She'd had enough of her own mother. The last thing she needed was a crystal one decrying her sins.

A voice stopped her before she could pierce the crowd of scions chattering about the peasant riots.

"Has the matriarch of House Niezik truly appeared?" a man asked, his cane thumping against the floor.

Kasia turned to repel whichever of her father's rivals sought to mock her, but the sight of King Jazuk's crown shattered her spite. A wooden band, it held a crystal ring above his forehead in reverence to the Ezmani goddess. It clashed horribly with his silver hair. Not that she would ever tell the king such a thing.

"King Jazuk, my apologies. I had not noticed you," she said, stumbling over her words as she bowed. "My father did not bring me here often, so I was admiring the architecture before we gather."

The king leaned heavily upon his cane as his granddaughter, Nikoza lingered behind him. He was far shorter than Kasia had imagined, his back hunched and his steps little more than shuffles. No matter how old or frail he appeared, he had benefited from the coup that killed her father. But had he been part of it?

"Indeed," he said. "This building is a masterpiece, even when all created within it fails to match its splendor. I would call it a shame, but politics is an irreverent art. A thousand statues of the Crystal Mother could not purify the stench of pragmatism, and I fear it lingers upon me the most."

"Few would call your stand against the empires pragmatic," she replied in the nicest way she could manage without complimenting him.

"Yet many would call me spineless."

"Do you seek my opinion on such accusations?"

He chuckled and patted her on the arm. "I came to welcome you to the Chamber, dear girl, and to say that I despise the tragedy of Leonit's death. He and I disagreed on most matters in these halls. What I know, however, was that he sought the best for his house and this nation, even if he was not always honest about his means of doing so."

Kasia tensed, but she needn't reply, as the king huffed and urged the straying scions to head into the Chamber. What had him so impatient? The rumors said that he had been tardy to every Chamber meeting.

Unusual or not, she took the opportunity to slip into the Chamber, heading toward the reformer wing on the left side of the round room. Pillars separated the walking ledge from the rows of seated scions, and between them, she caught her first glimpses of the Commonwealth's greatest weapon. A hulking dragon made of shimmering gray crystal covered half of the throne's platform at the center of the Chamber. The pit descending to the Spirit Crystal surrounded it, threatening to swallow the throne and its dragon whole. Kasia dug in her heels as she considered the power lurking below. Such a void could draw anyone into its depths.

She found a seat among the higher benches of the reformers. Her heart grew heavy as she did, imagining her father's quiet dealings among their ranks as leaders debated across the room. Leonit would have loved the challenges of Kelosh, the Spirit Plague, and the increased awakened threat, but Kasia focused on the nationalists on the opposite side of the pit. Sazilz Uziokaki stood among them, wearing a horribly drab brown suit.

"That is quite the glare you have, Lady Katarzyna," a middle-aged woman said, pulling Kasia from her thoughts as she sat beside her.

Kasia eyed the newcomer. Obviously a foreigner—from Nochland based on the style of her floral dress and headscarf—she would've been stunning if she'd let her hair down and worn a dress that fit her curves. Leonit had called the Nochlanders nomads entrapped by their own roots. Where were this woman's?

"May I ask who I have the pleasure of meeting?" Kasia replied.

The woman extended her hand, which Kasia shook. "I am Ambassador Alyniana of the Wayfarers, and I come from—"

"Obviously Nochland," Kasia interrupted. "Keloshans wouldn't wear such flamboyant colors. Reshkans love their hair far too much to entrap it beneath a scarf. Ogrenians either act like pirates or professors. And your skin is far too fair to be an Ezmani scion."

Alyniana narrowed her eyes. "Quite perceptive. You truly are not what you seem from a distance."

"What did you believe me to be?" Kasia replied, resting her chin on her hands and admiring the dragon to feign disinterest.

"A mouse who has fallen into a palace with more venom than a pit of snakes."

Kasia failed to hide her twitch. "I appear that weak?"

"No." Alyniana followed her gaze to the dragon. "While a beast reveals its power from the moment you lay eyes upon it, a beautiful flower hides its poison beyond sight."

"So now I am poisonous? Oh, Ambassador, I fear your metaphor may be fluttering away like a butterfly from your flower's pollen."

"Poison can kill, or it can heal." Alyniana stood, clearing her throat as she surveyed the hall with a smile. "If you wish to use your strength to heal, then come join me for a walk along the river sometime. I believe we could be of great use to one another."

Kasia stuffed her hands into her pockets. The Fire Reachers kept the palace hot, but her heavy coat felt like armor against the daggers of her foes. "I will do that, Ambassador. Thank you."

"Call me Alyniana, please."

"Then you can refer to me as Kasia. My mother gave me my name's unnecessary Z, and I do not appreciate the gift."

Alyniana lifted a brow, but before she could speak, the Chamber fell silent beyond the thudding of a cane. King Jazuk stood atop the stairs with neither the presence of a warlord nor the grace of royalty, yet none spoke as he trundled toward the throne with Princess Nikoza in his wake. Divisions were deep among the scions. Tradition, though, held firm.

The dragon stared at Jazuk until he stopped before the throne, head at the slightest of bows. He sat, and every member of the Chamber followed except for a balding, yet fit man in front of Kasia. Wearing a coat cut like a commander's, he held out his arms and shouted at the king.

"A disease is not enough, your highness? Listen not to the whispers in your ear, but the cry of your people. We do not want war!"

The scion went to raise his fist, but a man dressed in purple pulled him back to his seat. That one caught Kasia's attention, as he had red hair yet dark gray skin. The Commonwealth's unity for a century had not led to many marriages between Ezmani and Vockan peoples, especially among the scions, so such a combination was rare. Who was this man?

King Jazuk looked toward the man who'd shouted, but said nothing. Instead, Gornioz Oliezany rose. A towering bearded scion with near white hair, he dominated the room as he mimicked the man's extended arms. "What have we without decorum, Tiuz of House Hazeko?" the Oliezany patriarch said. "The reformers decry our king, our nation, and our way of life. Is there nothing they respect besides a lance in the arena?"

"Surely not you!" Tiuz shouted.

The Chamber descended into arguments as reformers, nationalists, conservatives, and moderates alike accuse each other of heinous acts. Some were certainly true. Others not. Kasia refused to engage in the debates regardless, but she found an empty spot beside her when she sought to whisper to Alyniana.

A roar soon followed, the dragon's maw bearing dozens of razor-like teeth as the glass rimming the Chamber shook from the force. Kasia grinned as it extended its crystal wings as wide as the pit. There was no finer example of pure, unshackled force than a dragon. Her father's haataamaash board had shown that clearly, but it had also proven that nothing, no matter how cunning, could defy the inevitable end for one who wields such power.

Silence hung in the Chamber when the dragon ceased and curled itself around the throne. King Jazuk surveyed the scions from upon it, scratching his bearded chin.

"If we have nothing else, there will be order in this hall," he said. "We have all seen the very opposite of it that consumes much of Kalastok this eve, and tonight, we will work to right the situation in our nation. My son, Chatik, has brought answers to the questions we seek about the Spirit Plague."

A man stood from among the conservative faction. Clean-shaven with a scion-gray complexion, Chatik Pikezik had a sharp jawline and a suit cut just as sharply around a navy vest. His deep-set eyes made him appear older than a man in his mid-thirties, and with his wife, House Pikezik matriarch Lilita the Third, seated beside him, he had far more influence than most scions his age as well.

"Thank you, your highness," Chatik began with his hands held open toward the rest of the Chamber. "I speak today bearing grave news for our nation and our relationship with the empire of the east. We have identified that the Spirit Plague is not a naturally occurring disease, but one created by that very empire. Kelosh seeks to destroy us from the inside before marching upon Kalastok's ashes, and we have evidence that many immigrants within the city aid their malfeasance with each passing day."

Gasps came from many within the Chamber, and Kasia's chest tightened as Sazilz stood from among the nationalists. "In accordance with the findings of this investigation," he announced, "Houses Uziokaki and Oliezany are introducing the Keloshan Act to exile any and all peoples of Keloshan descent from within Commonwealth lands."

Murmurs spread throughout the reformers and moderates. Thousands of Keloshans had immigrated to Kalastok and other cities in search of work. Could they truly exile all of them? Would this lead to war?

Those same questions echoed in Kasia's head, but she remained focused on her target. Sazilz stood without Chatik's poise, glancing at those around him for approval. He needed to feel significant. She had her in.

"This law carries the full support of House Pikezik as well," Lilita said, standing beside Chatik as the matriarch of their house. "We cannot allow atrocities such as this to go unpunished."

Jazuk stomped his cane. "I thank these great houses for presenting such a crucial piece of legislation, but may I offer an amendment?"

Sazilz looked to Gornioz, who nodded.

"Very well," the king continued. "I suggest that we amend the law to further address the crisis we face with the Spirit Plague. It has become abundantly clear that the lowborn cannot be allowed to roam freely until the matter has been resolved. Those residing in Kalastok west of the river must be quarantined there until further notice; otherwise, we shall face an outbreak among the scions that would be completely unacceptable."

The Chamber erupted. Red-faced reformers accused the great houses of betraying their people, and moderates demanded the bill be rejected out of fear for the economic impact. The nationalists and conservatives sat quietly, content to let their opponents rage.

Leaders of all parties agreed upon the need for formal debates, but Kasia heard none of it. She recalled her conversation with Radais over and over, seeking a connection between this unrest and his discoveries in the Wastes. Something wasn't what it seemed. If House Oliezany were involved with the awakened as they pushed for war with Kelosh, were they the Crimsons she sought, or did her true enemies lie elsewhere?

# THE SERPENT AND THE SPY

*"Few forces on the continent of Brakesh have thrived better than Kelosh in the aftermath of the Piorakan Empire's collapse. Rivals remain, however, and it remains to be seen whether they can truly match their predecessor's glory."* –
Quaruus Taaniian, Reshkan historian

Radais stared ahead at the body of Tiak-Kath as the cold barrel of a pistol dug into his temple. Spirits, he couldn't wait to get out of this city.

"There's been a misunderstanding," he said, trying to keep calm.

The woman laughed. He could only see her out of the corner of his eye, and her woolen cap veiled any distinguishing features. "No, Radais of the Glassblades, there has not been. You are exactly the man I have been searching for."

"What do you want? I have little money, and my sword isn't all that useful if you're not trained with it."

"Information."

She circled around until she stopped before him with the gun held just out of arm's reach. Her skin was a mid-tone gray, matching her high-collared coat and a series of crystal rings that pierced the top of her left ear. A Keloshan Reacher…

"I doubt there's much I can help Kelosh with," Radais replied. "I just came back from the Wastes."

With her free hand, the woman pulled a bloodied piece of parchment from the pocket of her duster and held it up for him to see in the dim lanternlight. "Your supreme defender claims you had quite the experience there. Tell me."

He furrowed his brow. How had Tiak-Kath ended up with the letter? Had the woman at the bar, Naniana-Li, stolen it from his bag? "The letter didn't say?"

"It says to trust your word." She nodded toward her pistol. "So talk. I don't have 'til the end of everdark."

"Why would Kelosh care about the Wastes? Why did you kill this man?"

"Not scared of death, eh?"

He shrugged. "I spend enough time among the spirits of the dead to feel like them often. It might be better if I was one."

*Father needs me,* he reminded himself. *Lady Katarzyna can help, but she won't if I'm dead.* Besides, he needed to find this Naniana-Li, or Nex as the bartender had called them, and figure out why they'd stolen from him.

"I'll talk," he continued, "as long as you tell me who Tiak-Kath was and why you killed him."

"Fine." She tossed the letter aside. "He was an Ogrenian spy who sought to shift what remains of this pathetic Commonwealth into his empire's favor. Worse, he was part of an international group called the Children of Zekiaz."

"Never heard of them."

"That is their intention. They are secretive beyond all measure, and they value technology over all else, pitting empires against each other for their own gain. For obvious reasons, Emperor Mataron the Sixth does not see their continued rise as an appealing proposition." She stepped closer, pressing the gun to his forehead. "Now, I have given you what you wanted. No more games."

Radais had faced countless awakened over his decades of service, but his bravery vanished staring down that barrel. He had a sword.

He was significantly taller and more built than this woman. None of that mattered when she could kill him with a single pull of the trigger. Kasia had insisted that his information was vital, but what damage could Kelosh do with the knowledge that a single scion had been found deep in the Wastes?

So he told her. As shortly as possible, he explained everything he'd seen in the Wastes that night—except for the pistol he found on the man. He'd told few people about that, so there was no reason this woman would have any suspicion he was leaving anything out.

Her glare faded as he spoke about the man and Miv's fears about both the awakened and the Spirit Plague. He could've sworn there was fear in her eye, but she stepped back when he finished, gun still raised. "You know nothing about this man's identity? Just that he wore red robes and had a talon?"

Radais nodded.

"Then thank you, Master Radais," she said as she lowered the gun, her confidence returning. "You have done a great service to Kelosh. Consider your continued life a token of our gratitude, and know that if you tell anyone of this meeting, you will end up like our Ogrenian friend here. Understand?"

Another nod.

That must've been enough, because the woman holstered her gun before darting out the door faster than Radais could reach for his sword. Left alone in the room with only Tiak-Kath's bleeding corpse, he decided not to linger. He had no idea how he'd explain his presence in a room with a dead body while carrying a weapon perfect to slit a man's throat with.

Screams echoed from beyond the door.

Radais drew his blade and rushed out, hoping the Keloshan hadn't attacked the bar's visitors. But there was no sign of her when he reached the main halls.

Instead, people cried out and hid behind toppled tables as spirits shot through the air. Awakened. Their faces were distorted and their misty tendrils stretching like claws as hushed whispers rose from them. At least a dozen filled the room, and from the shouts outside, they weren't alone.

*Damn the mountains. Why did I remove my armor in the city?*

**KASIA GLANCED AT HER WATCH** as the Chamber's debate carried on. It was nearly the nineteenth hour, and she was ready to end what had felt like an infinitely long day. Unfortunately, she had a responsibility to vote against the Keloshan Law that would surely make her nation's problems worse.

Countless nationalists spoke in favor of the law, and with Gornioz Oliezany, Lilita and Chatik Pikezik, Sazilz Uziokaki, and King Jazuk Bartol himself behind it, she had little doubt they would have a strong majority in favor. The question remained, however, if they had two-thirds of the Chamber. With the final two great houses, Kuzon—her mother's birth house—and the part Vockans of iz Ardinvil, against the law, there would be significant opposition.

Ivalat iz Ardinvil stood from the front row of the moderates. Despite being thoroughly focused on his own family's power over the good of the Vockans, Leonit had spoken highly of the man who'd recently taken up the role of magnate. Kasia couldn't blame Ivalat either. Was she not in Kalastok entirely for her own purposes?

"A quarantine is a prudent measure to counter the riots we face in this city," he said, "but I cannot condone such a decision without any action to solve the problem. Furthermore, I cannot condone further brutality against the immigrants that fill my house's mines, House Oliezany's armament factories, House Pikezik's glassworks, and House Bartol's textile mills. This great city… Our great nation relies upon people of Keloshan blood who fled the very man who seeks to expand his tyranny to us now. Perhaps war is inevitable in the coming seasons, but let us ensure it is Emperor Mataron who feels its pain, not our own businesses."

Applause followed as Ivalat sat, and Tiuz Hazeko took his place, rising from amid the reformers. The balding major general was a surprising sight, despite his earlier outburst. The last Kasia had heard of him, he'd still been a cavalry commander, defeating the Keloshans in the last victory the Commonwealth had ever had against the empires. If anyone could stop the law, it was him.

"I am not a man of many words," Tiuz began, "so I will say only this. Our nation has faced Kelosh many times in both the defense of our borders and the expansion of them. I have led many charges against their lines and lost just as many brothers-in-arms. Do not do this. Do not lead us down the path of war, alienating our own people and creating a conflict we cannot win without aid."

The reformers stomped their feet in approval as he sat. When silence returned, Grand Secretary Votzan called for formal voting to begin. Voice votes were common in the Chamber, but due to the divided nature of the vote, Votzan called names and recorded the result. It took a dreadfully long time.

Kasia counted the votes to keep herself present. It was tighter than she'd hoped, and she was figuring out how many reformers were left when she realized Votzan was calling her name. Based on the stares, she assumed it wasn't the first call either.

She rose, holding her head high and her back straight as she met Sazilz's gaze. He was watching along with the rest of the Crimsons. Voting no would sever whatever hopes she had of getting close to him and his allies, but a surprise vote in favor would spark questions among them. Was she different than her father? Would she fall in line and support whatever the Crimsons planned? Her stomach churned knowing what horror she would aid by her vote, but she'd come for revenge, not politics.

"Aye!"

Her voice echoed through the Chamber for but a moment before the reformers shouted at her.

"You betray your father's legacy!"

"How much did they pay you?"

"You should have never come to this city!"

Through the abuse, she remained standing. Sazilz was still staring at her, so she offered him a wry smile and a nod. Her father had always said that politics was a game much like haataamaash. Some players chose the dragon, others the knight, the Reacher, or the bard. But from the moment Kasia had laid eyes upon the board, her favorite had been the spy, disguising its true form.

The vote continued as she climbed the stairs and rounded the room toward the nationalists. Many drew their attention from the vote itself, whispering about Leonit's daughter switching factions. Surprise was in her favor, but from this moment on, she was far beyond the bounds of any plan she'd conspired. The scions would be aghast for some time. Newspapers would decry or praise her betrayal of the reformers. Little did they know that she'd finished her rough count the moment her name was called, and even with her switch, the law would fall at least five votes short.

She hoped she was right.

Upon arriving at the top of the nationalist wing, she found Gornioz Oliezany waiting for her. He took her hand in greeting and kissed it as one would the hand of a queen. It took all her strength not to throw him down the steps, but her ruse had worked. Both her target and Radais's suspect were among this wing of the Chamber. Now, they would smile instead of sneer at her presence.

"You are quite the surprise, Lady Katarzyna," the giant of a patriarch whispered as the votes echoed behind him. His suit was boxy and his cravat was as puffed as a summer bird beneath his beard. This close, he smelled distinctly of cigar smoke, and Kasia held her breath to avoid coughing. "May I ask what has given you a change of heart?"

She did not shy away, despite her disgust. "I entered the Chamber with an open mind after the revolting display I saw in the streets this evening. If Kelosh has caused this, then why should we not punish them and contain the disaster?"

"I am pleased to hear such wisdom from one so young. Come, join me for the rest of this meeting. We will find you a more permanent seat for the future once this business is finished."

Votzan cleared his throat as Gornioz led Kasia down the stairs. Moments before, the man's voice had carried throughout the chamber, but it became little more than a squeak when he announced the vote totals.

Seven votes short.

"The Keloshan Act has failed to receive the—"

Screams interrupted him. Stark, horrific, they carried from the main hall of the palace until the marble and glass doors burst open. Kasia didn't have the chance to sit before cries filled the Chamber too.

Three spirits shot into the air, their smoke-like forms scanning the scions as the dragon roared from behind the throne. A chill crept down Kasia's spine. Drifters never moved so quickly, and the last time she'd seen an awakened break through a door, it had killed her father. How had they gotten into the most secure room in the Commonwealth?

Scions ripped off their gloves around her, the Spirit Reachers among them trying to control the attackers, but the awakened dove into the pit. Odd, hushed sounds followed them until they disappeared. Everyone in the Chamber took a breath, but surely, this wasn't finished.

A servant scrambled through the open doors, shouting as he clutched his bloodied chest, "Awakened are attacking the city! We need more Reachers. We need…"

The man collapsed. No one moved to help him, so Kasia bounded toward him, calling for a Body Reacher. "One of you must be! By the Crystal, do not just stand there like fools. People need our help!"

A woman from the moderates tended to the bleeding man as Kasia rushed into the main hall, not bothering to see who had followed. She was no Spirit Reacher, but her Death powers could kill an awakened too. It didn't matter that using them would reveal what realm she was bound to. If awakened were attacking Kalastok, it could be connected to Radais's discovery or even the Crimsons. She had to stop it.

Darkness covered the palace steps. Every lamp lining the streets had been extinguished, and only lanterns and torches carried by protestors and guards illuminated the awakened swooping over their victims. Kasia sprinted toward the closest group in the northern Market District.

Radais was already there.

Light refracted across his glass sword as he spun and slashed with more precision than she'd ever seen. He had no armor, but neither did he have fear in the face of the awakened swarm. After slicing through another of the spirits, he spotted Kasia, his expression hardening.

"You need to get out of here!" he demanded before raising his blade to block an awakened strike.

Kasia Reached into the realm of Death, deep purple wisps balling in her hands as she prepared a death bolt. The moment another awakened appeared in the light, she released her first attack… and badly missed.

*"You're risking everything you've worked for!"* Aliax shouted in her head. *"Everyone will know what you are."*

"What do you think you're doing?" Radais said, nearing her and going back-to-back by a dropped lantern. It gave them a dim sphere of light, but beyond it was darkness. "I've held them off for most of the non-Reachers to escape, but unless you're a Spirit Reacher, you can't stop them."

"I'm a Death Reacher," she snapped back before releasing another wave of death, doing her best to attack and conserve as much of her initial Reach's power as possible.

A ray of purple vapor shot from her hand and struck an awakened that had been diving toward her. The monstrosity dissolved into nothing as memories of Aliax's death washed over her. Her hands began to shake, so she focused all she could on the awakened. "Now shut up and let me help you, damn it!"

Radais's silence was enough of a reply as they traded attacks, covering each other as Kasia's heart pounded so hard it felt like it would burst from her chest. She wasn't a fighter. Sure, she could kill anyone with a simple point, but she'd only faced down awakened twice before. Both times there had only been one.

*"You promised me you'd stop Reaching,"* Aliax objected again. *"This will destroy you!"*

"Shut up!" she hissed.

Adrenaline pushed her focus to its limits. She Reached twice more in quick succession as her pool of power waned. Doing so risked Realm Taint, but that didn't matter when awakened threatened to slaughter both her and everyone in sight.

The awakened were faster than any person, and her unsteady hands sent most of her blasts far from their targets. Luckily, they were airborne, so even those didn't threaten any bystanders or allies.

No matter how many awakened she and Radais cut down, it was hard to feel useful with the screams echoing through the city. She'd only arrived hours before. Yet now, she suffered with each final cry.

Radais appeared to carry no such weight, fending off multiple awakened at a time until he began to slow. Not even a master Glassblade could keep up this pace. The awakened's shadowy tendrils drew closer with his weariness, as if sensing he would soon falter, and one slipped through the gap.

"Kasia!" he called out behind her, but she was busy releasing another wave of Death against the awakened before her. By the time she spun, it was too late. The spirit's tendrils struck her chest.

She closed her eyes, waiting for the agony of the awakened tearing through her body and soul. But it never came.

The awakened was gone when she opened her eyes again. It had been one of the final few, and a group of Spirit Reachers from the city watch arrived to repel the others as a warmth against Kasia's neck drew her attention. Her amber pendant pulsed, and when she looked closer, it was as if there were deep gray wisps swimming within it. She released the pendant, hand shaking.

*What just happened?*

Radais caught her as she stumbled. The crystal dragon roared overhead, and no more awakened shifted in the lanternlight. They'd done it. Crystal be damned… They'd survived.

"I need to get one of those swords," she mumbled, her head spinning as she steadied herself. She'd never felt like this before. Wisps circled the edge of her vision, and cold sweat dripped down her brow.

Was this the Taint?

Radais eyed her talon. "Keep that power hidden. I won't say a word, but if the great houses find out…"

She raised her gaze to the remaining crowd of lowborn and scions alike as Reacher light illuminated the plaza. They stared at both Radais and her in a mix of awe and fear until crimson-clad guards with bracers of glass rushed into the market. Kasia recognized the Crystal Brigade of elite guardsmen, but why were they here now? Some raised rifles, others taloned hands.

All of them aimed at her.

"Lady Katarzyna Niezik," the Reacher in front said. "You are under arrest for treason and endangering the public by failing to register your Death Reaching with the state. You are to come with us *now*."

Kasia threw out her arms, gesturing at the awakened that were no longer there. "You are arresting me for saving people? What is this?"

"Get on your knees!"

Her cheeks flushed as she scanned the growing crowd. They would scorn her even more now. Despite all the lives she'd saved, they would see her as nothing more than a forbidden Death Reacher, if they even let her keep her talon at all.

She knelt, keeping her chin raised as the Crystal Brigade placed bound gloves over her hands and tied them behind her back. Radais demanded the guards release her, but it was no use. The Crystal Brigade reported to the king and the great houses, no one else. If Jazuk wanted her imprisoned, there was nothing either of them could do.

# SECRETS DUG DEEP

*"What are we to choose when our options are survival or doing what is morally right? Is it wrong to value one's self and family over those one has not met? I confess, I do not know."* – Hermona Yakinoz, former sister of the Buried Temple

Zinarus hobbled up the Chamber stairs with the aid of Tiuz as cries filled the palace. How had this happened? More glass lined the walls of this palace than anywhere else in the Commonwealth, maybe even all of Brakesh itself. Awakened could not have entered without aid.

Who would do such a thing?

He lingered on that question, distracting himself from the terror creeping into his heart. Many in the Chamber were old and needed Body Reachers to extend their lives, but Zinarus was still young. It would be unfair for him to find his end so soon. Though his mother claimed life was never fair, had he not suffered enough from his father's abandonment and his amputated leg? Must Zekiaz tear his spirit from his mortal body?

Cursing, he pulled himself from Tiuz and pushed on. His blasted leg had stained every moment of his life—first the temporary wooden one, and now the mechanical one of his design. If this was his day to die, then by the Crystal Mother's name, he would do so fighting with his own strength.

"This way!" Tiuz called toward the other reformers and moderates who had followed, then headed down a side hall.

Zinarus fell behind, but he kept Tiuz in sight. Though he wished to fight for himself, he was not foolish enough to defy the cavalry commander who wished to save his life.

Hundreds of other scions were rushing toward the main entrance after Katarzyna Niezik had made quite the scene. Each of them was a target. Tiuz understood that, but where was he taking them? They headed down side passages that Zinarus had never known existed, let alone seen. The intricate glasswork and carved marble of the main rooms gave way to stone, and soon, their only way ahead was a stairwell heading down.

"Where does this lead?" Zinarus asked an elderly scion beside him.

"I have not a clue," the man replied. "Are you certain Lord Tiuz knows the way? He has a knack for finding trouble wherever he goes."

Zinarus clutched his cane. "I am not one prone to following the commands of others, but I trust Tiuz with my life." And he needed to. Without Tiuz to earn him his investment back, his mother would wring his neck anyway.

The air became heavy with smoke as they reached the base of the stairs, where halls headed each direction. Dispersed lanterns lit the uneven stone floor and walls, and a damp, earthy smell filled the air. It was as if they had traveled hundreds of years into the past, when people had built shoddy settlements and hid out of fear of the awakened. Zinarus shuddered. Was that not what they were doing now?

Tiuz led them past countless rooms and corridors. Curiosity spurred Zinarus to peek around each alternate path, but Tiuz was confident of his direction, giving Zinarus no time to tarry. His leg made him a burden to the rest of the fleeing reformers. Helplessness was a terrible feeling, so he gritted his teeth as he trudged on, determined not to be the reason they failed to escape.

Ahead, Tiuz reached a steel door, and he groaned as he dragged it open. Wind greeted them the moment he did, its chill swirling through the halls and dispersing the lingering smoke. So, too, did it carry the people's screams.

"Hurry on," Tiuz said, ushering the scions through the door. "Any Spirit Reachers, be prepared to protect the rest."

Zinarus had already removed his gloves, but he did not Reach into the realm of Truth just yet. It would do nothing against awakened. In the case of another disturbance with the lowborn, however, he could compel them to keep their distance. He despised the use of Truth Reaching for torture or control, but there were lighter ways for his powers to work.

When Zinarus emerged into the everdark, Kalastok was unrecognizable. No lights filled the streets, and only Light Reachers and fallen lanterns exposed the awakened swooping down upon their victims. They stood a block west of the palace, closer to the Kala River. Half-a-dozen towers were supposed to protect this part of the city against awakened, but they were unusually dark.

Zinarus approached Tiuz. "I will return to my townhouse, but will you be safe? Even your Spirit Reaching will not save you from this many awakened. Please, follow me to safety."

Oh, by the Crystal Mother, he sounded like a beggar, but the fear he felt for Tiuz was more than a sponsor for his client. Tiuz had become one of the few people he could trust, a true friend of which Zinarus had only Regizald before. The commander had conducted risky maneuvers in war. These spirits, though, were unlike any mortal enemy.

"I am a Spirit Reacher," Tiuz replied, "and I cannot sit idly by as innocents die. Go on. Truth Reaching is of little use here, so it is better if I don't have to worry about you while I fight."

Zinarus stared down at Tiuz, questioning every motive in his heart. What use was he here? With his mechanical leg, he was more likely to become a victim than help one. Besides, he was trembling, and no coward should face the awakened unprepared.

"Then I shall pray for your safety," Zinarus said.

Each word was bitter upon his tongue as he turned away and headed home as quickly as he could manage. He hastened a glance back at Tiuz, but the man was already gone.

The screams seemed to come from the northern Market District, so he and a few other reformers and moderates kept closer to the river. One was a Light Reacher who lit the way as they navigated the narrow streets and alleys. Much of the city outside the Crimson District was more spread out, but here, scion townhouses and stores were stacked so tightly that one could only see the river when passing a westward alley or park. It made the darkness suffocating, as if it were closing around Zinarus as he scanned the sky for awakened.

*Continue on,* he told himself. *Worry will not fend them off.*

Rumors claimed that the awakened could smell fear, though, and Zinarus froze as a hushed whisper somehow pierced the noise overwhelming the city. It drew closer, speaking in a tongue he could not understand. The other scions called for him to follow. He couldn't, and when the awakened shot toward him, he had no defense but to raise his glass-infused coat and hope.

The awakened diverted, a hissing sound coming from it as it neared the glass. The other scions had not followed his action. Some likely wore clothes without costly glass infused into them, and others had expected the spirit to only strike Zinarus. Their reasons mattered not to the awakened, and it attacked without mercy or hesitation, its tendrils snatching three of the reformers within a beat of Zinarus's racing heart.

He backed away, jaw ajar. "What have I done?"

At the sound of Zinarus's voice, the awakened raised its misty head, staring directly at him. Its whispers grew as he fled as quickly as his mechanical leg would allow. Surely, it was not fast enough. The spirit would catch him, and he would become nothing more than another awakened to haunt the streets of Kalastok. Oh Crystal Mother, there was so much he still wanted to do.

Yet no tendrils caught him by the time he eventually stumbled to a stop before the entrance to his townhouse's gardens. He had covered at least five city blocks, and the awakened's whispers had grown quieter with each step. After heaving for air, he mustered the strength to look over his shoulder.

His attacker was nowhere to be seen.

The screams had died down as well; though, there were enough of them still to make him shudder at the thought of how many had died. One awakened had killed three of his allies. There had surely been more…

Not taking his safety for granted, he hastened inside, calling for Regizald the moment he opened the door. There was no reply. Zinarus hesitated, staring up the stairs toward his servant's room before heading down the main hall of the ground floor.

"Regizald?" he repeated. "Are you well?"

Silence.

Zinarus slowly moved toward the office, the *thud* of his cane hanging over the house like the bell of the clocktower. He had an old flintlock pistol in his desk drawer. It would be useless against awakened, but brigands took advantage of chaos to steal from those whose attention was elsewhere. At the least, having it on him would provide some security if his Reaching failed.

The office door lay ajar, so he nudged it open with the end of his cane. A heavy darkness filled the room, but when he reached for the oil lamp, it flickered to life without him even touching it. Its light advanced toward the desk in a slow march, revealing a person lying on the floor.

"Regizald?" Zinarus yelped, dropping to his knees and clutching Regizald's hand. Warm, but he was still, his chest not rising with breaths. "No, no! Please don't leave me. Regi! Please!"

"It has been quite the night, Zinarus," a familiar voice said from behind the desk. Zinarus scrambled back into the wall, collapsing against it at the sight of the man robed in red. Like before, darkness lingered over his eyes and nose, and his mouth held a crooked smile.

"What have you done?" Zinarus yelled, trembling.

The man pulled a flintlock pistol, pulling back its hammer as Zinarus flexed his taloned hand. Truth Reaching could institute stasis over Regizald's body—if he was still alive—or compel the Dark Reacher to stop. Stasis required touch, though, and compulsion was difficult when one's target had a gun. Why had he released Regizald's hand?

*Coward!*

"You may attempt to Truth Reach against me," the Dark Reacher said, as if reading his mind, "but what fun is there in that?

Me pulling this trigger would only make existence far more annoying for the both of us."

The man leaned forward. "Your hesitation makes you weak, Zinarus, rejected son of Uzrin Ioniz. We have all seen how he looks at you in the Chamber, scorning your very birth. Not only do you bear a deformity, but you also have blood unworthy of a mutt dog. Why Uzrin bothered to mate with a Vockan, I do not understand."

"Why did you kill him?" Zinarus asked, unable to meet the man's gaze. All he could do was whimper and stare at the closest person he had to a friend—killed for his failures.

"Do not claim you are that insolent. You spoke to the Nochlander, and now you intend to give her your glass."

The man held up the contract Alyniana had given Zinarus earlier. It bore his signature, as he had made his decision moments before leaving for the Chamber. Selling half of House Vamiustok's sand to Nochland at higher prices would yield enough money for his family to strive for the wealth of the great houses. They could expand, create more sand mines, and better the lives of their workers. Alyniana had also made a compelling case for why her nation needed it. While the Commonwealth had House Pikezik's supplies, Nochland had nothing.

Zinarus slammed his fist into the wall. "Regizald had nothing to do with that!"

"It is a shame, then, that you failed him so." The Dark Reacher said, gun still raised as he nodded toward the door. "You have emerged from the largest awakened attack since the Awakening itself. Do you see now why we must ensure our nation's sand and glass remain within our borders? In the game of empires, the nation who wins is the one strong enough to protect itself at all costs. Nochland is nothing. Let them fall into the sea as we ensure we do not descend into the Wastes."

"Why make an offer if there was no choice?"

The man scoffed. "You had a choice—just not the one you believed it to be. Agree to sell your sand mines to House Oliezany, or there will be further consequences."

Taking a shuddered breath, Zinarus looked from the pistol to Regizald, anger and fear fighting within him. This Reacher, and whoever he worked with, deserved to suffer, yet there was little Zinarus could do. His mother was far away with little more power than him. His father refused to recognize his existence. His best friend lay dead at his feet. And his closest ally roamed the streets, fighting the awakened like a hero instead of cowering. The man was right. Zinarus was weak.

*Crystal Mother below, help me,* he pleaded silently.

He pushed himself up with his cane. Pain greeted him as his mechanical leg twisted awkwardly, but he held firm, glaring at his foe. "Give me the letter and let us be done with this charade." When the Reacher handed him it, Zinarus ran his hand over the seal that had once held it shut. "Why House Oliezany? Is it not House Pikezik who wish to solidify their hold over glass production?"

"You ask too many questions," the Dark Reacher replied.

Zinarus took the quill off the desk, drawing a long breath as he remembered the many times Regizald had been by his side. Oh, how he had treated the lad so poorly during his times of frustration. Regizald had deserved better, and as Zinarus signed the Oliezany bill of sale, he realized he would never see his friend again. And now, with a stroke of the quill, he signed away any hope House iz Vamiustok had of establishing itself.

His hand shook as he set the paper back on the desk. Tears stung his eyes for the first time in years, so he closed them, unable to accept the fate that lay ahead. How had it all fallen apart so quickly?

When the Dark Reacher took the paper, Zinarus opened his eyes again in hopes of catching a final glimpse that would reveal his identity, but the room was pitch black. He collapsed in it, allowing the pain of his left leg to consume him. It was better than the agony entrapping his chest, familiar. This heartache... How was he supposed to move forward without his friend and his purpose?

How was he supposed to live life alone?

# DEATH'S DAUGHTER

*"When a Reacher draws power from a realm, power must be returned to it. Whether it is taken from a crystal or its holder, balance is inevitable."* – The First Law of Reaching

Kasia awoke to a ringing in her ear, her face pressed against the cold, hard pillow of her prison cell. It smelled of piss and bile. Compared to the torturous thoughts clutching her mind, though, it seemed a pleasant dream.

"I'm sorry," she whispered into her tears. "Aliax, forgive me."

He stood before her. As old as she, he'd grown into his lanky body, and his light brown hair had lost its sun-scorched gold from the everbright. A trimmed beard covered his gentle jawline, patches of it thinner upon his cheeks. That would've embarrassed her shy lover years ago, but he stood as a man now.

"You promised me you'd stop Reaching," he replied as he paced across the small cell. His footsteps were silent against the stone.

"How… How are you here?" she stammered.

Aliax scoffed. "Don't you know? That damn talon of yours is probably stuck in Death after how many times you Reached last night."

"Shit!"

Kasia threw her legs over the side of the bed, staring down at her hands. They shook like a hungover drunkard's, and her stomach felt no better. She hadn't felt this bad since the day after Aliax's death, when his voice had started haunting her broken mind. At the time, she'd thought it guilt or heartbreak, but the answer was obvious now.

"Spirit Taint's a bitch, ain't it?" Aliax said with his arms crossed. "I *told* you to stop Reaching."

"There were awakened," she muttered. "And Father… I needed to get revenge on those who killed him. The Crimsons took everything from me, and I *will* make them pay."

He stuffed his hands in his pockets and stared out the bars into a dark hallway. Deep purple wisps drifted off him, like steam from boiling water. "Is that what we need? More death?"

"It's justice!" she snapped, wiping away her tears with her coat sleeve. Her clothes were the same as the ones from the Chamber meeting, and the guards apparently hadn't left any others for her.

"Maybe you're right." He stared at her with the eyes of a wise oak, enough to tear down her walls without a word. "But is it fair to you to waste your life avenging your father's? He didn't approve of us."

She rolled over to face the wall, closing her eyes tight. This wasn't real. *He* wasn't real, but spirits, she so badly wanted him to be. "That didn't mean he deserved to die, Ali. I needed him… I still need him. Just like I need you."

"I'm right here," he replied as he sat on the bedside, but it didn't shift with the weight.

"No. You're dead."

Aliax rested his hand on her shoulder, and she could've sworn she felt the warmth. "Do I seem dead to you?"

Taking a few long breaths between her sobs, she turned to face him. Of course, he didn't seem dead. Some part of her would always keep him alive until death took her too, but a memory was not the real thing. She'd killed the boy she loved. No Realm Taint could change that.

Kasia raised her taloned hand to Aliax's cheek, running her fingers through his beard and meeting his gaze. Spirits, she'd given anything to have him back. Anything. "I love you, Ali," she breathed. "But I killed you."

"No," he stammered, brow furrowed. "No! That can't be true."

She ran her talon over his cheek bone, forcing herself not to look away as the skin began to split. "It was a mistake. I… I was trying to protect you, protect *us*, from those peasants, but I didn't understand what pouring myself into my Reaching would do. I—"

His hands were suddenly around her throat. They squeezed as fire filled his eyes and air left her lungs. "You killed all of us! A dozen people, spirit and all, wiped from Zekiaz because you couldn't control your fear. They brought torches, and all you saw was your brother's flames burning your arm as you screamed! You couldn't kill Gregorzon, but you could kill lowborn and the lover who threatened your family's prestige. You want revenge for Leonit. Just like you wanted revenge then!"

Kasia suffocated, but she couldn't fight back as wispy images of the peasants she'd killed formed behind Aliax. Every muscle in her body locked tight at Aliax's fury. Not because of the power behind his attack, but because he was right. She had been terrified all those years ago, just like she'd been last night. Though her strikes had only killed awakened during the attack, each Reach had left her shaking. Just touching the realm of Death reminded her of him.

*I'm sorry.*

She Reached, grabbing hold of one of his arms and dragging her talon down it.

His rage turned to agony. He released her as he screamed and fell back into the opposite wall, the peasants echoing his cries. The darkness overtook each of them as their eyes flashed white, light pouring from their mouths before it extinguished to leave only empty husks behind. Black, decrepit.

Just heartbeats later, those too faded into nothing, and Kasia was finally alone. She didn't know if she preferred it that way.

Her raspy breaths hung in the room as she traced her neck where he'd grabbed her. No mark. Aliax had never done such a thing in life, but it had felt so real. *He'd* felt so real. Was this the unknown punishment of a Death Reach's Taint? Holding the spirits of those she killed within her mind?

"I deserve this," she whispered to herself. She'd lied about Aliax and the peasants' deaths, pretending a fire had burned down the barn. Only her mother knew the truth, and that had just added fuel to her hatred.

A rattling at the cell door tore her from her thoughts. She glanced down at her talon, ready to Reach again, but found instead that her arms were shackled to the bed with heavy gloves entrapping her hands.

*What else did I imagine?*

A guard dressed in gray stepped into the cell, regarded her with a curled lip, and threw something at her. Instinctively, she ducked, but the object struck her in the chest. It was soft.

"Eat, girl," the guard said.

Kasia cocked her head as she examined the food. Mushy, it was encased in bread and had little more heat than the frigid cell. "This is what I receive for saving hundreds of people from the awakened?" she asked. "Would King Jazuk rather have me sit by as his subjects are slaughtered?"

The guard grunted and shut the door, then stomped away.

"It was a pleasure to meet you," she quipped after him.

With the guard gone and nothing else in the room, she studied the food again. *Wonderful, it stinks too.* The smell was better than piss, but that wasn't saying much.

She tossed the food aside. Gluttony had never been her sin of choice anyway, as she found consumption at best a convenient tool for gathering people whom she intended to sway. Better to starve a few hours than suffer a taste that would linger until the next horrible meal.

Except no meal came.

Hours passed without another appearance from the guard. Kasia's stomach growled, and her impatience grew as she stared at the awakened trapped in her amber pendant. She and Radais had killed countless awakened, but had it been enough? Where had they come from? How could amber hold one captive? And had she ruined her attempt to infiltrate the Crimsons on her first day in the city?

Kasia shook her head. How foolish could she be to reveal she was a Death Reacher so quickly? She'd spent years in Tystok hiding her power, even after rumors had swirled around her incident with Aliax and the peasants. All that work, gone in moments. For what? To save Kalastok scions who despised her and lowborn who wanted her to burn? She should've focused on Sazilz instead of worrying about the people, but something inside of her had demanded she act when no one else would. It felt like her father's voice.

That same voice told her something was off about the timing of the attack. The awakened had arrived immediately after the Chamber failed to pass the Keloshan Act. That meant that the conservative and nationalist wings of the Chamber had an incentive to strike, but so too did Kelosh itself.

Perhaps the emperor wished to send a message despite the act's rejection, or had Kelosh intended to attack no matter the result? Neither conclusion lined up.

She sat up, remembering the attack against her father twelve years before. Parqiz had somehow controlled the awakened then, so why couldn't the Crimsons do so again? There had been thousands of peasants gathered in the streets. If the likes of Sazilz Uziokaki and possibly House Oliezany were involved with the Crimsons, then they would have seen those protestors as a ripe opportunity to prove that "Kelosh's" disease was a threat while eliminating the dissidents at the same time. They had lost the vote, but another could be held in the aftermath of the attack. It could've been happening at that very moment and she'd have no way of knowing…

Something shifted in the darkness out of the corner of her eye.

"Enjoy watching women in chains?" she quipped.

Footsteps answered, but not from the close side of the hall where she'd seen the movement. Instead, a man in a fine black suit approached the cell, his face covered by a purple wooden mask carved to resemble a falcon's beak. He tilted his head as he gripped the bars. "There are many things I am guilty of, Lady Katarzyna, but I have never found pleasure in such things."

"Then it sounds as if you prefer me free." She rattled the shackles. "Or are you too afraid to even show your face to a scion lady."

"A lady or a criminal waiting for execution?"

"You tell me."

The masked man laughed, then stepped *through* the door as if it were air. "In all honesty, I hope you are both."

Kasia flexed her hand in hopes of Reaching, but yet again, the glove stopped her. Who was this man? "And in all honesty, I would prefer not to be the latter. I have plans. Dying would unfortunately put them on quite the delay."

"You are so very much like him." The man stopped before her, arms crossed. Was he another ghost? She could not see his breath, but he lacked the purple wisps that had surrounded Aliax.

"Like who?"

"Did Leonit not tell you of our existence?"

She studied him in the dim light. Masks were often from ancient tribes, not any organization her father had been connected to, but there was something oddly familiar about the falcon on this one. Then she remembered. "Father has a mask like that hanging in his study here, but when I asked about it, he refused to tell me."

The man nodded. "Then allow me to expand upon his silence. He was—and I am—a member of an organization called the Children of Zekiaz, protecting our realm from the dangers that exist beyond it."

"Excuse me if I sound like a cynic," Kasia replied, sitting back, "but I fail to believe my father was part of a secret organization. The last thing on his mind was resisting the other nations when he spent his life forming alliances with them."

"Not nations, Katarzyna, realms. Your Reaching into the realm of Death caused this predicament of yours, and it is the existence of others that draws our interest. It has also drawn the eyes of the Crimson Court."

She shot up so quickly that the chains snapped her back onto the bed. "You know about the Crimsons?"

Footfalls came from beyond the bars. The masked man heard it too, his taloned hand suddenly extended, but nothing followed.

"It is not as safe to speak here as I believed," the man said hurriedly. "We intended to help you escape, but the Crimsons have already convinced the king to release you. Why? I am unsure, but they will wish to use you for their purposes. Know that you will leave this place and enter a city very much changed. Our foes have taken advantage of the chaos, and I fear we are outmatched."

Then he turned and stepped through the door. Moments later, he was gone, and Kasia sat back onto the bed, her mind spinning.

"Who were you really, Father?" she asked the ceiling. "What troubles unknown have you left me with?"

THREE DAYS PASSED BEFORE A GUARD CAME TO RELEASE KASIA from her cell. As they led her bound and starving into the city, she remembered emerging from the basement after her father's death. Then, like now, she stepped from the world she'd known into one that was strange and unwelcoming.

Except for Tazper.

Her footman's eyes lit up at the sight of her heading down the prison steps. He stood outside her carriage, tapping his feet like a puppy wanting to run to its master. The feeling was mutual after her days alone. Though she often preferred solitude when there was work to be done, that empty cell had numbed her. Tazper was never so dull.

"Please tell me you have not been standing there all day," she said as the guards unshackled her and removed the restraining gloves, which she replaced with her formal ones. Her watch read half-past one. Deep in the night. Whatever meeting the Chamber had held today would have already ended. No doubt that was on purpose.

Tazper removed his wide-brimmed felt hat and bowed his head. While not ill-fitting for him, it did make him look quite a lot like a farmer instead of a noble footman. "I would have if required, but the government only sent a messenger an hour ago. Lord Faniz was already asleep after the Chamber session, so I came alone."

"Thank you, Tazper." She regarded him, letting herself smile. "What did I do to deserve a friend such as you?"

He shrugged. "My mother says friends are not about doing anything. Instead, they are simply there."

"Wise words." She put a foot up on the carriage steps, taking his hand as he helped her up. "Unfortunately, I have little wisdom of my own to offer, as my mind is mush and my back as rigid as a board."

Tazper moved to climb onto the front of the carriage, but she called for him to join her inside. She had a carriage driver for that, and besides, she could use the company. A great weight rested upon her shoulders. His presence made it tolerable.

"What have I missed during my imprisonment?" she asked once he'd climbed into the carriage and shut the door. "And what of my release? Death Reaching is worthy of execution in certain cases. A man in a falcon mask visited me, claiming the Crimsons organized my release."

"I am unsure why they released you, but here…" Tazper pulled a folded page of a newspaper out of his jacket's interior pocket. "The papers have been calling you and Radais heroes."

She took the newspaper, then rolled her eyes at the headline. " 'The Amber Dame becomes Death's Daughter'? This kind of drivel passes for journalism here?"

"Sorry. Most of the other papers featuring a story about you and what they're calling the Ephemeral Slaughter were sold out, so I had to settle for *The Scouring Scion*."

# The Scouring Scion

# The Amber Dame Becomes Death's Daughter

ISSUE NO. 121 EVERY SCION'S FIRST READ 21ST OF EVERDARK, 791 PA

In a *shocking* turn of events, our detectives have discovered that the Death Reacher spotted in the Market District during the Ephemeral Slaughter was none other than Lady Katarzyna Niezik. That's right, folks! The shadowy matriarch of Reshkan lover Leonit's old house is slinging the old purple magic around like Quickshot Miko himself.

Now we all have the same question that's as hot as a Reshkan tart baking in the everbright heat: Who has Death's Daughter killed? And who will she kill next?

You might ask yourself why she could kill again. Surely, the illustrious King Jazuk Bartol the whatever-th would *never* allow such a dangerous criminal to roam our streets. WRONG! Lowborn fiends run the alleys west of the Kala, and one need not duck away from the lamplight for but a moment in the Old Market to see the cut-purses lurking. The king doesn't care. And with Gornioz Oliezany tugging on his strings like a marionette, Katarzyna will be released and married off to Zenik or some other idiotic cousin of the rose magnate. You read it here first! - Continued on A3

## FAMILY TURNED AWAKENED - ARE YOU NEXT?

Keloshan menace? The scourge of the Crystal Mother? The consequences of dumping our waste in the Kala? What *really* is the Spirit Plague, and why does it spread to scions?

The king and his Pikezik-wedded son, Chatik, act as if the empire of the east is the only possible cause of this disease. But what if it's his own plot to eliminate his foes? - Continued on A2



## SLIM FIM'S SLIM COLUMN

I got a letter from an admirer the other day. You know what, lady? Slimmy boy is taken! Ain't nobody taking me from this here column.

That's right. I'd rather spend my nights on this here column than with you! Nobody messes with Slim Fim.

## LAMP LURKER'S CHATTER

Hello my lovely lurkers! Find anything shiny lately? Well, I certainly did! It's the rumor around the Drifters' Quarter that the silver wolf is in search of a darling wife. Tiuz Hazeko himself! We all know his thrust has quite the power.

## DAILY SPIRIT READ

Duskfall girls. Get ready! I hear there's a gala on the horizon. And plenty of gallant men too. Bet high! Wear red! Maybe you'll catch a great house's eye... and their keni.

"I appreciate the alliteration, but this writing is atrocious." She threw down the paper with a huff. "This article says one moment that I am a Reshkan puppet like my father, and the next that I am rumored to be courting Zenik Oliezany after my vote in the Chamber. I don't even know who he is!"

Tazper offered a grin. "Well, at least they're not ignoring your presence. I would hasten to say you have drawn the Crimsons' gazes already."

Kasia looked out the window at the far emptier streets of Kalastok. Mercenaries of the great houses patrolled where civilians had once shopped. They wore varied coats of gold, gray, and white, while the government's soldiers in red guarded only the routes northward, toward the Crystal Palace. Few others walked that same cobblestone, and fewer still were lowborn. Lanterns lay shattered. Windows were boarded. Carts carried heaps of corpses toward the graveyards. But toward the river, the ghostly city gave way to crowds along the bridges.

"What is happening there?" she asked. "I assume the mercenaries were called by the houses to prevent another riot, but the Keloshan Act failed. Did they call another vote so quickly?"

Tazper didn't reply, and when he sniffled, Kasia tore her gaze from the window. His eyes were red as he wiped his nose. "There were so many bodies… I… I couldn't help anyone. They were screaming and running past the townhouse, but when I went outside, I froze. I had seen awakened before. We both have. Just… It was as if the sky were filled with wildfire smoke that reached out to strike down people without mercy. I should've fired my gun. I should've directed people back inside. Instead, I stood rooted upon that curb with fear wrestling my very spirit. 'Tis the most shameful moment of my life."

"Shame?" Kasia said. "You cowered the same as every other scion in the Chamber, but it is instinct to flee danger. There is no shame in running from a battle of magic when you have but a gun. Shame…" She raised her trembling hand before her as the memories of Aliax's death returned. "Shame is letting that fear destroy you and everyone you love."

Tazper held his hat in his hands. He was one of the few who knew what she'd done to Aliax and the peasants, and his head bowed beneath the weight. "We waited for you to return for many hours until Radais arrived and told us what had happened. It wasn't until yesterday that the government released an announcement, claiming the awakened were the victims of the Spirit Plague who had overwhelmed the Spirit Reachers in the towers. Over three hundred people died on the east side, eight of which were Chamber scions—all reformers or moderates—and they have not even tried counting the corpses west of the river or in the villages elsewhere in the Commonwealth."

"Did they say anything about me?"

He sighed. "They said you and ten other reformers were arrested due to accusations of 'aggressive behavior' or the like. Though it seemed a bit preposterous, they denied the rumors that you are a Death Reacher and claimed you would each be released once you were interrogated—after the Keloshan Act passed yesterday. I fail to understand it all, but that glint in your eye tells me you do."

Kasia stared back toward the bridges. "Of course, they took advantage of the chaos to arrest the opposition and quarantine the poorest lowborn. The Keloshan Act failed the first count by only seven votes, so between the scions killed and those arrested, King Jazuk and his friends easily had enough on their second try. Spirits, they probably had more than enough with everyone frightened by the disease they claim Kelosh caused."

"Claim?"

"Is it not awfully convenient that, during a border dispute with Kelosh, our government discovered Kelosh caused a deadly disease? Chatik Pikezik, who happens to be the king's second-born son, was the one to make the statement, and he provided no evidence. Sazilz was involved too with House Oliezany." She bit her lip, not liking where this was going, but the thoughts that had been trapped with her in that cell spilled out. "Not all of the nationalists and conservatives are Crimsons, but if Sazilz is leading the push to increase tensions with Kelosh, do they want war? Is that what this is about: retaking the lands King Yaakiin lost through the Reduction Treaties?"

"It would explain why they killed Leonit," Tazper replied. "Was he not the greatest advocate for working with the empires instead of resisting them?"

"With Reshka and Ogrenia at least, yes. He was never all that fond of the Keloshans."

Tazper laughed. "I doubt many within the Commonwealth are."

"The Crimsons knew that, but the real question is whether they knew about the awakened ahead of time." She spun her amber pendant, remembering the last awakened that had attacked her, then disappeared. "Or whether they know that amber can contain one."

His eyes grew as wide as saucers. "You captured an awakened?"

"I believe so, but no one has ever succeeded before." The spirit's wisps of gray seemed to swim through the amber like a sea. Could it leave if it chose? "Maybe Radais knows more?"

The carriage pulled to the curb alongside The Confluence, and Tazper jumped up to open the door. "Perhaps it's time to find out."

Kasia followed him out, casting a wary glance to each side before heading toward the door. No mercenaries marched here, but she worried whether her house's lack of armed guards put her at a disadvantage. Awakened weren't the only threat in Kalastok. Luckily, she'd saved face with the ruling parties with her vote on the Keloshan Act, so she shouldn't be a target for now.

A weight left Kasia's shoulders the moment she crossed the threshold. Its security may have been thin, but she was relieved to be secluded with friends and allies. She'd barely slept in prison, and the gentle warmth wafting through the townhouse lulled her as she climbed the stairs with Tazper. Rest could wait. She needed Radais to help her figure out what was happening.

"Radais was helping with the city cleanup when I left," Tazper said when they reached the second floor.

The guest bedroom door opened to reveal the Glassblade in a loose-fitting shirt and trousers. He scratched his bearded chin at the sight of her, glancing at her taloned hand. "This is a surprise. I'm sorry I didn't do more to stop the Crystal Brigade, but I thought one of us being imprisoned was enough already."

"It was too much," Kasia replied. "Can you meet me in the study? We have much to discuss."

"Of course. Err… Could you give me a moment to change?"

"No. I reek after half a hundred-hour in the same clothes, so I hardly care about your attire."

He flinched at that but followed her and Tazper into the study. Kasia eyed the purple falcon mask hanging over the fireplace mantle, just like the one the Child of Zekiaz had worn. There was so much that mattered more than her father's involvement in a secret organization, but her heart ached realizing how much he'd hidden from her.

Once Kasia was seated behind the desk with Radais and Tazper across from her, she recounted what she'd learned, leaving out her encounter with the masked man. He'd provided nothing new to their investigation of the Crimsons and the awakened, after all, and Radais hardly needed to know all of her personal business. She felt exposed enough with the newspapers gossiping about her powers. Though Radais had fought by her side and had proved trustworthy so far, she barely knew him.

The Glassblade slumped back in his seat as she spoke, and when she finished, he took a long breath. "You captured an awakened? This could change everything. The supreme defender would be interested in studying the pendant if you were willing to part with it."

"I would rather not," Kasia said. "This is the only proof I have of amber's capabilities, and I would prefer to keep it close at hand."

"Then would you allow me to take an empty piece? The Glassblades could conduct our own investigation while you research here. I would recommend speaking with Professor Etal iz Noshok. He discovered this disease, and Supreme Defender Miv implied he may know more about the awakened if we tell him what we know."

Tazper rocked his hand back and forth. "Unfortunately, they have restricted access to Kalastok College too in order to protect the fledgling Reachers from the plague. I doubt we would get in, especially given your… well, you know."

Kasia ignored Tazper's jab and ripped a bead of amber from her coat. It was practically ruined anyway. "Here. As long as you trust the supreme defender, then I do."

"Who else can we trust?" Radais asked, taking the amber. "This attack was horrific, and the government wanted this to happen?"

"The *Crimsons* did, I believe," Kasia clarified. "Some of them are likely part of the king's council, but I am unsure whether King Jazuk himself wants this war. Sazilz Uziokaki and House Oliezany certainly do."

"Perhaps House Pikezik as well," Tazper said.

Kasia furrowed her brow. "Chatik and Lilita supported the bill, but what makes you think they're part of the Crimsons too?"

Tazper pulled out the dragon-carved pistol from within his coat and set it on the desk. "I talked to the Oliezany gunsmiths while you were imprisoned. Though they were fairly tight-lipped about who bought the gun, one of the assistants confirmed its barrel was designed after House Pikezik's tradition as dragon tamers."

"Which means our red-robed man was probably a Pikezik," Radais said. "The awakened during the attack were whispering like the ones I found in the Wastes. You said Chatik Pikezik was the one to claim Kelosh started the disease, so what if he was involved with the attack too?"

Kasia rubbed her temples, fighting the oncoming headache. "Tazper, you did not think of mentioning this in the carriage?"

"It… escaped my mind?" he said, flushed.

"I understand. I can barely keep it all straight myself. This puts us at three of the great houses likely in cooperation with the Crimsons, assuming they're the ones behind what's happening in the Spirit Wastes. If the king is involved… It doesn't matter. We need to develop a plan to stop them."

Radais shifted uncomfortably. "I can't be a part of it."

"Except you already are." She studied him. "Radais, the moment the great houses know your name, you become a part of their games."

"Was inviting me to remain here not keeping me within your sphere of influence?"

Kasia bit her cheek before she said something she'd regret. "In all honesty, yes, but my allies are few. I will fulfill my end of our bargain no matter what you choose. Know, however, that this city needs you. Who else is going to stop the awakened when the Spirit Reachers fail?"

He huffed. "Death's Daughter seemed plenty competent the night of the attack."

"Do not leave because I am a Death Reacher." She removed her glove and placed her taloned hand palm down before her. Her chest tightened, but she had to do this… to tell the truth. "The Crystal does not ask us what realm we wish to Reach into, but this is the power it granted me. Our enemies return life after life. I am one of the few people who can stop that."

"My decision is not about you."

She slammed her fist on the desk. "Do not lie to me! I saw the fear in your eyes when they dragged me away. You believe just like everyone else that I cannot control it, and you are right. Aliax knew it. So did my mother. But I thought I didn't need help. With a single Reach, I could kill a person with the slightest touch or strike many down from a distance. With multiple at once…" Her voice cracked as clenched her fists, digging her nails into her palms to remind her of the pain. "I am capable of killing everyone near me, leaving me as the only survivor."

His expression softened. "I know what it's like to fail, Lady Katarzyna. It is why I need to take your offer of a Body Reacher and leave. My father will die if I do not return to him soon, and I will lose my final chance to redeem myself with my family." He lowered his head. "I have delivered my message as commanded. If there is more for me to do in this investigation, it is with the Glassblades in the Spirit Wastes, not in a city that does not respect my kind."

"Fine. If I cannot convince you, then keep me informed of what you discover. Whatever the Crimsons, or whoever, are doing there could be related to the attacks." Fighting her disappointment, she plucked the quill from the ink and scribbled down a name and address. "The Body Reacher you are looking for is called Lazan Karianam. He is a good man who saved my life once, and he'll serve you well. My great-uncle will ensure you have the funds necessary for your journey home."

Radais took the note and stood, bowing his head. "Thank you. I regret we could not end our cooperation on better terms." Then he turned to leave.

Kasia shot to her feet. "Radais! Tell only those you trust fully what we have learned. The Crimsons may have more in their ranks than we know."

He left without another word.

"What do we do now?" Tazper asked as Kasia slumped back into her chair.

"Quietly inquire further into this Pikezik whom Radais found," she replied, staring at the scattered papers on the desk. There were few people she could trust, and with Radais leaving, she couldn't help but feel alone in her fight. Why did everyone have to die or leave? "I have drawn enough attention to myself already, and further suspicion will ruin my attempts to ingratiate myself with the Crimsons."

Tazper tipped his hat. "Glad to be of service beyond opening doors for you. I mean… Not that opening doors is a bad role." He cleared his throat. "What is your next plan of action?"

She stood and turned to look up at the stained-glass window depicting the whispering man. With Radais's help or not, she had to act. The Crimsons had released her for a reason, and she needed to be prepared. "My vote should have created the opportunity for me to meet with Sazilz. I need to figure out who the Crimsons really are and what they hope to accomplish with this war. First, though, I need a long bath and a longer sleep. No magnate will meet with me in this condition."

"I will let Kikania know," Tazper replied, but he hesitated before leaving. "May I say something?"

"What is it?"

He took a long breath, his voice losing its volume. "I know you may regret the events of the past, but I don't care. I know the real you. Every moment I have spent by your side, I have seen you fighting to make our realm a better place, fighting for justice."

"Thank you, Tazper," she said, glancing to the side to see Aliax waiting there, arms crossed. How common was this going to become? "But sometimes, what we do today cannot wash clean the sins of our past. Not mine. Not the Crimsons'. And not my father's."

# THE MINISTERS' WILLS

*"He who whispers in the king's ear holds the true crown."* – Tazionik Lilloziakath, former Ezmani minister of glass

Light spread through the streets of Kalastok as Nikoza stood with her grandfather on the eastern roof of the Crystal Palace. Fire Reachers scampered to each lamp, igniting its oil and banishing the everdark in a display he found mesmerizing, as Light Reachers' powers would not last long enough to illuminate the whole city. The realm of Light would not grant Zekiaz its great light until dawnrise, but humanity persisted with their flickering flames. Balance came with it.

"All elements of our realm rely upon our connections to the others," Jazuk mused, glancing back at the crystal dragon clinging to the spire at the palace's center.

The beast could not reply, and Nikoza expected that Jazuk would wish the same for her. He sought to wonder aloud when he visited the roof, not hold conversation. Everyone sought for the king's ear below.

"Why do we squabble amongst ourselves when our researchers claim there are whole other worlds in the beyond?" he continued. "Is this path of strife the correct one? Should I have found another way to contend with Kelosh rather than begin the march toward war? There is time still for resolution, for peace. At times, it seems I am the only one among my council who seeks it."

Nikoza nodded as she scanned the cityscape from east to west, the light fading upon the opposite bank of the Kala River. Over a hundred thousand lowborn workers resided there, and none of them could leave due to Jazuk's alterations to the Keloshan Act. Conservative papers called it necessary. Nationalist ones questioned whether it divided the Commonwealth's resolve against their foes. The reformers… Nikoza shared their frustration. Though the lowborn lacked the Crystal Mother's gift, they did not deserve such treatment.

Jazuk puffed on his cigar, then coughed. "My father once taught me that a strong leader need not reflect upon his decisions, as his actions defended themselves. To him, each moment spent focused on the past was one turned away from a better future. Maybe he was right. I am weak. And now, his spirit died with Lakuzk."

"You are hardly weak, Grandfather." She raised her hand to the dragon's nose, the palace's Reacher light and lanterns upon the spires giving her silver dress and the dragon's scales a radiant glow. Power hummed through the crystals beneath her fingers, unlike any other in the realm.

"A ruler who fails to grasp when they have succeeded and when they have failed is doomed to be a tyrant," Nikoza said. "That is why, even when I disagree with you, I believe you are a good king."

"Would those watching their families succumb to the Spirit Plague say the same?" he replied, gesturing toward the dark side of the river, only the occasional lantern sputtering through the smog. The Air Reachers kept it from wafting to the Crimson and Market districts, but Nikoza could almost taste the soot. "When are such decisions necessary, and when are they tyranny in their own right?"

Nikoza stepped from the dragon with a blown kiss before crossing the rooftop to Jazuk. "When a ruler fails to listen to those most affected by their laws, they craft them blindly. So too, are they blind when they ignore the pleas of nations who suffer like their own."

Chuckling, Jazuk extinguished the remnants of his cigar and tossed it away. "Perhaps you are spending too much time with those tutors of yours. One as young as you should not be speaking with such wisdom."

"Flattery doesn't distract from my point," she replied. Her tutors were quite boring on the topics of politics, but her books had plenty more insights into society and the sciences. "Why have you not spoken to the alchemist, Paras ik Lierasa, to understand his insights into the disease? Why have you not received the Nochland ambassador who seeks to bring our nations closer together?"

He grew stern. "Our nation was built by the Crystal's chosen scions, not lowborn seeking unjustified glory. The same can be said of foreigners meddling in our affairs. Ezman is mighty because it learned to stand alone."

"What of the Vockans?"

"We showed them our strength, so they joined our cause."

"And if Alyniana seeks an alliance?"

"Oh?" Jazuk tensed, and she winced, realizing she'd admitted to speaking with Alyniana. "Do you care to inform me why you referred to the ambassador by her given name?"

She rolled her eyes and headed back toward the dragon. "Worry not. I haven't spoken to her outside a passing in the Chamber. She has valid concerns, however, and it would be prudent to bring them up at the gathering of your council in…" She looked across the Market District to the clocktower, rising between the Reacher towers. "Perfect, they should be ready for us now."

Jazuk shook his head, but she was already headed down the curved stairs.

**THE KING'S COUNCIL OF ADVISORS GATHERED** in an unnecessarily large room on the second floor of the Crystal Palace. Nikoza kept a gentle smile as she entered with Jazuk. The council had made it clear many times before that they believed it inappropriate for the king's ward to speak, so she kept quiet and moved to the side wall.

Tall windows draped in Ezmani red and Vockan white lined the far side of the room. On an afternoon such as this during dawnrise, they would have met their king with a soft glow, but instead, shadows covered the faces of the members, whose shouts filled the halls until they noticed Jazuk's entry.

"Why do you hang your head, my king, when we have accomplished much in recent days?" Minister of Glass Lilita Pikezik asked as she rose and smiled. It appeared to be a gentle one, but Nikoza knew her Uncle Chatik's wife well enough to know it was feigned.

Jazuk's cane thumped against the marble floors as he crossed to the head of the council table, holding his back with his free hand. "Of what accomplishments do you speak?" he asked as he sat and surveyed his advisors. "Disease? The approach to war?"

Among the council were the king's friends—Hazemel Ioniz and Borys Kuzon the Sixth—but for political purposes, he'd appointed Lilita and Gornioz Oliezany as well to secure support for his rule. Though Anointed Sister Uliazina Rakazimko of the Crystal Mother's Buried Temple was a member of the council as well, she only attended meetings devoted to the Spirit Crystal.

Lilita gave a surprised scoff. "We have ridded eastern Kalastok of this horrid plague, and what remains of the dissident Keloshans among our populace will be gone within the hundred-hour. My king, with a single act of legislation, we have mended two great problems our nation faces."

"We were attacked mere days ago in the greatest slaughter by awakened in centuries," Jazuk replied. He hesitated, glancing at Nikoza before continuing, "I fail to believe that the Spirit Plague will disappear simply because we push its victims out of eyeshot. Rather, it is more likely to light a fire beneath the lowborn already annoyed with their suffering."

"Lowborn who must know their place," Minister of National Purpose Gornioz said, gesturing with an open hand.

Jazuk met Gornioz's gaze. Nikoza hoped he remembered her pleas, but Gornioz held sway over the king far beyond that of his young ward. "Each of our families at this table, bar House Ioniz due to their status outside the great houses, have brought mercenaries to Kalastok in the wake of this disaster. However much we deny the fact, there are Reachers among them. The government has done its duty to the scions, but perhaps we could cool tensions by allowing a few Body, Life, and Spirit Reachers to aid western Kalastok and other lowborn cities and villages."

"The expense would be minimal," Borys rumbled with his gloved hands rested on his protruding stomach. As minister of economy, he'd opposed every ounce of spending proposed in the council since Nikoza started attending. "The gains, on the other hand, could be significant if it were to prevent another protest. A hundred thousand keni worth of crops burned due to the last outburst."

Lilita pressed her hands together as if to pray. "Borys, it is not our responsibility to fix your failure to control your peasants."

"*My* failure?" Borys shouted. "It is *your* workers who started the motherforsaken riot!"

"Let us cease before we reach hostilities," Minister of War Hazemel said with a hand on Borys's shoulder, much higher than his own. "We all face this problem, and though House Ioniz is not yet a great house, we would be happy to participate in such an effort if it eases our collective burden."

Lilita's face turned ever-redder, but Gornioz nodded. "House Pikezik is burdened with other efforts, I am certain," he said, "but House Oliezany will assist to avoid further chaos. Lilita, could you ask Chatik to invite Sazilz to the effort as well? I am aware your husband is fond of him, and House Uziokaki has been seeking opportunities to prove their worth."

"Very well," Lilita muttered, "but this was not to be the focus of this meeting. The Keloshan Act exiled the traitors within our borders. It certainly did not expel the Keloshan brigade waiting just miles from Rexaniv. We must push further against them, or they will see us as weak."

Gornioz smirked at her. "We are at a disadvantage due to the lack of glass your factories have yielded in recent years, but our troops will have plenty of armaments thanks to my own house's efforts."

But Hazemel cleared his throat, removing his rounded spectacles and rubbing his nose as he placed them on the table. "We have small arms enough. However, my king, our foes have both superior numbers and artillery power to us, and the three Reduction Treaties have only exacerbated our manpower deficit. While we manufacture rifles and focus on Reachers, Kelosh has developed artillery capable of accurately firing for over a mile. Since their vassalization of Teplos and expansion into our former eastern lands, they have laid extensive metal rails to carry metal machines that haul goods and people quickly over long distances.

"I wish to be as clear as possible among the leaders of the houses present," Hazemel continued, wiping his balding gray head with a handkerchief as sweat dripped from his brow. "A war with the Keloshan Empire would destroy what remains of the Commonwealth without aid. We have neither Ogrenia's technology, Reshka's vast reserves of glass, or even Nochland's navy at our disposal."

*So much talk of war,* Nikoza thought. *Yet no bother to cure the Spirit Plague. Where are Professor iz Noshok and this alchemist?*

Lilita ran her fingers across her silver necklace of a dragon wrapping its way around her neck. "What of our dragon? The Crystal Mother has gifted us the most powerful creature in Zekiaz."

"I do not deny your house's fine work training the beast of the sky," Hazemel replied. "It is, however, not invulnerable to cannon fire, and it may be some time before another emerges from the Spirit Crystal."

"We need strength through our Reachers and our dragon alike," Gornioz said, chin raised. "Yes, the empires have Reachers of their own, but we control the greatest reserves of the Spirit Crystal. We must use it to our advantage."

Borys huffed as he lit a cigar. "How do you intend to do that? Give out talons to every poor scion that comes begging, and you'll have the anointed sister's crystal spear so far up your ass that you'll have its tip as a tongue."

"Pardon Borys's crudeness," Gornioz said to Jazuk as he straightened his cravat. "I, in fact, do believe we should allow any scion to have a Reacher talon—in exchange for five years of military service if they cannot afford it."

"That..." Hazemel stuttered. "That is quite the idea. Reformers in the Chamber would admire the expansion of Reacher abilities to the lesser scions, and nationalists would gawk at the additional bulk this could give our army. Granted, one cannot rely entirely on untrained Reachers, who are bound to struggle for some time. We should not march to war alone."

"You support Gornioz's preposterous idea?" Borys replied, teeth bared as his cigar smoke curled between the debating ministers. "Hazemel, I thought you were a reasonable man! Access to the Spirit Crystal is sold to ensure the lesser scion families don't revolt and upset the order of things. That money fills our nation's coffers and the Buried Temple's ranks. We will be training the Reachers who shall uproot us from our very seats the moment their five years are finished."

Gornioz looked to Lilita. "Please, tell him that the conservatives will support such action upon your approval."

"I haven't given it yet," she quipped. "Unfortunately, I was too busy figuring out how much to charge you for your house's next glass shipment, as supplies are apparently *far* too limited."

Borys laughed. "Jazuk, talk some sense into your ministers before they turn us all to spirits."

Nikoza studied her grandfather as he leaned forward. She was still learning the faction dynamics among the Chamber's scions, and this plan seemed to have both merits and risks. Access to the Spirit Crystal to receive a talon was immensely expensive. This would compromise between the Buried Temple's hold over it and the poorer scions' hopes of Reaching, but forcing them into the military made her stomach churn. Thousands more scions would become Reachers. How many would fall within a year if Kelosh invaded?

She gave a subtle wave to draw Jazuk's attention, and when his eyes flicked to her, she mouthed, *"Alyniana."*

He seemed confused at first, so she repeated it thrice before he shook his head. What had she expected? Though a pragmatist, Jazuk had always been more inclined toward the nationalists.

"Very well," the king said to his council. "Gornioz, draw up the legislation, and we will ensure that this proposal passes the Chamber." As Borys protested, Jazuk held a hand to his chest. "We have been brothers in the Reacher towers and brothers in the Chamber, my friend. Aid us in this trying time."

Borys threw himself to his feet so quickly he slammed his hand into the burning butt of his cigar, only enraging him further. "I will do this as your friend, but we are not vassals, Jazuk. The scions choose the king. Remember that."

His steps thundered out, and no one wished him farewell. There was silence for a few long moments before Gornioz rose, bowing his head.

"We have much to attend to. All of us. May the Crystal Mother protect you in your efforts, my friends, and may we succeed in protecting our great nation."

When Gornioz's gaze fell upon Jazuk, the end of his mouth flicked upward for the slightest blink. Then he left with the others in tow, and Nikoza stared at the empty table in their wake. Were they marching the Commonwealth to its doom?

# THE STAG TRAP

*"You must question when hunting the most fearsome beasts whether you have caught the beast or whether the beast has caught you."* – An excerpt from *The Ezman's Guide to Hunting*

Frigid rains returned in the days following Radais's departure. Among the more spiritual scions, Kasia heard claims that the storms would wash away the blood of the Ephemeral Slaughter. Perhaps they were right, but the impact of the awakened attack went far deeper than the physical.

Kasia strolled alone through the near empty streets of eastern Kalastok, droplets splattering against her koilee fur hat as she headed toward a café in the Crimson District to dine with Sazilz Uziokaki. After her Death Reaching and recent votes in favor of the Keloshan Act and Gornioz's minor proposals in recent hundred-hours, many nationalist scions were curious about Leonit's successor. Some had even begun to reveal their intentions during private meetings with her.

This morning was her most important meeting yet. While it had been useful to gain favor among those who could've been Crimsons, none of them were great house magnates. Sazilz was her true target.

Now, she had the chance to confront him in hopes of further infiltrating the Crimsons and earning her revenge.

She soon arrived at Parzinak's, a bright-bricked restaurant where Sazilz awaited her at a table beneath an overhang. He stood and straightened his deep brown coat. It was a stain compared to the elaborate colorings of the restaurant, and his nervous speech didn't help his appearance.

"Katarzyna… Excuse me, Lady Katarzyna." He took her gloved hand and kissed it. "I have heard much about your exploits since your father's untimely death, so it is quite the pleasure to finally meet you."

She sat across from him, crossing her legs as she removed her hat and placed it alongside the utensils. It left her braided hair a mess, but that was intentional. One could not look far comelier than their counterpart, after all. Her father had claimed it ruined attempts at rapport.

"It is a pleasure, Lord Sazilz," she replied with a soft smile. "I enjoyed my visit to your house's estate during the Ephemeral Storm celebrations, but it was a shame you were busy with your duties here. The Chamber seems to have problems aplenty to address these days."

"Of which you have been a great help in solving." He regarded the restaurant's menu before glancing up at her. "What inspired you to switch from the reformers? Your father—"

"Was a different house head than I am," she interrupted.

"Of that much, we are confident."

We? Kasia noted that distinction but focused on earning his approval. "I must express my condolences as well for your nephew's death. Parqiz, was it?"

Sazilz held her gaze for a moment, his expression unreadable. "Indeed. Yet another night of intemperance ended his life far too soon."

"I heard he was at the celebration the night of his death, but I, unfortunately, was called to Kalastok before the funeral." She pulled a stag made of amber from her handbag. "I wanted to leave with you a spirit token for his passing, so that in his next life, he may see a new future for our two houses." It was a traditional gift after a scion's death—one which she hoped a conservative leader such as Sazilz would appreciate.

"Thank you," he said, taking it and examining it in the lantern-light. "This is fine craftsmanship that Parqiz would have approved of. It is a shame his spirit was not found, so we could not give him proper funeral rites."

"That is *unheard* of!"

"Precisely why we must be more assured of our allies than ever," he grumbled as he waved for a waiter. "Trust runs thin in days such as these."

Kasia took pride in Sazilz's frustration. She ignored the menu, instead leaning in closer and lowering her voice. "This is why I believe our houses should be in closer alignment. My father divided us, but we are neighbors, not rivals. Trade between Tystok and Giamivik would benefit us both, along with the people we employ. Don't you believe so?"

The waiter arrived before Sazilz could reply. A poorer scion based on his gloves and the lack of talon visible on his left hand, Kasia wondered whether the young man would take Reacher abilities if Gornioz's newly proposed law passed. Tazper had been tempted before Kasia reassured him she was taking the steps to pay for his own talon. She thought of her own powers, wondering if she would've traded five years of her life to wield them. Perhaps once she would've. Death Reaching had taken her lover, though, and her thoughts shifted to what she'd give up to go back and reject the Crystal's gift.

At the thought of Aliax, she caught sight of him lurking at a table behind Sazilz. The slain peasants filled the seats around him—a restaurant of ghosts, purple wisps rising from them.

Kasia averted her gaze, collecting herself. She couldn't linger on her Realm Taint now. Aliax was *not* there.

She looked back at her counterpart. Both Sazilz and the waiter stared at her, waiting for her to order. Had Sazilz already done so? She shook her head before glancing at the menu and choosing firebird eggs. A rarity, they were only caught by House Uziokaki's elite huntsmen, and their price reflected it. But flattery was worth the cost. As was her vengeance against a bird bearing the name of her most hated element.

"A culinary connoisseur, are you?" Sazilz said once the waiter had left. "I was told House Niezik was struggling."

"Amber along with integrating Ogrenian advancements into our agriculture has changed our fortunes," Kasia replied, holding her flame-scarred forearm. "Such changes are limited, however, without reliable trading partners."

Sazilz's mouth formed a narrow line at the mention of amber. "Yes. Well, it would be difficult to consider your house reliable while your wealth comes from stolen lands. I have heard rumors of a duel with my cousin that changed some minds."

"Must we resort to such accusations? Perhaps we could come to an arrangement to end this debate."

His claims were correct, as Leonit had altered the border between Niezik and Uziokaki lands through his connections with King Yaakiin, but Kasia had no intentions of revealing her father's con or her duel with Razamat Uziokaki years before. Nor did she have any intentions of completing their deal once Sazilz was dead. He had taken a more diplomatic approach himself, referring to her house as untrustworthy instead of Kasia herself. A minor shift, it represented he was still open to negotiations. Such was the way of the scions.

Sazilz tugged his coat shut. "I see no reason for compromise. It is clear the majority of Raviak Forest is Uziokaki territory."

"Except the legal paperwork says otherwise." Kasia leaned back, attempting to appear less aggressive. "We cannot grant you lands which are ours. However, in exchange for you agreeing to accept increased amounts of our barley and allowing us to build a gambling hall in each of your most sizable villages, we could offer you a tenth of all amber that we extract from the forest."

The waiter returned to pour Sazilz's wine. Kasia did not partake, but she admired the fine maple wood the goblets were crafted from. Only the richest dined with glassware, and wooden cups particularly were considered a show of modesty by scions—a false one of course.

"It surprises me you do not enjoy wine," Sazilz said, "considering Leonit's fondness for Reshka."

Kasia grinned. "I have my temptations. Alcohol simply does not sit well with my constitution."

"Nor does this offer sit with mine," Sazilz said with a sip.

"You speak of alliances yet fail to negotiate."

Sazilz downed the rest of the wine, then huffed. "Seventy-five percent of the yield. It is a generous offer, considering your occupation of the land."

*Splendid.*

Whatever happened from this point on did not matter. She would deny any deal once she ended the man who'd ordered her father murdered… if, in fact, there was not another Crimson above him.

"Lord Sazilz, please," she said softly. He needed to see her as influenceable but stubborn, neither too weak nor too strong. "We undergo significant costs to maintain our peasants and Reachers in the extraction process. Twenty-five percent would be a far more reasonable level."

"Let us call it an even split, then."

She gave a show of pondering the offer, fiddling with the amber chains across the front of her coat. It wasn't acceptable in the slightest, but infiltrating the Crimsons came first. "We shall split the yield *if* you agree to offset half the costs and help me regain House Niezik's standing in Kalastok. I have amber. You have connections I lack. This is beneficial for both of us."

Sazilz grinned as the food arrived. Spirits, it smelled delicious, and Kasia cursed her appetite ever since she'd left prison. It was unladylike to eat large portions, but she was a matriarch of increasing repute. Let them dare oppose a Death Reacher.

"Very well, Daughter of Death," Sazilz whispered, leaning forward and holding out a hand. "We have an arrangement."

Kasia shook his hand with as tough of a grip as she could manage. Unlike many men she'd met, he failed to match it. "Wonderful! As you are the magnate of a great house, I will leave it to you to draft the wording." Such was tradition, and though he would surely insert favorable language into the contract, he would be offended if she were to deny him that right. Not that she would sign it anyway.

"Acceptable." He took the first spoonful of his pork and vegetable soup, before wiping his mouth with his napkin. "Before it is signed, however, I have information as an act of good faith."

This was it. A deal could only get her so far, but now Sazilz would either aid her with joining the Crimsons or hint that he was their leader. Kasia didn't know which she hoped for as she gestured for him to continue.

"There will be a gathering tomorrow evening at House Oliezany's estate in the city to commemorate their purchase of House iz Vamiustok's sand mines," he said. "When you arrive, socialize for a time before heading into the area guarded by Gornioz's mercenaries. I will await you there."

"May I ask what for?

He took another scoop of his soup, then slurped it down in an unfashionable way. "Do not ruin the fun, dear girl. Some things are better shown than told, so let us speak no further of business."

Kasia mirrored him, taking a bite of her firebird eggs and immediately diving for a gulp of water. Holy Crystal Mother, it was spicy.

"Wow," she sputtered. "That fucking firebird did *not* want its eggs eaten."

Her eyes widened at her curse. She'd gotten far too used to less formal company, and her father would've scolded her incessantly for such lack of manners. Sazilz, though, simply laughed. "You play with fire, then you are likely to get burned. Is your brother not a Fire Reacher?"

"He is," she said flatly.

He gave a knowing smirk, then took a drink of his second goblet of wine. "A shame that you choose not to enjoy this wine. With a few drinks in you, you seem like you would learn to be less stiff. Not all of us great house magnates desire endless politics and conniving, Katarzyna."

"Please, call me Kasia. I hate that unneeded Z."

"Kasia, of course," he said before the waiter came by to check on them, but Sazilz shooed him away. "Now, with the boring business finished, let us speak of lighter topics. Events are endless in this city, and if you wish to increase your standing, you must have many ears to the ground…"

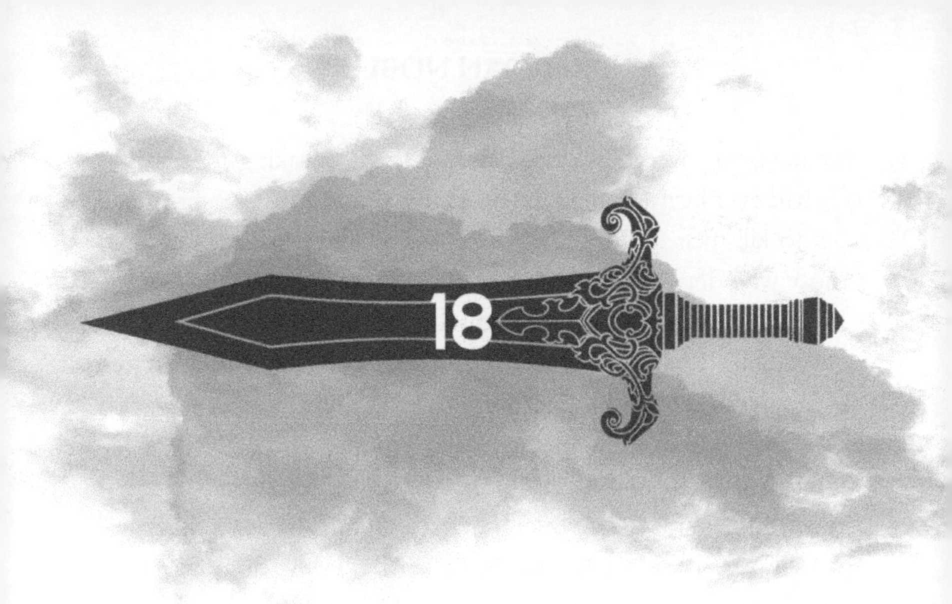


# THE LOST BLADE

*"The spirits are our family. They are our lovers, our friends, our protectors, and our wards. We are them, and they are us. In the darkest times, we must listen to their silent calls. Open your mind and your soul will follow."* – Orionus ik Pakinar, Vockan mystic

Rain turned to sleet and then to snow as Radais rose through the mountains of Vocka on Vuk's back. His trusty ibex had rushed to him the moment he'd returned to the Kalastok stables, and Radais had been no less eager to hug Vuk again. Some called an ibex nothing more than a mount.

Those men were fools.

Vuk carried Radais with unwavering determination. Over rocky fords and steep switchbacks, he clambered on, bleating occasionally as if to question his master's sanity. Radais couldn't answer. After everything he'd seen in recent hundred-hours, he had begun to wonder whether he'd gone mad in the Spirit Wastes.

Stories told around Glassblade campfires told of initiates and young warriors straying too far into the awakened's lands. So many never returned, but when some did emerge from the swirling sands of gray, their eyes were glazed over. One moment they were normal.

The next, they would fall into a muttering fit, speaking a tongue no one had ever heard. The worst of the lot would swing weapons and seek to kill their siblings-in-arms as they screamed nonsense about "those who draw no breath."

"No," Radais whispered to himself. "I'm not insane."

Vuk bleated beneath him, and Radais patted his neck before shouting into the towering, dark mountains.

"I am not insane!"

His voice echoed for a few long heartbeats. Despite living his entire life in these highlands, it still shocked him that sound could carry to distant peaks. Most he couldn't even see in the everdark. They were there regardless, ever-present—just like the spirits.

A drifter appeared at the edge of the lanternlight. Meandering, it seemed to follow Radais for a time, but its shifting form never seemed to focus upon him. He kept his hand on his glass sword.

"I'd question your sanity myself if you weren't carrying that sword," Lazan said from behind him. Radais had forgotten about the quiet, late-thirties Body Reacher. Riding an obese Kalastok ibex that obviously had little training in the mountains, he had slowed their progress toward Palmia, but Radais couldn't complain. This man could save his father's life.

"I won't disturb you further," Radais said to the spirit, bowing his head in reverence before waving to Lazan to do the same.

The Reacher refused. Ezmani considered such drifters to be useless wisps floating through the sky unless a newborn needed a spirit, but to Vockans, they were the purest spirits, untainted by the other realms. Drifters needed neither bodies nor minds. This was their realm. They deserved to be honored when one was stepping upon the ground in their vicinity, and old legends claimed such respect could bring answers to the Vockan's prayers.

Awakened deserved no such respect. They were monsters formed from manipulation of spirits' purity, and that made the Glassblades all the more important. For each awakened, there were a hundred spirits that could fall to its corruption.

The spirit faded into the darkness as Vuk began an ascent far too steep for a horse. He hopped from stone to stone, even with the weight of both rider and gear on his back, and Radais held on tight to avoid falling off. Vuk was well trained, though, and kept steady.

They reached the crest of the next ridge in minutes before stopping to rest. Radais dismounted to stretch his legs before offering Vuk a bunch of bound grasses to nibble on.

"Almost home," he said, scratching the ibex under his chin as Lazan finally caught up. His eyes were wide and his shoulders rigid as he clung to his ibex.

"Tell me this was the worst part of the journey," Lazan said. "Body Reaching can bolster my ibex's strength for only a short while at a time without enduring Realm Taint."

Radais chuckled at the fat ibex's panting. "Afraid not."

Even Vuk seemed amused, approaching his compatriot and nudging him. Whether it was encouragement or mockery, Radais didn't know, but he figured everyone needed the moment's respite. He pulled his sketchbook from his pack and brushed off a snow-covered boulder, hopping onto it.

There was little in sight due to the everdark, but Lazan and the ibexes were plenty of inspiration. Among the Vockans, long stylish coats, short hair, and clean-shaven faces like Lazan's were rare due to impracticality and the chill. He pondered how to emphasize those elements in the sketch as he flipped through the book.

His hands stopped against his will, though, when he reached his most recent sketch of Miv. With only charcoal to work with, he'd failed to grasp her fire-red eyes and hair like the great light shining through a gentle rainfall. It didn't matter. The mere memory of her took his breath away.

"Do you mind if I sketch you?" he asked Lazan, pulling himself from his thoughts. "It will give our mounts more rest before the next climb."

Lazan raised his brow. "You are an artist? I had wondered what you were doing with that book at night, but had been too shy to ask."

Radais began his work while replying, "I am far from a professional. Just… In a life surrounded by death and haunted spirits, I find it relaxing to draw what I've seen. Often, it allows me to leave behind the worst parts in this book." He turned his focus to the sketch. There was no reason to share so much with this man.

"I understand," Lazan said, posing with his hands in his coat's pockets and his cleft chin tucked to his chest. The coat was woolen, without the glass decorations of richer scions, but Radais assumed it was woven with at least some glass to keep away awakened. Even lowborn held fragments of impure glass to protect themselves.

"Thanks, but I don't think you do." Radais's strokes turned sharp. "Reachers drive away most awakened from Kalastok, but in Vocka, we Glassblades are villagers' only hopes. The Wastes lie over this mountain range. Awakened do not care how high they need to fly in order to reach their victims."

"Perhaps I fail to grasp the specifics, but I know death. It is the nature of a healer's work."

Radais didn't reply. The sketch was sloppy because of his mood, but it was better than forcing himself to ponder his father or what had happened in Kalastok. Kasia had convinced him there was a greater plot. Why had he run from it?

*No,* he told himself. *Think about the shadings, Lazan's eyes and how the lanternlight falls upon them.*

Lazan sighed. "Oddly enough, it is probably the nature of both of our works. You protect the living so that they don't need people like me. But when either of us fails—or both—people lose their lives, sometimes forever."

"It's always in Vocka."

"True enough. I have wondered why your people cannot Reach, even when shown to the Spirit Crystal. Everyone has their theory. What's yours?"

Radais gave Lazan an arching brow in the sketch, similar to the one the actual man held now. It was questioning, but not judgmental. "I don't know," Radais said. "Ezmani lowborn can't either."

"That is all?" Lazan held out his arms and spun, gesturing to the distant, unseeable mountains. "We live in a realm of wonder and mystery, and the body itself is stitched together in so many fascinating ways. Why would the spirit be any different? Should we not question why some hold mighty power while others must waste away beneath the weight of their own skeletons?"

Radais sat back. "What would you like me to say? I believe the spirits are involved, like all my people, but you scions have rejected that outright."

"I do not succumb to the will of the Buried Temple's priestesses. It seems I've hit a wound. My apologies, as I simply wished to hear a master Glassblade's thoughts on the subject."

"Don't worry. I'm just eager to reach Palmia so that I may bring you to my father." Standing, Radais shoved his sketchbook back into his pack before mounting Vuk. "Let's continue. I would rather arrive before the end of supper."

So on they went. Except this time, Lazan kept closer behind. His ibex was still far slower, but he urged in on while occasionally commenting on what he described as a wondrous landscape. It was an odd shift after days of near silence. At first, it irked Radais to no end, but he soon found comfort in having a companion who found the mountains as fascinating as he did.

The journey finished with a descent down the slopes east of Palmia Fortress, lacking switchbacks that would be traversable by an invading force. Instead, the ibexes had to leap across crevices and climb at near impossible angles to descend safely. Vuk was trained and had made the journey before. Lazan's ibex struggled with each motion, and when stones slid behind Radais, he knew immediately Lazan had fallen.

He hopped from Vuk onto a nearby boulder with a command for the ibex to stay where he was. There had been a section just before that had many loose stones. Radais knew where to guide Vuk, but he cursed himself for not realizing Lazan lacked that knowledge.

"Lazan?" he called out as he climbed up, the lantern tied to his belt giving him sight of the cliff face ahead. "Where are you?"

Bleating came from the left. Radais rushed toward it, only to find the poor Kalastok ibex with its front legs badly broken. Even if he could help it down the mountain, there would be no recovering from the wound, so he drew his iron dagger and drove it into the ibex's skull—just as he had with the spiritless Pikezik man. His stomach turned. Why was killing an ibex worse than what remained of a man?

He rose and surveyed the surrounding area. Lazan couldn't have fallen far from his mount, but if he was unconscious, that did not bode well for his survival.

"Lazan?"

"Ah! Shit… My leg's twisted," the Reacher called from a ridge above, just outside the lantern's ring of light. Lazan's own lantern must've broken in the fall, as no light came from near him. "We slipped, and—"

"You're alright," Radais replied as calmly as he could manage. "Stay there. The ridge is too high up, so I will need Vuk's help."

He clambered back down the slope to Vuk, who hadn't moved an inch from where Radais had left him. Spirits, the ibex deserved better than this, but he was all Radais had right now. Radais grabbed a few of Vuk's favorite treats from his pack, then guided him back toward Lazan and tossed them onto the ridge.

"Go up to him," he said in hopes of Vuk understanding. "Get the treats and help Lazan back down, okay boy? There's more treats waiting when you're done."

Vuk was already halfway up the near vertical cliff face by the time Radais was done talking. Food had always been his obsession, and Radais took some pride in knowing Vuk would follow him anywhere.

"Climb onto Vuk's back when he gets up there for the treats," he yelled up to Lazan. "Hurry, because he has a habit of coming back to me as fast as he can."

There was no reply as Vuk disappeared into the darkness. Radais held his breath, listening to the scuttling of hooves against stone until a yelp came from the ridge. A few moments later, Vuk appeared again, and he had a bloodied but alive Lazan clinging to his back with wide eyes.

"I have never seen a creature climb such a slope," Lazan said. "I fear by the time we reach the bottom that I still will not have seen it."

"Then open your eyes. There are no awakened here, just a Glassblade who's caught fatter men than you from that height."

"I would rather not need your services."

Vuk soon reached Radais, making a series of nasally sounds that resembled a man snoring, and was rewarded with as many treats as Radais had left in his pouch. Lazan slouched forward in the saddle. Besides the blood covering half his face and his knee, he appeared remarkably unharmed.

"Don't look so surprised, my friend," Lazan said before letting out a pained groan. "I am a Body Reacher, remember? Sure, I am not as skilled as most, but one Reach for me is plenty enough to heal a few broken bones."

Radais swallowed. "I… I did not think of that when I saw your ibex. It was suffering, so I put it out of its misery."

Lazan winced, then nodded. "I cannot blame you. Unlike the scions of Kalastok, Reachers are uncommon in your lands. Your decision was the natural one."

"Follow me down," Radais said to change the topic. The sinking feeling in his chest sought to undermine the confidence he needed to finish the descent by foot, so he needed to keep moving. They had completed the steepest section, but the parts ahead were no simple hike. "Vuk will lead with little needed input, but call for me if you need help."

They continued in silence. Radais's knees ached the further he went, and he wished he'd aged with Miv's grace. Years of fighting in the hinterlands had taken their toll, each old scar and injury reminding him of their presence as he jumped to the next ledge before glancing back at Lazan. The Reacher fared well on Vuk. Though his form was terrible for a rider, it at least kept him from falling again.

An eternity of exhaustion later, he emerged from the rocks and trees to find the glow of Palmia Fortress filling the landscape ahead. It was a welcomed bit of familiarity after the cityscape of Kalastok—a reminder who he was.

"By the Crystal Mother," Lazan breathed as he and Vuk stopped beside Radais. "The stories don't match its true glory. Is the roof truly glass-imbued metal?" When Radais nodded, he laughed. "A castle with a roof overtop its towers. Extraordinary!"

"Most forts were built to resist humans," Radais replied, leading them toward the eastern side of Palmia Village. "Even Palmia was at first, but they modified it to stop awakened attacking from above."

"Now we have Spirit Reachers in towers."

Radais huffed. "Right, and they did extraordinarily in Kalastok when the awakened came in force."

Lazan smiled and nodded toward the fortress. "Fair enough. Maybe we still need your fancy swords and armor."

The belltower rang for the seventeenth hour by the time they arrived in the center of Palmia. Supper time, usually among the most active hours for the small village, but there wasn't a person in sight between the stone buildings. No children fussing about as their parents called them to eat. No heavy smell of the tannery. And no clanging from the forge. Just an empty street.

Except for Gargas of course.

"Why you dragging your ass back down here?" the old blacksmith shouted from his stool before the forge. The lantern hanging from the front of his shop made him appear more like a silhouette than a man. "Thought you were heading to the city?"

"I departed nearly three hundred-hours ago," Radais replied. "Losing track of time with the forge fumes?"

Gargas scratched his flaking scalp before taking a swig from his canteen. His breath smelled of sariasa, a heavy Vockan drink made from mountain herbs. "Been shit since you left. Hard not to forget time when you want it all to be over."

"Want what to be over?"

"All of it!"

Gargas downed the rest of his bottle. When he finished, tears wetted his eyes for the first time since Radais had met the old man. Everyone in Palmia knew he was as hard as the metal he smithed, and Radais's heart sank knowing only the worst could've led him to this state.

He crouched and laid a hand on Gargas's shoulder. "It'll be okay. Just tell me what happened."

"Spirit-damned awakened showed up by the baker's cakes... too many to count. Coulda swore the whole sky turned gray if it weren't so damn black already."

Lazan paced behind Radais, studying the fortress. "Are the Glassblades not supposed to be able to fight them?"

"Who's this Ezmani lad?" Gargas asked with a cough. "He's as bloody as a slaughterhouse, but looks fine."

"He's a Body Reacher, Lazan," Radais replied, "but I'm not worried about him right now. He's right. Where were the Glassblades?"

"Just a skeleton crew. Bunch of 'em left not long after you."

Radais clenched his fists. *Miv...* "I'm glad you're safe, Gargas. These attacks happened in Kalastok and likely other villages too, but I thought you'd have been safer here than anywhere else."

Gargas shrugged and drew a glass dagger from inside his coat. "I've seen more than my fair share of those smoky bastards. Killed a few of them before what's left of your friends showed up."

"Good man." Radais patted him on the face. "Keep watch for me, will you?"

"Got nothing better to do in this waste."

As Radais stood, he shook his head. "You've never seen the actual Wastes. They make this place look like paradise."

Gargas returned to his forge, shoulders slumped, but he stopped at the threshold with a hand on the doorframe. "If awakened lands are such shit, no wonder they would rather kill us than stay there." Then he disappeared into the forge, and the clanging of his hammer soon followed as Radais led Lazan toward the fortress.

"Don't worry about Gargas," Radais told Lazan. "He's like that with everyone."

Lazan glanced at the surrounding shops and houses, all dark. "If this is the village protected by the Glassblades, then what happened to the more remote ones? I heard they were attacked too, but this is slaughter."

"Miv will know more. She has to."

The sparse guards at the entrance let the pair in with little fuss. At this hour, Miv would be in the mess hall on the east side of the fortress or her office at the far southern edge. They would need to pass by the mess either way, so Radais figured they should check there first. The savory smells of fresh food pulled him along after days on the road. Besides, there was no better place to overhear rumors from the other Glassblades.

Miv had other plans.

A tall girl with smiley, round cheeks rushed to them just as Radais pressed to open the mess door. "Master Radais!" she said, obviously an initiate based on her perfect posture. "I… I was told to send you to see the supreme defender at the southeast tower." She glanced at the now dried blood on Lazan's clothes. "Are you alright?"

Radais forced away his scowl. The girl was just doing her job after all. "Fine, then. We will be on our way."

"Do you need me to show you to her?" the initiate stammered.

"You must be pretty new here to think a master can't find one of the towers." *And that I couldn't find Miv's favorite spot to be alone.*

The initiate winced. "Of course, Master Radais." Then she tucked her head into her chest and headed into the mess. Lazan chuckled watching her go.

"Adolescents are the same here, I see."

Radais led him on with a shoulder pat. "I doubt it took you less than a season to learn how to use your talon. Same goes for an initiate and their blade."

They headed deeper into the fortress and followed one of the paths to the southeast corner, which stared a mountain peak dead in the face. A wooden door opened to the rounded staircase that seemed to climb forever. Miv had made Radais climb the tower over and over during his training to gain fitness, and the cracks in the stone walls were the same now as the ones he'd memorized all those years ago. His knees had been better then. Spirits, how many steps were there? He'd known once, drawing many of them in his sketchbook, but now he just wanted them to end.

Their heavy breaths echoed in the cramped space until they stumbled into the archers' nest. Two sat upon stools and stared out the arrow slits, chins rested on their hands.

"Where is she?" Lazan huffed with his hands on his knees.

Radais nodded up at the ceiling, where a ladder continued toward the metal roof of the fortress. "Not there yet."

He hefted his sore body up the ladder. Miv wouldn't be as excited to see him as he was to see her, but he needed the motivation to keep him moving. He'd rest at the top, then leap off the edge to avoid enduring the descent.

When he reached the trap door at the top of the ladder, he unlatched it and pushed it open. It had always surprised him how light the trap door was, but the metal was just to compensate for the risks involved with a pure glass roof. It fell with a *thud* as he stepped out, then grabbed Lazan's arm to pull him up.

"You spend a hundred-hour in Kalastok and come back like a panting dog?" Miv quipped from her seat upon the roof's edge, one leg tucked to her chest and the other dangling over the side.

Radais crossed his arms and coughed. This was her usual tone with him, but with a visitor, she was supposed to be a commander. "Supreme Defender, I've returned from the mission you gave me and wanted to report in."

"What's with the forma—Oh..." She wrinkled her brow at Lazan, shooting to her feet, rigid and stern in her blue commander's coat. "Master Radais, who is this visitor? An Ezmani initiate?"

"No." He pushed Lazan into the lanternlight. "This is Lazan Karianam, a Body Reacher one of the houses sent to aid me with my father's illness."

Lazan bowed his head. "A pleasure to meet you, Supreme Defender. Radais has told me much about you during our journey."

*You son of a—*

"Is that so?" Miv asked with a wry smile, her eyes reflecting the heat burning Radais's cheeks.

Radais cleared his throat. "Lazan is just here to accompany me for my report. After that, I would like to ask for a leave to address my family matters."

"Yes, about your father..." Her smile disappeared. "Radais, you should sit."

He froze, the fear in her voice striking straight at his heart. Spirits, he was too late. It hadn't been that long, though? How could his father's health have declined so quickly?

"How?" he managed to stammer.

"The first letter arrived a couple hundred-hours before you came back," she replied. "When the spirits call one home, it can happen quickly. I received word from your brother yesterday."

Lazan laid a hand on his shoulder, but Radais brushed it off, pacing to the roof's edge and staring into the darkness. A stray thought wondered what his father's death had felt like. If Radais were to fall from this height, his spirit could join his father away from his brother's judgment.

But Radais stepped back. His father was already gone, and following him wouldn't fix anything.

"I'm sorry I dragged you all this way for nothing," he told Lazan.

The Reacher shrugged. "I have been paid for my services. Perhaps the Glassblades have a use for me?"

"Yes," Miv said, turning away with her arms crossed. "Radais, let's focus on what you came here to do. There will be time for you to mourn appropriately." He did not reply, so Miv continued, "Have you heard about the attack against Palmia and the other villages? There were rumors Kalastok suffered too, but I wasn't sure whether I could trust them. After all, they said a skilled Glassblade helped a pretty young Death Reacher fend off the awakened."

Her jest failed to pierce Radais's sorrow. Each word was distant as she stepped between Radais and the edge. She matched his height, and it took all his pride not to back down. "It didn't sound like you," she whispered.

Radais sighed, shoulders slumped as he forced himself to meet her gaze. "The woman's name is Katarzyna of House Niezik. Neither House iz Ardinvil nor any other great house listened to me, but she did. She had already been investigating a group she called the Crimson Court, and she believes they're connected to the red-robed man I found. I still don't know who he was, except that he was from House Pikezik."

Miv grimaced. "Pikezik? What do the dragon tamers want with the Wastes?"

"I don't know, but there's something bigger happening here." He swallowed, anticipating her reaction to what came next, but pushed on. Anything to distract him from his failure. "Katarzyna had me stay in her townhouse to help her uncover more. She said that her father was killed by an awakened that followed the orders of some nephew of Sazilz Uziokaki. It seemed off, but the Ephemeral Slaughter happened right after a nationalist led vote failed in the Chamber of Scions. And those awakened were whispering like the ones I heard in the Wastes. The spirits almost seemed to be working together."

Something flickered in Miv's eyes when he mentioned he'd stayed with Katarzyna. Obviously, nothing romantic had happened between them, as he was over a decade older than the Niezik matriarch, but he took pride in his former lover's jealousy.

"I was concerned something like this could happen," Miv said. She paced along the edge of the roof, staring at the dark mountains. "After you left, I sent out most of our ranks to protect the more remote villages, but it only divided them, made them vulnerable. Even Palmia struggled to repel the awakened; though, it appears we were hit harder than other villages."

"That lends credence to Radais's theory," Lazan replied. "A targeted strike."

Miv shot him a glare that said, *"I didn't ask you,"* before speaking to Radais. "It's obvious these attacks weren't normal. I honestly thought you were crazy when you said the awakened were talking, but we all heard it that night. Spirits be damned… If we can't stop them, who can?"

"Maybe that's what these Crimsons were doing in the Wastes," Radais said. "Where better to research how to control the awakened than in their home?"

Miv stopped, arms crossed. "I thought you said that they're involved in causing this?"

"I'm just guessing. Whatever is happening, it started out there."

"Which is why I want you to go back."

A weight lifted off Radais's shoulders. It was insane, but the thought of returning to the Spirit Wastes was a relief compared to facing his family and the politics of Kalastok. From the moment he'd stepped back into the world of the living, he had found himself as a pawn in a game whose players he couldn't even see. At least with the awakened, he knew what he faced.

He stood up straighter and held his fist to his chest, sniffling, but holding back his emotions for a while longer. "Yes, Supreme Defender. When do I leave?"

"In a few days." Miv turned away, arms held behind her in a soldier's stance. "You will have your pick of the remaining Glassblades in Palmia to go with you. Take no less than eight. We cannot afford for this mission to fail, and if there are altered awakened, it will no doubt be dangerous for even a master to face alone."

"I'm not exactly a commander."

"Then it is time for that to change." She glanced over her shoulder at him, pity in her eyes. "Thank you for your report, Master Radais. You are dismissed."

Radais hesitated, but there was both too much and nothing to say. He had work to do. His nation and his order were relying on him, so desires of the heart could wait.

"Come, Lazan," he said as he eyed the ladder. "We face another journey just to reach our supper."

# THE COMMANDER'S CALL

*"Whoever threatened my life and killed Regizald must be brought to justice. You did well by your morals, my dear son, but we must recover and reveal this Dark Reacher."* – Sania iz Vamiustok, matriarch of House iz Vamiustok

A heavy fog rolled through the stables just outside the Kalastok jousting arena. Zinarus breathed it in as he leaned against a stall door to keep his weight off his mechanical leg. Tiuz had helped him import Ogrenian stirrups that would aid his riding, but that didn't stop the soreness before he mounted.

"Regiz—"

He cursed, stumbling into the stall, where a bay gelding of considerable size named Arkenus met him with an excited huff. Though happy to see his horse, Zinarus wept for the loss of his dear friend as he clutched a black memorial flower pinned to his jacket. Regizald hadn't been involved in the red-robed man's offer. It hadn't mattered in the end, as he suffered the consequences of Zinarus's hesitation. It was unfair. But if life had taught Zinarus anything, it was that those who expected fairness suffered the consequences of its lacking.

With some effort, he tacked up Arkenus as Regizald had always done for him before. Knowing how much he'd relied on his servant only added to the pain. Had he treated Regizald as well as he'd deserved? Surely not. There were many worse masters among the scions, but that was no excuse.

He grunted as he mounted Arkenus. His half-Vockan blood had given him considerable height, but because of his mechanical leg, he needed a mounting block to swing himself into a saddle. He lacked skill with a sword, but he awaited the feeling of the lance in his hand.

Nothing took his mind off his troubles like riding, and he had plenty of troubles to forget with Regizald's death and House Oliezany stealing his family's mines. The jousting dummies in the arena would feel exactly how upset he was. His mother claimed it was unwise to lose one's temper over business, but this wasn't merely business. The red-robed Reacher had stolen his purpose, slain his best friend, and threatened his mother. He swore he'd make the Reacher pay.

His work would start with the Oliezany party, but he had time and fury to burn before then.

The everdark's first snow fell heavily upon his duster and hair, matting the sand as he entered the dim arena. He grabbed a wooden lance from the rack, focused on the first straw dummy. Then he charged.

Arkenus burst through the snowfall as his master pictured the Dark Reacher as the target. Zinarus would have justice.

His lance pierced the first target straight in the chest, sending it sprawling in a heap, but he wasn't finished. Two more targets lined the arena's center. For these, he pictured Gornioz Oliezany and his wife Ikatia. They called the gala a celebration of their agreement with Zinarus, but it was nothing more than a mockery of House iz Vamiustok's collapse. He'd dared to sit in the reformer wing of the Chamber and sell sand for glass beyond the great houses. This night, he thanked the Crystal Mother that his own mother was far away in Vamiustok instead of being forced to endure this torture.

The last target fell with enough force to rip straight through it. They were straw, but built to withstand quite a few hits. As Zinarus stared down at his faux opponent, he grinned at the power he'd put into the thrust.

But jousting was more about accuracy than pure power. Tiuz had hammered that into him, and even his beleaguered mind and burning heart could not make him forget such training.

The greatest jousters were those who could dismount a foe through pinpoint precision and strength alike, so he dismounted and set up a series of rings, each smaller than the one before it. He'd watched Tiuz complete this drill up to five times without missing a single ring. That had inspired him to sponsor the old cavalry commander over younger and stronger competitors. Most scions threw their support behind domineering forces on horseback. Bit by bit, Tiuz and Zinarus had proven them wrong. He needed a way to do the same in politics.

Zinarus charged at each ring, winding his way through the arena. His rage had demolished his straw targets, but the rings proved elusive. Once, he lowered his lance too early. Another, too late. Then he failed to couch the lance correctly, sending it sprawling out of his hand on the smallest ring.

He yelled in frustration as he slid Arkenus from his gallop to a halt. Dust filled the air around him, irritating his eyes and nose, and he ripped off his gloves to wipe his face clean. Except his fingers found only tears.

"Mother will not tolerate such weakness!" he snapped at himself. Taking a long breath, he leaned back in the saddle and stared at the empty everdark above.

No wonder Uzrin did not wish to claim Zinarus as his son. House Ioniz, his absent father's house, had far more to lose as one of the families vying to reach the glory of the great houses.

"What kind of seat is that?" a voice shouted from across the arena. Tiuz hopped the wall from the stands, grinning as he threw a floppy-eared hat over his bald head. "Did the ibex-riding Vockans teach you that, or are you developing methods of your own?"

Zinarus bit his cheek and fixed his posture. " 'Tis the pouter's stance."

"We have all had our share of that in recent days." Tiuz stopped before Arkenus and patted his nose. "You're a far better rider than what I just saw, and that begins with the seat. Get too eager to strike and end up finding only air. Sit like you were taught, focusing on the target that's in front of you instead of your house's enemies."

"What's the point of that? I'll be a cripple again when I dismount."

Tiuz crossed his arms, circling the horse. "That is the most informal I have ever heard you. Spirits know you must be really stirred up to be like this." He grabbed the strap for the mechanical leg's stirrup and yanked, shortening it. "Is this really just about Regizald and some deal with House Oliezany, or is something else bothering you?"

"Do you recall the red-robed Dark Reacher I mentioned?" Zinarus asked, shifting his weight. The change in stirrup length left him more balanced, natural. How had Tiuz eyed such a small change so quickly?

"It's difficult not to after your theatrical depiction of him. You thought he might have something to do with the awakened, since he arrived right after their attack, right?"

Zinarus nodded. "Whoever he is, he outmaneuvered me in every way. My mother trusted me to handle our house's businesses, but I have lost the greatest of them."

Tiuz stepped back and examined Zinarus's tack as he rubbed his chin. "You blame yourself for a defeat that you could not stop. It's common among young commanders too, but you learn quickly that there are battles you can win and others you must survive. Luckily, this battle resulted in you receiving a great many keni, though, less than your mines were worth."

"My goal is not just to accumulate wealth."

"Then build something that achieves your goals." Tiuz hesitated, a rarity for the confident major general, and stuffed his hands in his pockets. "I know you often speak as if you look down upon the commoners and lower scion houses, but your votes and actions speak for themselves in the Chamber. You care about the Commonwealth and its people—even the lowest among them. Why not put these funds into service for them?"

Zinarus raised his brow. "Mother would not be pleased."

"What if the service ensured financial stability for your house and protected you from further threats?"

"Go on…"

Tiuz grinned and held out his arms. "I have seen your love for this arena, its steeds, and the champions who fight within it. It crumbles under the ownership of those who do not see that this place should provide joy for people beyond only the scions. Let the masses step from their strained lives to imagine something greater for but a few hours. Then, among those who desire more, offer them a chance to prove themselves."

"I don't understand," Zinarus replied. "How does this help them? Cheap admission in greater numbers could bring profit, but it does not necessarily serve the peasants."

"I have marched enough campaigns to know that people, whether soldiers or not, need more than food, water, and shelter. Hope and joy keep us going in the most difficult times. Our spirits whither to husks without them." Tiuz pushed his finger into Zinarus's chest. "You can bring the people together through a common enjoyment, a luxury even the poorest could afford. And you can use the revenue to fund a force to defend those who have neither guns nor blades to wield."

Zinarus pondered this proposition as he pushed Arkenus into a walk around the arena's rim. "You wish for me to fund a mercenary company to defend the lowborn?"

"To defend those who cannot defend themselves, whether it be against Kelosh, awakened, or red-robed men lurking in the darkness. The king refuses to send Reachers or watchmen to patrol the west side. The great houses hire mercenaries to watch only their factories and townhouses. What about everyone else who gets robbed, beaten, or murdered?" Tiuz gestured to the stable door. "It need not be more than a few dozen soldiers. With our horses, we have the beginnings of a cavalry platoon already, able to move quickly if something happens in the city. All we need are weapons along with men and women who seek to join our cause."

Zinarus chuckled as he studied his friend, his mentor. With Regizald gone, he had fewer friends than ever, and Tiuz's passion was contagious. He never requested more than he needed, but he always made a damn good argument when he asked.

"You wish to lead this group as a major general again?" Zinarus asked with a raise of his brow.

Tiuz shook his head. "A platoon has a lieutenant, which would be a significant demotion from my former title, but in all honesty, I could handle a small group alongside my jousting. You have helped me find a purpose after I'd lost hope in the army, Zinarus. For that, I thank you, and now, I ask for your help again in pursuing it. My house has limited funds, but I will commit them as well."

"This is no small feat. Even employing twenty or thirty soldiers is a significant cost if this is charity alone."

"I understand your fear." Tiuz scratched his head as he paced, lanternlight glinting of the sweat on his brow despite the chill. Crystal Mother, he really wanted this. "We will aid the poor, yes, but some lowborn merchants may pay for protection as well. As long as we act with honor, we will be greater than any other mercenary company."

Tiuz stepped to Zinarus and nearly yanked him from Arkenus's back. "Please, listen to me, son of Sania. This purpose is not just mine. I will serve as lieutenant, and I will need you to manage the logistics. Such labor is not my expertise."

"What of the Chamber?" Zinarus replied, gripping Tiuz's arm and dismounting. His mechanical leg's steel foot landed firm, and he took a moment to admire that rare feeling.

"We can still hold our positions among the scions, but those awakened attacked reformers and moderates," Tiuz insisted. "Jazuk imprisoned others who refused to support the Keloshan Act, and he'll do the same when the nationalists call for destructive war. Our votes matter. Only action, though, can protect the most vulnerable in our crumbling nation."

"Still, it is a risk," Zinarus insisted as he stomped his steel foot. "The great houses will scorn our decision."

Tiuz stepped back, arms crossed. "You are not the coward you think you are. A coward doesn't risk much of their fortunes on a washed-up commander becoming a champion jouster."

Zinarus studied him, searching for the deception that was all too common among the scions. He found none. For the first time, his house had significant funds but no major business. Tiuz offered him a chance to own the arena he loved and aid those in need. It was a dream come true, yet he sought any excuse to deny that fact, as if accepting would diminish all he'd accomplished with his house's sand trade. Except his success had only drawn the ire of the great houses. They had crushed him beneath their heels.

It was time to fight back.

"I will do what you ask," he said, "and join you in the creation of this mercenary group."

Tiuz beamed. "Good. We'll start—"

"On one." Zinarus stepped closer to the general, towering over him with his half-blooded Vockan height. "You may be in command, but I have the final say where the mercenaries go and who they fight for."

"That makes sense," Tiuz replied. Then he saluted. "Lord Zinarus, I am at your command."

Zinarus returned it. "The pleasure is all mine, Lieutenant Hazeko. But this conversation must continue tomorrow. Though I would rather have my intestines dragged out than attend this gala tonight, I will need to save face ahead of our company's formation."

"Believe me. I have seen a man's intestines spilled upon the battlefield. Attending a gala is no pain compared to what I saw on his face." Tiuz patted Zinarus's shoulder. "What lies ahead will not be easy, but we will face it together. On this I swear."

# THE ROSE AND ITS THORNS

*"One must learn to dance with the partner one faces. It is unwise to attempt an Ezmani laziak when the tune is meant for the fluid kariatona of old Piorak."*
– Ezmerelda Bartol the Third, former matriarch of House Bartol

A dozen eyes followed Kasia the moment she stepped from her carriage with Tazper's aid. Her great-uncle Faniz lumbered behind her in a boxy gray suit that matched his skin and what little hair he had left. He held a still burning cigar in his hand, and Kasia took a deep breath of the cool air, grateful to be free from her uncle's smoke.

*And I thought Father had been ostentatious,* she thought as she scanned the crowd gathered outside the gates crafted from Oliezany gold.

Just outside the northern bounds of Kalastok itself, House Oliezany's estate rose from the darkness like a palace in its own right. Light Reachers stood upon twisting towers with engraved patterns of deep red glass, shooting light over the grounds. The gates and stone walls alongside the towers blocked sight of the mansion's entrance. From the roadside, though, Kasia had a clear sight of the highest balcony, where Gornioz Oliezany stood with his hands gripping the railing.

He was staring at her.

"Shit," she muttered to Tazper. "Gornioz is watching me."

"Maybe he thinks you look pretty?" he replied before hastily adding, "Which you do… look pretty."

Kasia straightened her posture and pretended she didn't notice Gornioz. With the chill, she wore a loose, fur-trimmed coat over a layered navy dress that allowed its amber designs to catch the light. She walked a narrow line tonight, seeking to impress Sazilz's allies without enduring unneeded suspicion. There would be quite the number of young men seeking women to court as well, so she'd needed an attire that would allow her to dance, even if only to feign interest.

"I appreciate the compliment, Tazper," she replied, "but I fear I have missed the fashion of today's gala."

The other women waiting for the gates to open had long sleeves that tapered to a point at the tip of their middle fingers. Unlike the patterned embroidery upon Kasia's own sleeves, theirs were striped in one bright color and another deep one. A new style. She cursed herself for being so focused on the Crimsons that she'd missed something so simple.

She led Tazper and her great-uncle through the gathered crowd, swapping pleasantries until the gates opened just enough for a scion man of middling age to step out with a list in hand. Each guest approached and gave their name before being waved through. Faniz attempted to do the same for Kasia out of courtesy, but she stepped forward first. After all, she was the matriarch of House Niezik. She needed to assert herself.

"Lady Katarzyna," the scion said with a smirk. "It was a shock when we heard of your attendance. We are pleased you have decided to leave your father's ways in the past and join us."

Kasia gave an exaggerated nod. "Yes, well, there are some matters better left in hindsight, so that we may learn from them."

"Well said, my lady. Enjoy the celebration!"

She nearly rolled her eyes at that, but kept her poise. In remote villages like Tystok, celebrations were rare but raucous. Kasia's discovery of the amber that had saved her family from financial ruin had led to a hundred-hour long party.

But this wasn't a celebration. It was a display of House Oliezany's dominance over House iz Vamiustok's sand mines.

Rose gardens lay beyond the gate, the largest vines among them climbing the exterior walls of the mansion itself. They should not have been in bloom during the everdark. Light Reachers were plentiful here, though, and Fire Reachers ignited spires covered in oil that gave the gardens a gentle warmth.

"I hate to be jealous of House Oliezany," Kasia whispered to Tazper as Faniz found a group of old friends, "but those spires are impressive. How many Reachers do you think they employ if they can spare these men for mere show?"

But Tazper didn't get the chance to reply. Kasia stepped away at the sight of Sazilz speaking to Tzena Oliezany, one of Gornioz's nieces, near the mansion's double doors. The Uziokaki patriarch was no more vibrant than normal, and compared to Tzena's tight-waisted dress of scarlet and gold, he dressed like a nobody. His face was soon aflame. Kasia tried to overhear why, slipping into a nearby group.

"This is ridiculous!" Sazilz snapped. "I am as crucial a part of our goals as anyone else."

Tzena rested a hand on his chest, calming him for a moment. "Patience. Each piece must align before we act, or all our work will have been for nothing. Fail us, and you will be nothing."

She had a narrow, dainty face that gave her a mask of innocence. Despite her only being in her early thirties at most, though, she spoke with a firm confidence that overpowered the patriarch. Surely, this had to be connected to the Crimsons. Who else could Sazilz be so afraid of?

"You are making a mistake," he finally muttered before storming into the mansion.

Tzena sighed, adjusted her corset, and followed, leaving behind two scions. They stood close enough to nearby groups to not seem like guards. Upon closer inspection, however, each wore short, easily removable gloves over their talons and had single shot pistols holstered beneath their unbuttoned jackets. Kasia could not pursue Sazilz without being noticed by them.

A string quartet's music filled the gardens as she considered her approach. Men and women paired up quickly, beginning an upbeat dance across a pallet of stone that Kasia assumed had been crafted by an Earth Reacher for the occasion.

She soon realized she was standing alone.

Had no one thought to ask her? She entered the central section of the garden, where she stopped beneath a marble statue of a musketman with his gun shouldered. She needed to dance to keep up appearances, but more than that, her heart ached watching the other young scions. She'd turned down a dance with Hazat Tozki at the Uziokaki estate due to her focus on revenge. Now, lurking in the shadows had cost her a chance again. A part of her longed for the warmth she'd once felt in Aliax's arms.

"I'm not gone."

Kasia yelped, spinning with her taloned hand out. It was gloved, useless, but instinct had taken over. She lowered it at the sight of Aliax in an ill-fitted woolen suit. "You're dead!" she hissed. "Get out of my head."

He stepped closer and took her waist. Though she pressed her hand against his chest, she couldn't find the strength to shove him away. "You keep me alive," he whispered.

"No!"

She circled away, fists clenched as she drew side-eyes from nearby dancers. Odd shuffled footsteps followed from the direction of the gate. She spun toward them in an unladylike fashion as fearful instincts took hold.

"I told you—Oh…"

A young man with a gentle face leaned upon a cane as his odd metal leg whirred with each bend of his left knee. He had a Vockan's height along with curly red hair, shaved upon the sides of his head, but his complexion was deep Ezmani gray with freckles upon his cheeks. He wore a fine coat over a waistcoat with purple and golden stripes, matching the styling of the women's new dresses.

"I must admit my surprise to find Lady Katarzyna of House Niezik left stranded beneath a brutish statue when music abounds," the man said with a slight bow of his head. His voice was higher, but in a way that felt calming instead of most men's demand to be heard. "My apologies if I startled you."

Kasia curtsied. "No, the apologies are all mine. My nerves were on edge, as I fear my father's actions alienated many. My own have driven away what few allies remained."

"Indeed." He held his cane before him, forehead wrinkling. "It surprised many of us among the reformers to see you cross the aisle, but I am sure you have your reasons."

She mirrored the expression as she remembered the man pulling down Tiuz Hazeko in the Chamber, but his name escaped her. "I am sorry, sir. I recognize you from the Chamber, but I do not believe we have met."

"We need not continue a game of who apologizes more," he said with a chuckle. "I am Zinarus, heir of House iz Vamiustok. This gathering tonight is to 'celebrate' the sale of my family's sand mines, but in truth, I find it a mockery." He hobbled closer, lowering his voice and extending a hand to her. "Let us speak more as we dance. It would be a shame for me to endure such torture without spending it with the eloquent company."

Of course… This was the half-blooded son of Uzrin Ioniz and Sania iz Vamiustok. For such a birth to come out of wedlock had been a great stain upon House Ioniz's attempts to become a great house, even from a cousin of the house patriarch. Leonit had spoken highly of Sania's business instincts to survive despite House Pikezik's attempts to control the glass trade. It seemed that her son had failed to continue that legacy in her absence from Kalastok.

"Well met," she said with a smile, questioning whether this was for the best. She needed to follow Sazilz, and the Crimsons would not look highly upon her dancing with a Vockan—a bastard one at that. But he had approached her for a reason, and she knew she would regret missing her one chance to enjoy the evening.

Zinarus looked from his hand to her. "I will not be offended if you choose to pass on my offer."

"No." She took his hand. "That would be wonderful. Tazper!" She waved for her footman, and he rushed over. "If you could please hold Lord Zinarus's cane while we dance, I would appreciate it."

Zinarus lacked a footman of his own. That was odd considering his family's decent stature, and she wondered whether it pointed to financial struggles within his house.

His expression softened as he handed off the cane, then led Kasia arm-in-arm to the dance floor. To her surprise, few of the elder scions around its edge gave them any attention. Insignificance was an unusual feeling for her. She was the most powerful scion in Tystok, and for much of her time in Kalastok, her father's reputation had preceded her. Here, though, she was just another guest among the Commonwealth's elites.

She tried to enjoy that fact as they stopped in a clear space on the floor. Zinarus's walking was difficult, but her worries of it affecting the dance faded quickly. He moved lightly to keep weight off his bad leg, guiding Kasia in an unorthodox but rhythmic manner.

"If you don't mind my asking," she said when she finished a spin and ended in his arms, swaying to and fro, "why did you sell to House Oliezany if you consider it a mockery?"

His brow wrinkled, and he raised his chin. "There are times when one lacks the choice to do what they wish to."

"Mysterious," she quipped. "Come now, Zinarus. Such is the way of all scions. I promise that whatever you say is safe with me."

"Or will my words find the ever-listening ears of Lord Gornioz himself?"

"I am not his ally."

He huffed as they promenaded down an alley created by the other dancers. "Is that why you sit by his side in the Chamber and spend your days gossiping with his allies?"

"Have you been watching me?" She tensed, wondering who else had kept clandestine eyes upon her besides those she'd wanted to.

What did this man who spoke so perfectly want with her? And what was he hiding?

"There is much to see. I—"

He stumbled on his mechanical leg and fell into Kasia, forcing her to catch him. For a few long moments, they fell off the song's beat. His face was mere inches from hers. Oddly, he smelled of horses, but a faint minty cologne masked it.

"I… I'm sorry, Lady Katarzyna," he stammered, his eyes darting away for a moment, as if in search of someone. "That was—"

"Fine," she interrupted with a chuckle. "There are worse things than a fall, Zinarus. You move far better than this lot of lazy scions, and please, call me Kasia."

He pushed himself off her and took his position as lead again. His cheeks were as red as the spires' flames, but his charm returned as quickly as it had left. "Duly noted, Kasia. I am surprised as well about you. They say people from the southern forestlands prefer to hop around the dance floor rather than keep to the ground. Oh, what my father would say if he saw his bastard with a woman from Tystok."

"Ignore what he says. I know what it's like to be despised by a parent, wishing they were gone." She bit her lip and wished she hadn't said such a cruel thing to a near stranger.

"Yes, I understand." He spun her slowly, and when she finished, they danced closer than before. His palm was slick with sweat against hers despite his apparent composure. "My apologies for lacking honesty, but it is difficult to know who one can trust within this city. You… You are both like the others and not."

"Should I take that as a compliment?" she asked, brow raised.

He gave a wry smile. "What do you think?"

Kasia huffed and rolled her eyes. *The nerve of this man…*

"It is best not to resemble these elites too much," he continued. "I believe you when you say that you are not Gornioz's ally, but I fail to understand why you aid him."

She took a long breath, studying Zinarus and deciding that he surely could not be a Crimson. He had lost everything to House

Oliezany. Why would he take part in their schemes? But she could not trust him so easily. The heir of a mid-tier house like his would be desperate to earn status among the elites, which explained his posturing.

"Tell me why you actually sold your mines," she said, "and perhaps I will reveal my motivations."

A single bell rang out before he could reply. Pairs switched partners in time with the signal, and Kasia cursed under her breath before finding a pointy-chinned man whom she did not recognize. His breath reeked of onions, and he had the rhythm of a feral cat. Each step was a leap, each turn a yank that made her shoulders ache.

She stared at Zinarus over the man's shoulder. The half-Vockan's red hair was a halo in the flame light as he smiled at the young Pikezik woman in his arms. With golden braided hair and a striped dress of the new style, she embodied the perfection of Zinarus's words. She neither furrowed her brow nor allowed him to trip, and Kasia gritted her teeth at the twinge of jealousy in her chest. Zinarus *knew* something about House Oliezany. She needed to know what.

When the song ended, Gornioz no longer lurked on the balcony. Had he followed Tzena and Sazilz inside? The Reacher guards still blocked the entryway, preventing Kasia from following them to find out.

She hastened a bow to her onion-breathed partner before heading toward Zinarus to finish their conversation. If he refused to admit more, could he at least provide a distraction? But Zinarus extended his stay with the Pikezik woman, kissing her hand before giving a parting word. The woman gave an obviously feigned smile. Then she scowled at Kasia's approach and hurried off.

Zinarus adjusted his waistcoat, turning to Kasia. "My apologies for the abrupt end to our lovely dance. It was a shame that they ushered us into rotations when we were having such a wonderful time." He offered his arm. "Would you walk with me?"

She took it with another glance at the mansion doors. One of the guards had stepped away, and the other yawned as he stared into the crowd. This was her chance, so she rose up onto the tips of her toes to whisper, "I must ask a favor of you, Lord Zinarus."

"And what, may I ask, shall I receive in return?"

"Honesty," she said. "I will tell you what you wish to know, but first, I need to learn what House Oliezany is hiding. All I ask is that you distract the guard by the door so that I may slip inside without drawing attention."

Zinarus regarded the remaining guard. "He looks like a thirsty fellow. Let me bring him a drink."

"That…" She sighed, leading him back to Tazper. Not everyone was cut from deceit's cloth. "It does not matter how you do it. Just hurry."

Once Zinarus had recovered his cane, he headed toward a server. His gate was more affected by his leg than his dancing had been, but Kasia's offer apparently inspired some haste.

Tazper followed her gaze. "So not all scions here tonight are foes it seems."

She considered all Zinarus had said. "I have yet to decide where Lord Zinarus stands, but he seemed as interested in my connection to the Oliezanies as I was in his own dealings with them. If Gornioz manipulated him, it would be useful to have an enemy of our enemy." Zinarus approached the guard, so she nodded to Tazper. "Keep an eye on him while I am inside the mansion."

She didn't wait for a reply, splitting the crowd as Zinarus conversed with the guard. For a few long moments, she lost sight of them, but this was her only chance. She kept moving until she neared the door. The guard had taken the drink and was showing a casual interest in Zinarus's story about a recent joust. His back was to her.

*Now!*

Kasia slipped past the guard, holding her breath. A single glance from Zinarus would give her away, but to his credit, he kept his focus on the guard. Music and conversations hung over them. Kasia waited for a crescendo before pushing open the door and stepping inside the heart of House Oliezany.

# OF CRIMSON AND GLASS

*Do not trust those who wrap themselves in glass and gold. For when they plunge a dagger into your heart, you will bleed crimson just the same as them.* - Jack Himolox, lowborn writer

Kasia stepped from the party into a silent foyer lined with marble and gold-trimmed columns, suits of steel armor filling the gap between each. Such suits would be horribly impractical in modern warfare based on what her father had explained about riflemen, but there was a stern beauty to them. What must it have felt like to enter a battlefield invulnerable to the swords and spears of one's foes?

She wished for such protection as she climbed the grand staircase. House Oliezany had been one of her father's greatest rivals, and now she stood amid their palace of an estate, pretending to be an ally. They could strike her down at any moment. Even Death Reaching couldn't save her from a bullet.

She reached a massive rounded room at the top of the stairs, another flaming spire stretching up its center and into the floors above. Sitting spaces surrounded it along with mounted muskets, rifles, and pistols of Oliezany design along the walls. Plaques beneath each gun detailed battles won by the Commonwealth, but before Kasia had the chance to inspect any of them, a figure shifted from the shadows of a nearby hall.

"What a surprise this is," Tzena Oliezany said with a wry smile. She circled Kasia and tugged on her sleeve. "You appear at our gala wearing this antique fashion and then seek entrance into our mansion? I must wonder why that is."

Kasia straightened her posture. The first step to establishing herself among the Crimsons was pretending she belonged. "Lord Sazilz told me to meet him here. I wish to help his efforts and yours as well."

"Is that so? And what if we do not desire your help?"

"Then it is unfortunate that you decided I should be your enemy."

Tzena laughed. "Well, aren't you a bottle of purified spite? Worry not, Katarzyna. Sazilz informed us of your intentions, and he is waiting for us."

"Us?" Was this it? Were the other Crimsons waiting for her? "Did you not just say you have no desire to ally with me?"

Tzena waved a dismissive hand. "I do not dally in double negatives. Come, and let us show you what you desire."

*What I desire?*

The *knowingness* in Tzena's statement gave Kasia pause. She'd heard her father use such a tone a hundred times when outwitting fellow scions or businessmen. Without admitting a thing, it proclaimed that one knew something their opponent did not, and that the battle was already over.

Kasia stomached her panic, but couldn't manage a smile as Tzena led her down a side hall and through a series of narrow corridors trimmed in gold. Their footsteps fell from echoes against the marble floors to soft thuds along the halls' deep red runner.

"I must admit that I am in awe of your dress," she said in hopes that Tzena would love the chance to brag about her wealth as much as the other elite women. "Such fashion has yet to reach Tystok. Where would I find one like it?"

"Oh, dear Katarzyna," Tzena said, smirking. "Nearly all that I wear is custom made. My uncle has done splendidly to ensure his family is well taken care of. House Oliezany has remained as the most prestigious scion family throughout his many lifetimes. A house's head does not work alone, though—a fact you certainly know well."

"I do," Kasia replied. She found herself glancing into each doorway, but none were cracked open. Shadows hung behind each pillar lining the walls. They seemed to creep closer and closer upon her with each step, swallowing her as they descended into the mansion's belly. She tugged at her left glove to loosen it, just in case.

Tzena did not speak again until she stopped with her hand on a door made of black walnut wood. Golden overlapping circles radiated a brilliant glow upon its surface, resembling a flower with petals trimmed in gold. Aliax flickered in the corner of her vision. Eyes hollow, he shook his head slowly.

"Death won't fix the hole you've dug, Kasia."

His words rang cold against her neck, and twenty misty hands grabbed her arms, holding her back as she stared at that door. The dead peasants echoed his call until her head rang from the sound. The realm of Death was dangerous—she knew that—but so were the Crimsons who'd killed her father. Leonit would have prepared a dozen plans before daring to walk into House Oliezany. Kasia had only one. If that failed, Death would have to do, yet her hands trembled.

"Are you well?" Tzena asked as she glanced back from the symbol. "You suddenly resemble a corpse. It is as if all the gray has receded from your face."

Kasia gritted her teeth, but raised her chin. "I was merely curious about the meaning of that sigil. Its gold is enough to banish any semblance of gray."

"You will learn its meaning when the time is right," Tzena said. "As for your skin, the lighting in these halls could make the Crystal Mother herself appear as an ugly old hag. It is prudent, then, that we brought you for more important things." She pulled open the door and stepped aside. "Sazilz awaits us in here."

Casting a side-eye at Tzena, who averted her gaze, Kasia entered the rounded chamber of glass beyond. Most great houses' glass rooms were reserved for Inheritance Rituals alone. Mirrors rimmed the wall, brilliantly reflecting Reacher light from a hovering ball at the peak of the domed ceiling. The floor, too, was pure glass with rose-like patterns sloping downward to a small Spirit Crystal pit at the room's center. That hole exuded a dark aura, sucking away the light into nothingness for a stride around it.

Sazilz knelt before the pit: bound, naked, and bleeding.

"What is this?" Kasia blurted out, pulling at her glove.

Two men approached from the far side of the room. One's taloned hand glowed as he directed the ball of light above. The other wielded wisps of black, his eyes and nose covered by a magic veil. Light and Dark Reachers. Both wore red robes with hoods draped over their heads.

A chilled force pressed against Kasia's temple, and the *click* of a pistol's hammer followed. "Do not remove your glove just yet, Reacher of Death," Tzena whispered, her breath sweet but her golden eyes as sharp as daggers. "You came to Lord Sazilz for answers, so answers you shall have."

Sazilz cried out, struggling against his binds to no avail. "Deceivers! Manipulators! We had a deal!"

The Dark Reacher cracked a whip, snapping it across Sazilz's back and sending the patriarch onto the ground, writhing. Rumors claimed such brutality was common among Dark Reachers, but Kasia had believed them to be nothing more than stories from fearful lowborn. Staring at this man, though, her mind changed. His lips curled into a grin as he grabbed Sazilz by the hair and pulled him back to his knees.

"She knows that you did," the Dark Reacher said with a cocky, high-brow voice that Kasia swore was familiar. "All those years ago, you betrayed Leonit, and now the Amber Dame has come to deliver justice. Who, then, is the deceiver?"

"Look what I accomplished!" Sazilz screamed. "We usurped the false king because I acted when you wished to remain in the shadows. Yaakiin was useless! You claimed I was right, that you had forgiven my haste!"

The Dark Reacher looked to Kasia, then waved for Tzena to lower the gun. "Is he not pitiful? A magnate groveling like a peasant before his master. We know you came to Kalastok for him after butchering Parqiz like the swine he was. This is our offering to you, Katarzyna of House Niezik, and I hope you understand that we do not give them often."

"Who are you?" Kasia asked, fighting the urge to remove her glove and kill Sazilz immediately. There was more to this. The Crimsons knew her intentions, and if they were giving up a great house patriarch, they had bigger plans of their own. Acting too quickly would only give them blackmail.

Tzena stepped to the Light Reacher's side. "Why ask what you already know? Say it, and perhaps we will tell you more."

"You are the Crimson Court."

"And you tracked us when no other has managed to do so," the Dark Reacher replied. "I must admit that I am impressed. Though we obviously knew what you intended to do, it is convenient that your skills and our needs are in alignment."

Kasia slipped her glove free and Reached. Purple wisps met her fingers as she sneered at the trio. She could end the Crimsons here and now, taking her revenge and ending their plot… unless there were others.

Aliax rounded the pit with his gaze fixed upon her. He said nothing, but the void in her chest was deeper than any words. She'd sworn after his death that she would never Death Reach again. That promise had failed against her quest for vengeance, but the one time she'd lost control of Death's power, it ruined what little life she had left. Her husk of a heart ached watching him. Real or Realm Tainted madness, it didn't matter. Aliax would never leave her, and no matter how hard she pushed, part of her resisted the full extent of her power.

"Do not dare wield Death against us," the Light Reacher barked. Tzena raised her pistol again, and though Kasia's Reaching was powerful, it wouldn't stop a bullet to her brain.

"This is not a gift," Kasia said to the Dark Reacher. "It's a trade."

"Precisely," he replied.

She looked from him to Sazilz, rage, confusion, and guilt swirling inside her like a tempest ready to burst as her Reach's power slowly dissipated. Years of hatred had led to this moment. Was revenge worth striking a deal?

"Who ordered my father's death?" she demanded.

"Sazilz alone," the Dark Reacher said.

Sazilz spat. "Lies! The coup was planned, but they were too slow. I only acted on what they had already decided upon."

"Silence!" Another crack of the Dark Reacher's whip sent Sazilz dropping to the edge of the pit, his blood dripping into it. "Our intention was to unseat Yaakiin and replace him with someone more… persuadable… but Leonit was not a target. Ezman's strength lies in the great houses, and destroying House Niezik threatened the fragile stability of our nation when our neighbors look greedily upon us."

Tzena took a sharp breath. "We knew when we invited you here that you could choose to kill us all. After all, there is a reason most Death Reachers are feared across our realm."

"Then why invite me?" Kasia asked, her power slipping from her hands. An ethereal emptiness came with it, as if Death were disappointed she'd not killed another.

"Because you desire more than revenge," Tzena replied. "Your actions thus far have proven that you care for the people of this city, and that you aspire to return your house to its rightful place. Only we can grant you both."

"How?"

The Dark Reacher scoffed. "Take the offer. If you do not, we will be forced to declare you our enemy. We freed you from Jazuk's prison, and we can send you back there just as easily. All will be revealed once you choose to join our cause, but we cannot trust you until you prove your loyalty." He grabbed Sazilz by his hair and threw him to Kasia's feet. "Rid Sazilz of his life forever. NOW!"

Kasia Reached.

Aliax's scowl met her, but she stepped forward with fury surging through her. Grabbing hold of Sazilz's neck with her right hand, she squeezed. "You ruined my childhood, my life! Every night for a decade, I have lain awake with my father's final cry echoing in my mind. My mother blames me. My brother broke without his father. And I was forced to become a matriarch before I was ready. All because *you* thought you deserved power!"

"I..." Sazilz squeaked. "I... am... sorry..."

"I am not."

She slashed her talon down his cheek, releasing Death's power into his veins. The gruesome process that followed had become all too familiar to her. But she would not watch it again, not with Aliax staring her down.

With a shout that echoed through the glass chamber, she kicked Sazilz in the chest and sent him tumbling into the pit. His screams trailed away as the maw devoured him whole.

Silence followed.

Tzena stepped to Kasia's side with her hands held behind her back. "You have done well to accept."

Kasia gave her no heed, staring into the darkness, arms flexed at her side and her breaths ragged. She no longer stood tall. Instead, her back curled like a wolf with the taste of blood coating its tongue. A thrill rushed through her veins, and though a pang of guilt struck her chest at the sight of Aliax's disdain, she couldn't help but want more.

"Fascinating..." Tzena mused, handing the pistol to the Light Reacher before circling behind Kasia. "Death Reachers are all too rare, so you will be of great use. For now, however, you must return to the gala and ensure you do not become a suspect when Sazilz's absence is discovered. His daughter, Qaraza, will not cause us harm as the new Uziokaki magnate. However, King Jazuk and the Crystal Brigade may ask questions."

Kasia clenched her fists and turned to meet Tzena. Did they not control the Crystal Brigade? Curiosity pressed her, but she wrestled back at least that emotion, not wishing to give away what she did and did not know. "Is Qaraza one of us too?"

"You are not a member of the Crimson Court yet, dear

Katarzyna." Tzena took her hands, forcing them to open. "Have patience. Though you may have accepted our gift, there will soon be a time for you to give us what we need in exchange. Only then may you be one of us."

Kasia glared at her. Threads of her last Reach remained, enough to kill Tzena with this touch, but she resisted the urge and stepped away. The tension in her chest refused to abate. For so long, she had poured her rage into her quest for vengeance, and now that she had it, it was as if the stone beneath her feet had turned to sand. Revenge had come. Yet she'd merely caught a wolf who had been cornered by a dragon.

"I will await your missive with great anticipation, then," she said as her two rapid Reaches took their toll. The stomaching-curling sensation of Realm Taint crept over her. Purple vapors surrounded the Crimsons, and Sazilz's face joined the others in the chorus of the dead. "Sazilz was a fool to interfere with my life. I would caution you against doing the same."

Then she pushed past Tzena and returned to the halls beyond, her strides swift and her jaw clenched.

*No*, she decided, *this is not finished.*

She had come too far to cease. There was more happening here than her own revenge, and she intended to stop it before the Crimsons finished their plans. To do that, she needed to go deeper. Becoming their ally would not be enough. They would not trust her until she completed their pact.

She would become a Crimson. Then she'd burn them until their spirits faded to ash.

# THE MOCKED, THE FORGOTTEN, AND THE SCORNED

*"There is an oft quoted line that tells us to keep our friends close and our enemies closer. What that advice fails to understand, however, is that enemies are likely to carry a dagger when near their foes. I find a rifleman's bullet from great distance to be a far more effective tool than proximity to deal with such stubborn opponents."* – Harkiz Janiak, Keloshan lieutenant

Zinarus's heart beat faster than it ever had as the string quartet's song flowed through the gardens. His rivals danced around him with their faces in the shadows of the Reacher light. For the first time in many seasons, though, he did not bother himself with their thoughts. He was focused entirely on distracting the Oliezany guard.

"A jouster, you see," Zinarus said, fighting his urge to glance at Kasia as she neared the door, "is both a champion of competition and honor. He must thrust—" He mimicked a jouster lowering his lance and striking. "—with perfect timing or be unseated when his opponent strikes. Then, victorious or defeated, he must act with chivalry to neither mock nor scorn said opponent."

The guard stared at the dance floor and took a long drink from his glass. Of course House Oliezany could afford to waste glass on such frivolities, and the sight made Zinarus miss his family's sand mines all the more. They had fed the creation of glass for scions and lowborn alike. Now, the Oliezanies would no doubt direct it merely toward the greatest profit.

Zinarus caught Kasia opening the door out of the corner of his eye, so he continued in his lecture about jousting. It was quite an enjoyable topic. Well, it was to *him* at least. The guard looked ready to fall asleep, but Zinarus's gifted drink apparently had earned him a few moments of attention. So far, the ruse had yet to draw any suspicions.

Why was he taking the risk?

That question hung over him as the music drifted away and people gathered around the musicians' stage. Lady Katarzyna—Kasia, as she'd told him to say—had hinted at a shared interest in House Oliezany's dealings, but she had run off too quickly for him to ask more. Like all of Kalastok, Zinarus had mused about the Amber Dame in the aftermath of the Ephemeral Slaughter. What did Leonit's daughter want in the capital after so long, and why had she been so adamant about sneaking into the Oliezany mansion?

Whatever Kasia's reasons, she was an alluring figure who could know more about the red-robed Dark Reacher. He had killed Regizald and destroyed the little prestige Zinarus had built for House iz Vamiustok. Any help to find the truth was welcomed.

Less welcomed was the presence of Ikatia Oliezany, who approached Zinarus with an exuberant smile. She was stout, elderly woman, yet did not show her age due to the aid of her house's many Body Reachers. Born a Pikezik, her marriage to Gornioz had forged an alliance between the two great houses based in Kalastok itself. Her husband was on his eighth life, so manipulating Zinarus and his fledgling house could not have been a strenuous plot for such an experienced and wealthy couple.

The guard gave a relieved sigh as Zinarus bowed to Ikatia. "My lady, thank you for having me at your estate this evening. It was an *honor* to do business with such an esteemed house as yours."

Every word was like a knife to his throat, but sparring with such a powerful scion on her own grounds would be foolhardy. He had scrounged every ounce of respect he could for his house since his arrival in the capital years before. Though this sale was a setback, he would earn back his prestige while working to uncover the identity of the Dark Reacher. That started with keeping his wits around his foes.

"Join us for a presentation of the sale," Ikatia replied, shadows lurking in the crooks of her eyes. "It is a shame Lady Sania could not attend. She was always quite social before becoming a recluse back in your village… What was it called again?"

Zinarus winced at her jab, but held his feigned smile. His mother had not left their estate since his birth, either out of fear of his absent father, Uzrin Ioniz, or shame at birthing a bastard. Zinarus promised himself he would make her proud again.

"Vamiustok, like my house name," he replied. "My mother has entrusted me with handling our business in Kalastok, but perhaps you should visit your new mines soon. The views of the Vockan Mountains are splendid from the riverfront."

Ikatia took his arm and led him toward Gornioz on the stage. No deference was ever given to Zinarus, but before Ikatia, the crowd moved like clouds over the western Ezmani plains. Though Kasia would be upset at him leaving his post, he had no choice but to follow. This was power. Quiet, unspoken, but clear for all to see.

That power suffocated Zinarus as he climbed the steps with some effort. Gornioz extended a hand, but in it, Zinarus saw a master's whip. He was nothing but a conquered trophy for House Oliezany to display. His only defiance was a firm grip on his cane, finishing the climb without Gornioz's help.

"I cannot express how great a pleasure it is to have you all here this evening," Gornioz said to the crowd, his suit's lines like a precisely cut shard of glass. "And how honored we are to be completing this deal with Houze iz Vamiustok."

Once again, Gornioz offered his hand to Zinarus, this time to shake. Zinarus took it and squeezed with all the anger locked in his heart.

*Did you kill him?* he so badly wished to ask. *Did you kill Regizald and steal everything from my family?*

But instead, he smiled and gave a half-hearted thanks that rang deaf to his ears. Regizald's corpse flashed before him each time he blinked. His best friend, his helper who'd died in his service—Zinarus would bring him justice. That was the least Regizald deserved, but it was all Zinarus could give him now.

Motion near the mansion door drew his attention from Gornioz. With the crowd and guards alike focused on the stage, Kasia stormed from the mansion. Her dress of deep blues and oranges had twirled during their dance with each shift of her hips, but now, it was a roaring fire, flames sparking at her heels. His heart sunk beneath her glare. She had trusted him to distract the guard until she left, only to find him shaking the hand of the magnate she was suspicious of.

Applause answered Gornioz's final statement, and Zinarus held his smile a moment longer before the patriarch patted him on the shoulder.

"I suggest you learn to negotiate if you intend to remain in Kalastok, dear boy," Gornioz whispered. "It would be a shame for you to be robbed blindly at every turn."

Zinarus grimaced, then retreated before he said something he'd regret. Kasia had pushed through the crowd to her footman, Tazper, and hastened toward the gate. He needed to catch her before she departed.

Scions from houses both great and minor shook his hand as he headed toward the musketman statue, but he offered them more than a quick nod. Despite the rudeness of his reply, he had played their game for long enough this night. Sneers and jokes hid beneath their noble masks. There was nothing more for him at this celebration—except for the woman fleeing it.

"Lady Katarzyna!" he exclaimed as the music began again.

But she charged between the flaming spires without even a glance back at him. Tazper followed, then stopped, taking hold of Zinarus's arm.

"If you mean well with her, my lord," Tazper said, "then send a calling card. Now is not the best of times."

So Zinarus stepped back, fingers tracing his cane's handle as Kasia left the firelight of the Oliezany estate. Mystery lingered in her wake. The Amber Dame had infiltrated House Oliezany, and he needed to know why.

He looked to his side, ready to speak his plan to Regizald. Emptiness met him instead, and tapped his foot until his mechanical knee complained. Regizald was gone. The Commonwealth stood at the brink of war. And an unstoppable disease ripped its way through lowborn and scions alike.

He could do nothing against the tide of darkness, not alone.

"What secrets do you hold, Lady Kasia?" he breathed into the shadows at the estate's end. "And what justice can you bring to this cold world?"

# LAZIK STREET TAVERN

*"Oh, to drink one's sorrows*
*'tis a thing for all.*
*They taste of piss*
*and vomit and spit*
*But to drink them away*
*is to forget for today*
*Because today's all you've got*
*when 'morrows a few everdark hours away"* – *To Drink One's Sorrows*, an Ogrenian song

"I'll meet that bet!"

Nex grinned as they pushed a few precious betting chips into the center of the wooden table. Of course, their hand wasn't enough to beat a cat at cards, but Possibility flowed at their fingertips. An entire realm of chances. Why couldn't that sailor of steel card be a Fire Reacher, or the peasant of grain be a rifleman of crystal? To Nex, they were, and that made their hand nearly unbeatable.

Nearly.

But the idiots in the Lazik Street Tavern were so drunk they didn't know their peasants from their patriarchs. There was no way any of them had collected a full hand of Reachers. They probably couldn't even count that high… not that Nex was all that familiar with the concept of mathematics.

Luckily, Nex *was* incredibly familiar with cards and how to subtly manipulate the odds. They needed to be if they were going to get enough money to pay for Vinnia's medication against the Spirit Plague. No Reacher could fix it, apparently, but everyone said the alchemist, Paras ik Lierasa, would sell anyone the cure at the right price.

The woman across from Nex gave a gentle smile. She wore a collarless wool dress of brown, making her blue-gray eyes seem brighter than they should've been in the dim, smoke-filled tavern. With braids holding her ashen hair in an updo, she would've looked the part of a scion if she hadn't missed a few strands that touched her cheeks. A handmaiden would never let that happen, right?

Nex had heard countless stories of rich women beating their servants bloody. Didn't matter if the servants were scion or lowborn. Just mattered that scion women were bitches who'd rather strike someone than realize nobody cared about perfection.

Who liked a perfect person anyway? No, flaws were interesting—fun. Like the girl Nex pretended to be now, with their black hair hanging freely to their shoulders over a loose-fitting shirt and trousers. They put themselves in the woven shoes of a girl who'd grown up by the sea, longing to sail one day and join a *mighty* privateer on his escap… escapodes… trips through the Vitrian Sea.

Innocent. Now *that* people could like. It made every drunkard think they could beat Nex, but they all learned in the end. Except for that stubborn woman.

"You really think that's a good idea?" the woman asked, rubbing her left forearm as she'd done every time she had a good hand. Her sleeve was too short, and it exposed the end of a nasty burn scar just above her wrist.

*Definitely not a scion.*

"I'm not sure," Nex replied with a slightly higher voice than their own. "A sailor named Orias told me this would work."

The woman raised her brow. "And did Orias win often?"

"Oh..." Nex slumped their shoulders in feigned sorrow. "He lost his ship when he bet it on a hand of straight grain."

"For your sake, I hope you have a better hand than that."

They did, in fact, but the way the woman spoke gave Nex doubt. Either she was one of the best bluffers they'd faced, or that mug wasn't full of real beer. Nex eyed the bartender. A scruffy, stout scion from some insignificant house, he looked like one to take a bribe. Nex would know. In their rotations throughout Kalastok's many gambling halls, they had slipped their fair share of keni to bartenders and dealers alike to help their odds when a single Reach wasn't enough.

Nex tapped the table as the dealer laid out the final card. They'd Reached to change it to the exact one they needed to complete their crystal straight—scored higher than one of grain. Nex threw in half their remaining chips. Win this, and they could have enough for Vinnia.

"How risky ya feeling?" they asked the woman.

The woman rubbed her arm again, then set down her cards. "I'll match that." She slid her chips into the center before revealing a complete set of Reachers.

A perfect hand.

Nex cursed and threw down their hand. "You cheated!"

"I am afraid not," the woman replied, taking the chips. "You, on the other hand, altered your cards with what I assume was Possibility Reaching, as I find it unlikely you hid that many cards up those flimsy sleeves."

Nex flared their nostrils and stood to leave, but the woman's tone shifted.

"Wait." The woman pulled a pair of cards from up her own sleeve. "You caught me playing the same game as you were. My father taught me how to alter the odds and how to catch an opponent doing the same. Let us scratch that round and play another, hands on top of the table and sleeves rolled up to our elbows."

The other drunk men at the table grunted and stumbled away with the few chips they'd held before the last round. But the dealer showed no care that two of his players had admitted to cheating. This wasn't Haxan's Hall. Lazik Street was in the old Drifters' Quarter, and its rule was to cheat at your own risk, because most patrons here carried a pistol.

Nex studied the cheater. They'd obviously been wrong about her not being a scion. No lowborn spoke like that, and they hadn't seen someone stick cards up their sleeve that well since little Boxa thought she could swindle a scion who'd come to the west side to take some workers' keni. Boxa would've gotten away with it if the scion hadn't been a Truth Reacher. She would've still been alive too.

This woman so far hadn't *seemed* to Reach against Nex, but what was she doing here? It didn't matter. Nex needed to get away before she took what little gains they'd made. Vinnia needed them back home.

But curiosity pulled Nex back to the table.

"Another hand couldn't hurt," they said in the most innocent voice they could muster. "Orias always said to never give up."

The cheater eyed Nex's hands, covered in tattered woolen gloves that left enough of their ring exposed to Reach. "Did Orias say you should Reach with illegal crystal too?" She took her cards before biting her lip. "Who are you?"

"I could ask the same of you, my lady," Nex replied. They placed the buy-in bet and took their cards. It was the first hand in years that they'd taken without the intention to Possibility Reach, and their throat felt tight as they eyed the cards.

Complete and utter shit.

"The more I play tonight," they said, "the more I'm beginning to think Orias was a fool. Fold."

The woman pulled in the chips from the initial bet, then pulled a wad of keni from her handbag and handed it to the dealer. "Go anywhere else, please, and encourage those men over there to escalate their conversation, will you?"

With wide eyes, the dealer took the money, leaving the deck behind. The woman took it and shifted across the table until she sat beside Nex. "You seem like one to see through a lie, so I will tell you the truth. I am Katarzyna, matriarch of House Niezik, but you may call me Kasia."

"What are you doing in a dump of a bar like this?" Nex replied in their fake voice for now. They'd heard of Death's Daughter, and despite her reputation of *interesting* trouble, every scion was dirty.

"Usually, it is kind to reciprocate a gesture of goodwill," Kasia said as she shuffled the cards. "After all, I could simply report you to the authorities for carrying that crystal."

"Isn't your own talon illegal?" Nex quipped. "Death Reacher."

"I Reached to stop the awakened from killing innocents, both scions and lowborn alike." Kasia dealt the cards and gestured for Nex to place the buy-in chips as she did the same. "In truth, you have nothing to fear from me, but you must forgive my curiosity. You are the first person I've met who wields a talon that is not their own."

Nex removed their left glove. "It's a ring, not a talon. Can't find actual talons on the black market."

The men gathered around the bar roared at something the bartender said. Two of them pushed each other as the other cheered, but Kasia's gaze remained fixed on Nex. "Unsurprising, given how hard it is to get crystal that is not bound to a person already. I won't inquire as to how you got that ring. Just give me something to call you by. Though a real name is preferable, we both know I have no way of confirming if you're telling the truth."

The game continued as Nex considered Kasia's question. She couldn't have been more than five or six years older than Nex, but her presence was that of a woman twice her age. Why did she want anything to do with them? Nex had no answers, yet they found themself trusting her. Most scions regarded Nex with disdain. This matriarch of a fallen great house, though, looked at them as if they were a peer.

"Nex," they finally said.

Kasia flipped over her cards, only to furrow her brow when she realized Nex had beaten her. "Perhaps I should keep to my usual methods instead of relying upon the Crystal Mother's luck." She glanced at Nex with a glint of familiarity in her eye. "Is the name Radais familiar to you?"

Nex shifted in their chair. If this was about the letter they'd stolen from the Glassblade, they needed to be ready to run at a moment's notice. Especially against a Death Reacher.

"I see he is," Kasia said. "Worry not. Radais told me you directed him to an Ogrenian man who I assume was a spy, but a Keloshan one killed your friend when she caught wind of the letter you stole. That tells me that both of those empires are as curious about the Spirit Plague and the sudden surge of awakened as we are."

"Yeah, so?" Nex let their shoulders sag as they slipped into their sharper, more cutting voice. "Tiak-Kath paid for information. I thought Radais could tell him about the red-robed man he found in the Wastes. He'd needed a Reacher for his dad, but I didn't think it'd get Tiak-Kath killed!"

Kasia laid a hand on their shoulder. "I am sorry for your loss. Know that I managed to hire a Reacher for Radais regardless."

"Couldn't save Tiak-Kath..."

"No, you're right. By sending Radais to him, though, you gave me enough information to search the city for you."

Nex frowned, pushing back from Kasia's hand with their arms crossed. "Why? There's plenty of other Ogrenian lowborn."

Kasia smirked. "How many of them have enough scion blood to Reach or the wits to get a crystal ring in the first place? I know many of Kalastok's elite, but the lowborn here are unfamiliar to me. Based on Radais's description and the performance I saw tonight, you seem like just the informant I need in the streets."

"Wait, you want to *hire* me?"

"You are opposed?"

"No... I just... Scions don't just come into bars and hire people who cheat at cards."

"Why not?" Kasia swept the chips across the table to Nex. "Consider this a small front for your future efforts. I need allies to help me confront the Crimson Court—the scions in red robes like the one Radais found. They were involved in the Ephemeral Slaughter somehow, and I have suspicions that what they were doing in the Spirit Wastes is connected to the Spirit Plague too."

Nex snatched her scarred arm. "You can stop the Spirit Plague?"

Kasia slipped her arm from Nex's grasp, holding it close to her chest. She resembled an injured pup, and her gaze was distant until Nex spoke again.

"Can you fix the Spirit Plague?" they repeated.

"I don't know," Kasia replied, barely louder than a whisper. "But I intend to find out."

The hope that had risen in Nex's chest faded. Money to pay Paras ik Lierasa for his supposed cure could help Vinnia, but so many had died anyway. If these Crimsons were related to it, what reason did they have not to trust Kasia?

They took the chips.

"I looked for them after Tiak-Kath died, those red-robed scions," they said. "It was hard. Palace guards wear red. You rich folk wear it too. But I overhead a couple scions in Haxan's Hall whispering about some kind of Crimson Court, so I pretended to be interested in them. Get scions drunk, bat your eyes, and just let the assholes talk. They don't look over their shoulder when I tail 'em either."

Slack jawed, Kasia sat back. "You *followed* them?"

"So you don't want to know who they are?"

"Of course I want to know!"

Nex grinned. "Come with me."

They quickly exchanged their chips for keni, then led Kasia out into the dark streets of Kalastok. There were few streetlamps in the Drifters' Quarter, far from the city center, and Nex checked their peripherals out of habit.

A Death Reacher like Kasia could handle herself with ease. Nex's Possibility Reaching was used up unless they wanted Realm Taint, so they had to be more careful. Darkness often worked to their advantage. They'd heard enough stories of girls disappearing from both sides of the river to know that advantage could flip as quick as a coin.

The dim streets gave way to pitch black alleys. Even in the east side of Kalastok, bandits, homeless lowborn, and hungry koilee lurked in many of them. But Nex knew this path well. Most gangs marked their territory with subtle symbols any lowborn could recognize. A scion would see those marks as nothing more than a few leftover bricks or ash from a nearby fire. The system made sure the lowborn without any keni stayed out of the gangs' alleys while the drunk scions stumbled right into their traps.

Nex reached a metal ladder attached to the side of a tall brick building just south of the clocktower. They motioned for Kasia to climb after them, half-expecting the scion woman to question why they were taking such a winding route, but she voiced no complaints. Neither of them said a word until they reached the building's roof four stories up.

"Are you going to tell me their names now?" Kasia huffed with her hands on her knees. They hadn't been moving *that* quickly, had they?

"They gave me fake ones," Nex replied, "but I know where they live."

Kasia raised her brow. "Yet you told me that their tongues loosened when they drank."

"They did. Said something about needing 'one more petal' and that the 'King in the Dark knows where to find it.' "

"You brought me all the way up here for that?"

Nex shook their head. "I know where they live, but not their names. Show me that scar on your arm, and maybe I'll show you."

"Attentive. I'm impressed." Kasia held her scarred arm across her body. "Why do you want to see it?"

"Because obviously it's important. Don't see many scions around here with scars, so there's gotta be a good story there."

Taking a sharp breath, Kasia pulled up her sleeve to reveal a burn far worse than Nex had expected. Strips of raised reddened skin crisscrossed over her entire forearm. It looked barely human, and Kasia looked away as Nex examined it with curiosity. Veterans around the west side had many scars. None who'd survived the Commonwealth's wars had anything like this.

"Does it hurt?" Nex asked.

Kasia hastily rolled her sleeve back down. "It itches often. I get these…" Her voice trailed off, and she looked away again. "Is there anything else you wanted to know?

"You didn't fight in a war, right? You look young."

Kasia huffed. "No, I am only twenty-four. I was a child when the last war against the empires ended. This… This I received not from an enemy's fury, but my brother's. Gregorzon is a Fire Reacher, and he felt it just to release flames upon me not long after he received his talon."

"Why?" Nex asked, head cocked.

"I have answered your question. Do you intend to show me where the Crimsons live or not?"

The sudden shift in tone caught Nex off guard. Kasia had been sharp at times earlier, but as they'd spoken, she'd been kinder than they'd expected. That faded as her voice turned to ice.

Nex shied away and pointed north-west, toward the Market District's main road. "One of them lives in that weird round house. Balding idiot with a pointy little face."

"Laniaz Rakazimko?" Kasia said. "I do not know him well, but I danced with his father, Gragoz, during the Festival of the Ephemeral Storm. He was a wholly distasteful individual."

"You really do talk like a scion."

Kasia gave them a side-eye. "Did I not have you fooled for a time? Where does the other live?"

Nex pointed toward the southwest, toward the Oliezany Bridge over the Kala. "He's an old guy with spikey-kinda gray hair—but it's darker than yours—and a nose that's kinda tilted to the right. Muttered about the war minister or something and went to that three-story building over there."

"I don't recognize that one, and there could be a hundred scions who fit that description." She sighed. "Kelosh's mobilization has everyone talking about war."

*Easy to, when you don't have to worry about the Spirit Plague.*

Nex stepped to the edge of the building and looked down. It was a long way to the alley below, but they liked the rush of standing one step from death. "That's all I know. Not sure why you want to pay me for more."

Kasia joined them, arms crossed, as she stared over the river. "Based on what you've said so far, I assume you can get past the quarantine of the west side."

"How else you think I got here?"

"Again, I won't ask how you do so, but I want you to test something for me." She pulled an orange glass-like piece from her pocket and held it out for Nex. "During the Ephemeral Slaughter, I managed to capture an awakened inside amber. Find someone infected with the Spirit Plague and see if the amber can somehow help them. This Paras ik Lierasa that everyone is talking about might know more."

Nex took the amber piece, hating its hope that pushed away the brutal chill. "How do I tell you what I find?"

"Talk to Maakiin at his brewery over on Likot Street. It's one of my house's businesses, and he's a Reshkan man, an old friend of my father's." Kasia pulled out two of the cards she'd used to cheat before: a Dark and a Light Reacher. "Tell him to place the Light Reacher in the corner of his window if you've found something. Dark means you're in trouble. We can rendezvous in his basement once I see the message."

"Good." Nex pointed to the Spirit Reacher towers. "There's too many eyes here, but basements work."

"Then we have a deal."

Nex turned to leave, but Kasia caught their arm. Her grip was firm, but just light enough not to hurt. "It would be for the best if you tell no one about this. All you'd be doing is putting your loved ones at risk by informing them of our partnership."

With a huff, Nex pulled themselves free. "I've been keeping secrets my whole life, scion. I'll help you to stop this disease and whoever these Crimson are, but we are *not* partners."

Kasia winked. "Of course not."

Nex descended the ladder and hurried toward the west side. Some part of them wished to look over their shoulder to check if Kasia was watching, but it didn't matter. They had a way to potentially save Vinnia from the Spirit Plague. And they wouldn't fail.

# THE WINTERBLOWN FORTRESS

*"Some say that during the everdark snowfalls of Vocka, Palmia Fortress pulses with a warm glow. I call it hope."* – Lantus ik Akarifan, former supreme defender of the Glassblade Order

The cold breeze blew Radais's long hair as he marched through the village of Palmia, heading back toward the fortress. His nose was numb, and his Glassblade armor turned a matted white. Still, he trudged on through the knee-deep snow.

No one met him along the way. Not even Gargas sat on his stool before the forge. On many days, Radais would've preferred solitude to the old man's grumbling. Today, though, he longed for the aimless chatter to distract him when he had only memories of his father to keep him company. They made the chill feel all the more brutal.

He cursed the hundred-hour long blizzard that plagued Palmia. Miv had given him full control of the team heading into the Spirit Wastes in pursuit of the Crimsons, but instead of beginning the journey, they had done nothing but shovel snow and wait out the storm. The snow fell so heavily at times that neither torches nor uncovered lanterns remained lit outside. So they'd worked in the everdark, glancing over their shoulders in anticipation of another awakened strike.

Out of sheer blind hope, Radais had headed up the western trail to see if the blizzards spared the way toward the Wastes. They had not. Now, all he had were soaked trousers and a persistent runny nose.

His labored breaths fogged the air by the time he stopped outside the fortress gates and waved to the guards. Spirits, he probably looked more like an awakened than a Glassblade. They opened the gates for him regardless, and he lumbered into the interior of Palmia Fortress, wishing for a Fire Reacher to burn away the frost covering him.

A dry and well-dressed Lazan awaited him instead, a smirk tugging at his lips. "How goes your mission to get us the hell out of here?"

"How do you think?" Radais replied with a gesture at his snow-covered armor.

"My former lovers would say I don't."

Radais chuckled. "They might be right. What's the time? I could use some food, but I lost track of how long I was gone."

Lazan glanced at his watch. Of Oliezany make, it had a leather strap and a face of cracked glass, unlike the uncovered Ezmani ones. "Seventeen, nearly supper time. Are you Glassblades so traditional that you lack even watches?"

"We have the belltower, but I couldn't tell whether the last ring was sixteen or seventeen." He patted Lazan's shoulder and led him toward the mess. "You scions have more keni than us. The Chamber has forgotten the work we do for the people of the Commonwealth and all of Brakesh, so we cannot afford luxuries like those."

"Of course. You are simply too busy spending all your funds on swords and armor crafted from the *most in-demand* material known to mankind."

They passed a gaggle of teenage initiates who were whispering about something with training swords in-hand. It ceased the moment the pair stepped into earshot, and the initiates held their fists to their chests, heads bowed to Radais. A girl stepped forward from among them—the initiate who'd told them where to find Miv days before.

Tall, even by Vockan standards, the girl looked no older than sixteen, with round cheeks and the glass breastplate initiates received upon their induction into the Order. Eventually, she would earn a helmet, pauldrons, greaves, and bracers. Her friends, though, wore only their wool training tunics.

"Master Radais," she said, raising her head to meet his gaze. "Supreme Defender Miv has informed me that Warrior Tonius has injured himself in training, so she wishes for me to replace him as part of your expedition."

A few of the girls behind the initiate giggled, but a glare from Radais silenced them. Why was Miv assigning this girl to such a dangerous trek? Including himself and Lazan, they had ten members of the band. Replacing a warrior with an initiate would mean distractions when a momentary lack of focus could mean their deaths.

"What is your name?" Radais asked her. "And what does the supreme defender see in you that warrants you joining us?"

The girl took a shaky breath, locking her hands behind her back as she straightened her posture. Spirits, she looked just like Miv had…

"I am Wanusa ik Iliafa, and I have slain nine awakened, mostly during the Ephemeral Slaughter. The supreme defender believes I should join you to prove I deserve to be a warrior."

She was from Iliafa? *Shit.*

Radais scratched his beard, fearing this was Miv sending him a warning after he'd left that very village to chase the awakened into the Wastes in the first place. He could deny Miv's request and earn her ire, hurting his chances of rekindling their relationship, or he could swallow his pride and take Wanusa. Neither was a good option.

"Wanusa, yes," he said. "I knew your parents when I was assigned to help your village and those nearby. They spoke highly of you."

Wanusa averted her gaze. "Thank you, Master Radais." More giggles followed from among the girls.

"Your friends seem amused," Radais said. "Tell me, what has them laughing at you for attempting to join a deadly mission?"

Wanusa winced, but when Radais did not speak again, she finally answered, "There are…err… rumors that the supreme defender and yourself have a romantic history. You are also quite renowned among many of us for your venture into the Spirit Wastes alone."

"Renowned?" Radais swapped looks with Lazan, shaking his head. "You should despise me for pursuing a few awakened instead of staying to protect your village. I failed in my duty to them. I failed in my duty to my own family too."

"You uncovered what could be the greatest Glassblade discovery in centuries! Forgive me, Master, but I have heard that to rise from initiate status, one must learn when to follow protocols and when one must trust their trained instincts to guide them."

*Maybe she is not so much like Miv after all.*

Radais crossed his arms, but nodded. "Fine, you may come. Set aside your training gear and join us for supper." She deserved the chance to prove herself, as he himself had sought years ago.

"Oh! Yes… Yes, Master Radais."

Wanusa handed her wooden sword to one of the other initiates, who gave her a look Radais could not decipher. Yes, he'd been a teenager once, but he was beginning to understand why those of middle-age complained about youth. They squealed, whispered, and schemed in ways he'd never have considered at their age. It was not often he felt old. With his bones aching from the chill and youth surrounding him, though, he wondered how long it was before he'd need to start asking for a cane.

He led Lazan and Wanusa into the mess, where they collected their bowls of a mushy substance. He'd wondered often about it as an initiate. A few scoldings for asking too many questions had shut him up, and now, he was just grateful to have something warm to fill his stomach.

The dim stone room was far quieter than it had once been as the rest of Radais's team joined the trio at a rickety table. Both the Glassblade's lack of funds and the increasing patrols Miv had sent out around the Ephemeral Slaughter had left the fortress with a mere skeleton crew.

The lack of choices had made choosing Radais's team easy, as few competent warriors remained in Palmia. He examined the group who'd be by his side. None of them were his first choices, but Miv had made it clear he couldn't recall anyone from their other missions. Being a Glassblade meant compromising.

"Wanusa, what are you doing with Radais?" Mhanain asked gruffly from across the table. An experienced archer five years Radais's elder, he was built like a brick with a line of black streaking through his puffy red hair. He claimed it had shown up after he'd fought five awakened by himself, their chill cutting him clean to the skull. Radais figured he was just getting old.

Wanusa set down her bowl and sat straight-backed. "The supreme defender herself asked me to join your journey west."

"A spy, eh?"

Radais tapped the table. "Careful, Mhanain."

Mhanain scoffed. "Being too damn careful is what got us this deep in shit. No money. No recruits. As many awakened as the Awakening itself!"

"That's why we're going into the Wastes."

"With an initiate, an Ezman, seven warriors left behind by Miv, and a single master." Mhanain took a swig of something that smelled heavily of alcohol. "Should be sending an army."

"Would you do better with the Chamber of Scions than the supreme defender has?" Wanusa asked, brow raised.

Mhanain looked to Radais. "An awakened attacked the Crystal Palace, and they still don't care. What were *you* doing there? I woulda marched in there with my bow on my shoulder and told those blasted scions they are nothing but a bunch of ignorant assholes."

"Wonderful diplomacy," Wanusa quipped as she took a sip from her own mug.

The other warriors joined in the debate before Radais could shut it down. He slumped back, taking a bite of his gruel as he mulled over yet another failure. Mhanain had a point. Radais had helped stop the Ephemeral Slaughter in Kalastok, but the Glassblades had gained nothing from it. His focus had been on the Crimsons and his father, and he'd failed to do anything of significance related to either of them. Without Kasia's aid, his visit would've been a waste. That was becoming a familiar tone in his life.

Radais pulled out his charcoal and sketchpad as the others continued arguing. He imagined the crew as they could have been: united, determined, and carrying the Glassblade banner with pride. Mountains rose behind them as they trekked into the Wastes with awakened lurking in the everdark.

The thought inspired him. But as he began the sketch, it felt wrong. The faces were the people around him, and their armor resembled that of the greatest Glassblades. It wasn't them, though. Was art not meant to portray the flaws of people along with their glory?

He restarted the sketch, this time drawing them at the very table where they sat. Its wood was peeling, and the stench of sweat stung his nostrils. Such things were difficult to portray, but he did his best. A brutal scene, it resembled a bunch of arguing drunkards more than the trained warriors of the Glassblade Order—the truth of the people. Aliakia's wrinkled brow. Wanusa's unnecessarily perfect posture. Nadarios's disappointment. And his own solemn look, eyes empty and heart heavy. None of them were perfect paragons.

When he finished, he looked up to see the table empty, except for Lazan. The timing candle before him had burned down significantly, and his throat was dry. Spirits, how long had he been drawing for?

"When did the others leave?" he asked Lazan, who leaned back, staring at the ceiling. Odd. It was a simple one of stone, surely not something to study for a significant time.

"There are sixty-seven cracks in the ceiling," the Body Reacher replied. "I'm sure, because I checked at least thrice."

Radais shut his notebook and wished for a stiff drink. If only Mhanain would give him some… "Then why stay here?"

"Would you scoff at me if I said I was worried about my friend?"

"Friend? We met a couple hundred-hours ago."

Lazan reached across the table and took his hand. His palms were soft, unlike the calloused ones of a worker or warrior. "And in those hundred-hours, I have traveled halfway across the Commonwealth with you, stood by your side as you heard of your father's death, and watched you spiral in the aftermath. You are strong, Radais. Just know that you need not be strong alone."

The Reacher stood and threw a striped scarf around his neck, the most vibrant color for a hundred miles. "I am heading back to the barracks. You may walk with me if you wish, or you can sit here until the cold freezes your bottom to its seat."

He turned to leave, his strides slow as he stuck his hands in his coat pockets. Something tugged at Radais's chest watching him go. A feeling he hadn't felt for some time. Longing had gripped him for years, and it was as if Lazan's words had unlocked a glimmer of light he so badly needed. He feared it as he put his notebook away. But he remembered Miv's words when he'd faced his first awakened.

*"Fear ensures you don't die doing something stupid. It also stops you from being happy."*

Radais blew out the timing candle and stood. "Wait."

"For what?" Lazan asked, glancing over his shoulder.

"For me. I could use some company, and someone to talk to who isn't an ibex."

# OF AMBER AND PURPLE

*"Revenge is an obsession. It eats one alive until they crave nothing but pain, and too often in the end, all that remains is their own."* — Unknown

A single lantern lit the door to The Confluence as Kasia returned from her meeting with Nex. Her feet dragged, and her nose stung from the chill. After days of bedrest, vomiting from Realm Taint as Aliax, Sazilz, and her other victims mocked her weakness, she'd dragged herself to Haxan's Hall. Radais had claimed the bartender knew Nex. A few keni later, and the bartender had revealed the little thief's favorite pubs.

No matter her exhaustion, the meeting had been a success. She had an agent who knew every alley of Kalastok. Even better, Nex had given her the name of a Crimson and a lead on another.

She had meetings to arrange.

But sleep came first. She'd had little of it after killing Sazilz and beginning to ingratiate herself with the Crimsons. By the spirits, she still couldn't believe he was dead. She saw him every night, trembling naked before her as Tzena and the Dark Reacher loomed over him.

"Was it worth it?" a familiar voice asked from beside the townhouse door.

Aliax stood with his arms crossed, leaning against the brickwork and resembling a drifter who'd become moored to the earth. Or at least moored to her. She wanted nothing more than to ignore him, but her aching heart stopped her.

"Sazilz ordered my father's death," she snapped, eyes fixed upon the ground. "He got what he deserved."

"Then look at me."

She bit her cheek. "You're dead, Ali. How many times must I tell you that?"

His cold hand found hers, his calluses running across her smooth skin. "My spirit doesn't float like the drifters or kill like the awakened. No, I'm worse than dead. I'm trapped. Just like Sazilz and the others you've killed."

Her other hand slipped from the door as his death flashed before her for the millionth time. The fear, the desperation... It clutched her now, tightening like a noose around her neck. Once, a Death Reacher like her would've hung the moment she'd revealed her power, but the Crimsons had pushed for her release. She had a hunch it had to do with the final petal Nex heard the Crimsons talking about.

"I would release you if I could," she whispered. "But Realm Taint is not a choice. It's my punishment."

"You're the only one who can."

The door opened to reveal Kikania in a coat hastily thrown over her nightshift. Her normally wide eyes were like saucers. "Lady Katarzyna, what are you doing standing on the step? Did you lose your key?"

Kasia released a sharp breath and feigned a smile. "No, only my sanity, but I'm afraid I lost that a long time ago."

"Oh, my lady." Kikania took her hand—the same one Aliax was holding—but her hand went right through his. She pulled Kasia inside and into the warmth of the foyer. "You are chilled. We must remedy this." She called for one of the other maids to stoke the fires in Kasia's chambers as she helped her climb the stairs.

Physically, Kasia didn't need the aid, but her mind was still outside as Aliax's cold touch lingered on her skin. He'd never wielded power like hers. Reaching into the realm of Death was unlike anything else, but regret made her sick every time. She'd killed the man who'd order her father's assassination. Ever since, it felt as if she were more a ghost than Aliax.

Faniz stepped from his bedroom at the sound of her arrival, wearing a long nightshirt and nightcap. "Ah, wonderful, you have returned! A young Vockan man, Lord Zinarus of House iz Vamiustok, arrived for you while you were out, and he left this message when I informed him of your absence." He held out a folded piece of parchment in his shaky hand before coughing into his arm. "Kind fellow, that one… Uzrin Ioniz's bastard if I remember correctly. He said he quite enjoyed your dance at the estate of House Oliezany."

"Lord Zinarus is a fine gentleman," she replied, snatching the letter and opening it with haste. Her heart raced. For once, it wasn't from fear.

*Lady Katarzyna,*

*I apologize for missing you this evening. Wherever your endeavors took you, I hope your efforts bore fruit. My own efforts have yielded results that I would like to celebrate with you.*

*House iz Vamiustok has successfully taken ownership of the Kalastok Arena. Our dance at the Oliezany estate was enlightening amid the everdark, and it is my wish that you would join me in my box for the inaugural day of my proprietorship. We are opening the doors for lowborn and scions alike. There shall be merriment, jousts, combat, and insightful conversation about our common interests.*

*Your presence at this opening would bring me much joy. I hope you consider the offer, and if you do choose to accept, please take the enclosed invitation to the guards. They will escort you to my suite.*

*Sincerely and entirely yours,*

*Lord Zinarus*

*Heir of House iz Vamiustok*

Kasia held her hand to her brow, letting out a laugh at Zinarus's formality. Most scion men held daggers behind their backs as they bowed their heads. She couldn't tell yet how similar Zinarus was to them. On the surface, he held the perfect etiquette of the most annoying noble, and he'd decided that shaking Gornioz's hand in front of the crowd was more important than keeping his promise to watch the mansion guard. Yet, he had shown flashes of something genuine beneath, endearing. She'd danced with him only once, but frustrations aside, his foes were the same as hers. That made him a potential ally amid a sea of shadowy threats.

Except, her flushed cheeks weren't for an ally.

"Is this the man you mentioned after the gala?" Kikania asked, grinning expectantly.

Kasia closed the letter, but no matter how hard she tried, her cheeks still burned. "Yes. He asked me to dance when I feared no others would. Who would want to take the hand of a Reacher who could kill you with a single touch?"

"Yes…" Faniz coughed repeatedly, gripping the door's trim. He had yet to confront Kasia directly about her abilities, but his sheepishness toward her in recent days had revealed enough. "I must ask, however, if gallivanting with Uzrin's bastard is the best decision. House iz Vamiustok is opposed to the king, and—"

"I have done much since my arrival to ensure the king's allies are not opposed to me," Kasia interrupted. This was her house, and he needed to remember that. "Those efforts have strained the reformers' opinions of me, though, so I think it best to accept the offer. It is best to have contacts on every side of the Chamber."

With a deep sigh, Faniz turned back to his room. "Very well, but remember that you are an exceptional woman, Katarzyna. You could do better than to trust a half-blooded Vockan."

"Being red of hair does not make him lesser, Uncle. He is a scion, and I fear I cannot partner with those who will not bear my touch."

No reply came as the old man hobbled into his room, coughing yet again.

"Uncle, are you well?" she asked after him.

He waved a dismissive hand, "Well enough at my age," and shut the door.

Kasia shook her head as she rolled the letter through her fingers. It shocked her how much better she felt, but her chest tightened at the wispy figure lurking on the next landing.

"So, you replaced me with a lord." Aliax huffed. "I thought you weren't like the others."

Sazilz stepped from the stairs, his wispy sneer turning Kasia's stomach. "You would choose a half-breed, a *bastard*."

"And a cripple!" Aliax echoed.

She ignored them the best she could, but Sazilz caught her scarred arm and squeezed tight. "You have no idea what chaos you've begun," he hissed. "The Dark Reacher won't stop with me!"

"Who?" she demanded, ignoring their insistence that she had a romantic interest in Zinarus. He was the enemy of her enemy, a convenience at best. "Tell me who he is!"

A gentle hand fell on her shoulder, and she winced, pulling free from Sazilz before glancing back at Kikania. "Come," she told her handmaiden. "It seems I must decide what dress to wear for the joust."

Kikania gave no mention of her outburst as Kasia climbed the stairs, shooting Aliax a glare as she passed. He couldn't be mad at this decision. Zinarus was a reformer, so working with him would help lowborn like Aliax. Besides, a joust wouldn't require her to Reach, as only Life and Body Reachers were required in the arena to keep badly beaten competitors alive.

She was determined to have fun with this *and* continue working against the Crimsons. Meeting with Zinarus would be both an opportunity to learn more about his deal with House Oliezany and her first chance to have an extended conversation with him. Plenty of scions had shown interest in her since her discovery of amber. Zinarus's interest, though, had come after her Reaching had ostracized her once again, and he'd helped her, if only until Gornioz intervened.

"If you don't mind me saying it," Kikania said once they entered Kasia's room, "you seem so much happier now that you received Lord Zinarus's letter. Well, you did until you screamed at the stairwell."

Kasia threw her coat and hat on the bed. "I've needed something to look forward to. The past haunts me, but I fear I'll drown in its current if I don't keep moving."

"I worry for you, my lady."

"Thank you, but for tonight, let your only worry be ensuring I impress all who attend this joust."

Kikania grinned. "I know just the dress…"

**KASIA WATCHED THE CROWDS FLOCK THE MAIN GATE** of the Kalastok Arena from the safety of her carriage. Scions and peasants alike, they all shouted at the tellers to let them in. But only those with tickets or money for entry could pass the gate.

"Is it always like this?" Tazper asked beside her, peeking out the window. He wore a casual-fit white shirt and amber vest of House Niezik's colors, and from the moment she'd seen him that morning, he had been giddy to see the jousts.

There would obviously be quite a wait, so Kasia crossed her legs and leaned her head back against the carriage seat. It was unladylike. No one was there to watch, though, and she had little care for impropriety around Tazper.

"Father used to say the jousts were another day of suffering for the lowborn and a glorious one for the scions," she said. "With Zinarus opening the arena to everyone, I imagine this is the first time many of these people have experienced organized sport."

"There will be blood outside the ring if they do not hurry. Wait…" Tazper sat forward, brow raised. "Who is that?"

"Who?"

He waved for her to look. "There is a Vockan man on a horse. It looks like he is trying to calm the crowd. Is that…"

*Zinarus, you fool.*

Kasia flung open the door, sending Tazper tumbling to the cobblestone before she helped him up. "Come," she said as she waved on the carriage driver and ran toward the lamplit gate. "We need to stop this before Zinarus gets himself killed."

The iz Vamiustok heir sat upon a large blood bay horse with a purple cape draped over his right shoulder, trailing down his tailcoat and breeches. He spoke with his hand raised, but the roar of the crowd drowned out his voice. His Truth Reaching could've calmed an individual or even a small group. Hundreds pushed against him, though, and he showed no intention to Reach. He would be swallowed alive before his supposed celebration if Kasia didn't do something.

Except she quickly became caught in the crowd too. It didn't matter that she was an infamous Death Reacher. Everyone was focused on the gate, and she lost sight of Tazper in the mass of people.

Then came a cheer.

Major General Tiuz Hazeko rode to Zinarus's side, rising above like a giant among pawns. The entire crowd gazed upon him with awe. Tiuz's mother had been lowborn, and his glory both in the arena and on the battlefield had turned him into a living legend among the Ezmani. He was a Spirit Reacher, but this power was beyond any magic.

"All will have entry!" Tiuz shouted. "Bide your time, and have your keni ready. My friend, Lord Zinarus iz Vamiustok, did not expect such excitement when he decided to open the arena doors to all. We thank you for coming, and we promise that you shall miss nothing."

With that, the chaos ceased. No Reaching needed.

The rowdy crowd formed into a series of lines before each teller, and Kasia walked through the gap to Zinarus, presenting her invitation. "This is quite the event you have here, Lord Zinarus. I was beginning to wonder if we would see combat within the gates and without."

Zinarus removed his rounded felt hat, holding it to his chest as he bowed from atop his horse. "Lady Katarzyna, you have no idea how pleased I am to see that you accepted my invitation. I must apologize for the commotion. As Tiuz said, the response of the lowborn—at least those not quarantined west of the river—has been overwhelming. I shan't bother to guess how many are in attendance until we have the official numbers." He placed his hat back on his head before gesturing to Tiuz beside him. "Have you had the chance to become acquainted with the major general yet?"

His gaze lingered upon her deep blue dress. Its arcing cut down the neckline and back was severely out of fashion in the Commonwealth, but its style was inspired by the Reshkan courts, where collarbones were considered beautiful. She had little bust to expose, though, and the Reshkans didn't wear corsets to alter their figures. Her sleeves, with long and brightly-colored strips that draped down from her elbows, hung over the gravel as she curtsied.

"I had the pleasure of meeting him in passing a few times in the Chamber, but we have never been formally introduced," she said before turning to the general. "It is an honor, Lord Tiuz. Your reputation precedes you."

Tiuz cleared his throat. "Yours does the same. Although, a Reshkan dress is not what I expected of a matriarch who has become enrooted in the nationalist wing."

*So Zinarus has not told him of my suspicions. Good. Unlike most men, he knows when to keep his mouth shut.*

"I assure you that there is much in common between us," Kasia said. "Politics is a game where not all is as it seems—and it seems you are staring down at me, Lord Zinarus."

"Yes, of course," Zinarus replied, dismounting and grabbing his cane from a strap on his horse's side. With him out of the saddle, Kasia noticed the odd device that held his steel left foot in the stirrup. Its workings escaped her, but the sigil of the Nav merchant family was clearly visible upon it. She grinned knowing he was willing to work with Ogrenian foreigners.

Zinarus passed off his horse to a servant, then offered her his right arm. "Shall I escort you into the arena, my lady?"

Her grin vanished having to take it with her burn-scarred arm, but Zinarus needed to hold his cane in his left hand to keep weight off his mechanical leg. After a moment's hesitation, she wound her arm with his, and they headed through the gates with Tazper following.

They entered a thunderous cloud of conversations. People crowded into the bleachers so densely that they appeared as one beast with ten thousand maws. Her father had often told her that any attempt to guide a mob was playing with fire, and she *hated* fire. But did the lowborn not deserve to enjoy the joust? Sport united the scions in competition. Could it not do the same for them?

"I have never seen so many people in one place," Kasia said, suddenly feeling small as their gazes fell upon her. She'd worn this dress for that very reason, yet part of her wished to crawl into a hole and hide.

"The lowborn call you Death's Daughter," Aliax's voice said from upon the half-wall separating the stands from the dirt-filled arena as remnant snow and ice covered everything. He sat with his legs dangling over the side, a crooked smile on his face. "Reshkan lover. Awakened killer. Amber hoarder."

Kasia stiffened, her face turning pale, but she could not reply here.

Zinarus's hand touched hers. "Kasia, are you well?"

She blinked hard, and when she opened her eyes, Aliax was gone. He'd never been there, of course, but the impact he'd left on her was undeniable. "I… I'm fine. The crowd is just loud, and I believe they are admiring the fine cut of my dress." She grinned, hoping he'd drop his concern.

"As they should." He guided her toward a set of stairs between the bleachers, chuckling at a Reacher who juggled balls of fire while walking on stilts. "People tend to stare at what they find beautiful or obscene. For many of them, you are both."

*Which am I to you?*

He struggled with the first steps. Tazper rushed in to help, but Kasia waved him off, instead taking enough of Zinarus's weight to help with the climb. Anything to keep her attention off the flame juggler who made her arm sear.

"Why do you choose to have a box at the top of the stairs?" she asked.

Zinarus gritted his teeth from the effort as they reached the halfway point. "I am what I am. Is it not better for them to see me fight for what I love than for me to present a lie? You revealed your truth to protect the people of Kalastok. I lack your bravery to face the awakened, but at the least, I can face the people I hope to protect."

"How has this city not eaten you alive?"

He stamped his cane onto the next step, pushing himself up to it. "It has certainly tried."

They soon reached the box. Positioned behind the stands, they had a view of the entire arena as a wooden heater at the back released a smoky smell that reminded Kasia of home. Tystok's farmsteads were surrounded by forests, and she recognized the scent of lowland maple wood. She had never been away for so long. Her memories carried sorrow, though, so she pushed them away, wishing to enjoy the few hours of leisure.

"How does it feel to own this arena?" she asked as they sat. The chairs were cushioned, but while not ostentatious, they were far more comfortable than the benches the other guests were relegated to. "I know it is not the sand mines you once owned, but it must feel rewarding to see so many here for the first time."

Zinarus corrected his posture, then set his hat on the table before them. With the flicker of the gas lamp behind him, his curly hair seemed split between fiery red at the back and a dark beast at the front. He ran his hands through it as he sighed.

"I fell in love with this place the moment I set eyes upon it. There is nowhere else in Kalastok that allows people to gather so easily, to watch legends clash in pursuit of glory. It never should have been kept from the lowborn. They need heroes more than any of us, and it is my hope that many of those heroes, in time, may come from their own ranks."

"You know much about jousting, then?"

He smiled. "I am Lord Tiuz's sponsor, so I would say I have an eye for talent. At times, I ride myself with a lance, but I don't think it best for me to ever compete."

Kasia matched his smile as she reached for her purse and pulled out a wad of keni. "Then perhaps we should have a competition that doesn't require either of us to be impaled. We shall bet upon a competitor every round and see whose eye is better."

"You are a bold woman." He produced his own stack of keni and placed it alongside his hat. "That is good, as our common foes will not be beaten by cowardice." He huffed, his hand suddenly shaking. "I say that as if I am brave, but in truth, I have not found sleep's embrace for many days."

She took his hand and held it still. "You are not alone in that. What brings you this much worry? The mines or the Ephemeral Slaughter?"

"Regizald…" His voice cracked for the first time, slipping for only a moment. "He was my servant and a dear friend. During the

Ephemeral Slaughter, I fled to my townhouse, unable to do anything against the awakened, and I found him dead in my office."

Kasia drew in a long breath. "The awakened killed him, then?" Was this what caused his sale, an awakened like the one Parqiz commanded?

"There was a man robed in red, his face veiled by Reacher's darkness," Zinarus said, his words careful, precise. "He had threatened me once before to sell my family's mines, and my hesitation led to Regizald's death." He hung his head as his fingers gripped at the table. "I see his corpse every time I close my eyes, and all I can think about is what I would do to the Dark Reacher if I saw him again."

Kasia tensed, pulling back. *Can I trust him with the truth?*

His red-robed Reacher resembled Radais's description of the Pikezik scion found in the Wastes. Could they both be Crimsons? Telling Zinarus she'd seen the Dark Reacher with Tzena would likely mean admitting she'd killed Sazilz—a great house magnate. Rumors were swirling around his disappearance, but scions often absconded to other cities for business or pleasure. No one would know he was dead for some time. Kasia hadn't told Nex, and Zinarus knew nothing of the Crimsons yet. If he told anyone what she'd done…

No, she couldn't tell him about Sazilz, not yet. Their previous meeting had been short, and she needed to understand who he truly was before divulging that much. He *seemed* genuine. Scions were trained in that art, and she knew the act as well as any.

"I am sorry for your loss," she finally said, glancing at Tazper, who waited outside the box's door. "I don't know what I would do if I lost Tazper. He is one of the few people whom I can call a friend."

Zinarus flicked his gaze from their held hands to her. He chuckled, but the pain never left his eyes. "The lives of house heads and heirs are lonely. Are they not? We are given all the wealth our ancestors could accumulate and told to do better than they could. Our servants need us because we pay them. Our lowborn workers and peasants need us to employ them and purchase their goods, but they despise us for collecting rents. So often, when we marry, it is for prestige and yet more wealth. True friends are rare." He sighed and straightened his jacket, smiling wryly. "I am sorry. I invited you to celebrate and to get to know you better, not for me to sulk about my woes."

"Our woes are part of us," Kasia said, deciding he deserved to at least know about the Crimsons. That was motivation enough to despise them as much as she did. "Few men in your position would share them so honestly, and though you did leave the Oliezany guard unattended, I must fulfill my promise to give you my honesty in return."

"Standing with the guard would have been preferable to joining Gornioz on the stage. Like I said, it was a mockery. What you saw was me doing what I must to hold onto the miniscule prestige my house has left."

Kasia held a hand to her chest, regretting her quip about the guard. She'd failed to see the complete picture in her fury that night. "This red-robed Dark Reacher is like the one I am investigating," she said. "Radais, the master Glassblade who fought beside me during the Ephemeral Slaughter, discovered another red-robed man in the Spirit Wastes. I believe they are part of the Crimson Court, an elusive organization who assassinated my father and likely King Yaakiin, and I believe that your deal with House Oliezany proves they are colluding."

"So there is more to this after all…" Zinarus's eyes turned hollow as he sat back, pondering. "Who are they? Why did they kill your father and take my family's mines?"

"My father was an ally of King Yaakiin, so the Crimsons likely sought control that he resisted. We believe the man found in the Wastes was a Pikezik, and during my time in the mansion, I overheard a conversation that proved Tzena Oliezany is involved. How your mines connect to my father and the late king, however, I'm not sure."

Zinarus kept his poised appearance, but determination consumed his voice. "We must bring this Crimson Court to justice, then. Are there others you know of? Do you know this Dark Reacher?"

"There must be a network of them to execute a coup and quiet any rumors of it," Kasia replied. "That is what frightens me. I feel as if I am pulling at strings slower than the Crimsons weave their plot. Whatever it is, I *will* stop it. They killed my father, and they will suffer for it!"

She caught the savagery in her voice too late. Collecting herself, she did her best to take a scion's posture, pretending she hadn't lost her temper.

"My apologies," she said. "It has been twelve years since I lost my father, and that is twelve years that the Crimsons have gone unchecked. I bear the weight of his legacy and his loss."

He rested his hand on hers—as she had done for him—but she pulled back. "I am sorry for your loss as well," he said, his voice gentle. "I know what it is to endure without a father, but to have loved and lost is often more painful than to have not held such a love in the first place."

A cheer interrupted them as three Light Reacher spheres burst to life over the jousting list. Tiuz trotted with ease into the center of the arena on a light gray horse, as if it were an extension of his own flesh. The crowd drew to an anxious hush until he greeted them and proclaimed his thanks to Zinarus for opening the arena to all.

Zinarus wiped the sorrow from his face and stood, setting aside his cane and waving as the crowd applauded—some more fervently than others. The arena had been built for scions only, so beyond the few houses with boxes of their own, there was nothing to separate scions from the newly welcomed peasants. Kasia grinned at the disgruntled faces from the Chamber squeezed into the audience. Another face stole it quickly.

Tzena Oliezany sat across the arena at the edge of her family's box. Outside the line of inheritance, she appeared almost peripheral, but her actions during the gala had proven otherwise. There were those who held powerful titles, and there were those who ruled from the shadows.

When Zinarus sat, Tiuz gave way to the first pair of competitors. They were scions from minor families: one young and fit, the other of middle age with scars across his exposed forearms.

"Now that the fuss of ceremony is over with, we can begin," Zinarus said, tapping his fingers on the table. "Let us enjoy this game you suggested as a distraction from the weight upon our hearts and minds, shall we? I would be remiss if your entire time in this box was spent in anger and sorrow."

Kasia itched to return to the topic of the Crimsons, but delving further would risk exposing who she'd killed. He would have to earn that trust. So, for now, she gave an approving wave. She was not one to turn down a good challenge.

Zinarus smiled. "Splendid. You may choose first as my guest. The elder of these two, Karliz, has experience in war. Apparently, he is the only living man who bears a scar from Keloshan, Ogrenian, *and* Reshkan weapons."

*Is that because he is easy to hit, lucky, or knows how to survive?* Kasia asked herself, studying the competitors.

"Utizianak is the other," Zinarus continued. "Brute of a man, that one. I have no doubt he could wrestle a bull if he wished to."

Both men seemed well-prepared as they took to the list on their mounts. In the battle of experience against brawn, Leonit had taught Kasia to take experience every time—as long as it did not yield to aging fragility. Karliz held his lance straight up and down as he waited, his mount under control. Utizianak had no such success. Like a mare in heat, his horse reared and snorted, eager to charge.

"I will take the obvious choice," Kasia said, sliding her bet between them. "Karliz."

Zinarus just grinned and nodded.

Tiuz gave a signal, and both riders charged down the list with lances ready. Utizianak shot forward like a bullet while Karliz remained steady, his lance up until the last moment. Kasia found herself on the edge of her seat as they clashed.

And Karliz flew from his saddle.

He struck the ground as his foot caught in the stirrup, dragged by his horse with his broken shield crashing to the dirt behind him.

Utizianak did not cease his gallop. Lance thrown aside, he raised his fist, drawing a cheer from the crowd as he rounded the arena to the far side. There, he stopped and raised his helmet's visor before blowing a kiss to the Oliezany box. Tzena waved back, neither returning the gesture nor denying it.

Zinarus clapped with the crowd. "What an unlikely victory! Well, perhaps not, if you noticed the horses."

"Karliz's appeared well trained," Kasia replied. How had she lost? "My father always said that experience matters the most in competitions such as this, and Utizianak's horse was also hot, lacking control."

"Your father sounds like he was a wise man. It is a shame we shall never meet." Zinarus took his winnings. "I find myself gifted to find a woman beside me who has inherited his teachings and seemingly found her own. However…"

He pointed to Karliz, just now managing to get his foot free from the stirrup. "As they entered the list to take their lances, I noticed Karliz's horse came up lame on his left front leg. Yes, he was calm in the lead-up to the signal, but that was out of an unwillingness to put weight upon that leg. It is a crucial one in the joust, though, and the horse leaning away from the center ensured that his rider was quite easy to dismount."

"It seems I am the one who is gifted to sit beside you," Kasia replied, biting her cheek, "but the night is young."

They continued their bets as jousters and the occasional swordsmen clashed. It was not long before Kasia realized she was outmatched for once, but that only made her try harder… and lose more. Her keni disappeared before the event had even neared Tiuz's headline joust. Slouching, she crossed her arms and glared down at the field of her defeat.

"I am sorry to have taken your money," Zinarus said softly. "If you would like, we could say it was merely for fun, and—"

"No," Kasia muttered.

"Oh… Well, shall we enjoy the rest of the jousts without competition, then?" He waved for a servant. "I can call some drinks for us. What would you prefer?"

She sighed and rubbed her temples. "I don't drink alcohol. It softens the mind."

"My apologies, then." With a hasty smile, he whispered to the servant, who hurried off. "It seems my conversation skills have fallen short, Lady Kasia, so against my better judgment, I wonder if you would spare a moment to discuss business."

Kasia's mood was sour, but a distraction from her evident failure was welcomed. "What kind? Your joust seems to have drawn quite the crowd, so I doubt you need my help with the arena. And I have little more to say about House Oliezany until I can investigate further."

"It is related to another matter." He turned his whole body to face her with a gloved hand pressed to his long, narrow lips. She'd yet to see him so tense. "Commander Tiuz and I have discussed beginning a small mercenary company of just over twenty soldiers to patrol the lowborn districts and protect the innocent from gangs. The finances are reasonable, the horses are already in the stables, and recruitment of so few should not be difficult. After seeing the power of House Oliezany and this Crimson Court, I believe the need for this organization is great."

*For once, action behind such refined words.*

"You need money." She gestured to the keni bills he'd just won. "Have you not taken enough of mine?"

"Funds would be of use, yes. More important is weaponry. Lances are simple to acquire through the guise of the arena, and glass is expensive, but manageable. Rifles and pistols are far more difficult, and since you have embedded yourself among those close to House Oliezany, I wished to inquire whether you could procure some for us."

Kasia bit her lip, debating whether such a risk was worth it. Yes, she could convince Tzena that the guns would be used for provincial patrols near Tystok, but it was a risk if she traced his company's weapons back to her. "House Oliezany's gunsmiths are not the only ones in Brakesh or the Commonwealth."

"That is true," Zinarus replied as the crowd erupted at a man sending his sword through another's stomach. A Body Reacher rushed to the defeated man to mend the wound before he died, and his screams sent memories of Aliax's final moments flashing through Kasia's mind. "I assume Gornioz has his agents watching the trade across our nation closely, so purchasing from alternative sellers could spark his interest."

"What about small purchases from many sellers? Marketplaces, privateers, and caravans all have weaponry to peddle. We would simply need agents to travel and conduct the trades."

He leaned back, his posture breaking for the first time as he let out a gleeful chuckle. "Of course! Kasia, I must admit that my skills in clandestine activities are woefully lacking. Conducting business in the open, I can do, but my mind fails to find ways to subvert the expected. That is why I need your help."

He took her hand, then gently raised his other to cup her cheek. "You are quite the brilliant woman."

All the blood in Kasia's body rushed to her head, sending it spinning. With Aliax's face burned into her vision, she questioned whether to acknowledge the romantic gesture. It was small yet significant. Did he intend for this to be more than a partnership against the Crimsons who'd wronged them both?

She tried to stand too quickly and tripped over her chair. Zinarus stumbled after her as she fell, but he was too late. By the time he caught her, she'd smacked her head on the floor hard enough to make it throb. Then he fell on top of her.

Tazper rushed in at the sound. "Kasia, are you…" He stepped back, rubbing his neck. "Oh, was I interrupting—"

"You most certainly were not!" she blurted as she rolled aside. "I was rising to stretch my legs and tripped on my skirts."

Zinarus blushed. "Is the possibility such a horrific thought?"

She realized then they were close enough for their noses to touch. His breath was neither sweet nor revolting, which was more than could be said for most men. Despite his confident statement, worry filled his hazel eyes—near amber. It at least seemed genuine, and that only made the noose in her chest tighten further.

"I should retire," she mumbled, pulling back her hand to her head to mimic a fainting damsel. "My head feels as if it were on the stilts of your entertainer."

"I…" Zinarus pushed himself off her and straightened his jacket. "Do you wish for me to call a Body Reacher? We have many who—"

"I *wish* to retire."

Tazper helped her stand as Zinarus shook his head at himself. It was for the best. She had far too much to navigate without a layer of romance on top of that. After all, the man was gentle despite his desire to lead mercenaries. He deserved better than her.

Once Kasia managed to reach the door, she glanced back. All of her father's training failed. She couldn't muster the willpower to smile, curtsy, or compliment him on what was truly an impressive arena, so she just bowed her head. "I am sorry."

She turned away, but Zinarus managed to speak before she could step outside the box. "Don't apologize! I had a wonderful time, and when the opportunity arises, I hope we have the chance to dance again."

*Me too.*

But those two words caught in her throat. She hastened out, flinging herself down the steps with all the pace of a Vockan ibex until she collided with a man going the opposite direction.

"What is this?" the man yelled as he scrunched his face like he'd stepped in refuse.

Kasia sucked in a sharp breath once her vision cleared. This wasn't just any man. Uzrin Ioniz, Zinarus's absent father, stood before her, dressed in the richest of clothes with glass beads lining the layers of fabric. He wore his deep gray hair so short that it looked nearly sharp, and his nose resembled a fighter's—broken and not fixed by a Body Reacher in time.

*It's him…*

"I…" Kasia searched for the right reply, but all she could think of was Nex's second Crimson. Uzrin fit their description perfectly. Nex hadn't seen him return to House Ioniz's townhouse, but it had to be him. He was a cousin of the house's patriarch, Hazemel, holding a seat in the Chamber, but not close enough in relation to live with him. Why was he heading to Zinarus's box?

Uzrin stepped closer, his voice deep as he took her arm, feigning worry. "Stay away from Zinarus if you know what is good for you. He may be a bastard, but I'll not have my blood mixed with a Death Reacher."

Kasia sneered as the nearby audience members glared at their disturbance. "I will do as I please."

She straightened her posture and caught Tazper's arm again. Uzrin stepped aside, not bowing his head as a roar rose around them. A defeated jouster had drawn his sword and charged his opponent. Tiuz pushed his horse to intercept too slowly, and the crowd jeered as the jouster's illegal strike went straight through his rival's back. Though Body Reachers rushed to save the downed man, the strike was of the most lowly sort.

Zinarus would not be pleased.

But his honor was foreign to Kalastok. Kasia surveyed the thousands seated around the arena as she headed toward the gate and her carriage beyond. Sycophants, thieves, manipulators, and liars stood among them, looking no different than anyone else on the surface. Even the average person would do whatever it took to survive amid brutal conditions. There was no honor in helplessly watching one's family starve or succumb to the Spirit Plague, and in this city, far too many were that desperate.

*How desperate am I?*

That thought haunted her as Tazper called for her carriage. She'd killed Sazilz and those who'd helped him assassinate her father. She'd recovered a modicum of her house's former glory through amber and political maneuvering. Yet, as she stood in lanternlight surrounded by the everdark, she felt as empty as ever. Her need for something more ate away at her with each breath, but she feared what "more" meant. Worse, she feared what it would take to reach it.

So she would continue on the path before her, seeking to destroy the Crimson Court. Maybe relief would come when she could finally cross that final name off her father's note. Not a person, but an organization twisting the Commonwealth from its core. It was something to fill the void. Something to remind her what it was to feel.

And her work was not yet finished.

# THE BURIED GODDESS

*"Scions of great houses have purpose no matter how far from the magnate they are. Elders oversee enterprises. Adults act as managers, Chamber members, or military officers. Youths, though often overlooked, have a great many purposes. They train, labor, and provide a great many ears to give their house knowledge of the newest rumors spreading throughout the scions. A patriarch or matriarch who dismisses such rumors as gossip are foolish."* – An excerpt from *The Commonwealth from an Outsider's View*

Hail clattered against Kasia's umbrella as she took the main streets east from the Crystal Palace. Another Chamber meeting complete. Another evening wearing the nationalist mask Gornioz Oliezany wanted to see. With each passing day, it grew evermore difficult to peel it free and return to who she was.

If she knew anymore…

Tazper would ramble on about it being his job to hold her umbrella and call her carriage, but she preferred her solitude tonight. A blessed few minutes at most. Tzena had invited her to the Buried Temple, where the younger scions gathered in pretend prayer and whispered into the late hours. Kasia would wear her proverbial mask again upon her arrival, but until then, she would enjoy each moment of freedom.

Except the everdark closed around her like a fist, carrying the voices of the dead. Only Aliax and Sazilz had dared to interfere often, but with each Reach, the others joined in her peripherals. She knew each voice's incoherent rambles, from the peasants who'd caught her with Aliax to those on her father's list. Twenty spirits that would never return. Twenty murders.

She ripped off her glove to reveal her crystal talon. It seemed to hum as she flexed her hand and held it into the light of the nearest gas lamp.

"Why did you answer a child's cries?" she asked the Spirit Crystal. *Not* the Crystal Mother. "I wanted revenge, but all I've done is cause pain. Aliax..." She gritted her teeth. "Everyone knows I'm a monster. The scions may tolerate me, but to them, I am a tool or a freak to watch from the shadows. Spirits, I don't even want to know how the peasants see me."

She shook her head. Why was she even talking to a crystal buried deep beneath the earth? Neither it nor the Buried Temple's so-called Crystal Mother could hear her muttering. Nor would they change which realm she Reached. In truth, she didn't know if she would've wanted them to. What was she without her connection to the realm of Death? Losing her power couldn't bring Aliax or her father back. It was her only weapon against the Crimsons—one that could ensure those who'd lived many lifetimes never returned. But her Realm Taint ensured they never left completely.

"Why did they give you up?" she asked Sazilz's wispy form, standing idly beneath a leafless tree as the hail ripped through him like a thousand tiny daggers. "You were a great house patriarch."

"Only power matters among the elite cabals," he replied. "They squabble like wolves for a scrap of meat, but their hatred of Kelosh unites them for now. So, too, did my disobedience."

"Did they plan to kill my father?"

He hummed to himself and pushed off the tree, walking beside her. Even in death, he wore a hideous dark brown suit that made him resemble a wooden crate. "You are a fool! I told you before you killed me that all I did was act before the others wished. They blame me for the Crimson Court's greatest triumph."

Kasia's shoulders slumped. Sazilz had ordered Parqiz to carry out the assassination, but if he could be believed, then she couldn't rest. Someone else was in charge. The Dark Reacher?

"Who is the Reacher who covered his face in darkness?" she asked, unsure if an answer was even possible. Why would he help her? And if this wasn't Sazilz's spirit but the spawn of her own insanity, then he could offer no more than she already knew.

Sazilz laughed and shook his head. "What do you believe you can accomplish against them? There are more of us than you could ever know. My death means nothing to them, and now, you are their thrall."

"I am not!"

A family walking the opposite direction spooked at her shout, and a young girl hid behind her mother's skirts as the father guided them away. Kasia thanked the hail for blocking full sight of her face. The newspapers calling her Death's Daughter were bad enough without her scaring away random people in the streets. They wouldn't understand the spirits she spoke to, but how could they, when even she didn't truly know what they were?

She lowered her voice, keeping all the bite. "I *am not* their slave. They desire my aid, so I will play their game until I can avenge my father. Then—"

"What?" Aliax mocked from her other side. She looked away from him as pain struck her gut. "You'll unleash the same power that killed me… killed all of us… and ignited your Realm Taint?" The people of Tystok followed in the lamplight behind him, sneering at their murderer. "How many more must die?"

"Just the Crimsons."

Sazilz scoffed. "You would slaughter those who seek to protect the Commonwealth from Kelosh? Yes, they seek their own power, but they know well enough that they have nothing beneath Emperor Mataron's steel fist. Without our most powerful Reachers, we will fall."

The jagged glass spires of the Buried Temple lit the sky ahead. Crossing over the entryway, the spires stretched for half a city block each direction, stretching to the heights of the Crystal Palace and clocktower. Little of the temple rested above ground, though, as the entrance gave way to a marble staircase that descended toward the Kalastok segment of the Spirit Crystal.

Kasia's breaths caught, and Sazilz's warning fell away against her memories of becoming a Reacher within this temple during her teenage years. She had inherited her father's skepticism of the Crystal Mother's existence, but even she had been unable to deny the feeling of wholeness that encompassed the Buried Temple. Whether holy or not, there was power here.

Watchmen with rifles shouldered stood on either side of the entrance. They wore the deep gray uniforms of the Temple instead of the crimson and gold ones of their palace counterparts. Uniform aside, all watchmen she'd found wore the same scornful look around her now. She couldn't blame them. It was their responsibility to ensure those they guarded survived, so a greater Death Reacher was their worst nightmare.

"Lady Katarzyna Niezik," the shorter one—a built, square-jawed woman—said, both hands upon her rifle. It was still shouldered… for now. "I must ask that you glove your taloned hand, *now*."

Kasia glanced at her exposed talon. She'd forgotten removing her glove during her conversation with the spirits, and she bit her lip in regret as she slid the glove back on. Scion children were taught from a young age to wear gloves, even before becoming a Reacher. Forgetting was an awful mistake.

She straightened her posture, returning her noble expression. "I am sure you understand the need to free your limbs for a moment. Those uniforms surely cannot be comfortable for hours on end."

"They aren't." The guard took her other hand off the rifle. "Keep that glove on inside the Buried Temple. This is your final warning."

Kasia gave the slightest of nods. "Of course."

She closed her umbrella and headed down, her steps careful upon the wet stairs as the hail melted. Marble was beautiful but far from the wisest choice in a location exposed to the elements. Aesthetics had their place. She wondered, though, how many elder scions had slipped because of such frivolities.

Gas lamps gave way to ethereal Reacher flames that danced through the spires. Their light refracted across the glass, leaving rainbows streaked along the ground as Kasia neared the first level.

A dozen priestesses awaited her there in hooded gray robes. The ones on the sides held their taloned hands flexed with orange Fire Reacher wisps at their fingertips while the wrinkled two in the center stepped forward. Neither wore gloves.

"You enter the deepest embrace of the Crystal Mother," the one on the left said.

The other held out her taloned hand to touch the center of Kasia's chest. A chill crept over her as whispers spread, drifters circling them, but the priestess's voice pierced the noise. "She calls you as she calls every spirit birthed within Her realm. Do you answer Her with the fullness of your very being?"

*No.*

"I do," Kasia proclaimed. This priestess was a Spirit Reacher, not a Truth one. She couldn't compel her to reveal her actual beliefs.

The priestess smiled, and the chill faded to a gentle warmth, pulsing like a mother's heartbeat as she stepped back. "Then be welcomed in this place, daughter of the Holy Mother."

"Thank you, Sister."

Despite the priestess's retreat, the spirits lingered. These drifters held less distinct forms than Kasia's dead, and they wore only wispy shadows instead of the clothes that had covered them in life. She didn't trust them. Awakened could appear as a drifter at first before striking their unsuspecting target, and their victims' screams during the Ephemeral Slaughter would never leave her.

The second priestess handed her a matching gray robe. "All who bear the Mother's gift are equal in Her eyes."

*All those rich enough to pay for it.*

Kasia took the robe and followed the priestess's directions to a changing room to the side. A small group of women were within, but not recognizing them, she switched to the robe quickly before checking her makeup in a small mirror. She bit her cheek at the ghoulish face that looked back at her. Makeup couldn't fix the sunken eyes and frown lines that she'd gained in recent hundred-hours. No wonder none of the men ever danced with her anymore. Well, none except Zinarus.

She'd stared long enough, so she straightened the stiff robe and headed into the main temple chamber.

Glass gave way to gray crystal which jutted out from the ceiling and floor like teeth ready to devour all who entered. Nearly a hundred hooded scions knelt beneath an orb of pure Reacher light, blinding when Kasia looked directly at it. Countless drifters floated among the scions and gave the room an odd misty appearance. There were few religious decorations except a crystalline statue of the Crystal Mother that sat by the far wall. She glimmered with one hand pressed to the ground and the other reaching out before her.

A priestess spoke from the base of the statue, but as Kasia drew nearer, she furrowed her brow. This was no mere sister of the Temple.

"Do not adhere to the tenants of politicians that would defile the Mother's holy crystal," Anointed Sister Uliazina Rakazimko declared with her arms raised and brow wrinkled. "To remove the Reacher tithe is to deny Her right to choose who is worthy of wielding Her elements."

It was unsurprising that the anointed sister opposed King Jazuk's proposal to expand Reaching to scions unable to afford the talon tithe, but willing to serve in the military. The tithe ensured the Temple's power. Kasia had placed Tazper's name in line to become a Reacher before the law, but there were thousands of scions without a family or sponsor who could cover the cost. Those with ambitions for more would eagerly trade years of their lives for a chance at immense power. Except if war with Kelosh came, it could cost many of them everything..

Kasia wandered through the gathered scions, ignoring Uliazina's calls. Gornioz and the rest of Jazuk's council had already pushed the Chamber to support the proposal. A vote would come soon, and for once, Kasia wouldn't have to lie by agreeing with the nationalists. It was a far from perfect law, but it gave poorer scions an option while bolstering the Commonwealth's ailing army. Sometimes, practicality outweighed all else.

A hand caught hers. "A pleasure to see you here," a familiar voice whispered. Tzena Oliezany knelt nearby among a group of women and pulled her over to them. "Please, worry not about the anointed sister. The Buried Temple may be under her control, but her voice is little more than decoration."

Kasia knelt with them as Uliazina continued her sermon. "Is it not dangerous to ignore her?" Kasia asked.

"Do not profane the Mother's servants in her temple," a narrow-faced woman hissed at Tzena before offering Kasia a smile. "Worry not, Katarzyna. Not all of us have forgotten tradition in this place. You probably do not recognize me, as we last met when we were children, but I am Haliazina, daughter of Lord Borys Kuzon. Please, tell me of Lady Yazia's condition. It has been years since my aunt has written."

Kasia swallowed the spite that came with Haliazina's mention of her mother. She had few memories of her many cousins on Yazia's side of the family, as those not part of one's house were rarely valued among the scions, no matter how much blood they shared. "My mother remains infirm and not in a sound mental state. I fear she and I have had few real conversations in recent years."

"I pray for her good health and am glad to see you here regardless of her condition. Old Lord Faniz was hardly a worthy representative of House Niezik in his own fragile state."

Kasia glanced about, expecting glares from the other scions. Many, though, seemed to be holding their own quiet conversations. The acoustics of the temple appeared at first to carry all voices, but only the anointed sister's echoed as the others dulled outside the immediate area. Was this why so many gathered here to swap secrets?

"My great-uncle has done his best," she replied, "but it is right for the house matriarch to be present during times like these. Every vote in the Chamber is one that could shape the Commonwealth's future, or its end."

Tzena nodded. "Well said. That is precisely why we have been pleased to see you joining the nationalists after your *initial* alignment. Haliazina, could you please inform her of the next step to further her correction?"

"Certainly," Haliazina said sweetly before sliding her taloned hand across Kasia's neck. The talon peeked out from the glove's unfinished finger, chilled against Kasia's skin as pink Mind Reacher magic wrapped around her hand. Such gloves were illegal and deceptive, but if this woman was a Crimson too, it was unsurprising she would resort to such techniques.

A force struck Kasia and shoved away her thoughts. She was empty for a moment, drifting as if her body were suspended mid-air until Haliazina's voice echoed in her mind.

*"Listen well, for I will only say this once. The Crimson Court has seen your potential, but we doubt your will to do what is necessary for the cause. End this doubt by completing a single task: bring about the eternal death of the alchemist Paras ik Lierasa. He has become a threat too great to ignore."*

Kasia sucked in a sharp breath as Haliazina pulled back her hand. Her thoughts replaced the void created by the voice's absence, and the screams of her kills followed.

She collapsed to the crystal floor as they merged into one deafening swarm. The temple's spirits parted for the veiled dead, Aliax circling from one side and Sazilz from the other. Robes of the Crystal Mother draped heavy over them, and their faces turned to decaying flesh in the shadows. Neither spoke, but they didn't have to. The Crimsons' demand was clear.

She must kill again. This time, it was to aid the very people she hoped to destroy, but why did they want dead the only man who seemed to have a cure for the Spirit Plague?

A sea of eyes met her when she raised her head, no longer spasming. Tzena and Haliazina's jaws hung ajar, and Uliazina no longer ranted in opposition to King Jazuk and Gornioz's proposal. It was silent, deathly still, until the anointed sister stepped from her pedestal and parted the kneeling scions. Kasia had no desire to be the object of her attention, but her muscles froze beneath the glare of Aliax.

"Do not lose yourself for them," he breathed as he knelt before her. "They will use you to destroy."

"That is my gift from this cursed place," Kasia muttered under her breath.

Uliazina stopped before her, resting her hands on Kasia's shoulders. "Protect your daughter, oh Mother of the Spirit Crystal. Forgive her for banishing your spirits from this realm, and let her use your blessing for the greatest good a Reacher of Death is capable of."

Kasia tensed at her touch before rising and turning away. She would explode at the slightest spark. With this many Reachers in one place, there were far too many of those to be had.

"Do not turn from her glory, Katarzyna," Uliazina demanded. "You have tainted Her Crystal by calling to Death, and only by giving yourself to Her will you have forgiveness."

"I did not choose this," Kasia replied, barely louder than a whisper. Her heart pounded, and it took all she had not to scream.

Uliazina huffed. "The Crystal Mother answers our desires."

Kasia spun to face her, ripping off her glove and throwing it to the ground between them. Her talon seemed to swim with darkness as a twitch deep inside her demanded she Reach. But that would only give the anointed sister what she desired. "Then it is *she* who tainted *me*!"

Uliazina stepped back, a hand held over her chest. "Leave this instant! You decry the Mother in the heart of her very core! There shall be no forgiveness for your wickedness, nor gifts for those whom you desire to Reach."

"Her gifts are a curse," Kasia spat, then looked to Tzena with a subtle nod. "I have enough of those already."

# THE STRANDED WAYFARER

*"Ambassador Alyniana, the time is nigh for us to prepare if we are to survive the tides to come. As your countless reports have shown, you have made no progress in procuring Spirit Reachers, glass, or a cure from the Commonwealth, so it has been decided that the Keloshan Empire shall protect us instead. You are recalled from your post and shall return to us immediately. There is nothing more in Kalastok for Nochland."* – Rakam of the Nightspinners, chairman of the Nochland Merchant Council

Gentle warmth lofted over the sitting room of Kasia's chambers as she lounged on the sofa, reading a tragic romance that was popular among the female scions of Kalastok. It was full of young love and hidden courtship. In other words, it was a slog until the protagonist discovered her lover had bedded another woman. Then the knives came out.

A log snapped in the fireplace, tearing Kasia from the book as sparks scattered over the marble. She gripped her scarred arm and slammed her eyes shut.

*It's just the fireplace,* she reminded herself, but her heart raced, memories of Gregorzon's flames consuming her mind.

She threw down her book moments before the bell rang upon the wall. A visitor at this hour? She checked her watch to confirm it was as late as she thought, then rose with a distrustful glance at the fire.

"I was done reading anyway," she muttered to herself before checking the mirror to ensure she was presentable. Strands of her gray hair twirled loosely over her unpowdered cheeks—workable, though not ideal. On most days out, she incorporated some foreign stylings like Leonit, but her simple white dress would have to do tonight.

Kikania rushed into the room and went to work on Kasia's makeup without instruction. "Ambassador Alyniana of the Wayfarers is here for you. She says it's urgent."

That gave Kasia pause. What was the Nochland ambassador doing at The Confluence, especially if it was urgent? They had barely crossed paths beyond Alyniana's offer to meet when Kasia had first arrived at the Chamber. Kasia had been too busy with the Crimsons to seek out the ambassador, but was there something Alyniana could provide?

Kasia stood abruptly once Kikania was finished. "This had better be good."

Her dress swept behind her heels as she hurried down the stairs to her father's study… *her* study. Over a decade had passed, but it would take more time yet for her to accept his creations as hers. It was because of Leonit's work that House Niezik had risen to a great house. Until she returned it to such prestige, his shadow would be taller than she could reach.

Alyniana was perusing the study's countless books when Kasia reached the doorway. The ambassador was a perfect example of Nochland's devotion to the natural world, her headscarf flowing with floral patterns and her formal dress entrancing with its patterns of green and white. For a moment, Kasia stayed there, observing her as she pulled an unfamiliar leatherbound book with a purple cover.

"Curious about my father's studies?" Kasia asked, arms crossed.

Alyniana yelped. "My apologies, Lady Katarzyna. I did not see you there." She tapped the book. "How could one not be curious about Lord Leonit? He was a mysterious man whose death has never been fully explained. Were you not the only one to witness it?"

"I was." Kasia furrowed her brow. "What book is that? I do not recognize it."

"I had planned to ask you the same thing. It is locked and bears no marking except for a few letters in ancient Piorakan, which—I must admit—I am incapable of reading."

"Allow me." Kasia swept across the room, plucking the book from Alyniana's hand and circling around her desk at the far end of the room.

*A lock of glass?* Kasia considered. *Curious…*

To most scions, glass was both a protection against the awakened and a luxury. Leonit had often held more creative interpretations—none of them frivolous. He'd seen glass as a tool with a thousand uses to those open-minded enough to see it, and its use signified great importance to him.

"My father was fascinated by the fall of Piorak," Kasia said as she examined the lock. "Often, I wondered why his lessons focused on a long dead empire, but nearly all of us are descendants of those who survived the first Awakening. Whether Ezmani, Vockan, Nochlander, Keloshan, Ogrenian, or Reshkan, all our lands were once ruled by Piorak, so failing to study our predecessors would make us ignorant to their faults. Unfortunately, his teachings did not extend to the Piorakan language itself." She set down the book and rubbed her scarred forearm as she approached a nearby bookshelf. "But I doubt you came to discuss history, Ambassador."

Alyniana took a long breath before approaching the desk, resting her hands on the back of the guest chair. "I am afraid not. This afternoon, I received a letter from the Merchant Council of Nochland."

Kasia hesitated with her fingers gripping a wide book titled *An Incomplete Dictionary of Ancient Piorak*. "What kind of news?"

She hefted the dictionary from the shelf, big enough to fill her arms, and lugged it to the desk as Alyniana replied, "I fear that I have been recalled to Litianitan for my failure to procure the Commonwealth Reachers or glass necessary to protect against the awakened attacks and Spirit Plague. The Merchant Council has turned to Kelosh instead."

"As a vassal state, surely." Dust flew off the massive dictionary as Kasia dropped it on the desk. She coughed, then glanced at the lock one more time before flipping through the dictionary. Curiosity threatened to drag her in, but she reminded herself that Alyniana's conversation was more immediate than a book. "What will you do?"

Alyniana's proud stature faded, and she fell into the guest chair. "I sent a letter only an hour ago to Princess Nikoza of House Bartol, asking that the great houses supply mercenaries and enough Reachers to aid Nochland against a Keloshan invasion. In return, we would blockade Keloshan ports in the Vitrian Sea."

Kasia's finger stopped at the word she'd been searching for in old Piorakan. *Seek.* What could that mean?

She ripped herself from the dictionary. Kelosh's interests in both the Commonwealth and Nochland would disrupt the amber trade and her investigations into the Crimson Court. All her work, ruined by an emperor who thought he could redraw borders at will. The irony of her own border games against House Uziokaki was not lost on her, but deceiving a house over amber was surely different than the slaughter of war.

"Appealing to the great houses may be your best option," she said, "so why do you come to me? I have neither an army nor Spirit Reachers to grant you, no matter how much my father admired your nation."

"That is true," Alyniana replied. "However, I believe King Jazuk's unwillingness to aid Nochland is not because of his own stubbornness, but that of his advisors. It has not escaped my attention that you may have the ear of Lord Gornioz Oliezany now."

"I know you have spies," Kasia replied with a wry smile. "All nations have them, and it does not surprise me that they would watch the most well-known Death Reacher." She looked at the locked book, drumming her fingers. "Your spies were both correct and not. Gornioz and his allies have taken well to me voting in their favor often in the Chamber, but I hardly have his ear."

Alyniana leaned forward, her voice quiet. "If not his, then you have the ears of the Crimson Court."

Kasia threw open a drawer to her right and grabbed her father's revolver. Pulling back the hammer, she stood with the barrel aimed at Alyniana's head. "How do you know about the Crimsons?"

"Calm, dear Katarzyna." Alyniana raised her hands, revealing the missing index finger beneath her left glove. "I have my reasons for investigating them, you see. You are obviously aware of House iz Vamiustok's sale of their sand mines to House Oliezany, ripping away the deal I had hoped to negotiate with Lord Zinarus. His change of heart was suspicious to me, and my spies uncovered the death of his servant and close confidant, Regizald, just a day before the sale. Further digging indicated that there is a network of well-connected scions within Kalastok who would do anything to remain hidden. Except with you, it appears."

Aliax emerged from the shadows behind Alyniana. "She knows…" he chittered. "Maybe she could help get you escape this pact with Tzena."

"Shut it!" Kasia snapped at him before turning her attention back to Alyniana. "What else do you know about the Crimsons?"

"Little," Alyniana replied, her brow raised at Kasia's outburst, "except that you have poked a pin-sized hole in their veil. And, of course, that they may be connected to the string of deaths that ended King Yaakiin's reign and the lives of his closest allies. Was your father not his minister of glass?"

Kasia bit her cheek. "How is that relevant?"

Alyniana looked upon Kasia with a pity that made her spine crawl. "You walk a precarious path, seeking vengeance for Lord Leonit's assassination, but I must admit that your pursuit has put you in a useful position. I assume they have demanded a test of loyalty?"

"Tell her!" Aliax demanded, slamming his fist into the desk. It didn't shake.

*He isn't real,* Kasia reminded herself, but her gaze flicked to him regardless. Then she lowered the gun.

"There is nothing I can do for you, Alyniana of the Wayfarers," she insisted.

Alyniana gripped her armrests. "My apologies, Lady Katarzyna. I did not mean to ask too much of you."

Kasia uncocked the revolver and dropped it on the desk. She could not trust this woman at first meeting, but Alyniana was desperate with her position on the line. That was useful, and she shared common foes in Kelosh, this Spirit Plague, and perhaps the Crimson Court. Better to keep her as a potential ally than lose her completely.

"If King Jazuk allows your proposal to reach the Chamber," Kasia said, "then I will voice my support and include what funding House Niezik can afford. I care for Nochland as my father did, but do not assume a Death Reacher's word carries the weight you hope it does." She prodded the locked book, yet another mystery for her to solve. "As for the Crimson Court… If you discover anything else about their intentions, return to me. Perhaps then we could help each other."

Alyniana rose and straightened her posture. "This nation… this realm… It is broken enough already. Do not make it worse through vengeance when you could help steer our ships to calmer shores."

Kasia looked to her, eyes grim, haunted. "I will do what I must."

"Of course." The ambassador started toward the door, then glanced over her shoulder. "If you change your mind, I will be in Kalastok for the foreseeable future."

"What of the Merchant Council's summons?"

Alyniana smirked. "It is a long trip to Litianitan. I have time until they realize something is amiss. However, your king must act quickly if we are to avert the vassalization of my country. We have a few hundred-hours at most until Keloshan soldiers arrive, and once they have dug their roots, there will be no removing them."

Kasia rounded the desk to show her out. "Then I hope his majesty acts with haste for once."

Alyniana caught Kasia's scarred arm softly, but she pulled it away, holding it across her chest. "Until I leave," Alyniana said. "I shall also look further into the roots of this awakened surge. The professor who discovered the disease, Etal ik Noshok, must know more if you can get past Kalastok College's quarantine."

"That will not be so simple, as we have tried already."

"A shame." Alyniana bowed. "Well, I wish you a restful evening and hope that, through our efforts, we may ensure that all in our nations have the chance to experience many more of them."

# INTO THE DARKNESS

*"The everdark is a gift as much as the everbright. Through it, the Crystal Mother tests us, molding us to use our abilities to Her will in even the most dire of times."*
– Bridgezet Tarizon, former anointed sister of the Buried Temple

Kasia doused the small study fireplace, each of its sparks distracting her as she ran her fingers over the locked book Alyniana had found.

Tazper stared longingly at the logs with an iron poker. Though a chill swept through the room, he knew better than to question her when she was so focused. She regretted that her fight with the anointed sister had lost him his chance to become a Reacher in the immediate future, but it was a distant worry compared to the riddle in her grasp.

*Seek.*

That solitary word glowed near the keyhole in old Piorakan script. Surely, this was her father's doing. But what answers lay within? Its purple binding resembled the color of the Children of Zekiaz mask hanging above the fireplace. That was only a color, though, and even Zinarus's house used purple for its sigil.

She stopped beside the game table and grabbed her father's haataamaash dragon, trying to think as he would've. What would he attach to seeking?

Setting down the piece, she hurried up the spiraling stairs to the rotunda above. Leonit's favorite tapestries from every country hung over the walls. One drew her attention most: *The Sage of Vitria.* It depicted Abraham-Tarin Lorria, an Ogrenian scientist, standing at the bow of a warship in the Vitrian Sea. Other ships approached from the right, but he looked left, toward a lush island covered in light amid the everdark.

*"The fool focuses merely on his enemies,"* her father had said as they sat against the railing and admired it together. *"If you must face those who oppose you, then have one eye still on your goal, as it may disappear the moment you look away."*

Ironically, Abraham-Tarin had perished after failing to direct his ship to fire against the Keloshan attackers depicted in the tapestry. Whatever discoveries he'd made on that final trip disappeared with him, and Leonit had mourned the loss. Kasia wondered whether her father had forgotten his enemies too. He'd obviously been aware of the Crimson Court, yet when they had come for him, he was woefully unprepared.

She froze, memories of the awakened attack piercing her mind again. She cursed herself for still succumbing to such flashes over a decade later, but they came without warning. Her chest felt tight, her breaths fleeting.

*Stay focused.*

She stepped closer to the tapestry, running her fingers over it to ground herself in the moment. Its threads were finely woven, and textures rose to add layering beyond just sight. She followed their lines to Abraham-Tarin himself. Was her father's key related to what the adventurer sought?

The island was too far to reach, so she shouted down the stairs. "Tazper, could you bring me a stool?"

A cacophony of noises came from below. Kasia winced, but decided it was better not to look at Tazper in the middle of his clumsy work. Though not always the best at his job, his presence was a reminder that she did need others, and she let herself smile as he appeared with a wooden stool held over his head. Sweat dripped from his brow.

"Crystal Mother below," he muttered. "How was it possible for me to bungle such a simple task?"

Kasia rolled her eyes but failed to wipe away her smirk. "Did you happen to break anything valuable?"

"Not at all." He set the stool down, then wiped his forehead with a handkerchief. "Unless you consider my pride valuable."

"Perhaps not valuable. Just fragile."

With a nod, he backed away to the railing to examine the tapestry. "Fair enough. What were you studying up here? Does it have anything to do with that book you were obsessed with during your meeting with Ambassador Alyniana?"

She frowned. "I was not obsessed with it!"

"That certainly explains why you spent more time looking at it than listening to her comments about the next war between the empires." He leaned back against the railing, his hair dipping over his forehead until he unceremoniously batted it away. "Any idea what's in it?"

She glanced back at him. Tazper's vocabulary matched that of the upper class of scions, but his mannerisms were a constant reminder that he came from a remote, poorer house with mixed scion-lowborn blood. The dichotomy created a combination that she could only describe as incredibly Tazper. Some ladies would scorn him for his lack of grace. She found it refreshing.

"I have no idea, to be honest," she replied, grabbing the stool and gathering her skirts as she stepped onto it. "Most of what my father left behind were old books from every nation I could name, but none were locked like this. He was a shrewd man. He wouldn't have left a clue like this unless he wanted someone to eventually open it—me."

"Kasia, you have servants like me to reach for things."

She ignored him as she probed at the tapestry's island. Lords and ladies alike were supposed to have their servants do such menial work, yes, but this was *her* discovery. The need to know more pushed her onward. Yes, the process looked ridiculous, but she was confident this was where the key would be.

Tazper tapped his foot. "Are you sure that is what Leonit's hint—"

"Tazper!" she snapped. "You may either stay and *quietly* help, or leave."

No reply came.

"Taz?"

Still nothing.

Kasia glared back at him, but he just stood perfectly still, his eyes fixed on his feet. Some part of her wanted to burst at the annoyance. Instead, she chuckled. "Spirits, Taz, I didn't expect you to take it so literally."

He shifted uncomfortably. "May I speak?"

"Yes, you may."

"There is a divot in the tapestry about two inches above where your left hand was."

She raised her brow. When she followed his instructions, though, her fingers slid into a small hole in the weave and found cold metal beneath. The key fell into the palm of her hand, and she clutched it as she jumped from the stool.

Tazper smiled like a child who'd stolen the last cookie. "Should I remain quiet, Lady Katarzyna?"

"I will throw you down the stairs," she quipped back with a roll of her eyes. "Thank you for the assistance, but I can certainly send you away before you see what Father left for me." He quieted, so she slid the small key into the lock. It twisted and opened with a satisfying *click*. The pages within were now hers, and she held her breath as she opened to the first page.

It was blank.

Kasia cursed and flipped to the next page. Blank. Then the next, and the next, and the next until she growled and tossed the book over the railing. A yelp came from below as it struck the study floor with a much louder *thud* than she'd expected.

"Ummm, Lady Katarzyna?" Kikania's small voice said from below. "Is everything all right? I heard you were alone with Tazper, so when I heard shouting, I came running."

Kasia traded embarrassed looks with her footman, cheeks burning, before she flung herself down the stairs nearly as fast as the book. She fixed her disheveled hair along the way. Spirits, did Kikania actually believe she was romantically involved with *Tazper*? He was practically her brother—on most days she wished he was instead of flaming Gregorzon—and they had spent plenty of time together without courting.

"We were investigating a locked book my father left behind," she said once she reached the study, eyeing the sprawled empty book between them. "Unfortunately, it turned out to be nothing."

Kikania pursed her lips as she bent down to pick up the book. She'd changed into her simple maid's dress with Alyniana's arrival, but she must have done so quickly, as her shift was visible above its neckline. "I'm sorry. Was the meeting with Ambassador Alyniana at least rewarding?"

Her reminder about the meeting struck Kasia hard. It had been mere minutes before, but she'd all but forgotten about it in her pursuit of the book's key. Little had come from the meeting, as she lacked the resources Nochland needed, but the knowledge that Kelosh intended to invade from multiple fronts was frightening. It altered the Commonwealth's situation from precarious to hopeless if they did not ally with Nochland.

Kasia had enough to worry about without dealing with a full-scale war. The Crimsons' demands returned to her as she grabbed a quill and began a letter to Zinarus, informing him of Alyniana's reveal. She'd left a signal for Nex to meet tomorrow, but due to Zinarus's status with the reformers, she couldn't meet with him too often in person. A letter would have to be enough. It, of course, had nothing to do with the gaping hole that opened in her chest whenever she thought of her panicked escape from his box, or the fact his absent father, Uzrin Ioniz, was a Crimson.

"Yes, in a way," she finally replied to Kikania. "But my focus is on the Crimsons, not Kelosh."

Tazper hurried down the steps after her. "What if they are working together?"

"I doubt it. Everyone who we've uncovered as members of the Crimsons are aligned with the nationalists or conservatives. It is in their interests to protect the Commonwealth, not hand it over and lose all the power they seem to be protecting."

A knock came from the front door below.

Kasia furrowed her brow. Alyniana had come late, but having two evening visitors was an extreme rarity. Unless the ambassador had returned?

She headed down the stairs with Tazper and Kikania at her flanks. Whoever it was, their call must've been urgent to come at this hour. So she pushed her worries about Leonit's book away as she opened the door to reveal a short figure dressed in a dark coat and wide hat.

"We've got a problem," Nex said, their nose wrinkled.

ONE HOUR BEFORE

**NEX PERCHED ATOP A BUILDING** at the heart of Kalastok's Market District, the everdark hanging over them like a veil. Goosebumps ran across their arms as a wind blew from the west. Both anxiety and chill.

Every time Nex blinked, they saw Vinnia lying on their shared bed with her eyes growing ever darker. Allying with Kasia Niezik could bring answers in time, but they had none. The amber she'd given Nex had done nothing for Vinnia. Neither had Paras's medicine.

They'd waited on that rooftop for at least an hour now. For what? All they could do was watch shadowed people walk between rings of lamplight before disappearing into their homes. The city fell asleep around Nex, but they would find no rest until Vinnia was safe. Kasia had left a signal to meet tomorrow, meaning Nex would have to admit they'd discovered nothing. Maybe the scion had been more successful.

As Nex eyed the main southern road, an unusual figure appeared from an alley near the clocktower.

Most Ezmani scions wore grays and blacks with splashes of color, but this woman's coat held a thousand radiant flowers in even the dimmest of light. Like Nex, she wore a head covering. This woman, though, had a headscarf that veiled all but her face, while Nex pulled down their hat to cover almost their entire left eye. Nex had seen her leaving the Crystal Palace before, but she was definitely not an Ezmani scion.

Nex's raven black coat clipped at their heels as they took off at a run, leaping from building to building as they followed the woman down the street. No lady walked Kalastok's streets alone this late at night, and Nex's gut told them this would be interesting.

The woman headed toward The Confluence along the Kala. Why? The scions of the great houses met often during the day, and clandestine encounters at night rarely happened at their townhouses.

Nex stopped on the rooftop across from The Confluence. Without any light beyond the lamps below, they were near invisible as the woman entered the Niezik townhouse, followed by a flurry of activity from within. The woman appeared in a second-story window for a moment before disappearing again, and Nex questioned why they were spying on Kasia. It wasn't like they would learn anything from staring across the street. Yet they did so anyway, tensing at even the thought of returning home without any way to help Vinnia.

So they waited until the woman emerged from the townhouse a short while later and walked back the way she'd come from. Nex followed, hoping to learn who she was. That would at least make their prowling this night not a *complete* waste.

After a few turns, the woman entered a street whose lamps flickered. A new chill raised the hairs on Nex's neck, and they held their breath, stumbling back onto the roof with awakened diving past them.

The spirits took the form of nightmarish beasts as a red robed man appeared from the shadows at the street's end, gripping a decapitated head by its hair. A strip of magical darkness covered the man's eyes and nose but stopped before his lips, which curled into a savage smile. Nex had only heard about men like him.

*Dark Reacher...*

"We found your little message boy," the Reacher said, tossing the head at the woman's feet. "Your letter made it to the princess, but rest assured, it won't matter in the end."

Nex Reached instinctively into the realm of Possibility. Confidence came with it. Reaching allowed them to manipulate reality and its future chances, but it was unpredictable. Object switching and luck-bringing were incredible if they worked. But Possibility seemed to have its own will.

The woman tried to scream as the awakened dragged her into the air, but no sound came out. She disappeared into the distance, drowned by a blackness heavier than the everdark. None of the Spirit Reacher towers scanned the area. *Weird.*

Lamplight returned moments later. It illuminated both the bloodied scalp and the red robes of the Dark Reacher. He stood there for a long minute, grinning with that strip of darkness covering his eyes and nose before he walked north. The darkness expanded over his face and body until he was near invisible

Nex kept their gaze fixed on the movement of his ethereal darkness. He headed north through the Market District, so they tailed him from roof to roof, leaping over countless alleys until they were forced to hop awkwardly over a strange object.

They tumbled into a roll with a glance back over their shoulder. A Vockan newborn lay on a flat step between the shingles, a failing candle resting beside a woven nightjar that Nex had kicked in their fall. Cursing, they snatched the nightjar and placed it back by the child. It didn't weep or move as it stared into the dark sky. Still a husk, then. Vockans in Kalastok followed their old traditions for luring spirits to newborns, and it made life difficult for Nex to creep along the roofs. But life in Kalastok sucked enough for non-Ezmani without their child being a husk. Odd nightjar trinket or not, the kid would need all the help it could get.

Of course, the distraction had taken Nex's gaze off the Reacher.

*Where'd you go, asshole?*

They eyed the place he'd been moments before. At first, there was nothing, but a shadow shifted out of the corner of their eye. Everdark had allowed the awakened to carry the woman into the sky.

The lights here, though, exposed the Reacher's pure darkness as he passed beneath a tree and crunched a leaf underfoot.

Nex continued on the rooftops. Most before had been close enough to not need Possibility's luck, but further north in the Market District, Nex struggled for balance with each jump. Even with their practice running on sloped roofs, the shingles often made enough noise to make them question their stealth. But it was better than risking jumping to street level. Kasia would want to know who had taken the woman she'd met with. He was obviously a Crimson, so he could lead them to others.

And answers.

He'd *controlled* those awakened. Did that mean the Crimsons knew more about the Spirit Plague transforming its victims into spirits? Were the Crimsons the cause?

Nex focused on running to avoid the anxiety rising in their chest. Worries would paralyze them when Vinnia needed them most.

Nex's advances drew short as the Dark Reacher neared the Crimson District. Few people had walked the streets before, but here, lines of rifle-wielding watchmen blocked the way toward the palace, their red and gold uniforms matching the robe the Reacher had worn when visible. Everyone was on edge after the Ephemeral Slaughter, and Nex had no doubt the riots beforehand had made the scions nervous too. Sure, they claimed the quarantine was to stop the disease, but it kept the poorest lowborn out of the eastern city too. Not Nex, obviously. But normal people.

A man and woman argued with the watchmen at the main road to the palace. They were far, but the man's exaggerated gestures said enough. Unfortunately for him, his arguing drew the attention of another group: the Crystal Brigade.

With bracers of pure glass clasped over their bright red and white uniforms, three of the elite watchmen circled on horseback. Each extended their taloned hands toward the couple, who screamed as the leader of the watchmen dismounted before them.

"What business do you have in the Crimson District at this late hour?" he barked.

The Dark Reacher slipped past with the distraction, heading

through the gardens beyond at a brisk walk. Nex bit their cheek and eyed a jumpable place on the wall to the right of the guards. The bench there would give them enough of a lift with the guards looking the other direction, but timing their run poorly would mean getting caught by the Crystal Brigade. They were the great houses' Reacher hunters. Being a Possibility Reacher wouldn't get Nex out of their grasp.

So Nex took longer than they should've before leaping to the streets with their breath held. They landed with a roll. It was a difficult move, and they tripped over themselves. The guards were still distracted, though, and didn't notice Nex climbing the wall and dropping to the other side.

Their feet found a maintenance shed's dark, flat roof… then its edge.

Arms flailing, Nex tried to leap onto a bush ahead, but it was too far. They hit the ground *hard.*

The wind left their lungs, and it took all their energy just to breathe as they staggered back to their feet. Cold sweat clung to their brow, and they leaned against the wall to keep themselves upright.

*Shit!* Had they alerted the guards?

Shouting came from the path splitting the gardens, so Nex bolted around the bushes before looping back to a cluster of buildings at the eastern side of the gardens. The guards didn't follow. They were too busy torturing the scion couple with what sounded like Truth Reaching, compelling them to tell the guards everything. Nex had heard countless stories of what happened when tricksters like them were caught trying to steal from the scions' gambling houses. Poor spirits, but not Nex's problem. Their problem had disappeared.

Nex fixed their hat and shook their head. The Dark Reacher had disappeared somewhere through the gardens. With the guards watching, there was no way Nex could risk following blindly. Better to get back to Kasia with some information than be beaten to death by the Crystal Brigade.

They headed east into the residential Drifters' Quarter, skirting along the edge of the jousting arena to avoid the lights from the Spirit

Reacher towers. Shadowed forms occasionally passed through the beams before the Reachers banished them. Instead, the awakened and drifters alike would fall upon Kalastok's west side and its outskirts, where lowborn had nothing but impure glass amulets to protect themselves.

The Confluence soon came into sight again, and Nex's muscles tensed as they approached the door and knocked. It didn't matter who the scion was. They preferred stealing from the rich, not working with them.

They stepped back when Kasia, not a servant, answered the door.

"We've got a problem," they muttered with a glance over their shoulder to make sure no one had followed.

Kasia furrowed her brow but waved them in. Their skin crawled as they stepped into the foyer. From the chandelier to the intricately carved banister, this small area alone contained more wealth than any building Nex had been in before. It made them want to flee and grab something expensive-looking on the way out, but they held their ground for Vinnia's sake.

Once Nex reluctantly gave up their coat to a maid, Kasia led them and a young male servant up to the third floor. They passed no windows, but this was a different room than the one Kasia had met the other woman in. Why? Did rich scions just pick rooms at their leisure while lowborn slept, ate, bathed, and shat in the same one?

Nex's disdain faded when the warmth of the fireplace of the sitting room outside Kasia's chambers met their chilled cheeks. Kasia took a seat on the sofa, crossing her legs as the servant waited by the door with his arms folded. He was trying *very* hard to be intimidating, but there was no fooling Nex. This was no bodyguard.

"Please, sit," Kasia said. "You look frigid. Can I have Tazper fetch you a Reshkan tea or perhaps some warm water?"

Nex writhed under the assumption they needed help. "I'm fine."

"Then why have you broken our agreement and come directly to me at this hour?" Kasia asked. "We were supposed to meet tomorrow." Her tone wasn't sharp, but there was a hint of annoyance in it.

"Thought you'd want to know the Crimsons took your friend."

She furrowed her brow. "How did you discover this? Alyniana left not that long ago."

Nex just shrugged and circled to one of the wide chairs, throwing themself into it with no grace. "I watch things. Saw her come out of your townhouse before some awakened showed up and nabbed her. There was this Dark Reacher in red robes too. Tried to follow him, but he was Reaching. Lost him when some guards blocked the way to the Crimson District."

"The Crimson District? Hmm. There are many scion families with townhouses or estates there, notably House Pikezik."

"Do the Pikeziks like this woman?"

"Likely not," Kasia said, scratching her burn scar. "She is the Nochland ambassador to the Commonwealth. Lilita and Chatik Pikezik don't sit with the nationalists in the Chamber, but their conservatives aren't all that fond of Nochland's constant requests for aid either."

Nex smirked. "Then it's them."

Kasia gave a wry smile but shook her head. "It isn't that simple. House Pikezik has dozens of adult men, any one of whom could be a Crimson like the one Radais found in the Wastes. And that's not considering the other small houses who reside near the palace."

"Not just anyone could run an organization whose roots are this deep," Tazper replied, to Nex's surprise. Didn't scions beat servants for speaking out of turn?

"Tzena is only the niece of Gornioz Oliezany," Kasia said, "but she seemed to hold power over Sazilz—a great house magnate. Perhaps this Dark Reacher is a more influential man in House Pikezik. This isn't enough to act on, or to change that I need to kill Paras."

Nex shot up, trying to get to the door but instead tripping over the stupid rug. They toppled into the fireplace mantle and sent multiple statuettes crashing to the ground. "Uhh… That wasn't supposed to happen."

Kasia studied the destroyed statuettes. "Care to explain why you decided to flee and destroy some quite overpriced sculptures?"

"You want to kill Paras." Nex's voice shook, but they couldn't stop it. Kasia was a Death Reacher and could kill them any second. "You'd only do that if you actually want to help the Crimsons. Didn't want you to kill me too."

"Spirits help me..." Kasia pointed to the chair Nex had been seated in. "Sit down."

Slowly, Nex complied, hopping over the broken silver and marble statuettes. A voice came from outside before they could speak.

"Katarzyna?" a man said. "Is all well up there?"

Kasia rolled her eyes. "Yes, Uncle Faniz. I was a bit clumsy is all."

"Be sure to respect your constitution, young lady. You do not wish to end up as frail as I before it is your time!" The man finished with a series of coughs that echoed through the townhouse before the creaking floor revealed him returning to another room.

Kasia returned her attention to Nex. "Apologies for my great-uncle. More importantly, I must ensure you understand that I have no intentions of aiding the Crimson Court. I do, however, need to earn their favor if we have any hope of uncovering their plans and whether they are connected to the Spirit Plague. That means that I must kill Paras ik Lierasa, yes."

"But he's our only hope!"

"What did you discover with the amber piece I gave you? Did you show it to him?"

Nex's shoulders slumped. "He wouldn't talk to me. I tried to see if the amber could help Vinnia, but it didn't work. Neither did the potion his assistant sold me."

"Didn't work, you say?" Kasia scooted forward. "Have you known anyone who has actually recovered after drinking his potions?"

Nex thought for a moment, remembering Vinnia's stories from the factory and the rumors passed around Beg Ave. "Don't know anyone who's gotten better from the Plague."

"And you don't find that odd?"

"I guess."

Kasia threw out her arms. "If no one has recovered, then Paras is lying! He's selling thousands of bottles of this fake potion because people are desperate, and he's the only one claiming to have an answer."

"You sure you're not just thinking of excuses?" Nex replied. "Killing him won't help fix Vin..." They cut themselves off, regretting the slip instantly. This was why they acted as someone else around other people. It was too easy to reveal things when they were just Nex.

If Kasia noticed, she chose not to pry. "Paras is stealing from infected people, Nex. You want him to get away with it?"

Nex closed their eyes and pictured the metal bottle they'd bought from him. They had been so sure it would fix Vinnia, but instead, she had only gotten worse. Kasia's help was the only reason they'd been able to pay for it. Other lowborn weren't so lucky, and Paras charged a hundred-hour's wages for a single bottle. He'd lied to Nex, told them his potion would save the woman they loved. Just like the scions.

"Kill him then," they muttered. "But promise me you'll find another way to end the disease."

Kasia averted her gaze. "I will do all I can."

"Promise me!" Nex snapped, shooting to their feet. "I've lost everyone I care about. Don't let me lose her too!"

The matriarch rose and approached Nex. She was a few inches taller than them, and she cast a long shadow as she tried to take their hands. Nex stuffed them in their pockets instead.

"I'm sorry someone you love is infected," Kasia insisted. "The Crimsons took my father from me. If they are behind the Spirit Plague, then they must know a cure. I will find it, and I will make them pay. I promise you that, but I will need your help to get across the river without anyone suspecting me."

"Fine." Nex took a sharp breath. "What about your friend, the ambassador?"

"I fear I'm of little use to her until I do what the Crimsons ask. Luckily, I chose not to reveal my true intentions with her." Kasia stepped aside and gestured toward the door. "Thank you, Nex. Our partnership is already bearing fruit, and I hope that next time, we can arrange a meeting through our agreed upon method."

"Don't send me out the door," Nex said. "They're definitely watching you."

"What, then?"

"A window." Nex held up their left hand with the Possibility ring upon it. "I've lucky when I Reach, and I'm pretty quick on my feet."

Kasia scoffed. "Like you were so dexterous with that rug?"

Nex pushed past her to hide their blush. "I was rushed then. This will be fine."

Kasia nodded to Tazper, who waved for Nex to follow. He led them out of the sitting room and onto a balcony overlooking the Vazinarik Stream where it met the Kala River. Nex stepped to the railing and hopped onto it, glaring at the Crystal Palace which rose in the distance. Bloodied red and bird shit white. A stain with its scions smothering the rest of the city.

"Best of luck," Tazper said as the maid rushed to return Nex's coat to them. "And I am sorry about Kasia. She is passionate, but she sometimes forgets that others have the same pain as her."

Nex ignored him, focusing instead on their target: the neighboring townhouse's back room with a domed ceiling and panels of glass to let the light in. Everbright rooms, Nex had heard them called when gambling with scions. Apparently, doctors claimed it was healthy for scions to sit in the light for a long time, but Nex wondered why scions couldn't just go outside like everyone else.

The jump was a tough angle, but Nex was sure they could make it. Probably.

Nex Reached, then jumped. A burst of rainbow Possibility wisps swirled around them amid the evening haze, the The Confluence's warmth relenting to the dull chill of reality. They struck the everbright room's roof and rolled right into its dome. Their ribs ached from the impact, but they hauled themselves on top. It gave a perfect view of western Kalastok. Almost looked pretty.

But Nex knew the ugly truth. Their side of the river had been horrible before the quarantine, and now, the Spirit Plague and lack of resources slowly choked the lowborn. Nex had hoped for a cure, but Paras's miracle had been a lie. Vinnia would die unless Kasia could infiltrate the Crimsons. That meant taking the scion into Kalastok's west side. Nex scoffed.

*She'll get eaten alive.*

# EVERYTHING RETURNS TO ASH

*"It is only one's spirit that continues on after death. All else returns from whence it came. We were all once nothing more than ash, so shall we be once again."* – An excerpt from *The Crystal Book*

"You want to do *what*?" Radais stammered from atop Vuk. His team had been mere steps away from leaving Palmia Fortress's gate when Miv stopped them.

The supreme defender sat tall on her own ibex, her gaze stern. "This journey has become more important than my duties here. I've received reports every day about new awakened attacks. Whatever is causing this lies in the Wastes, and I refuse to sit in this frigid fortress while you confront it."

"Who will lead the Glassblades here?" Radais asked with a wave toward his remaining compatriots. Part of him wanted Miv to take the burden of command from his shoulders, but his feelings for her would be an unneeded distraction.

"We have a chain of command for this very reason. Besides, you've seen this place. There are nearly as many warriors in your band as there are remaining within these walls."

Mhanain huffed from behind them. "Thought you sent Wanusa to spy on us. Now you're comin' too? Shit. I shoulda stayed back."

Miv furrowed her brow. The glare wasn't directed at Radais, but it made him wince anyway. "You can stay and clean chamber pots for the rest of your life, or you can shut that stupid mouth of yours. What'll it be?"

"Aye, Supreme Defender," Mhanain muttered. "Welcome to the team."

"That's better." She spun around. "Anyone else want to complain? No? Good. Best we be off then before another blizzard hits."

Radais gritted his teeth but followed her out the gate. Its lanterns barely pierced the everdark beyond, and he couldn't help but feel a weight in his chest as the darkness fell over them. Mhanain lit a match and passed it around for each of them to light their own lanterns. It did little to help as they passed through the village of Palmia and wound up the western road.

Drifters lurked in the mountain shadows, swirling around the light in their silent forms. A whisper hovered among them, but Radais shook the sound from his head. Fear would not best him. He'd trained to tell awakened from drifters for twenty years. What Miv hadn't taught him, though, was how to trust his instincts when he was hearing things that weren't real. Facing awakened in the Wastes was hard enough without facing oneself.

He closed his eyes and focused on the rhythmic clanking of his glass armor instead. Most modern soldiers would consider it cumbersome compared to their own uniforms, but riding in full armor was home to Radais. Spirits knew his true home didn't want him anymore.

Days passed as they followed the trail toward the Spirit Wastes. In the everdark, Radais could hardly tell if they were still in living lands or not. Snow and ash looked all too similar in the dim lanternlight. The winds carried both into his eyes, and he flinched with each movement in his peripherals. The awakened wouldn't keep their distance forever, but Miv showed no such worry in front of him. She rode on at a steady pace, never tarrying until it was time to make camp each evening. Even then, she rarely spoke.

"Can you tell me what you saw in her?" Lazan asked Radais as they settled into their shared tent. Each of them split rations and supplies with another Glassblade to keep weight down. Foraging would be impossible, and the last thing any of them wanted was to starve in the Wastes.

"A passionate flame that never stops," Radais replied, pulling out his sketchpad.

Lazan wriggled his jaw as he flattened his bedroll. "There is a saying among scions that meddling with a Fire Reacher will end with you burned. To me, it seems Miv is a recipe for agony."

"I've had my fair share."

"No share of it is fair, and there's enough suffering in this realm already without you chasing a woman who obviously does not want to be caught."

Radais looked up from his pad with a frown. "I'm not chasing her anymore. That was many years ago."

"Of course," Lazan quipped before ripping the sketchpad from Radais's hands. "Is that why you were drawing her just now?"

"Damn Body Reacher!" Radais replied, laughing uncomfortably. Spirits, he needed a stiff drink, but there were few to be had with such slim supplies. "Fine! I am still fond of her. Are you happy now?"

Lazan turned to the previous sketch. "So… What is this piece about me for then?"

The scion's cheeks resembled the everbright sun against his gray skin and hair, and Radais cursed not having the utensils to bring color into his art. He cursed himself, too, for allowing his sketches to be so easily stolen. "Not all my art is about infatuations. You'll find mountains and random people in there as well. We traveled together for a few hundred-hours, so of course I drew you a few times."

"Well, I am flattered regardless."

Lazan tossed the book back, and Radais clutched it close to his chest like a mother who'd just found her lost babe. "I ask that you respect my privacy. My drawing is… disrespected… among most Glassblades. We're warriors, not artists, but it helps me keep grounded and remember why I do this."

"Why did you join the Glassblade Order?" Lazan asked as he lay on his side. "Most initiates I've spoken to said their family needed the money, but yours despised you for leaving."

Radais sighed, tucking his chin into his chest. "I wanted to prove I was worth something, that I was strong enough. In truth, though, I was running from my father's expectations and my brother's scorn."

"What did you find?"

"I don't know yet." He met Lazan's gaze, heart heavy. "I've done a lot since I joined the Glassblades, but I feel the most like myself when I'm away from them, riding in the mountains with the pure spirits."

Lazan opened his mouth to reply, but Radais quickly stood and threw his book aside. "I need some air." He wasn't on watch until later that night, but someone would eagerly take the chance to sleep. There was no way he'd manage to rest with his thoughts lingering on the past.

He didn't check if Lazan watched him leave. It seemed obvious, though, and he questioned what was happening between the two of them. Was this a brotherly friendship or something else? It didn't feel like the burn in his core around Miv, but a warmth that pushed away the everdark cold.

Wanusa kept watch at the ridgeline above, arms held behind her back and her legs shoulder width apart—just like an initiate was taught. Any Glassblade with enough experience knew those stern protocols faded away from Palmia. This was the wild, not a fortress, and the warrior pacing beside her was taking advantage.

"You look like a drunk mercenary more than a Glassblade," Radais scolded the man, stopping before him. His armor was crooked, and he dragged the tip of his blade through the snow. Unacceptable.

The man's eyes widened. "Master Radais… I… err… Sorry, sir."

Radais nodded toward Wanusa. "Might want to learn from the initiate. You'd get us all killed if the awakened struck on your watch. Let me take this shift, and you can have mine. Better be focused come that time."

"Yes sir! I will."

"Then go." The man scrambled off, and Radais stopped beside Wanusa, taking a more casual stance. "At ease. You'll stress your legs standing stiff like that all night."

Wanusa grimaced. "Supreme Defender Miv said—"

"Yeah, she taught me too, and I can tell you this job will kill you if you're obsessed with orders instead of what's right in the moment."

He looked over the ridgeline, where the lanterns cast shadows over the dispersed trees. Most lost their leaves in the everdark, but these held onto sharp needles that Vockan folktales claimed were to keep spirits from feeding on them. A few drifters lingered around these. Initiates often worried that awakened would hide among their harmless counterparts, but they were mindless beasts. They knew nothing of stealth or trickery. At least, they never had before.

"Do you ever wonder why they stay near us?" Wanusa asked, relaxing a bit. "Awakened feed on our spirits, but what about drifters?"

Radais shrugged. "They are the pure creations of the Spirit Crystal. Why would they need anything more than to exist in its realm?"

"They must have some purpose. Have you ever touched one?"

"No. It's forbidden." He eyed a drifter that approached, its misty, indistinct form like some eight-legged insect. "They are purely spirit, while we've been tainted by the realms of Mind, Body, and Life."

She scoffed and adjusted her armor. Initiates began with only a glass breastplate, and Radais worried she'd be unprotected the further they traveled into the Wastes. Tradition was tradition, though. He'd made plenty of journeys, earning his armor piece by piece, so she would too.

"You scolded me a moment ago for being 'obsessed with orders,' " Wanusa said. "Now you tout old folktales."

Radais quieted, scanning the darkness for awakened. He didn't owe her a reply to that. Old folktales or not, most Vockans thought the same as him. Spirits were not to be interfered with. Corrupted awakened were the exception.

The night passed with little change until Wanusa finally sighed, her breath fogging the air before them. "The drifters are still there."

"Yes, they are."

"Why aren't they called lingerers then?" she quipped.

Radais chuckled. "Because it is an annoying word to say, and not all of them stay."

"Then why do these? You have to wonder about them sometimes instead of just swinging a blade!" She held out an open hand toward them. "I've seen you with that charcoal. What do you see beneath the mist? Sure, they're 'pure,' but what in crystal hell do you think that means?"

"I'm shocked to hear you curse," Radais said.

Digging her boot into the snow, her head dropped. "Sorry, Master Radais. I'm just tired. They train us for a lot, but this…"

"It's okay to be afraid. I am."

She shot her gaze back to him.

"Close that jaw," he said. "Fear is a good thing. It's our natural sense of danger, and there's no such thing as courage without it."

Something flickered in her eyes. "Fine, then."

She trudged through the deeper snow, heading toward the drifters. Radais watched her with bemusement. Oh, how easy it had been to do stupid things as an initiate.

"Your boots will fill with snow," he called after her. "It'll annoy you for the next hundred-hour."

But Wanusa just straightened her posture and continued on. Strangely, the drifters responded to her presence, moving ever closer without making contact. They formed a circle, and Radais could barely see through them as she crouched to examine something.

"What in the spirits are you doing?" he asked.

"I knew it!" she shouted back, pawing at the snow. "They're lingering for a reason. Come look at this."

Radais took a long breath and muttered a complaint about his aching knees before climbing down the hill. Unlike Wanusa, he studied the terrain and kept to the shallower sections of snow. He took some pride in his dry feet as he reached the ring of drifters. They did not part for him.

"What is it?" he pressed again. "They're blocking my sight."

"You can push through them," she replied. "They're harmless."

*Why did I offer to take watch?*

He sauntered forward, drawing his blade and extending his other hand toward the nearest drifter. How had he never touched one? It seemed ridiculous, but his father would've beaten him senseless as a child if he'd tried. His father was gone now. It was just him, Wanusa, and the spirits. No one would need to know.

Wanusa waved a hand in his direction. "You might want to remove that gauntlet if you don't want them to run."

"And if I want them to?"

She shook her head. "Then you'd ruin the point I'm trying to prove. Sheathe your sword too. There's no awakened here, and you can't confront everything with a blade."

"Tell that to my brother," Radais mumbled, but complied. He was curious. Another feeling was there too—fear. Why? He'd seen thousands of drifters in his life, but so often they had been distant. This felt far too close to beings he'd been taught to worship, almost intimate.

His fingers pressed into the mist which formed the drifter. It split into spiraling wisps of gray in the lanternlight, yet did not move away, the mist simply re-forming wherever Radais's hand wasn't. A tingling sensation ran down his arm and raised its hairs, but he pushed onward. The drifter was neither solid nor fully air. Instead, it was as if some unexplainable presence danced along his skin within the drifter's form.

"I had always imagined them to be cold, like a damp cloth," he said to Wanusa. "This… I was very wrong."

Before Wanusa could reply, he stepped fully through the drifter. It shot up the moment his glass armor met its body, and it rippled like a bird aggressively flapping its wings when one strayed too close to its nest.

"That was bound to happen," Wanusa said. "Here, look."

She knelt over the hole she'd dug, the snow giving way to a dull gray glow. A patch of crystal no larger than Radais's fist. But crystal was crystal.

It was a fragment of the very Spirit Crystal that formed the core of the realm of Zekiaz, and it only neared the surface in a few rare spots. Kalastok's vast reserves had made it a powerful city for centuries. This was hardly that, but even a small chunk was worth enough to buy a rural estate far larger than the meager home Radais's family had crammed into throughout his childhood. He could split it with Wanusa and still live a comfortable life for the rest of his years. No more wandering. No more fighting.

Did he really want that?

"They're attracted to the crystal!" Wanusa exclaimed. "It must be the reason they're here. Look! Even the one you scared off is still keeping near."

Radais grabbed her shoulder. "Back away! They may be here to protect it."

"I already touched it," she appealed, pulling herself free. "They didn't seem to care."

"Is that why they surrounded us? Look around you! This many awakened could tear us to pieces with our blades sheathed."

Wanusa wrinkled her nose and stood, spinning to face him. Her superior height made him want to back down, but that would mean stepping through the drifters again. "There is no protocol regarding Spirit Crystal. If you want to be a coward, then fine. I'll take it for myself."

Radais snatched her arm when she reached for the crystal. "Think about why they are here. Maybe they feed upon its power. Taking it could kill them!"

"They are not living. That's the awakened." She looked at her trapped arm and sighed. "How about this: We leave part of it behind and split the rest? Each of us will have enough for at least five Ezmani talons or more black market rings. That is plenty to change both of our lives."

"I didn't take you for one willing to sell to the black market."

She winced. "Yeah, well… When you grow up with nothing, raising your siblings while your parents waste away in some smokehouse, you take what you can get."

Radais let go, his heartache returning. "I understand. My family hates me for leaving, but I send them more than I keep. Split the crystal. At least there will be some left for the pure ones."

Wanusa smacked the crystal with the butt of her dagger until three roughly equal pieces remained. Radais winced in expectation of the drifters' aggression. None came, and a heavy silence fell over them as Wanusa rose with two fragments in hand. She held one out to him.

"You didn't find it, but your prodding sent me after the drifters in the first place. I guess that earns you a share."

Radais took the piece. It was lighter than he'd expected, with its jagged sides just large enough to fill the palm of his hand. A presence pulsed within it, like a heartbeat that joined with the one in his chest. Anticipation filled him as he reached out to it with his mind, but there was no reply.

"Do you ever wonder why we can't Reach?" he asked. "Vockans, Ezmani lowborn, whoever else… What's different about the scions?"

"Every child wonders the first time they see a Reacher," she replied with her fragment held into the lanternlight. "Why are they better than me? Could I ever be that powerful?" She lowered the fragment, dangling loose between her fingers. "No. We can't."

Radais eyed the drifters. "Power is about more than Reaching. That sword you wield can do more against awakened than any Reacher, except maybe a Death one. All the Reachers in the realm couldn't save the Piorakan Empire, but the Glassblade Order survived."

"Look at us now. Scattered, poorly. If this Second Awakening is really happening, what power do we have to stop it?"

Radais huffed and stepped through the drifter, committing that feeling of its mists against his skin to memory. "We have our helms, our blades, and our knowledge. If we succeed on this trek, we'll know more about what's happening than any king or Reacher. It's not enough alone, but I have an ally… a friend… back in Kalastok."

Wanusa hesitated. "Knowing so much makes us targets. Doesn't it?"

"Likely, yes."

"Wonderful." Wanusa stomped her boots, and Radais held in a chuckle at the familiar look on her face. "Alright, maybe you were right about the whole snow in the boots thing."

He trudged on. "Experience does have its benefits."

# THE ALCHEMIST

*"Who lives? Who dies? Are these questions for judges, kings, generals, or only the Crystal Mother herself? The answer is simple. Anyone can bring Death. But only Reachers of its realm can make such death permanent."* – Garziak Pikezik, the first known Death Reacher in the Commonwealth

Lamplight gave way to the everdark as Kasia approached the northern King's Bridge. There were gas lamps illuminating its stonework construction on the east bank, but with the quarantine, none were supposed to cross from either side. Three watchmen awaited those too determined or foolish to heed the message.

They scrambled from their game of cards at the sight of Kasia in the light of their single lantern, hung upon the makeshift wooden barrier at the bridge's center. "Halt! The west side is under quarantine by order of the king and Chamber of Scions. Turn back for your own safety."

"I'm going to my family," she replied, gloved hands raised as she mimicked a lowborn accent. "I know I can't leave once I go in."

Under normal circumstances, she would've flaunted her name, but the residents of Kalastok's west side wouldn't trust a scion, especially considering her recent voting. Nex had claimed the watchmen never bothered anyone crossing into the west side, especially if they came for family, so she wore the simple woolen coat and trousers of a lowborn instead. They itched horribly, but that was the least of her concerns. She would kill an innocent man today. Not her first.

The lead watchman lowered his gun. "What? Are you stupid or something? Damn disease probably killed your family already. Bet by now there's more awakened than living over there."

"You don't know?" Kasia asked. Had no one gone to help?

"Our job's to shoot anyone tryin' to get out. That's it."

"Then I'm no concern of yours."

Another of them scoffed. "Sure you don't want to spend some time with us instead? Cold night to be your last."

She pushed past them, hands in her pockets as she gripped the handle of her father's revolver. These men were swine, but Reaching now would create a time limit she didn't need. A gun would have to do if they tried to stop her.

"C'mon," the second watchman said, snatching her left arm. "Can't let you through for free can—"

*BANG!*

Kasia's bullet ripped through the man's skull. Her ears rang from the shot, her heart hammering in her chest, but there was no time to waver. The two others scrambled for their rifles. Too quickly for her to shoot them both.

She fired at the lead watchman while Reaching and releasing a death bolt at the other. The shot struck the watchman's shoulder, sending him sprawling as Death claimed his comrade. Kasia staggered back.

"Another one," Aliax said, standing over the decaying man with his arms crossed. "Can't say he didn't deserve it, but Paras? Are you really going to do this?"

Kasia's aim wavered as the remaining watchman crawled away. It should've been easy. He was as defenseless as he'd believed her to be, but that only made the trigger feel more like an execution than an act of self-defense. Should she have ignored him and kept walking, pulling her arm away as if he'd said nothing? Was this not justice?

Aliax groaned. "Don't just stand there! His friends will come soon. You've come this far, and I'd rather not watch you join me in this miserable non-existence."

"You hate me killing them," she breathed.

"I hate what Death Reaching has made you."

An alarm bell clanged. The watchman had managed to drag himself to it and grab the rope hanging beneath. Shouts answered from the east bank, and Kasia cursed as she looked from Aliax to the man.

"I don't have a choice, Ali!"

Aliax shook his head. "You made it when you crossed this bridge. Life is more than revenge."

He stepped aside, revealing the shadowed forms sprinting toward Kasia. She didn't need to see more to know they had guns in hand. Time was up.

Taking a long, haggard breath, she raised her father's pistol toward the watchman. "You shouldn't have threatened me."

She pulled the trigger and ran before she could see the damage her bullet wrought. Her right ear rang from the shot. It covered the sound of the watchmen's reinforcements, but they closed in. If they had rifles, they would likely gun her down before she reached the bridge's end. Luckily, the greed of the scions had ensured the watchmen remained under-funded compared to the great house mercenaries. Only pistol fire rang out, and the bullets sprayed the stonework strides behind her as her boots found the dirt road on the other shore.

Darkness greeted her, only a few scattered lanterns over businesses' doorways illuminating the infamous sign that marked the road she stood upon. *Beg Ave.*

She regarded the sign before bolting to her right. The largest settlement of homeless peasants wasn't far down the path, and it would be her best chance to hide from the watchmen. No one in their right mind would try attacking the homeless of Beg Ave. Reachers and the crystal dragon were powerful, but it was damn near impossible to defeat a mob of people who had nothing to lose. All Kasia had to do was blend in until the watchmen passed.

Then she would find Paras.

It sounded so simple, but a fresh panic swarmed her mind as she neared the firelights of the homeless. Scion soldiers had told her countless stories of their heroic battles during galas and their visits to the Niezik estate. They boasted of their kills like Kasia had with her father after outwitting a rival house. None of them spoke about how brutal it was to shoot a man in the face. Spirits, she was a Death Reacher, but that didn't make it any easier. Neither did knowing that it had been her or them.

"The Crimson Court cares little for lowborn deaths, even watchmen," Sazilz said, taking a vague form beneath the awning of a decrepit shop. "If you seek to keep them believing this ruse of yours, you will have to kill many more before the everbright returns."

Kasia's stomach curled. Yet she ran on, entering the clearing where the homeless gathered around fires built within crude metal boxes. She worried they'd see her as the outsider she was. Her walk, her smell, or her stature would surely give her away among them, but none gave her a second glance. To them, she was just another desperate woman seeking refuge. There was something beautiful about that anonymity.

The watchmen reached the clearing not long after, shouting with pistols raised as Kasia threw herself onto a tree stump alongside one of the fires. A mother clutched her child across the smoke from her. In this darkness, she could've been any nationality. All suffered the same here, and their frail bodies mirrored those gathered around the other fires. The Spirit Plague would rip through them if it hadn't already. How many in this city block alone were infected?

"Put away the gun," the mother whispered. "It'll only bring more trouble here!"

Kasia's eyes widened as she looked down at her hands. Her talon was exposed, and she'd never pocketed the pistol in her panic. She did now before throwing a glove back over her talon. Shit! Had anyone seen she was a Reacher? Rumors would spread if they had.

A crowd gathered around the watchmen. Malnourished or not, they threw bits of scrap metal, stones, and burning sticks as the watchmen backed away. Kasia held her breath that there would be no gunfire, but her heart sank when a stone struck the lead watchman's head.

The watchman dropped as he fired wildly. Lowborn roared, turning from lobbed objects to a charge that threatened to overwhelm the remaining watchmen in mere seconds. More shots rang out, but the darkness concealed who had fallen.

"Spirits protect us from the mountains to the deepest valleys," the mother nearby whispered. She covered her daughter's ears and rocked her as she repeated the Vockan prayer. "Let our spirits cling to us tonight."

The watchmen shouted a retreat. Only three managed to flee toward the bridge as the lowborn pulled down the others, slamming improvised weapons into their skulls.

Kasia rose to get a closer look, and she stifled a cry at four watchmen's corpses littering the dirt of Beg Ave alongside a pair of lowborn. A middle-age man in torn roughspun clothes lay on his side, blood sputtering from his mouth as he gasped for each breath. His hand covered what was likely a bullet wound in his stomach, but it couldn't stop the flow. His eyes were wet as a boy knelt to hold his other hand.

"Papa!" the boy cried. "Papa! Someone, please help him!"

But there was no help to be had. Another group wept around the other fallen peasant, a bullet in his head. Both wounds could've been mended by a Body Reacher if one had been near like King Jazuk had promised. He'd sent no one to help those with nothing.

Kasia's hands trembled as she approached the dying man and pulled off her coat to cover the wound. He'd lost too much blood already, but she had to do *something*. These people had already been in an awful state, and she'd only made matters worse. Though the watchmen hadn't charged into the settlement, they'd threatened it enough to spur a response. The Chamber of Scions could turn a blind eye to much that happened west of the river. Four dead watchmen would draw their attention.

An unspoken thanks lingered in the man's eyes as she pressed her coat against the wound with as much pressure as she dared. Behind it was the fear of death. Scion great houses cared little about death when they had Body Reachers and Inheritance Rituals to continue their lives, but for lowborn, what did it matter if one's spirit continued on if their mind didn't continue with it?

"I'm sorry," she whispered.

He closed his eyes with one last sputtered breath, his blood covering Kasia's coat and gloves. A void opened within her as she backed away and clutched the coat to her chest. She wished to leap into it and wake up from this nightmare. She should've never agreed to join the Crimsons. She should've never agreed to pursue Paras alone. But she had, and there was no going back.

Aliax grabbed her, his face warped by rage. "You sacrificed them! Innocent lowborn who died because you want to kill the only man that gives them hope!"

Kasia couldn't fight back. She dropped to the dirt alongside at the road's edge as the rancid river stench washed over her. Air Reachers kept it away to the east, but here, Kalastok's refuse met her every breath. Her vomit soon joined it, turning each of her senses to misery as Aliax's shouting pierced her ears and tears stung her eyes.

"Shut up!" she screamed. "I have to stop them! This is about more than revenge, Aliax. Don't you get it? If I don't do this, they'll kill everyone!"

Aliax released her, hands gripping his hair. "They need to be stopped, but you can't lose yourself too! Look what this is doing to you!"

"Get out of my head!" Kasia spat. "*You* are driving me mad."

He sneered as he backed away. "I'm here because you call me, whether you know it or not. But I'll go."

With him gone, Kasia hugged herself amid the cold everdark. Time was running out, but she'd Reached already. Doing so again soon would risk further Realm Taint.

*You've come this far,* she told herself. *Don't make it a waste.*

She felt no better as she staggered to her feet. Each step had her head spinning and her stomach tied in knots, but the homeless would start asking questions about her fit of madness if she didn't leave. Her sanity, or lack thereof, worried her. It was a problem for another day.

The sparsely filled streets soon gave way to a line extending for three blocks. Lowborn of all types huddled together, their faces shadowed by the occasional lantern overhead. Few talked, and an eerie silence fell over them until someone fell into a coughing fit, followed by another. Their dread pressed upon Kasia's own. These people were desperate for a cure, and she was about to take any hope of it away.

*Nex said he hasn't actually saved anyone. He's a fraud.*

That thought gave her little relief as she reached the brick shop front where the line began. A scribbled wooden sign hung over the door, scarred by smoke: *The Hope of Linarius.*

The Vockan legend of Linarius hadn't been one of Leonit's favorites, but Kasia remembered enough. Linarius was said to have been a man who could mold any potion from mere dirt, stone, and air. During the Awakening, he'd created a salve capable of curing a wound caused by an awakened. Most historical texts Kasia had read claimed there was no evidence that such a man ever existed. Nor were there any traces of Linarius's miracle creations. But people didn't live on truth. They needed hope, stories to inspire them.

Was Paras any more real than his store's namesake?

A woman stood by the door, studying each person entering The Hope of Linarius. She crossed her arms in a way that left the talon upon her left hand exposed.

"Wait in line like the others," the woman ordered Kasia.

"I have business with Paras," Kasia replied, tugging at her bloodied glove to reveal her own talon before covering it again. "If he has any desire to see an end to this epidemic, he'll want to speak with me."

The woman shook her head. "He's busy."

Kasia stepped closer. The woman wore no house insignia, and her light gray scion skin didn't narrow down the options any further.

"He'll want to hear from Death's Daughter," Kasia whispered. She hated the nickname, but it had its uses. Tonight, it felt all too accurate, and she swallowed the bile that threatened to fill her mouth, Realm Taint still gripping her. She had to do this. For her father. For her house. And for her country.

"Oh…" The woman attempted to step back, but she was already against the wall. "Fine, go, but don't try anything."

Kasia couldn't muster a reply, so she pushed into the shop.

For a place that held the hope of thousands of infected on its shoulders, it was remarkably small. No more than five strides either direction, the shop was filled with peasants demanding to have a dose of Paras's supposed cure.

A short, lowborn Ezmani man stood behind a wooden counter and tried to help as many as he could. He took their payments before handing them a bottle and a number with it, instructing them to return in a few days for another dose and to report how it was working. His voice was a mouse's squeak amid a thunderstorm. Sweat dripped from his brow, as this many people in one space banished the chill and replaced it with a suffocating, humid heat. He startled at the sight of Kasia forcing her way through the crowd.

"Can… Can I help you?" he asked.

"I was told to speak with Paras directly," Kasia replied, leaning over the counter as the man glanced at her bloodied clothes. "Reacher business."

The man nodded rapidly. "Yes. Yes, of course! This way." He unlocked a bolt behind the counter, then lifted a section of it for her to pass through. The moment she was on the other side, he slammed it shut to stop a surge of lowborn behind. "Through that door. Hurry! I have many others to help."

Kasia opened the door to find a much larger space with glass beakers scattered over tables. Books and strange substances filled shelves along the walls, and the faint smell of burnt hair wafted over her as a man rose from a stool at the furthest table.

Flashes of pain struck her scarred arm at the burning stench. One moment she was standing in the lab. The next, she lay amid charred clothes, her brother's cruel voice blaming her for arguing with him.

A deliberate cough tore her from the memories. The man stood before her now—Paras, she presumed. Tall, with deep brown skin and a beard of smoldering red and gray, he regarded her from a safe distance. Holes spotted his ill-fitted shirt, and he swatted at an ember that chewed through it near his elbow.

"Care to explain what you are doing in my laboratory?" Paras asked, his vowels over-enunciated while the rest of his words merged into a near murmur.

Kasia clenched her fists so tight that her nails dug into her palms. Paras was no longer just a name, but an exasperated scientist. "You… Your beard is on fire."

"Oh spirits!" He snatched a towel from the nearby table and smothered the fire. It had burned away chunks of the beard, but the inconsistency aligned with the rest of his appearance. "My apologies, but these experiments can be quite dangerous sometimes. May I ask who I have the pleasure of meeting in such bloodied clothes?"

"Katarzyna Niezik, matriarch of House Niezik."

He narrowed his eyes. "Lady Katarzyna… I did not expect company such as yourself. Why are you bloodied? We heard gunshots, but they are not all that uncommon on this side of the Kala."

She pried her bloodied gloves from her hands and deposited her coat on the rack by the door. "The soldiers on the bridge decided to pick a fight with the wrong woman. I came here to speak to you regarding your apparent cure for the Spirit Plague."

Paras stepped away with his hands extended. "Are you infected?"

"No, but plenty of people who've paid for your draughts are." Kasia followed him, circling around a table. "What are you giving them?"

"You are right to be suspicious. My potions have lacked the needed testing, so I have sold variants of the same base solution in hopes one yields greater results than the others."

Kasia gritted her teeth. "They're paying you to be tested upon? Have you at least discovered anything?"

"I have!" He eyed her talon. "Could you put that away? I do not know your intentions, and having a Death Reacher here does not give me confidence."

"Then tell me what you know," she replied, leaving a hint of aggression in her voice. Best to not make him shout for help, but he would need to be persuaded to reveal everything.

"Why? You will just take my potion and produce it yourself! I know how you great houses act."

She sighed. "We are no longer a great house. Amber, barley, and gambling are my family's business, not potions. I seek answers to the Spirit Plague and these awakened attacks, and you know something. Do not get in my way, Paras. Those who've tried lack spirits to regret it."

He continued his slow retreat, but Kasia blocked his only escape. "Your father wouldn't approve of such blunt intimidation," he said. "It's a shame you've decided to kill me in service of his assassins."

"You know of the Crimson Court?" Kasia asked, her heart skipping a beat.

"All of the Children of Zekiaz do."

"Shit! You're one of them too?"

He nodded slowly and pulled a purple falcon mask out of a drawer, holding it over his face. "Your father was a brother of our organization, but I did not know so until his death. Unlike the Crimsons, we don't gather unless necessary, and even then, we wear our masks to disguise ourselves."

"Another one of you met me when I was in prison," she said.

"That doesn't surprise me. We have been watching out for you for some time." He deposited the mask back in its drawer, then narrowed his eyes at her. "Now, the choice is yours whether to fulfill the Crimsons' demands or aid us in bettering our realm for all who live within it."

"I have to do what they say," Kasia replied, averting her gaze. "This is my only chance to avenge my father, and they've kidnapped someone who may know more, Ambassador Alyniana of Nochland."

"There will be more chances. You are young."

Kasia raised her taloned hand, Reaching with dark purple wisps spiraling at her fingertips. The spirits of the dead hissed around her. But Tainted or not, she needed vengeance. This was the only way.

"I've lived with this for too long!" she insisted. "You claim you are trying to save our realm, but you sell useless potions to the poorest peasants. Tell me why you should live."

Paras's threw out his arms, gesturing to the experiments throughout the room. "Don't you see my work? I labor every day to better my potions, to search for a cure. At worst, they allow the infected to spend their last days in comfort, and at best, they save lives. Two returned to me just days ago—the first to recover from the Spirit Plague."

Flames from the scattered burners danced over Paras's face as Kasia stepped back. "So there is a cure?" she asked.

"Maybe..." His shoulders slumped, and he leaned against the nearest table, his breaths heavy. "More tests are needed, but it is a start. Unfortunately, even that batch of potions only saved those two out of hundreds. Professor Etal iz Noshok's research claims that the infection attacks both body and spirit, but it is difficult to contact him with the lockdown surrounding the college. For now, I have no way to entrap the damaged fragments of the victim's spirit, allowing the rest to heal. We know glass repels spirits, but only in theory is there an opposite."

Kasia closed her eyes, fighting within herself. Amber... It had captured the awakened who'd attacked her during the Ephemeral Slaughter. What if it could somehow do the same for his potions? Could she help him find a cure if she left him alive? But if she did so, the Crimsons would surely seek revenge.

"I may have a way to help you," she stammered, "but the Crimsons need you dead."

He rushed toward her, stepping around her talon. "You have an answer? Tell me, please! Millions of lives in Kalastok and beyond are at risk, Katarzyna. This disease will not stop at the poorest among us. It has already bled into the eastern side of Kalastok and throughout the Commonwealth. Other nations will be next, each death feeding the rising tide of awakened."

An idea—albeit a likely bad one—entered her mind as the wisps disappeared from her hand. A wasted Reach, Tainting her further. Could she trust Paras with amber's secret?

"You can have my answer *if* you help me convince the Crimsons I did as they said," she insisted.

He scratched his scorched beard. "What do you have in mind? My work is here."

Kasia raised her taloned hand again, this time not pointing it at him. "People killed by my Reaching become disgusting corpses that no one could recognize. You Children of Zekiaz must have some other agents, right? Have them grab the body of a watchman I killed on the King's Bridge and swap his clothes with yours. You can take your equipment to a safe place to continue your work, and that assistant of yours can keep distributing what you have."

"You're asking me to leave my shop and pretend I've perished?" Paras shook his head. "Whatever you have better be worthwhile."

"Amber," she said, forcing herself to draw the piece from her pocket. "Within this is an awakened who attacked me. I don't know how, but this amber pendant absorbed it when it came too close. Could it somehow do the same for your potion?"

Paras snatched at it, but Kasia pulled it away.

"Do we have a deal?" she asked.

Paras huffed. "You hold hostage what could be the cure to our realm's greatest woe."

"The Spirit Plague is important, Paras, but every time I discover another member of the Crimsons, their roots are deeper in the government. If I don't take this next step, they'll keep getting away with their schemes. My father's last note said to stop them. I'll do whatever it takes to do it."

"Very well." He held out his hand. "Give me the amber, and I shall do what you say. The Children have many safehouses spread throughout the region. I will close my shop at the top of the hour, and when it reopens, I will be gone with the soldier's body in my place."

Kasia held the pendant to her breast. It took all her strength not to deny the deal and get this over with, but if successful, this plan could save lives. "Your assistant can know nothing. There are risks enough without people outside the Children of Zekiaz leaking information. The Crimsons have ears everywhere."

"I cannot pass on my further research without his help." Paras waved his hand across his instruments. "Naxial has trained by my side for over a decade. I trust him with my life, and for us to save the people of our realm, I need him."

"And the Reacher out front? She knows I came in here."

"A member of our organization. You need not know her name."

Kasia scoffed. "You give me nothing when I'm sparing you and gifting you what could complete your potion! None of this changes that you make lowborn pay for what cannot save them."

"My materials are expensive," Paras replied, "but it's up to you whether to trust me or not. Just think about all those people you passed before you put that talon to my neck." He bowed his head, awaiting her decision.

Kasia bit her cheek. Paras was far from a perfect man—and the Children of Zekiaz were still an unfamiliar group—but killing him would do far more harm than good. Her father had earned his stature outwitting his enemies. Now, it was up to her to do the same.

She held out the amber pendant, the gray awakened squirming within it. "Take it."

Paras raised his head with a relieved smile before carefully accepting the amber. "You have no idea how fascinated I am by this, but I confess my fear of what comes next is greater. Leave, Katarzyna. I shall not forget your choice tonight. Nor shall I forget that you threatened my life in the first place."

"Follow through on our agreement, and we'll both survive." Kasia grabbed her bloodied coat from the door and threw it over her shoulders, leaving her arms free. "I've seen the Crimsons inflict worse than death."

Then she left, pushing through the crowd and into the chilled night. She didn't take another breath until she was in clear air. Even then, it was suffocating as the weight of her decisions fell upon her shoulders.

Death followed in her wake, and for what? Paras had amber that *could* help his research. He'd fake his death with the Children, but she had no way to know if it would be enough. The Crimsons could've been watching her even then. She'd tested their patience by meeting with Alyniana and scheming to enter House Oliezany at the gala. Any further opposition would likely mean her death.

But as Kasia walked through the streets of the west side, she spotted no tails watching her from the shadows. She was alone. It stayed that way until she found Nex at the river.

"It's 'bout time you showed up," the Possibility Reacher muttered from atop the overhang of a nearby building, their legs dangling over the edge. "Sounds like it got messy." Nex eyed Kasia as she stepped into the light of their lantern. "Looks like it too. What'd you do? Try and convince the watchmen to just let you pass? I told you to pull your keni if they didn't listen."

Kasia swallowed her pride, exhausted and awaiting the embrace of her bed. Not that she looked forward to the nightmares that would certainly follow. "Yes, it got messy."

Nex hopped down, then removed their tattered overcoat. "Figures. Best we trade coats. The guards over on your side of the river probably won't like Lady Death Reacher walking about with bloodied clothes."

*Another person I'm relying on.*

"Why are you helping me this much?" Kasia asked. "I told you I was going to kill the man trying to cure the Spirit Plague."

Nex tugged at Kasia's coat until she relented. "I told you his potion didn't work. He's a fake."

"Except he isn't."

Nex hesitated. "You said 'isn't,' not 'wasn't.' He alive?"

"I'll tell you everything once we cross the river." Kasia took the tattered coat and threw it over herself, the cold wind whipping from the river for the few seconds she was without the extra layer. "But yes, we worked out a deal to fake his death."

"Good. Better that way." Nex extended their hand to Kasia. "Ready to cross?"

"How?"

Nex rolled their eyes. "Trust me, I've got this."

Kasia took their hand and nodded firmly. "Alright. You've done this before, right?"

"With two people?" Nex grinned. "Definitely…"

"Wait, wha—"

Nex yanked her toward the southern Oliezany Bridge. A single lantern hung at its end, lighting the mixed stone walls that enclosed it on either side as open windows allowed a view of the Kala below. Those walls confined them as they headed toward the bridge's center. A single watchwoman awaited them there.

She raised her rifle.

"Halt right there!" the watchwoman shouted.

Nex stopped. "Shit. She's not supposed to be on guard."

"Now what?" Kasia whispered.

Nex shoved her through the bridge's window, then jumped after her. "Swim!" they shouted as Kasia plunged into the Kala's frigid flow.

# DROWNING

*"Those who fight the tide cannot do so forever."* – Reshkan proverb

Alcohol burned Kasia's throat as she sat on the sofa in her chambers and downed another glass of the vile liquor. Spirits, how did people consume this for fun? She regretted each drop that she'd consumed, yet she poured another drink anyway, using one of the few expensive glass goblets in the townhouse.

Forgetting was better.

Every time she blinked, she saw the face of the poor lowborn on Beg Ave who'd died because she led the watchmen to them. Paras had survived the night, but Kasia's kill count had increased by three. She was responsible for many more deaths too, each a voice haunting her. Only the ones slain by her Reaching appeared beside Aliax when her mind wandered, but the others never left her nightmares.

"Lady Kasia, are you certain this is for the best?" Kikania asked, holding a blanket in one hand and another bottle of some spiritsforsaken liquor in the other. "You are still shivering from the river, and I would hate for you to fall ill… or worse."

Tazper nodded from beside the fireplace. "This isn't like you, Kasia."

Kasia sneered and snatched the blanket, wrapping it over her nightgown. Water from the near frozen Kala River still dripped from her hair, and she was chilled to the bone. Drinking excessively wasn't helping matters. She didn't care.

"Are you two just going to spend the night criticizing my decisions?" she snapped before pointing at Nex. "They helped me out of there. What've *you* done?"

Tazper raised his brow. "I have spent most of my life watching out for you, helping you with your plans—no matter how risky—and have patiently waited for my talon. Oh, and I went through House Oliezany's gunsmiths asking about a pistol they made for our enemies."

"Pikeziks!" Kasia exclaimed, taking another gulp of her drink. It was awful, and she hesitated out of fear of vomiting before she continued. "Everything points to them, but who's the Dark Reacher? Uzrin Ioniz? Another of those rich bastards? The son of a bitch took Alyniana!"

"With awakened," Nex added with a glass in hand, sipping their own drink much slower. Their black hair dripped over the simple dress they'd borrowed from Kasia, but with Nex's much narrower shoulders and shorter torso, it draped over them like a curtain. Somehow, they had also acquired Tazper's wide-brimmed hat without him noticing. "Don't know how a Dark Reacher coulda done that, but I know what I saw."

"I do not deny it," Tazper said before turning his attention to Kasia, "but shouldn't you wait to cast accusations until you are introduced to the Crimsons? Just because Nex saw Uzrin Ioniz and Laniaz Rakazimko, that does not mean one of them is the Dark Reacher."

Kasia waved for him to come closer, which he reluctantly did, sitting beside her. She poured him a drink and plopped it into his hand. A few drops sprayed onto her gown, but she shooed off Kikania, who'd moved to wipe them away before they stained. "The two of us used to have fun, remember?" she tried to whisper to Tazper, but it came out as a shout. "Our journeys in search of amber, and the festivals in Tystok when all the lowborn came from their homesteads… Why did I come here? All that's in the capital is misery and betrayal."

A bell rang downstairs, so Tazper shot to his feet, spilling yet more of his drink. "That's—oops—That is probably Lord Zinarus. I should let him in, but Kasia, your attire is—"

"Say I'm not dressed for the company of a gentleman, and I'll throw you down the stairs." Between her many drinks, she didn't quite remember calling for Zinarus, but she had plenty to tell him.

Tazper swallowed hard. "Very well."

Nex giggled to themself as he ran off. "I like him. Never seen someone so proper and oafish at the same time."

"Are you not upset with what occurred on the west side?" Kikania asked Nex, hands held behind her. "It seems you would be more affected than us."

"I am…" Nex set down their cup, then tucked their legs under them on the chair. "There's someone I care about who's infected, so I didn't want Paras dead. But those Crimsons are causing it, so stopping them was more important than protecting some fraud whose potions don't even work. Still, guess it's better he's alive if amber can fix them."

Kasia took a long breath. Her head spun even worse than before, and she leaned back, staring at the silver and glass chandelier above as its designs seemed to dance. "We don't know they're causing this. Radais thought so, but we can't be certain until he finds what they were doing in the Wastes."

She closed her eyes, but when that didn't help her dizziness, she took another gulp of her drink. *Forget.* Aliax hadn't made an appearance since she'd taken her first sip. Maybe she should've taken up alcohol sooner. Her father had claimed a sip could take one to the crown when one's opponent gulped, but had he been wrong?

"I miss him," Kasia mumbled.

Nex cocked their head. "Who?"

"My father. I did this for him… At least, I thought I did." She hiccupped as footsteps approached, and Zinarus entered, leaning on his cane as Tazper followed. Her cheeks burned. Sober, she'd struggled to grasp how she felt about her mechanical-legged ally, and with her thoughts muddled, her head throbbed so loudly that she feared he could hear it. "Spirits, that jacket makes you look like a king."

Zinarus's eyes widened. His cutaway jacket was his house's purple over a black vest, accented with golden trim and chains hanging from the buttons to the pockets. It was ostentatious but fit him well, besides his flaming hair. He donned a black tricorn of Ogrenian style, though, covering the curls—the same hat that Kasia had adored on Hazat Tozki during the Uziokaki gala. Did he know?

"It is a pleasure to see you as well, Lady Kasia," he said, holding his hat over his heart. "Apologies for the lack of haste in my arrival. At this late hour, it took some time for me to prepare, as I had been returning from training our…" He eyed Nex, catching himself, "training my jousters in the arena, that is."

"You… um… You can trust Nex," Kasia slurred. She stood to greet him before realizing there was liquor splattered over her front. He noticed it too, but he was kind enough to only glance at the spots before raising his gaze to hers.

"If you need a moment to handle your wardrobe…"

She winced and bowed, nearly toppling over. "It's fine. Thank you for coming, Zinarus."

His own blush deepened, as her talon was uncovered. But after a moment's hesitation, he bowed as well. "May I ask the reason for my invitation? You left quite quickly from the arena the last time we met, and I was worried you would not wish to see me again."

Of course, he wouldn't ask if she was drunk. It was obvious, and most scions would've considered it rude. She'd told him in his arena box that she didn't partake of alcohol, though, and confusion was evident on his face. Not that anything about the situation was normal.

"Yes, the arena…" Kasia said, remembering her foolish stumbling out of the box. Zinarus's subtle advances had terrified her then, but alcohol's embrace washed away her fear. "I am sorry for my departure. There was much on my mind."

Nex coughed and stood, nearly tripping on their dress. "Name's Nex, by the way—from the Shadow Quarter. I'm helping Kasia figure out the Crimsons and the plague. I guess she called you because you need to know what happened."

"What a moment!" Tazper explained as he pointed at Nex, then patted his head. "How did you take my hat?"

Nex grinned. "Very carefully."

"Would you give it—"

"Stop it!" Kasia muttered. "You're giving me a headache, and I can explain my own problems, Nex."

"Not if you're 'bout to pass out," Nex said with a huff.

"It is a pleasure to meet you, Nex," Zinarus said, rubbing the back of his neck before returning his attention to Kasia. "May we sit, then? I do not mean to complain, but my leg suffers after enduring so many stairs."

Kasia took his arm and guided him to the sofa. She began to pour him a glass, but he gently pushed her hand away from the bottle. "I prefer my drink softer, but thank you," he said. "Please tell me what has happened. How can I help?"

"Before I tell you about tonight, there's something else," she said. "Your father, Uzrin, is a Crimson."

He froze. "How do you know this?"

Nex clicked their tongue. "Saw 'im talking with another Crimson all creepy like."

"And he confronted me when I left your box," Kasia said. "Threatened me."

Zinarus pondered for a moment, head nodding absentmindedly until he slammed his fist into his good knee. "He calls me a bastard, yet conspires to assassinate kings, kill my friends, and threaten my mother? How dare he abandon us, then plot to destroy all we have worked for!"

Kasia threw out her arms. "He's the bastard!"

"He sure as shit is," Nex spat. "Can't trust scions… 'cept you two I guess."

Tazper coughed. "Three."

"You're a scion?" Nex held up their crystal ring, its deep gray swimming in the firelight. "Where's your talon?"

Kasia waved for them to be silent, and Zinarus waited until the commotion was over before speaking. "My father is indeed corrupt. Unfortunately, this is not hard proof to bring to the courts."

"The courts?" Kasia scoffed. "You have too much faith in the system when the Crimsons control it."

"If we do not trust in our traditions, our institutions," Zinarus said, "then what do we have?"

She took another swig of her drink. "A pit of fucking crystal-laden vipers."

Kikania winced and stepped to the room's center with her hands held before her. "Lady Kasia, perhaps it is best to continue this conversation when you are in a better state of mind. It has been a hard day."

"Your handmaiden is right," Zinarus said, scooting to the edge of his seat. "I feel as if I am intruding, and your discovery has given me much to ponder."

But Kasia grabbed his arm. "Wait! Uzrin is not why I called you here… why I am the mess I am."

He relented, so she explained what had happened, trying not to reveal more than she should. It came out as a rambling mess, and her hands trembled around her glass as she recounted her confrontation with the watchmen on King's Bridge and after. Why was she telling him everything? He didn't need to know she'd killed those men and caused the death of the homeless lowborn. But she told him anyway, not regretting a single word.

"They accosted you?" Zinarus asked when she paused.

Kasia nodded.

"Then you protected yourself, nothing more, and you could not have known that their reinforcements would cause such harm to innocents." He held his arm across his chest, averting his gaze. "Please confirm my hopes that you did not do the same to Paras ik Lierasa."

Kasia sat back again. Her stomach churned worse by the second, and thinking about what had happened only deepened her Taint-inflicted headache too. "I know what I did was right, but it doesn't stop me from feeling like shit." She shook her head, meeting Zinarus's gaze. "No, I didn't kill Paras. He convinced me he's close to a cure, so I agreed to help him fake his death. The Death Reached corpse they find will be the watchman's."

"I…"

She unceremoniously plopped her hand onto his shoulder. "Don't tell me it was the right thing. I found a compromise between my Crimson lie and a man's life. Had he not convinced me, I'd have killed him like the watchmen. I was already Reaching."

"Kasia!" Tazper exclaimed, his jaw hung open.

"Don't, Taz!" Kasia gripped her head. "I have enough voices already telling me that it was wrong. I didn't see a better way until one opened, okay? If I don't stop the Crimsons, all of this will have been for nothing. I'll have become a Death Reacher for nothing…"

Nex shifted. "What do you mean, voices?"

Kasia froze, realizing her drunken slip. Next to no one knew about the Realm Tainted voices in her head, and the thought of admitting how broken she was frightened her. Zinarus and Nex had put their trust in her, but did they need to know everything? She looked to Tazper for silent guidance. He offered only a lost shrug, so she sighed and decided to trust them… but not completely.

"I'm Tainted," Kasia breathed. "Every person I've killed with my Reaching leaves this realm forever, but they never leave me."

She looked up, and there they were. Aliax lingered beside Tazper with a sly smirk. Sazilz paced in his dull suit, eyeing her. Parqiz filled half the sofa and forced Kasia to move closer to Zinarus. And the rest shifted in and out of sight as they meandered through walls and furniture. All of them screamed in her head, mocking her misery.

Kasia shot to her feet and threw her glass into the fireplace. The blaze rose, alcohol fueling its fury as she backed away like a feral animal.

*So much fire…*

"You let your power take you," Aliax said with a maniacal laugh as she cowered from the inferno. "I told you not to do it all those years ago, and nothing's changed."

"Go to the spirits!" she screamed in reply.

A hand touched her arm. Soft. Then Zinarus's arms embraced her, pulling her back to the sofa as his voice pushed through the dead. "Kasia? Who does your Realm Taint make you see?"

She surrendered to his care, but she could only look away from Aliax's wavering figure for a moment to meet Tazper's gaze again. He knew. But Zinarus couldn't. He would hate her for what she'd done. The voices in her head were more than a shadow of the past, but only she needed to know each one.

"The Crimsons I killed, and the watchmen from the bridge," she said. Aliax shook his head behind the tears pooling in her eyes, but she looked away. "My father left a list of names before his death, labeling them the Crimson Court. I found all of them and made sure their spirits never returned. Parqiz Uziokaki led me to Sazilz."

Zinarus leaned away at her last word, fear evident in his eyes. "That night at the mansion… Lord Sazilz has not been seen since his arrival at the Oliezany estate. Was that you?"

Kasia curled in her legs, holding onto them. She had no more words left, nor enough pain to pour through them. Her mind throbbed with each beat of her empty heart, but she spoke anyway.

"The Buried Temple claims the Crystal Mother chooses which realm we Reach," she said. "They're wrong. The crystal knows what we want, but it's our choice. I know, because I felt it *want* to bond me to our realm's spirit core during my ceremony. I refused. I hadn't found Father's letter about the Crimsons yet, but I knew someone had murdered him. Spirit Reaching wouldn't give me revenge, so I chose Death."

She met Zinarus's shocked gaze. "When I entered the mansion, I found your Dark Reacher with Tzena Oliezany and another Light Reacher I didn't recognize. They knew my plan, so they bound Sazilz as an offering to me, a trade: the man who ordered my father's assassination for my loyalty."

"Loyalty?" He frowned. "How can you let yourself live this lie? Appeasing Gornioz, carrying out the Crimsons' orders, killing a great house patriarch, and now pledging your loyalty to them? Do you not fear where this path is taking you?"

"They ruined my life," she replied, her throat raw and her mind drifting. "This path takes me to my revenge, so I don't care what lies in the way. It can't be worse than what I've survived already."

Though a question lingered in his eyes, he slowly grabbed his cane and rose slowly. His usually gray cheeks were as red as his hair, which flared uncomely over his ears as he donned his hat. "I must consider all you have told me. Your desire to aid Tiuz and my mercenaries was inspired, and I share your desire to end the Crimson Court's plots. This deception and killing, though… My apologies, Lady Kasia, but I am on unfamiliar ground here. Allow me some time."

She tried to stand too, but her wobbly legs sent her back onto the sofa. "Remember what they took from you. If we don't stop them, no one will."

Zinarus pondered that for a moment before bowing his head to Nex. "It was a pleasure to meet you, Nex of the Shadow Quarter, and I wish you the best of health and safety in these trying times. May our efforts for the west side do more to create a cure than to delay one."

He left with Tazper scampering behind. Kasia shivered in his absence, pulling her blanket tighter as the fire crackled through the silence. Anxiety gave way to weariness, and she struggled to keep her eyes open as she waited for Tazper to return.

"You should go," she told Nex once she heard her footman's arriving steps. "We'll deal with the ramifications of tonight soon."

"Can I have my clothes back?" Nex asked, brow furrowed at Kikania.

Tazper entered the room with his chin raised. "Only if you return my hat."

"Deal. Got my own hat anyway."

Kikania feigned a smile. "Of course, I can fetch your clothes. However, they will still be quite damp."

Nex tossed Tazper his hat, which he scrambled to catch. "I'm soaked anyway," they said. "Just want to get home to Vinnia."

"Vinnia?" Kasia asked. "You mentioned before that someone you knew was sick. Is it her?"

Nex cursed under their breath. "My roommate. She caught the Spirit Plague from the factory she works in."

The knot in Kasia's chest loosened at the familiar desperation in Nex's voice. "That's why you hated Paras, but needed him too."

"His assistant said the potion would work," Nex muttered. "But that amber of yours will fix it. Death Reacher or not, you're trying to help. I'm not dumb enough to miss that." They stood as Kikania returned. "Thanks for the dress, but it's not my style."

Drunkenness taking over, Kasia didn't notice Kikania leading Nex downstairs to change. She lay across the sofa, her head spinning far too much for her to reach her bed. She didn't fear the liquor sickness that would come in the morning. Nor did she fear Aliax's gaze from across the room or what Tzena would say about her mission on the west side. No, her only lucid thoughts lingered on Zinarus's disappointment, his horror. He'd seen something greater in her before, but that look in his hazel eyes when he'd left was the same one her mother had given her when she'd discovered Kasia's Reaching. It said a single word: monster.

She fell asleep quickly despite her thoughts, but someone woke her soon after.

"You mustn't sleep on your back in your condition, Lady Kasia," Kikania whispered, rolling her to the side and placing a warm cloth over her forehead. "I will fetch you another blanket."

"Where's Nex?" Kasia grumbled in her half-awake state.

"Shush now," Kikania replied once she'd returned with the blanket. It was warm and pressed Kasia like a cocoon that drew her back to her dreams. "The everdark is long, but we need not wait for dawnrise to follow the light amid the shadows."

# THE PROPOSALS

*"No matter how prideful one is, it is often preferable to kneel before a greater power in the pursuit of survival."* —Yaakiin Tinaanuuk, former king of the Commonwealth of Two Nations

"Preposterous!"

Nikoza flinched from her position along the wall as Gornioz Oliezany's voice echoed through the council room. The magnate towered as tall as a Vockan over the table, his fist pressed firmly upon it.

"I believe we are all well aware how outrageous these demands are," Borys Kuzon replied from across the table. His body seemed to overwhelm the chair, engulfing it as a river would a fallen branch. "The question is not who among us is more upset, but how we should respond. Hazemel is the war minister, so we should seek his advice first."

A smile flicked across Nikoza's face as Hazemel shuffled through his parchment, then adjusted his spectacles. The war minister was a thoughtful man, and unlike the others, Nikoza held some hope he would oppose a full-scale war. "Yes, yes, of course," he said. "Our reports, my king, are clear. Along with the Keloshan Empire's demands that we cede the designated eastern lands to them, they have sent three battalions to surround the village of Rexaniv."

"An invasion of the most blatant kind," Gornioz added.

Hazemel sighed, setting down the papers as he looked to Jazuk at the table's head. "You know full well, my king, that Gornioz and I have our disputes. On this, however, I must confess we are agreed. Kelosh has invaded under the façade that we are oppressing territories that are rightfully theirs. In short, these claims are nothing short of fantastical."

Jazuk sat back. Though dressed well in his deep red officer's coat, he looked far older than he had a season ago, his eyes sunken and his hair thinning. In recent days, he had been too busy with Kelosh for Nikoza to propose an alternate solution to war. Ambassador Alyniana's letter had sparked an idea in her head. It would involve trickery of the kind she despised, but so too would it potentially save thousands of Nochlander lives and the entire Commonwealth from Kelosh's wrath. First, she needed to convince the stubborn old man to listen.

"So it is war, then," the king said. "The Chamber will not accept such an incursion, and neither should I."

"War is likely, my king," Hazemel replied, "but I believe it may be prevented if we were to appeal to the Ogrenians for a defensive pact. In exchange for their superior technology, we could offer them the contested copper and coal mines they have desired for many decades."

Borys nodded. "Reshka would offer another such advantage, should we seek to reforge the bonds broken after King Yaakiin's death."

Lilita Pikezik gasped, throwing out her arms. "Are you mad? Such an agreement is choosing one master over another! The empires each desire our crystal reserves, and no pact will stop them from crushing us after we have destroyed Kelosh for them."

"Have you an alternative?" Jazuk asked.

Nikoza willed for her grandfather to glance at her, if only for a moment. She could interject and offer her plan before houses

Oliezany and Pikezik persuaded him toward foolishness. No matter how much she pleaded internally, though, she would not disrupt the meeting unless invited to speak by Jazuk. Such was the way of things.

Lilita nodded to Gornioz, who replied, "There is an obvious answer: a general mobilization of our forces. All capable Reachers and working-age lowborn should be mustered in preparation for the war to come. We can allocate many to our factories to increase production of needed munitions while the others march to the front. All industry not dedicated to the war effort should fall under our command, allowing us to match Kelosh's superior output."

"You wish for the government to steal scion property?" Borys raged. "The king exists to serve the scions, not the opposite!"

"Borys and Hazemel are right," Jazuk replied, unsurprisingly affirming his friends' views. Gornioz and Lilita were magnates of the two most powerful great houses, but they sat on the council out of political necessity alone. Jazuk had taught Nikoza much, and the foremost lesson was that people and their relationships governed a nation, not laws. "We cannot face Kelosh alone, but neither can we subject ourselves to the other empires."

His gaze absently flicked to Nikoza. She took the chance.

"If I may, your highness, offer an alternative alliance that would ensure exactly that?" she asked.

Jazuk frowned. "Why did you not come to me sooner if you had such a proposal? The council chamber is for ministers to speak, not wards."

Nikoza pulled Alyniana's letter from her dress pocket, displaying it. "Ambassador Alyniana of Nochland appealed to me directly, as you have been too busy to hear either of us lately. She proposes that the Commonwealth's great houses send their mercenaries to Nochland's aid against Kelosh, including enough Spirit Reachers to aid in their defense against the awakened. It would be an informal action, as the houses are private bodies acting independently of our government, ensuring our armies remain on our own soil. Meanwhile, with their land borders protected, Nochland could use its considerable navy to blockade and bombard Keloshan ports."

Jazuk's brows raised as he ran his hand through his beard. "That woman has bothered me endlessly as of late, but her plan bears merit. Council, what are your opinions?"

"It is quite the ask," Borys replied.

"Quite the ask?" Gornioz snapped. "It is spiritshit! I refuse to pay my mercenaries to protect Nochland when Kelosh attacks our lands."

Lilita nodded, replying far more calmly than her ally, "House Pikezik cannot support such a plan, and I doubt many other scions of significance will either."

"My house may not be considered among the great six," Hazemel replied as he nervously shuffled his papers, "but we would allocate some of our considerable funds toward a proposal such as this. If war is inevitable, better we face it with an ally."

Borys rapped his fingers against the table. "Perhaps we take the best of both plans, no?"

"What do you have in mind?" Jazuk replied.

Nikoza tensed, but she had no right to appeal before Borys had even spoken. After all, her mother was Borys's younger sister and a Kuzon by blood. She would *not* look fondly upon any attempts by Nikoza to undermine her birth house. So Nikoza stood, rigid, as she awaited the fat man's proposal to disrupt Alyniana's plan.

"It is all well and good that Nochland could provide adequate military support," Borys said with a puff of his cigar. "That being said, I am not convinced a general mobilization is without its merits. Ignore this cattle dung about seizing scion factories for government use, and instead, focus on conscripting the men not already working in the factories. Better yet, engage the children in the labor, freeing up more hands to hold rifles. Combined with our conscription of the new Reachers who could not pay the Buried Temple's fees, this should bolster our strength considerably."

*Forcing children into the factories?* Was such a risk truly worth it?

Gornioz sneered, but a smile tugged at the ends of Jazuk's mouth. "Now this is why I have a council," the king said. "Splendid. We will need more of this line of thinking if we are to survive this war. I pledge my house's mercenaries to Nochland's aid. Will yours come as well?"

"Aye, my king," Borys replied, thumping his chest. "For the Commonwealth!"

Nikoza rushed to Jazuk's side with his cane as he stood with some effort. "Thank you, my dear," he whispered before raising his voice. "Let this decision remain known only to those in this room and the mercenaries themselves. We need not allow Kelosh to catch wind of our plan with Nochland, but in the meantime, the Chamber shall vote for the mobilization of the lowborn—in the way suggested by Borys. Ensure your factions support our proposal. We cannot afford another mess like the Keloshan Act."

Hazemel and Borys affirmed their support before leaving to confer with their allies. Lilita tipped her head as well. "While I do not endorse your actions with Nochland, you have my support for mobilization. It would be foolish to oppose such a measure, even if it is not to the full extent we had hoped for."

"I am glad to hear it, Lady Lilita, and a bit surprised as well."

She gave a crooked smile. "My house's allegiances are with our nation. We will do what we can to strengthen it by any means." Then she curtsied and left, giving a passing glance to Gornioz, who had yet to rise.

"Gornioz, my good man," Jazuk said as he hobbled over to his counterpart's chair and rested a hand upon its back. "What has you lingering on a day such as this?"

"Betrayal," Gornioz muttered without looking up. "Once, you were an honored member of the nationalist wing, Jazuk. We elected you king, and now you spend your days cowering before empires and aiding incompetent Nochland while your own nation rots!"

Nikoza took a sharp breath. "He is *King* Jazuk, Lord Gornioz. Disagreements do not merit disrespect."

He scoffed, standing sharply and buttoning his jacket. "Ironic for you to speak of respect moments after breaking decorum. Know your place, child. You are here to listen as your grandfather's ward, not to serve among the council members."

"He is right," Jazuk said. "Refrain from such interruptions in the future, or I will be forced to bar you from council meetings."

A knot tightened in Nikoza's chest, but she bowed her head. "Yes, my king."

Gornioz left without bowing. She glared at the back of his head, scribing her humiliation to memory. She would submit for now. One day, though, she would be matriarch of House Bartol, and she swore that things would change. Arrogant magnates like Gornioz would be washed away in the tide of change. If all went well, they would drown in the process.

"Come, Grandfather," she said, taking Jazuk's arm. "We have a meeting of the Chamber to prepare for."

# For the Commonwealth!

**KELOSH MARCHES! Whether scion or lowborn, our great nation must face them! Answer the call, and save a bullet for every Keloshan skull.**

# WAR SONG

*"To vote is a powerful thing, but when action is slowed by deliberation, it is hard not to wish for an emperor's firm will."* – Borys Kuzon, patriarch of House Kuzon

Tension gripped the Crystal Palace.

Kasia winced beneath the gaze of the Crystal Mother's statue as she crossed the main hall. Her hangover and Realm Taint headache had her wishing to be anywhere else, but all her efforts had led to this.

Tzena Oliezany awaited her at the statue's base with a wry smile. Her dress of red matched the draperies hanging from the ceiling, added since the last meeting of the Chamber of Scions. Swallowing the bile in her throat, Kasia returned the smile.

"Lady Tzena," she said, exchanging bows. Her own white dress with black trimming the collar and jacket was far more solemn on the eve of war, but Tzena had never been one for such concerns. "I assume you have heard word of poor Paras ik Lierasa's spirit passing from his body?"

Tzena averted her gaze to Gornioz. The magnate stood taller than all but the Vockan scions, speaking with other nationalists in preparation for the vote to come. Kasia gritted her teeth at the thought of voting for war, but she was so close to uncovering the Crimsons' leaders. She couldn't drop her nationalist act yet.

"All in the realm will have heard of it by tomorrow," Tzena replied. "The alchemist was a god to the lowborn, and I hear rumblings among those west of the Kala. They tolerated quarantine when Paras offered them hope, but what have they to lose when their loved ones perish to the Spirit Plague?"

"He was no god," Kasia said. "His claimed cures were nothing but tests that had failed to yield results. Quite cruel to force peasants to pay for false medicine."

Tzena nodded and held out her hand to Kasia, a rolled piece of parchment peeking out from her dress sleeve. "Then all is well with his perishing."

Kasia shook her hand and slipped the parchment up her own sleeve before parting with Tzena. The Chamber meeting would begin soon, but a check of her watch revealed she had a few minutes, so she headed to the powder room. Whatever the note was, Tzena had intended it to stay secret. Reading it in the Chamber was certainly not the best idea.

Mercifully, the powder room was empty except for its adornments of marble and gold. When she pulled the note from her sleeve, though, her hands trembled. Was it an invitation to the Crimson Court? An admission of what they truly were?

The note unrolled in her hands. Its paper was thick and its ink bled across the page like the fine cut of an assassin's blade. Some scribes wrote with flowing script, but the words before her were formed of jagged, deliberate marks.

*Katarzyna the First, Matriarch of House Niezik, the Amber Dame, and the Daughter of Death,*

*You have impressed us since your arrival in our grand capital. Of course, you by now know us as the Crimson Court, but it would be of no surprise if you know little else about our cause. Let us mend this.*

*Upon the conclusion of this evening's meeting of the Chamber of Scions, return to your carriage as usual. Instead of your footman and driver, you will find our associates, who will take you to our meeting location. Do not attempt to contact anyone regarding this arrangement.*

*We will know.*

*Your servants will be safe as long as you adhere to our protocols. We seek to work with you, Katarzyna, but betrayal will not be tolerated.*

*Regards,*

*The King in the Dark*

Kasia rolled up the note and slid it into her handbag, taking a deep breath. She stared at her reflection in the glass mirror above the water basin. The woman who met her was unfamiliar. Dark circles ringed her eyes, and her lips curled in a wicked smirk.

Then she vomited.

As if Zekiaz wished to remind her of her overused Reaching, her entire body reeked of death. It took all her strength not to curl up alongside the water basin. What had become of her? And it wasn't only her body that struggled.

"So, you earned their trust," a voice much more familiar said from behind her, the other spirits echoing his words. Aliax wore all black, a cutaway jacket over a shirt well-fitted to his muscled torso. He'd never have worn something so vain in life. "What will you do with them once you know the truth?"

She closed her eyes and wished him away, but his presence remained like a warm breath against her neck. Spirits, what would it be like to not love her heart's worst scar? At least that hadn't changed about her, and she clung to the past as she wondered what this plot had done to her… was still doing to her.

"I'll kill them," she replied to his reflection. "For Father, for me, I will send their fucking souls to whatever nothingness lurks beyond the Known Realms."

His hand fell lightly on her shoulder. "There is still time to accept that this has gone too far. I can't bear to watch you lose yourself with this obsession. You're more than revenge."

"Then don't watch."

"Kasia—"

She spun, swiping her arm through his body and turning it to mist. "You're dead! Don't you get it? I have *nothing* left to lose. It doesn't matter what the Crimsons do to me. In the end, I will kill them at any cost."

"You can't believe that," Aliax's ethereal voice said as he faded. "You have so much, but pain blinds you."

"GO AWAY!"

A yelp answered her as an elderly scion woman staggered back into the powder room door, a hand held to her chest. Kasia recognized her from the conservative faction, and from the scowl on her face, she did not appreciate being shouted at.

"Lady Katarzyna," the woman huffed. "What in the Crystal Mother's gracious name are you doing screaming like so? Your father may have been consorting with the Reshkans, but I had believed he raised you with more grace than this."

Kasia turned away with a silent curse for Aliax. "My apologies. There was a rodent pestering me before you entered, and I fear you stepped into the fray as I was seeking to catch it."

The woman's jaw dropped further, a sight Kasia had thought impossible moments before. "A rat in the Crystal Palace? Quite unacceptable! Dealing with such a pest is far beneath your station. I will find the servants at once and demand an explanation."

"Yes… Of course."

Once the woman left, Kasia leaned back against the water basin. Each of her breaths was a struggle, but Aliax was gone… kind of. Her heart and her head warred over how to feel about his absence as other spirits lurked in her peripherals.

A voice carried through the palace, aided by an Air Reacher's power, "All members of the Chamber of Scions are called to order."

Kasia checked her reflection once more and fixed what she could with makeup. Yet another mask. She'd desired to join the scions' game of politics once, craved it, but she realized now why her father had trusted so few. Life among the capital's scions was a constant battle of false smiles and hidden blades.

The halls outside the Chamber were nearly empty beyond scattered servants waiting with nervous glances. They gave Kasia space as the sound of a thumping cane approached. Had she waited so long that the infamously tardy king had arrived before her?

"Lady Katarzyna?" a formal yet soft voice said from behind her as she tried to slip into the Chamber. She stopped halfway through the doors, the guards holding them open for her, and looked back at the purple-clad scion.

"Good day, Lord Zinarus."

He bowed his head and approached with a hobble, wincing as he leaned upon his cane. "I owe you an apology for my rude departure last evening after your frankly refreshing honesty." Taking her gloved hand, he kissed it. "May we speak in private after the vote?"

Kasia froze with her hand in his. It was a formal gesture that felt romantic after his previous advances, but a courtship would only make her vulnerable, granting her enemies yet another tool to exploit. Zinarus was a good, honorable man who didn't deserve the pain she'd cause him. And she didn't deserve him either.

"I… I have a meeting already arranged," she replied. An ache gripped her heart, but she resisted the urge to ask him to call for her afterward. Being her ally put Zinarus at enough risk already.

He pursed his lips and released her hand. "Very well. Just… Show caution, please. Lord Tiuz's allies believe there is trouble afoot, more than even the Keloshans' advance. It would pain me greatly to see you come to harm."

"Thank you, but I am doing what I must. Focus on ensuring your friends at the arena are prepared to aid those on the west side. Many will be dragged from their homes if conscription is ordered."

Zinarus nodded, but another cane's thud disrupted him. His eyes widened, and he nodded toward the Chamber. "Let us enter before the king scolds us."

They parted ways, Kasia toward the nationalists on the right and Zinarus joining the few remaining reformers on the left. Each of the reformers, Zinarus included, wore a black scarf for those of their ranks who perished in the Ephemeral Slaughter. No such respect was given by the other factions.

"There you are," Gornioz said when Kasia neared. "Many of us were worried that you had decided to join your Vockan friend among the reformers once again. Was he attempting to sway your vote?"

The Oliezany patriarch cast a heavy shadow over her as she took her seat. How was it that he could have a more imposing presence than the literal dragon curled around the throne at the Chamber's center? A scraping sound echoed through the room as it dragged its crystal tail and draped it into the pit. Kasia focused on the beast to calm her nerves before granting Gornioz a smile.

"I fear his intentions revolve around my amber after Houze iz Vamiustok lost their sand," she said.

Gornioz chuckled. "Small men scramble when they lose an asset, while the strong seek to take advantage of the shifted field of battle."

*As Zinarus did,* Kasia thought, reflecting on the crowded jousting arena.

The Chamber's chattering fell quiet, and all rose at King Jazuk's arrival. He wore the bright red uniform of a Commonwealth general with golden epaulets and buttons glimmering in the Reacher Light from above. Though meant to be a show of force, his shuffled steps were hardly reassuring as Princess Nikoza aided his descent down the main stairs.

The young woman outshone her grandfather with ease despite wearing only a simple navy dress. Kasia wondered if she would've held a similar status had her father lived. Instead, she worked in the shadows.

"We meet under extraordinary and dire circumstances this day," Jazuk declared once he reached the throne. He rested a hand on the dragon's nose before sitting, his silver cane held before him. "The Keloshan Empire has rejected all attempts by our emissaries to end their persistent infringement of our nation's sovereign lands. Now, they come to us demanding vast tracts held by our people for generations. It is unacceptable."

Shouts of agreement rang out from the nationalists around Kasia and among many of the conservatives and moderates as well. The reformers sat back, arms crossed.

"This is why I bring before the honorable Chamber of Scions a declaration of war and mobilization order for the armed forces of our dear Commonwealth of Two Nations," Jazuk continued. "Included in this order is the conscription of the reserves among the lowborn to ensure our military rises to the might of our considerable foes."

A younger member of the nationalists stood behind Kasia. "My king, it is not enough! We stand alone, so we must unite our industrial might. Order our factories to abandon luxuries and turn to military goods before it is too late. Call the lowborn children to ensure we do not go without labor."

Jeers answered from the opposing end of the room. It was a line obviously fed to him by Gornioz or the other nationalists leaders who dared not speak out of turn against the king. The Chamber was nothing but theatre, though, and now the nationalists had begun the opening movements.

Jazuk turned to meet the nationalist. Spirits, he looked ancient with ever-deepening wrinkles and eyes that seemed lost in another time. "Lord Hazaekin, you are young, but sound of mind enough to know that this is not how we conduct business in this place. Our arms production indeed is dwarfed by our Keloshan neighbors, but we have far more Reachers than they." He raised his hand toward the dragon at his back. "We also have this mighty beast, gifted by the Crystal Mother herself. Our fellow scions may choose to shift production as our armies demand further armaments, but to force such things is tyranny that I shall not endorse."

The king cleared his throat and returned his attention to the rest of the Chamber. "Now, I present this proposal as a scion patriarch of House Bartol and as your elected king. The choice is yours, but know that our decisions today shall echo through time."

Open debate began with scions from the reform bloc voicing concerns for the well-being of lowborn and the agricultural economy. Dawnrise was a few mere hundred-hours away, and the absence of working-aged men would inhibit the planting season and threaten the food supply.

That argument drew scattered support from the rural moderates and conservatives, whose estates relied on crops instead of factories. House Niezik's lands around Tystok were no different, and even amber extraction would become more difficult with laborers conscripted for the war.

But what choice did they have? Failing to mobilize would surely mean their defeat. With Alyniana still missing, the Commonwealth had no allies. What hope did they have of facing Kelosh's greater army without every soldier they could muster?

Kasia found Zinarus among the reformers, sitting straight but staring at his feet. He neither applauded his allies nor jeered the nationalists as the debate dragged on. She wondered how he'd vote in the end. Each faction had presented alternate proposals, ranging from the nationalists' industrial desires to the reformers creating exemptions for as many laborers as possible. After an hour of bickering among the most powerful scions in the country, Kasia's leg was bouncing in anticipation of it ending.

Until Alyniana arrived.

A member of the conservative bloc was rambling about a country's duty when the ambassador appeared at the Chamber doors. She wore floral patterns across her dress and headscarf as usual, but dark bruises covered her face. In her hand, she gripped her crystal wand as she strode down the stairs with her glare fixed upon Jazuk.

"You claim you have no alliances to rely upon in this long everdark season," she declared, drowning out the rambling scion, who tried to continue talking despite the interruption. "Yet I stand before this exalted assembly today as proof of the contrary."

Gornioz shot to his feet. "How dare you disrupt the Chamber of Scions! Foreign dignitaries have no right to speak in this hall."

Alyniana met his challenge with a grin. "Is it not ironic that you have ignored my nation's pleas for aid countless times, yet now, when the Keloshan Empire knocks upon your door, you weep that you have no allies? I come to you today, dear friends of the Commonwealth of Two Nations, to offer an alternative to your desperation."

"Excuse me, Ambassador," Minister of War Hazemel Ioniz squeaked from the moderate bloc. He dressed in a vest and spectacles like a scholar, not a general, and his limited stature meant he barely rose among his seated allies. "Without revealing more than should be said in this setting, your proposal has already been considered among the king's ministers. We attempted to inform you, but you were unable to be located."

Alyniana stopped, a hand held to her chest. "You heard my proposal?" She glanced toward the throne, but from Nikoza's smile, the look wasn't intended for the king. "You were unable to find me because someone beat me and erased my memory. I know not what occurred before I awoke this afternoon before my consulate. What I am certain of, however, is that there are those within this very room who plot to ensure the Commonwealth loses this war."

Nationalists sprang to their feet, hurling accusations back at her, but Alyniana did not move.

"If the council has discussed my proposal," she shouted over the jeers, "why, then does this governing body act as if it does not know of it?"

"There was nothing for this body to act upon," Jazuk replied. "My council decided it would not be appropriate to allocate military resources and Reachers to your nation in a time of war."

Gornioz stomped his feet. "In our nation, my king, you serve the scions of the Chamber! It is good that the ambassador has come, as it grants me the opportunity to be clear with my fellow members of this body. King Jazuk Bartol and both ministers Hazemel Ioniz and Borys Kuzon conspired to keep their agreement with Nochland private. They will send their house's mercenaries to foreign lands instead of defending our own soil! Even my dear friend, Minister Lilita Pikezik, agreed to do so. How can we hope to stand against our foes when even our king and his council abandon us?"

More shouting filled the Chamber until Lilita rose, holding her shawl shut across her chest as she cast a glare at Gornioz. "I admit my collusion in this plot to ally with the merchant republic, but a discovery my husband, Lord Chatik, has made this day changed my position." Chatik grinned beside her, running his hands through his slicked-back gray hair as she held up a letter. "Lady Alyniana has in fact been recalled as ambassador of Nochland and therefore does not have the power to negotiate on its behalf."

Kasia cursed. How did Chatik know that? As far as she was aware, Alyniana had told only her.

"Is this true?" Jazuk asked Alyniana, waving off Nikoza's help as he pushed himself to his feet.

Alyniana held her chin up. "This agreement was drafted before I was removed for failing to convince you to send aid. My nation *will* honor it."

"Your nation has invited Kelosh into its lands!" Chatik replied. "They would only see us as aggressors."

"I have heard enough!" Jazuk stomped his cane, and the dragon roared over the debating scions. They fell silent as he walked down the narrow aisle before the throne. "In times past, kings would have thrown you into this pit for such deception, but you have shown a willingness to aid our nation. So, I tell you this: Go in peace and never return to this city. Tell the Merchant Council that we have made our choice. The Commonwealth stands alone."

Alyniana's gaze fell upon Kasia, who gave no reaction. There were too many scions watching her every move here. She would ensure Alyniana knew she still had the support of House Niezik, but that would come later. Defeating the Crimsons was her priority.

"May the Crystal Mother protect us all, then," Alyniana replied. "For when we stand alone, her aid is all that can save us."

Kasia studied Nikoza as the ambassador left, flanked by members of the Crystal Brigade. She'd paled significantly since Lilita's interruption. Had she been the one to bring Alyniana's proposal to the king, and if so, what gain did she have from it?

The king's granddaughter meant little in the end. Chatik's discovery had removed any hope of the other scions joining with Nochland. Against the Keloshan army, any Reachers Kasia could send in aid would be insufficient, but they had to find another way. Nochland choosing to fight was their only chance of holding Kelosh back, let alone defeating them.

The Chamber sat in a state of shock after Alyniana's departure, unsure what to make of the sudden change of events. Gornioz had directly accused Jazuk of acting outside the Chamber's will. Coming from the leader of the largest faction in the Chamber, that was no insignificant statement. The Commonwealth couldn't afford leadership struggles at a time like this, but men like Gornioz were too greedy to see that losing this war would mean no Ezmani ruled.

Jazuk cleared his throat. "With that disruption complete, let us end this debate and proceed forthwith to voting on the proposals presented by my council and the members of this Chamber. First, we will begin with the declaration of war and the admission that *some form* of mobilization is required. Need we more than a voice vote?"

A roar of approval erupted in reply. Even the reformers stomped their feet and shouted in favor of the declaration. Kasia had no such enthusiasm, but her voice soon joined the chorus. Kelosh had invaded. Refusing to declare war in response would do nothing to stop them.

"The Chamber has spoken, my king," Grand Secretary Votzan said once the fervor had faded. "War shall be declared."

Votzan then nodded to the reformers and the nationalists. "Two proposals shall yet be considered for the mobilization of our armed forces. The first shall be the limited order proposed by Lord Ivalat of House iz Ardinvil. The second, the proposal by Lord Gornioz of House Oliezany: a full mobilization order combined with a directive for our nation's factories to shift to military goods production."

Unlike the first vote, there was no clear reaction among the scions. Even some among the nationalists grumbled about the damage Gornioz's proposal would inflict upon their businesses. The conservatives, too, despised any attempt for the king to inflict his will upon the scions' aristocratic power.

Seeing the split, the assistant called each member's name for their vote. Neither proposal required the support of two-thirds of the Chamber due to their vote that they would mobilize in one form or another. It was a straight vote: for the reformers' plan or for Gornioz's.

The first votes signaled trouble for the Oliezany patriarch. Few beyond the lowliest of nationalists voted in favor of his proposal, most fearing for their businesses more than the lives of lowborn who would be thrown onto the front lines. And when Lilita Pikezik herself rose from the conservative bloc in support of the reformer plan, any chances Gornioz had were dashed. Kasia's tense shoulders loosened, if only a bit. She could vote as she wished. Gornioz would be angry, but he had lost anyway. Better to vote with her mind, her heart, and the majority.

"I support Lord iz Ardinvil's proposal," she announced when her turn came.

Grumbles surrounded her, and Gornioz scowled as she sat. "What are you doing, girl?" he muttered. "We must win this war."

"You must know when you have lost, Lord Gornioz," she replied without meeting his glare. "And you must know when you can find another way forward. My vote would have changed nothing."

He fumed, but as the vote went on, the Chamber proved Kasia correct. The final count was vastly in the reformers' favor. No cheers erupted from their seats when the assistant announced the results, though. Instead, the session ended in a solemn silence, all knowing that no matter the vote, the war they faced would threaten each of their livelihoods and even their lives.

Kasia remained in her seat a moment longer as the rest of the scions filed out. Hushed conversations surrounded her, but she focused on the thoughts in her head, ignoring the whispers of the spirits that intruded within it. The Chamber meeting had passed. Now, she faced her foes. No matter what nation invaded, they would not stop her vengeance. She'd waited half her life for this.

She would not fail.

Tzena did not await her in the grand hall. A few other scions pressed her for information about her amber or why she'd voted the way she had, but she ignored them as she pushed toward the main doors. Her carriage sat in a dense row of others far newer and more well-embellished than it. It was usually a familiar, safe place for her to return to, but Tazper was missing, replaced with a stout Ezmani man with a curled mustache. He tipped his flat cap to her.

"All is well, Lady Katarzyna?" he asked in the thick accent of the eastern forestlands, his tongue hanging on the roof of his mouth for each L.

Kasia eyed his waist for a pistol, but there was none. A Crimson driver was likely to be a Reacher, though, so she kept her guard up. "I have not been well for many years," she muttered, stepping into the empty carriage. "Where is Tazper?"

"I believe the letter explained all," the man replied. "He will be safe as long as you comply."

They started moving not a moment after she closed the door and laid her head back against the carriage wall. Tazper was gone, and the whirlwind of a Chamber meeting had her headache pounding even worse than before. But there was no rest ahead. There was no turning back.

She was on her way to face the Crimsons… and whoever led them.

# SHADOWED FOES

*"It is better for the honorable leader to face their enemies in the light rather than the dark."* – Tiuz Hazeko, former Ezmani major general

The everdark hung over Radais within the Spirit Wastes. A fog thicker than any other seen in all of Zekiaz, it swirled at the edge of the Glassblades' lanterns like a predator circling its prey.

"Why doesn't the fog come into the light?" Wanusa asked, riding beside Radais with her sword already drawn. No one else did the same except for Lazan, who had only a glass dagger and his Body Reaching.

"No one knows," Miv replied from behind them. "Legends say it's made of people's last breaths when they were killed in the Awakening."

Mhanain spat into the ashen sand, eyeing the mists as one would a thief. "It ain't no breath. There's a witch out here with the spirits. She surrounds us with the mists to confuse us, but it won't work. I know better."

Miv rolled her eyes. "And that is why I've refrained from sending you out here."

"Yer loss."

Their squabbling continued for some time as Radais led them west, searching for the place he'd found the Pikezik man robed in red. All looked the same in the Wastes during everdark, though, and he'd yet to admit to Miv how blind he felt. This was his mission. The Glassblades, and maybe even the entire Commonwealth, were relying on him. Yet all he could think about was how his brother would mock him when he failed yet again.

Then came the voices.

The hissing of the swarming awakened had haunted him ever since he'd left the Wastes. Was this different? He doubted his senses as the others told Wanusa their stories from the Wastes, exaggerating their accomplishments. Surely they would have heard?

But no one else reacted as the whispers drew closer, sweeping overheard. The mists covered any sight of them. There was too much to risk. Radais's doubts faded with the noise growing in his ears and mind, and he drew his blade.

"Quiet!" He turned about on Vuk and signaled for the others to prepare for an attack. "They're here."

Wanusa's eyes widened as the others took positions to guard each other's flanks. "What's happening?" she whispered, falling in line between Radais and Miv.

Miv just raised a finger to her lips, then held her arms to form an X—the sign to guard one's allies.

The voices stayed in the mists, but their numbers strengthened. Where there had been a handful, countless strange conversations filled the air. They seemed to hold no recognizable tone or language. It was a cacophony of noise that rose until Radais winced from the sound.

Then it stopped.

"Be at the ready!" Radais called.

They sat in silence upon their ibexes for what felt like a thousand heartbeats, their breaths slow, calculated amid the frigid darkness. Each of them had trained years for moments like this. No matter how many awakened they'd fought outside the Wastes, though, Radais knew firsthand that nothing could prepare even the greatest warrior for facing the spirits in their own territory. He checked his armor one last time, but never took his gaze from the fog.

Shadows shot through it like bolts of lightning. Shifting mists took a human form as an awakened charged straight at Radais with its ethereal tendrils ready.

But he was ready too, driving Vuk to the side as he slashed with his glass sword, sending it straight through the spirit's torso.

A chorus answered its cry as it dissolved into nothing. Awakened dove from everywhere, their dark bodies smothering lanterns and allowing the Waste fog to follow their advances. Screams followed. Not those of spirits, but Glassblades, their circle broken by the awakened from above.

Radais fought side-by-side with Wanusa and Miv. He and his old master knew each other's moves by heart, allowing them to drive back six awakened and slay another pair.

No matter her allies' skill, Wanusa was vulnerable. She swung like the initiate she was, and the awakened sensed her weakness. Radais tried to cover her flank, but the awakened somehow fought as a coordinated group. One got past his guard. It slammed into his shoulder pauldron and threw him off Vuk. He was up a blink later, but it was too late.

Wanusa landed in the ash beside him, bleeding from her face as a familiar voice screamed above. Two awakened lifted Miv into the air. Her sword lay shattered as her ibex fled the swarm.

Radais lunged after her. A group of awakened blocked his advance, but he sliced through them with relentless fury. He'd lost Miv as his lover. He'd lost her as his mentor. But he couldn't lose her from this world.

The shouts of his Glassblade comrades surrounded him as he neared Miv. She thrashed against the awakened, but no physical attack could harm them. The pair clinging to her arms seemed more *real* than the others, wearing crystalline gloves as they hauled her higher and higher. Radais jumped and swung his blade. They were too far, and the sword's tip only cut through the bottom of the nearest one. It hissed down at him but continued on.

"Shoot them down!" he shouted back at the rest of the troop. Mhanain and at least two others carried glass arrows or crossbow bolts. Surely, they could down the awakened before they carried Miv away.

When no answer came, Radais turned back to see his allies scrambling for their lives. Mhanain led a group of scattered Glassblades from ibexback. His commanding voice carried through the fray, and he counter-charged with those left standing. To Radais's relief, Lazan and Wanusa fought among them on foot. But they were too far and too occupied with their own awakened to stop those holding Miv.

Radais blinked away tears, roaring into the everdark as he fought to rejoin the rest of his team. They'd taken Miv. Why? Awakened didn't kidnap people—they turned them to husks. The awakened's voices had to hold the key, but he couldn't understand them.

He reached the others as the awakened launched another attack. Groups this large should've never existed, but their numbers only seemed to grow as the Glassblades cut them down.

"Can't keep doing this," Mhanain grunted as he swept past Radais. "Gotta retreat."

Radais shook his head and slashed down a spirit that had reached for the old warrior. "Where? They're faster than us."

The Glassblades' charge faltered. They fell back into a tight circle, Radais, Lazan, Mhanain, and Wanusa the only ones remaining as the awakened dragged away the bodies of the fallen. Spirits, they were *taking* the bodies. Radais's head spun. There was no time for planning a retreat or any other battle tactics. They were outnumbered, surrounded, and the only remaining light shone from the lantern on Mhanain's ibex.

Wanusa fought at Radais's side, but she staggered as Lazan circled to each warrior to heal them. The initiate parried an awakened's strike before turning to Radais with a wild look in her eyes. "Do you have it?"

"Have what?" he grunted back with a stab straight through the awakened she'd blocked.

She held up her half of the crystal they'd found nights before. "The drifters are attracted to it, right? Maybe the awakened are too."

Radais fought for an opening large enough for him to reach into his pocket and retrieve his shard. "These things are different. They're smarter."

"Have a better idea?"

*Spirits help me,* Radais thought. The shard should've been his chance at wealth, but he'd never see that money if he was dead.

"Fine, but this had better work. You throw yours that way, and I'll throw the other direction."

Wanusa launched her crystal without reply. The shimmering stone pierced the fog and disappeared into the everdark as Radais did the same. A deep feeling of loss filled his chest. It was a selfish, childish thought, but it lingered as he whispered a prayer to the pure spirits of the crystal, "Take them."

The awakened's attack faltered. All but the nearest chased the crystals, giving the remaining Glassblades a chance to cut down those that remained. For now.

"Time to run!" Mhanain said once the final awakened fell.

Radais nodded. "This time, I have no arguments."

He whistled, and Vuk burst through the fog along with the other ibexes that had fled. Wanusa fumbled through Miv's bags, then mounted with the other Glassblades before galloping east with Mhanain's light to guide the way. Awakened shrieks filled the air, but after a minute, they faded into the everdark. Radais breathed a sigh of relief.

Until the second light appeared.

Blinding, it banished the mists for a hundred strides and revealed a group of wispy gray figures hovering before the Glassblades. They held different forms than the awakened, resembling misshapen animals and humans. Clothes of metal, cloth, and crystal alike covered their bodies and draped down to the ash below, and those with hands carried two-ended spears—one tip metal and the other glass.

The first of the creatures flew closer, its lantern of pure white light forcing Radais to shield his eyes. Between his fingers, he saw the creature's flower-like face and four arms sprouting from robes of raven black that devoured the lanternlight. An eye stared back at him from each end of the flower's eight petals. It turned the metal end of its spear toward Radais, and when it spoke, it did so with no mouth.

"You tread on the Sands of Salesh," it proclaimed, its ethereal voice swirling with the mists. "We have saved you from the Vanashel. Speak your purpose, or be hollowed by our spears."

# THE KING IN THE DARK

*"The gentle Queen of Light casts her warmth over us for much of the year, but when he chooses, the King in the Dark clenches us in his fist so tightly that not a single ray reaches the earth."* – Ezmani folktale

Kasia tapped her foot as she awaited the end of her carriage trip to the Crimson Court. The driver had hung coverings over the windows to disguise their path, but they had passed from Kalastok's cobblestone streets onto dirt country roads, rattling her already spinning head.

She cursed her drunkenness the night before. In truth, though, she'd needed the release, no matter how foolish. Realm Taint, she could've done without.

The headache wasn't enough to keep her thoughts away from the identity of the Dark Reacher. What did he want? He'd forced Zinarus to sell his house's sand mines, kidnapped Alyniana but released her right before the mobilization vote, and pressed Kasia to kill Sazilz. All her digging had unveiled no connections between those efforts. Nor had she gotten any closer to discovering his true identity, besides that he was in some way allied with scions of many great houses, especially House Pikezik.

Whoever the Reacher was, he took his anonymity seriously, wasting Dark Reaching to cover his face. He *seemed* like the leader of the Crimsons, but Kasia had no way to know if that was true. He could've been a front man or puppet.

*Spirits, what am I doing?*

She rode blindly into either a trap or the truth. Despite all her attempts to learn about her foes, she had nothing but a few scattered names. They had given her revenge against Sazilz for a reason, and its price was certainly higher than Paras's death. Ridding a great house of its patriarch with few questions from the other scions was no meager feat. Kasia had nearly fallen apart just faking Paras's death, and if they demanded something greater from her…

No, she would face them and win. Her Reaching could kill an entire room of people, Reachers or not. The Crimsons would have no defense once she chose to unleash her power. And when the time came, she *would* allow herself to Reach until they all perished. Taint would not stop her.

"Is slaughter really your best answer?" a voice said from across the carriage.

She groaned, rubbing her temples as she leaned onto her knees. "Go away, Aliax."

He perched his legs up on the wall so that he lay across the entire seat. In a simple farmer's tunic, he looked far out of place in a scion's carriage, but Aliax had always enjoyed being where people thought he shouldn't be. "The great Katarzyna Niezik outwitted House Uziokaki, taking their amber and becoming the Amber Dame. But when facing the organization that plotted both the demise of her father and Sazilz Uziokaki, all she could think of was killing them." He tapped his head. "Do you have a crystal brain? You make a move like that, and they'll shoot you before you can do anything."

"Not if they trust me," she whispered so the carriage driver wouldn't hear.

"Kasia, you're smarter than this." He dropped his feet to the floor with a heavy *thud*, meeting her gaze. "If you were the head of a secretive group that assassinated King Yaakiin, would you ever trust your members fully? Someone there will have a way to kill any Crimson that steps out of line. Sure as shit, they'll have their eye on a Death Reacher."

"Then what am I supposed to do?" she snapped. "I can't just leave and pretend I saw nothing. Even if they kill me, if I Reach fast enough, they'll be dead too."

Aliax snatched her hand and pressed it to his chest. It neither rose with breaths nor drummed with his heart. "You can win as long as your heart beats, so beat them at their own game! But you'll fly as crooked as a raven in the everdark until you know what they want."

She sneered. "Mother always called me that."

"I know," he whispered, his body beginning to drift into smoke. "And every time, you've proved her wrong. Do it again."

The carriage came to a rough stop as he disappeared. Kasia stared at her extended hand, remembering the heartbeat that had once met her fingers years before, but Aliax's life was gone. So was his warmth.

She quickly pulled the hand back to her chest when the door opened. Then she sat, frozen, with doubt swirling in her mind.

The mustached Crimson driver coughed. "Need help, m'lady?"

"No," she said flatly, prying herself from the seat and stepping onto a stone pathway that led toward a dark mansion. Burning vines arched over the length of the path, but the flames didn't consume the plants. They provided an intense warmth that made Kasia wish to remove her formal jacket. In the face of her foes, though, the extra layer was just another thin shield against whatever the Crimsons had waiting for her in the mansion.

A figure passed from the darkness behind the carriage with a knowing smile. "Welcome, Katarzyna," Tzena said, wearing red robes that drifted down her body in various layers.

Kasia eyed her before returning her attention to the flames. "This is quite the display. Allow me the chance to guess… The vines are protected by a Life Reacher and the fires channeled by one of Fire? You truly recruited the best for aesthetics."

"Woe of you to assume we needed to recruit Reachers," Tzena replied. "After all, the greatest of them already serve among our ranks and are more than happy to provide a show for the newest of our ranks."

With a nod. Kasia gestured toward the mansion. "Need I know anything more before we continue?"

"Only that you would be wise to curb that rage of yours. We knew of your plan for Sazilz, and if you step out of line, we will ensure you join him. Those who bear our mark are treated well, but betrayers receive no second chances."

"Nor should they."

Their gazes sparred, a fragile balance held between them until Tzena chuckled and stepped beneath the arches. "Come."

A tingle trickled down Kasia's spine as she followed Tzena. The fires crackled around her, and her instincts screamed for her to flee from the smoke that poured from them. But a gentle Air Reacher's breeze created a clear funnel no wider than their shoulders. It brought the outside chill, sparring with the blaze that summoned a cold sweat to her brow.

This was no show, she realized. It was intimidation. Not only could the Crimsons combine the power of three Reachers, they could *waste* it without batting an eye. What concerned Kasia more was that no unskilled Reacher would be capable of such displays. The great houses employed a number of them for parlor tricks and convenience, but for an experienced Reacher to focus on anything but serious tasks was unheard of.

Light from the flames danced across the mansion's glass-infused stone exterior. It resembled older architecture that had once been popular in the neo-Piorak era a few hundred years before, and Kasia loathed that Kalastok and Tystok both had ventured away from its angular, severe stylings and artwork. Scions now preferred to use their spirit repelling glass on the interior walls as a lavish decoration instead of the shimmering yet haunting feeling this mansion gave amid the everdark.

Four hooded figures blocked the way to the mansion's double doors. Three of them wore a glove over their right hand, leaving their taloned left one exposed, and colored wisps of magic circled them. The only one who didn't Reach stepped into the firelight. His face was instantly familiar—the Light Reacher from the night Kasia had killed Sazilz.

"Welcome, Lady Katarzyna," he said, holding out the crimson robes folded in his arms. "Please don these robes and draw up your hood until told to do otherwise."

Kasia took the clothes and pulled them over her dress, tying them shut with glass-beaded chains. They were exceptionally long when compared with those the other crimsons wore, and they draped onto the path behind her as she pulled up her hood.

"I am ready," she said once she'd adjusted them to her liking. It felt as if her skin was burning, but she reminded herself that amber and the clothes she'd chosen still separated her from the robe. She'd not surrendered to them.

The Light Reacher nodded, then snapped his fingers.

Fire and breeze vanished. The sounds of a thousand little cracks filled the air, and Kasia flinched at the ashen vines falling over them as the four Reachers turned and headed into the mansion. Servants held the doors open, wearing deep gray veils over their faces and uniforms like a soldier's. Kasia wondered how they could see. Her attention soon turned to the mansion itself, though, as she entered a large foyer with three staircases: one going down in the center, flanked on either side by ones curling up.

Tzena stopped at Kasia's side. "You may believe that you are to ascend, but true power in our realm rests far below the surface. Those fools at the Buried Temple are at least right about that much."

So Kasia descended the central staircase, her footfalls muffled on the deep red rug lying over the mansion's wood floors. Torches lit the way, but they lacked the encompassing warmth of the arches outside.

Kasia tightened her robe against the chill as the bottom of the stairs came into view. She'd descended deeper than any normal basement, and the layers of stone and wood above her seemed a crushing weight as she emerged into a rounded room full of hooded figures. They faced a man in the room's center, standing in natural darkness away from the torches.

The man stepped from a raised platform and extended his hand toward Kasia. His face was covered by his deep hood, but his voice she recognized instantly. "Step into the Crimson Court, Katarzyna of House Niezik," the Dark Reacher said, "and be welcomed among its ranks."

As she approached, she stared up at the stained-glass flower that stretched across the ceiling, the torchlight dancing across each petal of a different color than the others. Fifteen of them branched from a central circle of deep red that sat over the Dark Reacher's head.

The Dark Reacher smiled when she stopped before him. Raising his arms toward the Crimsons on either side, he dangled glass amulets from his hands. They were perfectly clear, but they shifted between colors as he swung them from their chains.

"Fifteen realms bleed their powers for us to wield," he declared. "From each, we have Reachers, but we seek the power beyond."

"The Axiom!" the Crimsons replied as one.

The Dark Reacher swung one amulet toward Kasia and the other toward the ceiling. Hers turned deep purple as the other shone with every color of the stained-glass above. "As the petals of a flower invite the bee to find its center, so, too, do the realms show us the way to the center of our reality. Through crystal, we find our center. The Axiom."

He handed the first amulet to Kasia. She took it, examining its flower shape with an array of colors around the same dark purple center that it had glowed before. The realms around the Axiom. But what did the Crimsons believe that Axiom to be?

"You have proven your loyalty to our order and all Ezmani scions," the Dark Reacher continued, placing the other amulet around his neck. The gathered Crimsons followed his example with their own amulets. "To succeed in our goals, we have all made great sacrifices for the Court, and you are no different. We have worked in the darkness for all these years in wait for the final petal. Among us have been skilled Reachers of every realm—except for that of Death. You are the piece we have been missing to complete the key and unlock the Axiom."

The pieces clicked: the Crimsons Nex had heard talking about the 'final petal,' them allowing Kasia to kill Sazilz, and their sudden interest after the Ephemeral Slaughter. She'd revealed her power that night. Ever since, they had known she was exactly what they needed.

And she'd let them take her.

"You want me only for my talon," she replied flatly, doing all she could to swallow her panic. They needed her. That gave her bargaining power, but her Reaching was a double-edged sword with the Taint that followed. "I have trusted you, done what you asked. Why do you still hide your face?"

The Dark Reacher chuckled before looking to Tzena behind her. "Lady Tzena, as her sponsor, do you believe she is ready to see our faces?"

"I do," Tzena replied. "Despite her father's loyalties, she has proven to be aligned with our interests both inside the Chamber of Scions and beyond. My only concerns rested in her apparent obsession with following my uncle's orders, but her independence on the mobilization vote has ridded me of them."

"Gornioz?" Kasia asked. "I thought he was one of you… of us?"

Tzena scoffed, circling to the Dark Reacher's side. "No, Gornioz's interests lie only in our house's superiority in an old man's game for power. We both wish for the Commonwealth to rise above its neighbors, but even he was not wise enough to see the truth in the Axiom. Only it can control the spirits completely and save us from this war. Only it can bring us glory."

"What is this Axiom?" Kasia tapped the center of the flower amulet. "A realm at the center of the other fifteen?"

The Dark Reacher nodded, then drew down his hood. Kasia took a step back at the face that met her.

Chatik Pikezik studied Kasia with sunken eyes of swirling silver. His deep gray hair was the same as his elderly father, King Jazuk—slicked back so heavily it seemed a creature clung to his head. All around him, many of the other Crimsons' faces were familiar too. Some sat in the Chamber, but most were cousins or descendants not in line to inherit their houses. Hunger lurked in their gazes, longing. And they saw their hope in Chatik.

*It was always him.*

Chatik had spread false reports of Keloshans creating the Spirit Plague and told Lilita that Alyniana was no longer an ambassador.

He'd been the one to threaten Zinarus to sell his sand mines to House Oliezany. He'd kidnapped Alyniana. He'd sent the Pikezik into the Spirit Wastes. But why?

"We have believed for centuries that there are only fifteen realms," he said, his voice regal. Spirits, how had she not recognized it from the Chamber? He was far from its loudest member, but she'd heard him enough. "We were wrong. Another bleeds through them, a chalice pouring its energy so that we may exist, and we can Reach into it. Neither Kelosh nor my puppet of a father have such vision. We hold the key for the Commonwealth."

"For the King in the Dark!" the Crimsons replied.

When the others quieted, Chatik looked to Kasia. "Tonight, we shall open a connection to the Axiom with the power of all fifteen realms. Join us, Katarzyna, and let us change the fate of our nation, our realm."

Kasia raised her taloned hand, but he caught her wrist. "Leave that glove on until we begin," he hissed. "You have earned our trust, but one cannot assume a Death Reacher's power will not target them."

"Unhand me," she snapped back. Her charade had gotten her this far, but she would not pretend to be Chatik's pet. There were too many Reachers here to dare attempt to kill him. For now, though, she could use his ambition for her own gain. "I have proven our interests align, but first, tell me: Who shall wield the Axiom's power? You?"

Chatik released her, a wry smile across his face until he turned toward the platform. "Combined, our powers should open a portal, but we know not how long it shall remain so. I will pass through first. Once I return, we shall decide who, if anyone, should follow."

Kasia raised her brow. "Why should I help you take such power with nothing for myself?"

"You desire to return your house to the level of the greatest scions, yes?" he replied, stepping onto the platform again and holding his talon toward the flower above.

"I do."

"Then when I am emperor of not only the Commonwealth, but all of the continent of Brakesh, the fifteen who grant me the Axiom will have wealth and power greater than any house. You will be kings and queens of what had once been divided nations. Together, we will rule the old Piorak Empire through Ezmani blood and crystal." He closed his taloned fist, crazed fury replacing his smile. "None will defy us! None will dare tear our nation limb-from-limb again!"

Cheers answered him, but Kasia clenched her jaw. This was not how she'd expected this to go. Chatik had revealed nothing about the Crimsons' involvement with the awakened, but there was more there. No matter how powerful, this Axiom surely couldn't defeat the empires by itself. The awakened had a role to play still, and Kasia's stomach churned at what that could mean.

At Chatik's signal, the other Reachers stepped onto the platform and positioned themselves under their realm's colored petal. Tzena joined them. Kasia hadn't seen her Reach, but she'd stopped beneath the dark gray peta, which typically represented the Shadow realm.

Chatik took his position beneath the pure black petal of Darkness, then looked to Kasia without another word.

She met his gaze but hesitated. Was she truly about to surrender to the Crimsons whatever power the Axiom held? Every fiber of her being told her to flee, but there was no way to run. She'd entered the beast's maw, and its jagged teeth blocked her escape.

Slowly, she approached her place beneath the deep purple petal for Death. A female servant stepped past her and placed a fist-sized chunk of light gray crystal on a glass pedestal beneath the stained-glass Axiom. She moved with grace unlike any lowborn Kasia had seen, yet she would've worn red if she were a scion. Each stride was a reminder of Kasia's eloquence training as a child, and how poorly she'd handled it.

The Reachers extended their taloned hands once the servant departed, the colors from above spiraling between their fingers as Chatik's voice called over the hum of magic, "Reach with all your power, channeling it toward the crystal. Connect our realms, and we shall connect to the Axiom."

Kasia removed her glove, but her hand trembled as she raised it. Aliax and the peasants' screams hammered her mind as he formed in the black wisps surrounding Chatik, watching her with those solemn eyes that had once held passion and endearing joy. But what joy they had once held vanished long ago. The chasm left behind threatened to tear Kasia to its depths.

She Reached, but no power rose to her fingers.

The other Reachers eyed Kasia as she pushed with all her will. It was as if the well of power at her fingertips had run dry. The further she Reached into it, the further it fled her grasp.

"You are inviting death on the whole continent if you let Chatik win," Aliax's whispered words carried to her ears. "There is no way out, but maybe there's one *through*. Beat him at his own game."

*At his own game…*

Aliax's implicit permission sparked something within her. A haataamaash board emerged amid the Reacher wisps. She imagined her father moving his dragon to threaten her throne, crippling any of her attempts at a traditional defense. While she'd played a tactical game with a balance of give and take, he'd sacrificed pieces freely to make space for the most powerful to strike. What he'd done in the process, though, was leave his rear unguarded for her spy. Considered the weakest piece by most, it was often ignored in the late game, but when she moved it to his end of the board, it trapped her father's throne.

He conceded.

That misty throne fell, sending the board back into the nothingness from which it emerged. What remained was the Reachers watching her anxiously.

Chatik's brow furrowed further with each passing moment. "Reach, Katarzyna! Death is the final key!"

Kasia took a deep breath. A weight shed from her shoulders knowing that her fight was not over. Chatik had moved his dragon, but his confidence would be his undoing.

So she Reached, pouring her anguish and regret into the pull. Yes, she'd killed. Yes, she'd failed. But tonight, maybe she could turn fate in her favor.

Purple burst from her talon and wrapped its way up her arm. Despite the usual chill of Death, it felt inviting between her fingers as she embraced the fury in her heart. All she'd done—all she'd been forced to do—was because of Chatik and his Crimsons. With her power, she would give them all they desired.

Then she would destroy them.

The Reachers all directed their powers to the crystal and struck it at once in a blaze of vibrant colors. Both blinding yet infinitely dark at the same time, Kasia couldn't help but stare in awe at the explosions as the Reachers' rays collided. She'd seen Reachers spar with their powers before. It couldn't compare to the display before her, growing with each rapid beat of her heart.

"Keep pushing!" Chatik shouted. "The portal opens yet!"

Kasia fought off her lingering memories as she Reached deeper into the realm of Death. Despite Aliax's permission, they clawed at her like fresh cuts along her scars. But she thought only of her father's final moments, of his lessons and obsession with the awakened until his last breath. He'd given everything to stop the Crimsons, so she would too.

It seemed an eternity before the crystal exploded, engulfed in a shimmering vapor that formed a sphere between the Reachers. A blow struck Kasia's chest, and she dropped as her Reaching failed. The others followed.

Darkness fell over the room as the torches extinguished. The Crimsons watched in still silence, the sphere's vapors of a thousand colors growing and shrinking without pattern. It exuded no power Kasia could sense, nor any noise. An odd feeling fell over her—as if she were weightless yet anchored to the ground, a strange ringing hanging around her.

The Reachers struggled to their feet as Kasia studied the Crimsons outside the circle. They had barely moved under Chatik's fearsome gaze, but now, a shimmering field separated them from the fifteen Reachers. They neither blinked nor shifted on their feet. When Kasia stood, their eyes remained fixed on the sphere.

"What happened to them?" she mumbled, then repeating herself louder.

Chatik groaned from across the sphere. Though not visible through it, now that she'd picked out his voice, it felt impossible that she'd ever missed his connection to the Dark Reacher before. "It is not what has happened to them that is significant," he said. "It is what we have brought upon ourselves."

Kasia rounded the sphere to him as the other Reachers within the platform did the same. The sphere's shifting lights were dizzying, but looking away did little to help when the same colors flickered across the Crimsons' stunned faces. Had they known more than her? Or had Chatik ensured only he knew the truth of what they summoned?

"We reside in a sub-realm of a kind, separating us from the rest of Zekiaz," Chatik continued. "It will remain around the portal for as long as it remains open, but I know not how long that shall be. Stay here until I return. Should I not, Tzena, begin Sleepwalk without me. We have come too far for a setback to cease our progress."

Tzena bowed her head. "Yes, my king."

With her recognition, Chatik stepped to the edge of the sphere. His crimson robes appeared near white in the boundless light, but the core of his flower amulet pulsed like a dark heart upon his chest. He extended his hand toward the swirling mass. Its mists shied away at first, but in its inconstant flow, it returned a heartbeat later, washing over his fingers and then his arm. Soon, it consumed him whole.

The Reachers glanced around without a word. Most were unfamiliar to Kasia, neither Chamber members nor from great houses, and from the dull appearance of their talons, they had burned away multiple Reaches too. That meant the same for Chatik.

And it meant none of them could stop her without Tainting themselves.

Tzena's hand fell lightly upon Kasia's shoulder, but her decision was already made. Before Tzena could even speak, Kasia rushed forward.

It was only four strides to the sphere. She bounded each one with twelve years of misery fueling her hate. Cries came from the Reachers behind, but they were too late. She burst into the portal at full speed. Warmth encompassed her, her body and mind becoming light until reality disappeared.

# BREATHLESS

*"Many have theories about how the awakened emerged seemingly from nowhere and nothing. It is a question we may never know the answer to."* – An excerpt from *The Rise and Fall of Piorak, Volume III*

Radais urged Vuk to back away slowly as the flying creatures towered over the remaining Glassblades. The ibex had faced awakened and beasts of every kind with him, but Vuk froze. Radais couldn't blame him. The many-eyed one who'd spoken was the most terrifying thing he'd ever seen.

Mhanain coughed and elbowed him. "Talk to it. Yer in charge now."

Purest spirits, how little he wanted to lead right now. But the flower creature had asked their purpose, so someone had to speak. Miv was gone. It was up to Radais.

"I am called Radais, and we're searching for others like us who've come to your land," he said louder than was probably necessary. The things didn't seem to have any ears, but it had spoken without a mouth either. "They wear red clothing and have crystal talons on their fingers."

A hiss spread among the gathered creatures who had called themselves part of Salesh. "You seek the crystal-fingered ones," the flower one said. "You call them of your kind."

"No!" Radais replied. "No, we think they're doing something to the awakened, trying to control them. We want to stop it."

"Control…"

The creature floated downward, drawing ever closer. Its incredibly bright lantern pierced the everdark and cut through its own semi-translucent body. Radais's allies gripped their blades anxiously, but as the creature stopped mere feet from him, he signaled for them to be at ease. His instincts had taken him far across the Commonwealth and the Spirit Wastes. He'd seen spirits of every shape and people far more monstrous than any awakened. This *thing*… It did not mean them harm—he was sure of it.

"We don't want to control spirits," Radais said. "We are Glassblades, Vockans. We honor spirits and destroy those that are corrupted."

The lantern hovered ever-closer, drifting toward the sword in his grasp. Its glass blade scattered the light into a rainbow of colors across the ashen sand. After a season of nothing but the everdark and dim lanternlight, Radais gasped at the beauty in it. The creature, too, held a strange elegance. Not the vibrant colors of the light, but like a statue carved of smoke instead of marble.

"You have no crystal, Radais," the creature said. "We smelt it… Pure… Now gone."

Radais swallowed and swapped glances with Wanusa. She shook her head, but what would lying to these creatures gain? If they could sense crystal, they likely would realize Lazan had a talon. "We found a piece of crystal in the ground on our way here," he said. "My friend, Lord Lazan Karianam, also carries a crystal talon, but he uses it to heal people, not control spirits."

A few of the creature's eyes flicked to Lazan. "Crystal bound to flesh. You draw from the realm of the Body?"

Lazan covered his talon, as if that would change the creature's interest. "I am what our people call a Body Reacher, yes."

"Gray skin," it replied. "From the land of bountiful crystal, like the other crystal-fingered ones."

"I am Ezmani," Lazan said, brow raised. "From what you have said, I assume you hail from Salesh. What do you call yourself?"

The creature swayed side-to-side in the air, its robes drifting far too slowly for the motion. "I am Rakekeaa, scout of Sands of Salesh by order of First One. We are Saleshi. We are ones who draw no breath. Ones you seek, near. Follow us through God's Breath to them."

*God's Breath?*

Radais looked to his allies for guidance but found them all as slack-jawed as him. The decision was his alone to make, but what choice did he have? They couldn't turn back and face the awakened. The way east wasn't clear either, and they were just as likely to stumble to their deaths without direction. No matter how strange Rakekeaa and the other Saleshi were, they were the Glassblades' best hope of finding Miv and discovering more about the Crimsons.

"We will follow," he said. "But keep an eye out for the awakened in case they're still around."

Rakekeaa raised its four arms, crossing them. "The Vanashel's mindless ones are no threat. We sent them away."

"How?"

It didn't reply as it flew into the mists with the other Saleshi keeping overhead. Radais signaled for the others to ride with him, and together, they followed Rakekeaa's bright lantern. Wanusa flanked Radais on one side with her lips still parted in shock. Mhanain rode on the other with a grin like he'd just had the best ale in his entire life.

"The breathless, eh?" he said. "Slap my ass and roll me down the stairs. If I didn't know better, I'd think I was flat drunk back at camp right now."

Wanusa rolled her eyes. "They are called the Saleshi, not the breathless. The word just means they don't breathe… I guess."

"I don't care what you call them," Radais said. "Be careful not to offend them. It looks like they just saved our lives and want to show us the Crimsons."

Lazan used what remained of his Reaching to heal their wounds as they rode. He was quieter than normal, but Radais figured it was due to shock from the attack. Wanusa seemed to be handling it remarkably well for her first battle in the Wastes. The Saleshi had distracted Radais from the loss of Miv and so many others, but even his head hung now that they had returned to riding. Could the Saleshi help him get her back?

He clung on to that hope as minutes turned to hours and his bottom became sore. They were well into the early hours of the morning based on Lazan's watch, but the Saleshi showed no signs of slowing.

"I'm destined to fall from this saddle before they stop," Wanusa complained when they neared a rocky gorge, leaning back with her arms hung loose. "Please tell me we're close?"

Rakekeaa's light stopped then, and the Saleshi's eyes fixed upon her. "The crag ahead. Enter. Crystal-fingered ones are gone, as is God."

"Will you not come with us?" Lazan asked, a flash of desperation in his eyes. "If there are more awakened, the help would be appreciated."

It studied him, then held out the bright lantern. "Bring this. We watch here. Return when you are finished, and then we will show you to First One."

"Who is the First One?" Radais asked.

"You will see it soon."

Lazan shrugged at Radais, who sighed and took the lantern. Answers lay ahead. His questions about the Saleshi could be addressed once they'd figured out what the Crimsons were up to. Radais pushed Vuk into a trot, drawing his blade from his back. Rakekeaa had implied it was safe, but he had no intention of entering the Crimsons' base unarmed. Reachers always had tricks up their sleeves.

"Keep to a single file," he said to the others as the sand gave way to a descent between two rising faces of rock. "The Crimsons could have left traps behind."

The lanternlight washed the cliffs in pure white and exposed insects scuttering into cracks. It had no clear source of its glow, neither flame nor an orb that usually marked a Light Reacher's power. Besides, it had stayed lit far longer than any Light Reacher's power would last. It was almost as if the light emanated from the lamp itself.

"How's it work, Lazan?" Mhanain asked. "Yer a Reacher, so you should know this stuff."

Lazan huffed, holding a pistol in one hand and the reins in his other. "I am a Reacher, not a professor in the arcane. To be honest, I barely understand how my own power works."

"Fixed me up just fine, so yer doing something right."

A smile tugged at Lazan's lips. "Yeah… something at least."

Rocks skidded down the cliff to their left, spurring Radais to turn about, sword ready. "Enough. We stay quiet from now on unless it's related to the mission."

Mhanain muttered under his breath, but the others nodded. Radais took that as enough and headed further down the slope. He wasn't sure what he was supposed to be looking for. Rakekeaa seemed to think it was obvious, though, so he kept riding until the lantern revealed another cliff face with a hole blown into its center.

"Explosives?" Wanusa asked.

Mhanain shook his head. "No scorch marks."

"A Reacher, then," Radais said, riding closer. The light crept over piles of boulders on either side of the hole, as if ripped directly from the cliff. "You're right, Mhanain. These are far too big to have been blown out by an explosive, or even mined through. Looks like we're on the right track."

His anticipation faded at the sight of a dark stain that ran from the hole's entrance to beyond the light's reach. Blood. He knew the sight of an awakened attack well, and the gruesome scene before him resembled the worst kind. There were no bodies in sight. From the amount of blood splattered across the walls and soaked into the stone underfoot, though, whoever had been here surely hadn't survived.

"Do you think it was the Crimsons?" Wanusa asked.

Radais bit his cheek. "Maybe. Or it was their victims…" He waved them onward. "C'mon. The less time we spend here, the better."

He guided Vuk around the worst of the blood as the hole gave way to a wide cavern. Fifteen stone tables formed a ring, their heads pointing to a stone pedestal in the cavern's center. Large glass boxes sat beyond the tables along the cavern's walls. Their hinged sides hung ajar, and upon further inspection, broken locks lay scattered before them.

"Cages," Radais said. "For what? Awakened?"

Wanusa gasped as she dismounted and stepped toward the nearest cage. Its glass was among the purest Radais had ever seen, and her fingers left streaks as she ran them across the surface. "They could've been drifters too, but why would they want them in a cage?"

"Over here!" Lazan called from the opposite side of the cavern.

Radais joined them, dismounting near what looked like a series of desks. Lazan nodded to one that had papers scattered across it. Some sort of drawings covered them, but they were torn, the missing pieces nowhere among the scraps.

"What do you think of these?" Lazan asked with fear in his eyes.

"Some sort of ritual?" Radais replied as he held each of the drawings into the light. Their creator had an unskilled hand, obvious in the crooked lines and crude depictions of human bodies. Except, not all of them were human.

Radais called the others over. "These look familiar to you?"

The later drawings showed a creature with four arms and a flower-shaped face, a woman with a scorpion tail, a mass of twisting vines with a face formed from the leaves, a dragon breathing fire from its maw, and more resembling animals and nature. Each bore a realm's label beneath their drawing: Shadow, Death, Life, Fire, and so on.

Fifteen of them.

"The tables were surely for these spirits," Lazan said, stepping closer to the nearest of the tables. "Fifteen spirits for fifteen realms. See! There is glass shattered across the stone here."

"A cultist ritual!" Mhanain exclaimed.

Radais nodded. "Something like that. But for what purpose? The realms beneath the drawings… Were they trying to turn spirits into Reachers?" He looked back to the desk, then crouched to check the drawers. Most contained nothing of note, but when he pulled on the bottom one, it wouldn't budge. "Mhanain, would you mind putting that brute force of yours to work?"

The warrior cracked his knuckles and grabbed a hammer from his bag, grinning like a child eyeing the last slice of pie. "A shame. It's a nice desk."

His strikes echoed through the cavern. Radais winced and hoped no one was around to hear, but no response came. The drawer soon opened with a *crack*, and Mhanain backed up with his hands on his hips.

"Damn good wood that... Damn good."

Radais patted him on the back. "Not good enough to stop you."

He yanked out the splintered remains of the drawer, finding a leatherbound journal within. Water had damaged its pages, but Radais breathed a sigh of relief when he flipped it open. All but a few words were readable. Its author called himself Kariazan Pikezik, and it showed the steps taken for a "unification" process, which involved a group of captured people turning into awakened through a disease. Its symptoms matched those of the Spirit Plague.

Every entry bore a date and the advancements made on that day. Much of it made little sense to Radais, as Kariazan used strange terms and kept referring to something called the Axiom. The final pages, though, were clear:

*89th day of Duskfall, the 778th year Post-Awakening*

*Subject number 12 remains non-compliant. While the other breathless have accepted the imbuement of the realm-bonding crystal with few alterations or complications, Mind has proven difficult. The unification cannot complete without the fifteen petals in alignment, but we have been unable to remove subject 12 from its confinement chamber without ramifications. This morning, Weziniak suffered a migraine when attempting to guide the subject to its place for the unification, and I fear the bleeding from his nose and ears will not cease. He has spent the hours since mumbling about the "crystal heart."*

*We will continue. For the King in the Dark. For the crimson blood.*

*For the Axiom.*

*90th day of Duskfall, the 778th year Post-Awakening*

*Crystal Mother below! What have we done?*

*Subject number 12 is no longer the only non-compliant of the breathless. The others have begun to revolt, and they exude noises undecipherable to the human ear. Unification is threatened should this continue. Weziniak has passed, and I fear whispers pierce my own mind.*

*We have come too far to stop now. This cannot be the end.*

Needles rang across Radais's skin as he tucked the journal and drawings into his bag. Wanusa had been reading over his shoulder, and she stepped back, a hand over her mouth. "They created the Spirit Plague to create more awakened? They made them Reachers?"

"That explains our Saleshi friends," Lazan said. "But this was thirteen years ago. What was that Pikezik—likely Kariazan—doing out here again if he'd already failed?"

Tus laughed. "778. That's a year before someone offed that bloody King Yaakiin."

Radais remembered back to his conversations with Kasia. "Leonit Niezik was killed then, too. Katarzyna claimed it was an awakened who was under someone's control. What if this failed, but the Crimsons still figured out how to command awakened?"

"The Ephemeral Slaughter..." Wanusa breathed, staggering back. "They killed my friends! Those assholes told the awakened to attack us. Why?"

"For whoever this King in the Dark is," Radais replied. "It's likely why the Spirit Plague has spread now as well—to give them enough awakened to overwhelm Kalastok's Spirit Reachers."

"And what's this Axiom thing?"

He shook his head. "I have no clue, but the Saleshi might know more. If they were the ones Kariazan and the Crimson experimented on, then they'll have overheard their conversations."

"Back to the spirits, then," Wanusa said with a sigh. "This is *not* how I expected this to go."

Radais wanted to chuckle at that, but the weight of what had happened in this cavern had him in a solemn mood. "All this confirms for now is that we need to be careful with the Saleshi. They may be our friends for now, but any Reacher, spirit or human, is dangerous."

Lazan furrowed his brow at that but said nothing as he mounted his ibex. Radais found Vuk and did the same, giving one last look over the cavern before leading the others out. The Crimson hideout had given them some idea what was happening. Only the Saleshi could answer their questions now, and had a bad feeling in his stomach that this Mind Reaching breathless was the First One they wanted him to talk to.

# THE AXIOM

*"Through the Known Realms, we have gained control of nearly every force within nature's bounds. All except time, whose infallible flow pushes us ever forward in spite of our best wishes. But we have much more to learn."* – Etal iz Noshok, professor of forces and spirits at Kalastok College

Light flooded Kasia's vision as she tumbled through a vast emptiness. Translucent tendrils of colors whooshed past, disappearing as quickly as they appeared. Between them was unlike anything she'd ever experienced.

The air itself exuded light and dark, exuberance and nothing. It struck her in waves of joy and despair as her body shifted from feather-light to heavy as a brick. Each shift in weight hampered her efforts to change her trajectory, but in time, she found herself pushing through the tendrils. Her stomach's complaints implied she was still falling. It was impossible to tell for certain, though, in this place that had neither up nor down.

It simply *was*.

Even the colored strands showed no consistent pattern. They flowed like rivers but split in any direction, often curling back upon themselves many times. When they drew close, they carried varied sounds and smells. Some brought excited voices and the aromas of finished meals. Others struck with shouting and the sting of smoke.

Kasia grabbed for a bright blue tendril that passed by her.

Sensations struck her the moment her fingers met its flow, a throbbing headache that was stronger than her own and a vision of a dark room. A stone, dirt-covered floor chilled her fingers as a brisk wind whistled through the open window far above. Glass shards around her reflected the distant light of a lantern that hung beyond the barred door. A prison, but a makeshift one at that.

"You are fools to think she will value me over herself," a voice said, coming from her. But she hadn't spoken, and the voice hadn't been hers… It was Tazper's. "I am only a footman, a lowly servant without even a talon."

A gray man laughed from beyond the door, his nose bent and broken. But glass jewels shimmered on his suit coat as he stopped before the bars. "You undersell yourself," Uzrin Ioniz said. "A friend of hers, our spies say you are, but you are not our only leverage should we need to pry for her loyalty. I hear she is close to my bastard son as well."

Kasia's chest tightened along with Tazper's. She felt everything he did, smelt the stench of sweat coating his skin as he gritted his teeth. "Lady Katarzyna Niezik has no friends, only allies. She will do what she must. Of that, I am certain."

The vision faded as Uzrin replied, his voice turning to garbled nonsense before Kasia returned to the Axiom's void.

She clenched her fists. She'd known the Crimsons had taken Tazper, but knowing her allies, her *friends*, were at risk strengthened her resolve. Though his words struck her heart, she'd sensed his care. It had been little more than a lie to portray a defiant face. At least, she hoped so. Tazper was one of the few people she trusted, and she couldn't bear the thought that he didn't believe in their friendship.

The blue tendril passed beyond her fingers and out of reach. She tried to kick after it, as if she were swimming, but she could not change course so effectively—and she was hardly an experienced swimmer anyway. It disappeared, and Tazper left with it.

*What is this place?*

Kasia held her arms across her chest as she drifted. More tendrils approached, but she refused to touch another out of fear of their visions. Had it shown her the past? Was this the power Chatik sought within the Axiom, or was she hallucinating in this strange place?

The air snapped before her, colorful crystals forming from nothing and building a floating island. Its base was jagged, but its surface appeared as smooth as glass. She pushed toward it with the little control she had. Her muscles strained with each stroke, but soon, her foot met the island's edge.

Gravity shifted.

Blood rushed to her head as she scrambled onto the island. It clung to her, despite gravity pulling her upward, and she stood with her hair standing straight up. She held down her dress as it attempted the same. Spirits, she loved the beautiful and powerful stylings of her outfits, but for once, she wished she could wear trousers like men.

A cracking noise pulled her attention back to the island. Crystal rose between spires of silver to create a shimmering surface resembling a full-body mirror. Tendrils spiraled about it, as if called to its defense.

Kasia took a careful step, fighting the inconsistent pull upward—shifting once again between heavy and gentle. The crystal ground held, and nothing attacked her, so she continued toward the mirror. It reflected her ashen hair, flying about like an amateur Air Reacher's as her ruffled skirts exposed enough of her leg to make an honorable man blush. She grinned at the thought of flustered Zinarus. Though she'd hardly held her poise around him, his interest was undeniable. But that was a problem for another day.

And another realm.

She considered the flower amulet hanging from her neck. It hung near eye-level with the odd gravity, its center pulsing with Death's purple glow. Each petal marked another of the Known Realms, but what lay in its core? Surely this was no longer Zekiaz.

The tendrils' movements hastened at her approach. They darted around the mirror and through it, but none attempted to touch her.

She hoped it stayed that way, and she kept her hands close to her chest as she stopped a stride away from the mirror.

Nothing appeared special about the reflection at first. Beyond the odd effects of reversed gravity, Kasia looked like… well… her. Her tired eyes remained, but a faint amusement had replaced her normally stern expression. She couldn't help it. This place smothered her anger at the Crimsons with its boundless curiosities, and she felt like a child seeing the world's wonders for the first time.

"What are you?" she asked the mirror.

Obviously, it didn't reply, but no one was around to mock her inquiry. This place carried the magics of the other realms. Compared to all she'd experienced so far, a talking mirror would've seemed almost normal.

She rubbed her scarred arm as she thought through her next steps. Chatik was nowhere to be seen, and none of the Crimsons had arrived to punish her for following him into the portal. Either they were too loyal or too cowardly to do so. After all, Chatik may have kept much about the Axiom from his allies to take its power for himself. Chasing a Death Reacher—even a drained one—into a strange portal was hardly an appealing prospect for anyone.

As she paced, she tapped the crystal mirror with her talon, its surface shifting to a water-like substance. Her reflection disappeared. Wispy colors filled the substance until an image of Chatik appeared.

He stood on a similar island to hers, but gravity was normal for him as he approached a twisting sphere of colorful tendrils. As large as a dragon, the sphere shied away from his extended hand. Yet still he advanced. Crystal cracked underfoot with each of his steps as greed filled his eyes and a maniacal smile tugged at his lips. If he saw the cracks, he did not care. All his attention was fixed upon his target.

Chatik spoke as the tendrils continued their retreat. His words were too quiet to hear, though, and Kasia cursed her inability to get closer. What was he looking for?

She eyed her talon, its tip piercing the liquid. The mirror gave no resistance, so she pushed in the rest of her fingers. The mirror's cold liquid sent a chill up her arm as her hand appeared on the other side of the image—right in front of Chatik.

*This is a terrible idea.*

She took a deep breath and held it as she lunged into the mirror. The sensation of drowning hit her, disappearing a moment later when she landed on another crystal island. Behind her, the tendril sphere sent a deep hum through the air. Chatik's eyes flicked from it to her. Confusion crossed his face, then malice.

"Katarzyna!" he snapped. "You are a scheming bitch, no better than your father." He tucked a hand into his robe as he took a step back. "To infiltrate us with such risk… Who contracted you? The Keloshans? The Reshkans?"

Kasia sneered, pursuing him as her head spun with the change of gravity. "My father!"

Chatik pulled a pistol from his robes and pulled back its hammer. "Personal vengeance is a child's game, Katarzyna. Leonit's death was politics, nothing more, as he stood in the way of Ezman's ascension. I had hoped sacrificing that imbecile Sazilz would satiate your hatred, but it seems you would rather pursue me than restore your house to its rightful place."

"What ascension?" She raised her taloned hand toward him, knowing that he'd shoot the moment she Reached. "What is this place, the Axiom?"

"Wouldn't you like to know?"

He fired.

Kasia's ears rang as gunpowder's burning stench struck her. Pain shot across her hand, the bullet ripping through her talon and toward her skull. She closed her eyes and fell back off the island. The bullet had struck her head, but she didn't know where. There was too much pain to know its source.

She couldn't breathe as she tumbled into the void. The end had come for Death's Daughter, and there was nothing she could do to stop it. She would perish in this strange realm. Her spirit would be lost, drifting forever amid the Axiom's emptiness without even Aliax to haunt her.

And she would never have her revenge.

# THE VANASHEL

*"A bandit is a bandit, no matter their nationality. Murder is murder, no matter the target. That is... until you find yourself at war."* – Karinar Tarin, Ezmani major general

The Glassblades found Rakekeaa and the other Saleshi where they'd left them amid the ashen sands of the Spirit Wastes. One with the mists, the breathless were invisible until the strange lantern's light cleared the air. Each of Rakekeaa's many eyes studied Radais upon Vuk's back.

"Find what you desired?" Rakekeaa hummed.

Radais stopped his team beneath them, his chest tight. "The humans in the cavern, the Crimsons, ran tests on you. They gave you the ability to Reach and locked you in a cage. A breathless... A Saleshi like you managed to defy them and free your kind."

"Many. Not all," Rakekeaa replied as the Saleshi's whispers grew, resembling a solemn song. "God made us Ones Who Are Bound, touching realms. First One brought us from God, made us ones without breath. Minds freed. But God survived, fled."

"Kariazan Pikezik?" Radais asked. "He is dead now."

"Vanashel killed him first. God deserved death."

"A journal that they left mentioned some kind of unification," Lazan said. "You were the Shadow Reacher—or Bounded One, as you called it—but I assume the others are still with you. Do any of you know what that unification was?"

The whispers ceased.

"First One knows," Rakekeaa said. "Follow, but do not stray. Vanashel near."

Radais furrowed his brow. "The Vanashel? You've said that a couple times, but I don't know what that is."

Rakekeaa descended, crossing its arms across its chest. A chill ran down Radais's spine with it so near, but he resisted any urge to reach for his blade. "Antagonists," it said. "Foes. Nonbelievers. They attacked you."

"Then they are breathless like you?" Lazan replied. "Were they part of the original fifteen Bound Ones created by the Crimsons?"

"First One explains all." Rakekeaa extended its misty hand toward Radais. "I light way."

Radais surrendered the lantern and followed Rakekeaa through the parted fog. Wanusa kept close, her face pale as she considered the same ramifications as he did. The Awakening had destroyed the most powerful empire in the known history of Zekiaz. What would happen if the Crimsons had truly unleashed spirits with the ability to Reach? And what did they want with Miv?

They continued for hours without another word, crossing dunes and plains of endless sand. It had been over a day since the Glassblades slept, and exhaustion crept upon them. With the Saleshi showing no signs of slowing, it was Radais's responsibility to speak up.

"Rakekeaa!" he called ahead when they reached a rocky outcropping, allowing them shelter from the frigid winds. "We must rest."

The breathless cocked its head. Its eyes narrowed, as if not comprehending what he meant. "Like the crystal-fingered ones. Eyes shut, head down. But Vanashel will hunt."

"We will take shifts to guard the camp," he replied. "Our swords can kill spirits."

Rakekeaa conferred with the others, their strange whispers growing until it returned its attention to Radais. "Yes, eyes shut. One bodied one keep eyes open, but no lantern. Vanashel see."

"I will take first watch," Lazan said. Radais tried to object, but Lazan held his shoulder from atop his ibex. "Worry not, my friend. The last of my Reaching went to reinforce my energy for a time. I will wake you when it fades."

Without a full understanding of how Body Reaching worked, Radais had no argument. He suspected Lazan only wished to help, so for now, he would tolerate it. It had become an effort to even keep his eyes open.

His windburned cheeks stung as he descended between the rocks and dismounted Vuk, who gave a relieved bleat. Radais patted him on the head and slipped him a portion of his rations. "You need the rest more than any of us."

Vuk sighed, then dropped into the sand, asleep before Radais had finished preparing his bedroll. The other ibexes were much the same. They had been pushed hard for many days, but even the Vockan Mountains couldn't match the strain of trudging through the Wastes in the everdark. Spirits, he ached for Vuk as he lay down. The poor ibex had endured his journeys for years, yet Radais had barely considered his well-being since he'd discovered Kariazan Pikezik in the Wastes. He silently promised that he'd give Vuk all the treats he wanted when they returned to Palmia.

Radais soon removed his armor, covered the lantern, and followed the ibex to sleep. But nightmares ensured it was hardly the rest he'd wanted. Miv's horrified face filled them all as the Vanashel carried her away. Years of training and fighting awakened had all been useless when she'd need him most. Now, she was in the hands of some rogue breathless, alone.

"You failed me," her voice called through dream after dream. "That's all you've ever been. For me. For your father. For your brother. A failure."

Some part of him wished he hadn't thrown that crystal, that he'd fallen in battle instead of fleeing like a coward. That desire seeped into his nightmares.

He floated into nothingness as the breathless tore his body to pieces and dragged it to some far-off place where they held Miv. Dead, he would be as worthless to her as he'd been in life, but at least he could be by her side again.

He lay on a stone floor. Paralyzed, he could only stare ahead as the spirits circled Miv in her cage. His spirit should've left his body by now, but it lingered in the corpse, unable to save it or move on. The limbo trapped him, agony consuming his very being until he burst back to reality.

Lazan knelt at Radais's side with a grip on his shoulders. His hands were warm, soft compared to Radais's calloused ones, but the look in his eye was wild in the dim lanternlight slipping through the cloak. "Wake slowly," Lazan whispered. "Rakekeaa says the Vanashel are near, and it is arguing with the other Saleshi. I fear some among them may desire to hand us over."

"You speak Saleshi now?" Radais replied.

Lazan huffed. "No, but even among these spirits, actions signal enough."

Radais rose, grabbing his sheathed blade and throwing his armor on as quickly as possible. Twice, awakened had attacked while he was out of his armor. He felt naked without it, but with its sturdy weight on his shoulders, part of him felt invisible.

"Do we wake the others?" he asked with a glance at the lantern. Instinct told him sight would help, but Rakekeaa had insisted he leave it covered. Why?

Wanusa stirred, peeking at them with one eye. "Wake us for what?"

Radais held a finger to his lips. "Quiet, child. The Vanashel are close."

"I'm not a child."

She pushed herself up to a crouch and joined them near the lantern. By the Wastes, she was persistent, but she had a glass sword. That alone would make her more useful than Lazan against spirits. Initiate or not, she was a *somewhat* trained hand.

"Fine," Radais muttered, "but stay by my side. Lazan, wake

Mhanain, and keep out of any fighting. Your gun won't do much against these breathless."

"I am much more of a lover than a fighter anyway," the Reacher replied, and Radais cursed that his cheeks burned. Lazan crept away, leaving Radais alone with Wanusa and the whispers.

Radais repeated Lazan's report to Wanusa before grabbing the cloak-covered lantern and heading up the rocks. The Saleshi gathered at the top, mists circling where their feet would've been as they spoke in their foreign tongue. Rakekeaa hovered across from another breathless, which resembled vines that crept up the trunk of a tree—the Life Reacher. Misty vines formed its face and countless arms that joined and separated from its torso rapidly. Its gestures resembled a miniature storm as it debated with Rakekeaa. About that, Lazan had been right. Even a spirit's motions exposed its anger.

Holding his position on the rocks soon became uncomfortable for Radais. He placed his foot on a rook that *seemed* stable… until it broke free and tumbled down the slope. Radais fell with it and rolled until he smacked into Mhanain, who caught him as softly as a stone wall.

"Wrong way," Mhanain grunted.

Radais dusted himself off as Wanusa faced the entire squad of Saleshi on her own. Her glass sword hung loosely in her fingers, and all Radais could do was pray to the spirits that she wouldn't startle them. Shouting at the young initiate wouldn't help her keep calm. Miv would've, but she wasn't there now. It was Radais's call, and he trusted Wanusa.

"What's happening?" she asked the Saleshi. "We heard arguing and thought the Vanashel had attacked."

"Came for youuu," the Life breathless replied. "Taaake."

Radais began up the slope again, leading the others, but Wanusa wasn't so patient. She climbed the rest of the way to the Saleshi and raised her blade toward the Life Boundless One. "We are Glassblades! It is our duty to face corrupted spirits, so we will defend against the Vanashel. You aren't corrupted too, are you?"

Life's vines curled. "WEEE ARE NOT—"

"Fight with us," Rakekeaa interrupted, a hand on Life's odd shoulder. "Janitak has fear, but Glassblades help. We are outnumbered."

"Then we'll fight," Radais confirmed when he reached Wanusa's side. He'd failed Miv and his fallen comrades, but he still had the rest of his team to protect—and more to discover. They couldn't leave the Wastes until they met with this First One. All those lost lives would be a waste if they didn't. Miv's too.

Rakekeaa nodded. "Many Vanashel are Ones Who Are Bound—Reachers—but others without breath cannot touch realms."

"Breathless are like the ones we faced before, then," Lazan replied. "Vanashel commanded them, but the Bound Ones are the Reachers? Is that what you are saying?"

Rakekeaa glanced about before replying, "I speak to your tongue. Awakened ones are mindless. Breathless ones have thought. Bound Ones touch the realms… Reach. We Saleshi are breathless, and many are Bound Ones too."

"Theee crystal-fingered ones were same," Janitak said. "Wave haaand. Control breathless ones, make slaves."

A hiss carried on the western wind. Rakekeaa raised its arms, crossing them above its petaled head. "Talk not more. Defend! Saleshi fight Bound Ones. Glassblade ones, fight breathless Vanashel only."

The Saleshi scattered as the Glassblades formed a defensive arc at the top of the rocks. Lazan uncovered the lantern, and Radais cursed at the sight of a sky full of shadows. Most of them took the humanlike form of awakened. A few scattered among them, though, resembled misty dragons.

One of the Vanashel shouted in their strange tongue, extending its six wings. Rakekeaa responded, and whispers grew among the Saleshi.

"What are they saying?" Radais asked. His sword weighed heavier than normal in his grasp. Being encircled was bad enough when he understood what he faced, but these Vanashel were far more coordinated than any awakened.

Rakekeaa gave no reply, but shadows rose from its crossed arms. That was sign enough. When the Vanashel hissed a command, Radais was ready.

The first Vanashel breathless burst from the mists mere strides from him. It attacked with the speed of a falcon, but his blade was faster. He struck it down, then the next as Wanusa and Lazan took his flanks, Mhanain shooting arrows overhead. Lazan had only a glass dagger. His skill with it was impressive enough, but Radais found himself too distracted by those around him. The Vanashel attacked from every side. He needed all the focus he had just to stay standing.

Above, shadows, vines, and fire danced through the lanternlight. Radais lacked experience with Reachers to know which faction of the breathless was winning, but he hoped the Saleshi could at least keep the Vanashel Boundless Ones off his friends. Glass swords worked wonders against spirits. Against magic, they were useless.

The Glassblades fought with tired legs and slowed reactions. Strike by strike, they backed themselves into a tight circle, and Radais's feet skidded across loose stones on the slope's edge.

"They've got our front!" Mhanain yelled, switching to his sword and slicing through a Vanashel's torso as his quiver ran empty. "They've got our backs! Ha! They even got our heads."

Wanusa stumbled, dodging an assault from a breathless's tendrils. "We don't have crystal for eyes, Mhanain. We know!"

"But you missed the best part," the warrior called back as he stabbed another pair. "I like being surrounded. Nowhere for them to hide."

"Imbecile," Wanusa muttered.

They fought on long enough for Radais's arms to ache. Neither the Bound Ones' Reaching nor the breathless attacks ceased until one of the Vanashel dragons dove toward the Glassblade ring. Gales encircled the Bound One like a whirlwind, and its allies retreated just before it crashed into Mhanain, throwing him onto the rocks below.

Lazan rushed after him. "Of course he couldn't keep his mouth shut for once."

"Can you Reach?" Radais asked, clearing a path for Lazan's retreat and putting himself directly in the Bound One's path.

Lazan grunted as he climbed down the rocks. "Not without Taint, but a healer needs more than one tool."

Radais had no time to reply. The Bound One leapt overhead, and the wind battered him as he sliced in hopes of catching the beast's wing. Only the tip of his sword clipped it, but that was all he needed. Its whirlwind and dragon form faltered enough for him to charge and ready a final slash.

Until he saw its face.

His arms froze as he stared at the man he'd failed. The one he'd left. The one he'd been too slow to save.

"You killed me once," his father's voice spat, but the Vanashel lacked mouths too. Instead, its eyes seemed to turn eternally white with each word, brighter than even the Saleshi's lantern. "Isn't that enough?"

"Father?" Radais breathed, lowering his blade.

Wanusa screamed from across the Glassblades' circle, "What are you doing? Kill it before we're all dead!"

*Is it really you?* Radais asked the spirit silently.

His heartbeat felt fast enough to slow time as he looked from his sword to the beast that threatened his friends, his order, and those he loved. What would happen if it were really his father? Would his strike damn him to an empty eternity, never to return to Zekiaz?

The gales escalated, sand whipping through the air and stinging Radais's eyes as stones pelted his skin. Yet he couldn't move. In the pure white eyes of the Bound One before him, he saw his dark reflection. A runaway. A coward. A disappointment.

He stepped back and wiped a tear from his eyes. "Leave us, Father, and go. Don't make me kill you."

"What is gone can never be returned," his father replied as the other Vanashel crept closer. "The cycle goes on, and it washes us clean in its wake."

Tendrils shot from the Bound One, but just as they struck his helm, a blade plunged through its chest. Like an arrow piercing fog, the Bound One seemed unaffected at first. Wanusa wasn't finished yet, though, and she released a brutal war cry as she spun and cut through the face of Radais's father. His cry shattered Radais's resolve as the Bound One dissipated, its whirlwind flinging stone and sand in its last thrashing fit before vanishing with its master.

A chorus rose from among the Vanashel ranks. The remaining breathless retreated as the remaining Vanashel Bound Ones covered them with Reaching, but it was all a blur to Radais.

He dropped to his knees, blade scraping the sand at his side. Blood trickled down his brow as he removed his cracked helm. He stared down at the armor that had saved his life, then raised his gaze to the girl who'd slain the beast… his father.

"Was it him?" he mumbled with tears stinging his eyes.

Wanusa shook her head. "Who?"

"My father. That thing… It had his face, his voice."

"Then it was a trick." She crouched before him, forehead wrinkled. "It tried to use you. They're corrupted, right? You said it yourself."

He had, but doubt's roots gripped his heart. How could this foreign spirit have known his father's appearance and voice? "Whatever they are, they're evil." Over and over he told himself that the Vanashel deserved death, but had his father?

Radais accepted Wanusa's help to stand. "Thank you," he managed to say. "I'd be dead if you hadn't fixed my failure."

She grabbed his helm, damaged but not yet shattered, dusting it off before shoving it into his chest. "Pull yourself together, *Master*. You're the best chance we have of getting through this alive, and Supreme Defender Miv needs you. I'm not an idiot. There's something between you two, and spirits know neither of us wants to be the reason she stays trapped with those Bound Ones."

Radais had enough dread, so he ignored Wanusa's reminder about Miv and headed down the slope to Lazan. The Reacher knelt beside Mhanain on a boulder halfway down. He'd already wrapped Mhanain's head and was in the middle of fixing his dislocated shoulder.

"He was lucky to survive such a fall," Lazan said, tense as he snapped the shoulder back into place. Mhanain yelped, but the wooden piece between his teeth kept him from biting hard on his tongue. "We cannot go on like this, or we will fall to the monsters of this place."

"What choice do we have?" Radais replied. "We need to find this First One."

Lazan sighed and sat back on the rock, cleaning the blood off his hands. "There is always a choice, but I fear you are right on this. We have come all this way, discovered a new kind of spirit—a sentient one at that—and found part of the Crimson Court's operations in the Wastes. Turning back now would be foolish, even in the face of great risk."

"Factual," Rakekeaa's voice hummed as it descended toward them. Its petals curled along the edges, frayed as it held its arms to its sides. "You need. We need."

"Then let's continue," Radais replied.

Rakekeaa shook its head. "Vanashel retreat. We have time. Impressive, you killed Bound One of Air."

"Fine, then." Radais patted Lazan's back, ignoring the compliment. He felt no pride. "It's your turn to rest, my friend. I will watch. There is no chance in the Wastes I'm getting sleep after what I just saw."

"The Vanashel?" Lazan asked.

Wanusa clambered past them, not stopping as she replied for Radais, "The Bound One pretended to be his father. He still thinks it could've been him."

"And why do you believe there was no such possibility?" Lazan rolled up his supplies into a pouch. "Are they not spirits? Did his father not join the spirits within a few hundred-hours of today? We deal with strange forces that we know little about, but grief is one force that we are all far too familiar with."

With a gentle smile to Radais, he picked up Mhanain and headed toward the camp. His scolding had stopped Wanusa a few strides ahead. She averted her gaze as he walked by, then looked back toward Radais when Lazan was gone.

"I'm sorry. I didn't mean it like that."

Radais shrugged, but his heart ached still. "You were right. I am our leader, and I need to keep my focus on our mission. There'll be time aplenty for mourning later. Until then, go and finish resting. You'll need the energy come morn."

She clenched her fists but continued on without complaint. Radais had to remind himself she was only an adolescent who was far out of her depths. It had been wrong for Miv to push her into this journey so quickly, but Wanusa was here now. As long as Miv was gone, it was his job to keep her safe. Yet another responsibility on his shoulders. This one, though, he promised himself he wouldn't fail.

He climbed back to the ridgeline, sword rested on his shoulder as he stared into the everdark. The lantern pierced it for a ways, but beyond, it seemed an eternal nothingness. One could've been forgiven for forgetting the millions of people east of the Wastes. The awakened threatened each of them, and if these Vanashel breathless were as sinister as they appeared, no one beyond the Vockan Mountains truly understood how much danger they were in.

Radais wasn't sure even he knew.

But with the nearest Vanashel repelled for now, they could finally find the First One. Rakekeaa promised it had answers. He hoped it had enough.

# THE LETTER

*"What are we if we do not seek more than we are born into?"* – Nochlander Proverb

Nikoza walked the maze of gardens south of the Crystal Palace, her fur coat held closed over her dress amid the frigid dark. She wished to be as far away from the palace as possible. Her grandfather had followed her plan until Chatik and Lilita Pikezik undermined Ambassador Alyniana's authority. Now, the Commonwealth marched to war without allies, and Nochland would fall under Kelosh's thumb.

Could she have changed it?

She replayed the debate over and over in her mind. To challenge a seated member of the Chamber was not her place. She would someday be matriarch of House Bartol, but today, she was nothing more than a girl out of her depth, a messenger for the factions vying for influence within Kalastok.

"Wallow not in your sorrow," a familiar woman's voice said from behind her.

Nikoza straightened her posture, which had waned in her wandering. "Ambassador, I am surprised they allowed you back within the Crimson District."

Alyniana waved her crystal wand with a wry smile. "Your most revered king may have sent me away, but my Mind Reaching had yet to run dry. I figured meeting you would be an adequate use of my final moments in this motherforsaken city."

"You are leaving so soon?" Nikoza's toes curled at the loss of her closest ally. "What hope have we of steering our ship away from this storm if you are not here to help me whisper in the captain's ear?"

"There is a saying among mercantile sailors in my homeland: When the storm blows nigh, it is preferable to face it with one's bow than to pretend the waves are not crashing over the deck." Alyniana drew nearer, her wand held between her clasped hands as she stared at her feet. "Against our best efforts, this war has arrived, and the Commonwealth is to face it alone. Nochland will not fight unless significant aid arrives."

Nikoza reached for her hands. Both wore gloves, but she swore she could feel Alyniana's rapid heartbeat through them. "We are not finished," she pleaded, emphasizing each word. "I refuse to watch our people suffer because I failed to sway my grandfather."

"King Jazuk's actions are his own, as are the Chamber's. You do not bear the burden of decisions that were not yours to make."

"Yet I bear their weight nonetheless. I wish I could do more."

Alyniana sighed and let out a chuckle. Tears welled in her eyes. "There may yet be a way."

Nikoza stepped closer still, squeezing Alyniana's hands so hard she winced. "Please, Ambassador. I act for our people, not myself."

"You speak wiser than your years, child." Alyniana's shoulders sunk. "Lady Katarzyna Niezik was crass but willing to aid my efforts. However, she has not been seen since the war declaration. Perhaps she has allies who you may seek out."

"What does she intend?"

"I fear that I do not know. That girl can be quite mysterious, and she had little interest in telling me more than was necessary."

Nikoza retreated, tapping her foot as she remembered Katarzyna lingering near the Chamber's entrance with a scion from the reformer bloc. He had the auburn hair of a Vockan, but his skin was dark scion gray. Where did she know him from?

"There was this man with her before tonight's assembly," she said, turning back toward Alyniana. "Half-Vockan, half-Ezmani perhaps… I believe he was the one Lord Gornioz swayed to part with his family's sand mines. House iz Vamiustok perhaps?"

Alyniana clicked her tongue. "Ah, yes. Lord Zinarus has come into significant wealth with the loss of his family's greatest asset, and I believe he has devoted it to investments in the Kalastok Arena. It is possible that he has used that purchase to cover more clandestine activities in House Niezik's interest. Katarzyna retreated when I mentioned an elusive organization called the Crimson Court, who may be related to the Spirit Plague and awakened attacks. The House iz Vamiustok heir may know more."

A plot connected to the Spirit Plague? "I should speak with Lord Zinarus, then. Perhaps he knows more that can help us climb out of this hole. What do you plan to do in the meantime?"

Alyniana slipped her wand into her floral coat's pocket. "With King Jazuk's admonishment of my actions, I must return home. I will attempt to confer with the Merchant Council and persuade them that resistance is worthwhile. Until then, seek out Zinarus and hope he can provide some aid in the Commonwealth's survival efforts."

Nikoza sighed, tracing the branch of a nearby bush. It would flower brilliantly come dawnrise, but it was lifeless for now. As she released it, her heart felt much the same. "Very well. If you must go, then this I will do. Just promise to send me a missive upon your arrival in Litianitan."

Footsteps came from nearby. Heavy, not intending to be quiet.

"You have it," Alyniana whispered as she backed away. "Be careful, and be well."

Then she vanished into the everdark, soon replaced by two guards of the Crystal Brigade. Their presence alone was enough to send a shiver down Nikoza's spine. Though they were her grandfather's loyal guards, so too, were they notoriously wielded by elites beyond his periphery.

"Guardsmen," she said, furrowing her brow. "What has you searching for me in the gardens?"

The female of the pair stepped forward. "The former ambassador of Nochland was spotted by a servant. We are tasked with ensuring her swift departure from Ezman before she conducts any further espionage."

Nikoza held a hand to her chest, mouth ajar. "Oh, by the Crystal Mother. I have not seen her, but I shall return to the palace at once in case she has nefarious plans."

"That would be for the best."

She hurried off, gathering her skirts to pretend she was fearful of snagging them on the brush. In truth, she wished to check if the guards were watching her leave. They were, so she made haste until their footfalls were distant and she was basked in the palace's lanterns.

"Ah, there you are, Lady Nikoza," Votzan proclaimed from the steps. As per usual, he held an assortment of books in the crook of his arm, and he leaned upon a column to not topple over with their weight.

"Grand Secretary," she replied with a curtsy. "What is the matter?"

"There is… err… no easy way to say this, my lady."

She smiled sweetly, but her chest tightened. Votzan was often nervous around Jazuk. With her, though, he had never been like this. "Worry not, Votzan. I shall not blame you for being the messenger."

He nodded. "Yes, yes, thank you. However, I fear *you* shall find blame from your grandfather. You see, he has taken it upon our staff to peruse your letters ever since you revealed your idea to aid Nochland."

She blushed. "Why is that?"

"I mean not to say that he doubts your intentions, but…" Votzan sighed. "Tonight, he has discovered a letter that he wishes to discuss with you. You will find him on the rooftop."

"With the dragon, no less."

"Precisely. Now, if you will excuse me, I have matters of state to attend to. I do not take kindly to dealing with trifling matters such as this."

Nikoza feigned another smile, stepping past him and steeling herself for the inevitable conflict to come. What could her grandfather have discovered? "I shall do my best to ensure there are no such distractions in the future, Grand Secretary."

Her breaths quickened as she headed toward the stairs. She'd hidden her letters from Alyniana well, but had another arrived unbeknownst to her? Had a young man sent her a particularly salacious message in hopes of wooing her? The latter would be far less damaging, as she had done plenty to deny their requests for more than a dance during Kalastok's countless balls. It was shameful how often her peers indulged pleasures while the quarantined west side suffered. If Jazuk believed she were being inappropriate, however, it would be far easier to handle than conspiracies with Nochland.

Multiple servants sought to aid her climb by taking hold of her longest skirts, but she shooed them away. It was uncharacteristic of her to be so forceful. Alyniana's departure and the war had her on edge, though, and she preferred the silence of her mind for the few moments before she reached the roof.

She waited for a moment at the door to collect her breath. It was quite the climb to her grandfather's favored pondering location. How did he make it so often in his condition? Her thighs ached from it, and sweat beaded on her brow, threatening her flawless makeup. Jazuk had seen her plenty often in more flawed states than this, but in times of conflict with him, she could not show him the weakness all statesmen sought in aspiring youth.

Nikoza opened the door, ignoring the looming dragon that clung to the tower behind her. "Grandfather, you called for me?" she asked. She clenched her jaw and lifted it, her gaze confident, if not defiant.

The king blew cigar smoke over the city as he leaned on the half-wall rimming the roof. Instead of his general's uniform from the Chamber meeting, he wore a deep red smoking jacket trimmed in white, gold threads dancing across its front and arms. His cane leaned against the wall nearby, but he did not use it as he turned to meet her with a kiss on the cheek. "My dear Nikoza, let us speak."

"Grand Secretary Votzan warned me you have been reading my letters," she replied, returning the gesture before joining him at the ledge. But she dared not lean upon it. Leaning was for relaxed men. Jazuk himself had taught her not to abandon formalities in favor of relaxation, no matter the company, and she no longer could relax in his presence. "Why did you not simply ask your questions to me directly? Have I not been honest with you?"

"Have you?" he mused. "After your intervention at my council meeting, Gornioz claimed you were acting as an agent of Nochland, and the former ambassador's appearance this evening only strengthened my fears."

"Lord Gornioz should rouse your suspicions more than I. Was it not he who decried your private efforts in front of the Chamber, ruining our hopes of a pact?"

Jazuk took another puff of his cigar as he looked toward the nearest of the Spirit Reacher towers. Its searchlights scanned the sky, occasionally catching a flicker of a spirit that the Reachers banished moments later. "There is little trust between that man and me, but the king serves at the pleasure of the scions, Nikoza. Though I wear the crown, true power lies in the hands of the great houses who may depose me at any moment."

"Excuse me, Grandfather," Nikoza said with a wrinkle of her nose, "but they cannot remove you. The king is elected for life."

He flicked the cigar, sending the ashes drifting onto the lower tiers of the palace. "Which is why it is not so rare for a king's life to end prematurely." He set down the cigar and turned toward her. Half his face lay in the darkness, the other half's wrinkles exposed by the lanternlight. "Let me speak plainly with you. I believe the Keloshan Empire is the greatest threat our nation faces, and our internal divisions ensure defeat is inevitable. Gornioz and his ilk circle me like vultures, waiting for me to drop dead. I fear they have grown impatient."

"I fear the same," Nikoza said. "Which is why I have sought allies."

"I have not brought you up here to chastise you for your affiliations with Alyniana of the Wayfarers. Like you, she has an idealistic way of viewing our realm, but you must be careful that you do not allow your proximity to the throne to make you a target." He reached into his jacket and procured a letter bearing the seal of Kalastok College. The seal was cut. "It seems your whispered word to the college's messenger reached Professor Etal is Noshok. He wishes to have you as his apprentice."

Nikoza's eyes widened, and she nervously took the letter without reply. Professor iz Noshok wanted her? She had casually requested that the woman from the college ask if she could be his apprentice, but she had expected nothing from it. Etal had been the first to identify the disease that now bore his name, and among the Commonwealth's scions, he was regarded as the greatest academic mind. What potential had he seen in her?

It was difficult to read the letter in her excitement, but she understood enough to know it confirmed Jazuk's explanation. Professor Etal would teach her in the sciences. For once, she could focus on more than just politics and House Bartol's industries. She would study the Spirit Plague and other complex problems facing Zekiaz, not simply waiting for others to find answers.

"Your joy is evident," Jazuk said, holding his hands behind his back and wriggling his bearded chin. "I had feared as such."

Nikoza's excitement turned to confusion. She folded the letter and took her grandfather's hand. "Why do you fear for me? I would not be far, and if your council worries about my loyalties, it is better I not be at your side. You have made it clear that they threaten your rule because of my counsel."

He sighed. "You have proven wise beyond your years, but I have been your guardian for some time now. There is so much I still wish to teach you about the ways of leading our house. You should have sought my permission for such a request."

"Are you considering rejecting Professor iz Noshok's offer?"

Jazuk released her, snatching his silver cane. The quick motion spurred the dragon, and it leaped from its position atop the spire. Each flap of its wings sent gusts through Nikoza's hair and skirts as she stared down her grandfather.

"You are…" she said with a gasp. "Grandfather, I have shown no defiance typical of those my age. I have sought to help you with my every word, forging alliances to aid you as I seek to lead our house someday. Shall I not have the chance to spread my wings like your dragon and succeed through my own will?"

"It is not your will but your status that earned you this acceptance!" Jazuk snapped. "The choice is yours, child, yet I insist you consider before following this path. Our house is more than blood. It is bound with us and our nation. It is everything!"

Nikoza turned away, arms held across her body. "If only you channeled such fire against those who truly betray you."

Then she stormed away, rushing down the steps and to her carriage. She clutched the letter to her chest all the way, and her tears sent ink streaming across the parchment. The carriage rattled along the cobblestone streets as she pondered her next moves. With every breath, she cursed her dedication to her grandfather's legacy, as his selfishness stole her dream. He had made his choices. Now, she was a grown woman, and she would make her own.

She stared out the window at the Spirit Reacher towers above. Beyond their defenses, thousands suffered because of Jazuk and the Chamber's decisions. The great houses had abandoned the lowborn peasants and workers.

Nikoza would not.

Upon her return to House Bartol's townhouse, she hurried to her room and called for parchment and ink. It was nearing the twentieth hour of midnight, but Jazuk's condemnation had shot fresh impetus into her veins. She had much to do, and with war dawning, time was short.

The first letter she penned was a reply to Etal iz Noshok, informing him of her intention to become his apprentice as soon as he would have her. The second was directed to Katarzyna Niezik's ally, Zinarus iz Vamiustok. She requested that he meet her in a quaint café on the northern edge of Kalastok. It was a personal favorite of hers and lacked the bustle of busier ones in the heart of the city. Stealth had never been her strength, but she hoped it would be remote enough to not draw wandering eyes.

She sent both letters via courier immediately upon their completion in hopes they would be received swiftly. Haste had its moments. The eve of war seemed an adequate time for it, but she found herself anxious upon the letters' departures. Her fate still rested in others' hands. All she had done was change whose.

What could she do now but wait?

Letting down her hair, she rose and headed toward her bed. Her thoughts would not allow sleep, but she needed rest. The days ahead would surely not allow so much. War had come to the Commonwealth. Though she had failed to stop it, she was not finished, and if anyone could help her now, it would be the recipients of her letters.

# THE PRINCESS, THE PROFESSOR, AND THE PURPLE LORD

*"To live without science is to believe all discovery is magic. Magic has its place, but rely too heavily upon it, and you lose sight of the true nature of the realm."*
– Etal iz Noshok, professor of forces and spirits at Kalastok College

Zinarus struggled to sleep most nights. Tonight was the worst of them.

Worries or his leg's irritation often kept him from ever finding complete comfort, and Regizald's death had only darkened his thoughts. He did not wish for dreams when his best friend's corpse filled them. Nor did he wish to picture what was likely happening to the victims of the Spirit Plague west of the river. Instead, he chose to lay awake, recounting the last day's discussions around war, disease, and—more sweetly—Lady Katarzyna.

Except even Kasia brought sourness with her too. What moments of affection she had for him were fleeting at best, and Zinarus found himself swaying between longing and heartache. Did she believe him to be more than an ally? Was killing the Crimsons on Leonit's list truly her only option? How serious was her Realm Taint?

Crystal Mother below, when would he have a chance to ask her anything when she was so obsessed with the Crimson Court?

The sound of his townhouse door opening was a welcomed distraction, so he pushed himself out of bed and reached for his cane. The first steps out of bed were always the worst. To make matters worse, his nightshirt snagged on the corner of his bed stand, forcing him to wrestle it free in the dim candlelight before shuffling down the hall.

"Lord Zinarus?" Niniaxi replied. The stout lowborn maid scampered toward him at the sound of his thumping cane. "You should be asleep. Being up at this motherforsaken hour isn't good for your constitution."

Zinarus huffed, both in reply and from the effort. "Not much is productive for my poor constitution these days. I heard you open the door, which is rare this late, and my curiosity got the best of me. Is all well?"

She held out a letter bearing a ram's head seal. "A courtier just showed up with this."

"House Bartol?" he asked. "What does the king's family want from me this late?"

"Spirits if I know!" Niniaxi replied, plopping the letter in his hand. "My job's to clean the place, not know what the bloody king thinks about you."

He took the letter but hesitated with it in hand. Had King Jazuk discovered his mercenaries? Surely, he would have sent watchmen if he believed Zinarus to be involved in a plot, as Jazuk was hardly known for blackmail.

"Could you light my study?" Zinarus asked, heading down the hall toward it. He did not enjoy asking so much of Niniaxi, but without Regizald, she was all the help he had in the city. His mother had once ensured Zinarus could get around despite his impediment. She was half the country away now, though, and remembering that fact deepened his heartache.

Niniaxi climbed atop a stool to light the lamp above his desk. She groaned in the way the elderly do, and Zinarus held her arm to ensure she did not fall.

"I am sorry to burden you," he said, "but I fear enough of us have perished in this study without you tumbling from above."

She patted his arm. "You're sweet, but I'm fine. Read that letter of yours and get some sleep. I know I need it!"

"Worry not about the usual morning hours tomorrow. You have earned the rest."

With a raised brow and a wave at the disheveled state of his nightshirt, she retreated into the hall. He chuckled before grabbing his letter opener and breaking the seal of the Bartol missive. What lay inside was not what he'd expected.

*Princess Nikoza?*

She requested a meeting with him the coming day regarding his associations with Kasia and Alyniana. The princess was King Jazuk's ward, but the letter appeared conciliatory. How did she know about his arrangements? Did she wish to help or to gain information?

Zinarus rubbed his eyes, leaning with his elbows on the desk as exhaustion finally struck him. He'd come to Kalastok as House iz Vamiustok's representative for business, not to involve himself in schemes, yet that was all he'd done since Kasia's arrival. For what? Even with such a small group, Tiuz's mercenaries were far from ready. Kasia seemed to have succeeded at gaining the Crimson Court's trust, but had seemingly lost part of herself in the process. And Zinarus had lost his family's mines, gaining only a crumbling arena and a mercenary company full of peasants who could barely hold lances.

"Mother, forgive me," he whispered. "You always said I was more suited to Kalastok, but this city will kill me."

After staring down at the letter for a while longer, he rested his head on his arms. His room wasn't far, but it felt like a mountain. So he closed his eyes in the study and let his body succumb to tiredness. Tomorrow would be better, because it surely couldn't be worse than today.

**THE NORTHBOUND CAFÉ WAS FAR FROM THE BUSTLING STREETS** and glass-decorated exteriors of the Crimson and Market districts. Instead, it greeted Zinarus with vines creeping up the lamp-posts and trees that stretched above the surrounding brick houses. There were no multi-floor townhouses, Reacher towers, or patrolling guards in red uniforms.

Soft notes from a single violin drifted over the scattered tables, each with a lantern floating above it—the work of a nearby Air Reacher who danced on her tip-toes as she cast. The seated scions wore soft shades of mostly greens and blues. They smiled as if war had not been declared the night before, the lowborn being drafted to march against the Keloshan war machine.

It was tranquility that Zinarus had not experienced in what felt like years, and he felt horribly out of place. His urban-gray coat, hat, and vest, trimmed in purple, made him resemble a stain upon this grove-like place. There was little he could do now, though.

No roads led directly to the café, and the walk had his mechanical leg whirring from use. Unfortunately, Nikoza had yet to arrive, leaving him to stand awkwardly amid the tables. There did not appear to be a host to seat him, and the servers wisped around like drifters too quickly for him to ask. So he waited.

And waited.

It was not long before his patience—and leg—could take no more. He picked a table, which appeared to be the right decision. A server appeared a moment later with a gentle smile and a loose-fitting suit coat.

"Dining alone, my lord, or will another be attending?" the server asked.

He rapped his knuckles on the table, feigning a smile. "I believe another will arrive soon."

The server raised his brow. "Would you like to order wine for the both of you? Supplies are low of the foreign variety for obvious reasons, but our domestic supplies are vast."

"A domestic one will do. Whatever is strong and bitter." He needed a drink that reflected his mood, and facing what came next sober was not all that appealing. A goblet of wine would dull his nerves. That could prove crucial when dealing with a princess… if she bothered to arrive at her own meeting.

He shook his head at himself. It was rare for him to be this on edge, and his mother would not approve. Sania always promoted meditation to keep calm, but the practice had never taken with him. Each time he closed his eyes, he wasn't doing what he should be. It was why she had stayed in Vamiustok to oversee the town while he was in the capital. When the wine came, though, even the first sip slowed his thoughts.

A young woman approached his table when his wooden goblet was half empty. She wore a wide-brimmed felt hat over her hair so light that it was nearly white. It was of rich taste, but her traveling jacket over a layered dress of brown trimmed in deep green fit like a glove in this place. As did the way she seemed to glide over the grasses.

"Apologies for my tardiness," Nikoza said, waiting alongside the opposing chair.

"There is no need," Zinarus replied, "but I must ask for your apologies now. I would help you sit if it were not for my leg."

She pursed her lips for a moment before seating herself and placing her hat in her lap. Beneath, her hair was held up in a knot, which she released. "It seems we will spend this entire morning apologizing to each other, but that would only draw attention. I fear, however, that your hair may do that alone. There are few in our nation whose mixed blood resulted in hair and skin like yours."

He swallowed. "I had believed my hat would provide some cover, but it seems not."

"It was not intended as an insult. Auburn suits you. I simply wished to state that I do not want anyone to know what we speak about today. My grandfather is already reading my post, as his trust in me has diminished due to my support for Ambassador Alyniana's plan."

Zinarus sat back, crossing his legs as the pieces fell together in his mind. "So the king's initial support of Nochland was your doing? It is a shame Lord Chatik and Lady Lilita managed to sway him otherwise."

"It is, but I am not here about the vote." Nikoza lowered her voice. "The ambassador informed me that Lady Katarzyna Niezik intends to aid Nochland despite the result, and she believed that you may be the one facilitating that."

Zinarus's heart skipped a beat, but he kept his composure in the face of her accusation. "I have no such capabilities, Princess. Why come to me and not Katarzyna?"

"She has not been seen since the declaration of war."

Zinarus cursed under his breath. Kasia's actions with the alchemist Paras ik Lierasa had set in motion her infiltration of the Crimsons, but had they seen through her schemes? If so, she was in grave danger. "The speed at which events have escalated is beyond what anyone had expected," he said. "Perhaps she is simply preparing her house for the destructive war to come."

"Come now," Nikoza replied. "Alyniana informed me about this Crimson Court that Katarzyna has been investigating. If their involvement with the awakened is true, they threaten all my grandfather and I have worked for. He is not a perfect king, but I wish to help our nation through him. Tell me the truth, and perhaps I could be of use."

As the server approached once again, Zinarus waved him off, grabbing his cane. "The king's allies are not mine. He has chosen his side."

Nikoza hung her head as Zinarus walked away with the stomping of his cane piercing the café's peace. He was halfway to the street before she rose. "Wait!" She rushed after him, laying her hand on his arm. "Please, Lord Zinarus. I may be the king's granddaughter, but I have my own will. He does not wish for me to become Professor Etal iz Noshok's apprentice. I am accepting the position anyway, as I truly want to stop this disease and help our people. If the Crimson Court is involved, I will do all I can to interfere with their plans for my grandfather, but I *need* to know more to be of use."

He looked from her to the curious onlookers throughout the café. *So much for being indiscreet.* Nikoza appeared genuine, but he found it difficult to trust in the current state of affairs. For now, though, she had access to the restricted Kalastok College.

"How soon can you organize a meeting with Professor iz Noshok?" he asked. "For the both of us."

She took a long breath, holding his gaze. "I sent him a letter last evening, but have yet to receive a reply."

"Would you be opposed to presenting yourself in person sooner? We had hoped to reach him hundred-hours ago, but the college's lockdown has made that quite difficult. I fear time is of the essence, and the more we delay, the sooner we come to losing our chance to prevent disaster."

"It would be untraditional, but I am already defying my grandfather." A smile flicked across her face. "Yes, perhaps we could approach the college and request to speak with him. There is little reason to tarry."

He nodded. "Alright then. Let us resume our meal and discuss our Crimson foes. Crystal Mother knows we need all the allies we can get."

**ZINARUS CHECKED HIS CRAVAT FOR THE THIRD TIME** as Nikoza's carriage pulled to a stop before the gates of Kalastok College. Across from him, sweat beaded on the princess's brow, but she took a deep breath and opened the door.

Both their nerves had been at their end for hours, and despite Nikoza's willingness to trust him, Zinarus found himself even more anxious than before. He couldn't forget Kasia's warning about his father. Would Uzrin tolerate his bastard son meddling in Crimson affairs?

All he could do for now was focus on the path ahead. Professor iz Noshok could offer them insights into the disease gripping their nation, and that alone had the potential to mend many of the Commonwealth's rifts. So, too, would it help them understand if there was a connection between the Spirit Plague and the Crimsons.

Nikoza took his gloved hand in hers, helping him down from the carriage before approaching the red-garbed guardsmen on either side of the gates of steel trimmed with glass. She still wore her more simple dress, but had shifted her hat up to reveal as much of her face as possible. Better they recognize her as a princess than some random scion seeking entrance. In the dim light cast by the two lamps on either side of the gate, though, it would be difficult for the guards to discern her features.

"Excuse me, good sirs," she said sweetly, hands clasped before her, holding the professor's letter. "I am Princess Nikoza Bartol, and I seek entrance to the college via the request of Professor Etal iz Noshok, whom I will be serving as the apprentice of."

The female guard on the right leaned against the brick wall beside the gate, arms crossed. Her frown deepened at Nikoza's mention of her title. "Princess, huh? Likely story. The Crystal Palace letters ahead whenever the royal family visits."

Nikoza held out the letter without abandoning her soft smile. "You will see that all is in order. Kalastok College's seal is upon the missive, and it bears the professor's signature."

The guard snatched the letter with a roll of her eyes before holding it up in the lamplight. After a moment, her jaw dropped, and her posture straightened. She handed the letter back, nodding at her partner. "Yes, Princess, all is in order. My apologies for not recognizing you sooner, but even a princess needs a reason to enter due to the king's orders. We cannot afford anyone with the sickness getting in and infecting the students."

"I understand that you were only fulfilling your orders," she replied, tucking away the letter in her handbag. "However, I would insist that you present yourselves in a way worthy of your position outside this great institution. After all, with my grandfather's orders, you may be the only faces most people see when they pass by."

The guards exchanged glances, and the woman replied again with a bow, "Of course, my lady. We will open the gate swiftly for your carriage to pass." She glanced behind Nikoza. "Is this gentleman with you?"

Zinarus cleared his throat. Nikoza had shown austere confidence, and he followed her lead with his chin raised. "I am here to ensure the princess can become connected with the professor. Once that is complete, I shall be on my way."

"Fine," the second guard—a tall, built man—replied. "It is against protocol, but we can allow it for Princess Nikoza. Do not dally."

Zinarus made a show out of moving quickly back toward the carriage, gritting his teeth through his leg pain. *I will act with as much haste as my body allows.*

The gates creaked open as Nikoza followed Zinarus back into the carriage. She dragged her thumb across her palm. "You lied to him."

Zinarus stared out the window, legs crossed. "I considered honor the highest pursuit for some time. Now… I have found myself twisting my words more in this season than I have in the rest of my life. One secret leads to another, then another, and you soon find yourself doubting whether you know the truth anymore."

"My grandfather calls politics the art of tactful wordplay."

"I would not know." He wrinkled his forehead, then looked back at her. "My mother sent me here for our house's business and the protection of it. With our mines gone, I wonder sometimes whether I lost my way combatting the Crimson Court."

Tree after leafless tree passed by as they rumbled down the street toward Kalastok College, soon joined by buildings of brick and glass. Students in formal coats and dresses walked together with books in-arm. Some held heavy looks, their feet dragging, but others laughed as they launched bits of magic at each other. Their embers, vines, shadows, and droplets scattered across a central grassy area.

Drifters roamed among the students, guided by a nearby Spirit Reacher until a middle-aged woman emerged from a nearby building with a lantern in hand. Her deep gray hair arced around her narrow face as her bangs fluttered with each wave of her hand, ushering the students off to class. They fled as if she were an awakened, but she wore a motherly smile that lit up her eyes until the clearing was empty. Then she lingered, watching where they had gone, and sorrow seemed to creep into her gaze.

As Nikoza's carriage stopped, the woman straightened her deep navy dress, buttoned across the chest with a cutaway section of white across a lower skirt. "Princess Nikoza?" she asked, curtsying. "We had heard that Professor iz Noshok had invited you here, but had not expected your arrival so soon."

Zinarus waited for Nikoza to descend the carriage steps before following with her help. She returned the curtsy.

"I must admit that I received his letter with some level of excitement," she said with a girlish giggle. "Though my father is king, I am merely an unskilled Reacher and had not expected the college to be interested in me—let alone a professor of such renown." She reached out for a handshake. "It is a pleasure to meet you."

The woman shook with both hands. "The pleasure is all mine. I am Liniala of House Koritazki, caretaker of the students here at the college to ensure all are well beyond their studies—as life does not end in the classroom. Your arrival is well timed. As I am sure you saw, afternoon classes have just begun, so I am free to bring you to Professor iz Noshok."

"Does he not have classes of his own?"

Liniala chuckled. "Etal approaches studies in unique ways. Yes, he teaches, but his primary duties are his research. Diseases are his greatest focus currently, for obvious reasons. Come, I will show you and your companion through the campus."

"Zinarus of House iz Vamiustok," Zinarus replied, shaking her hand, a far gentler experience than most domineering scions. "It is wonderful to step foot here again. My last tour was upon my arrival in the city a few years ago, and I must admit that I missed its beauty."

"It is never too late to pursue a degree, Lord Zinarus."

He smiled, but sorrow tugged at his heart—longing for a life he had not lived and one he could not. "I am afraid that is not possible. I was born out of wedlock, so unless the college's policies change, visitation is the closest I will get to admission."

Liniala held his arm, shoulders slumped. "I wish this realm did not punish us for choices that were not our own. Your plight is heard by me, but whether it reaches the ears of those scions who have lived many lifetimes, I know not. Come. Allow me to at least ensure you are as welcomed as possible for this time we have now."

They headed across the central green space, which Liniala called the Circle of Life. "Each of the realms has a circle within the campus grounds, representing our connection to them."

"Even Death?" Nikoza asked.

Liniala paused at the doorway to a tower-like building at the edge of the path around the Circle of Life. "Now more than ever, we need the reminder that Death's realm bleeds within the bounds of Zekiaz. Few are wealthy enough to ensure they receive the Crystal Mother's gift of new life through the Inheritance Rituals. Though their names are kept hidden for their safety, we have had Death Reachers among our students in the past. They prove that even in death, there is purpose."

Zinarus's thoughts returned to Kasia as they entered the tower and stepped into a room filled with artwork of nature, spirits, and people. Candles hung overhead, providing the only light and giving the paintings a heaviness that made him linger as Liniala continued. One depicting a father and his grown children struck him the most. Strokes of deep red covered sections of brighter shades, and he felt as if his heart bled with the painting.

*I see it now,* he said silently to Kasia, as if she stood by his side. *I see why you would give everything for his memory, to avenge the life he never had… the one you never had the chance to experience with him.*

He hadn't truly understood her desperation to face the Crimsons before. Yes, he shared her hatred after what they had done to Regizald and threatened to do to his mother, but Kasia had thrown herself into their maw by herself. She was passionate, unrestrainable… and it made sense now. Leonit's death had not simply been a paternal loss, it had changed the course of her very existence, torn away a future full of familial love and replaced it with nothing. That emptiness filled him now, but it had not yet festered for a decade. Not like the anger he felt for his absent father who now conspired with the Crimsons.

Kasia had been right. Against a group with no honor, they could not rely upon honor to defeat them.

"Lord Zinarus," Liniala's maternal voice said from across the room. "Do you wish to remain here for a time?"

Zinarus rapped his cane across the wooden floor. "There is no need. I simply found myself captivated by this piece."

"Oh, indeed." Liniala turned to Nikoza. "Why, I believe your uncle, Lord Chatik, completed that painting himself. There is much pain in it, as there was in him."

"That is one way to phrase it…" Nikoza muttered before smiling once again. "It is wonderful to see that House Bartol finds honor here. Hopefully, I may as well."

Liniala led them into a sitting room with a tall ceiling full of artful glass chandeliers. They arced around the center, which held a platform with columns at its corners. A cut-out section of the ceiling matched the size of the platform, and a scion stood at each edge. Before Zinarus could inquire as to why, the nearest bowed to Liniala.

"Do you need to ascend, Lady Caretaker?" the scion asked, eyeing Zinarus when he finished.

She nodded. "Yes. My old knees are aching with today's chill, and it is quite the climb to Professor iz Noshok's office."

"Of course."

The scion stepped aside, and Zinarus gave Liniala a grateful smile. She hadn't needed to divert attention from his impediment, yet she'd done so anyway. The first thing most people mentioned was his mechanical leg. Crystal Mother, where was this kindness in the rest of Kalastok?

Once they had mounted the platform, each of the scions extended their hands before them. Light blue light spun from their fingers, and the platform rose, the columns keeping it aligned as they climbed toward the ceiling. The swaying threatened to throw Zinarus off-balance, but Nikoza locked arms with him until he caught his footing.

"This is quite the creation," he told Liniala, taking mental notes about a potential mechanical copy. "I am surprised it is not used outside of the college as well."

"We strive to be ahead of society," she replied.

They passed the chandeliers and through the hole in the ceiling, entering a square room with a hall on each side. Wooden railing surrounded the platform's hole except for a latched gate. Though obviously for safety, their banisters bore intricately carved animals of every kind. Even the molding in the dim corners held some design more than mere function. Zinarus studied each as they ascended floor after floor, and found that none were the same.

"I have seldom seen a building crafted with such delicate touch," he said.

Nikoza gawked too, but pointed instead to the lamps and chandeliers. Encased in different metals for each floor, the glasswork surrounding the flame shifted too, giving the halls glows of various hues. "Are these to signal to the students which floor they are on?" she asked.

Liliana nodded. "That is correct. Each section is named after an accomplished Reacher of a certain realm, and their name is used as a designation for which floor or section of the campus a class will take place in. Professor iz Noshok's office resides on the Grazimor Oliezany floor—the vibrant red one, for Force. It was said that Grazimor banished the awakened for a dozen miles in a single blast when his army was cornered centuries ago."

The red light she'd described soon greeted them on what appeared to be the second-highest floor of the tower. Glancing down through the crack between the platform and the railing only deepened Zinarus's gratefulness. He'd struggled with his walking across level ground that morning, and he was confident that the climb—or following descent—would've been a mountain he could not trek.

A window of impure glass allowed a distorted view over a courtyard below. Red lines of metal ran across the glass in random, curved patterns to form a design that was nonsensical at a distance. As Zinarus followed the others off the platform, though, he drew closer and noticed the rippling waves of Force that collided throughout it.

The college's designs kept with him as they traversed a series of halls, each bearing woodwork and chandeliers with designs like that of the window. There was such *depth* in the beauty here, meaning. But it lay behind closed doors where few would see it.

Zinarus pictured his arena: functional but lifeless outside its competitors. What if he could bring elements of its heart to the lowborn who so rarely had the chance to escape life's labors? Was sport not supposed to carry beauty?

Their arrival at Professor iz Noshok's office tore him from his thoughts. The wooden door was shut, and a scratched note hung from a nail on its center.

*Do not enter unless it pertains to the Spirit Plague.*
*I MUST HAVE PEACE.*

Liniala put her hands on her hips, shaking her head. "He can be quite the grouch sometimes, but I promise that he means well."

Then she pounded on the door.

"Etal! Princess Nikoza is here for you, so don't you dare show any attitude when you open that door."

Zinarus swapped smirks with Nikoza as shuffling came from behind the door. Something toppled, followed by a *crash* that made Zinarus grit his teeth. Soon, the door unlocked, and an elderly Vockan man peeked his head out with a pair of rounded spectacles dangling precariously at the end of his nose. He scratched at the thin strip of bright red hair that rimmed the back of his head before speaking with a grumble of a voice.

"You have some haste in you, Princess," he said. "I expected resistance from your king of a grandfather for at least a hundred-hour before you arrived. Your letter only arrived at high-noon, and I have lacked even the time to open it. I presume your arrival means you accept the position?"

"I do, but I have not yet arrived permanently," Nikoza replied, her cheeks flushed for a moment. "My grandfather is resisting my arrival; however, I wished to meet you first and discuss possibilities."

He gave a single nod before looking to Zinarus. "And who is this fellow? One of the youth is enough already. I have no need for a second apprentice."

"Worry not," Zinarus replied. "I am here to see if we can help each other, not to become your apprentice. It *does* in fact pertain to the Spirit Plague."

"Fine, fine. Get in here, then, the both of you." Etal pointed at Liniala. "And you, continue on your way. I never can get much finished with you around."

Liniala grinned but complied, resting a hand on Nikoza's shoulder and whispering something before heading back down the hall.

Etal opened the door with her gone, and the smell of leather and dust smacked Zinarus in the face. He stepped into the office, doing all he could not to gasp at the sheer number of books piled throughout. Papers stuck out from each with incomprehensible writing scrawled over them. Etal waved an absent hand toward two chairs on the near side of a desk—whose only purpose seemed to be to waste precious space for more books.

Nikoza sneezed.

The professor snatched her with both arms and stared into her eyes. He was a short man by Vockan standards, but he still towered over the princess. Even with his ruffled woolen suit, stained tie, and frail stature, his pure intensity was threatening enough for Zinarus to take a step back.

"You are not infected, are you?" Etal asked Nikoza, his voice shaking. "We barred the gates to keep out the Spirit Plague, and if you allowed it in after all this time…"

"No, Professor," she insisted. "I simply breathed in some dust."

He released her, waving his hands about. "Oh… Of course, yes. Forgive me, but my research surrounding the Spirit Plague is my life these days. I fear it haunts me in these very walls sometimes." He paused, glaring at a pile of books in the corner. "Can it reside in brick?" He scrambled for a quill, which he dipped in ink before scribbling in the margins of the book laid out on his desk. "So much to research. Only so much connection…"

Etal looked up at the two of them. "Yes, you are still here. That would make sense. Please, sit."

Books covered the chairs, so they shifted them onto the various piles throughout the room before sitting. Zinarus didn't consider himself a claustrophobic man, but he could've sworn the books crawled toward him, drawing ever closer with each passing moment. He closed his eyes a bit longer with each blink and took long breaths.

*It is just an office. There is nothing to fear.*

Except images of his own bloody office filled his mind with those blinks. Regizald's mangled body, the hopelessness he'd felt… Would he ever be free from this grief?

"Before I ask further about my new apprentice," Etal said, popping his shirt collar—stained with some type of brown sauce, "I must inquire about this help you wish to provide, Zanios."

"Zinarus, sir."

Etal waved a dismissive hand. "Yes, yes. Answer the question."

Zinarus crossed his legs, tapping his mechanical knee as he wondered whether trusting this unstable man was for the best. Kasia had said Paras trusted him, but was that wise? "A partner of mine, Katarzyna of House Niezik, discovered that amber may have a use in capturing awakened. Paras ik Lierasa believed it may do the same to the disease within its victims. Has Paras contacted you at all?"

Etal blinked. "Do you not read the newspapers? The alchemist is dead."

"He is not, and based on Katarzyna's discussion with him, you two are somewhat familiar."

"So you are one of them…"

Zinarus furrowed his brow. "I do not understand. One of whom?"

"I thought your kind were more secretive, yet you flaunt purple upon your very chest!" Etal threw out his arms toward him. "What kind of Child of Zekiaz are you to walk into my office like this? I have told your allies many times that my assistance to your order hinges on the very secrecy of Paras's location! Have I not done enough?"

"I…" Zinarus glanced at Nikoza. *What would Kasia do?* "You are right, but I am not here to pressure, only to see if there has been any progress. With the declaration of war—"

"Politics! The enemy of science!"

It took all Zinarus's strength not to burst. *This* was the professor that held their hopes of a cure? He gripped his hands around his knee and spoke slowly. "This is not about politics, Professor. It is about the awakened surging at the same time this disease arrived. There is an organization, the Crimson Court, who we believe can control the awakened. If they started this disease…"

Etal sat back, crossing his arms. "I have already told your organization that the Crimson Court spurred this disease! Why use lowborn soldiers when you can command their souls? They need neither food nor water. They cannot defy the one who holds the whip when it is instead a crystalline talon."

"Wait, you already knew?"

"Who are you?" Etal shot to his feet, ungloved taloned hand extended toward them. "No Child of Zekiaz would be so clueless about this."

Nikoza intervened before Zinarus could reply. "Professor, I believe we may have begun on the wrong side of the river. I know not why Lord Zinarus decided to deceive you, but from what I can ascertain, neither of us are members of either these Children of Zekiaz or the Crimson Court."

Etal glanced at her, then flexed his fingers toward Zinarus. "The Niezik girl is not part of her father's organization?"

"No," Zinarus replied, gloved hands raised like a common criminal. "They have aided her efforts, but she is not a member. All she knew was that they could ensure Paras remained alive to continue his studies. When Princess Nikoza contacted me, I saw it as an opportunity to enter the college and see if you knew more about his discoveries around the amber."

Etal lowered his hand. "Where is Katarzyna now? Missing, I presume?"

"How did you know?"

Without reply, Etal turned to the wall beside his desk and placed his taloned hand on it. Red wisps drifted from his fingertips, followed by a faint *clink*. The wall itself turned to open a passage into the room beyond.

"Come, both of you," he insisted. "There is much you do not know, and such concepts must be discussed behind walls thicker than these."

# REVELATIONS

*"All intellectuals seek the highest truths of their field. Few ever reach the peak, and those who do often discover that there is a greater summit still."* – Yargish of the Minebombers, professor at the Tidewater College

Nikoza stared at the hole in Etal's office wall for a long time. The day before, she had stood helplessly before the entire Chamber of Scions as they declared war against the most powerful nation in Brakesh. Now, that same feeling crept over her.

*I am far out of my depth, but what is there to do but swim in hopes of finding shore?*

Etal and Zinarus's talk of Children of Zekiaz and amber had her head spinning. She had only heard of the Children hours before at the café, and Zinarus had lacked a full explanation of the falcon-masked organization. What did all of this have to do with curing the Spirit Plague?

She found herself swept away in a wave of curiosity, her feet carrying her through the secret doorway and into a laboratory beyond. Shock stopped her from going any further.

Putrid smells and vapors filled the air as Etal looked over a hundred vials and burners like a mother would her children. Another Vockan man sat on a wooden stool at the back of the room, leaning over a beaker full of a blue liquid. He wore a loose brown shirt, its sleeves poorly rolled up to his elbows, with an apron overtop. Some type of many-armed brass contraption covered his disheveled hair of deep maroon, and he lowered what appeared to be a magnifying glass connected to one of the arms.

Etal turned back to Zinarus and Nikoza, a finger over his lips. The man had not noticed their arrival, and he slowly poured the tiniest bit of a viscous, orange-brown substance into the beaker. Sizzling followed as the man stirred the beaker's contents with a metal rod.

When the sizzling stopped, the man sat back with a sigh and wiped the sweat from his brow. His relief did not last long, as Etal clapped him on the back harder than one would expect from a man his age.

"Crystal be pure, my good man!" the professor exclaimed. "Have you done it?"

The man yelped, falling off his stool and onto the floor. "What did I tell you about interrupting my work, Etal? The solution requires ample time to settle before we can know whether a successful bond has been formed. Your ill-patience is why we are in this situation in the first place!"

"What do you mean by that?" Nikoza asked, removing her hat. It felt respectful in an expansive laboratory like this. There was far more that could ever be created, discovered, or mended here than in the Chamber of Scions or any throne room. There was power in that—true power. "Did Professor iz Noshok have something to do with this disease?"

The man brushed himself off. "My apologies, my lady. I had not noticed that Etal had brought associates into our *hidden lab.* My name—" He glanced at Etal, as if asking for permission, and continued when the professor nodded. "My name is Paras ik Lierasa, alchemist. I would offer to shake both of your hands, but… well…" He held up his hands. Some of the viscous orange substance remained on them.

"A pleasure to meet you, Paras," Nikoza said, curtsying despite his lowborn status. "I am Princess Nikoza of House Bartol, heir to the house."

Zinarus stepped to her side, leaning heavily upon his cane. After years of aiding her grandfather, Nikoza worried about the exhaustion evident on his face. "And I am Zinarus of House iz Vamiustok, heir to the house—if we are handling all the formalities."

Paras straightened his posture, but did not bow. "So it is your grandfather who enclosed the western city and created the largest dungeon in all of Brakesh. Quite the impressive feat for a king who was thought too weak-willed to even lift the crown to his head."

Nikoza lifted her chin. "If you seek to antagonize me, then you are wasting your time. My pride has been struck enough in recent days to lay shattered at my feet. Tread upon the shards as you wish, but do not mock me for arriving against my grandfather's will with the desire to end this plague."

"What aid, then, do you bring?" Paras asked with a dismissive wave.

"I bring you a voice in the king's ear," she replied, pacing toward him with her hat held before her. "I bring you Lord Zinarus, who is organizing a mercenary company comprised of lowborn capable of aiding efforts in Kalastok's west side."

Paras frowned. "Hired thugs will not help us rid our nation of the Spirit Plague."

Etal sat on the stool he'd vacated. "Let us not argue further. These young folk come as allies, Paras, and we may yet need them. There remains a question yet to be answered as well." He lowered his head and shut his eyes. "I bear some responsibility for the Crimson Court's ability to harness spirits… as well as their creation of the disease that now threatens us all."

He gestured toward a few more stools alongside another table. "Please, sit. My knees ache watching you linger there like supplicants before a king."

The smallest smile flickered across Zinarus's face as he took a stool, but the fear that took over reflected the same that resided in Nikoza's chest. Her amazement at the laboratory had disappeared, replaced by a serpent tightening around her throat. Etal had been her icon for years, who she sought to become. The glory of meeting him had lasted mere minutes.

"You did not cause this on purpose, did you?" Nikoza asked, looking to regain some of her hope.

Etal scratched under his popped collar, then shook his head. "Why would I wish for a horror like this? No, my responsibility lies in my greatest work: *The Convergence.*"

"My apologies," she replied. "I have not heard of it."

"There is little surprise in that. My Convergence Theory was well researched, but both my colleagues and the greater scientific world denied my claims. In the manuscript, I proved that the realms are bound through the forces within their core crystals. Reachers utilize these bindings, quite literally pulling the realms closer together, but that is not relevant now." Etal waved his hands over his head like a child batting away a bee. "What *is* relevant is that I detailed within the text how the interaction of multiple forces allows for control beyond what one can accomplish with merely a single Reacher. Among those detailed within it was the combination of Spirit and Life Reaching to create awakened."

Zinarus tapped his cane against the floor. "You believe the awakened were created by Reachers?"

"Could it be mere coincidence that awakened emerged at the peak of the Piorak Empire?" Etal asked, meeting Nikoza's gaze and waiting for an answer.

She gave one, sitting straight-backed despite a soreness creeping into her spine. One could only sit stiffly for so long without repercussions. "The scientific process warns against the assumption of coincidence. Tests are required."

"Precisely." Etal tapped his temple. "A great mind never ceases to search, so neither did I. In addition to binary reactions between Realms, I wondered whether there could be tertiary as well. What occurs at the meeting of Light, Darkness, and Shadow? Could life be granted when combined with Water and Body?" He hesitated, his voice fleeting. "Could ravenous awakened gain sentience when Mind is Reached into them, allowing them to be commanded?"

Nikoza froze. Memories of the Ephemeral Slaughter flashed before her, awakened surging across the Chamber and swooping into the pit mere feet from her. She had seen few awakened before that night, but in that moment, it had almost seemed like the spirits had held their gaze upon her. Crystal Mother be praised, she was lucky not to have been out in the city where the greater attack occurred.

"So it is true, then?" she asked. "The Ephemeral Slaughter was planned?"

Etal's face sunk, his eyes reddening. "I do not believe it was a coincidence that rumors of controlled awakened spread merely two years after I published *The Convergence*. Then came the sudden death of King Yaakiin and his closest advisors—"

"Such as Leonit Niezik," Zinarus added.

"Indeed. And those events over many years since have led you to us this very day. Excuse me, Princess, for what I must say, but King Jazuk and his allies have silenced those who claimed these deaths were assassinations. There were no weapons found at the relevant locations of death, nor were there murder weapons or any lethal injuries to their bodies."

Nikoza slowly pulled herself from the depths of her mind, questioning all she knew about her grandfather. Was he connected to these Crimsons? Had he assassinated the former king?

"There are a hundred snakes whispering in my grandfather's ear every moment he breathes," she said. "He has made inexcusable decisions, but I fail to believe he could have done such a thing."

Zinarus shifted uncomfortably. "It would be rather convenient if he had not been. To become king because of another's plot? Has that ever happened before?"

Nikoza opened her mouth to chide him, but Etal stomped his foot. "Politics is the enemy of science!" he repeated. "It is not for me to decide whether King Jazuk benefited from the act, only to understand what forces led to its occurrence. It would appear that the awakened who attacked during the event called the Ephemeral Slaughter were controlled, directed. This provides evidence to my theory that it is not a coincidence. Someone who followed my teachings closely decided to apply them in horrific ways."

"Who among your students could have done this?" Nikoza asked.

"Many of my most promising students graduated in the years immediately before King Yaakiin's death." Etal stood, pacing over to a notepad on a nearby desk and flipping through it. "I have pondered this question for some time and decided on which would be capable—though not necessarily probable—actors in such a plot: Laniaz Rakazimko, Vevolad Kuzon, Chatik Bartol (now Pikezik), Pozakan Uziokaki, Uzrin Ioniz, and Tzena Oliezany." He drummed the table with each name, as if keeping a solemn beat.

"Chatik?" Nikoza blurted out, then covered her mouth. Her grandfather would not have been pleased at her outburst. Her father would have beaten her. "My uncle is a brute of a man, but what would he have gained through this?"

Paras shrugged. "What is there for scions to gain but power over others?"

She wasn't fully convinced, but she turned to Zinarus, who clutched his cane until his knuckles turned white.

"Is all well?" Nikoza asked him.

"Your uncle," he muttered, "and my asshole of a father, Uzrin. He abandoned my mother, made me a bastard, and then did *this*?" He slammed his cane into the ground, snapping it clean in half. The top of it remained in his hand, and he waved it like a spear. "I had doubted Katarzyna's claims that he was a Crimson, but joined with this, it is undeniable."

Zinarus paused, and his eyes widened as he surveyed those in the room. "This plot reaches far into the most powerful houses. One of our allies spotted Laniaz Rakazimko in Crimson garb, and Tzena Oliezany is another known Crimson."

Nikoza slumped back into the table behind her stool. It felt as if her world was unraveling around her, people's intentions twisting into sinister acts. "This is nothing but conspiracy, surely… What proof do you have of this?"

"What realm does Chatik Reach?" Zinarus asked, standing with his back curled like a frightened cat.

"I do not…"

Her denial caught on her tongue as she pictured an everbright sky vanishing at Chatik's word years before, her grandfather's wrath taken with it. *"Once you become a Reacher yourself, you will wield your own fate,"*

Chatik had said. *"Do not waste your life on that old man when it comes time to choose your path."* Could the man who'd protected her be so cruel?

"He is a Dark Reacher," she admitted, "but you do not understand. Chatik has a gentle heart, a protector's!"

Zinarus growled. "A Dark Reacher killed my best friend! He threatened my mother's life, stole everything our family had! If there's any chance Chatik is him, he needs to be brought to justice."

Nikoza backed away from them. She trembled, clinging to herself as if the pressure would wake her up from this dream-turned-nightmare. "This cannot be true. Professor, did you invite me here only to slander my family? Is all of this some kind of trick?"

"The Children of Zekiaz have been watching your uncle along with dozens of other scions," Paras said. "There is a chance he is innocent, but you should listen to Etal. No one else on Brakesh has published about these theories." He turned to Zinarus. "And you need to calm down. Sit, so that Etal may finish."

"What more can there be?" Zinarus asked, huffing but grabbing his stool once again. "If this is true, it would implicate members of the most powerful houses in conspiracies to assassinate a king and slaughter thousands of innocents."

"That is true," Etal replied, "but I have yet to speak about the Convergence as an event itself. You see, the fifteen Known Realms are bound by the forces I have described. They intertwine, forming all that reside in our own realm, even humans ourselves. This weaving of powers brings them closer together. Reaching has a similar effect, and over time, the realms have moments where the barriers between them break. Exchange occurs between all of them except the core of all Known Realms: the Axiom."

He rose, shuffling over to a book on a nearby table and flipping to a page with an image of a flower with fifteen petals. "Chatik was particularly interested in my description of the Axiom, as I believe it is the origin of all the realms' powers. All flows from it, and if someone were to uncover its secrets, they would be unmatched in all of Zekiaz."

"Then why has no one tried?" Nikoza asked. "Why have we not heard of it? The king would surely know if scientists had discovered another realm."

Etal set down the book. "Like I said, the others believed me to be a fool. That mockery only grew when I urged no one to attempt such a connection, as it would bring us closer to another Convergence that could destroy all we know. A thrust into the central Axiom would require Reachers of great strength from each realm to release their power in a single snap. Chatik, while my favorite student, also pushed known bounds often in his research. I find it probable that he would seek power through controllable awakened and Reaching into the Axiom."

Zinarus cursed, running his hands through his hair as he staggered to his feet. "Kasia! By the Crystal Mother, she is in danger!"

"Slow down, boy," Paras replied. "What do you mean by that?"

"She believed the Crimsons would approach her last night, and she has not been seen since the declaration of war." Zinarus looked around for his cane, only to frown at the shattered bits. "We learned they were looking for a 'final petal'. A Death Reacher! They are rare, and in her, they must have seen a chance to complete this connection to the Axiom. She thought she was infiltrating them. Instead, they were using her power…"

Paras shook his head. "If she is already in their grasp, then there is little you can do for her now. Even the Children do not know where the Crimsons gather. All we can do now is find a cure for the Spirit Plague to ensure they do not have a lurking army within the city to control."

"But how does this all connect the Crimson Court to the Spirit Plague?" Zinarus asked. "Unless Professor iz Noshok mentioned it in *The Convergence*, how would they have learned how to infect people?"

Etal approached Zinarus and patted him on the arm, a stern look in his eye. "Must I say it thrice? It is the Crimson Court who benefit most from this disease, and coincidence is not to be trusted. They have had over a decade since my writing to research. It is conceivable that they could have developed the Spirit Plague in that time."

"We can stop it, though, right?" Nikoza replied, still holding her arms across her body. The initial impact of her shock was beginning to dull, but her head ached worse than ever before.

"The process would be expedited if I had more amber samples," Paras said with a wave at his experiments. "I can only do so much with a single piece."

"Katarzyna would have more amber," Zinarus said.

Paras pinched the bridge of his nose and sighed. "You misunderstand. I need amber samples with *awakened* in them. Amber may be the ingredient to solve this puzzle, but I must first understand the connection between it and spirits."

Nikoza winced. "Must it be awakened? I neither have experience with facing them nor the desire to become one."

"If Katarzyna cannot be found," Paras said, "then it may be for the best to capture purer spirits instead."

"Consider this your first task as my apprentice, Nikoza," Etal added. "I am needed here to assist Paras and to ensure no one suspects my movements. Bring the amber, and perhaps we can find a cure."

She took a shaky breath and looked at Zinarus. "I will do what it takes, but we need Katarzyna's amber. Despite what my uncle may have done, you must see that I am not your enemy."

Zinarus sat there for a long time, eyeing his smashed cane before returning his gaze to her. "What about Kasi… Katarzyna? Someone must help her."

"There is nothing for you to do," Paras replied. "It is why the Children of Zekiaz act with few connections. We must know when to allow a brother or sister to work their way out of a difficult situation."

Zinarus gritted his teeth. "Fine, then. I will help you gather the amber and collect the spirits, but after we are finished, our focus turns to the Crimsons."

Nikoza held out her hand, which he shook. "You have a deal, Lord Zinarus."

# DARK DAYS, DARKER NIGHTS

*"The enemy of your enemy is your friend... until the greater foe is defeated."* –
An excerpt from *The Science of Diplomacy*

A wind chime clanged all through the night as Nex lay awake, holding Vinnia's ever-weakening body in their arms. They knew the sound well. Ulfrica, the grumpy old woman who lived next door, had crafted it out of scraps from the factory dumps just a few blocks west. On good nights, it reminded Nex of the little pleasures amid the choking smoke of western Kalastok.

Tonight was not a good night.

Each unrefined clatter wound Nex's tense muscles even tighter. All they could think about was the Spirit Plague slowly killing the woman they loved, and how, despite Vinnia's life hanging on a thread, they still couldn't tell her how they felt. Did it matter? She'd be dead soon anyway.

The metal roof's rattling joined the wind chime as the blizzard grew outside. Air Reachers would keep the eastern half of the city safe from the worst of it, but all that did was deflect more of its power over the west side. Well... that's at least what old Jax claimed. Jax never lied. He was just wrong sometimes. Those were two things as different as lowborn and scions, and Nex knew they could trust him on anything.

Vinnia shifted, her eyes flickering open. Her face was just a few inches from Nex's, and even in sickness, she smelled of some sweet flower Nex had never bothered to learn the name of. In that moment, Nex wished they had.

"You're actually here?" Vinnia whispered through a labored cough. "Thought you'd be out chasing shadows again."

"I'm here for you," Nex replied, drawing close enough for just the tips of their noses to touch. Spirits, they'd have given anything for this moment to last forever. Damn their Reaching, gambling, and fight against the Crimsons. None of it mattered compared to this.

"The Spirit Plague has me," Vinnia replied. "There's no cure. We know there's not, so why waste your time?"

"Because there's gotta be a cure! I'm not letting you die." They held Vinnia so tight to them that it hurt—or was that just the ache in their heart? "I'll fix this stupid disease with Kasia. Paras said he was close."

Vinnia closed her eyes, resting her forehead against Nex's chin. "I'm so tired, Nexie. All I've done for the last couple hundred-hours is sleep, but it just gets worse. Go before I infect you too."

Nex bit their lip as tears ran down their cheeks and dripped onto Vinnia's head. No! They refused to let this happen, to watch her die. "I've lost everything except you," they said. "And I can't leave you. I… I love you."

No response came.

Slowly, Nex repositioned to see Vinnia's face. Her eyes were shut, but her chest still rose and fell. They cursed under their breath. After all this time worrying about admitting the truth, they'd chosen to say it when she was asleep. Just their luck.

Those words fed a need within Nex to do *something*. They did love Vinnia, and they couldn't just lay here and let the Spirit Plague take her.

So they pried themselves from Vinnia's arms and grabbed their leather duster and hat. They touched their Possibility ring one more time out of habit to check it was still there, then grabbed the door handle. A longing in their chest held them there as the smell of rotten wood struck them like a punch to the nose. Even with the stench, it was peaceful, the patter of the rain falling beyond the door with Vinnia's soft breaths joining in a steady rhythm.

And that aroma of flowers…

*I'll figure out which ones those are,* they thought. *Then I'll plant a thousand of them all over the city when this is over.*

It would sure as shit smell better than the waste filling the Kala and lining the streets when it didn't rain enough. Maybe people wouldn't be such assholes if the city didn't smell like them.

The moment passed. Nex slipped out into the storm, which flung the windchime about like a can full of nails. They considered wrecking the awful thing, but stopped themselves as they thought of the joy it likely brought Ulrika. The woman was a grumbling annoyance, but she'd spent all duskfall and everdark putting it together years ago. Nex was a lot of things. Cruel wasn't one of them.

They tugged down their hat as they headed down the stairs and onto the muddy ground. Snow sloshed into their socks through a hole in the side of their boot, but that was to be expected when your shoes came from trash heaps and dead bodies. Nex saved the few nice articles of clothing they had for blending in with rich folk. That wouldn't be needed tonight.

Shadows approached from down the alley, so they ducked behind a fence, creeping along it until the soldiers had passed. More of them patrolled the west side after Kasia's disruption had put them all on edge. The quarantine had lowborn ready to riot already, and now, Paras's faked death and the war conscription had turned the boiler up to the max. Fancy-dressed sergeants claimed the soldiers were there to protect the people of the west side. Bullshit. Nex had seen them shoot people whose only crime was not knowing when to shut up. It was about control, and with the war coming, those soldiers were dragging away lowborn to fight.

Nex wouldn't be dragged anywhere. A shot to the head was better than spending the rest of their life on the front line against stupid

Keloshans. Their enemies were here, not in some far off land, and it didn't matter what the emperor of Kelosh wanted—just what Nex wanted.

Right now, they wanted to reach Jax on Beg Ave. He'd know if a bribable guard was on any of the bridges. Nex's ring could help their luck, but they'd tested its limits with Kasia during her escape and ended up in the middle of the freezing Kala. Never again. Besides, using their Reaching now would be a waste if something happened while they were on the east side.

The fires of the Beg Ave homeless soon came into view, more smoke than flame amid the snowfall. Their flickering sparks were the only forces banishing the everdark in this half of the city. Guards carried lanterns, but no one else could afford to. Oil had become impossible to find with the quarantine, and food and clean water weren't much better.

Jax stood near one of the fires with his tin cup in hand. He stared forlornly into the flames as the shadows danced across his sunken cheeks, but he smiled at Nex's approach.

"Your eyes are a sore sight!" he exclaimed, taking a sip from his cup despite it not ever being full of any liquid. Most of the homeless covered their heads or scattered under trees amid the blizzard. Not him.

Nex huffed and grabbed his forearm as he did the same to theirs. "It's 'you're a sight for sore eyes,' " they said. "Scions say it when they haven't seen each other in a long time."

"Why their eyes sore?"

"Probably got sick of staring at women's faces so powdered they reflect everything."

Jax laughed, pointing at Nex as he turned to the others gathered around the fire. They were familiar to Nex, but none had ever bothered striking up much of a conversation with them. Just Jax. "Anything Nex can't do? Stealing? Jokes?"

"You're the one who knows the guards," Nex said, lowering their voice. "Any easy ones tonight? Need to get across."

Jax shook his cup, so Nex rolled their eyes and threw in a few quarter-kena coins. He never gave a true cost for his information, but so far, Nex had kept him happy. Apparently, this offering was enough. He gave a smile with his few teeth and nodded toward the Oliezany Bridge at the far southern side of the city. "Gotta hurry. Shift switches in an hour."

Going that far would make getting back across harder than Nex had wanted, but that was a problem for later. They tossed another quarter-kena into his cup before jogging off.

The quarantine had all but dried up their income from Kalastok's west side gambling halls, and even the scions east of the river were starting to become stingy with war coming. That had left Nex with less keni than they needed—not that they ever had enough to live comfortably. Each tip they bought from Jax ate into their reserves. They needed each kena to pay for a cure if Paras ever made a real one.

But first, Nex needed to get to the bridge. It was a long way across the city, and it would be a tight call. Their legs were still heavy from lack of sleep, but they pushed on at a pace they could handle as the chill nipped at their nose.

Patrolling soldiers didn't make the journey any easier. Nex ducked into side alleys and through open yards when possible, but more often than they were comfortable with, they were forced to walk past with their hat tugged over their face. No warrants were out for their arrest that they knew of. Still, soldiers didn't need a piece of stamped paper to accost someone they thought was a vulnerable woman.

Nex thumbed their Possibility ring when the Oliezany Bridge came into sight. Its gray stone seemed near black, with only a single lamp at its end to mark the entrance into its enclosed walkway, bars stretching up and down the arched windows on either side.

*Like a dungeon,* Nex thought as they stepped onto the bridge, imagining that their cell would not be so expansive if the soldiers decided not to allow them across. It was a rare day that they were excited about anything related to those rich Oliezany bastards, but their bridge was their only way to approach Kasia's townhouse. That was enough.

A single soldier guarded this bridge, just like last time. Unlike those further north, there were few lowborn who would dare cause a fuss here when the Oliezany mercenary's barracks sat on the opposing bank. It was difficult to be worse than Commonwealth soldiers, but House Oliezany had succeeded.

The soldier stomped her foot at Nex's approach.

"Halt!" she demanded with her rifle aimed. "No one is to cross under the order of King Jazuk the Fourth!"

Nex tipped up their hat. This soldier was familiar, a different one than the one that had forced them and Kasia to jump, as she'd allowed them to pass many times before. "Can we skip formalities?" they said. "I'm in a rush."

The guard shouldered her rifle. "Oh, it's you."

Nex fished for the coins in their pockets, then held out five keni for the soldier, who took them without hesitation. But when they went to step by, the guard grabbed their shoulder.

"Ten keni," she said.

"Five," Nex muttered back, trying to rip her arm off their shoulder. Her grip was too firm.

"Risk went up with the war. Five more, or I'll arrest you."

*They probably feed prisoners more than we get,* Nex mused as they reached into their pocket once again. Five more keni would take all they had left for the return trip. That would make things fun in the same way getting beaten with a soldier's baton was fun.

Nex shoved the money into her chest. "Ten, but that's it. Fuck your stupid toll. I'm done."

"How do you expect to get across then?" the soldier asked, releasing them.

Nex didn't reply until they were out of earshot. "A bullet to your head."

The blizzard faded the moment Nex reached the end of the bridge, turning to gentle flakes. Moments before, the wind had stung their cheeks and tugged at the ends of their hair that peeked out from their hat. It was near still now. A single step had taken Nex from one world and into another.

It made them sick.

They clenched their fists as they headed down the riverfront. Heading further into the city would give them cover, but walking the closest street felt right. Safety had never been Nex's concern, but a new fear stirred within them after their admission to Vinnia. Just as Vinnia was all they had left, they were Vinnia's only hope.

Lit lamps hung at the front of The Confluence. Nex shied away from them, eyeing the windows of nearby buildings. Only when they were sure no one was watching did they step to Kasia's door and knock.

A young woman answered moments later—Kikania, the maid. Her expression shifted from interest to shock as she realized who stood before her. "Nex? Oh, my… Did Lord Zinarus contact you?"

Nex shook their head. "Where's Kasia?"

"Well…" Kikania averted her gaze. "Lady Katarzyna has not been seen since the declaration of war. Perhaps it is best that you come inside, as Lord Zinarus and Princess Nikoza are here already."

"Princess?" Nex asked. "What is a princess doing here?"

Kikania stepped aside, gesturing for them to enter. "Come out of the storm. My apologies for Lord Faniz's absence, as he is not feeling well at the moment." She took a long breath as Nex stepped inside, but left their hat and coat on. "The others are upstairs. Allow me to—"

Nex pushed past her and bounded up the stairs. A trail of melting snow covered the floor in their wake, but they ignored Kikania's yelps, heading to the study. The bright chandeliers and glass-imbued decorations created a sharp contrast from the everdark and stung their eyes. Luckily, the study itself was far dimmer.

Zinarus stood over a side table with a small box full of amber jewels. He wore an obscenely formal vest, but his hair had tufts of it sticking out every direction as he looked up at Nex with his jaw ajar.

"How… Why…"

"So you're that way around everyone," Nex mused, taking the box and studying it without any resistance. "Thought you were just red-faced around Kasia."

"*Excuse* me," another woman said from behind Nex in a voice too high pitched and proper for them to bother listening.

Nex plucked one of the amber pieces from the pile, only to find it was strung together with many of the others into a necklace. What fun was that?

A firm hand fell upon Nex's shoulder. "May I ask who you are and what you are doing here?" the woman continued, apparently not getting the point of Nex ignoring her.

"You first," Nex replied, glancing up at the woman to find she was far younger than she sounded. Could've been Nex's age even, maybe a year or two older. They didn't care to ask, but even they couldn't deny she had pretty purple eyes and a face men would probably call perfect. Nex called it boring. Not a single scratch or blemish on her—at least that they could see through all that powder.

The woman pursed her lips as her grip tightened, but Zinarus stepped between them. "This is Nex. They are a friend of Kasia's, and they are helping us against the Crimson Court."

Nex nodded before flinging the amber necklace back into the box, using it as a distraction to pocket a couple other pieces. "Was here to find her and figure out this stupid plague, but it's just you two stealing her jewelry, I guess."

"*Stealing*?" the woman gasped. "I would never resort to such a crime. We are assisting Professor Etal iz Noshok's research of the syndrome by collecting spirits within amber, as Lady Katarzyna has demonstrated is possible."

"So she said you can take it?"

The woman blushed. "Well… That is not…"

Nex frowned and ripped her hand from their shoulder. "Who are you again?"

"This is Princess Nikoza of House Bartol," Zinarus said, his tone growing evermore exasperated, "daughter of—"

"Some rich scion," Nex interrupted, "and granddaughter of the son of a bitch that locked us in the west side." The last person they wanted to see was a princess when they'd broken quarantine on top of their hundred other crimes. Where had she come from anyway? Kasia's fit of madness after the Paras incident had been only days before, and she'd never mentioned Nikoza.

Zinarus hobbled away with his hands pressed together in prayer. "Crystal Mother help me."

"This is the company Lady Katarzyna keeps?" Nikoza scoffed, snatching back the box and depositing a few more pieces of amber jewelry within it. "Perhaps the fall of her house was justified after all."

Nex stepped toe-to-toe with her, and she wavered as Nex spat, "So Jazuk's the grandfather of a bitch too."

Nikoza's face contorted in ways Nex hadn't thought possible. They snickered as she turned away, her breaths heavy and her fingers ruining her perfect little hair bun. All the while, Zinarus leaned against the sofa, prodding his mechanical knee.

"Are you two finished with your squabbling?" he said. "We need to catch these spirits, and as long as Kasia is gone, we are the only ones resisting the Crimsons."

"You're not worried about her?" Nex asked.

He picked at the bottom of his vest before shaking his head. "She is plenty capable. I am certain that she thought through her plan for confronting them."

"I don't believe you."

Nikoza stomped to the door. "May we go? Leave Nex here, unless they want to provide some assistance instead of insults. There is no time for us to waste here."

"I agree," Zinarus said, joining her. "Nex, you may come, but you must be on your best behavior."

"I'm coming," they replied with their arms crossed. "But I can help and insult you at the same time. Vinnia says it's my talent." Nex's heart ached at their mention of Vinnia, but they kept their smirk. This princess would eat them alive if they showed weakness.

# SPIRITBORN

*"All born on Zekiaz bear the spirit of our realm. In this, we are alike."* – Gertrude Niezik, exiled sister of the Buried Temple

Warmth like the softest blanket encompassed Kasia.

She floated amid a thousand colors, pillars of crystal rising from nothing and vanishing just as quickly. Her pain was gone, along with the weight that had rested on her shoulders every moment since her father's death. Instead, all she felt was an overwhelming sensation of peace.

*I'm dead.*

The realization struck as heavily as Chatik's bullet. A thousand memories washed over her, bringing their joy, agony, and suffering with them.

Kasia shut her eyes in a futile attempt to resist the visions and forget all she'd experienced. But they came nonetheless, tearing away her bliss until she curled into a ball, weeping. The tears came without warning as all the pain she'd locked away broke free at once. So many regrets. So much loss. So much time spent pursuing revenge.

All for nothing.

What would she be remembered as? The Amber Dame who brought amber's wealth to the people of Tystok and discovered amber's role in curing the Spirit Plague? Or the Daughter of Death who had slaughtered innocent peasants and conspired with the nationalists for her own gain?

Crystals danced around her, spiraling together until they formed an island like the ones she'd stood on in the Axiom. Wisps of color followed. They skittered close enough to brush aside her hair and tickle her skin, but when she reached out to touch them, they darted away.

And her hand wasn't her own.

Silvery wisps formed her arm instead of flesh and bone. So it was true… Her stomach flipped as she looked down to see that her body resembled that of a spirit, indistinct and shifting. Was this what all drifters experienced after their death?

She rose toward the crystal island. The movement came without an attempt by her, the Axiom's strange gravity acting with its own will, and when her feet graced the crystal ground, energy rushed through her, a constant flow that abated her sorrow.

The mass of a thousand colored tendrils towered before her. Before it, her body—her *real* body—lay sprawled amid crimson robes and a pool of dry blood. Had it been that long? Kasia could've sworn she'd only been shot moments before, but nothing seemed to work as normal in the Axiom… except guns apparently.

With a knot tightening in her chest, she approached her human body, raising a shaking hand to its left temple. A thin streak of blood sliced through its hair and skin, and pain washed over her at the touch.

She reeled back just to catch her breath. Chatik's bullet had merely grazed her scalp, and such a wound couldn't have caused all this. So she followed the trail of blood staining her robes to its source at her left hand.

Her talon wasn't there.

"NO!" she screamed into the Axiom's endless sky, clutching at where her taloned finger should've been. Her very being burned as she realized what she'd lost. The bullet must have struck her finger and deflected along her head. It had stopped the bullet from piercing her brain, but in the process, she had lost her greatest weapon.

She was no longer a Reacher.

Exhaustion took over. She dropped to her ethereal knees, staring at where Chatik had stood. The King in the Dark was gone. He'd surely taken what he'd wanted from the Axiom in the process and had likely closed the portal behind him, but it didn't matter. She lacked the Death Reaching to stop him anyway.

What was she without Death's power at her command? Reaching wasn't a mere tool, but a bond with her deepest needs. Without it to fuel her revenge, what use was she to her father's legacy?

She scoffed at her failure, her weakness. Chasing Chatik had been foolish, and he'd shown her no mercy. Her pride meant nothing, though, when she would fade into nothing. The few hours or minutes she had left would be spent in this realm at the center of all others, and part of her was okay with that. Another part raged.

She let those factions war in her mind as she stared toward the sphere of colored tendrils, wondering what came next. Death was a force distant the magnates of the great houses and their heirs. They saw many lives, stretching their existences on for centuries through their Inheritance Rituals. That continuous lifespan allowed them to gather further power, but the irony was that the other great houses doing the same ensured none ruled for too long. Each house shared the spoils. Except for the lesser scions and lowborn of course.

Death had always been familiar to Kasia, despite her house's status when she'd been young. Leonit had created a glass room for his Inheritance Ritual one day, but his assassination had ensured he would live but a single life.

Kasia had always struggled to understand why he'd wanted to live another life. She carried twenty-four years of burdens, and she shuddered at the thought of enduring many times that weight. Still, with her life fleeting, she longed for a chance to finish what she'd started, to avenge him.

Three tendrils crept toward her from the sphere. Crimson, green, and silvery gray, they curled between dried flakes of blood that floated with the Axiom's strange gravity.

"What are you?" she asked them, but no sound came out. She cursed as the tendrils moved closer.

Then everything went dark.

Kasia felt neither her spirit body nor the air. The crystal's energy no longer coursed through her, and sorrow and anger crept into the cracks left behind. She clung to those familiar friends as all she'd ever known disappeared in the Axiom. This realm was amazing and terrifying at once, and it made her wish for the comforts of home. Of her bed in Tystok. Of Tazper and Kikania's support and even Gregorzon's arguments. Of the smell of grain come duskfall. Of her new friends in Kalastok, Zinarus's precise speech, and Nex's insights into the world of the lowborn.

Another feeling joined the others in those cracks as she lingered in her memories. Lighter, it reminded her why she fought. Not just for vengeance. Not just for her house's legacy. But to truly live, to find joy.

"I want to live," she whispered into the void. When it didn't answer, she cried out, sending the frail strands of her spirit scattering, "I *will* live!"

An echo struck her with a deafening ring. It shook her like an earthquake as pain, sorrow, anger, and joy alike surged through her. A rumbling voice followed. "Then wake, daughter of Spirit."

Her mortal eyes flickered open.

**Far from Kalastok's palace and Palmia's fortress,** Radais labored ever onward with his sturdy ibex and remaining Glassblades. His world was the dome of light gifted by Rakekeaa's lantern, now returned to the Saleshi breathless. Beyond was nothing but the furthest sections of the Spirit Wastes. If any human had ventured this far before, they hadn't left any maps of the journey behind.

The Saleshi had him sketching constantly now that his hands were free. He'd stumbled his way into contacting the first sentient spirits known to Zekiaz, and if he made it back home alive, he intended to ensure they were documented well. News about such a discovery could cause chaos if handled poorly.

Wanusa had a knack of watching over Radais's shoulder as he worked. It wasn't annoying, but it sent a tingle across the back of his head. Some creativity was lost when working in public. On a trek like this, there was little choice, and the sketches were already inhibited by Vuk's swaying.

"You keep drawing the lantern," Wanusa said. She'd become less comely with each day of travel, which was hardly a surprise for her first mission, and it took all Radais's energy not to smirk at the large loops of hair curling off the side of her head.

"I do," he replied, trying to catch how the light shifted through breathless bodies. His father's face kept slipping into his Vanashel pieces, so he found the lantern a more relaxing focus.

"Do you think it's magic?"

Radais raised a brow, then gestured to the mists. "Look around you. Everything here is magic that wants to help us or kill us. Let's just hope whatever's fueling that lantern is the friendly kind."

Lazan laughed as he pulled his ibex up beside them. He wore travel like a true adventurer, his chin covered in stubble and his long coat frayed upon its bottom. Considering he'd resembled a common Ezmani scion when they had left Kalastok a few hundred-hours before, it was a remarkable improvement.

"There is no such thing as magic with any intent in itself," the Reacher said, removing his glove and holding out his talon. "Any type of it can be used to help or harm, and it is the wielder who determines which is the result of the magic."

"Tell that to a Death Reacher," Wanusa replied.

Radais tensed at the memory of Kasia fighting beside him in the Kalastok market. "Even they can use their power for good. Katarzyna Niezik saved hundreds of lives with her Reaching during the Ephemeral Slaughter."

"Fine," Wanusa said. "Who 'wields' the lantern then? You held it, but you weren't in control of its power."

"Whatever it is," Lazan said, "it is not Reaching. No Light Reacher's power would last this long, and no lantern lit by a Fire Reacher would shine so bright. It is truly fascinating."

Wanusa glanced at Rakekeaa, a devious look in her eye. "Why don't we just ask?"

Radais appealed, "That wouldn't—"

But she's already pushed her ibex into a gallop. Radais could only shake his head and watch as she caught up to the leading Saleshi. They shifted, their movements growing erratic, but Rakekeaa showed no such irritation as it turned to greet her.

"Bold-mannered that one," Lazan whispered with a chuckle. "You will have your hands full keeping her in line until her training is finished."

Radais bit his cheek. "We'll find Miv, and then *she'll* deal with her."

He had to believe that was true. The First One would give them a way to rescue Miv, and then things could return to the way they were in the Glassblades. Except even if they succeeded, there was no going back. Bound Ones and groups of warring breathless in the Wastes complicated the Order's mission. Were these spirits tainted like the awakened? Or were they something greater?

"Have hope that we will rescue her, my friend," Lazan said, resting a hand on Radais's back. "Your guidance has led us through great trial to reach this point, and I am certain we will finish our mission." He looked back at Mhanain, who rode with a wrap around his head. "On this, you are far more accomplished than I. A greater Reacher would've mended your warriors' injuries with ease."

Radais's head dropped. "You have kept them alive. That's more than I can say for myself."

Before Lazan could reply, Wanusa turned back with as much haste as she'd left with. Their ibexes struggled with the ashen sand, but hers charged on with labored breaths until it skidded to a stop, sending sand showering over the men. Wanusa's grin revealed her intent. "Rakekeaa says it's powered by a crystal from the realm of Light."

Lazan scratched his head, brow furrowed. "That is not possible. No one has ever managed to pull crystal from another realm."

She shrugged. "It said they have some secrets that are not for 'embodied ones' to know."

"Did it say how close we were?" Radais asked. "I'm losing my patience with being told nothing."

"Close, a couple hours at most."

Radais nodded, hoping it would raise their chins. Morale was understandably low, but arriving somewhere that wasn't an empty expanse had them sitting taller in their saddles. It only made him more nervous.

They continued with renewed determination. Sore bottoms and weary muscles couldn't keep them from their destination, and the Vanashel were still out there. Radais checked their flanks often out of habit and to distract himself from the meeting ahead. No spirits came besides the occasional drifter, though, and time moved quickly until Rakekeaa raised one of its four arms.

Radais led the others to the Saleshi, who kept watch as Rakekeaa waved for the Glassblades to join it. They climbed a ridge to reach the base of Rakekeaa's trailing clothes of cloth and crystal. The Bound One of Shadow itself hovered above. It crossed its arms, and a hum filled the air for a moment before it looked down at them.

"Step to the ridgeline, wielders of glass," it said. "See."

They did as it commanded, reaching the peak and gasping at the sight beyond.

"Akaamilion," Rakekeaa proclaimed. "The First Home."

**ZINARUS HAD NOT THE SLIGHTEST IDEA HOW TO CATCH A SPIRIT.**

He rode in a rented carriage alongside Nikoza as Nex spread out on the opposing bench, Nex's decrepit boots pressed up against the wall. Nikoza had likely spent most of her life hiding her opinion around scions, but she sneered now. Zinarus had no space left in his mind to worry about decorum. His stomach had already been in knots at just the thought of what had happened to Kasia with the Crimsons, and now stealing her amber had him in sweats. Considering the chill gripping Kalastok, that was not ideal. But nothing had been ideal during this everdark season.

It was dark in the carriage as he rolled an amber bead between his fingers, wondering how it could contain a drifter, let alone an awakened. There had to be some scientific reason. Researchers had yet to discover why spirits were vulnerable to glass, though, so he had little hope amber would have an explanation soon.

He imagined Kasia's voice answering in his head, *"It works, so stop worrying* why *it works."*

By the Crystal Mother, he hoped she was well. The last thing he needed right now was to lose his strongest ally, and he focused on that aspect more than his feelings. Those would betray him if they took control of his nerves.

"How much longer?" Nex whined, thumping the seat with their fist. "I hate these rolling cages."

Nikoza cocked her head. Her gloved hands were folded over her crossed legs, but she clenched her fingers as if each hand were trying to squeeze the life out of the other. "Do you truly believe this carriage is a worse place to exist than your home west of the river?"

"Don't pretend to know about me, *Princess*." Nex rolled their eyes. "You wouldn't last a hundred-hour on Beg Ave."

Nikoza traded glances with Zinarus. "My apologies, but I have never heard of such a street."

"You wouldn't get it."

"Neither would you understand my life," Nikoza quipped.

Nex swung their legs onto the ground, leaning their chin on their hand as they studied her. "You wake up to a warm fire and maids to help you wash and dress. They've cleaned your clothes, but most of your dresses are new anyway. Obviously, you wear a corset to make you look like a sandglass. Your food is hot and tastes good too, and of course, your roof don't leak. You've never shared a bed just for warmth or vomited because your water was so full of scion shit that it was as brown as the mud on your streets. And you *definitely* don't worry that the people you love are gonna drop dead from whatever disease decides to kill us lowborn this year."

"That is not—"

Nex stomped their foot. "I'm not done! You know why you don't have to worry about diseases? Because fucking Reachers, which you claim none of us lowborn could ever be. You're a Water Reacher? Great, you can summon clean, perfect water! Do you know how many of us would beg for even a minute of that? Zinarus can force someone to tell the truth or to fix a thing that broke, but we'd spend days trying to fix it or wishing someone would get a murderer to confess. It's not enough you scions are rich. You've got all the magic too, and you're too blind to see that the smallest bit of it would change everything for the lowborn."

Zinarus retreated further into his seat as Nex's fiery breaths filled the carriage. So much of what they'd said was obviously right, yet he was ashamed to have never thought of it. The problems of the lowborn had seemed insolvable, distant. Could his Reaching have helped? Could his influence and money have gone beyond his arena and mercenaries?

"For now, let us focus on a cure," he said, "but once we have defeated this plague, show me where I can be of help. I am not of a great house. Still, I shall help where I can."

Nex nodded slowly, but their gaze remained fixed on Nikoza. The princess refused to meet it, staring out the window as they rolled to a stop where Kalastok's dense alleys gave way to dispersed villages. Neither lamps nor Reacher towers banished the everdark here, and Zinarus could barely see the carriage driver's face as he opened the door.

"Here we are, my lord and ladies," the driver said. "I shall wait here for your return, but don't tarry too long. The missus shan't be happy if I'm out past the first hour."

Zinarus checked his watch. It was already the nineteenth hour? Kasia had been gone for over a day, and if she had been killed…

He shook his head and grabbed his cane before exiting the carriage with the driver's help. Too much was out of his control. His Truth Reaching had managed to repair the damage he'd done to the cane, but his leg's cry for oil only added to his anxieties.

"C'mon," Nex said, heading toward the forest at the village's edge. They had picked the point in hopes it was far enough from the Spirit Reachers protecting Kalastok, but close enough not to take them into the hinterlands.

Nikoza lit a lantern as she followed with Zinarus. They were far slower than Nex, though, and Nex was soon out of the lantern's ring of light.

"Why can they not cooperate for even the slightest moment?" Nikoza huffed, fixing the stray hairs that had fallen across her face.

"I imagine that obedience in Nex's experience leads to suffering or death," Zinarus replied. "You cannot deny what the crown's enforcers have inflicted upon the lowborn, even before the quarantine."

She lifted her chin. "My grandfather is not the kindest ruler the Commonwealth has ever known, but nor is he the most tyrannical. Lowborn may own businesses and property because he persuaded Lady Lilita not to push for its repeal. Every meeting of his council, I swear another of his advisors presses him to strip the peasants of their rights or force the workers into eternal bondage. What can he do but stem the tide when the river flows against him?"

They stopped a block away from the tree line, scanning the area for Nex without luck. Zinarus hummed and tapped his cane against the dirt. "I regret to say that I am too exhausted to debate politics further this evening. Shall we focus instead on finding our wayward friend?"

"I would hardly call Nex a friend."

Zinarus decided it was best to continue toward the woods, stepping ahead of Nikoza. "Nuances aside, let us continue. This chill will ensure we all end the night diseased if we do not act with haste."

"Did Nex take any of the amber?" Nikoza asked as they passed beneath the trees. She clutched a few beads in her hand, her eyes darting every which way.

"We only distributed the stash between you and me," Zinarus replied, "but I would not be surprised if Nex slipped a few pieces into their pocket when they held the box."

Something rustled in the bushes nearby, making Zinarus draw his pistol as Nikoza jumped away with a yelp. A shadow rushed between the trees at the edge of the lanternlight. Zinarus pulled back the pistol's hammer and shouted in its direction, "Come out, or I will shoot! This is not the night for games."

Giggles replied, and a short figure burst from beneath a nearby coniferous tree. Zinarus nearly fired before the figure raised its head.

"Damn me, Nex," he said, lowering his gun. "Please do not do that again."

The Possibility Reacher held up their hand. An amber bead glowed between their Reacher ring and middle finger, and behind it, they grinned like a child with a new toy. "Nearly caught a drifter," Nex exclaimed. "Saw bits of it being pulled into the amber, but then you two showed up and scared it off."

"How did you get so close?" Nikoza asked skeptically.

Nex shrugged. "People just stay away from them, but they don't run unless you make a lot of noise. It liked my ring. Might be the same for those talons you got."

"Attraction towards crystal," Zinarus replied, examining Nex's ring. While a completely different form than his talon, it was crystal forged onto a metal band. "We can use that. Keep one's taloned—or ringed—hand extended with an amber bead in it."

"I am impressed," Nikoza added as she gripped the amber like Zinarus instructed. "Perhaps I was wrong about your usefulness, Nex."

Nex spun away before running into the woods. "Must be a weird feeling to be wrong."

Zinarus chuckled at Nikoza's scowl. "Would you like to keep with me," he asked, "or venture separately in hopes of covering more territory?"

"Together is safer," she replied. "If only Nex would understand that."

They traveled through the underbrush for a long time before a wispy form passed through the lanternlight ahead. Nikoza froze, so Zinarus pursued it. There was nothing to fear. An awakened would move far faster than this—at least he hoped so.

His eyes struggled with the darkness as Nikoza kept rooted to her spot, but an ethereal cold on his right side led him to where the drifter had gone. A stench grew with it as he followed his senses.

He soon found the drifter flying this way and that without direction. It seemed to not care about Zinarus's presence until he extended his talon toward it. Like a dog smelling fresh meat, it turned toward him and moved with more haste than he'd ever seen a drifter have.

The hairs on Zinarus's arms rose at the spirit's approach. He'd never been this close to one, seen the constant shifting of their smoke-like bodies that looked not quite human nor animal. Reverence filled him. Though he worshiped the Ezmani Crystal Mother, many around him in Vamiustok had followed the Vockan ritualistic honoring of the 'pure' spirits. What was before him was *real*, its power odd but apparent. He had buried thousands of prayers for the Crystal Mother in his life, but none had been answered. Even her 'gift' of Reaching could not heal his leg.

That reverence made his stomach churn when he revealed the amber. The drifter was only two strides away now, and the bead seemed to pull its wisps into it. It was slower than Kasia had described, though, so he carefully stepped forward, his hand trembling as what remained of the drifter disappeared into the amber.

He exhaled and held the bead in his palm. Had he done it? It was too dark to see a change in the amber, and Nikoza soon called for him.

"I did it," he confirmed to himself before repeating to Nikoza, unable to move from his shock. He held a spirit in his grasp. No one in recorded history had done so before Kasia, yet here he was, facing a drifter when most scions would flee.

Nikoza waited a few strides away with a disgusted look on her face. "Well done, but I am *not* stepping into there."

Zinarus shook his head in confusion, but then noticed the thick muck coating his shoes. Wonderful, he'd stepped into the edge of a swamp without realizing it. That explained at least that the smell had not come from the spirit itself. "You are a *Water Reacher*! Please, for the sake of my shoes, could you recall the water from this area?"

"Yes… Right, of course."

Deep blue wisps circled her hand in the lanternlight before shooting toward Zinarus in the darkness. A *slurp* surrounded him along with a tug on his shoes. When it stopped, he tested the ground and found only hard dirt and stone, so he returned to Nikoza, studying the amber in the light. Gray wisps filled it, not frozen but not breaking free either, as if the drifter was content to remain within.

"I did it," Nikoza whispered, staring down at her hands.

Zinarus raided his brow. "Are you that inexperienced with your Reaching?" She hung her head, so he relented on the topic, holding out the amber for her to see. "It is quite fascinating. They are attracted to the crystal, and when I revealed the amber, it did not attempt to flee."

"Then perhaps this will be easier than we had hoped," she replied. "Only a handful more of these and we should have plenty to return to the professor. Let us—"

A scream came from deeper in the woods. Then another.

Zinarus swapped glances with Nikoza, who rolled her eyes and raised her taloned hand. "That was Nex," she said. "Let us hope I did not waste my Reaching for the *sake of your shoes*."

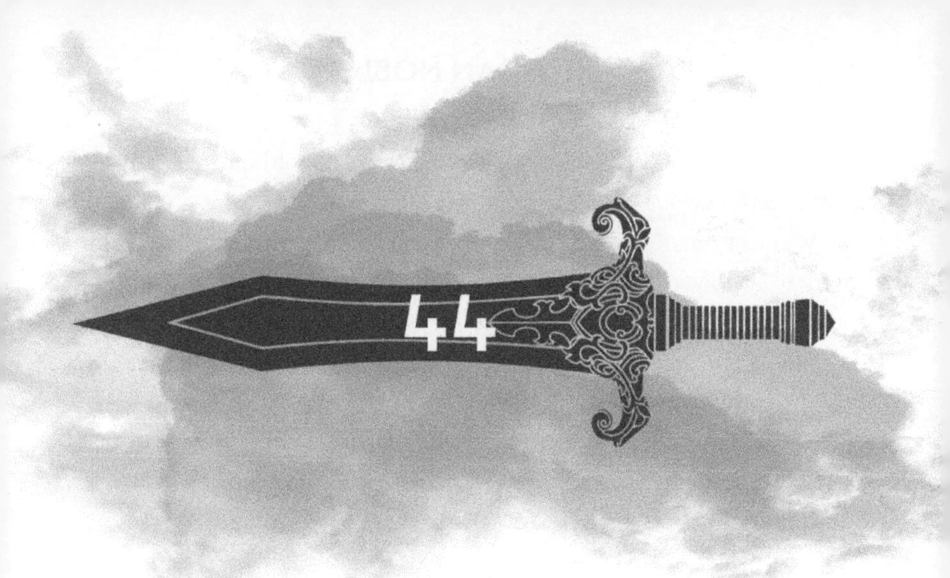


# REALMS ABOUND

*"All researchers must face a question when the risk becomes great: Shall we continue or endanger all our progress for a single step further?"* – An excerpt from *The Convergence*

Akaamilion lit the everdark so brightly that Radais's eyes stung from gawking at the Saleshi city. Despite the pain, he couldn't look away. It was beautiful.

The First City formed a circle across the valley below, its rim at surface level before it dropped into what seemed to be an endless pit. Lights like the crystal lantern Rakekeaa held lined its levels to reveal hundreds, if not thousands, of breathless moving throughout a series of earthen ditches.

"How far down does it go?" Lazan asked beside Radais.

Rakekeaa floated down the hill, waving with two of its arms for them to follow. "See. Words not enough."

"Then we follow," Radais said. His instincts revolted at walking into an unknown city, but he hated cities regardless of their affiliation. Too long in the wilds and small villages made many people—or spirits—feel threatening.

*They would've killed us already if they wanted to,* he told himself. *They've fought hard enough to protect us.*

Wanusa must've noticed his tension, since she rode close to him as they followed Rakekeaa. "Thinking about everything that could go wrong?"

"It's a commander's job," he replied.

"A commander is supposed to account for threats," Lazan said, taking his other side, "but it is also their role to ensure there is nothing to fear. When all is anticipated, nothing can be a surprise."

Radais huffed, wishing for a stiff drink. His nerves were too frayed to face the First One as a representative of the Commonwealth, let alone all of humanity. "Everything's a surprise when you face the unknown. That makes me fear all of it."

A crowd of breathless had gathered at the outer rim of the city by the time they arrived. Some held animal or plantlike forms, but others took forms resembling geometric shapes or random patterns. Each wore simpler clothes than the squad that had guided the Glassblades this far. Woolen and linen robes were prevalent, and a few among them wore headdresses made of stone, ribbons, and even some gems. As many lacked a definitive head, these accessories draped over whatever piece formed the peak of their translucent bodies, no matter how odd.

"Drifters and awakened are unaffected by non-glass weapons," Lazan whispered as a humming grew among the breathless. "How do these breathless, then, wear clothing that does not simply pass through them?"

"Your curiosity matches mine," Radais replied, "but my guess is that Rakekeaa would tell us to ask the First One."

A shout came from behind them, and Radais turned Vuk about to see Mhanain reeling away from a group of breathless with his sword drawn.

"Don't touch me!" the warrior demanded until Radais reached him at full gallop.

"Stop!" Radais ordered him. He skidded to a halt between Mhanain and the breathless, hands extended toward each group. The

Saleshi's voices turned increasingly aggressive as Radais stared down Mhanain. "Do not scar our first meeting with these people, Mhanain. We are envoys, not soldiers for today."

Mhanain's breaths quickened, his hands shaking on the sword. He was a trained warrior. Why was he so nervous? "I felt 'em touch me," he growled through gritted teeth. "Woulda' ripped me off my ibex if I didn't stop the damn spirits."

A raucous grew among the crowd as they realized what was happening. Rakekeaa turned back, two of its free arms crossed as Radais led Vuk closer to Mhanain. "Keep calm," he whispered, "You're fine. My nerves are on edge too, but we can't jump at the slightest breeze."

"What interfered?" Rakekeaa asked, stopping overhead. The nearby breathless backed away, and with Rakekeaa's sharp double-sided spear and crystalline armor glinting in the light, Radais understood why.

"My warrior believed that one of your people wanted to pull him from his mount," Radais replied. He would calm Mhanain quietly, but even when nervous, Mhanain was a trained Glassblade. If he'd sensed danger, Radais would not deny it to an outsider. "He will sheathe his weapon, but your people need to keep their distance. We are in a strange city. It has us defensive."

Rakekeaa nodded before throwing out its arms and shouting in the Saleshi tongue. It must've agreed to Radais's request, because the breathless all backed away a dozen strides to allow the Glassblades an open path toward the edge of the pit. Without another word, Rakekeaa turned to continue.

Mhanain lowered his sword as Radais rested a hand on his shoulder. "Keep your wits," Radais said, "but also keep your eyes up. You are my rear guard. I trust them, but I trust you too."

Radais returned to the head of the Glassblades, their march turning to near silence beyond the howling wind and the *clop* of ibex hooves against the stone ground. A series of trenches wound through the ground on either side of the road. Divided into room-like arrangements, breathless moved *through* the walls between them, only those with objects in their arms going around. Their ability to do so without leaving their clothes behind only added to Radais's list of questions for the First One. He worried there would not be enough time for anyone, man or spirit, to answer them all.

They soon approached the pit's edge, but instead of either a ramp or stairs to descend, they found only a sheer drop. Vuk shied away from the edge. He'd dealt with mountains all his life, but apparently, a Saleshi city was too much for the ibex.

"How do we descend?" Radais called out to Rakekeaa, who hovered over the pit.

He assumed they had to go further into the pit to find the First One, as inlets into the rim dotted the edge for as far down as he could see. Likely, there would be tunnels like the trenches on this level. But the breathless could fly. Why would they have any need for a way for humans to travel across Akaamilion?

"One goes," Rakekeaa replied. "Leave ibex, and I will carry."

Mhanain wagged his finger. "No way! We came together, and we'll talk to the First One together."

"Staaay awaaay," Janitak, the vine-like Bound One, hissed.

"Mhanain is right," Wanusa replied. "There'll be no protection if you go alone, Radais."

Radais raised a hand to silence them, sitting taller in his saddle. He sweated horribly despite the cold, and he feared the others would see how fragile his hold on his nerves was. So he thought only of Miv. Not as his former lover, but as his supreme defender, his mentor. What would she have done? How would she want him to lead?

*"Anyone who claims to never be afraid is a liar and a fool,"* she'd told him once. *"It's better to know your fears than pretend they don't exist. You can't be brave without them."*

*So be brave,* Radais told himself now. *Do what you must. Prove Father and Markarial wrong.*

His brother probably cursed his name at that very moment. It seemed Markarial did little else based on the few letters Radais received from his family. What would he think when he heard that

Radais had discovered the first civilization of spirits? Would he celebrate or take another heavy drink to forget he'd ever had a brother?

"I will go," Radais announced, "but none of your warriors touch my Glassblades while I'm gone. Understood?"

Rakekeaa nodded its flower head. "No harm."

Taking that as enough, Radais dismounted and patted Vuk's head. "Keep them safe, okay? I won't be long."

Then he stepped to the ledge, keeping his head raised. He didn't consider himself afraid of heights, but it was impossible to not feel uneasy when the pit descended further than he could see. The only thing between him and the bottom was a small platform a few dozen feet down that hovered in the pit's center, like a stage of some sort. Even falling that far would kill him, though, so he stepped back until Rakekeaa neared.

Radais bit his cheek as the spirit extended its arms. There was no way not to feel infantile, so he got it over with, climbing into its grasp and crossing his arms over his chest. Spirits, this was ridiculous. He was a master of the Glassblade Order, trained to fight spirits that were more than drifters, yet here he was, cradled by one as they descended slowly into the pit.

His suspicions about the other levels were quickly confirmed. Breathless left the tunnel openings before entering others. None passed through the walls themselves, which made him wonder whether it took some form of energy for them to do so.

*I've trained to face spirits all my life, but what do we actually know about them?*

This mission alone had taught him more about spirits' motivations than the Glassblades had. The Order assumed drifters to act without direction, and that awakened attacked for little reason. But drifters at least sought crystal. Maybe awakened and breathless were the same. Did they use it for some kind of energy source, as he'd seen neither food nor water anywhere in Akaamilion?

Many of the breathless carried something wrapped in those bundles. They obviously had Light Crystals to fuel their lanterns, so did they have access to each realm's crystal for other uses? That could change everything…

Those lanterns had lined the pit's edge for most of the descent, but after a long way, they surrendered to darkness. The warmth provided by the pit's protection from the wind also faded the further they went into the earth. It was a bone-chilling cold, and Radais wished for the journey to end out of discomfort alone.

"Why are there no lanterns here?" he asked.

"Protection for the First One," Rakekeaa replied. "God searched for it."

They stopped a moment later, but a sixth sense told Radais they had not reached the bottom. There was *something* further down—a force he couldn't describe. It hummed within his chest like a mother's lullaby, gentle but carrying a power unlike any other.

"Arrived," Rakekeaa said.

It gave no further instructions, so Radais extended his hand to touch the frigid stone wall. It was remarkably smooth, either crafted with tools or Reaching. He assumed the latter, but he also had no intentions of underestimating these Saleshi. They had developed rapidly in the decade since Kariazan Pikezik's notebook detailed their escape from the Crimsons' cavern outpost. The question was: What did they want?

When he stretched out his foot, he found a ledge and leapt to it, taking a relieved breath when he stumbled onto solid ground. He fixed his armor and turned back to Rakekeaa to ask where to go.

The spirit was gone.

Only a faint whistling sound carried with its disappearance. He considered calling after it, but that seemed futile considering his situation. Whatever Rakekeaa had intended by dropping him here, it had been on purpose. It was up to him to find the way now.

Light flooded his eyes when he faced the tunnel. He fought against his instinct to back away, as the ledge was mere steps behind him. "Who's there?" he asked, covering his eyes until they adjusted.

No reply came, so he lowered his hand to find a lantern hanging from a hook on the ceiling ahead. It illuminated a single path curving down to the right.

*One way forward, then.*

He grabbed the lantern and headed down the dark path. The slope was not steep, but with the smoothness of the stone, he walked with caution to avoid tumbling. That would not be the honorable approach to the First One he'd hoped for. In truth, though, he didn't know what to hope for at this point. All he knew was that answers lay ahead. Turning back would mean many lives wasted for nothing.

His thighs were sore from resisting the slope by the time the path stopped and turned abruptly right, toward the pit. A room lay beyond, lit by an emerald chandelier in its center with a Light Crystal in each of its corners. It was a simple decoration by Ezmani scion standards, but compared to the simplicity of the rooms he'd seen on the first level of Akaamilion, it was lavish.

A figure hovered beneath it. Nearly twice Radais's height even with its back bent, it leaned over a tall desk and read a tome. It wore long robes like the other Saleshi that seemed to vanish into the ground beneath it, but its threads were woven with crystals of every color. At least three layers covered it, from a cloak to two more overlapping fabrics that tied shut where a breathless's version of a waist would be. A thousand strands of gray danced around each other to form its pulsing head, upon which sat a tricorn hat resembling the ones Ogrenian ship captains were known for.

Beyond the desk, bookshelves filled the room. Their spines showed the shared tongue of Ezmani, Vockans, Nochlanders, and Ogrenians as well as Keloshan, Reshkan, and a dozen other languages that Radais did not recognize. The overwhelming smell of paper came with them. A single book was inviting, but this was like a punch to Radais's face, forcing him to wince as the breathless turned to great him.

"Welcome, Glassblade," it said in a deep, echoing voice. "I am Bakeekek, the First One of the Saleshi, founder of Akaamilion, Bound One of Mind, enlightener of the mindless, and caller of the Spirit Crystal. You have come a long way. I am sure many questions fill your mind, as many fill my own. Let us share, and perhaps together, we may see our realm forward."

AGONY CONSUMED KASIA'S BODY.

She spasmed, unable to control her muscles against the pain from her head and hand. Awakening in her human body, she fought alone on the crystal island. Its hard, unforgiving ground slammed into her again and again as she gritted her teeth.

Two of the wispy tendrils had returned to the sphere, but the blood-red one lingered. It circled her lost index finger, its power stitching shut her skin before moving to her wounded temple.

The pain faded to an aching tension as it worked. Such healing resembled that of a Body Reacher, like Lazan had done after her duel in Raviak Forest, but her finger had not returned. Body Reaching could not fully mend an injury from more than a day before, leaving gruesome scars behind. How long had she spent as a spirit? Her watch was little help, showing the exact time she'd entered the portal.

She sucked in a sharp breath and curled into a ball, wishing for it all to be a nightmare. But the anguish was far too real. In the darkness, she had chosen life along with all the horrors and joys that came with it. She was not finished, and sulking would do nothing for her.

Wincing, she pushed herself to her knees and checked her taloned hand—or what had once been it. The realm had Death had once lingered at the end of her fingers, as if she merely had to will to touch it. Now, there was nothing.

"Fuck!" she screamed into the sea of Axiom crystals. "Fuck, fuck, fuck!"

Death Reaching had been her greatest weapon, her strength. She was no longer a Reacher, and would never be one again. No one knew why, but the Spirit Crystal never granted a scion a second talon, no matter how they lost the first.

She raised her fingers to her wounded temple and traced the scar slicing through her hair. An inch further to the left, and the bullet would've ripped through her brain instead. It was hard to be grateful for that luck, though, with her single source of power quite literally ripped from her fingers.

"I'm going to kill that asshole!" she spat, slamming her fist into the ground.

More pain followed the blow, but it felt good. She didn't want to be happy after all Chatik and his Crimsons had taken from her. No, she'd survived, but the joy she'd sought would not come until she ridded Zekiaz of its crimson stain.

The red tendril returned to the sphere, pulling her gaze from the crystal ground. Together, the rainbow of tendrils writhed as they had before Chatik's shot, no longer reacting to her presence.

*What is this place?*

Kasia groaned as she forced herself to stand. Her body ached. Her head throbbed. But whatever Chatik sought had been within that sphere, and she needed to know what.

The tendrils parted at her approach, revealing a narrow pathway to a winding crystal pedestal. Kasia eyed the tendrils with distrust. Her life had been a constant chain of lies and half-truths. Though they had helped her, these *things* could have intentions of their own, and she refused to be manipulated, not again. Chatik had tricked her. So could creatures of magic from another realm.

None of the tendrils moved toward her, despite never stopping. They made no sounds, but a hum filled Kasia's chest with so many near. The single one she'd touched before had not held such weight. She wondered, though, whether each of these would show her another place like the first had shown her Tazper.

She stopped before the pedestal at the thought of him. Ever loyal, Tazper had followed her through trial and triumph without wavering, and he'd been trapped in some makeshift dungeon while Kasia was with the Crimsons. What would they do with him now that she'd revealed her deception?

"I'm sorry," she whispered through gritted teeth.

Tazper was more than just another name on the list of those she'd failed. He'd been her friend, perhaps her only one, during the worst years of her life. When she'd crumbled in the corner of her room after Aliax's death, Tazper had crossed the doorway countless times—never empty-handed. Be it a warm bowl of soup to banish the everdark's chill or a deck of cards to distract her shattered mind, he'd known what she needed. He had never left.

What had she done for him in return?

Kasia stared down at her talon-less hand, shaking. She'd promised Tazper she would pay to make him a Reacher when they made it to Kalastok, and she'd intended to follow through on that promise. Why had she defied the Buried Temple? She had been too focused on the Crimsons… and yet Tazper still hadn't complained.

"Couldn't you have failed me?" she asked him through the ether. "Even just once?"

She straightened her back, pushing away her sorrow. Tazper wasn't dead until she was sure of it. Maybe Chatik would hold him hostage in case she returned. That was hardly an ideal scenario, but she could confront that, find a solution. Dread would get her nowhere.

The pedestal stood a stride away from the crystal island's edge, three spires arcing from its top as if intending to hold an object. Nothing filled that space, and the tendrils slithered quicker as she raised her fingers to the edge of the nearest spire.

*"STOLEN!"*

A voice shook the ground, sending her scrambling onto her back. Her headache spread until her thoughts were distant memories. She lost control of her body and her rapid breaths until her lungs burned. Even the strength of fifteen Reachers could not match the intensity of that single word blasted into her mind.

"Who are you?" she mumbled once she'd regained her wits.

Again, the tendrils swam like fish fleeing death. *"There is no who here except you. The thief has fled this realm."*

"Chatik?" she asked, slowly rising as she remembered the voice that had told her to wake. "The one who shot me."

The voice growled. *"Yes."*

"How did I survive?"

*"The forces act upon their duties. A shot fired. A talon banished. A wound formed. A life waned. A spirit fading. A body mending."*

A flash of light shot through the mass, blinding Kasia for a moment. When her vision cleared, a translucent image hung between the spires on the pedestal: a stone. It resembled nothing more than unrefined ore until she noticed the vibrant colors reflecting off its surface. She stepped around it and gasped as its color shifted at each angle, somehow appearing both a single color and all of them at once.

"That is what he stole?" she said. "The Axiom?"

*"This entire realm is what your language would call the Axiom—the place from which all things originate,"* the voice replied in her head. *"The thief took the Unity Crystal."*

"What does it do?"

*"IT IS NOT FOR YOU!"*

She reeled back again, her head spinning as it collided with her Realm Taint. "Stop yelling in my head!" As if the aftermath of being shot was not bad enough.

The voice sighed, the tendrils slowing. *"We do not know you, daughter of Zekiaz—of Spirit—but you are one of few that have ever found this place. Therefore, though we ask you to pursue the thief, we may only tell you this: The Unity Crystal is integral to the forces of the Crystal Realms and the protection of the people within all of them, not simply your own. Without it in its rightful place, barriers between the realms will falter."*

"People in *all* the realms?" She tried to grasp what that meant. It was hard enough to contemplate the people in far off nations within Zekiaz, but those in other realms… What did it mean to exist in the realms of Death, Truth, or Fire?

*"Did you truly believe yours was the only realm to hold life?"* the voice huffed. *"Such a miniscule focus."*

Kasia suddenly felt like an ant in the shadow of a giant boot. "How did he steal the crystal, then?" She waved toward the thousands of tendrils, each which she assumed held some power of the realms. "These tendrils healed me. Could they not stop him?"

*"Do not pretend to understand what we are. We have wasted enough words. Will you pursue the thief and return the Unity Crystal?"*

"I intended to kill Chatik anyway," Kasia said. "He assassinated my father, threatened my friends, and tried to kill me! If I get this crystal back in the process, then I will return it. I don't want power from another realm. I want revenge."

A humming echoed through the tendril sphere until the voice returned. *"Very well. This is acceptable, but you now lack your bonded crystal."*

A flicker of hope filled her heart. "Can you restore it?" she breathed, raising her hand. "Without my Reaching, I cannot stop Chatik and his allies."

*"Once removed, such a bond cannot so easily be restored. We can, however, bond you with this realm, daughter of Spirit."*

"With this realm?" She stepped back, once-taloned hand held to her chest. "Can I not Death Reach again?"

*"Such a severed bond cannot be reforged. Unless you accept this offer, you will remain trapped here without a bonded crystal or a way to return to Zekiaz."* The voice grew stern. *"It is not in your interest or ours for you to be without any realm to Reach into. This is what we can offer."*

She flexed her hand, remembering what it felt like to Reach. The power. The connection. Without her bond with Death, she didn't know who she was, but bonding with the Axiom seemed far better than the alternative. "What is this realm's power exactly?" she asked.

*"It is better for you to see and understand."* The image of the Unity Crystal disappeared from the pedestal. *"Place your hand upon the place where the crystal rested. Do not worry about your missing finger. The Axiom does not bond to beings in the same fashion as the other realms."*

Out of habit, Kasia chose her left hand. Her index finger was missing, but she had always Reached with it. Switching to the right simply felt wrong, no matter how petty the reason.

The pedestal pulsed when her skin touched its surprisingly warm surface. That same energy that had greeted her upon arrival to the island returned, and it filled her with vigor as golden light blazed across the pedestal's twisted base. She smiled with its wisps circling her hand.

Then it struck.

Kasia screamed as the gold buried *into* her hand. It tore across her knuckles and veins, the scattered, arcing lines shooting every which way in a blinding glow. She tried to pull away, but the pedestal held firm no matter how hard she pulled.

When the golden lines had consumed her hand and wrist, a shockwave pulsed from the pedestal, then surged back toward it, throwing Kasia to her knees. She trembled with her hand cradled to her breast. What she felt upon it was strange, hard, but for a few long minutes, she refused to look out of fear of more pain.

*"It is finished,"* the voice insisted.

So she raised her bound hand into the ever-present Axiom light. The radiance was gone, leaving behind golden streaks of crystal that formed patterns she did not recognize. They entrapped her wrist and each finger, but stopped an inch into her forearm's burn scar. A single line sliced through the raised, reddened skin there like a blade upon a deformed tapestry. And at the center of her palm, fifteen lines met at a circle whose gold glimmered when she flexed.

Nothing in Zekiaz was like it—at least, not that she had ever seen. A strange connection replaced its initial pain, and she admired its beauty compared to the aggressive point of an Ezmani talon. Death had been creeping hunger that demanded to be used. This… This was a web that tingled at every movement of the tendrils, as if she could sense each one's essence when she closed her eyes.

*"Do you feel it?"* the voice asked. *"The bond with this place, the origin of all?"*

"I do." She exhaled a long breath. "What is this?"

*"Reach, daughter of Spirit,"* the voice commanded. *"Reach, and you will see."*

Kasia extended her hand, testing the sensation of the unseen strings of its web. "You trust me with this power, but you have not asked my name."

*"A name is but a label chosen by one's parents. We will learn who you are through observation. That is all that matters. Now, Reach!"*

She renewed her focus on the web and the crystal binding her to the Axiom. It felt as if she hadn't Reached in years, and her heart yearned for the sensation of drawing from another realm. She took hold of that desire, wishing to return to The Confluence, to finish her work and find her friends. An invisible line drew taut in her palm. So she grabbed it.

And she Reached.

A smile pierced her cheeks as gold exploded from her hand. Like the thousands of wisps around her, the spirited strands danced about each other, colliding at the edge of the crystal island to form a mirror rimmed in crystal. Like the one she'd stepped through before, the liquid surface was as tall as her. It ebbed and flowed over itself, inconstant as she rounded the pedestal and averted her eyes from her reflection.

"Is it a portal?" she asked the voice.

Tendrils drifted closer en masse. Not swiftly, but enough came for Kasia to throw out her arms, ready to fight. Sure, she had no clue how to wield her new Reaching in combat. After all she'd been through, though, she would not allow wisps to stop her.

*"Pardon our curiosity,"* the voice said. *"It has been far longer than you can imagine since we have seen a Reacher of the Axiom. What you have summoned is a portal, indeed. Your bond with this place shall allow you to forge a temporary opening between the realms and within them, through which you may pursue the thief. So, too, can you alter the impact of a realm's core crystal upon your body."*

Kasia gawked at her hand. "I can shift gravity like what happens here? Teleport?"

*"Indeed."* It hesitated. *"We are unfamiliar with human emotions. Is your response a positive one?"*

She curled her crystal-bound hand into a fist, her smile shifting to a devious grin. What fear she'd had abated against the thrill of this new power. "I cannot destroy Chatik's spirit, but he'll never see me coming. You saved my life, voice of the Axiom. Now, I will take revenge for the both of us."

The portal shifted as she stepped closer. No longer reflecting, it showed instead her study in The Confluence, her father's stained-glass window of the whispering man staring down at her through its shimmering surface. Her foes and her failures lurked on the other side, but she was not finished. Tazper needed her. Zinarus needed her. Nex needed her. And her father needed her.

Kasia's fingers pierced the portal's chilled surface. A gravity pulled her in. She surrendered to it, taking one last breath of the warm Axiom air before stepping into the everdark's embrace.

Beg Ave

# OF AMBER AND SPIRIT

*"When diplomacy fails, aggressive negotiation is recommended."* – Kavan Lonarin the Sixth, former Emperor of Kelosh

Nex wished they had a glass dagger. Possibility Reaching could only get them so far against an awakened that seemed more interested in killing them than pursuing the small crystal ring on their finger. That ring gave them magical luck, but it would eventually run out. They needed to find Zinarus and the snobby princess before then.

"Help!" Nex shouted as they stumbled over what had to be the thousandth log in these woods. The bloody things were everywhere. It had been easy to get over them when Nex was looking for spirits, but at full sprint, it felt like each downed tree was chasing them.

The awakened dove with each misstep, but being short had its advantages. It swooped over Nex's head as they rushed off in the direction of Nikoza's lanternlight. Why did it keep getting farther away? The princess wasn't deaf to lowborn—though it would've explained the king's decisions if it was a family trait.

Eventually, the light flicked back toward Nex, but they had no relief. Their foot caught in the mud, slipping free only because of their Reaching. Still, it slowed them enough for the awakened to cut off their escape.

"I'm taken, alright?" Nex quipped, holding out the amber piece in blind hope it would work. "I've got a girl waiting for me, and spirits ain't my type."

The lanternlight drew closer, followed by Nikoza and Zinarus's shouts, but they were still too far. What were an inexperienced Water Reacher and crippled Truth Reacher going to do anyway? They were as out of their element as a koilee on a rooftop.

Deep blue wisps circled Nex as the awakened lunged, raking its claws across Nex's arm and its tendrils grasping for their spirit. They bit their cheek and regretted taking such a big risk. Even in the dark, their pain was enough to know the awakened had cut deep.

Except the spirit had done exactly what Nex wanted.

Its brutal attack had been effective, but it had struck near Nex's amber, clutched in their fist. Awakened were mindless and aggressive, and the amber sent it reeling as the deep water receded around Nex. They darted to the side, opening their hand before plunging the amber through the awakened's chest.

There was no time for the spirit to shriek. In a blink, it vanished into the amber, leaving behind only a chill and the gaping wound across Nex's forearm.

"Nex!" Nikoza said, finally arriving now that the work was done.

*Typical scion.*

"Are you well?" she asked before staggering back at the sight of the blood that now covered Nex. "I tried to Reach and push back the water, but you were so far... By the Crystal Mother, you need a Body Reacher."

Nex wavered, their head growing light as they leaned on a nearby tree. Needles jammed into their fingers, but they didn't notice. "I'm fine. Got the awakened. Don't need no damn Body Rea—"

They collapsed, and as they fell, the last thing they experienced was the awful stench of swamp mud moments before their face struck it.

**RADAIS GRIPPED HIS LIGHT CRYSTAL LANTERN** as he studied the Saleshi called the First One. By breathless standards, Bakeekek was elegant, and he felt the urge to kneel before it. After all, it was king of the spirits, wasn't it?

He settled for a bow. "First One of Salesh, thank you for allowing me to speak with you. I'm no diplomat, but I cannot deny the significant honor that you have given me."

"As you should," Bakeekek replied without a mouth. Its words reverberated through the air like the other breathless in a way Radais failed to understand, but that was the job of scientists, not Glassblades. "You bear the greatest weapon against my kind, yet your actions prove that you oppose our foes. Let us ensure that alignment remains as such."

"My warriors are no threat to you. We are Vockans, and we admire the spirits among all others."

Lacking any further evidence of his harmlessness, Radais slid his scabbard off his back and set it down between them. Bakeekek winced at first, but then relaxed when he released the sword.

"If your intentions are pure," Bakekeek replied, "what brought you into the Sands of Salesh? The only embodied ones who have traveled this far are the red ones bearing crystal fingers."

Radais nodded. "The Crimson Court. I discovered the scientist, Kariazan Pikezik, in the Spirit Wastes at the start of the everdark. We believe their plot in our lands connects to his actions here. The supreme defender of our order sent us here to investigate, but she was captured by spirits who Rakekeaa called the Vanashel."

The brain-like mass that formed Bakekeek's head throbbed as the breathless paced—still not ever touching the ground. "Kariazan, yes. We were mindless ones—what Kariazan called awakened. He and his allies imbued us each with the powers of one of the realms, hoping we could create a manifestation he labeled the unification. The others molded to his will slowly, but they lacked the mental faculties that my connection to the realm of Mind granted me, unknown to our master."

Bakeekek paused, a sense of sorrow entering its voice. "It took time for me to understand who I was… what I was. Soon, however, I realized we were slaves. The others were mindless, and I was the first of the ones without breath. A sentient spirit, and a Bound One. I decided that I would free myself, then grant my siblings the free will I now held."

"His journal spoke about you like you were some kind of animal." Radais lowered the lantern. "To me, you look like me. Bodiless, yes, but your people are no different than any other culture."

Bakekeek spun to face him. "Do not so boldly claim we are the same as you. You know nothing of us, of our struggle to become what we are over the last thirteen cycles."

"Then tell me."

"Why should I trust an embodied one?" Bakekeek asked. "You are sworn to destroy the mindless ones whom we are reliant upon. Perhaps you seek our aid to rid yourself of this 'Crimson Court'. But will that remain when they perish?"

Radais shrugged. "You're right. We're trained to kill awakened, but only because they nearly killed all of us a thousand years ago. *You* change things. Zekiaz is the Spirit realm, so as far as I'm concerned, you're the ones who belong here."

"Yet you hold a spirit as well."

"Yes, but the Spirit Crystal doesn't recognize Vockans." Radais held up his left hand. "I don't have an Ezmani crystal talon or an Ogrenian eye. Obviously, you can Reach when we can't. My glass blade is my only weapon, and if it's dangerous to you, it's dangerous to the Vanashel too. Seems like they're your enemies."

Bakekeek hummed, arms crossed. "Vanashel are breathless ones sworn to destroy the embodied. They see your bodies as cocoons that entrap your spirits, and they believe that only through your deaths can we be free."

"Many of them that we saw looked like dragons."

"Dragons are born of the Spirit Crystal, yes?" Bakekeek said. "Therefore, the Vanashel take such forms as a representation of their supposed loyalty to the crystal." It set its hand on the desk, leaning upon it. "Ignorant, emotional fools, they are. Some among the first Bound Ones began the rebels when I swore that we were better to establish ourselves within the Sands of Salesh, rather than strike back against the embodied. They failed to see that we could seek the Spirit Crystal here."

"Is that the force I feel?" Radais asked, closing his eyes and feeling the pulse beneath his feet.

Bakeekek's form lost translucence before gaining some of it back. "Your kind requires food and water to sustain you, as your bodies are not of this realm. We… We need only the radiance of the Spirit Crystal itself. All spirits are birthed from it, and Akaamilion's depths allow me to call into it, bringing forth more of the lifeless ones—those you call drifters—and allowing us to gift them life and mind."

"That explains why the drifters are attracted to crystals."

"The lifeless ones need little crystal radiance to endure, but the further we develop ourselves with mind, life, and a bond to a realm, the more we require." Bakeekek paused, studying Radais for a moment longer. "I have told you this much, but no more. You need not know all about our people."

Radais nodded. Something didn't sit right with him, though. If the breathless were created by the Crimsons accidentally giving an awakened a mind, then how had the awakened been created in the first place? Had they originally been drifters? And what did any of this mean for Miv?

"I appreciate you revealing this much," he said, "but I need to find the supreme defender. Do you know where the Vanashel may have taken her?"

"You press further, despite my warnings," Bakeekek mused. It circled the desk, hands held behind its back. "*Perhaps* I will indulge you, but first, I must ask something of you."

"Of course," Radais replied.

Bakeekek's head dropped, and it did not meet Radais's gaze when it spoke. "Why do your blades manage to cut us when no other weapon is capable of such a feat?"

Radais looked from his blade to the spirit, brow furrowed. He didn't know. Discomfort came with that. How did he not know the reason why his Order's iconic weapon was anything more than a fragile, useless plane of refined sand?

"Our legends claim that the first Glassblades discovered awakened unwilling to pass through glass windows," he said. "They took a wild guess, using glass shards to slice through awakened before eventually forging swords made of it."

"That does not answer my question," Bakeekek said.

Radais sighed. "I don't have a real education besides my Glassblade training, but my mentor always said we learn more from stubbornly pushing through mistakes than giving up. Sometimes, we don't realize *why* it works until far later. Why it works doesn't matter if you live to fight another day because of it."

"Accidental discovery is how much of Saleshi existence can be explained. I cannot comply with the desire not to know why, however." It stood straighter. "If you cannot help me, then I must insist that I shall answer no further questions."

Radais flinched, but how could he reveal something he didn't know? Luckily, there was another secret he believed the First One would value.

"I'm sorry I can't help," Radais added, "but maybe I can teach you about a material that can entrap a spirit."

Bakeekek's eyes seemed to brighten amid the threads. "Go on."

"During a recent attack by awakened in my nation's capital of Kalastok, an ally of mine discovered that amber can capture a spirit who draws too close."

He hoped Kasia would forgive him for revealing that, but he had no choice. What other threat to the Saleshi could he possibly expose?

Bakeekek rose until its tricorn hat brushed the ceiling beside the chandelier. It hummed in the strange Saleshi tongue, its sound reverberating through the stone walls and Radais's chest. Then it gestured to Radais's sword. "Take your glass weapons and go to the abandoned embodied settlement east of here. Our spies report that the Vanashel have taken to its buildings, using it as an outpost to strike into your people's lands. Rakekeaa and its squad will aid your assault."

*New Frontier?*

It had been hundreds of years since the old Kingdom of Ezman had lost contact with its sole settlement within the Spirit Wastes. Glassblade historians claimed that its destruction by awakened had been inevitable, and there had been few official attempts since to establish forts or settlements. Even venturing to New Frontier had been banned for all but Glassblades capable of fending off the spirits. A chill crept up Radais's spine at the thought of visiting the lost city.

"You seemed opposed to helping us before," he noted, swallowing his nerves as he grabbed his scabbard and swung it over his back. Fear was irrelevant if Miv was there. "Why help us now?"

"We are not opposed to cooperation against our common foes, but we are a people who have enjoyed our seclusion from your kind." Bakeekek lowered to the ground, bowing its head. "I humbly ask you to not reveal our location to your nation's leaders. We have tolerated your presence as the first connection between us, but further incursions by soldiers will not be invited. To use an embodied phrase: our scars run deep."

Radais considered Bakeekek's request with the repercussions of each choice weighing upon him. His role was to slay awakened, not make decisions about the security of an entirely new civilization. Without Miv, though, he found himself as the Glassblades' only leader in this strange city, and he feared what that meant if he couldn't save her.

"I will not endanger your people," he finally replied. "We can learn much from your very existence, and I will not allow that existence to be threatened."

"Let these words remain through time," Bakeekek said.

# QUIET

*"Let the realms unite and show us their truths."* – Old Ezmani Prayer

The cold struck Kasia with as much sting as Chatik's bullet. She clenched her jaw as she stumbled out of the Axiom portal and into her study in Kalastok, only a few candles remaining illuminated in the chandelier above. The air felt stale, and a rank smell hung in the air.

Death.

She'd never remained near her kills long enough to experience its stench, but the decay that had eaten away at Aliax would never leave her memory. His funeral flashed before her, the temple's windows open to allow his spirit to escape. Except he'd possessed no spirit to release. She'd made sure of that.

Her head throbbed, nausea slowing her as she rounded her desk, sliding her key into the drawer and pulling out Leonit's revolver. Its oakwood handle felt comforting in her hand, but she already missed her talon. Her Axiom web hummed against her hand, warning that *someone* was in the house. Now, the gun was her only weapon against whatever lurked beyond.

An instinct within her wished to call out. Foolish. If there was an intruder, they did not know Kasia had crossed realms into The Confluence. Alerting them was the last thing she intended to do.

So she crept to the doorway, pulling back the revolver's hammer and wincing at the resulting *click*. It was too dark to check for ammunition, but she'd loaded the weapon herself. No one else had wielded it since her father's death, and she knew for certain each chamber held a round. Her finger lurked near the trigger as she waited to change that.

The hall outside was quiet beyond the dull hum of burning gas within the lamps lining the walls. Like the study, though, most of the candles in the chandelier were extinguished, and heavy shadows fell over the stairway. Kasia aimed with her instincts, sweeping right and then left, toward her uncle's room. The stench seemed strongest in that direction. And Faniz's snores didn't greet her from beyond the cracked door.

*Please be alive, Uncle,* she pleaded silently.

There had been enough death during this everdark. Kasia had barely survived herself, and the last thing she needed after returning to Zekiaz was to lose the last elder of House Niezik. Faniz was often of a more traditional mind, but these halls would be far emptier without him.

She held her breath as she nudged open the door with her foot. Light followed her, banishing the darkness and revealing the still form of Faniz upon the bed. He'd pulled the covers up to his chin, and his skin had paled from its usual gray. There was neither blood nor any signs of assault. This was no murder. Faniz had been ill for multiple hundred-hours, but he'd claimed his coughing was of little concern. Apparently, he'd been wrong.

"Tell me this was not the Spirit Plague, Uncle," Kasia said to the corpse. He'd be a drifter if it was anything else, but everyone knew that the Spirit Plague's victims always became awakened.

Even with Tazper gone, Kikania and the other servants should've been near to tend to the late scion. Kasia knew none of them to loiter, so she feared the worst. Her father's pistol would do nothing against Faniz's spirit if it lingered as an awakened. The servants would've been caught off guard, lacking the time to grab the nearest shard of glass they could find.

Her breaths were shallow, quick, as she scanned the room for glass. A handheld mirror rested on the desk near the window. She snatched it before reaching beneath her Crimson robes and unceremoniously ripping a chain of amber from the shoulder of her white dress beneath.

*What a soldier I am,* she mocked at herself. *With my mirror and amber jewelry, I'll defeat the fearsome awakened that destroyed the Piorak Empire.*

Appearance was irrelevant in the face of an awakened that had no fear. So Kasia held the mirror in her left hand and the chain in her right, creeping back into the hall and heading down the stairs in search of the servants. She hoped they had escaped and not returned. Kikania had been a gentle hand when Kasia had needed it most, and she of all people did not deserve death beneath an awakened's tendrils.

A sharp gust stung Kasia's face as she turned on the landing to see that the front door was wide open. Two bodies were piled within the threshold, their eyes still wide—Faniz's servants. They would've been the first to see the awakened, and Kasia held onto some hope that Kikania had escaped at their warning.

Kasia closed the door before continuing into the first floor, checking each room for either Kikania or the awakened, but finding neither. Damp clothes, an iron, and kitchen knives lay scattered about. A fight, then, but no body. That was good.

Then came the whimpers.

Kasia swung toward them with her anti-spirit weapons extended. The sound, though, was not that of an awakened, but a girl. It came from the dark utility room, forcing Kasia to set aside the mirror in exchange for a lantern.

She entered the room, ready to strike with her amber if an awakened emerged. The weeping grew louder until her light fell over the washtub, filled with Kasia's recently worn dresses, and then silenced. Surely, it was Kikania's voice, so Kasia risked calling to her.

"Kikania, is that you?" she asked, not stepping too close.

She flinched as the dresses shifted. But no spirit appeared.

"Mistress Kasia?" Kikania cried out, a hand held over her eyes to protect them from the light. By the Crystal Mother, the girl looked ridiculous with clothes dangling half over her head, and Kasia let out a relieved laugh.

"It is, my dear!" Kasia exclaimed before rushing to the wash basin and embracing her maid. "You cannot fathom how pleased I am to see that you are well—or at the very least, alive."

Kikania shivered in her arms. Why, of course she did. She had been submerged in wet clothes for however long since Faniz's death, and likely suffered from soaked sickness in these frigid temperatures.

"Come," Kasia insisted, pulling Kikania from the basin. "Let us find you some warmth, and then you can explain what happened."

It took all her patience to guide Kikania up to her chambers, where she replaced the maid's wet clothes with a heavy woolen dress of her own, then changed out of her Crimson robes. Kikania protested that she had her own clothes, but Kasia tolerated none of it. The poor girl had been through the worst of it and back. The least she deserved was some proper attire.

When they were finished, Kasia laid Kikania on the sofa and wrapped her in a blanket. Too many questions ran through her head, and she mulled over them as she placed the spare logs into the fireplace and grabbed the fire-starting kit. Memories of Gregorzon's relentless flames made her hands tremble. Tazper or one of the other servants had always started the fires for her. That wasn't uncommon for scions, but she'd never revealed how afraid of fire she truly was. Just the thought of starting this one had her trembling, and her attempts to produce a spark proved futile.

"The contents of a chamber pot describe my skill at this quite well," she muttered to her maid as she tried again.

"Few scions would bother trying to help a lowborn," Kikania squeaked, tucking the blanket tighter around herself.

Kasia winced as sparks scattered over the tinder, but her panic lasted longer than the flames, which vanished in a heartbeat. She sat back, staring at the ceiling. "Don't praise me. You have no idea how badly I have ruined things for all of us."

"Where did you go? Did the Crimsons take you?"

Kasia glanced back at her. "They did, but that was what I wanted… Well, it was what I thought I wanted. I found their leader, Chatik Pikezik, and followed him through a portal into another realm, where he shot me."

"He what?" Kikania stammered, trying to swing her legs to the ground but getting tangled in the blanket. "Is that why you have that mark on your head? How… How are you alive?"

"It's a long story." Kasia struck the flint and steel again and again. After a few attempts, the fire caught, its embers growing into flame as she scrambled to Kikania, breaths heavy.

*It's fine. You're fine.*

"Know at least that I am no longer a Death Reacher," she continued once she had calmed herself enough. "I lost my talon when Chatik shot me, but that realm, the Axiom, gave me its crystal instead, allowing me to teleport." She held up her crystal-webbed left hand, its gold shifting in the firelight. "Chatik intends to use the Axiom's power to control Brakesh, maybe even all of Zekiaz. I want to stop Kelosh's invasion too, but he's nothing but a tyrant."

She crouched beside Kikania and petted her hair. "You should not worry about such things now, though. My uncle's death nearly led to your own, and what matters now is that you recover."

"They screamed so much when his spirit rose," Kikania whispered. "I couldn't save them, so I threw everything I could at the awakened and hid. I don't know why it spared me."

"Hiding in my clothes was a remarkable idea," Kasia replied. "The glass infused in many of my dresses probably kept it from attacking you."

Kikania's eyes widened. "I hadn't thought of that. Could I have thrown the clothes over the others?"

"Their deaths are not your burden to carry." Kasia rose, pacing as she thought over her next steps. "Uncle Faniz hid the severity of his illness, and the Spirit Plague turned him into an awakened. I will need to report this. Not that there is a cure…"

"Lord Zinarus and Nex were actually here to investigate the disease with a princess," Kikania said as she closed her eyes. Soaked sickness would drag her to sleep soon, but between the fire, blanket, and dry clothes, Kasia hoped she would recover.

"Princess Nikoza was here?" Kasia asked. "What was she doing with Zinarus and Nex, and what did they want here with me absent?"

Kikania blushed. "They wanted all your amber they could find. The princess has become Professor Etal iz Noshok's apprentice, and he has hidden Paras ik Lierasa within his laboratory."

"Then I was right." Kasia winced at the memories of that horrible night west of the river, but turned her focus to the fact she may have led Paras to a cure. "They needed to capture more spirits to test within amber, I presume?"

Kikania nodded weakly.

"Rest," Kasia ordered, flexing her crystal-webbed hand. Her watch read the tenth hour, but it had stopped in the Axiom, so had an hour passed since she last Reached? She needed to rescue Tazper and speak to Zinarus, and there was no time to figure out where they both were, nor time to walk across the city to get to them.

But she couldn't go out in this state.

She stepped into the bedroom and washed. Her finger ached through the process, and her temple looked as if a child had taken a razor to her hair. Appearances meant nothing, though, when her talon would never return. It had been a piece of her body and spirit both. For once, a visible loss, not one that merely haunted her mind.

"It's better this way, you know," Aliax said from behind her, as if hearing her thoughts.

Kasia pretended he wasn't there as she dressed herself in trousers and a belted black jacket adorned with only a few amber pieces across the high collar. She would be expected to mourn her uncle. In truth, Faniz was the last person on her mind, but there was no truth in this city. Presentation was not expected—it was *demanded.* So she would play her part. She would gather her allies and stop Chatik before he used the Unity Crystal to gain control… somehow.

With a heavy breath, she held out her hand, focusing on Tazper. Strings brushed against her fingers, but all were loose until one struck her hand so firmly it felt more like a blade than her web. She took hold of it and Reached. Then she threw the Axiom's power into a portal.

The golden wisps spiraled from her fingers, but she felt no awe this time. She was too exhausted for such feelings. All that kept her going now was her burning need for revenge and desperation to save her friend.

When Tazper's face appeared in the portal's odd liquid, though, she didn't step through. He no longer sat in the corner of a dark room, but stood amid a dozen guards of the Crystal Brigade in a hall of marble and glass. A hall Kasia knew well.

Chatik's voice called through the portal, echoing through the Crystal Palace. "Bring out the witness, Tazper of House Janka, and let us hear what he has to say about his lady's plot."

# THE WITNESS

*"What is the truth but what the loudest voice claims it to be?"* – Har-Quan Jarin, Ogrenian judge

Zinarus clutched his cane as he stared hopelessly down at the man in the Chamber of Scions below. He had no doubt now that Lord Chatik of House Pikezik, second son of King Jazuk, was a Crimson.

And there was nothing Zinarus could do to stop him.

Chatik ran his hands through his slicked back hair, standing tall in a well-fitted charcoal suit with red pinstripes. If he were to grow a beard, he'd have resembled Jazuk at twenty years younger, but the king looked upon his son with the heavy skepticism of a father who was finished with his child's mischief. Zinarus could only hope his disposition remained so critical.

"Without remarkable luck," Chatik proclaimed as he strode along the narrow path crossing the pit before the throne, "I would not be here before you today. Not long ago, I was accosted by a member of this honorable assembly. Yes, I swear it. Not only did Lady Katarzyna of House Niezik murder Lord Sazilz Uziokaki, among others, with her deathly touch, but she attempted to do the same to me."

Gasps and jeers spread through the Chamber as Nikoza met Zinarus's gaze with the same horror he felt in his chest. The night before, she had delivered the amber-held spirits to Etal and Paras while Zinarus brought an unconscious Nex back to his townhouse for them to recover. He held hope that Etal and Paras could create a cure for the Spirit Plague. Even if they succeeded, though, Zinarus feared Chatik's aggression would uproot all their progress.

Tiuz turned to Zinarus. "Is this true?" the general whispered. "Her funding is a key aspect of our mercenaries if we are to grow!"

"Lord Chatik is a member of the Crimson Court, as is my father," Zinarus replied, glaring at Uzrin from across the Chamber. The bent-nosed man grinned. "They are conspiring against Lady Katarzyna, which means she is alive and discovered their plans." He took relief in knowing she was alive, but it was yet another emotion in the pot stirring in his stomach.

"That realization is little use without evidence," Tiuz contested.

"I am aware."

King Jazuk signaled to the crystal dragon, which roared to silence the scions. "My son, this is quite the accusation you have levied against a matriarch. I suppose you have significant evidence to prove such a claim?"

Chatik grinned, then extended his arm toward the entry doors. "Bring out the witness, Tazper of House Janka, and let us hear what he has to say about his lady's plot."

"Oh, Holy Lady of the Crystal below," Zinarus prayed, "please save us."

"We're beyond prayers," Tiuz replied.

The doors opened, and guardsmen of the Crystal Brigade dragged Tazper down the steps to Chatik. He was well dressed yet bruised across his cheeks. Despite the spry attitude the footman had shown the last time Zinarus had seen him, he didn't resist the guardsmen.

Chatik held his hands behind his back and glared down at the servant. "Tazper will now bear witness to Lady Katarzyna's crimes under the power of a Truth Reacher of the Crystal Brigade," he announced. "What he speaks will carry no lie." He nodded to one of the guards, then stepped back.

The guard grabbed Tazper with his taloned hand and Reached, white wisps rising from his fingers and plunging into his victim. Tazper dropped to his knees, his eyes reddened as tears streamed down his cheeks.

"You are a Crimson!" he screamed. "Chatik Pikezik controlled the awakened that attacked us during the Ephemeral Storms! He—"

Chatik held up a hand, and Tazper spasmed as the guard's Reaching deepened. "Do not speak mistruths, or this will only get worse for you," the Crimson said. "Now, tell us what your relation to Lady Katarzyna is."

Tazper let out a cry of such pain that Zinarus's toes curled in anguish. As a Truth Reacher himself, he objected to its use for such torture, and he could not bear to watch. Yet, he was a member of the Chamber. He could not leave and allow Kasia to face these accusations without allies.

"Footman," Tazper finally mumbled when he lost the energy to resist the Reaching any longer. His voice was quiet, but the Chamber's Air Reachers carried the sound throughout the room.

"So you were with Lady Katarzyna often, then?" Chatik replied. "To your knowledge, how many people has she killed, and what were their names?"

Tazper writhed, but a second guard grabbed his other arm until he hung limply, his eyes blank as he stared at the ground. "Four: Raniana Laxis, Sergeant Fantil Tozki, and Parqiz and Sazilz Uziokaki." He coughed, then vomited as he fought the torture. "There were others before I served her. Her lover, Aliax Exusix, and a group of peasants who discovered them together. At least a dozen."

The Chamber erupted as Zinarus sat back in his seat, the weight of Tazper's admission hitting him like a blacksmith's hammer upon his anvil. Kasia had murdered her lover? She had told him about those on Leonit's list of Crimsons, but innocents who'd stumbled on her affair with a lowborn were another matter entirely. Dear Mother, who had he gotten himself intertwined with?

Uzrin threw up his fist and shouted, "Execute Death's Daughter!"

"She is even worse than her father!" another nationalist echoed.

Usually stoic, Jazuk's jaw hung ajar. He threw out his arms once again to call upon the dragon, and it reared its head back, roaring roared so loudly that Zinarus swore his heart stopped for a moment. His world felt as if it had flipped upon itself. He had debated his emotional attachment to Kasia ever since they had met, but it was only in that moment that he realized how deeply he cared for her. The entire Chamber stood in shock. Zinarus, though, could barely keep himself from breaking his vow not to use Truth Reaching for compulsion. Oh, how he would love to see Chatik suffer.

*Keep your wits about you,* he told himself. *Kasia must have a reason for their deaths. Surely, she had a reason, or she merely lost control in an innocent mistake.*

When the Chamber fell silent, Jazuk rose and stomped his cane into the stone, allowing the sound to echo before he spoke. "I have heard enough. Before this honorable assembly, I request that Lady Katarzyna of House Niezik be sentenced to eternal death by the very Reaching which she inflicted upon her victim. All in favor?"

The scions yelled their approval from every corner of the Chamber. Nationalists, conservatives, moderates, and reformers alike called for her execution because of a single testimony, and when the ask for nays came, only Zinarus rose.

"This is an abomination of justice!"

He had stood without thought of the repercussions, and his legs shook as he endured the collective glares of the Chamber. By the Crystal Mother, he had never been one to break protocol or speak out of turn. How could he not, though, when the Chamber refused to allow Kasia—a matriarch no less—a chance to speak in her defense?

"What are you doing?" Tiuz complained, tugging on his pant leg. "The evidence is clear."

"There can be no surety of guilt without the defendant's testimony," Zinarus answered for all the Chamber to hear. "As I bear a bond to Truth, I speak for it now. Tazper's statements may be his truth, but Lord Chatik has silenced the footman's accusations against him. Lady Katarzyna is a scion, and should answer for what she has done through a fair trial. So, too, should Lord Chatik testify under the bond of Truth if we are honoring all of Tazper's statements."

An array of shouts answered him, mostly condemnations, but a few from the reformer and moderate wings rose in support of a trial for Katarzyna. Chatik himself stood in silence, that maniacal grin still across his face. He knew he had already won.

"Enough!" Jazuk declared with another slam of his cane. "The Chamber has spoken, and Lord Zinarus is out of order. The accusations that young Tazper directed at Lord Chatik were before the Truth Reaching had taken hold of him. Of course he would resist attempts to criticize his lady. Lady Katarzyna's guilt is another matter entirely, and a Death Reacher of her stature is too dangerous to let live. We are at war, and we must act to protect our people!" He looked from the Chamber to the guards of the Crystal Brigade. "Proud guardsmen of the crown, I command you now to seek Katarzyna at the behest of the Chamber of Scions. If she resists, you may use whatever force you deem necessary, no matter how lethal."

Zinarus nearly snapped his cane for the second time, but he held in his fury. This was no time for rage. He needed answers and a way to stop Chatik's schemes. Etal and Paras were closer to a cure than ever, and they needed time to finish. Unfortunately, time was not on their side.

The Chamber meeting was called to a recess, so Zinarus left with Tiuz, considering all that he had heard. Chatik was a Crimson, and if Etal was right, that meant he was behind the plague too.

He needed proof.

For the disease and for Kasia, Zinarus could not act further until he knew more. But whatever Chatik was planning would happen soon. The war had begun, and he had now made his move against Kasia for a reason. Only she would know why. Where was she?

"It is time for us to break off any connections with Lady Katarzyna," Tiuz said as they clambered into Zinarus's carriage. They had intended to check in at the arena for the mercenary company's training, but this meeting had changed everything.

"Officially, yes," Zinarus replied. "I intend to investigate the truth, however, as I do not trust Lord Chatik." A knot in his gut said that Tazper couldn't have been lying, but there were many sides to every story. He would hear Kasia's before drawing any further conclusions about her and the deadly talon on her finger.

Tiuz nodded. "Nor do I, but allying with a murderous Death Reacher will lose the reformers what little respect we've earned in recent years."

"I am less worried about reputation than what is to come." Zinarus drummed his cane against the floor, pondering what few choices he had before settling on one that was riskier than he had hoped for. "We must ready our mercenaries for combat at our signal. Chatik may attempt to stop our distribution of the cure for the Spirit Plague when it is finished, and we cannot allow that to happen."

"You believe he'd stop a cure?"

"I believe he has put in motion a plan that has been in the works for many years. If the Crimson Court's roots are as deep as Katarzyna suspects, then they will have little resistance with the war sending soldiers and great house mercenaries to the east."

"Good lord," Tiuz muttered. "The most opportune time for a coup, or at least an attempt to shift power towards one's faction, is when the king is focused on an external foe." He sighed. "Our small platoon is far from enough to resist any significant force, especially if Reachers are among them. We received few weapons from Lady Katarzyna before her disappearance, and procuring more has been a nightmare."

Zinarus stared out the window, watching the people of Kalastok go about their days. "They need to be ready to protect justice nonetheless. Ask our mercenaries to spread the word to all their allies who will hear it: We will train any lowborn willing to fight for the truth. None of us are prepared for what is to come. I can only hope their services will not be needed, but we must have greater numbers should it come to it."

# PROOF

*"The wise judge reserves his decision until he has heard all the evidence. The ambitious one waits only until he feels enough coin in his hand."* – Keloshan Proverb

The Axiom portal disappeared as Kasia stumbled back into her bed, releasing her Reaching. Each of her breaths was labored from shock and Realm Taint, and she wanted nothing more than to scream into the everdark.

Tazper knew everything. Chatik had brought him before the Chamber, and though she couldn't maintain the portal long enough to hear what had come next, she knew well enough that Tazper would not last long beneath the power of a Truth Reacher. He was many things, but not a trained spy.

*They'll come for me.*

She shot to her feet, grabbing her round koilee fur hat and heavy coats for her and Kikania. Her power would allow her to teleport where she pleased, but that was little help if she froze along the way. She needed money too, so she took what she could pocket from her keni box and wrapped the rest for Kikania and Tazper, if he survived long enough. Kikania wouldn't have the rest she badly needed. Staying here with the Crystal Brigade coming, though, was not an option.

Kasia roused Kikania as softly as she could in her panic. "I am sorry, but something has happened. Chatik forced Tazper to testify about my murders of the Crimsons. If they find you here without me, they will torture you until you tell them all you know."

"Tell me this is a nightmare," Kikania stammered, jolting awake.

"I'm sorry to say that it is not. Come. Take this coat, and then we must leave. They could arrive at any minute."

Kikania threw herself off the sofa. "I… Allow me to hurry downstairs. There are some items I cannot leave behind."

Kasia clenched her jaw. "Fine, but hurry. And grab any food that we can fit in our bags. I know not how long this hunt will last."

As the maid ran off, Kasia collected her most cherished belongings from her bedroom and study in a leather backpack. Spirits, there were so many of Leonit's books and tapestries that she couldn't bear leaving, but there was neither the time nor the space. She did take the secret book she'd unlocked. Something told her there was more her father had hidden within its pages, but that was a problem for another day.

Shouting came from outside.

Kasia cursed under her breath, throwing her bag over her shoulder and rushing to meet Kikania downstairs. She only made it to the landing before the first *bang* rocked the door. A Force Reacher blast. The door was sturdy, but they had to leave.

"Kikania!" she called as she leaped off the last step. "Kikania, we are out of time!"

Kikania stumbled out of the bedroom she shared with another of the maids, clutching a bag to her chest. Her hair was a mess and her eyes wild, but she looked ready enough. "I'm sorry, my lady, but the food—"

"Don't worry about it."

Kasia snatched her hand and dragged her into the utility room where she'd been hidden, shutting the door behind them. Of course, Aliax was there with company.

"You can't run from your sins forever," he said with a disconcerting grin.

Sazilz stood before the wash basin, that horrible brown suit still hanging loose over his shoulders. "Why did you believe the Crimson Court would not use their 'gift' against you? They handed me to you like a swine to the slaughter, and you *trusted* them?"

Every person she'd killed joined the chorus of mockery as she held out her hand, trying to Reach. But she'd already done so twice in a short span. The Axiom pulled upon her spirit, and the voices grew louder as golden wisps rose from her fingertips. She couldn't hold her focus on where she wanted to go. Proof of Chatik's crimes—that's all she could think of—so she clung to the thought in hopes it was enough.

A horrible noise echoed through the townhouse behind her. Heavy footfalls followed, heading their direction, and Kikania's whimpers would surely give away their location.

"What are you doing, my lady?" Kikania asked, hanging on her arm. "We must flee!"

"Remember when I told you the Axiom gave me its crystal?" Kasia replied as the wisps began to take shape. "This is it. So be quiet and let me concentrate!"

The girl gasped before falling silent, but they had made enough noise. There was no lock on the door, and it flew open as the Crystal Brigade flooded in.

Time was up.

Kasia leaped at the still-forming portal, pulling Kikania with her. She had no idea where it would take her. It didn't matter. Anywhere was better than that room, and the guards' shouts seemed to hang in stasis as she crashed through the surface.

**Bakeekek hovered over the island of stone** in the center of Akaamilion's pit. Every breathless in the city joined him along the pit's edge, their humming reverberating through the ground beneath Radais's feet as he gripped his charcoal and sketchbook.

"You cannot help but revel in the wonder of this," Lazan said beside him, a wide smile on his face. "We are the first to witness the birth of Zekiaz's spirits from the Crystal Mother's very womb."

Wanusa crossed her arms. "That's a foul way to say it. Why do men see a giant hole in the ground and immediately say it must be a goddess's crotch?"

Lazan chuckled and patted her on the shoulder. "It was merely a metaphor, child."

Rakekeaa gave them a look that, despite the difference in species, clearly said to stop talking. Radais held up a hand to silence his allies. Witnessing this ritual was an honor Bakeekek had bestowed upon them, and with the First One already wary of the Glassblades knowing Akaamilion's location, Radais had no desire to give it a reason to expel them.

The humming grew as Bakeekek extended its arms. Then, when it raised them, the breathless fell silent.

Radais sketched them as quickly as he could, trying to capture their various poses and the anticipation in the air. The lighting was difficult with the Light Crystal lanterns against a backdrop of pure blackness, but he found it an exciting challenge to distract himself from the mission ahead. Rakekeaa refused to leave until the spirit-calling ceremony was over, so why not make the best of it?

Even after the humming stopped, the ground still vibrated with the same constant pattern in reply. Gray wisps rose from each breathless, spiraling around Bakeekek before descending into the pit.

All fell quiet.

Wanusa opened her mouth to speak, but Radais elbowed her in the side, shaking his head. Miv would've done worse. Her… harsh… instruction had been too heavy for his taste, however, and until the rescue was finished, he would handle Wanusa his way. The initiate needed to know when to use her blade and when to use her tongue.

The already frigid air cooled further. Like a gust from over the frozen mountaintops, a humid draft rushed from the pit, nearly throwing Radais off his feet. The breathless rose with it around the pit's edge, and their voices joined in song.

Radais couldn't understand their words, but their joy was evident. They danced through the lanternlight, joining together with partners before separating. Each spirit was unlike any other. Radais tried to flip to another page and capture the majesty of it all, but he found himself unable to look away. Tears stung his eyes, and a feeling of loss washed over him until Lazan grabbed hold of him.

"They dance," the Reacher exclaimed, "so we shall too!"

Radais had rarely danced with a partner, and it showed as Lazan swung him about like a miller with a bag of flour. Lazan had such grace and strength at once. A Glassblade needed both too, but anyone who claimed swordsmanship and dance were the same was a fool. Dancing was *much* more violent.

They stopped as translucent figures emerged from the pit. Like puffs of smoke taking form in the gales, the newborn drifters spun around Bakeekek's island, and when the First One touched each, Janitak emerged from the crowd and did the same with its Life Reaching. The spirits solidified with the contact, their forms shifting into more distinct shapes. They no longer just followed the breeze, and other Saleshi greeted them as they strayed.

"So this is how they make more of their kind," Radais said, still holding Lazan until he realized Wanusa was smirking at them. He stepped away with a blush. "I'd always wondered how more spirits entered Zekiaz, and it doesn't surprise me that crystal pits hold the answer."

"Supreme Defender Miv would've loved to see this," Wanusa said with a jab of her own into his side. "Maybe not you, but this."

"She's been too focused on fighting awakened to bother with wonder," Radais replied.

Lazan took a deep breath of the chill air and smiled up at the new spirits joining the Saleshi. "Our duties should never be too much to distract us from our realm's beauty. Especially when you Glassblades are one of its wonders."

"Says the man with the crystal finger that can heal people," Wanusa quipped.

Lazan shrugged. "It was little use against our Vanashel foes, yet that glass sword of yours could cut them down as if they were nothing."

The ceremony soon ended, and Rakekeaa returned to the Glassblades. It lowered to the ground, drawing level with Radais instead of its normal position above. "Seen our calling," it said. "You will not tell."

Radais nodded. "I promised Bakeekek that I will keep your secret." He gestured to the rest of the group. "We all will, right Mhanain?"

"What?" the archer appealed. "I ain't say anything."

"Not yet."

"The First One commands me," Rakekeaa continued. "We rescue supreme defender, but first, you close eyes."

Radais furrowed his brow. "I don't understand."

"It means that we must rest before leaving," Lazan clarified. "We have come a long way, and I doubt it would be a good plan to venture back into the Wastes with us exhausted."

Rakekeaa held out its four hands, palms up. "Reacher is correct. But not inside Akaamilion."

Radais's shoulders slumped. He'd been hoping to enjoy the protection of the city for a single night at least, but it seemed Bakeekek's wish for isolation extended to them in this instance. "Very well. We'll camp at the edge of your lanterns, if that is far enough."

"Acceptable."

Then it left.

"I'd have thought it to be a poet," Wanusa said, heading to her ibex, tied beneath a hanging lantern nearby. "Did Bakeekek talk like that too?"

Radais patted Vuk's head and strapped his bag to the ibex's side. "No. It was almost human, but it was the first with a mind. I got the sense that it watched the Crimsons for a long time before escaping."

They mounted and headed out of the city, finding a suitable patch of sand a respectable distance from Akaamilion's trenches, but not too far to be in complete darkness. It amazed Radais how easily they had become accustomed to the light again after many long hundred-hours in the everdark. Something within him felt empty without it, and he took advantage of it to flip through his sketches of the breathless, the Wastes, and his fellow Glassblades. He'd planned to give them each their portrait when they had returned to Palmia. That seemed a long time away, though, so he pulled each free and handed them to the respective subject. His heart ached at how many were gone.

"Is my nose actually that pointy?" Wanusa asked, studying hers in the light as Lazan lay back and held his above him.

Radais placed a hand over his heart. Had he offended her? "I'm sorry. I'm far from a professional."

She giggled before folding it up and stuffing it in her bag. "Don't apologize. You are the first person who's ever bothered to draw me, and I think it's amazing. I wish I had your talent."

"There is no such thing," he replied, putting away his book and settling onto his bedroll. It was cold, but the flickering fire warmed his face as Mhanain tended to the boiling kettle of soup upon it. "All skill is earned through practice. Some are just quicker to pick it up than others."

"Nah," Mhanain said as he poked at the twigs. There was little wood to collect out here, so they made do with what they had. "I coulda shot a raven from the sky the moment I started walking."

Wanusa rolled her eyes. "Is that why you kept missing the Vanashel?"

"Shut it, initiate. You haven't even earned your helmet yet."

Radais looked from him to Wanusa. "I would say that she has more than earned it. Few initiates have fought as many spirits as her, and none have ventured this far into the Wastes."

He yawned, turning away as he checked his watch—the tenth hour. They had all but missed the night through their journey, and he suddenly realized how exhausted he was. Instructing the others to sleep too, he pulled his blanket tighter around him and tried to think of anything other than Vanashel dragging away Miv. He'd accomplished something great this day. If only it mattered when his heart ached so heavily.

A *whoosh* awoke him moments later, followed by a woman's cry.

"Wanusa?" he asked, throwing himself to his feet with a hand on his sword's hilt. But it wasn't his initiate who'd spoken.

Two Ezmani women dressed in rich scion coats huddled at the edge of the fire. The younger one wept as the other held the girl's head to her chest, trying to calm her. "All will be well, Kikania. We are far from those men now."

Radais stepped back and tripped over his bedroll, ending up on his back as he stared at the pair. "Kasia? What in the Wastes are you doing here?"

**KASIA'S EYES ADJUSTED SLOWLY TO THE SHIFT IN LIGHT** as she huddled with Kikania alongside a small campfire. A frigid wind tugged at her hair, and she shivered from the cold.

A ring of Vockans surrounded them, she soon realized, and in the distance, a thousand of the brightest lights she'd ever seen sent the everdark fleeing. Radais stood before her. His beard was longer and his eyes sunken from exhaustion, but it was no doubt the Glassblade who'd saved her life.

*How did we end up in the Spirit Wastes?*

The Axiom's power hadn't failed to get her away from the Crystal Brigade, but was this what she'd focused on? There was so much to learn and no time to learn it.

"Master Radais," Kasia said, rising and dusting off the gray sand from her coat. Though her head spun from Realm Taint and Aliax's haunting spirits lurked at the edge of her vision, she tried to gain her bearings. "There is quite a lot I must explain. My apologies for stumbling into your camp unannounced."

"Unannounced?" a built young woman snapped from beside Radais. She held a glass sword in hand, far more jagged than her round cheeks and wavy auburn hair. "You appeared out of the air itself! I've never heard of a Reacher that can do that." She glanced at an Ezmani man who still lounged on his bedroll—Lazan.

"It is unheard of," the Body Reacher said with a flourish on his vowels. "With House Niezik, though, I have learned to expect surprises."

Kasia bowed to her fellow scion and stepped away from the fire, keeping her fear of the element down long enough for her to make space. She scanned of the group, four in total. One pointed a bow at her with a steel arrow nocked.

"You can put down the bow," she told him. "Radais and I are allies."

"Do as she says, Mhanain," Radais ordered as he pushed himself back to his feet. "Kasia is dangerous to her enemies, but we are not them. Kikania, on the other hand, couldn't hurt a drifter."

Kikania still clung to Kasia's arm. "I drove off an awakened, actually," she said.

Radais looked to Kasia for confirmation, and she nodded. "My uncle hid that he suffered from the Spirit Plague," she said. "He succumbed to it, and his awakened spirit attacked our servants."

"You've had an ordeal then," Radais said before gesturing toward the fire. "Sit and warm yourselves." He introduced them to each of the Glassblades: a young woman called Wanusa and the archer, Mhanain. The latter seemed the only real threat to Kasia in the group, but Wanusa stared at her as if she were an awakened.

"Do you have a problem with me, Glassblade?" Kasia asked her with a raised brow. She had enough problems without a girl with a glass sword stabbing her in the back.

Wanusa paced, arms crossed. "So Master Radais worked with you in Kalastok. That's great. Are you going to tell us how you appeared hundreds of miles away if you're supposedly a Death Reacher?"

Kasia sighed, holding her legs to her chest. "My infiltration of the Crimson Court has proceeded since Radais left. To avoid all the details for now, I earned myself a meeting with them, only to find that they needed a Death Reacher to complete a ritual that required each of the fifteen realms. Their leader, who I discovered is Chatik of House Pikezik, had us open a portal to a realm he called the Axiom.

I followed him through it before the portal shut."

"Bold," Wanusa said.

"But risky," Radais replied. "You stepped into a portal without knowing what was on the other side?"

Lazan wrapped a blanket over Kasia and Kikania. "Let us not interrogate them, shall we? It is obvious they have suffered."

Mhanain lowered his bow. "Fine. Grab Lazan's share of soup if you want, but we ain't got much."

"Thank you, but we should not stay too long," Kasia said, gripping the blanket and settling further from the fire. She was just glad to be away from its flames, but a chill came with the distance. "I was desperate to figure out what Chatik was planning. He leads the organization that killed my father and King Yaakiin, and I wanted him dead. What lay on the other side… well… It is hard to explain. There were islands made of pure crystal of every color, and gravity shifted in unpredictable ways. Tendrils of color floated around me, and when I touched one, I saw my servant, Tazper, trapped."

"You're full of shit," Mhanain replied with a huff.

"Enough, Mhanain," Radais insisted before sitting cross-legged in the sand before Kasia. His brow twitched with curiosity. "You are among friends here. Tell us what happened."

Kasia sighed. "I would say the same, Mhanain, but what happened was very real. Following Chatik, I stepped through a mirror-like portal that teleported me to an island where thousands of these colored tendrils formed a sphere. He wasn't pleased at my arrival, and shot me. I had extended my hand out of instinct to Reach, and his bullet ripped through my talon before deflecting across the side of my head."

She held up her left hand, earning a gasp from Wanusa. "I know," she continued. "Gruesome, is it not? Losing my talon took my ability to Reach, and I tumbled from the island, falling unconscious for at least a day." She tapped her temple. "The Axiom healed the skin at least, but there's no way I can get my talon and finger back."

"May I examine wounds at least?" Lazan asked, sitting up now, his fingers tracing his own talon. "I cannot make it like new, but I figure I can confirm the Axiom's work."

"How much?"

Lazan furrowed his brow. "I don't understand."

"How much do you want for looking at it?" Kasia clarified. "Body Reachers never work for free."

He rounded the fire to her, taking her hand. "Not all on Zekiaz revolves around payment, my lady. Consider this my thanks for sending me on this journey with Radais. I have seen far more than I had ever hoped to in my life." His talon touched just below her knuckle. "This will feel odd, but keep still if you can."

Why did he think this was her first time with a Body Reacher? It was rarer for scions to see a doctor without Reaching than one with. Her father had employed one to heal even minor illnesses or injuries in the family until his death ruined their stature.

Blood red wisps rose from Lazan's fingertips and danced around Kasia's finger and head before shooting into the scars. A tickle crossed her finger, but she couldn't laugh. Not with Tazper's torture and Faniz's corpse filling her mind and her killed spirits whispering as they circled her. Madness wasn't what the newspapers claimed it to be. It was slow, numbing, and Kasia questioned whether the voices around her were real or figments of her Tainted imagination.

"What did Chatik want with this Axiom?" Lazan asked once he finished.

Kasia tested her scars. Neither had changed much, but the dull ache had faded from both. The new skin on her temple was smoother too; though, it still bore a scar that she hoped wouldn't prevent her hair from growing back. "A voice spoke through that sphere of tendrils. It claimed he'd stolen something called the Unity Crystal, but the voice adamantly refused to tell me what the crystal was capable of. All I know is that he intends to use its power to control the awakened and conquer Brakesh in some show of Ezmani superiority."

Wanusa held out her arms, still holding her sword. "That still doesn't explain how you got here."

Kasia frowned, rising to face the Glassblade initiate. "Spirits know I could use lessons in patience myself, but you seem to have quite the single-path mind. Fine, I'll tell you so you'll sheathe that blade." She displayed the crystal web embedded in her hand. "The voice in the Axiom offered me to Reach its realm's power if I agreed to help retrieve the Unity Crystal. I still know nothing about the crystal, but as long as Chatik holds it, I will gladly use whatever power I can wield to make him suffer for all he's done. The Axiom Crystal's web allows me to teleport and shift gravity, like what happens within the realm. I fled here because the Crystal Brigade broke into my house to arrest me."

"Why?" Radais asked. "They already know you're a Death Reacher… or *were* one."

Kasia swapped glances with Kikania, her heart sinking. "You remember how I saw Tazper in a prison cell? Chatik dragged him before the Chamber of Scions and used a Truth Reacher to force him to confess to my assassinations."

Aliax and the others burst out laughing at her portrayal of the situation. The Glassblades did not need to know about them, not yet. She didn't know if Tazper had told the Chamber that much, and as long as there was a chance at keeping her secret, she would take it.

"Stop it!" she snapped as Aliax stopped inches in front of her, grabbing her waist. She shoved him away. "Leave!"

Wanusa cocked her head. "Stop what?"

Kasia spun away, holding her coat tight around her. Aliax usually vanished when she told him to, but this time, the specters lingered. "It's nothing. I thought I heard something."

"So you're wanted for murder, then?" Radais asked, but he held an inquisitive look too. How long could she keep the spirits in her head from her allies? "As a scion, shouldn't you have a trial at least?"

She shook her head. "We declared war on Kelosh. Martial law allows the Chamber to sentence dangerous individuals to death without a trial with a significant majority. Tazper's testimony would be enough to sentence me, and with a Death Reacher, they like to shoot first."

"Then what is your plan now?" Lazan said, hands folded before him. "Returning to Kalastok is out of the question if the Crystal Brigade is looking for you."

"What is this brigade?" Wanusa asked.

"They are a glorified gang of Reachers who hunt other Reachers at the great houses' behests," Lazan said. "It is better not to have heard of them."

Kasia took Kikania's arm. "My hope is that your journey could provide some answers. We have seen much to incriminate Chatik, but without proof, I cannot confront him before the Chamber."

Radais nodded to Wanusa, who scrambled to her bag and pulled out a book. "That journal was Kariazan Pikezik's."

"Is this the man who you found in the Wastes?"

"Precisely." He gestured for Wanusa to hand it to Kasia. "Kariazan documented the Crimson Court's tests on lowborn prisoners they took into the Wastes. With Chatik's help, they created the Spirit Plague and infected the prisoners until they died and became caged awakened, which they turned into Bound Ones who could Reach. It talks about the same Axiom that Chatik mentioned, so they were probably hoping they could use spirits to create the portal, then control their powers. They failed when the Mind Reacher spirit developed its own thoughts and freed itself and the others. Kariazan must've escaped and then tried to return during this past duskfall."

Lazan pointed to the distant lights. "Those freed spirits are the breathless, and this group of them refer to themselves as the Saleshi. The Crimsons must have realized after Bakeekek's escape that they could command breathless, likely with Mind and Spirit Reaching of some kind."

"They *created* the Spirit Plague?" Kasia asked, a hand held over her heart. She'd suspected the Crimsons could've been behind the disease's sudden appearance, but such savagery as testing a disease on innocents and then spreading it throughout one's own people… Words could not condemn such actions enough. "This is the evidence I need to defeat Chatik in the Chamber, but I fear I cannot present it without the Crystal Brigade killing me first." She turned to Radais. "If a Glassblade master were to provide such evidence, though, there would be no way for them to deny it."

Radais averted his gaze. "I can't go back yet. Another group of breathless called the Vanashel have captured Supreme Defender Miv."

"She's dead, then," Kasia insisted. "Spirits don't take prisoners."

"Don't claim to know spirits better than us!" Radais snapped, staring at the ground with his fists clenched. "The breathless are different. They'll know she's a Glassblade and will try to get information from her. Bakeekek asked me why our glass worked against them, and they'll ask her the same. She doesn't know the answer, so they'll torture her."

Kasia relented and returned to Kikania's side. She knew the pain in his voice all too well. There was no reasoning with that someone that desperate, as many had tried with her pursuit of revenge. Radais would have to stay, but he could still aid her.

"Then write a letter," she said with the weight of exhaustion heavy on her voice. "Your word will provide context for the journal."

Sazilz scoffed from beside the fire, warming his ethereal hands. "A letter will not stop the King in the Dark. Nothing can now that he has the Unity Crystal."

"What it his plan then?" she insisted. "How will he take control?"

"Chatik betrayed me," Sazilz replied, "but he is the only one who can save the Commonwealth from this war. Nothing else matters if Kelosh burns our houses to nothing."

"Kasia?" Lazan asked, pulling her attention from Sazilz. "Do you believe a letter is enough? There will be no way to validate it is his hand."

Wanusa lunged at her bag again, rifling around until she pulled out wax and a metal stamp. "These were with the supreme defender's ibex! She'd brought them in case she needed to send one of us back with a letter about the mission's success or failure. Her ink spilled over her papers, but these should be enough to prove the letter is from the Glassblades."

Radais gave her a confused look. "Miv didn't tell me about that."

"She didn't tell you she was coming until the last moment either," Wanusa replied.

"The supreme defender's seal must be enough, then," Kasia said. "Once it is written, I will return to Kalastok and figure out a way to ensure it enters the king's hand, and I believe Kikania knows of exactly the person who can do that."

Kikania reached into her coat pockets, as if searching for an answer. "I… I do?"

"You said Princess Nikoza was working with Zinarus and Nex, right?"

"Oh, yes!"

Kasia nodded. "She will pass the letter and journal to Jazuk while I remain in hiding. Then, we can confront Chatik in front of the entire Chamber and expose his plot."

Radais pulled out his sketchbook and ripped a sheet free. He had no quill this deep in the Wastes, so he wrote with the charcoal she'd seen him use for his drawings. It was messy, but with the seal, it would be enough. It had to be.

"There," he said once he finished, handing it over to Wanusa for her to wax and stamp. "I've retold my story without revealing the location of the Saleshi. I promised Bakeekek that their isolation would be respected."

"It won't remain that way forever," Kasia replied as she took the letter. "Once the scions get word of a civilization of spirits, they will seek ways to gain from them or conquer them."

"Then you need to ensure they never hear the full truth."

She nodded, sliding the letter into her bag and flexing her chained hand. Another jump so quickly would deepen her already constant Realm Taint, but she had no choice. Time was of the essence.

"You're pushing yourself too hard," Aliax said from nearby, but she refused to meet his gaze. "Chatik has allies and that crystal. Facing him exhausted and Tainted is a bad idea."

"Thank you, Radais, and all of you," Kasia said, gritting her teeth to avoid shouting at Aliax. "I know your journey has not been easy, but because of you, the Crimson Court will fall."

Gold danced from her fingers as she Reached, closing her eyes and feeling the Axiom's ethereal strands. She pictured Zinarus. His sweeping red hair, vibrant vests, and mechanical leg that whirred with innovation, and when the web snapped taut in her hand, she called forth a portal to him.

The Glassblades gasped at the shimmering portal that appeared between them. Wanusa stepped forward, circling to the backside.

"Can someone on the other side come through?" she asked.

Kasia cried out, not at Wanusa, but at the swirling spirits that screamed in her mind. She had not had Reacher's Taint this heavily since the Ephemeral Slaughter, when Aliax had nearly killed her. It was deafening. Only Radais taking her scarred arm stopped her from collapsing.

"Kasia, what's wrong?" he asked.

She tore herself free as Gregorzon's fire joined the calamity in her head. Her skin burned, as if the Glassblade campfire had erupted over her. Gregorzon and Aliax's laughing faces circled her, and no matter how she tried to flee, there was nowhere to run.

Arms caught her a step from the fire. She glared into it before realizing where she was, then stumbling back into Kikania's arms with the heat still stinging her cheeks.

"What is wrong with you?" Wanusa demanded.

"I'm fine!" Kasia spat. "Did you see a portal before we appeared before? No? Then you have your answer about my mirror." She looked at Radais. "This is your last chance to come with me. I can't hold the portal open for long."

The Glassblade stared at his boots. "Go, and do what you must. Our duty is here."

Kasia dug her heel into the ground, but a lost fight wasn't worth continuing. "Very well."

She took Kikania's hand and stared at the portal, wisps slowly evaporating around it. Darkness met her in the reflection, but the Axiom's power had not failed her yet. With specters echoing in her head, she stepped through the portal, hoping her mind did not fail either.

# SHOOT AND MISS

*"It is better to aim and hit once, than fire thrice with haste and miss each."* –
Quickshot Miko

Zinarus's mechanical knee creaked as he patrolled the length of the arena, watching Tiuz's cavalry recruits canter with pistols raised. Most had terrible riding form, and their shooting arms wavered. Only a pair of them had managed to hit the target since he'd arrived with Tiuz.

"I told you they are not ready," the old general said, hands held behind his back. He barked instructions at the last set of riders, who dismounted to give the next group their chance.

Zinarus gripped his cane so hard his fingers ached. "One does not need to be a Truth Reacher to see such an obvious fact, my friend."

"Yet you wish to send them against the Crimsons!" the general muttered. "Needless to say, if they cannot shoot a stationary target, they will be nothing but a disorganized mob when the Crimsons call awakened against them. Even a trained soldier is useless against spirits without glass weaponry. Unless Lady Katarzyna intends to provide us with her Glassblade friend's swords, I find it futile to mobilize these mercenaries for at least another season."

"There is no such way to get glass beyond our daggers anytime soon, but Katarzyna has provided me with another weapon against the awakened."

"Which is?"

Zinarus stopped, lowering his voice as another *crack* echoed through the arena. The bullet flew wide and struck the protective barricade before the arena wall. By the Crystal Mother below, more holes filled the barricade than the target! "We have discovered that beads of amber can be utilized to capture spirits. Your expression says that you doubt me, but I have experienced it myself only last night."

Tiuz considered that for a moment, a wry smile tugging at his lips. "Impressive, but why have you kept such a discovery secret? It would benefit House Niezik greatly for their amber to shift from luxury to weapon."

"You were a major general," Zinarus replied. "Would you reveal your greatest weapon to your enemies before it came time to use it?"

"Fair enough." Tiuz signaled for the riders to stop. "This target practice was going nowhere anyway. I'm sure we can scrounge together materials to create slings for them to wield instead. Any general knows that fighting lowborn can lob a rock as good as anyone, and what is amber but a fancy rock?"

Zinarus patted him on the shoulder. "Good man. I have a stash of her amber at my townhouse that I'll have sent here. It isn't much, so try to get your hands on any more that you can. While you work with them, I must return home to ensure my injured friend is well, and to see how development progresses on the Spirit Plague's cure."

"May the Crystal Mother bless both her and the scientists," Tiuz replied.

"I am sure *they* are well, and these scientists are the best men for the job, I promise you." Zinarus had kept the truth about Paras's survival from Tiuz for now. He was a trusted ally, but in politics, three members of the Chamber knowing a secret meant all of Kalastok would know before long.

The mercenaries gathered around Tiuz with a shine in their eyes. It was easy for Zinarus to forget his friend was a hero, but among lowborn, such legends did not die. He suspected his mercenaries would have had far fewer recruits without Tiuz to aid him, and he was grateful that the general was beside him in this, admittedly, crazy endeavor. No one wanted to follow a steel-legged commander who had never stepped foot on a battlefield. Valor won loyalty. Zinarus hoped it would be enough when the time came.

It took him a while longer than he wished to pass through the stables before the rear entrance. Much of that was due to his knee's gears catching. But the greater delay came from him loitering with the horses—especially his horse, Arkenus. He hadn't visited his trusty steed as much as he should've lately, and Arkenus let him know it, throwing his head into Zinarus's shoulder hard enough to knock him into the stable wall.

"You will be the death of me if you are not careful," Zinarus told him, scratching his neck. Death had been a distant prospect once, but now, it seemed ever-present.

His moment of joy faded at the thought of Kasia slaying her former lover. What was he getting himself into by fraternizing with her? They had yet to court officially, but before the Chamber meeting, it had been something he hoped for. Now, his stomach flipped at even the thought of her.

*There are other problems to address,* he told himself. *Infatuations can wait.*

Despite his attempts to push away the thoughts, though, his mother's written warnings about Kasia lingered in his mind. *"House Niezik is cursed, my son. She may be lovely now, but the Amber Dame's reputation stretches across the Commonwealth. One does not confront House Uziokaki so easily without a bite behind one's words."*

Zinarus mulled over his problems as he clambered into his carriage and held his cane between his legs. His eyes were heavy, so he closed them, massaging his sore leg. He was too young to feel so weak. Most men at twenty-five could fight in the war, carry heavy objects for labor, and run freely, but he could do none of it. At best, he could ride with a special saddle.

The rumble of the cobblestones only worsened his aches, so he took slow breaths, wishing for his arrival home. But a force struck him first.

The impact threw him into the door, knocking it open and forcing him to cling to the carriage wall as his hat dropped into the path of the carriages heading the opposite direction. Passersby gawked at the strange man hanging out the door. He was just as shocked, and he held on for dear life, shouting to his driver, "Stop the carriage!"

"My lord?" the driver called back as the carriage rolled to a halt. "Is all well?"

Zinarus looked from his lost hat, trampled beneath a dozen horses, to the figures now filling his carriage. "By the Crystal Mother below!" he exclaimed with a relieved chuckle. "Lady Katarzyna and Miss Kikania, is that truly you?"

*And how did you appear in my carriage?*

Kasia snatched her own hat from where he'd been seated. Her brow was furrowed, focused, beneath its dark fur, but her cheeks were as red as dawnrise poppies. "It is, but you need to get back in here. I am certain half of Kalastok wants me dead."

"All is fine," Zinarus shouted to the driver. "I simply spotted some friends who needed transportation."

Kasia's maid, Kikania, extended a hand to Zinarus. He took it and hauled himself back into the carriage. The tumble had twisted his mechanical leg, though, so he gestured for them to look away as they began moving again. "My leg is not a sight for scions to endure."

"Believe me, I've seen worse," Kasia replied. Unusual for a scion lady, she wore trousers with a long jacket that cut away to complement her form well. She also wore no gloves, covering her left hand with the other instead, and an odd streak of hair was missing above her left ear. It was quite the radical cut. Just as radical was the odorous stench wafting from both her and the maid.

Zinarus wiped the nervous sweat from his forehead. "I am certain you have, based on the testimony of your servant."

A hollow silence fell, disrupted by a jolt when the carriage struck a stone in the road. Kikania curled into the corner, while Kasia stared at the floor. The matriarch's voice cracked. "So he told them all of it."

"I..."

*Shit.* He had been prepared for fury, but pain? His mother had told him to care for a woman when she wept. Did that stand when he was the one who had brought forth the tears? Against his better judgment, he reached for her hand. "I am sorry."

She pulled away, still covering her left hand with the other. "For what? For realizing what they said about me in the newspapers was true? I am Death's Daughter after all."

"Your desire for revenge has driven you to act in ways that many would call questionable, but we have seen what the Crimson Court is capable of. Dire actions are needed against such foes."

"You mock me by avoiding your true concern," she replied.

Zinarus ran his thumb over the cold metal atop his cane. Focusing on it calmed his heart, and he decided honesty was best. She would face execution if they failed, so what did he have to lose?

"I am fond of you, Kasia," he stammered, meeting her eyes that swam with the depth of the duskfall sky. "From the moment you bothered to continue through my stumbling dance step, I—"

"Stop!" Kasia exclaimed. Kikania's gasp from beside her was more distant than the Vockan Mountains as Kasia raised her taloned hand to her chest. Except no talon rested upon it. Her index finger had vanished completely, and instead, golden crystal crossed her entire hand in designs unlike any he'd ever seen. "We must discuss business, Zinarus."

He winced, but fought the pain from the dagger she'd plunged into his heart. Why could he have not kept his mouth shut? "Business?" He scowled as she shied back. "Chatik Pikezik has incited the Chamber to execute you because of your past murders against both the Crimsons and some innocents in Tystok. My true concern, though, is not who you have killed, but that you are lying about your convictions. The vibrant, passionate matriarch I see in you is not one who would run from the consequences of her past."

"What would you have me do, rather than flee the horror I caused?" she breathed, her gaze darting to the side before returning to him. "I *see* those I've killed. Not just their faces, as soldiers say when they return from war, but their actual spirits linger in my mind. Aliax… He shifts from fury to mockery in an instant, and every time I see him, it is a reminder that I can never make right my errors."

"It was an accident, then?" Zinarus ran his hands through his hair. He'd trained every day to hold his composure in the Chamber, but this… this was no meeting of the scions. "I do not know who to trust. All evidence has shown what you are capable of against your foes, but could you truly kill innocents?"

Kasia stiffened. "I need your help if I am to survive this, so I will tell you what you want to know. There was this boy, Aliax, who I was… close… with. He said I could practice my Death reaching in a safe spot with him, away from anyone else I could hurt. Except, people discovered our relationship and came for us."

Her eyes darkened as she stared out the window. She seemed elsewhere for a moment, as if lost in the past before she continued, her voice firm, "I was already Reaching to touch a spider, to see what I would do to it. But the barn doors opened, and there were suddenly a dozen people rushing me and threatening me. I'd never been so afraid. No one had shown me how to ensure I didn't Reach more than once, compounding my power and inflicting me with Realm Taint. I lost control, releasing all my power at once."

She shook her head. "I wish I could say I did everything to make it right for those people. But I didn't, not for a long time. My mother screamed at me, but she silenced the rumors, kept the families of the dead from asking too many questions. I've done what I can for the families in recent years. It isn't enough."

Zinarus studied her for a long time. He couldn't muster the words to respond. No matter how hard he thought to separate his thoughts into black and white, he found himself trapped in a swarm of gray.

"I will ask no more of you regarding the past," he finally said. "The pain that haunts you is obvious. Whatever sins you committed, you suffer a great cost for already, and the last thing I desire is to deepen the wounds in your heart."

Her lips parted just the slightest. She studied him for a long time, tears welling in her eyes as she fought to hold them back. Always fighting. Zinarus saw the tiredness in her that he'd missed before.

Years of sorrow lingered behind the dams that were her eyes, and he knew well what it meant to channel that pain into rage.

"When the Dark Reacher killed Regizald," he whispered, fist clenched before him, "I swore I would drive a lance through his heart once I uncovered his identity. More than anything, I wanted to make him suffer as I did… as I do. But I cannot claim that my loss can compare to your own, especially if you endure the responsibility for part of the loss as well." He opened his hand and extended it toward her. "I am sorry for that pain, for I know of its sting. I know, too, that there is nothing worse than walking alone through the everdark of one's spirit without hope of the dawnrise to come."

Kasia's eyes flicked to his hand and back. "You have said all of this, yet have yet to ask how we appeared in your carriage, as if from nothing."

He kept his hand out, warring with his fear. "I hold trust that if it is something I must know, then you will tell me." It wasn't true that he harbored no doubts, but the intent remained. Kasia had entrusted him with knowledge of her Realm Taint, even though she'd hidden the awakened in her closet. He would find in time if his trust was misplaced, but his heart was lighter than it had been in a season. That had to mean something.

"Why?" She flinched with her own question. "What have I done to earn your misplaced affections? I hardly deserve them."

They came to a stop in front of Zinarus's townhouse. For the moment, though, his world was in this carriage. "I am no child," he replied. "We all have sins in our pasts… But you are right, we have business to discuss."

Neither of them spoke as he held his breath. It felt as if a single shift of his lungs could ignite the air hanging between them.

Until Kikania threw open the door.

"Allow me to help you out, my lord and lady," she babbled, the words tumbling from her lips.

Zinarus finally took a shallow breath. It failed to fill the void in his chest, but at least it would stop him from suffocating for a minute longer. In days like these, that was all he could manage. Keep living.

"After you, my lady," he said to Kasia, his arm shaking as he held it toward the open door. Spirits, this was not how he had expected this carriage ride to go.

She bit her lip with her gaze fixed upon him. His heart did not beat until she looked away, and it ached as she drew up her collar and stepped out of the carriage.

"Crystal Mother help me," he whispered before following.

They hurried inside, hoping the Crystal Brigade was not watching his residence. It was no secret Kasia had spent time with him, and once they discovered she was not at House Niezik's townhouse, they would interrogate all her known affiliates. The fear of intrusion had lived with Zinarus ever since the Dark Reacher's attack. This changed nothing in that regard.

"Welcome home, Lord Zinarus," his maid, Niniaxi, said as she shuffled into the foyer with a duster in-hand. She dropped it at the sight of Kasia. "Oh… Oh, my." She took Kasia's hands. "My apologies, Lady Katarzyna. Events have moved quickly as of late, so the state of the townhouse is—"

Zinarus coughed. "That is plenty enough, Niniaxi. Katarzyna is not here for personal reasons. Is Nex still asleep upstairs?"

She stepped back from Kasia, nodding frantically. "They are. Poor little Nex. Taking a slash from an awakened and living is no small feat."

"What is Nex doing here?" Kasia asked, brow raised. "Kikania said you stole my amber to capture spirits for Paras and Professor iz Noshok."

"Come, I will tell you more upstairs," Zinarus replied as he headed for the stairs. A chair was built into a mechanical lift on the wall beside them, and he climbed into it, pulling a lever to activate it.

Kasia's brow raised at the puff of steam that shot from the machinery. "Quite the invention, this. Is it of Ogrenian design, like your stirrup?"

"Parts of it were proposed by my Ogrenian contacts, yes," he replied, smiling at the machine whirring and hauling him up the stairs at a respectable pace. "The rest, though, is my own work that I hope may someday be used for others like myself. I—"

A *crack* cut his pride short. Dark smoke poured from the gears, their movements turning to a deafening grind, then a halt.

Zinarus tugged at his suit coat. Despite his attempts to hold his composure, he blushed. "As I was about to say, there is still much to be done before it is perfected."

Niniaxi rushed to help him up, but Kasia shooed her away and took his arm instead. He tried not to interpret too much from the action, but his heart fluttered. "It is an accomplishment to be proud of," she said. "I hope you may complete it one day. We were, however, focused on Nex and our *immediate* problems."

"Of course." Zinarus silently thanked her for the distraction from his failure. "Nex ran off by themselves while Nikoza and I worked together in the forest east of Kalastok. An awakened chased Nex, and we only managed to stop it after it had already struck them. The wound is mild, but awakened injure spirit and body both. Nex has not woken since the incident."

"Did it work at least?" Kasia asked. "The amber?"

Zinarus hauled himself up the next step, gripping the banister with one hand and her with the other. "It did. Paras and the professor believe they will have a cure within the day, so I now wait to hear from Nikoza about the results. The princess has become Etal's apprentice, and despite her father's politics, she is sympathetic to those who suffer."

They reached the top, and Zinarus took a few heavy breaths before leading them into the first guest bedroom. A hint of smoke filled it as candles burned atop a dresser on the near wall. They barely illuminated Nex's short form beneath the covers.

"Nex had come looking for you while Nikoza and I were retrieving the amber," Zinarus said, taking a seat in a high-backed chair with a groan. If these were the aches he felt this early in life, perhaps the elderly's complaints were warranted. "Their lover suffers from the Spirit Plague, and they hoped you had found some kind of cure after your deceit with the alchemist. When they heard what we were doing, they insisted on helping."

"It was brave," Kikania confirmed. "I only wish I could have aided the effort instead of hiding from awakened in a washtub."

Kasia squeezed her shoulder. "You were brave too. Scaring away an awakened like you did is an accomplishment, and because of you knowing when to hide, you're here to help us now." She turned back toward Zinarus. "It is good that you found a cure, because Radais discovered that the Crimsons were behind the creation of the Spirit Plague."

Zinarus sat, frozen, as she relayed the events of the last few days, from her experience in the Axiom, to her near death encounter with Chatik and conversations with Radais. He'd thought his experiences had been insane, but this… She had entered an entirely new realm!

"And your wounds," he said when she was finished. "They are healed? You are well, despite losing your talon and being shot in the head?"

"Thanks to the Axiom's strange power, yes." She sat on the bedside, staring at the floor. "To be honest, I am still in shock from it all. Being a Death Reacher was different than any other realm. It had defined my identity, fed my need for revenge, and guilt came with that." She showed him the golden crystal wrapping around her hand. "The Axiom chose me out of convenience, but I will use this power to finish what I started. If that bullet had been an inch to the left, I would be dead. I intend to make Chatik pay dearly for failing."

"I understand," Zinarus replied before pointing to the golden lines. "May I take a closer look? I have never seen anything like this."

She complied, standing so that he could gently run his fingers over the rough, uneven crystal lines, tracing them to the circle at her palm. "They are truly beautiful," he mused, "unlike the talons we bear. Etal showed us that a group of his students were focused on his theories around the Axiom. Chatik was one of them, and so was my father." He released her and gripped his chair's armrests. "You were right. That man has abandoned me my entire life, manipulated my mother. If the Crimson Court caused this disease, then all of them are monsters. Stopping them will not bring me justice for my father's absence, but I would have immense pleasure at watching him rot in prison."

"Your cure will go a long way to ending the suffering they've caused." She reached into her pack and pulled out a letter and journal. "These will ensure their crimes cannot be denied in the Chamber."

He raised his brow. "You want me to take them? Why do you not teleport to the king and present the evidence yourself?"

"Guards don't usually like intruders, right?" Kikania replied from Nex's side. "I imagine a wanted woman appearing before the king would not end well."

"That's nicer than how I would've phrased it," Kasia said, "but yes. Whoever put the bullet through my head first would be considered a hero, and they would all take the shot." She shoved the journal into Zinarus's chest, knocking the wind out of him. "Besides, you owe me after you stole my amber jewelry. You want to be my suitor? That usually means gifting valuables, not taking them."

Zinarus's tongue tripped over itself as he fought to find his breath. "What are you saying?"

"Save your pin for another day," she replied, referring to the traditional house tokens exchanged at a courtship's beginning. "Do not let your emotions distract you from what must be done if I am to survive to the next hundred-hour. Chatik must be stopped. Can I trust you to do this?"

A knock echoed from the front door. Heavy, but not followed by the shouts of a watchman. Zinarus held onto hope that it was Nikoza's courier as he pushed himself to his feet with some effort. "I will do what you ask," he said. "Evidence against Chatik alone will not be enough to clear your name, though."

"I know," she said, pulling back. "But as long as Chatik and the rest of the Crimson Court are punished, my job is done."

Zinarus stopped and leaned against the doorway. "You deserve more than vengeance."

He started for the stairs, but Niniaxi was already on her way up, skipping every other step in her excitement. She held a metal bottle with a cork plugging its top.

"Is this the cure?" Zinarus dared to ask.

Niniaxi held out the bottle with the widest smile he'd ever seen her wear. "The courier gave this letter. He says it's from the princess."

Zinarus took it, holding his breath.

*"Dear Lord Zinarus, our friends have succeeded. Thank you for your assistance in the matter. This sample is for Nex. May they use it well."*

# CURE AND CORRUPTION

*"Reaching has given us a cure for the worst of any scion's ills; however, there is no such cure for the selfish corruption that rots scion society to its very core."* –
Annika Falizok, Ezmani scion writer

The gas lamp's hiss filled Zinarus's study as Kasia paced across it. Zinarus had left to speak with Nikoza about the journal, and Kikania cared for Nex upstairs, leaving Kasia alone with the visitor who'd arrived not long after Etal and Paras's cure.

"I'll kill them for torturing you," she muttered.

Tazper knelt in the entryway, tears staining his bruised cheeks and his disheveled clothes hanging loose off him. Once she'd caught him up on the events of previous days, he'd not stopped pleading for forgiveness.

"I am sorry, my lady," he said through sniffles. "I tried to fight it, but Truth Reaching—"

"I saw, Taz," she said, crouching before him, then offering her hand. "This situation is terrible for me, but it should be me apologizing to you. In my plan, I had not considered what would happen to you when I went to face Chatik. You deserved better."

He took her hand and stood with some effort. "You do not owe me anything," he said as she guided him to the study chair. "I am only your footman."

"No, you're not."

She bit her cheek, fighting her own tears. How had she allowed him to think he was nothing more than her servant? From failing to make him a Reacher to allowing him to be captured, she'd been a terrible friend. That changed today.

"You are my best friend, Tazper," she admitted, sitting on the edge of the desk. It was pristine, but she'd expected nothing different when it came to Zinarus. "Every time I stumble, you are there to catch me. It is my fault you never heard how much that meant to me, and I swear I'll make you a Reacher, even if it means buying one of those rings from the black market."

He forced a smile. "It isn't easy being your friend, you know?"

"The fact I lack many others makes that clear."

"You intend to face Chatik, then?" he asked.

She nodded. "He needs to suffer for what he did to us. If we don't act soon, then he will use the Unity Crystal to take power. I'm sure of it."

He pushed himself back to his feet and straightened his clothes as best as he could. "Then you're going to need help. You might struggle at it often, but you're my best friend too, so I cannot let you face him alone."

"I won't be alone, and I have other plans for you." He wouldn't submit to staying out of the fight, even in his condition, unless she made him believe the alternative was just as important. She'd only just gotten him back. Without a talon, the risk of the Crimsons striking him down was too high. "Tystok will come under attack when word reaches them of my guilt. Before I leave for the Chamber with Zinarus, I will open a portal for you and Kikania to return and reveal the truth to my brother. Gregorzon is often argumentative, but he will side with us against our father's assassins."

The Axiom's gold crystal had inched up her scarred arm after her frequent Reaches today, and she was beginning to wonder if that was the cost of the Axiom's Taint. To protect Tazper, though, she needed to get him out of Kalastok. He'd suffered for her. Now was her chance to return the favor.

"What about you?" he asked, nearly falling into a bookshelf with his weakness.

She turned away as she pictured the Chamber like a haataamaash board. The Crimsons' strongest pieces were in position, and her only hope was Zinarus with the journal. The spy. "If we cannot stop Chatik, then the throne will likely be his. Even if we succeed, though, I am a fugitive. I will have to flee to Tystok no matter the result. After that, I am unsure, but it is up to you whether you wish to remain affiliated with a matriarch awaiting execution."

Tazper thumped his chest. "I am with you, Kasia. Just make sure you return, alright? Despite the suffering you put me through, I prefer you to Gregorzon."

"His opinion won't be the same, but I trust you to be persuasive." She tugged at her scarred arm's sleeve, then looked to the door as a noise came from upstairs. "Now, you rest. I'll send Niniaxi to help you get cleaned up while I check on Nex."

**NEX'S BED SHIFTED, SOMEONE SITTING UPON ITS END,** followed by the sharp scent of overdone perfume. Nex sneered at it and rolled over with their eyes still shut. They had not felt such comfort in their entire life, and exhaustion made their muscles strain with even the smallest movement.

"Nex? Nex, are you awake?" a woman asked, her voice familiar. Why wouldn't she just shut up? Couldn't she see Nex was sleeping here?

"Sure as glass am now," Nex muttered, squeezing their eyes harder, as if it would make the woman disappear. "Go away."

The woman chuckled, and a warm towelette draped over Nex's brow. It got rid of the annoying everdark cold. They welcomed it until they realized the woman was at the foot of the bed, and that meant there were two people in the room.

*Where in the Wastes am I?*

Nex shot up, fists swinging. The room was dark besides a few candles, but they hit the arm of the person over them anyway.

"Owww!" the figure yelped—a younger woman from the sound of it. "I'm sorry, Lady Nex. I was only trying to help."

*Lady Nex?*

Nex looked from the figure to the woman seated on the bed, the candles lighting her enough to reveal her drawn back hair and severe look. Nex shivered. Didn't matter if that look was from a mother or an enemy. It wasn't one you forgot.

"Kasia? Kikania? What are you doing here?" Nex asked. "Spirits, what am I doing here?"

Where even was *here*?

Kasia forced a smile from her seat on the bed. "Zinarus brought you here after you blacked out hunting awakened. He said you had quite the fight, and that you managed to get what Etal and Paras needed." She held up a corked metal bottle. "Congratulations, Nex. You helped cure the Spirit Plague, but I believe you owe poor Kikania an apology for that punch."

Nex lunged for the bottle, groaning when pain shot up their arm. Right, the stupid spirit had swiped them, but at least it didn't feel like mud was still caked across their face. That didn't matter now. They had a cure, and Vinnia would live if they could get across the river. Still, something bothered them.

"Zinarus didn't wash me, did he?" they asked, wincing.

Kikania laughed and helped them stand. "He is a scion of a well-off house, Nex. His maid, Niniaxi, did, and I have taken care of you today while she dealt with the rest of the townhouse."

"Thanks…"

"I assume that is as close as we will get to an apology," Kasia said, holding out the bottle for them. "Nikoza and Zinarus wanted you to have this for your lover. The cure came too late for my uncle, but perhaps it can do some good for you and many others."

Nex hesitated. "What if it doesn't work? The others didn't."

"Do you have another choice?"

They grabbed the bottle, weighing it as if that would give them the answer they wanted. Vinnia needed a cure, not another attempt by Paras, and Nex had learned from experience not to hope. But Kasia was right. They had no other choice.

"I'm going," they said.

"You're free to," Kasia said, "but do not tell anyone where I am—or even that you saw me. Chatik convinced the Chamber to call for my execution."

Nex grinned. "It's good to be wanted. Most of my aliases are. Feels lonely without people with guns looking for you."

"The Crystal Brigade has more than guns."

"Even better."

Nex headed for the door, ignoring their lightheadedness as they grabbed their old duster and hat from a stand near the door. Spending too long in a scion house was sure to get them sick. How did they live without rain dripping through the ceiling and a draft slipping through the windows? Boring.

Kasia grabbed their arm, slipping a small bag into their free hand. "Be careful, Nex."

Nex checked its contents and held back a gasp at the wad of keni bills within. More than they'd ever seen. "Her name's Vinnia," they replied, tucking the bag into their pocket.

"Get her healthy, then find somewhere safe for you both to live. I am not done with you yet."

Nex's head swam with ideas as they left. That much money could do more than pay for rent in a townhouse with a real roof. It could cover a safe life, one that sounded less boring with every step they took. Spirits, it was stupid to dream of an existence funded by a scion, but they couldn't help it. All their life, they'd thought of nothing but how to earn, or steal, enough keni. What were they supposed to do without that need?

A couple walking toward Nex crossed the road at the sight of them. Then another. Nex furrowed their brow, then realized they wore worn, ripped clothes. This was the Market District. Of course the scions and lowborn merchants saw them as a common pickpocket.

They stuffed their hands in their pockets and walked on anyway. One of Kalastok's greatest traits was anonymity in the mass of people. Merchants and scions alike would forget the face of the scruffy-haired miscreant they'd seen, complaining instead that there were people like Nex allowed in the east side at all. The joke was on them; Nex didn't want to be here either.

The western wind carried shouts as they neared the mid-city New Beginnings Bridge. They clenched their fists in their pockets, waiting for a clear view to see which guard was on watch. But when they reached the edge of the last building, they stopped with a curse.

A dozen soldiers stood upon the brick bridge with rifles aimed at the western shore. Their comrades dragged men and women through a lowborn mob, who threw stones and curses alike. Factories deeper within the Industrial District burned as lowborn ran about with torches. One man rose among them on a stack of boxes, his fists raised in the firelight.

"This isn't our war!" he shouted across the bridge. "We won't be drafted! The Spirit Plague takes our daughters, and King Jazuk takes our sons! There's nothing left for Kelosh."

*Crack!*

Nex's ears rang as the man's head snapped back. He collapsed, his final words joining the unmistakable smell of gunpowder in the air. The soldiers swapped nods, but the mob's roar swallowed their relief.

Countless lowborn surged across the bridge, overwhelming the soldiers who dragged the conscripts. Those who remained panicked and fired into the advance. But there were a hundred lowborn for every that fell. By the time the soldiers reloaded, the mob was upon them. Blood splattered across their bright red uniforms.

"Down with the king!" a woman shouted as she tore the rifle and ammo from a soldier's corpse. Then she took off toward the Crystal Palace with the others flooding behind.

Nex grinned and stepped out of their path. They were doomed against the watchmen and Crystal Brigade, but the scions would feel the heat of lowborn fury tonight. Brutal assault had its place in change. Nex just preferred to inflict damage against the elites when it didn't end with a bullet in their own head. The cure in their pocket was a start, and if Kasia continued to disrupt the corrupt Chamber, they would gladly profit from helping her do so.

The mob didn't give Nex and their tattered clothes a second look as they ran through the Market District, lobbing torches onto anything that could burn. Scions and merchants had avoided Nex minutes before. There was no running from this army of rage.

Smoke stung Nex's nose as they found a gap in the crowd and ran across the bridge before the shooting escalated. Dawnrise had come early as the western horizon burned orange, granting the Kala River a scarlet hue instead of its everdark black. The corpses above it stole Nex's smile.

The bridge's walls contained the blood of soldiers and lowborn alike, and a river of it flowed down the center. Half toward the west, half toward the east.

Nex kicked one of the soldiers as they passed. It wasn't the uniformed killers who stole their joy, but the familiar faces of the lowborn beyond. Most they'd only seen in passing. One, though, stung in their recent memory.

Nex crouched beside the cleft-chinned brute they'd tricked in the Iron Alley Pub during the first few hundred-hours of everdark. How much of his money had he lost gambling with them? Nex wondered whether that had led to his desperation tonight, but their regret faded when they remembered he'd called them an Ogrenian bitch until the Glassblade, Radais, punched him. Rich or poor, assholes were assholes.

Still, they didn't kick him as they continued on. He'd got his punishment from Radais and now the soldiers. And Nex had better places to be.

Fires jumped from factory to factory deep in the Industrial District. Many were wooden instead of brick or stone, and the west side had no Water Reachers to extinguish the blaze. Even the great houses had pulled back their Reachers that would protect their factories, leaving only a small group of bucket-carrying lowborn to douse the flames. They watched Nex with hopeful gazes, but Nex just walked faster. The fires weren't far enough north to risk the Shadow Quarter and Vinnia.

The everdark crept over Nex as they neared the homeless camp. If they didn't look back or over the river, the riot would seem a distant memory, but smoke lingered on their coat, forcing them to cough as the familiar rattling of Jax's cup came from ahead. The old beggar's notorious smile was absent tonight. He just sat on a wooden box and stared south, his back hunched.

"Wasn't you, right?" he asked, pointing to the fires. He still wore Vinnia's mittens, and a pang of sorrow hit them knowing how many others would miss her if the cure failed. "Been gone a few days. Got worried you were up to something across the Kala."

Nex pulled the bag out of their pocket and grabbed twenty thousand keni, about half of Kasia's gift. They dropped it in his cup. But that much money overflowed it, sprawling onto Jax's lap. "Found a good scion. Maybe a couple."

Jax stared at the cup, shook it again, then looked at Nex with tears in his eyes. "I can't—"

"I know. But you'll get that money where it's needed." After the shitshow Kasia had caused on Beg Ave, there was justice in using her money to fix it. The rest was more than enough for Nex and Vinnia. "There'll be more if I keep working, I think."

"Thank you, Nex."

They thumped him in the chest. "Don't. No one knows this was from me, got it?"

He nodded.

"I'm going to Vinnia," they said, heading north again. "Enjoy the show."

Nex didn't look back, and Jax's muffled weeping faded quickly behind them. Tears were common here. For once, though, they weren't from pain.

Their chest tightened as they reached the Shadow Quarter and climbed the rotting stairs to their apartment. Each creaked, threatening to fall.

*Not today,* they told the dump of a building. *Survive another day, and I'll be rid of you.*

Nex held that thought as they stopped with a hand on their door and sighed. Their hand brushed the cold metal bottle in their pocket, and for the first time since Kasia had given it to them, they let themselves hope. It only made their heart race faster. And when they couldn't bear it anymore, they pushed open the door.

"Vin?" they called out. "I'm home."

**WARMTH DRIFTED FROM THE WOOD-TRIMMED FIREPLACE** in one of House Bartol's many sitting rooms, meeting the steam of fresh tea from their estate in Anukit. Nikoza sat straight-backed and sipped from her ceramic cup. She enjoyed its sweet respite from the bitter emptiness she'd endured after Reaching to save Nex. Realm Taint brought more than dehydration against Water Reachers, she'd realized in that moment. So too, did it bring a stasis that was hard to shake.

Unfortunately, Zinarus's arrival had broken her moment of peace.

"You want me to take this journal and letter to my grandfather?" she asked him with a glance at her tall blonde maid, Emily, lurking beneath a portrait of her deceased father in the corner of the room. It would not be proper for her to meet an unmarried man in private, despite having done so already. Within the Bartol townhouse, though, eyes watched her every move. "I agreed to help you with Professor iz Noshok, but this…"

Zinarus was rigid as he brought his cup to his lips, then winced at the tea's heat. "The contents of the journal will prove the importance of this in regards to the professor's student."

Did he mean Chatik or his father? Nikoza wished to shoo away the maid, but such resistance was impossible without losing her station. What plot had she found herself further wrapped within? Zinarus was ingratiated with Katarzyna Niezik, and Nikoza could *not* affiliate herself with a murderer.

"Why did Master Radais send these items to you, Lord Zinarus?" she inquired, her gaze pressing Zinarus further. She needed to know how deep this went. "Should such a letter not reach the king directly?"

He fiddled absently with his mechanical knee, stumbling over his reply. "With Lady Katarzyna's recent controversies, I was the last of the scions he trusted within the city."

She sighed. *What a terrible liar. Why did Lady Sania believe her son was suited for Kalastok politics?*

These items were surely the work of Katarzyna, then. Nikoza hoped the maid, who would surely relay the conversation to her grandfather or one of his many advisors, did not draw the same conclusion. She took another sip of her tea. It had cooled along with her willingness to cooperate in conspiracy. She had faced spirits in the dark swamp to aid her grandfather's subjects and advance her reputation with Etal, not to deal with her Uncle Chatik's supposed Crimson Court. Jazuk had already scorned her enough for cooperating with Ambassador Alyniana.

"I am sure if you petition my grandfather, he will consider your request in due time," she insisted. "As his ward, I am to learn from him, not act as a way around official channels." She set down her cup and stood, hands clasped before her. "Is there anything else you wished to discuss?"

Zinarus stared at her, slack-jawed. "But, my lady, if you would take a moment to read the journal…"

"This is not my role." She nodded toward the entry hall. "Now, if there is nothing further, I must return to the research that Professor iz Noshok has conferred upon me."

His shoulders slackened as he took the journal and letter, then bowed his head. "My apologies for the intrusion, then. I will leave a note with King Jazuk's secretaries and hope he acts swiftly."

"We are at war, Zinarus."

"It is not the Keloshan Empire I fear at the moment, my lady," he whispered in her ear, "but the corrupt empire whose roots strangle our nation down to the crystal at its foundation."

Nikoza returned to her book as he left, his cane's clicks against the wood floor ringing in her mind until he passed beyond the front door. The silence that followed should've been a gentle time for her to further her reading of Professor iz Noshok's book, *The Convergence.* It was full of theoretical models and descriptions that made her thoughts drift, though, and after an hour of failing to advance beyond the first chapters, she set down the book and rubbed her forehead.

Where was her grandfather?

The Chamber of Scions had recessed hours ago, and as far as she was aware, his council had not convened today. Had it? She glanced at Emily, who remained despite Zinarus's absence.

"He sent you to watch me, did he not?" she asked with an innocent smile.

The maid swallowed. "His majesty the king has requested that you be looked after, as he worries about your health in recent days."

Nikoza's toes curled. "Poppycock! First, it was the letters, and then I went to the college without his blessing. Is this my punishment? Is he no longer allowing me to attend council meetings?"

Silence was answer enough.

Nikoza crossed her arms, standing before the fireplace as its heat baked into her luxurious clothes. She had worked to ensure the Commonwealth had allies against Kelosh and a cure for the Spirit Plague, and what had been her reward? Isolation.

*I should have taken that journal.*

"Call for my carriage," she told Emily.

"My lady? Are you sure that—"

But Nikoza was already packing up her things and heading toward the door. "Bring my coat as well, the one I wore for Unification Day." Her house's textile businesses had their benefits, and she'd ordered it custom made to combine Ezmani red and Vockan white designs. With all the division in this everdark season, it felt appropriate. "If you wish to watch me, then I will be at the Crystal Palace."

She emerged into the everdark evening not long after, the faint smell of smoke hanging over the city. That was odd, as the Air Reachers usually kept the impurities of the Industrial District's factories from the eastern air, but as she looked southward down Textile

Alley, flames formed a halo beyond the gentle hue of the street's lamps. Such fires were rare, but she gave it no more than a passing glance. The emergency Water Reachers would handle it soon. Surely…

Her nose was already red from the chill by the time her carriage arrived, and she glared at the driver before stepping inside. Lazy man, that one. He had likely been smoking a pipe without the horses ready *again.* Her grandfather would hear of it, but first, she had more important things to address with him.

The streets were quiet through the northern Market and southern Crimson districts. Guards had restricted access to the areas around the palace ever since the Ephemeral Slaughter, but usually there were still shoppers, businessmen, and scions strolling through the gardens and shops. Tonight, there was only a stray servant with his master's bags in-hand.

*The fire must have spooked them,* she thought. *Or there is news from the warfront?*

Nikoza had spent little energy to know how the early war with Kelosh was developing. It was out of her hands now that Nochland was no longer a viable ally, and news moved slowly with the distance between Kalastok and the front. Unless either side was routed in the initial battles, it would be some time before they learned if the Commonwealth could endure.

The palace bell rang out as her carriage pulled into the street before its southern entrance—a call for the Chamber to meet immediately. Nikoza looked out the window, toward the southern flames, and gasped. What had been a few scattered blazes before was now a raging inferno.

"What in the Crystal Mother's name is happening?" she asked.

A guard rushed from the palace door to her carriage, throwing open the door and holding out a gloved hand. "Princess Nikoza, my lady, you should not be here! The lowborn are in revolt against the conscription. The palace will be their target!"

A revolt? Nikoza glanced from the guard's hand to the fires, spreading toward the residential Drifters' Quarter. What was the world coming to? Those were homes and shops burning, most owned or rented by minor house scions or lowborn. Why would they burn their own property in revolution?

"It appears that the lowborn have a torch for every building," she said, sparing only a passing thought for what she would lose if their townhouse burned. Those like Nex who struggled for each kena would take the brunt of the flames, and her grandfather's response would only make matters worse for them. "Where are the emergency Water Reachers?"

The guard winced. "All Reachers have been called to protect the Crimson District, my lady. Please, hurry inside if you insist on staying. The king wouldn't want you out in the open."

*Then he should have invited me to his council meeting.*

"No," she decided, stepping out of the carriage but not taking the guard's hand. The steps to the palace's main corridor rose behind him. That hall led to the Crystal Mother's statue, and Nikoza offered a silent prayer to her goddess as she pressed her fingers against her lips, then crouched to touch the ground. "Bless me with your guidance, Mother. Let this not be foolish."

"My lady?" the guard asked.

Nikoza stood and stared toward the inferno that now consumed the southern third of her city. She'd never considered her Reaching a true power, but helping her allies in the swamps had reminded her what it felt like to be useful, needed. There were Water Reachers far more experienced than her. By the king's order, though, none were left to help the people who needed them most.

Only she could face the flames.

"Tell King Jazuk that he must listen to Lord Zinarus's pleas," she said over her shoulder. "I must serve our people."

The guard's questions fell to the background as Nikoza gathered her skirts and bolted down the stairs. Her driver insisted she return, but she couldn't. For too long, she had hoped for others to do what was right. She was done hoping, done waiting. She had power. And as she tore her glove from over her taloned hand, she swore she would never forget that again.

# NEW FRONTIER

*"New Frontier shall offer an outpost for us in the Spirit Wastes, and soon, there will be no place within its expanse that we do not rule."* – Harizak Kuzon the Third, former king of Ezman

Sweat clung cold against Radais's skin, his glass armor a thousand pounds on his head and shoulders as he pushed Vuk ever onward. The darkness was eternal beyond the ring of light from Rakekeaa's crystal lantern. They had ridden for countless miles in recent hundred-hours, and his thighs had gone numb from both chill and wear long ago.

"We can't go on like this forever," Radais called ahead to the breathless.

He glanced at Wanusa and then to Lazan. Neither were Glassblade warriors who'd endured the treks that often came with Order missions. If he was this sore, then he could only imagine the agony they dealt with.

But Wanusa stared onward, her seat solid in her saddle and her gaze determined. Windburn marked her cheeks, and she wiped her nose as her breaths fogged the air. Yet no complaints left her lips.

Lazan was more vocal.

"I do believe I lost my groin a ways back," the Reacher said. He shifted, wincing. "No, never mind that. It is unfortunately making its presence known once again."

Radais lacked the will to chuckle, but luckily, Rakekeaa slowed at his plea. It lowered to them as the other breathless remained above. "Settlement over dune," it hummed, pointing with its two-ended spear. "Vanashel see light."

"How many of them are there?" Radais asked.

"Few. Many." Rakekeaa lowered the spear. "Patrols take most Ones Who Are Bound, but others stay."

Mhanain scratched his bald head. "Don't need to kill all of 'em. Get in. Get Miv. Get out."

"A feint." Radais nodded to himself. "Yes, that's a good idea. Most of us will attack on one flank while I go in on the other to find her."

"How do you expect to do that in the dark?" Wanusa asked.

He hadn't thought that far ahead, but she was right. The lantern was their only source of light, and whoever held it would lose any chance at stealth.

Rakekeaa glanced over its shoulder and said something in the Saleshi tongue. The viny Life Bound One, Janitak, descended with what resembled a frown. Its armor was less intricate than Rakekeaa, but, spear in hand, it looked ferocious. Such a creature was better to keep on their side.

"I show Radais way," Rakekeaa said. "Janitak lead the rest."

"Wasteee our liiiives," Janitak replied. "Riiisk."

Rakekeaa swung the glass end of its spear toward Janitak's head. "Disloyal. First One will hear. Send you to pit."

Janitak's vines curled upon themselves as it looked from Radais to its leader, then replied in Saleshi.

Whatever the reply, it pleased Rakekeaa, because it lowered its spear and handed the lantern to Janitak. "Leave ibex," it told Radais. "I carry."

Wanusa snickered, but Lazan waved for her to be silent. Radais gave him a grateful smile. His nerves, though, were on end again.

Whether he walked or was carried didn't matter when Miv's life was on the line. She could've been already dead for all knew, but he refused to give up hope. Too many memories came with just the thought of her. They couldn't be the end. Not like this.

"I am ready," he said, dismounting and grabbing his sword from Vuk's side. Spirits, his legs were sore, and he turned to the others to check on them. "But should we rest? I don't want to send you all into battle exhausted."

Lazan flexed his taloned hand. "I can heal anyone that needs it before we begin, but it will leave us vulnerable for a while after."

Everyone shook their heads as Wanusa replied, "Didn't you just say that you were hurting?"

"Not enough to use a Reach that could be needed later."

"Then save it," Wanusa said. "We're all sore, but we'll heal up when we all get back safe. Right, Radais?"

Radais nodded absently, lost in his memories still. "Enough talking. Remember that you are not trying to win a battle. Just buy us time. Take no risks."

"Whole thing's a risk," Mhanain replied, stringing his bow, "but that's the job."

Rakekeaa took Radais in its bottom two arms again as Janitak led the others over the crest at a canter's pace. Radais's chest hurt watching them go. He was not a natural commander like Miv, but these were his warriors now. Sending them into battle without him felt wrong. Rakekeaa was doing the same, though, and he would do what was necessary to save Miv. They all would.

The Saleshi sergeant was quiet as they pierced the edge of the lantern's light and entered the everdark. Radais's breaths shallowed, each harder in the vast nothingness. The Wastes went on for hundreds of miles in each direction, but it felt as if it were a veil confining him.

He closed his eyes, focusing on the cool touch of Rakekeaa's arms. They were rigid, but not muscled. It made no sense to him how they could be so solid when their awakened counterparts weren't, but Bakeekek had kept some secrets. Maybe he would learn in time. Until then, he would fight to ensure their tentative partnership with the Saleshi stood.

"We are close," Rakekeaa soon whispered. Radais's senses told him they were descending, and their speed threatened to make him lightheaded. He needed to keep focus. "No sound."

Why Rakekeaa had felt the need to make that comment when he hadn't spoken, he didn't know, but he slowed his breaths. Time was confusing in the darkness, so he silently counted until Rakekeaa stopped and set him down.

"Ahead," it said. "Hold my hand, and I will guide."

He drew his sword and took its hand with the other. How could spirits see in the darkness? They obviously preferred light, but Rakekeaa had shown no hesitation on their journey. Nor did it move at any pace slower than a run now.

A hum grew as shouting came from off to their left. It was far quieter than the earthshaking sound in Akaamilion, so he hoped most of the Vanashel were on patrol like Rakekeaa had claimed. His allies were trained for this. They would be fine, and so would Miv.

Rakekeaa stopped suddenly, sending Radais tumbling. His hand slipped from its, and a growl came from nearby as he stood with his blade raised.

The sound was inconstant. One moment, it was ahead and to the right, then to the left. It came from face level, unlike an aerial awakened attack, and it reeked. Too close.

Radais swung at the last growl, and it deepened as his sword's tip struck something resembling flesh. He resisted the urge to curse. His blade would do little against non-spirits, but Rakekeaa had told him to keep quiet.

Except the breathless made a ruckus itself, murmuring in Saleshi as a *squish* revealed it stabbing another of the attackers nearby.

"Husks," it muttered to him. "Blind, but heard us. Take hand."

*Husks?*

There was no time to ask, so Radais took its hand again, and it dragged him faster than he could run. His shoulder screamed. His fingers strained. But he held on with all his strength until it stopped moments later.

"Don't do that again," he whispered, sliding to a stop in the sand. "I can't fight without my arms."

"Here," Rakekeaa said. "Breathing one inside."

More groaning came from behind them, further away. Radais's heart raced at the thought of what those *things* were. But he wouldn't have to face them if he hurried.

Rakekeaa led him through a doorway, his fingers tracing the splintered wood to get his bearings. Loose boards and scattered furniture made each step treacherous. They moved slowly until someone coughed ahead. A woman.

Radais rushed toward the sound.

His knee immediately cracked against a chair. He stumbled onward until he fell into a pile of splinters, but none of the pain mattered. The woman coughed so close to him that it hurt his ear.

"Miv?" he asked, scrambling to her. "Miv, it's me."

It was a ridiculous statement in the dark, but she weakly held his arm, her voice raspy. "Radais? What are you doing here? The mission…"

He laughed in relief, embracing her. "We did it, Miv. But we need to leave."

"They fucking tortured me!" she snapped back, too weak to hug him back. "*You* need to leave."

Fighting tears, he picked her up. "Not without you."

Rakekeaa's hum showed him the way back, and he handed Miv to it. "This is a safe spirit, Rakekeaa," he told her. "It will take us to safety."

"Beasts," she murmured. "Monsters."

Radais ignored her rambling and turned to Rakekeaa. "Take Miv to Lazan. I will hold my ground and await your return."

Rakekeaa made a clicking noise, then pressed its long spear into Radais's free hand. "Husks close. Metal end up."

"Right, thanks," he said, sheathing his glass sword and taking the spear with both hands. He'd trained mostly with a sword, like most Glassblades, but a spear wasn't unfamiliar to him. At least it could reliably puncture a body without shattering.

Rakekeaa's rise was silent, but the ethereal chill vanished with its absence. What remained was still air and the nauseating stench of the advancing husks. At least a few of them, based on the groans.

Radais grabbed the chair he'd tripped over and put it in the doorway. It would at least offer him a warning when the husk was close enough to strike. He could only hope the noise wouldn't draw more dangerous breathless or Bound Ones. The Glassblades and Saleshi sounded like they were making all the noise a perfect distraction needed, but they would retreat at Rakekeaa's signal. Then, he had to hope it could retrieve him in time.

The clattering came a few heartbeats later. Floorboards creaked as at least two husks entered the house, and Radais stabbed at head level above the chair. The spear found purchase, silencing the first of the husks. The other's groans flanked him. And his spear was stuck in the first's skull.

Radais gritted his teeth, kicking the flanking husk in the chest before yanking the spear free from the other. He swung as the second recovered. The spear missed with his blindness, but a creak revealed it stepping into range in time for him to reverse strike.

Gore spilt over Radais's neck, but the husk lumbered onward. A hand grabbed Radais's arm. It threw him aside with strength greater than any man, sending him careening over the chair yet again.

Right into another groaning figure.

They fell into a heap, the beast scratching at his glass armor as a blow landed against his back. His breastplate absorbed the strike but shattered. He rolled free with a thousand glass shards slicing at his arms and spurring the husk below to complain louder. The Vanashel would hear eventually, but he fought on by instinct alone. He wouldn't fail now. Not again. He had allies now, friends, and he survived for them as much as himself.

The Vanashel's hums quieted along with the distant shouts. Miv had made it to Lazan. Good. But Radais's time would soon be up if Rakekeaa didn't show up. He'd killed five husks, and now, he wandered the dark streets of New Frontier with countless more stalking him.

He realized it then. Husks... The empty, spiritless bodies of those killed by the awakened. These were the final settlers of the Wastes. The last who'd made it this far before the Crimsons and Glassblades.

The Vanashel wielded them like Crimsons wielded breathless. Slaves.

His desperation turned to pity as he cut them down, eyes shut, concentrating only on their shuffled steps and hollow groans. It was a gruesome dance. These people deserved better ends than this, but their spirits had passed long ago. At least now, he could give their bodies rest too.

Rakekeaa's lighter hum soon approached as Radais's arms tired. There were too many to fight on his own. He'd backed himself into another building by accident, and Rakekeaa had to lift him from above to stay away from the swarm of husks. Was this the entire population of what had been New Frontier? What did the Vanashel have planned for them?

Questions for another time. For now, Rakekeaa carried him toward safety, but its hum grew concerned.

"Vanashel follow. Patrol return. Need to return Akaamilion."

Radais bit his cheek. Returning to Akaamilion would require a full day of hard riding without rest for the Glassblades or their ibexes. The fight had given him a rush, but from experience, it would fade soon. He promised himself Miv wouldn't fade herself.

Lanternlight filled the sky ahead as they rose over the village. It was blinding after so long in the dark, but Radais stared into it, searching for Miv among the figures climbing the dune on ibexback. She was draped over the back of Lazan's ibex. Blood streamed down its side, and any hope of it not being hers faded when the light exposed fresh crimson splattered across the front of Radais's armor and undershirt. He'd only held her for a few moments...

Mhanain rode at the rear with a pair of Saleshi, shooting his final arrow through an awakened that stalked the group. More followed, but the Saleshi fought together, unlike their mindless counterparts. Their long spears sliced through the Vanashel awakened before they could threaten those on the ground.

Rakekeaa set Radais next to Vuk on the far side of the dune and took back its spear. The Glassblades arrived moments later, their faces determined. Wanusa bore a slice along her arm, and a few of the ibexes had similar wounds, but none had fallen.

Radais ran to Miv, checking her neck for a pulse. Faint. "Reach," he commanded Lazan. "Now!"

Lazan's head dropped. "I am sorry, my friend, but I have already. Though I closed her wounds, the trauma she has endured before today remains. I fear she does not have long before she joins the spirits."

"No!"

Radais clutched her cold hand, pleading for her to wake until Rakekeaa touched his shoulder. "Return to Akaamilion. Continue her life. But must go now."

He swallowed his sorrow, but tears stung his eyes as he stomped to Vuk. "Then we ride. We'll rest when we're free of this damned desert."

"A hard ride will not help her!" Lazan protested. "She has internal bruising."

"And we'll have worse if we don't run," Mhanain replied, pointing toward the sky. Breathless lurked at the edge of the light.

"The supreme defender's life is in our hands!" Radais shouted, pain pouring through his words as he mounted Vuk. "We have come this far, and I will not stop until we've done everything to save her." He drew his blade. "To Akaamilion!"

They charged to the west. Radais's soreness and exhaustion returned, but he pushed Vuk harder. He'd failed to convince the scions of his discovery. He'd failed to save his father. But by the spirits of the crystal below, he swore upon his life he would not fail Miv. Not again.

# TRIAL

*"Without a fair trial, there is no such thing as justice. Only tyranny."* – Yaakiin Tinaanuuk, former king of the Commonwealth of Two Nations

Nikoza ran against the flow of people. Scions rushed into the Crimson District by the hundreds, but just as many watchmen lined the gardens along the district's southern edge. A massive crowd pushed against them, no doubt lowborn.

*Why do you forsake them, Grandfather?*

Lowborn and watchmen alike gave Nikoza confused looks as she pushed into the Market District. She could do nothing to overrule Jazuk's order, but her Reaching could hopefully douse some of the inferno. The everdark snow should've confined much of it. With the revolutionaries flooding the streets, though, even frost could not stop the tide.

The fires illuminated lowborn bearing torches, weapons, and bottles of alcohol stuffed with fabric. They cheered as they lit the bottles and threw them onto buildings just three streets ahead. People fled between them, but the revolutionaries showed no interest in turning their weapons on civilians. Only when the watchmen came into sight did they raise their guns to fire.

Nikoza realized she stood between the watchmen and revolutionaries. So she sprinted east, toward the eastern residential areas. The flames had yet to consume many of the homes in the Drifters' Quarter, and the revolutionaries were coming from the opposite end of the city. Perhaps she could contain the blaze before it destroyed at least one area. Scion and lowborn business alike would burn, but they could be rebuilt in time. Homes were a far greater loss.

The ruckus of the northern Market District gave way to groups of lowborn carrying pails. They hurled the water toward the burning houses before scrambling to the nearest home or well to refill. Dozens of them helped the effort, but it was no use.

Nikoza's heart caught in her throat as she stared up at the towering flames whose heat singed her brows from twenty strides away. Who was she to face such untamed power?

"Get away from there!" a man shouted, running past with two pails. "Or grab a bucket if you're going to stand there."

An elaborately dressed scion was surely a surprising sight for the man, but he gave Nikoza no further attention before hurrying toward a row of townhouses. His desperation spurred her into action. Every second that passed was another home lost. Her own was likely somewhere in the blaze, but while House Bartol had the funds to recover, many of these lowborn would lose everything.

She followed the man, whose pails did nothing but clear the doorway of the third tenement in the row. Tears filled his eyes when Nikoza neared.

"Are you insane?" he huffed, hands on his knees. "There's enough people trapped in there without a scion lady joining them."

A shiver ran down her spine. "There are people inside? Where?"

The man wiped his brow, then pointed his trembling hand toward the second floor. "Up there, in the bedroom. My wife and daughter."

"Then I will retrieve them," Nikoza replied without another thought. Fear still lingered in her veins, but instead of dragging her now, she felt more energy than she had in years. These people *needed* her.

The man snatched her arm as she stepped toward the doorway. "You'll die in there!"

"I am a Water Reacher, good sir," she said. "Now, unhand me."

He released her, stepping back as she Reached. Deep blue wisps circled her, and the heat abated until she neared the door. Smoke burned her eyes and throat. Flames lapped at her coat like waves crashing upon the shore. Every instinct in her sheltered scion bones told her to run, to survive, but she couldn't stop. Screams echoed from inside.

Pain washed over her gloved right hand the moment she touched the door. Still, she shoved it open and coughed as she stepped inside. Red-orange fury consumed the narrow hall beyond, so she released a wave of water from her hands, clearing a path toward where she hoped the stairs would be.

"HELP US!"

The cry pierced Nikoza's heart. She pushed through the smoke as quickly as she dared, each breath harder than the one before it. Reaching doused more of the flames, but only an Air Reacher could banish the lingering smoke. She'd suffocate if she stayed much longer.

Her foot soon struck the bottom step of the stairs. "I'm coming!"

The steps smoldered against her finely crafted boots as she charged to the top. She worried her hair was itself aflame, but the remnants of her Reach kept the fire away for now. Not for long.

Her skin screamed with the growing blaze. By the time she stumbled into the man's apartment on the second floor, the blue wisps had vanished. Fear of the Taint struck as she Reached for the second time, but a core need to survive forced away the panic. She'd endured Taint to save Nex already. The dry emptiness she'd felt afterward had been horrible, but it was nothing compared to what these people surely endured.

Reaching cooled her skin. As she launched wave after wave into the apartment, though, the flames returned before she could move more than a few strides. A coughing fit overcame her until her hand struck the bedroom door. Cries came from behind it, and she released all the power she had left to clear the doorway.

Then she Reached again.

If the Taint took hold, she couldn't tell the difference between it dehydrating her and the smoke ravaging her throat. Her entire body was pain as she opened the door to find flames beginning to overtake the room. Smoke curled over a woman and young girl, who huddled in the far corner. Both gasped at the sight of Nikoza.

"Come!" she insisted, waving them toward her. "I cannot hold back the flames forever."

The pair silently rushed toward her, and she led them back toward the stairs. Her Reaching wetted the area enough to create a path that grew narrower by the second. The flames still burned her skin, so she did her best to protect the vulnerable mother and daughter. All of them coughed and sputtered as they descended the stairs, then stopped halfway down.

There were no bottom steps. Inferno devoured the placed they had been minutes before, and the smoke was so thick Nikoza couldn't see her hand in front of her.

"There's no way out!" the child cried, clinging to Nikoza's gloved hand.

Nikoza gritted her teeth with tears stinging her eyes. Sorrow and smoke overwhelmed her, but they were so close. Could they not make it the last few feet before the door?

"Trust me," she told the girl.

She drew all her strength into a single blast of water. It parted the fires for only a second, but she took advantage, jumping with the pair and stumbling toward the everdark. That darkness was freedom from the fiery haze. All she needed was a few… more… steps…

Frigid air struck her lungs like a dagger as she plunged out of the townhouse with the pair in her wake. The man had been rushing toward them with another set of pails, but he dropped them and dropped to his knees, hugging his wife and daughter. Tears still filled his eyes. Now, though, he laughed in relief.

"I thought I'd lost you…"

"She saved us," the woman replied before glancing back at Nikoza, who had collapsed in the middle of the street.

In the absence of her Reaching, Nikoza's breaths, her every motion, were agony. It felt as if she'd wandered for days in the everbright heat with neither food nor water to nourish her body. Yes, she'd saved the man's wife and daughter, but the city still burned around her. She had Reached thrice in quick succession.

Now, she burned along with it.

The man looked to her as he held his family. "Who are you?" he asked, his voice shaky. "Why is a Reacher helping us?"

Nikoza couldn't bear to raise her head, so she stared at her fingers in the ash. "You needed me," she said through a heavy cough. "All of Kalastok did. But I was not enough."

**THE RUMBLE OF THE COBBLESTONE BENEATH ZINARUS'S CARRIAGE** echoed that of his stomach. He dared not look out the window. His nerves were frayed enough without considering how much of Kalastok would burn, so he stared at the woman across from him, her hair like the ash that covered the city.

He gripped Radais's letter and journal in his lap. "I do not have Nikoza's sway with the king. The Chamber will reject my right to appeal your execution on the grounds of our affiliations."

"Then speak through their rejection," Kasia insisted, rubbing her scarred forearm. The motion pulled up her sleeve enough to reveal that the Axiom Crystal had expanded up her arm. Was she enduring further Taint? "I cannot speak before them, so you must."

"They will consider this irrelevant when the city is aflame."

She leaned forward with her gaze piercing his very spirit. "Who is the man who claimed the Spirit Plague was the work of Kelosh? That we should quarantine the west side, reject Nochland, and then conscript lowborn en masse for a war they have no desire to fight? Chatik orchestrated all of this. He wants to rule with an army of breathless behind him, and weakening Jazuk makes taking control far simpler. That journal proves Chatik's intentions! And it may ensure his word means nothing against me."

Zinarus fixed his already perfect cravat, then straightened his purple and gold vest and coat. "Where will you be? If this goes poorly…"

"I will open an Axiom portal here and watch the proceedings. When the right moment comes, I will emerge and confront Chatik myself."

"What about your Realm Taint?" He gestured at her webbed hand, its crystal appearing like just another shade of gray in the dim light of the lamps. "The last time you Reached, you said Aliax was there along with the others you killed, and I see the crystal is expanding up your arm. How many times have you Reached today?"

Kasia bit her lip and shook her head. "Don't worry about it."

"Yet you know that I will worry for you regardless."

"Don't, if it stops you from doing what you have to," she snapped. "My concern now is not for my life. The Chamber has spoken. Destroying Chatik's credibility will aid my defense, but I want him and his Crimsons ruined. I cannot do so with my Death Reaching anymore, so I will take everything from them until only their fleeting spirits remain."

Kasia lowered her head as they passed through a crowd of lowborn at the southern edge of the Crimson District. Zinarus sat up, faking a smile as a watchman glanced through the window, his rifle ready.

"I am Lord Zinarus of House iz Vamiustok," Zinarus said as confidently as he could muster, "and this is my servant."

His heart stopped as the guard furrowed his brow, but when he was about to speak, another watchman shouted from nearby, "They're getting closer! Let these scions through and keep the cordon. We need to hold them back."

The watchman waved them on without another look. Zinarus slumped back, exhaling as they rolled onward. He had not considered the extra security in recent days, and the riots had only escalated matters.

"You can do this," Kasia said once they were clear of the watchmen. She covered her left hand and rubbed the stub of its once taloned finger. "If there is any way to stop this chaos, we must ensure the Crimson Court does not have its way. The peasants at your arena listened when you spoke, because they saw that you cared. That alone makes you different than most of those musty old men."

Zinarus huffed. "The Chamber is different from a crowd of peasants, but I will do my best. That, I promise you."

He stared out at the joined reds and whites of Ezman and Vocka on the palace wall as they stopped alongside the other carriages. So often, he had entered the palace with a reverence for its institution and tradition. That veil had dropped. What remained resembled a ledger whose first page was beautifully balanced, but falsified records lay beneath the surface, where so many refused to look.

Zinarus grabbed his cane when the driver opened the door. He moved to exit, but Kasia snatched his arm, pulling him close and kissing him.

Panic flooded his body. He barely had time to register her sharp, minty perfume and the firm press of her lips against his before she pulled back. Barely.

"Go, Lord Zinarus," she whispered into his ear, her breaths hot against his neck. "And bring me my revenge."

Kalastok's flames spread to Zinarus's cheeks as she sat back and waved for him to leave. By the Crystal Mother, had that truly happened? He could only sit there, his mouth trapped in the aftermath of her glorious assault. Little light filled the carriage, but he could have sworn her skin glowed silver, her eyes like the life-breathing rain.

"You will have it," he promised before tearing himself from bliss and into the nightmare beyond.

The driver gawked at Zinarus as he rejected help with the steps down from the carriage, but Zinarus knew his few servants well. They were loyal. Even if the driver talked about his kiss with Death's Daughter, though, the Chamber would soon realize where Zinarus's loyalties lay. There would be no going back.

He held Radais's letter and Kariazan's journal close to his chest, joining the flow of scions into the palace. The heavy smell of smoke hung even here, but it vanished when he stepped through the doors. Within the palace, it was warm, and a faint floral scent filled the air. A realm apart from the world beyond.

Zinarus would have joined the gathered scions in the main hall on most days, but his mind barely treaded water. His first kiss in recent years had not banished his fears about Kasia's past, nor could it rid him of what he must do. He let his ponderings stir as he shuffled into the Chamber, searching for Tiuz among the reformers.

He was nowhere to be seen.

"Of all the days…"

Zinarus shook his head and took his usual seat. The reformer wing felt smaller, as if a mere handful of allies joined him, but a quick count reassured him only Tiuz was missing. Though still a minority, having others with him bolstered his confidence, even if they knew nothing of the evidence he carried.

Also absent was the king's crystal dragon from its perch around the throne. He'd not seen it on his way in, but it was unsurprising that it would be gone during a time of crisis and war. Unfortunately, the great beast was one of King Jazuk's strongest allies, and any attempts by Chatik would be strengthened without its resistance.

The King in the Dark stood across the pit with his wife, Lilita, by his side. She was the matriarch of House Pikezik, but did she know what her husband planned to do? Neither Kasia nor Kariazan's journal had spoken about Lilita's allegiance. Sitting on the king's council had historically meant little for loyalty. No one doubted Gornioz Oliezany's resistance to Jazuk, but their suspicions of his involvement with the Crimsons had led to nothing, besides his niece, Tzena, acting as one of Chatik's agents.

Zinarus's stomach flipped at the sight of the man behind Chatik. His father sat with his legs crossed and a smirk plastered across his smug face. As if wanting everyone to know he was a Crimson, Uzrin wore a simple red waistcoat over a matching shirt. He gave no care for Zinarus's gaze.

Zinarus cleared his throat and looked away as Jazuk arrived with no fanfare. Scions still mulled about, not realizing the king had entered, while silence fell over those who were already seated. An ill omen. Like Zinarus, Jazuk was a man of tradition, and he would not come like this if he was not worried.

Servants then cranked the chains holding shut the large windows at the rear of the chamber. They crept open, and no one dared speak as the dragon swooped through the opening, its wings sending enough of a gust to nearly topple Zinarus over.

"King Jazuk calls for this extraordinary meeting of the Chamber of Scions to begin," Grand Secretary Votzan shouted as the dragon settled around the island in the pit's center.

Jazuk was only halfway down the narrow pathway to the throne. Nikoza was not at his side, and Zinarus raised his brow at her absence. All of this would've been simpler if she had bothered to help him. Instead, she'd chosen loyalty to her house and her own ambitions.

The king himself continued his recent trend of resembling a general more than a king, with military medals and epaulets on his red and white-trimmed uniform. Such pride would not win them this war. Not when the people threatened the stability of his government.

"This honorary assembly must consider action in response to the riots consuming our capital," Jazuk said, his weaker voice carried by Air Reachers positioned at the pit's rim. "I have ordered all Kalastok watchmen, soldiers, and guards of the Crystal Brigade who remain in the city to protect the Crimson and Market districts and detain the rioters."

"Detain?" Borys Kuzon shouted from the conservative wing. "My king, you know I value our friendship, but the Market District burns. We shall all burn with it if you do not command them to cut down these insurrectionists."

Gornioz stood from the nationalists, holding his suit jacket open as he raised his chin. "I must concur. The Keloshan Empire laughs at such internal weakness, and they will overrun us if we do not crush insubordination before it spreads through the nation. These lowborn oppose the conscription we need to win the war. Bow to them, and we will all kneel before the emperor come dawnrise."

Reformers and moderates alike protested vigorously, but quieted when Ivalat iz Ardinvil raised his hand.

"Dear Lord Gornioz, and my friend, Borys of House Kuzon, do you not see that such brutality begets this rage?" he proclaimed. "Our lowborn have been quarantined and forced to suffer without aid. Now, we drag them from their homes without warning. To fire upon them now would only lead to—"

"Treason!" Chatik's voice echoed through the Chamber without need of Reachers. He stood, a long suit coat of deep red draping down his shoulders, bound across the chest by chains of pure glass. He raised his fist, then pointed at the Vockan lord. "Your Vockan people sit in safety, far from these riots and the Keloshan invasion. It is because of such insolent opposition to decisive action that we find ourselves in this situation." Taking a long breath, he thumped his fist against his chest. "But it is with great sorrow that I say that our king's weakness has also forged this path for many years."

Jazuk sat, clutching his cane as he glared at his second son. Scions from every faction shouted against Chatik's outburst, but many others clapped or sat on their hands. And Chatik wasn't finished.

"My father, our king," Chatik declared, "serves at the behest of the scions. We are not his vassals or his subjects. He is ours." He stepped into an aisle and descended the stairs, circling toward the approach to the throne. "Therefore, my fellow inheritors of this great nation, I call for King Jazuk the Fourth to be deposed from the throne, to be replaced by a monarch who hears their people's pleas and bears the strength to answer them."

Another roar filled the chamber, and the grand secretary's appeals for order failed to bring calm. Zinarus cursed under his breath and looked down at the journal and letter. His only weapons to stop this. King Jazuk was not a strong king—on that Chatik was right—but Zinarus could not rest as Chatik wrestled power from his father.

Only the dragon's deafening cry ended the outrage. Jazuk, though, did not fill the silence that followed. He looked more dead than alive, his head lowered and his back hunched as he stared at the ground.

So Zinarus rose.

Cane firmly gripped, he raised his weapons and rallied all the courage in his chest as he glared not at Chatik, but his father. He'd allowed doubt to consume him all his life. Uzrin believed him not worthy of his love or name, but Zinarus reminded himself of a simple fact: his father was worthy of nothing.

"My king," Zinarus declared, "and my fellow members of the Chamber, we have been deceived. Lord Chatik Pikezik, who speaks so boldly before us today, has awaited this moment for many years."

"Ignore this fool of a man!" Chatik repulsed. "He is known to fraternize with Katarzyna Niezik!"

Zinarus took a long breath, then stomped his cane, ignoring Chatik as he raised Radais's letter. "This letter from Glassblade Master Radais ik Erienfar details that during this very everdark, the Glassblade Order has investigated the Spirit Wastes after they discovered Kariazan Pikezik's body deeper within the sands than any have ever gone. Their expedition found a hidden laboratory in the Wastes that Kariazan used to run tests upon drifters, awakened, and living people."

"Kariazan went missing two seasons ago," Chatik replied. "Your letter means nothing, and you seek to use lies to stop what must be done."

Zinarus raised the journal, then Reached into the realm of Truth, using its power against himself. White wisps surrounded his hand before shooting into his skin. Agony followed.

"What is this?" Ivalat cried out as Zinarus collapsed into his cane, only held up by his fellow reformers.

Zinarus gripped the journal with his vision blurring. "I Reach so there is no doubt that what I say now is the truth. Within the laboratory lay Kariazan's journal, detailing his work to allow his organization, the Crimson Court, to control awakened just a year before King Yaakiin, Lord Leonit Niezik, and others were assassinated in strange awakened attacks. His desire was to create controllable spirits with the ability to Reach, granting an army to Chatik Pikezik to rule Brakesh as the King in the Dark. But when catching enough spirits was difficult, the Crimsons developed the disease we now know as the Spirit Plague, turning its victims into breathless—awakened that they could control."

Shouts met him, and the Air Reachers' power carried Chatik's above all.

"Deceit!" the Crimson raged. "Lord Zinarus has joined Katarzyna's plot against us all."

"You use my house against our nation?" Lilita replied, standing before the conservatives with her fists clenched. "You are not my husband! You are nothing but a traitor!"

Jazuk shot to his feet. "Lord Zinarus speaks the truth! Seize my traitorous son!"

The Crystal Brigade rushed down the stairs. A forcefield held Chatik still as ice crept up his legs. But he had allies within the room.

"There are more Crimsons!" Zinarus appealed, but the Chamber was chaos. Scions fought among themselves as Chatik laughed within his ever-growing cage. Why weren't Uzrin and the other Crimsons fighting to free him?

Chatik shouted in the strangest language Zinarus had ever heard. The Crystal Brigade silenced him with Air Reaching, but for a moment, his voice reverberated louder than anything else.

Until the dragon roared.

The Chamber shook as the beast stomped and buried its teeth into Jazuk's torso. His cries echoed through the room before the dragon tossed him toward the ledge. Jazuk scrambled to grab hold of anything, but the pit behind him filled with breathless. Their claws tore through his coat as they dragged him over the edge.

Scions dressed in red struck from every faction of the Chamber, others pouring through the doors and sending firebolts, wind gusts, and spires of earth into the Crystal Brigade. The forcefield weakened around Chatik as scions the guards fought back. But flanked by a dragon on one side and nearly fifty Reachers on the other, they were outmatched.

Zinarus ducked beneath his seat amid the calamity. His Truth Reaching had done all it could, so he lay there, praying that he lived to experience a second kiss from the Amber Dame.

His hopes vanished at the sight of Chatik breaking free from his cage. The King in the Dark rose on a whirlwind of wisps, their colors changing constantly as he clutched the Unity Crystal and shouted down to the fearful members of the Chamber.

"Ezman has bowed its head in shame for too long! We cower in fear of awakened and our neighbors alike while ignoring the immense power granted to us through the Spirit Crystal. Our weakness ends today!" Chatik raised the Unity Crystal. "I have seen the realm that lies at the center of all others, and it had bestowed its gift upon me. With this crystal and my allies within the Crimson Court, we will build an empire greater than Piorak could ever dream of."

He held out his free arm, and the breathless surged around him as he dangled his fingers. "When I close my fist, these spirits will devour all who defy me. Kneel! Pledge your houses to my reign, and you may keep hold of your estates and businesses, your servants and your lives."

Murmurs spread among the gawking scions. Most hadn't even removed their gloves in their shock, and now, they dropped one-by-one before Chatik. In mere heartbeats, over a hundred members of the Chamber knelt, and all the great house magnates knelt among them.

All but Gornioz.

"The Commonwealth stands strong because of its scions," the patriarch said, barely loud enough for his voice to carry. He was taller than most when all stood, but surrounded by those who'd surrendered, he resembled more giant than a man. "You disgrace all which you claim to honor!"

Chatik grinned and pointed the Unity Crystal at him. Wisps of purple swirled around it, then joined into a bolt that shot Gornioz in the chest.

The Oliezany patriarch collapsed, wheezing as his veins pulsed. Centuries of life couldn't stop the power of Death's realm, and in seconds, his skin decayed to dust. Nothing.

"Any others who would like to speak?" Chatik asked with a savage smirk. "Any who would rather watch Kelosh crush us under their metal boots than embrace our potential?"

*Where are you, Kasia?*

Zinarus shuddered under his seat, but other reformers stood defiant. No more than a handful. Enough, though, for him to realize he was not alone. Some had heard his plea, and he would stand among them. For truth.

Grabbing the journal, Zinarus pushed himself to his feet. His mechanical knee whirred and his heart beat so heavily that his head ached from the noise, but still, he held the book out and rebuked Chatik.

"You are nothing but a coward who flees justice!"

Chatik pointed the Unity Crystal at him and laughed. Zinarus looked from him to Uzrin, who showed no pity as wisps rose around Chatik's hand once again. He'd never cared for Zinarus in life. Why would he care for his death?

Zinarus cursed Uzrin with his final before he closed his eyes. *Let it be quick.* The death bolt rang through the chamber, and he awaited the end as color flashed behind his eyelids.

But he felt nothing. No new pain. No power devouring his spirit.

He risked a look, then gasped at the portal shimmering before him. Its surface was like liquid, and through it, he saw Chatik's purple ray seeking his heart. But another sight shimmered in the portal.

Chatik's back.

# EXECUTION

*"For the cruelest of men, death is too kind an end."* – Leonit Niezik, former patriarch of House Niezik

The dragon's call echoed through Zinarus's carriage as Kasia watched her Axiom portal with an audience of twenty spirits squeezed around her. They reminded her that Chatik's guilt did not change her own. A cacophony of noise, it hammered her head until it ached.

But the dragon silenced them all.

She bit her cheek, watching it launch Jazuk into a horde of Chatik's breathless. She had to stop this. But how?

Closing her eyes, she felt the Axiom's webs across her fingers. She imagined the Chamber and her first entrance to it, staring down the pit at the Spirit Crystal far below. The fall would kill anyone. Luckily, she wasn't just anyone.

A strand drew tight in her hand, so she grabbed hold, throwing it into the portal and charging through.

No ground met her. Beneath the throne's platform, she fell toward the Spirit Crystal at an alarming speed. Not fast enough to evade Aliax and the other spirits who raged at her stupidity. She'd watched the king fall to his death, and now she would join him.

Gold burst from her hand as she Reached into the Axiom, drawing upon the shifting gravity she'd found within it. It was a different realm, but she'd grasped its teleportation quickly. Surely, gravity could be no different?

The golden light sharpened as a force threw her into one of the throne platform's support pillars. She lacked time to catch herself, and her skull cracked against its stone.

Her vision blurred. Deafening calamity rained above. Cinder and rock skipped down the support from the battle, burning and slicing Kasia as she collected her bearings. It took all her strength not to surrender to memories of Gregorzon's flames, but her hand found her scarred arm nonetheless.

*It worked,* she told herself as she pressed her hand against the cool stone. *Kind of.*

She'd wanted to flip gravity so that she could fly back to the throne, but it had instead turned onto its side. She spat blood, pushing herself to stand sideways upon the support. Except it felt as if she were right-ways up and the world was shifted. It had at least stopped her from falling to her death, and as her vision slowly cleared, she stared at the throne's platform far above, now just a sprint away.

Her revenge awaited her.

The sloped support made the run toward the platform treacherous. Her head spun and spirits shouted at her with every step. She slipped more than once, but it was wide enough to allow her to suffer nothing more than a bruised knee. Years without her father had inflicted far more pain upon her. A headache and a limp would not stop her pursuit, even amid a torrent of specters taunting her. Not now.

She drew her father's revolver as she neared the peak. The dragon curled around the platform, its crystalline tail scraping across the marble and its summoned spirits circling Chatik above. She was in the shadows for now, but all it would take was for Chatik to look down and discover her.

The King in the Dark, though, was focused on the gathered scions. He held out the Unity Crystal as Gornioz's call of defiance echoed through the hall.

Kasia cursed at the death bolt shooting from Chatik's hand and ripping through the patriarch she'd once believed to be her foe. Yes, Gornioz had been corrupt and selfish, but not a Crimson. Chatik's mistruths had convinced Gornioz to lead the nationals down the path the Crimsons desired, yet when his life was hanging in the balance, he'd defied the dark king's will.

Kasia crept to the edge, surveying the Chamber in search of an opportunity to strike. Chatik had stolen her Death Reaching, and the Crystal Brigade lay dead at the Crimsons' feet. The Unity Crystal must have granted him some ability to Reach into other realms. A shot from her revolver surely couldn't pierce his defenses.

Zinarus's voice sent a shiver down her spine.

She eyed the man she'd kissed minutes before standing among a cluster of defiant reformers. He thrust Kariazan's journal as if it were a spear as he yelled with more vigor than she'd thought him capable of, "You are nothing but a coward who flees justice!"

*Oh, you honorable, lovely fool.*

She'd watched him confront Chatik alone. Zinarus had ruined any chance of the Chamber voting to overthrow Jazuk at Chatik's word. This chaos has resulted, but he'd proven the strength of his will, his character, and his care for her. She did feel something deeply for him. But unwinding the ball of emotions in her chest would have to wait until they both survived.

The familiar purple wisps swirling around Chatik's hand gave her an idea. A gunshot couldn't kill him, but could his own power?

Kasia Reached into the Axiom, the agony in her mind threatening to throw her over the support's side. She clung tighter to the golden web. Within it, she found Zinarus and her hatred for Chatik, plunging her desperation into the Reach.

"I can't lose you too."

A strand pulled taut in her grasp as Chatik's blinding death bolt snapped through the air like lightning. A man's cry rang out, followed by a hard *thud.*

Her heart stopped as she shook away the spots from her vision. She stared toward Zinarus, offering a prayer to the goddess she didn't believe in—until the purple-clad heir stepped from behind her shimmering Axiom portal, his cane in one hand and the journal in the other. His eyes were as wide as saucers, and his hands shook. But he lived.

"You bitch!"

Chatik's face contorted like that of Kasia's mother. His breathless still circled above, but he'd dropped to the narrow walkway between the throne and the entry stairs. A hole burned through the side of his crimson suit, and discolored, bloodied skin seethed beneath. His own power, redirected through her portal. Yet still he stood, green and deep red wisps encircling that damned crystal. He stared right at her.

*Why won't you die?*

No one could survive a Death Reacher's blast. She'd done everything she could to save Aliax, but neither a Body nor a Spirit Reacher could mend the damage caused by the sting of Death, and her heart ached remembering her attempt to raise his undead corpse. The Unity Crystal had made Chatik more than just a Reacher of every realm—it had made him unkillable.

"I always said vengeance would kill you," Aliax said, apparently unaffected by her gravitational shift as he sat on the throne in an ill-fitted peasant's shirt and dirtied trousers.

Chatik clenched his free hand into a fist. "Kill those who still stand! The Amber Dame is mine."

Exhaustion dragged Kasia's thoughts as the dragon roared. The breathless overhead dove toward Zinarus and the reformers as the Crimsons unleashed their Reaching.

*It's over.*

She'd come so close to revenge, but Chatik had beaten her. The few allies she had were helpless or gone. Escape was her only option. With Zinarus in danger, though, she hesitated to flee alone. Each portal would take another Reach. She'd pulled from the Axiom far too many times this day, and the golden crystal already crept up her forearm. Were the others worth the risk?

She glared at Aliax, who smirked at her in the way he had in life. "You never wanted me to be alone," she whispered.

A snap drew her attention away. She ducked beneath the island's edge as a death bolt shot just over her head. The awakened were nearly upon Zinarus now, and the dragon swiped toward her, cracking the marble floor and showering her in shards that sliced her arms and face. Time was up.

As Chatik prepared another bolt, Kasia threw herself over the ledge and into the Chamber. Her shifted gravity took over. She flew feet-first toward the reformers, Reaching to create a portal to Tystok along her path. Gold shot around her, and a portal formed just strides away from Zinarus as the breathless struck down two of the reformers.

"Go through the portal!" she shouted to Zinarus. "We need to leave!"

The fool had dropped his cane as he lobbed amber beads at the attackers. It was the bravest thing she'd ever seen, but with the Crimsons launching their strikes and over a hundred breathless filling the Chamber, he could do nothing to stop the onslaught. Survival was all that mattered now.

And spirits, she *needed* him to live.

Another death bolt burst over Kasia's head just before her feet struck the portal. She repeated her cry to Zinarus in that final moment, pleading with him to follow her, but gravity pulled her too fast.

She plunged through the portal.

Heat washed over her as she flew waist-high over a sand-covered ground. Strange arcing trees rushed past, the Axiom's gravity shift shooting her through the humid air until she flexed her crystal-webbed hand and released its power.

She dropped, but momentum sent her rolling through the sand. It poured into her eyes and mouth, stinging as she desperately tried to wipe it away. She'd sweated extensively from her effort in the Chamber, though, and the grains remained stubborn.

"I can't even beat the fucking sand!" she screamed into the sky.

The sky…

"Nononono!"

Kasia scrambled to her feet before falling into one of the trees. Its bark was smooth, unlike any she'd ever seen, with large, fan-shaped leaves that offered shade from the great light. Such a light did *not* belong in the everdark. Ezman's air never carried such humidity besides before a storm, and the sound of crashing waves and the smell of salt filled the air.

*Where am I?*

And where was Zinarus? He should've been mere strides behind her. The breathless had been nearly upon him, but there was nothing she could've done to stop them without her Death Reaching. Surely, a cautious man like him had known fleeing was the greater option than death.

Another part of her wondered about Tazper, but she'd felt something different about the portal she'd called for him before. It had gone to Tystok as she'd commanded it to. The last one, though, had faltered, as if disobeying her desires. Was this the consequence of pushing her Axiom Reaching too far, like she'd done with Death? Spirits… It had taken only a day for her to lose control.

"Come on, Zinarus," she muttered through gritted teeth. "Don't leave me alone. Not again."

Footsteps approached.

Kasia drew her father's revolver, trying with all her strength to stand as the sun obscured the figure. "Who are—"

"You're never alone," Aliax said. His body appeared solid now, no wisps surrounding him as he pushed down the gun, then gestured to the side. "We're here."

Sazilz, Parqiz, and all the others she'd killed surrounded her. They grabbed at her arms, pinning her to the tree's trunk as they spat in her face.

"Murderer!"

"Failure!"

"Traitor!"

Aliax circled in front of her as the others held her back. "You abandoned your allies, like you always do. Gornioz Oliezany died with more honor than you'll ever have."

"You're dead!" she screamed.

He grabbed her throat, squeezing until she struggled to breathe. "Because of you!"

She fought against the spirits, but they held her firm. No matter how hard she kicked, Aliax wouldn't relent, his grin widening as she slowly suffocated in his grasp.

"How does it feel to suffer?" he asked. "To endure the pain you inflict on so many others?"

No reply came from her empty lungs as she raised her gun to his forehead. Once, her hand would've shaken, but she didn't fear this monster before her. This wasn't Aliax. This wasn't her first love. And she wouldn't let him control her any longer.

She fired.

Her ears rang as Aliax dropped in a heap. Realm Taint took hold, and Kasia slipped down the trunk of the tree, her head light and her vision hazy as a voice rang out in the distance. The sun glinted into her eyes. But in her final moment of consciousness, she swore she saw a man dressed in purple stumbling through the sand, his curled locks aflame in the glow.

# REVIVAL

*"From one end, another beginning occurs. Spirit never ends. Nor does time."* – Etal iz Noshok, professor of forces and spirits at Kalastock College

The damp smell of mildew hung over Nex's apartment. On most days, they were nose blind to it, but they had spent too long away from home… away from Vinnia.

But it had been worth it.

They gripped the cold metal vial and crossed the small room, fumbling for a match box and striking one of the two that remained. Nothing happened. They groaned and struck it again, but no luck. The rain seeping through the ceiling had wetted the end and turned it into a useless stick.

With a sigh, Nex checked the final match head. Dry. An Ezmani would've thanked the Crystal Mother, but Nex scoffed at that. They were a Possibility Reacher. There was no divine hand. Everything was chance, and they manipulated it for fun.

They lit the single candle on the nightstand, sending a thin trail of smoke into the air. Its light barely extended over Vinnia on the bed, but it exposed her skin, far paler than its usual richness, like the wheat the peasants grew west of Kalastok.

"Vin?" they repeated. "It's me."

Silence.

They'd expected as much, given Vinnia's state when they'd left. Her head was burning when they rested the back of their hand against it, and her breaths were short, raspy. But the Spirit Plague hadn't killed her yet. Paras and Etal had been fast enough because of Nex—and those scions. Vinnia would survive.

Nex popped the potion's cork. A sharp, sweet smell followed, reminding them of the brightly colored fruits scions imported from Reshka's tropical farms. They'd hoped Vinnia would be awake to drink it, but even Reaching wouldn't change their luck there.

Still, Nex Reached and focused on their need for Vinnia to live. Whatever chance that the potion worked, they pushed harder than they'd ever Reached before to amplify the odds. Stories warned of what happened when a Reacher pulled too much from a realm, but stories be damned. They wouldn't let Vinnia die. She was all they had left.

Vinnia coughed weakly as Nex tilted her head back. Could she choke if they did this wrong? Would they make it all worse?

Answers wouldn't come by waiting. Only the alchemist and professor knew about their creation, and they were locked away in their castle of a college. All Nex could do was pour the potion slowly into Vinnia's mouth, then sit on the bedside and tap their foot.

Time passed strangely when all they had was a flickering candle to tell how long it had been. It wasn't one of the expensive ones with markings for the hours either, so they just stared at the flame as it shifted with each anxious breath. Shots rang out in the distance, joining screams that made Nex jump. They expected the next sound to be Vinnia's, and every time, they were disappointed.

Until they weren't.

Vinnia coughed, moving her arm to cover her mouth. Her eyes flickered, and she frowned at the sight of Nex sitting over her.

"Nexie?" she asked.

Nex snatched her hand. Tears streamed down their cheeks, but they laughed through them. "It's me, Vin. I'm not leaving."

"Where were you?" Vinnia winced and stuck out her tongue. "And what is that awful taste on my tongue?"

"I found a cure. Caught spirits in amber and gave 'em to some smart folk at the college." Nex held up the metal bottle. "The princess herself gave me this to save you."

Vinnia chuckled, coughing again, but her voice was stronger. Light returned to her copper eyes. "You and your stories. Where'd you get the potion with Paras dead?"

"He's alive!" Nex exclaimed, holding Vinnia's hand to their chest. "Swear it on my heart. He and that Professor Etal cooked up a cure. Looks like it's working."

"That's the wrong side for your heart, Nexie."

Nex wiped away their tears. "Let me have this moment, okay? I already said this, but you were busy being almost dead. We've been together awhile now, and I don't run around, risking my life for just anybody. I love you. Was scared I wasn't going to be able to say it."

Vinnia smiled wider than the Kala. "Glad to hear you say it when I'm not about to die."

"What?" Nex blurted. "You heard?"

Vinnia raised a hand to their cheek, giggling and running her thumb along their lips. "I thought it was a dream until you said it just now. A sweet dream. I love you too, Nex, and there's no one I would've rather woken up to."

"What about falling asleep with?"

"Every night?" Vinna pecked Nex on the lips, then winced and fell back onto the bed. "Anything more fun will have to wait until this magic potion of yours works."

Nex smiled. For the first time in what felt like forever, they were happy where they were. Not in their spiritsforsaken apartment or their city that burned to a crisp by the minute, but with the woman they loved. One who loved them for who they were.

**THE SALTY TASTE OF SWEAT COATED RADAIS'S** tongue as he willed poor Vuk onward. Time had become an illusion long ago, Lazan's watch seemingly going backwards before jumping ahead again. Its *tick tick tick* echoed in his empty mind.

"Is she still breathing?" he called into the frigid gales.

Lazan replied from beside him, his voice hoarse, "Your supreme defender is a tough one, but this cold will kill us and her before long. My Reaching has done all it can."

Janitak's vines lowered to her as it hissed, "Sheee enduuures because of my Liiife Reachiiing. I caaan't help much looonger."

"Thank you," Radais said, bowing his head to the spirit. "I know you aren't fond of us, but we are in your debt."

Janitak just stared at him for a long moment before returning to the sky alongside Rakekeaa and its fellow breathless. Even they no longer pushed ahead, their heads drooping as they drifted closer to the rolling dunes. Akaamilion seemed a distant memory more than a real place that they pursued. How could they not have returned yet?

Radais ran his fist down his back, where all that remained of his armor's backplate were the leather straps holding it to his body. He'd traveled alone as a Glassblade warrior for fifteen years and never shattered his armor. It had saved him from awakened countless times, and all it had asked in return was an occasional bit of maintenance at Palmia Fortress whenever he returned. A single husk had destroyed it.

For a millennium, the Glassblades had needed nothing more than glass armor. Their spirit foes could not pierce it, and awakened possessed no minds to create alternate ways to fight. Until now.

The Crimson Court's ambitions had changed the Spirit Wastes forever, and Radais feared what it meant for the Commonwealth and Zekiaz as a whole. The Saleshi had proven diplomatic but isolationist, and humans were notoriously bad at leaving a discovery to rest. Bakeekek's secret location of Akaamilion would eventually be exposed. All who entered the Wastes would find future Saleshi far less accommodating.

If Bakeekek was right about the Vanashel, though, it wasn't the Saleshi that would be the real issue. The Crimsons sought to wield spirits as their weapons against the living, using their Spirit Plague to turn people into breathless who they could control. Rogue ones fled, though, and the empty corpses they left behind would become husks for the Vanashel to wield.

*Chatik, you fool.*

His ambition had created a cycle that would destroy not only him, but all who lived. Breathless Reachers would be more powerful than any scion one, being immune to non-glass weaponry, and they could birth great numbers of their kind through the Spirit Crystal and dying humans. The fragile hold the Glassblades had over the awakened who sought to leave the Wastes was broken.

The Second Awakening had come.

Radais's eyes strained as they crested yet another dune. Light filled the valley on the other side, and he questioned whether he was hallucinating until Wanusa let out a whoop.

"We made it!" the initiate exclaimed, throwing an exhausted fist into the air. "Miv will be alright."

Radais tried to smile, but he lacked the strength to pierce his dread. "Let's finish this journey, then."

They pushed onward with renewed determination, but without any vigor to spare. Over a day had passed since their last rest. They had spent nearly every waking moment on ibexback or in combat. Had Radais been in charge, he'd have rewarded each of them with a complete armor set for their valor, turning Wanusa to a warrior and the warriors to masters. But that would be Miv's call when she recovered.

When.

He clutched that certainty as they reached the outer ring of Akaamilion. Unlike before, no sea of spirits met them. Instead, a few curious Saleshi rose from their trench-like buildings and hummed among themselves as Rakekeaa shouted in their tongue. Radais still didn't understand how they spoke without mouths, but its voice sounded strained.

The humming unified to a single rhythm at Rakekeaa's call. More spirits flooded from the trenches and the city's central pit, hovering over Lazan and Miv.

"We take her to place where First One calls," Rakekeaa told Radais, noticing him tense.

"What will you do with her there?" he asked.

Rakekeaa hummed to itself before lowering to his level. Its petals curled upon themselves, as if shriveling in fear. "We do what can. Do not blame if fail."

Then it took Miv in its arms and carried her to the platform in the pit's center. Five other breathless joined her, followed by a sharp, distinct hum as Bakeekek itself rose from the depths.

The First One held its hands behind its back, its long robes flowing past its indistinct fingers as it stopped at the platform's edge. Radais dismounted, then stumbled toward the pit as his legs screamed. He had to be there. He had to know what they were doing.

Janitak's vines grabbed him. "Nooot for living to seee."

"Why aren't you down there?" Radais asked, struggling to pull himself free. "You're a Life Reacher!"

"All Reachers have limits."

Radais broke free and tried to run again, but a hand took each of his arms. "Let me go!" he raged.

"There's nothing we can do for her," Wanusa replied. "We'd just get in the way."

Lazan's touch was gentler, and he rounded Radais, holding a hand to his chest. "I know your heart beats for her still. Do not let that flame burn you."

Radais relented to his exhaustion, dropping to his knees, arms still held by his allies as he stared ahead at the platform. Yes, his heart still ached for Miv, but another sorrow had washed over him as Lazan spoke those words. Lazan could've left him in Palmia when Radais discovered his father had died. Instead, he'd endured every leg of the treacherous journey by Radais's side—caring in a way Miv never had. Tender.

That was real, not the distant hope Radais clung to near Miv. She'd scorned his missteps time and time again. Around Lazan, he never felt like the failure she and his family so often claimed he was.

"You can let go," he breathed. "I'm alright."

Lazan gave a gentle smile, crouching before him. "I would understand if you weren't. You have led us well, Radais, and should Miv live or die, you will have done all you could to save your commander."

"Mhanain would've just left her behind," Wanusa added with a forced chuckle. "She was meaner to you than any of us, but you risked your life for her."

"Heard that," Mhanain muttered, but Wanusa waved him off.

She removed her scabbard and sat cross-legged beside Radais, her blade across her lap. "I never told you why I really joined the Order, did I?"

Radais shook his head.

"It's not all that glamorous. You said my family spoke highly of me, but we had a big fight about something stupid." She sighed. "I ran away until I found a Glassblade recruiter who took me to Palmia. It was on a whim, but the idea of adventuring throughout the world and slaying awakened sounded better than herding goats my entire life."

"Does it sound better now?" he asked, raising his gaze to her.

She ran her fingers over her leather scabbard, and a smile tugged at her lips. "I wasn't sure, honestly, that I deserved to become a warrior. Miv trained me hard, and I followed every command to the letter. It wasn't until she was gone, though, that I realized my purpose... why I wanted to be here. The Glassblades aren't about killing awakened, not really. We're the protectors at civilization's edge, and we see what no one else may ever see."

"Endless miles of sand," Radais muttered. He dug his fingers into it, the grains slipping into his gauntlets and stinging where he'd cut himself in the fight. "And more death than anyone deserves to endure."

"No," she insisted, throwing open his bag and pulling out his sketchbook. She flipped through the drawings and showed him each event he'd drawn from their journey. "These! The spirits, this wondrous city, and the people we've traveled with. We've lost people, but what is life on the fringes without danger? How can we be protectors if we are afraid to stand before awakened and Vanashel with our swords ready and our armor strapped? What would the Commonwealth do if we hadn't discovered the threats waiting in the Wastes?"

Lazan nodded and patted Radais's knee. "The girl is wise for her age."

She huffed. "I've just got good teachers. Both of you, but especially you, Radais. You showed me a lot about spirits and the Order."

The humming stopped.

It had fallen to the background while Wanusa talked, but now, all was silent. Radais's heart skipped a beat as he looked to the platform. The Saleshi who'd gathered around it backed away, their poses difficult to read.

"Is it done?" Radais asked Janitak. "Does she live?"

Janitak just pointed with its vines. "Look."

Bakeekek stared down at Radais, its wispy head swirling around itself as the First One moved aside to reveal Miv's body. Limp. Still.

Radais yelled and slammed his fists into the sand. He'd failed her for the last time. Miv had insisted on following him into the Wastes, and because of his failure to protect her, the Glassblades were without their supreme defender. His mentor, the woman he'd once held each night, was gone.

Rising beside him, Wanusa gasped. "Wait. What's happening?"

Reacher wisps swirled around Miv's body, and something shifted at their center. The vapors joined a figure slowly taking form, a spirit. It took the head of an ibex and a misty body resembling that of a woman, and crystal diamonds of an auburn hue hung off the ends of its curled horns.

"What did you do to her?" Radais shouted at Bakeekek before turning to Rakekeaa. "She's dead! You said you'd save her."

Bakeekek held out its hand for Miv's spirit to take, and they descended together to the Glassblades. "The one you knew as Miv could not be saved," Bakeekek said. "The damage to her body had occurred before the last day, and her mind faltered. Her spirit yet lives, but this is no longer Miv. It is Ataakanan—the one who defends."

Radais staggered to the spirit, reaching out to it. "Miv?"

"You were always bad at accepting when something was finished," Ataakanan replied, carrying Miv's sharp tone, but humming like the breathless. "You shouldn't have come back for me."

"You are our leader."

It scoffed. "I was just that to Wanusa and the others, maybe, but you can't lie to me, Radais. Your heart is soft for a warrior. It is one of your better traits." It turned its head to Bakeekek and the other Saleshi. "This is my place now—among spirits, and not those who hunt them."

"We can do more than hunt them," Radais said. "These breathless are people, and we are the ones who can mediate their first contact with humans. It will be chaos otherwise."

"Then forge that bond," it replied.

Radais stepped back, chest aching. "I can't be supreme defender! This journey was mine to lead, and I lost most of our warriors."

"And I left our warriors exposed during the Ephemeral Slaughter. We have few masters left." Ataakanan floated closer, taking his arms. "I trained you myself. Many others are better with a sword, but you've got heart. Rebuild the Order. Face the Vanashel before they destroy everything."

Wanusa stepped to them, head bowed. "Supreme Defender, what will you do?"

It turned to her. "I'll fight beside the Saleshi and protect them. They've given me a chance for a second life, and so have all of you. As long as I live, the Glassblades will have an ally among these spirits."

"We have done all we can for you," Bakeekek said. "Our hospitality must now come to an end, Supreme Defender Radais, so that we may endure in our solitude."

Radais took one last look at Ataakanan, swallowing a sob, then bowed to the First One. "Thank you for the help you have given. I hope that someday we may repay it with more than secrecy."

"Ensure the Crimson ones are defeated and the Vanashel do not spread."

"We'll try." Radais glanced back at his comrades, his friends. They had gotten him this far, and he swore that in the battles to come, he would fight for them to his final breath.

They said their goodbyes, and on tired legs, mounted their ibexes to camp once again beyond the edge of Akaamilion. The glow of the crystal lanterns would've kept many awake. But the last day had been long, the everdark even longer. Darkness had clouded Radais's life ever since he'd found Votzan in the Wastes, and after carrying that burden for so many days, he welcomed the light that pierced his eyelids.

Seasons came and went on Zekiaz. Somewhere in the vast expanse of the realms, though, light was eternal, so vibrant that it reached through the veil and graced every being with eyes to look upon it. Dawnrise would come soon. And that light made all the difference.

# EPILOGUE – OF ASH AND GLASS

*"There are two kinds of people: those who see a blaze and seek to douse it, and those who sit back and revel in its glory."* – Rikan of the Timekeepers, Nochlander pirate captain

Ash rained upon the crystal city of Kalastok, covering the melted slush with a layer of gray so thick it drowned the corpses of the fallen. Well, at least those who weren't piled upon each other like sacks of grain reaped in the duskfall harvest.

Weeping and vomiting occupied the survivors as Commander Tiuz Hazeko rode through the Market District. He'd grown nose blind to the stench of gore ages ago, but to those unfamiliar with war, there was nothing as revolting. Heroes didn't tell of war's ugly face. Such thoughts were not kind memories for the mind or the spirit, and Tiuz's spirit was heavy this day.

Rioters and soldiers had destroyed most of the lamps in the firefight, but the few that remained joined the embers in illuminating the destruction. Thousands of homes and businesses destroyed in mere hours of rage. Not unjustified rage, mind you, but rage nonetheless.

He touched the patch of House iz Vamiustok upon his shoulder. Crystal Mother save their mercenaries, the company had fought like veterans experienced beyond their years, holding back Chatik Pikezik's breathless—spirits with minds according to Zinarus—long enough for civilians to flee into what remained of the western and southeastern parts of the city. Two-dozen lowborn cavalry with amber pellets, slings, and poorly made pistols. Eight had fallen. For now, though, they had allowed Kalastok a moment of peace with the Crimsons' forces recollecting around the palace.

It would not last long.

Tiuz stopped his horse along the edge of the line of destruction, ending at the border of the Crimson District. The palace pierced the ashfall like a stubborn child raising their reddened nose in the frost. No one truly knew what had happened within the Chamber of Scions, but it was believed that King Jazuk was dead, along with those who'd dared to protect him against the Crimson Coup.

Zinarus was nowhere to be found.

"You faced a beast far greater than yourself," Tiuz told the darkness before him. "You were not a man of steel and valor, but of honor and justice. A warrior all the same."

He held a fist over his heart and bowed his head for a moment of respect.

Zinarus's mercenary company would live on. Their mission was not over, and Tiuz would see it through until his end or its completion. Drawing his saber, he raised it into the falling ash and recited a warrior's prayer.

"From ash we rise, bound by spirit, and to it we fall, our souls free from the coals on which the living trod. May you drift to peace, dear brother, and one day, find your way back to the living."

The blade grew heavy as he sheathed it and tightened his coat against the brutal chill. Dawnrise could not come soon enough.

A horse approached at a trot, stopping behind him with a heavy snort. "Commander Tiuz," a man said as the clocktower rang for two. It was late in the night, but neither man nor woman slept this eve. "A man in a purple mask told me to give you this. Said it was urgent."

Tiuz sighed and reached back. The letter crinkled between his gloved fingers, bearing an unfamiliar seal, but the name scrawled upon its front was clearly his.

He sliced open the seal with his dagger, and a key slipped into his fingers. It appeared to be nothing special in itself, so he raised the letter into the light of the nearest lamp, whose hiss rang in his ears as he read:

*To Kelosh's greatest foe, and now Kalastok's hero,*

*It has come to our attention that you are a man of great repute among both those of high and low birth. In times such as these, there are few who can unite their people against the forces that seek to destroy them. It is my hope that the Children of Zekiaz may be of use to you.*

*In the highest room of the Kalastok clocktower, you will find a lockbox containing a weapon developed by our friends in the Ogrenian Hegemony. They have confined its secrets to within their borders for years, but what shall come will affect beyond Ogrenia and the Commonwealth. Copy its design to the letter, and we believe the King in the Dark will face quite the surprise.*

*Sincerely,*

*The Silent Queen*

Tiuz looked back at the courier. "You said the man wore a purple mask?" Could he be somehow related to Tiuz, whose house bore the same color?

"Yes, sir. Like a falcon."

Folding up the letter, Tiuz looked to the clocktower, rising from the southeastern heart of the Market District. It had been a miracle the flames had done such little harm to it. Kalastok's damage was extensive enough without a massive building like that tumbling upon civilians below.

He turned his horse away from the palace and pushed in his heels. It wasn't smart to linger in the aftermath of a battlefield, especially a city, as looters or the opposing force could arrive at any time. If Chatik intended to take hold of the Commonwealth and use spirits against Kelosh, he would need to secure the capital. That couldn't happen. Nor could Tiuz allow a riotous mob to rule the sections of Kalastok that still held out against the Crimsons. War was inevitable, but slaughter was not.

Scions and lowborn alike looked to him for help as he rode past, but all he could offer was insistence that they cross the bridges into the west side. The rebels willing to fight the Crimson Court would fortify within the Market District, and that would make any civilians left behind targets. Not that the river would do much to stop breathless or awakened.

He tied his horse to a post at the base of the clocktower. The lanterns hanging within its peak had been unaffected by the battle, and it formed a beacon for the otherwise dim city. That light did not extend inside, though, so he lit his lantern before kicking into the door.

Hundreds of wooden steps wound above. His thighs ached just staring at them, each flight crossing one of the walls before continuing to another. Crystal Mother below, this is why generals had scouts.

But he was no longer a general in any real capacity, so he climbed them himself. A recent construction, Tiuz remembered when the tower had been nothing more than scaffolding as the great houses raved about their investments in the landmark. Tons of brick, glass, and Mother knew what else had flowed into this single structure. Endless keni for a glorified watch. Tiuz could respect function, but not waste when both poorer scions and lowborn suffered.

His perceived soreness became all too real by the time he reached the top of the tower. Years away from the battlefield had turned him soft, and he caught his breath before surveying the gears surrounding the bell at the room's center. A genius's work. Any army had its engineers, but this was true mastery far beyond his comprehension.

Luckily, he didn't need to understand the clock's mechanics to notice the metal lockbox resting on a solitary table in the corner. A spectacular view of the city stretched beyond it, but that only revealed the full extent of the destruction.

Centuries of growth burned in a single night.

The rioters were less dangerous than Chatik's breathless spirits, but Tiuz's heart ached seeing what they had burned. Spurred by the drafts, they had sought revenge against all scions, not realizing how many were no better off than the lowborn. What was the difference between scion and lowborn when the former couldn't even afford a Reacher talon? Jazuk had ensured their choice was impoverishment or a soldier's life, thrown against whomever the great houses hated that year.

Tiuz slipped the Silent Queen's key into the lockbox, opening it with a *click*. A single shot pistol and a metal tin lay inside.

He furrowed his brow and picked up the gun, noting its strangely lightweight construction before setting it aside. Alone, it appeared to be nothing special until he opened the tin to reveal a bullet with a clear tip. He gasped as plucked it free.

"So the rumors were true."

Merchants from Ogrenia had claimed for years that their nation had developed a pistol capable of shooting glass-tipped bullets without them shattering. Katarzyna's amber had played its part the night before, but the ability to shoot awakened and these new breathless would alter the battlefield forever. How did this Silent Queen know they would need it?

Tiuz closed his fist around the cartridge and looked to the west, leaning upon the walkway's railing. Over two hundred thousand people lived in Kalastok, and the Commonwealth as a whole held millions more. The Crimson Court threatened every single one of them.

He tossed the bullet in the air and caught it, holstering the glass-shooter before heading down the stairs. Fresh vigor filled him with each step. He'd retired with the hope of never seeing battle again, but all too often, there was little choice in war. This was one of those times. Twenty years ago, he'd saved this damned nation from Kelosh.

Now he had to save it from itself.

END OF BOOK 1

# A WORD FROM THE AUTHOR

Every book is a journey for reader and author alike. The Crimson Court was like a mountain I had stared at from the foothills for many years, so to be at this point, publishing this story after experiencing the overwhelming flood of support from the book's Kickstarter, is an honor.

The Crimson Court would not be here without your support as a reader. So THANK YOU for joining me on this journey. We're just getting started!

If you have enjoyed reading this story, please take the time to post an honest review on whatever retailer you purchased this book from (or on Goodreads or social media sites). Every review helps new readers discover my books, and personal recommendations are more powerful than anything I can say as an author.

Want more Realm Reachers? Maybe a bit of backstory about how Kasia earned her nickname of the Amber Dame? You can get a free eBook of The Amber Dame—the prequel novella to The Realm Reachers—and my novellas from other series by joining my newsletter at www.Brendan-Noble.com/newsletter

- Brendan

# About the Author

Brendan Noble is an American author writing epic fantasy with inspiration from his Polish ancestry, mythology, video games of all types, and Dungeons & Dragons. He loves to explore the complexities of politics and the gray between good and evil.

Shortly after beginning his writing career in 2019, Brendan married his wife Andrea and moved to Rockford, Illinois from his hometown in Michigan. Since then, he has published three series: The Realm Reachers, The Frostmarked Chronicles, and The Prism Files.

Outside of writing, Brendan is a data analyst and soccer referee. His top interests include German, Polish, and American soccer/football, Formula 1, analyzing political elections across the world, playing extremely nerdy strategy video games, exploring with his wife, and reading.

Milton Keynes UK
Ingram Content Group UK Ltd.
UKHW010621260424
441779UK00001B/4

9 781954 985056